CARREÑA 3:

Imperative Birth

BY

K GERARD MARTIN

Shouldercat Books

Contents

Chapter 1:

Shock

2110 Dec 29, Mon Morn. 376 Grey Road, Hamilton, New Zealand.

"The fog is worse out here than in Hamilton," Kristi said.

"I can barely see," Margaret said. "It's near white-out conditions. And there's mud everywhere. Fortunately, this van has four-wheel drive."

"Do you think we'll get stuck in Jonara's driveway?" Kristi asked.

"If we can make it back to the road, we'll be fine. But I don't trust that dirt road. Mud could get deep. If only this news van had tank tracks, then we'd make it without a problem," Margaret said.

"We might have to call a tank to help us," Kristi said.

"It would never fit on the narrow road," Margaret laughed. "This fog is making it hard to find the entrance."

"I can't see a green light," Kristi said.

"Can or cannot?" Margaret asked, unsure of what Kristi had just said.

"Cannot," Kristi said.

"Wait a minute, what am I doing? I should get the stupid award for the year," Margaret said.

"Why?" Kristi asked.

"We have a GPS location from the last two times we were here. I can use GPS to navigate our way back in. I can't believe I forgot. Everyone uses GPS nowadays," Margaret said.

"I think I know why you forgot," Kristi said. "Everything about the dirt road and Jonara's house is like a trip back in time before GPS or anything was invented."

"You got that right," Margaret said. "Here—this is the dirt road. As long as we don't slide off, we'll be fine."

They arrived at the elderly Jonara's house. Kristi helped Margaret with the equipment as before, but they kept it covered up until they reached inside.

"Now remember," Margaret said. "Don't take for granted that she remembers us. Lead with our full names so she'll think we're the heads of state."

"Okay," Kristi said.

Kristi pressed the doorbell and knocked on the door. Kristi heard the sound of the chain being unlatched. Jonara opened the door fully. She wore a cooking apron and hat.

"My name is Kristi Fernandez, and this is Margaret McAleese. We're from the Channel-A television—"

"Kristi! Margaret! It's me! Don't you remember? I'm your Mamma Maffet! Come in! I've been expecting you!" Jonara said.

Jonara was much more lively than in previous days. Kristi and Margaret picked up on this behavior immediately. They walked into the lobby area and noticed all mail had been re-moved from the floor. Further, all tables with mail in the hall-way were also gone. Jonara led the two women into the dining room where a large breakfast had been arranged—eggs, toast, bacon, breakfast rolls, waffles, pancakes, syrup, fresh fruit, ce-real, milk, juice, tea, coffee, soft drinks, and chocolate squares.

"Wow!" Kristi and Margaret remarked.

"Are you expecting company?" Kristi asked.

"Yes," Jonara said. "And my company has arrived. Oh, I'm so glad you're here. I haven't had this much fun in years. Please, have a seat. Enjoy some breakfast."

"Thank you," the younger women said.

"I can't get over what a sudden change this is," Kristi said as she helped herself to some food.

"Yeah," Margaret said. "It's like the world has changed. A bit of a shock, if you ask me. You're so alert and chipper this morn-ing. One would think you've already had coffee to start the day."

"Oh yes, I've had many cups of coffee today," Jonara admit-ted. "I'm so eager to tell you more of my experiences that led to my career choice. I don't get that many visitors. Did I say you're like grandchildren to me? I'm just so overcome with emotion."

"Aw," Kristi said. "We love our Mamma Maffet."

"I'm so glad," Jonara said.

"Should we do it here?" Kristi asked. "The interview, I mean?"

"Of course!" Jonara said. "This is a celebration, after all."

Margaret set up the video equipment and turned it on.

"So we left off at the sidewalk with Nekara the Red," Kristi said.

"I know precisely where we left off," Jonara said. "And this is what happened next."

Kristi narrated Jonara's story as follows:

2023 Oct 8, Sun Morn. Corpus Christi, Texas.

"Good morning," said a familiar voice.

Jonara opened her eyes. She rolled over and saw Evanita in the doorway.

"Mommy!" Jonara cried as she jumped to her feet and hugged her expectant mother.

"Oh, wow! I've never known you to be so happy in the morning," Evanita said.

"You're home! They let you out! You must be fully healed!" Jonara celebrated.

"Silly girl," Evanita said. "You must be still half asleep. Come downstairs and have some breakfast!"

"This will be the best breakfast I've ever had," Jonara said. "My mommy. My mommy!"

Evanita blushed. She didn't know what to make of Jonara's excitement.

"Assigned seating as usual," Evanita said as the two entered the dining room.

"Huh?" Jonara asked. "Oh, something new."

Jonara looked at the table. Six places were set with fancy tableware, a large plate of scrambled eggs, lean bacon, cinnamon rolls, fresh fruit, croissants, orange juice, coffee, and milk.

"Wow! Why the celebration?" Jonara asked as she sat down.

Evanita smiled and stood behind her chair. She motioned Jonara to do the same.

"Huh?" Jonara asked.

"It's rude to sit down before everyone else, dear," Evanita said. "Stand up behind your chair."

"It is? I should?" Jonara asked.

"You know better, Jonara. Now stand up," Evanita said.

Jonara stood up behind her chair. Something was different. Her mother never spoke to her like that. Why the formality? Why the food? How did she get out of the hospital?

"We're ready," Anna said as she led the others into the dining room.

Anna walked in followed by Johnny who had gained considerable weight, Eva who wore a crucifix choker around her neck, and a man with medium-dark skin a bit older than Eva—a man Jonara did not recognize.

"Let's say grace," the unknown man said. "In the name of the Father, and of the Son, and of the Holy Spirit. Amen."

The family except Jonara made the sign of the cross during this first part of the grace. Jonara looked around in shock. The man continued with prayer.

"Bless us O Lord, and these thy gifts which we are about to receive from thy bounty through Christ our Lord, Amen," the man said, and he led the group in the sign of the cross to finish:

"In the name of the Father, and of the Son, and of the Holy Spirit. Amen."

The group took to their chairs. Jonara remained standing.

"Jonara, you didn't say grace," Eva said. "You have to say grace before eating."

"Jonara is out of it this morning," Evanita said.

"Could be the bump on the head she had last night," the man said.

"Go on, Jonara, say grace," Johnny said.

"God is great, God is good, let us thank him for our food. By his hand, we are fed, give us Lord our daily bread. Amen," Jonara said.

"Blasphemy!" Eva said. "That's not the Catholic grace. That's a Protestant prayer!"

"Jonara," Johnny said. "Why are you saying a Protestant prayer? We're all Catholic."

Jonara's eyes lit up in terror.

"Sit down, sugar," the man said.

"Yes, sir," Jonara said as she sat down.

"Is that any way to speak to your grandfather?" Eva asked. "What about, 'Yes, Grandpa'?"

"Grandpa?" Jonara asked.

"She must have a little amnesia to forget me," Jonara's grandpa said.

"Well," Eva said. "We can't spend all morning talking about it. We have to eat quickly to beat the one-hour mark before Communion."

"Communion?" Jonara asked.

"Yes. We're all going to Mass this morning," Eva said. "You do remember your Catholic faith, don't you?"

Jonara looked around the room like a rabbit caught in a corner. She looked for clues or help. Evanita wore a bracelet with a crucifix. Jonara's "grandpa" wore a lapel pin with a crucifix. Eva had the crucifix necklace. Johnny was overweight. What had happened? Everyone had become Catholic, Grandma Eva was married to a man, and Jonara's mother was out of the hospital. Was she still asleep? She pinched herself to wake up. No, she wasn't asleep. Afraid to say, do, or eat much of anything, Jonara poured a small amount of orange juice into her cup. The faint image of Nekara appeared in the juice's reflection. Nekara winked and promptly disappeared. Jonara swished the juice and looked for Nekara again, but Nekara did not reappear.

"Don't play with your juice, Jonara," Evanita said.

Jonara took a sip of juice. It was the best orange juice she'd ever tasted.

"Eva, as usual, your cooking is out of this world," Grandpa said.

"A woman's place is in the kitchen. She should cook the best food for her husband and family—in that order," Eva said.

"She should never wander. A Spanish woman's legs are best bound and kept in the husband's home."

"What?! Who are you?" Jonara blurted out.

"Jonara!" Evanita said. "Shame on you! Give your grandmother an apology."

"Apology for what? She's turned into a traitor," Jonara said.

"That's enough, young lady," Evanita said. "Go upstairs and get ready for church! We're going a little early so you can go to confession. Two sins in one morning is a record."

Jonara pushed the chair back and stood up.

"Jonara!" Evanita said.

"What?" Jonara replied.

"You're forgetting your manners, dear," Evanita said. "What are you supposed to say?"

"I'm sorry?" Jonara said.

"No, besides that. Where is your thinking cap today?" Evanita asked.

"Go easy on her," Grandpa said. "She has a concussion."

"I'll have obedience in my family," Evanita said. "Jonara— ask to be excused."

"May I be excused?" Jonara asked.

"Yes you may," Evanita replied.

Jonara ran from the dining room and up the stairs.

"Don't run in the house!" Johnny yelled after her.

Jonara rushed into her bedroom and closed the door. She looked at the window. There was no evidence of glass being broken or recently repaired. Very few books in the room. No diary of Nanna Geneva. Jonara searched around frantically for any evidence of the relics—anything. Then she patted her upper chest and found the Moissan Ruby around her neck.

"The Water Ruby!" Jonara said with glee. "So there is something that wasn't removed. I bet Nekara did this to me. I'll set things right. I need a cell phone. Good, there's mine. Now I'll set it to vibrate. Water Ruby, do your stuff."

But nothing happened for Jonara. She pressed the vibrating cell phone against the Moissan Ruby but was unable to sense anything. She reached for the candleholder as she was so used to doing, but it wasn't there.

"Nekara's doing again. She got rid of the candleholder. Now she's blocking the Water Ruby's power. But she can't block a Miramish chant."

Jonara kept the cell phone vibrating and attempted to say something in Miramish, but each time she tried, the words came out in English: "Water Ruby, get my life back...Break this journey in time...Release me...release, release!...A curse on Nekara...Bring Cerafina back to me...Felifia, help me!"

Nothing. She looked at the Moissan Ruby. It had a greenish tint to it.

"I've forgotten Miramish. I can't remember a single word. And the Water Ruby is green now, not cerise. What happened? Everything is broken! And I'm Roman Catholic! What is this madness?!"

"Are you almost ready in there?" Evanita called through the door.

"Coming," Jonara called back.

Jonara quickly threw on some church clothes. She finished slipping her feet into shoes as Evanita knocked and cracked the door open.

"Good, you're ready. Let's go," Evanita said.

The six entered a minivan and proceeded to Candlewood Catholic Church.

"What happened to Nanna Geneva's car?" Jonara asked.

"She hasn't had a car in ten years," Eva said. "This is her minivan. We'll use it for now until we're ready to fly back."

There was a brief silence in the minivan. Jonara stared out the window and noticed the street signs were in two languages—Catalan and English. The cars looked European, like from France or Spain.

"Mommy," Jonara said. "Were you in the hospital?"

"When I was younger," Evanita said. "I was running through the woods behind my house and stepped on a rock the wrong way. I ripped my Achilles tendon and had to get it stitched up."

"No, I mean later," Jonara said.

"No, I don't think so," Evanita said.

"What about last week? Didn't you have preeclampsia at Corpus Christi Hospital?" Jonara asked.

"Why would you ask such a horrible question? You know I've been with you the entire time either at your Nanna Geneva's house or at a restaurant," Evanita said.

"Never mind," Jonara said.

"Marcus, this is it. Turn in here," Eva said.

"Marcus?" Jonara said. "Who's Marcus?"

Everyone but Jonara laughed.

"Your grandfather's first name is 'Marcus'," Eva said. "But you might not know that. You're used to calling him 'Grandpa'. Isn't that right, Mr. Cracbern?" Eva asked Marcus.

A huge fireball of horror, like the Castle Bravo explosion, welled up in Jonara. She choked on her own throat and beat it with her hand for air.

"What's wrong?" Evanita asked. "Quit playing. Church is a serious affair."

Jonara turned and faced the side of the car—away from human eye contact. She looked down, coughed, and gasped for air. When she looked up at the car window, Nekara's face appeared.

"So, how do you like your new life?" Nekara asked.

"This is wrong. Take me back," Jonara said.

"There's nothing wrong with weekly Mass, young lady," Evanita said, thinking Jonara was speaking to her. "No, we won't take you back until after Mass and the reception. You know, with all the sins you're piling up this morning, we won't have time to get you into confession before Mass. You'll have to skip Communion until your slate is clean. It's a shame, really."

"She can receive Communion," Marcus said. "The restriction is only for mortal sins, not venial sins."

"The way she's been denying her faith, it's practically a mortal sin," Evanita said.

"Oh let her take Communion," Eva said. "It will do her good. Then we'll all receive hosts as a family."

Jonara couldn't believe what she was hearing. Her entire family was against her.

"I'm your only friend," Nekara said in the window. "Don't worry—no one else can see me—except Marcus when I want him to. But he doesn't need me anymore. I trained him quite well when he was younger. Now he's an adult—financially successful, full of vice, and ready to abuse the less fortunate to maintain his wealth. If you're wise, you won't say anything else just now. Your family will think you're crazy."

Jonara wanted to say something, but unfortunately, Nekara was right. Jonara reached for the Moissan Ruby around her neck and shook it in hopes of getting it to activate.

"That's right. Try using your moisharn," Nekara said. "Unfortunately for you, it's been drained of power. Oh you Earth people—you expect things to last forever, and when they don't, you cry foul. Yes, it was you who drained it. You used the last of it while fortifying that De Havilland aircraft as it crashed into Les Agudes peak in the Montseny Mountains."

Nekara disappeared. The minivan arrived at Candlewood Catholic Church. The six exited and entered the large vestibule. Jonara looked around and saw Cerafina in a corner conversing with her boyfriend—the one Jonara had seen the day before.

"She really is different," Jonara said. "But she's still a Catholic."

While Jonara stared, a young boy a year older than her approached her.

"You're new here," the boy said.

"What?" Jonara said, not paying attention.

"Tony is already taken," the boy said.

"Tony?" Jonara asked, still staring at Cerafina.

"Yeah. He's got a girlfriend. Her name is Cera Vagatti," the boy said.

"I don't date...I mean, I'm not really...I'm just going to church," Jonara said. "Who are you?"

"Greg Dannerstadt. Nice to meet you. And your name is?"

"You're Greg Dannerstadt!" Jonara said.

"Jonara Pindus!" Evanita called. "Quit dawdling and follow us."

"Nice to meet you, Jonara Pindus," Greg smiled. "You can be one of my girlfriends. I'll let you."

"No thanks," Jonara said, and she followed her mother.

"You'll be back," Greg said.

Jonara could see why Cerafina hated Greg. He was a cad, a snake in the grass, slippery as a fish, cute and well-polished physically, but lacking in self-sacrifice and humility.

"Jonara!" Evanita chided. "Did you forget something? Holy water!"

Jonara looked around and saw other people dip their fingers in a bowl of water and make the sign of the cross. She mimicked them.

"Finally," Evanita said.

Jonara sat with her mother. This was her first Catholic Mass—second if Saint Stellan counted. However, there was no lifting bench seat in the very back. Candlewood Catholic Church was quite conventional.

Jonara realized she could fake knowledge of the Mass by simply mimicking other behavior. The people knelt when they first arrived and clasped their hands together. Jonara did the same. Next, the people sat and waited for Mass to begin—as did Jonara. The Mass started, and the people stood—as did Jonara. Then at various points in the Mass, people sat, stood, or knelt. Jonara followed suit. Later in the Mass, the people shook each other's hands. Jonara shook their hands back and started to leave the pew to shake hands with people in other pews, but Evanita grabbed onto Jonara's arm and pulled her back. To Jonara's shock, Greg sat in the pew behind her. He reached out to shake her hand, and Jonara—thinking nothing of it—shook his hand in reply. As she did, Greg took his middle finger and drew it across Jonara's palm several times, winked his eye, and grinned. Jonara pulled her hand back in disgust and turned back around.

Greg leaned forward and whispered into Jonara's ear, "I know you want to be my girlfriend."

Jonara pulled forward to avoid his foul breath on her neck. She looked around the church for Cerafina and saw her on the far side. Greg reached out and pulled Jonara back by the collar.

"Tony is taken. I'm available," Greg whispered again.

Jonara pulled away from Greg and switched places with Evanita. Another few minutes of Mass passed, and the moment of Communion came along. Beginning with the first rows and working progressively back as directed by ushers, people filed out of their pews and stood in a line down the aisle toward the priest and other Eucharist providers.

"Just do what they do," Jonara said to herself as she entered the aisle.

"Let's share a host together," Greg whispered behind her.

How did Greg get behind her? Jonara thought her mother was behind her, but Evanita took a different line. Jonara didn't understand the nature of his suggestion, and she didn't care. She would simply do what others did in front of her. She watched, and the priest placed either a host in the person's hand followed by the person placing the host in his or her mouth, or he placed the host on the person's tongue. How did the priest know which method to do? Was there some secret freemason code? Jonara had a vague memory of Nanna Geneva at Saint Stellan trying to receive communion, but Jonara couldn't remember the details. She shook the Moissan Ruby in hopes of getting insight into how to deal with the situation, but the Moissan Ruby remained quiet.

Jonara turned around and asked Greg, "What do I do?"

"Here," he said, "let me in front."

Greg jumped in front of Jonara in the line. When it was his turn, he held out his tongue, and the priest placed the host on Greg's tongue. Greg stepped aside, broke off the host, ate the one half, dragged Jonara to the side with him, and placed the other half in her mouth. Jonara reacted in shock, removed the half-host from her mouth, and held it in her hand. The priest pointed sternly at the two and then motioned for them to leave the building. The congregation in the front pews gasped. Greg led Jonara back to the pews, and as Jonara entered her pew, Evanita swatted her on the butt.

"What mischief are you up to, young lady?" Evanita said. "Stop clowning around. This is a serious sin you've committed. That was the real flesh of Christ you desecrated! And you're holding it in your hand! Swallow it quickly!"

"But it's been in Greg's m—" Jonara started.

"I said swallow it!" Evanita demanded, and she forced the host from Jonara's hand.

Jonara swallowed the half-host.

"Quick! Say an Our Father and ten Hail Marys. Pray!" Evanita demanded.

Evanita forced Jonara down to the kneeler. Jonara didn't know how the Our Father or Hail Mary went. She couldn't remember if she'd read it in Nanna Geneva's diary or if someone said it during one of her trips back in time. Something in the back of her mind said, "Yes, someone said it," but Jonara couldn't remember who, and she certainly didn't learn while growing up—at least not in the timeline she remembered.

The Mass ended, fortunately for Jonara, in just under an hour. The six exited, but once the family left the main church area, Evanita led Jonara out a side door while the rest of the family socialized with church friends.

"What was that stunt all about, Jonara Cracbern Pindus?" Evanita said. "You know you're supposed to receive your own host. You don't take part of someone else's. That's like cutting the Body of Christ in half. Is that what you're trying to do, cut Christ in half?"

"No," Jonara said. "And my middle name is Carreña, not Cracbern!"

"What? Who said you could start pretending your name is something else?" Evanita said. "Your middle name honors your grandfather. After everything he's done for us, it's the least we could do by naming his first granddaughter after him."

"It's the least they could do after everything Marcus has done to your family," Nekara said as her head popped out of nowhere.

"Shush," Jonara said to Nekara.

Evanita slapped Jonara across the face.

"Don't tell me to shush, young lady. You're going straight to Nanna Geneva's house. You'll go to confession when we return to Portland. And no going out to lunch for you today. You can make yourself a cold sandwich at Nanna Geneva's house. We're dropping you off."

The party arrived at Geneva's house.

"I'll stay here with Jonara," Marcus said.

"Are you sure, Marcus?" Eva asked.

"Sure. You all have a good time. I'm going to have a little chat with Jonara," Marcus said.

"Very well," Eva said.

Eva, Evanita, Anna, and Johnny left Marcus and Jonara at Geneva's house. Marcus led Jonara inside.

"Have a seat, Jonara," Marcus said. "I need to make a few phone calls first before we begin."

Jonara and Marcus sat at the dining room table. Marcus dialed a number on his cell phone.

"This is Marcus Cracbern. Status report," Marcus said.

Long pause.

"That's not acceptable," he said. "You are to have the last dry-run complete by Wednesday. Mach 3.5 isn't good enough. We must have Mach 4. We fly live on Saturday. No, you continue working them the weekend and nights until they're caught up. This event will not wait for us. I don't care about the union. That's right. Tell them their jobs will be outsourced permanently if they don't put in extra effort. Yes, give them all the free coffee and colas they want. Decongestant meds too. And pizza, with lots of grease. Right. Dry-run Wednesday, Karl, Wednesday. You will be rewarded, yes. Saturday will dawn a new era for the company and the Church. Definitely. Global expansion of the largest kind. Yes. Yes. I'll check later. Twist the tail, Karl. Twist it 'till it breaks."

Marcus hung up his cell phone and stared at Jonara.

"What?" Jonara asked. "You're staring at me. Why?"

Marcus continued staring at Jonara.

"I'm sorry. Please, stop staring at me," Jonara begged.

"He won't stop staring at you," Nekara's voice said.

Nekara appeared in full form and stood behind Marcus.

"I froze time. All because I love you, Jonara," Nekara said.

"You don't love me," Jonara said. "You can't. You don't know what love is."

"Oh but I do," Nekara said. "I love men—everywhere. They are my prized soldiers. They are my work, my obsession, my *raison d'être*. Is this not love?"

"You are full of hate. You create misery and death for others. That's not love at all," Jonara said.

"Hate is love with a final goal. Love is never-ending hate. I love you, Jonara," Nekara said with a laugh. "I want your hate to last forever."

"Stop it, stop it!" Jonara yelled. "Your words are poison. I want my life back. I want it back now. This is torture."

Nekara laughed again.

"This torture pleases me. You see, Jonara, you created this situation. You had a goal—the protection of your family. You love your family. You succeeded in the goal. Now you hate it. Hate is love with a final goal, remember? You love it, I love you, we hate and love each other," Nekara said.

"Everything is your doing," Jonara said.

"Your lies are weak, Jonara. I can help you fortify them. Simply chant your Miramish word for *indurate*. You'll harden your lies such that you believe them," Nekara said.

Jonara returned a look of bepuzzlement.

"Yes, you issued the *indurate* chant," Nekara said. "Quite powerful. Even I avoid it when possible. Makes things strong by giving them uniformity. Spreads beyond the original target. This is expected, Jonara. Uniformity is like a domino chain—once the critical structure is achieved, the disorganized, the hapless, and the vulnerable fall victim to authority and order. Their 'culture' as they call it cannot hold up to the might of the structure. And you issued this structure. On Les Agudes. Do you not realize what you've done?"

"I was strengthening the aircraft body. I was saving my grandma and great-grandma," Jonara said.

"Les Agudes!" Nekara reiterated. "I've said it before, and I'll say it again—Earthlings think nothing of consequences. You used up the charge of your moisharn, but you also changed the course of power on Les Agudes, albeit for a different time. But moisharns are like that—they affect different times at the same time."

"I'm not listening to this hogwash," Jonara said.

"It doesn't matter if you listen or not. What matters is what you did. And now I have you to thank. Yes, Jonara, you. This is another reason I love you. Your temporal induration gave me the advantage I needed to defeat Felifia on that mountain range. Yes, Montseny Mountains. You strengthened and liberated me," Nekara said.

"Lies. You're trying to recruit me," Jonara said.

"There's no need to recruit you," Nekara said. "You're already mine. Felifia's women in the Caves of Healing? In 1492? Never happened. Those women stayed in Spain. They never left. Their identities were reshaped before they were born. Their families converted to Catholicism over two hundred years prior. All."

"It can't be the reason. It can't be," Jonara said.

"Oh but it is. It's exactly why Eva is Catholic, Marcus is Catholic, Johnny is Catholic, and you, Jonara—it's why you're Catholic too. Uniformity. That's what the induration chant does. You did my work. You did my job. You're my best helper, my slave. Congratulations, you recruited yourself!" Nekara bragged.

Jonara ran out the door and screamed in the front yard. Passersby remained frozen in place.

"They can't hear you, Jonara," Nekara said as she popped into the front yard before Jonara. "Scream more, Jonara. Let misery overwhelm you. It's addictive, like love. Obsess with misery. That's right. Now look at me. You want to choke me, to alleviate your misery. Hate is love with a final goal. That's right. Love me, Jonara, love me!"

"Why don't you kill me and get it over with. Isn't that your goal, your final 'love' for me?" Jonara asked.

Nekara laughed.

"Joni, Joni, Joni!" Nekara ranted. "Look at the world around you? It's as static as the people itself—endlessly feeding on their own vices and accomplishing little or nothing. Your grandpa, Marcus Cracbern, for example."

"He's not my grandpa," Jonara said.

"Oh but he is. Perhaps not biologically, but legally he is," Nekara said.

"Then Evanita's father isn't Marcus Cracbern. He isn't in this timeline and wasn't in the other. He could never be the father, because that would change me. But I'm the same person now as I was before," Jonara reasoned. "You only made him my grandpa because you knew that would aggravate me."

"You're forgetting who the causal factor is here. You are the factor, you changed the timeline, and you take the responsibility," Nekara said.

Jonara stared intently at Nekara, and Nekara stared back. For a brief moment, a symbol appeared on her forehead.

"It was you!" Jonara said. "You were in those other places. The Vice of Christ! The cat in the parking lot. The oak tree! You! You split me into Modern and Victorian. What is your secret? Build up a structure in absolute uniformity and slice it down the middle? Build and divide?!"

Nekara laughed in approval. She clapped her hands and bowed to Jonara.

"This is why I love you. You're an excellent student," Nekara said. "Look at your grandpa in there."

"He's not my grandpa!" Jonara reiterated.

"He wants power. That's it. An easy vice to feed. He's been that way since I first corrupted him as a child, when he began using my *duavirt*."

"It's a *duavisha*," Jonara said. "Not a *duavirt!*"

"I explained this before. *Duavirt* is its name in my language—Dahmek," Nekara said. "I don't lower myself to using that Miramish language as you do. But details aside, there are many other men like Marcus I've corrupted over the millennium, but all are extremely limited. You, Jonara, you have excellent potential. Imagine a world at your beck and call. You would be Queen Jonara. I would be your consort and adviser. Forget this world where you live—there's no hope in it. Together—you and I—can set things aright as they should be. We need only work together and build our planet of people."

"Planet of people?" Jonara questioned.

Nekara laughed.

"Excellent, you didn't question our working together," Nekara said. "Excellent."

"I won't work with you," Jonara said.

"But you already are," Nekara said. "Each moment we spend together increases the bond between us. Love or hate—it doesn't matter. The bond is increasing."

"Even if we did work together," Jonara said.

"Yes, yes!" Nekara acknowledged with glee.

"I said *if*. You would want me to build up some orderly empire only to divide it later on. Civil War," Jonara said.

"Oh piddle-paddle," Nekara said. "Don't use words like *civil war*. They imply reunification. Of course I would have you divide the empire—one for you and one for me. That's how a regime procreates. You would like procreating with me, Jonara Carreña Pindus."

"You called me by my correct name!"

"Because I love you," Nekara said.

"I don't believe that lie, and I won't help you. Go back to your planet or whatever Hell you're from and stay there. I'd rather love someone like Felifia than you."

"Felifia!?" Nekara rebuked. "Indeed! Felifia the Wise. Felifia the Good. Felifia the Healer. Felifia the Leader. I'm tired of hearing about Felifia. Felifia is a weak woman who wouldn't take the reins of the horse with me when we needed help the most. Felifia wouldn't catch the ball when I pitched it. She was on a pilgrimage to spread fairness and hope to women on this Damiriak dumping station you call Earth until I trapped her. For what? I've molded this human society in my evil image. And she believed she could come along late in the ball game and change the rules into something ethical. How dare she! No, you won't have any dealings with her."

Jonara wanted to ask Nekara about Felifia. And what was that about a Damiriak dumping station? No, Jonara would not ask. It would only encourage Nekara. And who knew if Nekara was capable of telling the truth. Jonara looked around. Every street and store sign was bilingual—Catalan and English.

"Yes, yes!" Nekara said. "This country is bilingual. See the signs?"

"I see them," Jonara said as she tried to hide her shock.

"The Catalan words use a larger font. This country was a colony of Spain at one time, administered by the Kingdom of Aragon," Nekara said.

"Another lie! The Revolutionary War was fought against—" Jonara started.

"The Catalans," Nekara finished.

"The British!" Jonara said.

"Now how can you say that about these United States of Amerigo Vespucci, an Italian under the command of Fernando the II of Aragon?" Nekara asked.

"It's history!" Jonara said. "I learned history in school."

"Your old school, from your old life. But that has changed. Look around you, Joni. The cars—do they look like the America you know?" Nekara asked.

"No. They look like European cars," Jonara said.

"Look at this building, Jonara. Read the English title," Nekara said.

"Corpus Christi Detention Center for the Sexually Insane," Jonara read. "I don't remember this here before."

"Because it wasn't," Nekara said. "Let's go inside. Oh silly me, we can't go in until I unfreeze time. Here."

Nekara made some hand signals against her abdomen. Cars drove past, trees moved in the wind, and pedestrians continued walking.

"There. Come along, Joni," Nekara urged.

"No. You're trying to trick me further," Jonara said.

"And you have something better to do?" Nekara asked. "As I said before, I'm the only friend you have. Besides, this building can't hurt you. You're not one of the sexually insane. Oh wait— there was that thing with Cerafina. Hmm."

"What is that supposed to mean?" Jonara asked.

"Oh nothing. Come along then, Joni," Nekara urged.

Jonara heaved a big sigh.

"Yes," Nekara said. "Enjoy the misery. The frustration. The futility."

"Whatever you say I am, I'm not," Jonara said.

"A telltale sign of a love-hate relationship," Nekara said. "I accept your words of affection. I can read you oh so easily. Come then and visit the detention center. It will enlighten you."

"Enlighten, yeah, right!" Jonara said sarcastically.

But Jonara had nothing better to do, as Nekara stated.

"I hate it when she's right," Jonara mumbled.

"I know you do," Nekara said with a grin.

The two entered the detention center.

"Welcome," said a tour guide. "Are you here for the tour?"

"Yes, we are," Nekara said before Jonara could say anything.

"Very good. Follow me, please," said the tour guide. "We like to keep our patients happy in their confinement."

"I don't understand," Jonara said. "This looks like a zoo, not a jail. Why are these sexual predators on display for us? Why are they behind bars like monkeys or something?"

Nekara laughed.

"Your little friend lives a sheltered life," the tour guide said to Nekara.

"Very sheltered," Nekara said.

"I will explain," the tour guide said. "This is not a jail. This is not a prison. There are no sexual predators here. That means no rapists, no pedophiles, none of that. This is a psychiatric hospital. Our patients are sick. They believe they are attracted to people of the same gender. Some are simply confused. Others have mental impairments. Some respond to simple therapy. These two men in this cage, for example. They're practicing what to say to a woman, how to take her on a date, and how to be attractive to her."

"You can't learn how to fall in love," Jonara said.

"You have much to learn about this world," Nekara said. "Love is taught. The Church decides the proper guidelines to follow. Some simply need extra tutoring."

"That's right," the tour guide said. "You understand the process well, Miss...Miss..."

"Nekara Redding," Nekara said.

"Miss Nekara, I don't mean to sound forward, but we have a shortage of staff at this facility. If you should find yourself in need of work or—"

"Thank you," Nekara said. "It's good to know I'm needed."

"You would be well loved and appreciated here," the tour guide said. "Our patients have the utmost respect for those in authority."

"As it should be," Nekara laughed.

"It's all wrong! Men and women should be free to love whoever they wish!" Jonara blurted.

The area hushed into silence. The tour guide frowned on Jonara, looked up at Nekara, and nodded her head in affirmation.

"I understand," the tour guide said. "You already have a patient. A field trip?"

"Yes," Nekara said. "It's her alternative therapy."

"I'm not a patient!" Jonara blurted again.

"Early stages," the tour guide said. "You have a long way to go."

"Yes, but we'll get her retrained, won't we Jonara?" Nekara grinned.

Jonara held silent.

"Why don't you protest again?" Nekara said.

"Good," the tour guide said to Nekara. "Challenge her beliefs."

"Yes, Jonara," Nekara said. "Look closely at your beliefs. Look around you. Do you wish to continue living like these poor deluded folk? Or do you wish to live a healthy and happy life in society, free of this confinement?"

"Society is already confined. You confined it!" Jonara said.

"Reversed poles and delusional," the tour guide said. "Have you pursued drug therapy yet?"

"No," Nekara said. "But I'm sure we won't need to go that far, will we Jonara?"

Jonara eked out a smirk.

"I applaud your positive attitude," the tour guide said.

"Oh, I'm full of positive thoughts," Nekara said. "Isn't that right, Jonara?"

Jonara smirked again. The tour guide continued leading the two through the detention center. Cages alternated between gay men and lesbians. The "patients" were sullen and downtrodden as if resigned to their fate.

"They need education, enlightenment," Jonara thought to herself.

"We provide them with the best educational materials available," the tour guide said. "Here—I'm sure you recognize this book."

"Procreation and God's Plan," Nekara read. "A standard read."

"Procreation and someone's plan," Jonara said. "It's rigged!"

"Paranoia?" the tour guide asked Nekara.

"Of course," Nekara replied.

"Rethink the drug therapy. It does wonders for her type," the tour guide said.

"I'm not a type!" Jonara said.

"It's amazing how drugs control outbursts," the tour guide said. "You'll be doing her and the Church a favor. Trust us."

"Shall we go, Joni?" Nekara said.

Jonara held silent again. The two exited the detention building and walked down the sidewalk.

"Okay, Nekara. You've had your fun. I know this is fake. Gay people don't live in zoos," Jonara said.

"I know. They should be killed immediately," Nekara said.

"That's not what I said," Jonara said.

"You didn't have to," Nekara said. "Only recently has the Church changed its stance on gay people. The Church shows mercy."

"This isn't mercy!" Jonara said.

"Isn't it though?" Nekara continued. "Gays were executed routinely until they gained rights ten years ago."

"What!? That's impossible," Jonara said.

"Shall we go back inside the detention center and ask the tour guide? What do you suppose she'll say?" Nekara asked.

Jonara did not answer.

"That's right. You know I'm right. And I love you, Jonara."

"Stop it!" Jonara demanded. "You're making me sick."

"You're already sick, but it's not my doing. You love that Cerafina girl, am I right? No, don't answer. But she doesn't love you. She can't. She has a boyfriend. And she knows as should you that her immortal soul would be damned to Hell if she strayed from God's Plan," Nekara said.

"I won't be coerced," Jonara said. "No institution can force me into anything."

Nekara grinned.

"You're talking with me, aren't you?" Nekara asked.

"What is that supposed to mean?" Jonara asked.

"You know what it means. You don't need coercing. But why remind you? You can deny all you wish, and it won't change a thing. But back to the homosexual issue. Times are changing, Jonara. These rehabilitation centers are about to be closed down. No, not in a year. The existing patients will live their lives out here, but once they die, that's it."

"What are you talking about? Even if I believe this nightmare—which I don't—you would have to make room for new patients," Jonara said.

"There won't be new patients—not after October the 14th," Nekara laughed.

"Oh I get it. This wretched society will go back to executing gays," Jonara said.

"Oh you don't get it," Nekara said. "There's something better than this messy business of execution. Don't get me wrong—there's nothing better than a prolonged death. But Americans can be too compassionate at times. They'll put a person to sleep mercifully. I say this—bring back the Nazi methods of death. No, not Nazi—ancient Roman. Crucifixion. Misery and suffering *in extremis*. Jonara, some sacrifices must be made for the greater good. After the 14th, the Roman Catholic Church will have achieved its ultimate goal in saving souls—that of controlled procreation."

"No church can legislate life," Jonara said.

"How naïve you are. Good. The more ignorant you are, the more helpful you'll be with The Plan. It's my plan, Jonara, and yours too now that I'm your faithful servant," Nekara said.

"The universe isn't like that," Jonara said. "The birds and the bees—"

"Could also be under our control, if we want them. Think of it. We can eliminate mosquitoes. We can promote endangered species like the bald eagle and the passenger pigeon," Nekara said.

"The passenger pigeon is extinct," Jonara said.

"We can bring it back," Nekara said.

"It would be hunted to extinction again," Jonara said.

"We can prevent those types of people from being born," Nekara said. "You see, Jonara? You and I will remake the world for the better. For the good of all."

"Your monologue is getting really old," Jonara said. "My Water Ruby has no power. I have no power. Everything you're saying is a lie. You know what I really think? I think I'm in a catatonic state. Yeah, I'm in a nightmare. And you're torturing me. I may or may not wake up again. I don't know. But the world is in the waking world. It's safe. And that's it. Period. I'm stressed out and tired. Nanna Geneva died, and I've spent too much time looking into the past. Yeah, that's it. I'm just going to go back to Nanna Geneva's house and take a nap. And I'm not talking to you anymore, Nekara. If I'm going to spend the rest of my life locked up in this world, oh well, hogwash happens."

"As you wish—for now, Jonara. But you'll call for me again," Nekara said, and she vanished.

CHAPTER 2:

The Induration Event

2023 Oct 8, Sun Afnoon. Corpus Christi, Texas.

"There you are, Jonara," Marcus said. "One moment you were there, and the next you were gone."

"I went out for a walk," Jonara said. "But I'm back."

"Good. We're expecting company. Bishop Tárrega of the Corpus Christi diocese is on his way over here. He'll accompany the family to Corpus Christi Bay where new vitacepticals are being built," Marcus said.

"Huh?" Jonara asked. "What are you talking about?"

"Your amnesia must be very bad. Eva wanted to put you in the hospital, but I talked her into keeping you with us. It's important, I think, that you see for yourself the future of the Church and the human race," Marcus explained.

The doorbell rang.

"That must be him," Marcus said as he walked over to the door.

"Hello, Mr. Cracbern," a young male said.

"Good afternoon, Greg," Marcus said.

"Greg Dannerstadt? Oh, no!" Jonara said.

"Come in, come in," Marcus said.

"Thank you, sir," Greg replied.

Greg held a hand behind his back as he entered Geneva's house.

"These are for you, Jonara," Greg said as he produced a bouquet of flowers.

"I see you've met Greg," Marcus said.

Jonara stood and stared at the flowers, not knowing what to do about them.

"Take them," Greg said. "They're for you."

"Jonara? Your manners!" Marcus said.

"I don't think I should accept them," Jonara said.

"Jonara—Greg isn't the Anti-Christ or anything like that," Marcus said.

"No," Greg grinned quite devilishly, "not the Anti-Christ."

Greg moved toward Jonara and whispered in her ear, "But I could be your Anti-Christ."

"Get away from me!" Jonara said as she pushed Greg away.

"Jonara. Greg is our guest. You should treat him as such. Offer him something to drink."

"Grrr," Jonara muttered. "Would...you...like...something...to drink?"

"Yes, thank you," Greg said. "I'd like a cola, if you have one."

Jonara disappeared into the kitchen and returned with an open bottle of cola. Greg extended his hand to accept it, but Jonara flipped the bottle and poured the beverage onto Greg's shirt.

"Jonara! That's rude! You know better than that," Marcus said.

"That's okay, Mr. Cracbern. When a girl gives a guy attention, it means she likes him, no matter what kind of attention it is," Greg said. "Did she tell you she's my new girlfriend?"

"No, she didn't. When did you two start going steady?" Marcus asked.

"At church this morning," Greg said.

"He's not my boyfriend!" Jonara protested.

Voices carried from just outside the front door.

"More guests," Marcus said.

In through the front door walked Eva, Evanita, and Johnny.

"No sweat, just family," Marcus said.

"And what does that mean?" Eva asked as she gave Marcus a kiss on the cheek.

"Eva, darling. This is Greg Dannerstadt. Greg, this is my wife, Eva Cracbern, her daughter Evanita Pindus, and Evanita's husband, Johnny Pindus."

"Nice to meet you," they all said.

"Greg is Jonara's new boyfriend," Marcus said.

"You're the one from church," Evanita said. "That was a naughty trick you pulled."

"Yes, ma'am, and I apologize. But I only wanted to share the moment with my girlfriend," Greg said as he stood next to Jonara and threw his arm around her shoulder.

Jonara pushed his arm away.

"So where is the bishop?" Eva asked.

"He's on the way," Marcus said.

"Bishop? What bishop?" Greg asked.

A knock at the door interrupted the conversation. Johnny opened the door.

"Bishop Tárrega," Marcus said. "Please, come in."

"Thank you," the bishop said.

"Tárrega?" Greg asked. "Are you related to Francisco Tárrega, the Spanish musician?"

"I wish I were," the bishop said.

"Excuse the lad, Bishop," Marcus said. "May I introduce my lovely wife, Eva Cracbern, and her daughter, Evanita Pindus?"

"Pleased to meet you," the bishop said.

"Also, here is Evanita's husband, Johnny Pindus, and their daughter, Jonara Pindus."

"And me," Greg said.

"Yes, the lad's name is Greg Dannerstadt," Marcus said.

"Another one of the family?" the bishop asked.

"Not yet!" Greg grinned.

"Greg is Jonara's boyfriend. He's Catholic," Marcus explained.

"Very good," the bishop said.

"He's not my boyfriend," Jonara said.

The bishop smiled.

"Jonara is suffering from a concussion and isn't thinking clearly," Marcus said. "She seems to have forgotten her Catholic faith."

"Oh, that won't do at all," Bishop Tárrega said. "We must help you with your spiritual recovery."

"And there's no better way than by visiting Corpus Christi Bay and the site of the new vitaceptical," Evanita said.

"Vitacepticals," the bishop corrected. "There are many people in Texas. One vitaceptical by itself couldn't possibly address all their needs. The entire perimeter of the bay will contain vitacepticals. Come. We should go to the bay now. I intend to address the crowds on this very subject. You are my special guests, of course, and you will ride in my bus."

"Wow!" Evanita said.

Bishop Tárrega led the group outside Geneva's house and into a tour bus decorated with crosses and images of Jesus wearing a thorned crown.

"Hop aboard!" the bishop said.

Marcus, Eva, Evanita, Johnny, Jonara, and Greg followed the bishop onto the bus. The driver closed the bus door and drove the bus to the Vagatti house. He beeped once. The Vagatti family exited their house and entered the bus—Davino, Marina, Leo, Cerafina, and Cerafina's boyfriend—Tony. Cerafina and Tony sat behind Greg and Jonara. Jonara sat by the window and wasn't happy about sharing a seat with Greg.

"So which hussy number is this?" Cerafina asked as the bus drove toward Corpus Christi Bay. "Is she six or seven?"

"Now now, Cera my love," Greg said. "You know I only have eyes for you."

"You can cut out the crud," Cerafina said. "Tony's my boyfriend now."

"Yeah, Greg. Leave my girl alone," Tony said. "Isn't it bad enough you get your girls to do your pranks?"

"Me? Never," Greg laughed.

"No?" Cerafina continued. "What about when you sent her to my house yesterday? She called me a dyke."

"No, I didn't," Jonara said.

"Yeah, you did," Tony said.

"Joni, my love, is it true?" Greg asked.

"I went to Shlifa's house yesterday," Jonara started.

"Shlifa?" Greg asked.

"Yeah, see? She called me that too," Cerafina said.

"You shouldn't call people names," Greg said. "It's rude, my sweet little girlfriend."

"Quit calling me your girlfriend," Jonara said. "I'm not."

"Everyone knows you are," Tony said. "At least you're one of them. But I'll never understand why they all fall for you, Dannerstadt."

"Because I'm a special and sensitive kind of guy," Greg grinned.

"Greg, you make me want to puke," Jonara said. "Tony, you don't know what you're talking about. And Cerafina—I wish you would dig deep in your heart for what is pure and right in this world, and see that these guys next to us are a bunch of jerks."

Greg slapped Jonara.

"Hey!" Jonara said. "I'll sue you for that."

"You ain't got no rights," Greg said. "A guy can slap a woman to keep her in line. It's a dogma from Vatican III."

"Vatican III? There's no such thing," Jonara said.

"You see? She's nuts!" Cerafina said.

"Her grandpa said she's suffering amnesia from a bump on the head," Greg said.

"You mean the one I gave her when I kicked her off my front porch?" Cerafina said. "But she got that bump after I kicked her. What about her crazy talk before that, when she called me a dyke? How do you explain that?"

"You really are a crazy girl, carrot-top!" Greg said to Jonara. "Here—let me massage that bump on your head."

Greg moved his fingers through Jonara's hair.

"Yuck, yuck, and triple yuck!" Jonara said. "I wish someone would get me out of this bus!"

1263 Jul 15. Montseny Mountains, Iberia.

"Isn't the view beautiful?" Nekara asked Jonara.

Jonara stood at the end of a dirt road with Nekara the Red. It was a sunny warm day, but clouds loomed from the west.

"What is this? Where am I?" Jonara asked. "Send me back."

"You wanted out of the bus," Nekara said. "So here you are."

"I never said to take me to these mountains," Jonara said.

"You recognize them, don't you?" Nekara asked.

"How can I? The Water Ruby doesn't work anymore. And this place seems different. The trees, the plants. That stone hut over there looks old, very old."

"That hut is someone's home," Nekara said. "The year is 1263, it's July 15th, and you are on the Montseny Mountains."

"Spain!" Jonara said.

"No, not yet," Nekara said. "At least not the collection of regions you know as Spain. But it will be. And there's an old man approaching on the road. See him in the distance?"

"The one riding the half-wagon?" Jonara asked.

"You Americans are pathetic," Nekara said. "The least you can do is learn a little history! That's not a half-wagon—there's no such thing."

"But it has two wheels. Where are the other two?" Jonara asked.

"It has two wheels because it's a cart!" Nekara said. "A one-horse cart! But that's not important. What is important is the man riding in the cart. Do you recognize him?"

"Santa Claus?" Jonara asked.

"And Jonara is the chosen one? The one who could cast Miramish chants? The one who indurated this mountain slope? But she knows absolutely nothing. Nothing!" Nekara said.

"That's not true. I know lots of things. I know how to read and write. I know math. I know the Presidents of the United States," Jonara said.

"Oh the agony of isolation! But I love you, Jonara. Your ignorance is a fuel for misery. Knowledge is power, and power overcomes misery, but since you have neither knowledge nor power, your misery is self-fulfilling. Now before I begin my triumph over Felifia..."

"Felifia!" Jonara burst. "You and Felifia? Here? In these mountains?"

"Of course! These are the mountains where your grandmother and great-grandmother crashed in the De Havilland jet. You cast the indurate chant—a chant that spread through time and unified collective thought. The old man there? His name is

Rabbi Nachmanides. A Jewish scholar from Girona. You remember that name, don't you?"

"Not the scholar, but Nanna Geneva was born in Girona and
grew up there in the abbey," Jonara said.

"Yes, but before—before my sweeping arm eradicated variety
and diversity, Jewish people had a great educational center in
Girona, and Rabbi Nachmanides was their leader—for his time,"
Nekara said.

"You could be lying, of course," Jonara said.

"I could, but why lie when the truth is more enjoyable? The
rabbi is actually on his way to Barcelona to defend his Jewish
faith against Friar Pablo Christiani—a Roman Catholic," Nekara
explained.

"I had a feeling you were going to say that," Jonara said.
"Seems I can't get away from the Catholic religion."

"And why should you?" Nekara said.

"Because I want to be me and live my life the way I want,
not the way—"

"The Church wants? Or God wants?" Nekara laughed.

"That's the Catholic god," Jonara said. "God could be a
woman."

"She is a woman. She's me," Nekara said.

"No, if you are to be a deity, you'd be the devil," Jonara said.

Nekara grinned and said, "It's more fun being the devil."

Jonara paused for a moment.

"If he's on his way to Barcelona," Jonara asked at length,
"then why is he here? These mountains are out of the way."

"Ah, something intelligent," Nekara said. "Yes, the mountains are out of the way. He diverted from the main road at Sant
Celonia to take this road. And here he is."

"But why? What good is it?" Jonara asked.

"Why?" Nekara asked. "Look around you. Isn't this a great
place to sit and have a think?"

"I guess," Jonara said. "You're saying he's come here to
think?"

"Yes. He's here for Jewish meditation as a way to grow closer to God. That's me, you know."

"You're lying again," Jonara said.

"Perhaps. But he is here for Jewish meditation. See for yourself!" Nekara said.

Rabbi Nachmanides stopped the horse and tied the reins to a tree. He produced a small table and stool from the cart and placed them on the ground in a soft patch of grass. Next, he placed a candleholder with two candles on the table and lit them. He placed a covered breadbasket on the table, a bottle of wine, a cup, and a small plate on the table. The rabbi sat on the stool, cut some bread, poured the wine in the glass, wrapped a prayer shawl around himself, and spoke a prayer in Hebrew. He then ate the bread and drank the wine.

"He's having lunch," Jonara said.

"He's alone," Nekara said. "Haven't you ever lost yourself in thought while eating alone?"

"I can't remember such a time," Jonara boasted.

"Observe. He is looking around and reciting additional prayers," Nekara said.

"Nekara—what is your game?" Jonara said. "So far you've shown me these mountains and this rabbi eating lunch. So what? You can't tell me that somehow this man has something to do with the future and why all of my family is Catholic. He's Jewish. I don't see the connection."

"My dear, it is because he's Jewish that your family is now all Catholic," Nekara said.

"What does he do, dump Judaism for Christianity?"

"No, just the opposite!" Nekara said. "He defends Judaism so well that the Jewish Expulsion is delayed until 1492!"

"Delayed! What are you talking about?" Jonara asked.

"Just this. I'm about to battle the precious and almighty Felifia of Eho Miriam. Me, Nekara the Red of Eho Dahma. This is the mountain where she beat me and forced my spirit to wander in the shadows of men's desires. But now things are different. Your indurate chant will change everything. There! Look at that light! So ethereal, so spiritual. A human form of light without flesh! Behold, the battle begins!"

The dark clouds approached from the west.

"God," Rabbi Nachmanides said. "Hear me now on these mountains. The storm clouds roll in. You warn me of peril, and I listen. In five days, I defend your name against those who would split you three ways and claim that a messiah has delivered us. I ask for insight and strength. Allow my free speech before the king and friar. Hear me now, O Lord!"

The rabbi looked up and saw a bright light on a mountain peak. A voice spoke from the light, but he did not understand the words. The voice spoke to the dark clouds, and the clouds responded with thunder.

Jonara stood by the trembling rabbi and hugged him. This hug connected Jonara to the rabbi's world, and he saw her.

"Little girl? Where did you come from?" he asked.

There was no time for introductions. The conflict between Felifia and Nekara began and captured Jonara's and the rabbi's full attention. The rabbi understood nothing of the conflict—hearing thunder when words were spoken. Despite Jonara's loss in ability to speak Miramish, she was able to understand all that was spoken between the bright light—Felifia, and the dark cloud—Nekara.

Felifia in Miramish

Nekara, Nekara.
Hiu kail e zhioko ishu shai feriaifa?
Bilefo tienu di Elesha.
Nia pelefo di tefiko di kail e voshara
Dhaku pilamefifa.

Translation

Nekara, Nekara.
Why do you hide in the sky?
Come down to Earth.
I wish to offer you love
And friendship.

Nekara in Dahmek

Kail tefirsk nau pamelfif?
Dhark voshar?
Tefirsk e kail dir nau voshave
Dhark sharlf deniu, Felifia?

Translation

You offer me friendship?
And common-love?
Do you offer me deep-love
And pleasure-love too, Felifia?

Felifia in Miramish

Wei, wei!
Ulu tefikao di kail e shishu voshari
Felito kail e tienu
Veletu kaish e gelafika
Opeifu keloriku pelaufu depi,

Translation

Yes, yes!
If offering you these loves
Brings you down
From your brew
Of dark cloudy thoughts,

Felifia in Miramish

Dhaku kelorithu felunaku paliti
Opeifu yuakata,
Dodu nia tefiko tiren e loreifu!

Translation

And impulsive lightning acts
Of wickedness,
Then I offer them all!

Nekara in Dahmek

Nui garfk!
Yosh ule nia pliurstyot e tilen!
Nia flifstyot Eho Miriame
Velt shair shkavat orp tupoit.
Eho Miriame narzgyot e nau,
Shair Rolarme narzgyot e nau,
Dhark e kail narzgyot e nau!
Halk vol nui rifat
Yarme flaursh lukaimespyot
Velt kiart?
Nia dhai artharaskyot.
Weir, nau.
Yarme flaursh luausnyot,
Nia kiarstyot.
Nia dhai tuyoislyot e dir Eho Dahma.
Kail tuthuke kodi glersk,
Kail friorskyot nui tuyoil.
Vede nia oir belveskyot.
Nia vorastyot flaursh
Lieme Eho Dahma,
Nui miolfu laurk.
Yosh Eho Dahma fiulotelsfyot,
Nia dhai miafskyot okuan
Vu kail dhark nui plornyek.
Nui lepalu rifat vol tuyoil
Dir tshunu Damiriaku tairgu buarnk
Dhai glersk vu tilesh mirshu brienf,
Elesh.
Kail vol fersh orp nui tuyoil,
Dhark mahir kail kemirsp
Nui pamelfif?
Hiur tuthuke kodi nia orshirsp
Zhesh e zhaukaik?
Litarsne kail dir brels nau,
Shair garfk e kail pliurstyot,
Lieme fruirt yosh dhor liaik
Vivoan shair e rolarme,
Shair plornyek,
Dhark shair Damiriaku Andauf?
Dotirseit kail nui toirkyek

Translation

My brew!
As if I created it!
I brought Eho Miriam
From the brink of extinction.
Eho Miriam made me,
The Council made me,
And you made me!
What was my thanks
When life returned
From death?
I was inverted.
Yes, me.
When life flourished,
I died.
I was exiled to Eho Dahma.
You should know,
You witnessed my exile.
But I didn't concede.
I built life
On Eho Dahma,
My new planet.
As Eho Dahma prospered,
I was chained again
By you and my people.
My final thanks was exile
To this Damiriak garbage dump
Known by its other name,
Earth.
You were part of my exile,
And now you want
My friendship?
Why should I accept
Such treachery?
Do you plan to place me,
The brew you created,
On display as a trophy
Before the council,
The people,
And the Damiriak Empire?
Will you pick my bones

Nekara in Dahmek

Dir grelirst kaish garfk
Dhark parzve nui ranirp
Dir nuish Damiriaku plornyek?

Translation

To stir your brew
And feed my flesh
To our Damiriak people?

Felifia in Miramish

Niai koro feshinatui.
Niai koro voshavovui.
Nia liutiro di voshavovo kail.
Nia makoiu taukio.
Nia kemipo shai kufeweka mafu kail.
Vedu nia oi ferepa kodi
Kofo kail e bupeliuto
Shai fiada nuish e peloni
Kiokio zhau kelitiu di rukofito.
Bilefo tienu, Nekara.
Rupo kaish e geraka
Ishu shai feriaifa.

Translation

We were partners.
We were lovers.
I continue to love you.
I never stopped.
I want the best for you.
But I can't
Have you destroy
The beauty our people
Worked so hard to preserve.
Come down, Nekara.
Leave your anger
In the sky.

Nekara in Dahmek

Kail kemirsp shair kufwerk maf nau?
Halk yarke kodi kail
Tefirsk dir nau mahir?
Dhark e hiur kail gloifst e nau
Borsh dhor nuarn?
Nia bupliurstyot
Halk nirske kodi dhai bupliurstyot
Dir luvorast e nuish plornyek.
Nia dhai grusfyot bierpu ofelarve
Dir blersk shair vimorlyek
Orp sharlorp
Hirsh vaufirstyot e nuish plornyek
Ishe nuatshyek orp shair flairth.
Shirsh nuatshyek e ganlarsfyot
Shair belurt e dhark veidon.
Nui trafirt vol piuvoradu, weir.
Vede til nirshke kodi dhai tiskyot.
Nia tiskyot shair galirku kiork,
Kairsh galirku kiork.
Kail plushirspyot flenift
Maf shair Andaufange luvashil,
Dhark nia plushirspyot e trupaf
Maf lor yarsh dhai bupliurstyot.
Vede tshade vil kuden e nau.
Nia narzgaut e tshunu halrelt
Yosh nia loirsf.

Translation

You want the best for me?
What would you
Offer to me now?
And why do you charge me
With a crime?
I destroyed
What had to be destroyed
To rebuild our people.
I was given full approval
To break the bonds
Of sentiment
Which imprisoned our people
In rituals of the past.
These rituals ignored
The present and future.
My job was unpopular, yes.
But it had to be done.
I did the dirty work,
Your dirty work.
You received credit
For the Empire's rebirth,
And I received blame
For all that was destroyed.
But that is behind me.
I am making this world
As I desire.

Nekara in Dahmek

Taursk beirshaskaut e nau, Felifia.
Tirida-iri tash klorshyek
Vil deniu ralzhu maf zhesh beirshak.
Virsf e vark dir Eho Miriame.
Virsf e vark dhark rufsp nau
Dir nui klaifirf,
Tshunu laurk—Elesh.

Translation

Stop pursuing me, Felifia.
Fifty-three hundred years
Is too long for such pursuit.
Go back to Eho Miriam.
Go back and leave me
To my kingdom,
This planet—Earth.

Felifia in Miramish

Nia kofo baimata, Nekara.
Nia kofo baimata mafu shai firodi
Yashu gokio
Nui ferupu zhumanu sharifa,
Dhaku kaimio shan ishetu
Dho gaifiku boritu sharadala.
Nia pelefo nia ferepa kodi
Lutiko dauna.
Nia pelefo Eho Miriama
Makoiu utivifio
Shai zhaura-opeifu-felaushu beroika.
Nia pelefo kail e dhaku nia
Ferepa kodi koto deiludu felaushi,
Opiolu veletu shai pelatha
Yashu sheliakio shai Daufika
Ishetu shai Ehoi
Opeifu Miriama dhaku Dahma.
Nia yaka kodi tiko inodizha
Mafu kail,
Nui zhumanu sharifa, Nekara.
Vedu nia oi ferepa kodi ferilako kail
Di kuariko dhaku kauvuto
Vu kaishfal e liemu Elesha.
Buliriko veletu shai koili
Opeifu kaish gaifika,
Dhaku lepo nau thoisha-di-thoisha.
Niai hemefu koto litani
Mafu dho felianua.
Hiu oi ferepa kodi niai
Kuno nuish e felianua okuanu?

Translation

I have sorrow, Nekara.
I have sorrow for the events
That took
My sweet junior wife,
And turned her into
A bitter vicious woman.
I wish I could
Redo time.
I wish Eho Miriam
Never underwent
The loss-of-life crisis.
I wish you and I
Could have had quiet lives,
Away from the controversy
That split the Empire
Into the Ehos
Of Miriam and Dahma.
I would do anything
For you,
My junior wife, Nekara.
But I cannot allow you
To sulk and suffer
By yourself on Earth.
Descend from the heights
Of your bitterness,
And meet me face-to-face.
We once had plans
For a family.
Why can't we
Begin our family again?

Nekara in Dahmek

Baimart oir tuarsne
Shair Andauf.
Mahil til hausf
Nui grulirkyek orp luterpuet.

Translation

Sorrow does not change
The Empire.
Nor does it heal
My wounds of rejection.

Nekara in Dahmek

Kail e lorilf kodi voshazve nau,
Vede nia oir frelp kodi voshazve
Inowel.
Klorip e velt e nuish plornyek
Kokyot klairshskyot e nui dralt
Ishte braizhganor.
Shair thrishk orp nui walirsh
Dhai ushkausyot.
Voshar oir kloraskeit lieme kiart.
Vede yosh dir dhor fliarnwan,
Kail glersk yarsh
Niai mauak frelp kodi zhuverst
Borsh heme.
Nia dhai busheifstyot.
Nui thuvapyek dir frelsp
Miramishu shardanyek dir belshisp
Kokyot oir gailaskyot nau.
Nui thuvapyek dir frelsp
Dahmeku shardanyek dir belshisp
Kokyot oir gailaskyot nau shartu.
Zhaul halk luvaurs, nia fasp?
Nia prelsteit kail halk luvaurs:
Tshunu laurk brienfyotu Elesh
Vil nuime.
Shirsh vir nui luartyek,
Maf nia vorastaut dhor sholarf,
Velt shair klairshkyek orp nui dralt:
Tiauzhu, gufirku,
Pilapu, drukartu,
Kaiftu, dhark bushlerku.
Nia bietriesleit e nui nirshk
Maf e fiupliurt,
Dhark e kitrulis nui zhuarl
Lieme shirshu voashku raufpyek.

Translation

You might love me,
But I cannot love
Anymore.
Scorn from our people
Has scorched my heart
Into charcoal.
The forest of my youth
Was arsoned.
Love will not grow on death.
But as to a family,
You know that
We never can succeed
With one.
I was sterilized.
My efforts to enable
Miramish women to conceive
Did not help me.
My efforts to enable
Dahmek women to conceive
Did not help me either.
So what remains, I ask?
I will tell you what remains:
This planet named Earth
Is mine.
These are my children,
For I am building a humanity,
From the scorches of my heart:
Envious, lustful,
Obsessive, predatory,
Hateful, and destructive.
I will fulfill my need
For procreation,
And imprint my spirit
On these waste lands.

Felifia in Miramish

Ulu kaish e darala kilo kelaishokiou,
Dodu kerilapo nuime.
Nui darala dauteio
Mafu rau peishei.
Ulu kail oi ferepa kodi liushipo,
Dodu kerilapo nui shelada.
Nui biatha liushipeio
Mafu rau peishei.
Ulu dho haloreta

Translation

If your heart is scorched,
Then borrow mine.
My heart will beat
For us both.
If you cannot conceive,
Then borrow my body.
My womb will conceive
For us both.
If a world

Felifia in Miramish

Kail e pelefo di peliuto,
Dodu kelugo nau kaish e kapa.
Nuish e kapi thoritheio zhaishu,
Dhaku nago teshunu lauka
Ishetu dho beresha opeifu luthuka
Dhaku pelafa.
Fienara kilo oi kufu
Mafu fiupeliuta,
Mafu kiterulishaola,
Ilu mafu biebupa.
Nia gerutho di nui dereifa.
Gerutheio kail e di nau kaish?

Translation

You wish to create,
Then lend me your hand.
Our hands will hold fast,
And make this planet
Into a place of respect
And grace.
Loneliness is not good
For procreation,
For imprinting,
Or for fulfillment.
I give you my trust.
Will you give me yours?

Nekara in Dahmek

Kail e lorwak brelsyot e nau
Utine kiash e shpursh, Felifia,
Yosh kail kokyot ishe shair flairth
Borsh kaish lialirtyek orp diave.
Vede nia vil oir zhaul niarfu
Yosh nia vol ishe nui walirsh.
Maf walirsh vil leisheifa,
Vede shirft vil zhaukaik.
Nia hemf koiarskyot
Shair "dreirf" kutirp
Yosh lor walirshu kelerfyek
Dhai dalirs.
Vede shair yutharaf
Oir kauvurst e dreirf
Maf ralzhwelu tshome shair yaurp
Orp ome iwashreide.
Nia vil Nekara shair Fiesht.
Nia vil arfwelu
Dhark wel zhurnityotu.
Nia oir frelp kodi piutirsk
Halk shair yutharaf dalirsyot e nau.
Nia grusf kail tshunu viurtaut,
Felifia:
Naf kaish theiftu zhurde,
Lukaimesp dir shair Andauf,
Dhark oir blersf e vark.
Koko oir.
Nui morth vil kraltyotu e dinarlu,
Dhark tshunu laurk
Oyalirsf nui kiork.
Nui biorat klorask viurlu

Translation

You almost placed me
Under your spell, Felifia,
As you did in the past
With your words of melody.
But I am not so naïve
As I was in my youth.
For youth is exuberance,
But maturity is treachery.
I once worshipped
The "trust" deity
As all young girls
Are taught.
But the universe
Does not suffer trust
For longer than the whip
Of an eyelash.
I am Nekara the Red.
I am older
And more experienced.
I cannot undo
What the universe taught me.
I give you this warning,
Felifia:
For your own safety,
Return to the Empire,
And don't come back.
Don't.
My patience is worn thin,
And this planet
Awaits my work.
My power grows daily

Nekara in Dahmek	**Translation**
Dhark voilunirstaut kaish.	And is surpassing yours.
Nia oir plersf dir vaugast kail,	I do not wish to fight you,
Vede nia kokeit ule dhai fiushairsk.	But I will if provoked.
Virsf e vark, Felifia.	Go back, Felifia.
Virsf e vark dhark e kufliau!	Go back, and goodbye!

Rabbi Nachmanides prayed during this time. The winds picked up strength, the light of Felifia changed from steady to pulsing, and the rabbi's horse reared in fear.

"Easy, boy," the rabbi said, but his horse could not be settled.

"*Felito Nekara veletu shai feriaifa di shai beranita!* (Bring Nekara from the sky to the ground!)" Felifia chanted.

Beams of swirling and twisting light, like quickly growing branches of a tree, leapt from Felifia's arms and surrounded Nekara's clouds in the sky. In response, the winds increased with a fury like a gigantic wild bird flapping her wings with all her might to avoid being captured. Leaves swirled into creature-like figures and danced around the mountain. Several danced into Rabbi Nachmanides and parted in half to swirl around him. One such leaf-creature spooked the horse and chased it down the mountain. The rabbi took three steps toward the horse as if to follow, but his achy bones reminded him he was too old for such pursuit.

"*Krairzge Felifia borsh traishku thelirnyek orp e bushlerk!* (Blast Felifia with straight winds of destruction!)" Nekara shouted from the clouds.

A single, powerful blast of wind shot down from the clouds and into the mountainside. The trees leaned back from the wind. Dirt, leaves, and other debris shot across the slope as if a bomb blast had motivated them. Rabbi Nachmanides and Jonara were picked up by the wind and carried a dozen meters before being dropped.

"The storm grows worse," Rabbi Nachmanides said. "Yet the hut remains standing. I must seek its shelter."

Jonara and Rabbi Nachmanides ran for the hut. They reached the door, and the rabbi opened it.

"No one here," he said.

The hut was clean and lived-in, but the occupant or occupants were not there at the moment. In one corner stood a cylindrical tube with one end open and the other end egg-shaped and resting atop support rods connected to an unlit oil lamp. A green glass—much like a hand mirror—lay next to it. The rabbi and Jonara peered through holes in the wall and watched the storm between Felifia and Nekara.

"*Fepo biofu keriopi ivemu tireshfar!* (Set random eddies upon themselves!)" Felifia chanted.

Nekara's straight winds broke into eddies, like straight hair diverging into large, swooping curls. The curling air bounced off trees, boulders, the ground, and many landed blows into one another, canceling their effect. The curls grew and rebounded into the clouds where they engulfed Nekara, but only temporarily. Nekara halted her wind assault and launched another weapon.

"*Brutasp shair kavolaryek emde Felifia borsh dialirkyek orp heidorn!* (Burst the heavens onto Felifia with trunks of water!)" Nekara shouted.

The clouds opened up with an intensified downburst of rain. The rain beat on the hut like thousands of squirrels scampering across the roof for their lives. The scampering sound gave way to a steady blast, like multiple fire hoses pouring tree-trunks worth of water down at a time. Several holes opened up in the ceiling, and water poured into the hut as if the hut were suddenly sinking in a lake.

"I'll drown! My Lord! Spare me from this storm!" Rabbi Nachmanides cried.

The hut filled with water like a swimming pool. The rabbi and Jonara stood on stools to catch air above the waterline. Various items in the hut floated about—not in idle up-and-down bobbing, but along with a strong flow of water such that the rabbi and Jonara were knocked off their stools several times and had to fight with all their strength to get their heads back above the waterline. The two stood on a table in the corner where a small water eddy held them against the wall.

"Felifia, help us!" Jonara called.

Jonara wished she could help the rabbi and herself with a Miramish chant of her own, but as hard as she tried, she could not remember a Miramish word. She shook the Moissan Ruby, but it remained dark and unresponsive.

"*Moitho feluana liemu heidona, lukaimo di biufita!* (Shine light on water, return to vapor!)" Felifia shouted.

The water level dropped in the hut. The air became hot, humid, and heavy. Jonara and Rabbi Nachmanides choked on the thick vapor.

"I can barely see," Jonara said. "The fog is too thick."

Fog poured out of the hut as the water evaporated. Rabbi Nachmanides opened the hut's door to the outside, and the last of the water and vapor poured out, but into what? Neither could see more than a half-meter in front of them.

"I shall be lost if this fog does not clear," Rabbi Nachmanides said. "I cannot see the way back to the road."

"Then I will help," Nekara boomed from the clouds above, although Nachmanides only heard the sound of thunder.

Nekara in Dahmek	**Translation**
Keirzge Felifia	Overwhelm Felifia
Borsh bioratyek orp leirde:	With powers of nature:
Thelim, heidorn,	Wind, water,
Fluarnk, dhark diuvart.	Lightning, and vortex.
Kliaushsk shair braft	Scour the ground
Yosh nui dralt dhai kliaushskyot.	As my heart was scoured.
Vutharsk shorsh	Purge those
Lowe dafirsk nau	Who challenge me
Velt e tshunu niugiuftu shkroilk.	From this mountain slope.

The fog lifted away into the clouds above. Water and other light debris lifted from the ground and ascended to the sky. Jonara's and Rabbi Nachmanides's hair flew directly up as if a huge vacuum cleaner were above their heads. He and Jonara felt light on their feet, and a dangerous sense of euphoria overcame them. For this reason, the two did not seek shelter in the hut but instead remained in the open and witnessed a funnel cloud of many hues weave and sway in the air as it migrated to the earth, like a huge tentacle of a squid or octopus.

The tentacle reached for Felifia, but she held up her hand as if slicing a rope in two halves and cried, "*Kifiaisho ishetu alisha!* (Divide into emptiness!)"

The tentacle-like funnel slit long-ways, creating two tentacle-like funnels—both leading up to the master cloud—Nekara. The tentacle funnels reached for Felifia and lifted her into the air.

"*Paumubo di kaishfar e dhaku oliriko ishu tufipi!* (Bind to yourselves and ascend in knots!)" Felifia cried.

The tentacles crisscrossed paths and entangled each other, but they maintained their grips on Felifia and continued lifting her into the air.

"*Oi di nau! Lununo nau!* (Not to me! Release me!)" Felifia cried.

Felifia pointed a finger at the closest knot. A brilliant cherry-red light leapt from her finger and penetrated both tentacles. The tentacles stopped ascending, loosened their grip on Felifia, and released her. She fell back to the earth and shouted:

"*Mumatho nui zhaila!* (Cushion my fall!)"

Felifia never landed on the earth. Nekara sent a lightning bolt down through the tentacles. The tentacles jerked as if resuscitated back to life. They swept down and re-lifted Felifia into the air. The lightning attempted to shock Felifia, but she held out her hand and repeated the word:

"*Moiko!* (Shield!)"

Felifia gasped for breath. One tentacle gripped around her neck, restricting her trachea. The other tentacle encircled her abdomen and squeezed. Her face turned cherry red from the increased blood energy. Felifia was not dying, but her position was seriously compromised. She summoned her strength and made a last effort to reason with Nekara.

Felifia in Miramish	Translation
Kail e nishoko di goko	You need to take
Dho kelitu reigina idu kaishfal,	A hard look at yourself,
Nekara.	Nekara.
Teshunu beriaka opeifu leidu viuki	This use of natural forces

Felifia in Miramish

Okuaneku felausha,
Okuaneku kaish theifu guafita,
Dhaku okuaneku
Kaish e voshariou ona,
Golisheio kail e feraikelu
Teshomu inei kelaishaola
Kail e pelushipio
Vaka ishu nuish e daufika.
Kail e sharo kail e teranito
Shishu viuki,
Vedu tir e teraniteio kail
Ulu tir e kokio oi lorudoliu.
Lukaimo teranita
Opeifu Eleshanga shelada
Dhaku shash e viuki
Di shashfal.
Dhaku kail e lukuaneio
Opeifu kaish theifu zhiuna
Ishu shai tuanita.

Translation

Against life,
Against your own kind,
And against
Your loved one,
Will scar you worse
Than any scorching
You received
Back in our Empire.
You believe you control
These forces,
But they will control you
If they haven't already.
Return control
Of Earth's body
And her forces
To herself,
And you will regain control
Of your own self
In the exchange.

Nekara in Dahmek

Maur!
Nia kokeit oir!

Translation

No!
I will not!

Felifia in Miramish/Mirsua

Dodu nia ishaiko
Koilu Miramishu Biorita:
Nias kilos Talithas Felifias
Opeifus Miriamas.
Serisus Bioritus Uferthuas
Maias-alifas-elifas-ilofas-orifas-
Urifas-hemes-hemes-hemes.
Nias gubelasos kailes, Nekaras.
Nias gubelasos kaises e zualas
Dhakus...

Translation

Then I invoke
High Miramish Power:
I am Princess Felifia
Of Miriam.
Serisian Power Identifier
M-A-E-I-O-
U-one-one-one.
I compress you, Nekara.
I compress your spirit
And...

"*Maur!* (No!)" Nekara boomed.

Nekara in Dahmek

Zhairsp yuarnu shriauk
Velt shair friaift, dhark e kriarsk
Lor Miramishu biorat!

Translation

Send white fire
From the sky, and shatter
All Miramish power!

Sustained lightning bolts carried through the tentacles (which maintained their grips on Felifia) and electrified Felifia. Felifia fought with all her strength to say the last words that would contain Nekara once and for all—words Jonara had never heard before, but words Jonara understood. They were a form of Miramish, but every word ended in the letter *s*, and most *sh/zh* consonants were replaced with *s/z*. The words sounded terrible—worse than Dahmek, and Jonara shuddered as Felifia pronounced each word ending, with the hissing seeping through her flesh like snakes writhing under her skin. Jonara referred to the altered version of Miramish as *Mirsua*.

Felifia was determined to end the conflict. She clutched something in her fist, held up her fist to Nekara, and uttered the last Mirsua words to complete the chant:

Felifia in Mirsua	**Translation**
Nias berelikos	I complete
Hakus nias e sokalitios.	What I started.
Nias e seloikas	I command
Kaises gaifikas dhakus kaifas	Your bitterness and hatred
Dis e selukos isus e sais pelaufis.	To stay in the clouds.
Nias gubelasos kaises e zualas	I compress your spirit
Dhakus dhausos kaises naikas	And transfer your psyche
Veletus tesunus haloretas	From this world
Dis e sais lamatis	To the origins
Opeifus nuises omalalikuis.	Of our ancestors.
Orinokos kaises naikas	Submit your psyche
Dis tesunus duavisas.	To this duavisha.
Kirus kails luvauseios	Here you will remain
Iutaunus daunas	Until time
Hethetos misefeluikus.	Judges otherwise.
Nias weifos tesunus e seloikas	I sign this command
Talithas Felifias opeifus Miriamas.	Princess Felifia of Miriam.
Dosikos!	Execute!

The tentacles and lightning bolts stopped their frantic movements and held fast—frozen in time. Felifia's beams of light that she first sent up after Nekara now converged on the tentacles and lightning bolts and converted them to additional beams of Felifia's light. Stripped of her weapons, Nekara shrieked in desperation, like a tired, spoiled brat being forced to bed for the night. Jonara and the rabbi saw what appeared to be an explosion in reverse—the clouds shrank and withered into the beams of light with the light growing stronger and brighter yet narrower. The clouds and beams of light shrank from sky-sized to tree-sized to bush-sized to football-sized to grape-sized and smaller all the while attached at its base to the pebble-sized duavisha in Felifia's hand. The last of the clouds and light, along with Nekara, slipped into the duavisha, and Felifia closed her hand into a fist.

"*Tiles dhais tikos!* (It is done!)" Felifia yelled in Mirsua.

Rabbi Nachmanides and Jonara looked around. The sky cleared. The sun beamed down and warmed them. Felifia walked down from the mountain and greeted the two.

"Go now and defend your faith," Felifia said to the rabbi.

"Who are you?" the rabbi asked. "Are you an angel of God?"

"I am Felifia. Do not worship me. I am a living being, similar to you. I am here to help, not destroy. You are a good man, Rabbi Nachmanides. Help and do not destroy. Here, your horse returns to you."

As Felifia said, the rabbi's horse returned from wherever it ran, pulling the cart behind it.

"I thought I would die on this mountain. But I am spared. I feel like a man given an extra life to live. I defend my faith and speak the truth no matter what consequences are pressed before me," the rabbi said.

"Good. All the best speed," Felifia said.

"Are you coming with me, little friend?" the rabbi asked Jonara.

"No, she cannot," Felifia said. "I have something to show Jonara."

"Jonara," the rabbi said. "Such a lovely name. I will remember you both. Thank you! Shalom!"

The rabbi rode down the mountain path on the way to Barcelona. Felifia turned to Jonara and took Jonara's hand.

"You will come with me. I will show you where Nekara's spirit must go," Felifia said.

"You won! Nekara said I made you lose! I don't understand. She said she would win."

"Nekara says many things. I won and lost. I didn't want to imprison Nekara like this, but it was necessary," Felifia said.

"Then my life will return to normal? Cerafina and I will be good friends again?" Jonara asked.

"It's not that simple," Felifia said. "Nekara's powers are still at work."

"Why don't you destroy her?" Jonara asked. "She's evil. You know it, and I know it."

"Even the worst cases may heal in time," Felifia said. "I won't destroy my junior wife."

Felifia snapped her free hand, and the two vanished from the Montseny Mountains.

Jelana's Cave. Mountains East of Asmara, Eritrea, Africa.

Felifia and Jonara arrived at the same cave opening where Jelana, Quadri, and Hakim stood in the 1950s.

"I've been here before," Jonara said.

"Yes. So have I," Felifia said.

Felifia led Jonara inside along the same narrow passageway with a wall-face to the left and a steep drop-off to the right.

"You can't place her here," Jonara said. "She'll be discovered."

"I know," Felifia said.

"You know? I don't understand," Jonara said. "She'll be discovered by Jelana Margo—the duavisha. And Marcus will get hold of it. And Nekara will corrupt him. And—"

With Felifia's power, the two traveled much more quickly than Jelana, Quadri, and Hakim had. The two were now crossing the bridge next to the sulfur pool.

"Don't think too much about it," Felifia said. "As I said, time will judge Nekara. I know of everything you speak."

"And still you'll place her in these caves? That's crazy! There must be another way," Jonara said.

The two arrived in the chamber where Jelana would fall in 1955.

"This is the place," Felifia said. "This is where my spaceship crashed."

"You? A spaceship? In here? Crashed?" Jonara asked.

"Well, not really a spaceship. An efferite sphere. The main portion crashed here, but three fragments broke off during entry into Earth's atmosphere and crashed elsewhere," Felifia explained.

"Where? Where did they crash?" Jonara asked.

"I'm surprised you have to ask. You should know at least one of the places if not two," Felifia laughed.

"Rome?" Jonara asked.

"Yes. The smallest fragment landed in Rome. The next largest fragment landed—"

"In Athens? Greece?" Jonara asked.

"Not quite. The Pindos Mountains. Samarina," Felifia said.

"That's where Fantina and her father lived!" Jonara said. "And the largest? Where did it land? In the United States? In Portland, Oregon? That's where my father found the Water Ruby."

"No," Felifia said. "The largest landed a kilometer east of Carreña, Spain. St. Renata's Abbey?"

"Of course! What was I thinking!" Jonara said. "But what about the Water Ruby? What about this?"

Jonara held the Moissan Ruby up to Felifia. Felifia took the stone and held it in her other hand, the first hand still holding onto the duavisha. Felifia closed her eyes and took two deep breaths.

"I remember the last time these two stones met," Felifia said.

Jonara looked into Felifia's eyes and saw tears welling up.

"You're sad," Jonara said. "Don't be sad."

Jonara hugged Felifia, and Felifia reciprocated.

"Thank you for the hug, Jonara. I was younger, so was she. We exchanged these as gifts before her exile from the Damiriak solar system. She gave me this unlocked duavisha—a special duavisha that has no restrictions, and I gave her the moishiana—what you call a *Water Ruby*. We had high hopes and plans. None of them came true."

"Then the Water Ruby belongs to you," Jonara said.

"No, not anymore," Felifia said as she returned it to Jonara. "It is in your possession now. You are destined to have it."

"Me? How? But if you gave it to Nekara...but you crashed here...wait a minute...does that mean Nekara crashed here too?"

"Nekara crashed on this planet, but not here," Felifia explained. "Her spaceship—also an efferite sphere—crashed and created Corpus Christi Bay in Corpus Christi, Texas. Two fragments broke off from her efferite sphere while entering Earth's atmosphere. The largest landed and created a bay in the Willamette River in Portland, Oregon. That bay is surrounded by Ross Island, Hardtack Island, Toe Island, and East Island. A smaller part broke off and landed at a point where four of your U.S. states meet—Utah, Colorado, Arizona, and New Mexico. Jonara—Nekara would do anything to corrupt all people on this planet. It would give her great power—power that could lead to worse things."

"What's worse than someone ruling this entire planet?" Jonara asked.

"I know that seems like the worst possible thing, but if she should accomplish world dominion, she could mount a threat against the Damiriak Empire again. And I don't know if we could stop her. It was all we could do to exile her the first time to Eho Dahma, the second time to this planet, and now the third time to this duavisha," Felifia explained. "And as strongly devoted as I am to Nekara, I cannot keep this duavisha with me. I must cast it into the pool below where time will judge it."

"No! Felifia, I mean, Princess Felifia, please! She'll be discovered! She'll grow again! There must be a better way. Take her back to your Empire. Get rid of her there. Don't leave her on Earth. We have enough problems," Jonara begged.

"Your suggestion is tempting," Felifia said. "How I would like to take her home and keep her in a small jar on my mantelpiece where she would be safe. That's the easy way. But something would happen. I would feel sorry for her and let her out. She would grow large again and wreak havoc on the Empire. And I would protect her to the detriment of my people. No, I cannot."

"But she's not safe here either," Jonara said. "She'll get out again."

"I know Doctor Jelana finds the duavisha. I know Nekara gets loose and torments men. And I know what she has done to you," Felifia said.

"Have you no heart? You can spare this world of her. You can get my life back," Jonara said.

"You Earth people have such short vision. Miramish women have deep vision into the future and can see how the ends work out. I do not cast this duavisha into the pool with a light heart. I know the havoc she will wreak on this world. But for the ends to work out properly, this is the only way, as ugly as it may seem. Someone once taught me that the hardest part about achieving success is knowing that one must suffer incredibly for a portion of the journey. I do not advocate needless suffering. This is not a haphazard decision. But it is the best one for the distant future," Felifia said.

"Whose future? Yours? What about mine?" Jonara asked.

"Some people will suffer more. Some will pay with their lives. I know this. Nekara taught me that lesson when Eho Miriam nearly lost her population of women. I'm willing to make the sacrifice," Felifia said.

"Well I'm not," Jonara said. "Give me that duavisha. I'll watch it."

Jonara reached for the duavisha, but she was too late. Felifia cast it into the pool of water below where it sank to the depths.

"It's not fair!" Jonara said. "It's not!"

1263 Jul 20-24. The Disputation of Barcelona. The Kingdom of Aragon, Iberia.

Jonara appeared in the royal palace of James I of Aragon. In attendance were the king, his court, knights, Jewish and Christian dignitaries, Friar Raymond of Penyaforte, Rabbi Nach-manides, and Friar Pablo Christiani. Friar Raymond made last-minute preparations as those in attendance engaged in light discussion.

"As I promised before, my Lord," Friar Christiani said to King James, "based on the Talmud and other Jewish writings, I can prove that Jesus is the Messiah."

"Let us begin," Friar Raymond said. "There are three subjects to be discussed. One—has the Messiah appeared or not? Two—is, according to Scripture, the Messiah a divine or a human being? And three—do the Jews or Christians hold the true faith? Friar Pablo Christiani will answer for Christians. By order of the king, Rabbi Nachmanides is summoned from Girona to answer for the Jews. Conditions have been set that Rabbi Nachmanides will not debate with the king, and the king will not participate in the debate."

"If I may speak," Rabbi Nachmanides said.

The palace rumbled with concern that the rabbi was seemingly speaking out of turn.

"Yes, what is it?" Friar Raymond said.

"I will do as the king commands, if you permit me to speak freely. I hereby request the permission of the king and the permission of Friar Raymond of Penyaforte and his associates who are here."

"So long as you do not utter blasphemies," Friar Raymond said.

"I wish to observe your law in this regard," Rabbi Nachmanides said. "But I also wish to speak freely in debate, as you speak freely. I have the wisdom to speak properly in debate as you indicate, but it must be according to my will."

King James and the friars gave permission.

"You may as well begin," Friar Raymond said.

"Thank you. The debate between Christians and Jews concerns many matters of custom which are not essential. In this revered court, I wish to debate only matters that are essential."

"You have spoken wisely," Friar Raymond said. "We will speak first about the Messiah. Did he come as the Christians believe, or will he come as the Jews believe?"

"I will prove from the Talmud that the Messiah has already come," Friar Christiani said.

"Before we debate this, I ask him to tell me how this is possible," Rabbi Nachmanides said. "I heard that he said this to many Jews while he was in Provence and other places. This surprises me. Is he saying the Talmud sages believed Jesus was the Messiah and divine? It is well known that the Jesus situation occurred during the period of the Second Temple. His birth and death were prior to the destruction of the Temple, while the Talmud sages were after. The Mishnah was compiled many years after the destruction. If these sages wrote that Jesus was the Messiah and that his faith and religion were true, then how did they remain in the Jewish faith? Why did they not convert and turn to the faith of Jesus, as Friar Pablo did? He interpreted their words to mean that the faith of the Christians is the true faith—Heaven forbid—and as a result, he converted. If these sages believed in Jesus and in his faith, how is it that they did not convert as Friar Pablo, who understands their teachings better than they themselves do?"

"These lengthy observations are meant to cancel the debate," Friar Christiani said. "No matter. You will hear what I have to say. Scripture says, 'The scepter shall not pass from Judah, nor the staff from his descendants, until Shiloh comes,' meaning the Messiah. The prophet says Judah will have power forever, until the coming of the Messiah who will descend from Judah. Today, you Jews have neither scepter nor staff. The Messiah has come. He is of the seed of Judah, and his is the power."

"It was not the prophet's intention to say the rule of Judah would never be suspended," the rabbi replied. "Instead, he said it would not pass away and be canceled completely. This means any monarchy in Israel belongs to Judah. If suspended because of sin, it would eventually return to Judah."

Rabbi Nachmanides backed up his claim with evidence of such suspensions before Jesus lived.

"During those suspensions, the Jews had authorities, even if they were not kings," Friar Christiani said. "According to the

Talmud, 'The scepter shall not pass from Judah,'—these are the exilarchs in Babylonia who control the people—'Nor the staff from his descendants'—these are the offspring of Hillel who teach the Torah publicly. You do not have the ordination today as known in the Talmud. That authority has been annulled. There is no one among you worthy of being designated *Rabbi*."

"It was not the intention of the rabbis to explain this verse other than meaning actual kingship," Rabbi Nachmanides said. "You do not understand law and halakhah. You only understand a little aggadah. The sages say no man should judge a case on his own and be free of liability to pay in case of error, unless he receives permission from the patriarch, who is like a king. They said that during the period of exile, they have the right to confer permission and ordination. This took place among the sages of the Talmud, more than four hundred years after Jesus's death. It was not the view of the sages of the Talmud that this would constitute the scepter and the staff which come from the seed of Judah. The prophet promised Judah that actual kingship over Israel would be his. This promise was suspended for a long period, as I have mentioned. During the period of exile in Babylonia, there was no scepter or staff whatsoever, neither exilarch nor patriarch, for authority was held by the priests, the judges, the officers, or whoever they chose."

"It is said in the Talmud that the Messiah has already come," Friar Christiani said. "There is a story in Midrash Lamentations about a man plowing, and his ox mooed. A passing Arab said, 'Jew, Jew, unhitch your ox, plowshare, and plow, for the Temple has been destroyed.' He unhitched his ox, plowshare, and plow. The Arab said, 'Hitch your ox, plowshare, and plow, for your Messiah has been born'."

"I do not believe the story, even if it is proof of my view," Rabbi Nachmanides said.

"Behold! He denies their books," Friar Christiani said.

"It says that on the day of destruction, after the Temple was destroyed, the Messiah was born," the rabbi said. "Thus Jesus was not the Messiah, as you claim. For he was born and killed two hundred years prior to the destruction of the Temple. According to your reckoning, he was born seventy-three years prior to the destruction of the Temple."

Friar Christiani stared with hostility toward the rabbi. He opened his mouth as if to say something, froze in the moment, closed his mouth, and turned away. Rabbi Nachmanides motioned toward Friar Christiani to reply, but the friar waved him off.

"The dispute does not concern Jesus," the royal judge, Master William, said to break the silence. "The question is if the Messiah has come or not. You say he has not, but your book says he has."

"The sages did not say that the Messiah has come. They said that he was born. On the day that our teacher Moses was born, he did not come and redeem us. However, when he went before Pharaoh at the command of God and said to him, 'These are the words of the Lord—send forth my people!' then he may be said to have arrived. Likewise the Messiah—when he goes before the pope and says to him at God's command, 'Send forth my people,' then he may be said to have come. However, to this day he has not yet come and is in no sense the Messiah. For King David on the day that he was born was not the anointed one. Only when Samuel anointed him was he the anointed one. On the day that Elijah will anoint the Messiah at God's command may he be called the Messiah. On the day that he will subsequently come before the pope to redeem us, then he may be said to have arrived."

"Behold the passage in Isaiah," Friar Christiani said. "Chapter fifty-three tells of the death of the Messiah, how he was to fall into the hands of his enemies, and how he was placed next to the wicked as happened to Jesus. Do you believe that this section speaks of the Messiah?"

"In true meaning, it speaks only of the people of Israel which the prophets call 'Israel my servant,' or 'Jacob my servant.' Yes, the rabbis in the aggadah explain it as referring to the Messiah. However, they never said he would be killed at the hands of his enemies. No book of the Jews says he would be killed, turned over to his enemies, or buried with the wicked. I shall explain for you this section properly and clearly, if you wish."

Friar Christiani and the others ignored the rabbi's offer of enlightenment.

"In the Talmud, Rabbi Joshua ben Levi asked Elijah when the Messiah would come," Friar Christiani said. "Elijah answered, 'Ask the Messiah himself.' Joshua asked, 'Where is he?' Elijah replied, 'At the gate of Rome with the sick.' Joshua went to Rome and found him. Thus the Messiah has come, is in Rome, and is Jesus who rules in Rome."

"It is clear from this the Messiah has not come," Rabbi Nachmanides said. "He asked Elijah when the Messiah would come, not when he came. Further, he asked the Messiah himself when he would come. Thus he has not yet come. These stories say simply he was born already, but I do not believe this."

King James could no longer hold back his interest, and he questioned the rabbi.

"How will the Messiah arrive, if he was born when the Temple was destroyed over a thousand years ago? No human can live a thousand years," King James said.

"Conditions were set that I not debate with you," the rabbi said. "However, I will reply. Early men such as Adam and Methuselah lived almost a thousand years. Elijah and Enoch lived longer than that."

"Where is the Messiah now?" King James asked.

"This is not important for the debate, and I will not respond. Maybe you can find him at the gates of Toledo, if you send one of your couriers there," Rabbi Nachmanides said jokingly.

The group rose. King James set the debate to resume the following Monday. Jonara turned to say something to Felifia, but Felifia was nowhere to be found. The world swirled around Jonara, but instead of the usual grays, the world swirled in cherry-reds and cerise-crimsons.

Monday arrived. The debate resumed—officially or otherwise—amongst a gathering of people in the city. Friar Christiani rose to speak to the people, the clergy, sages, and King James, but Rabbi Nachmanides pleaded with the king to be heard first. King James granted the rabbi's request. Rabbi Nachmanides rose and spoke to the people. He explained the different Jewish books, their purpose, and their merits, emphasizing that the Jewish Bible was to be accepted as truth, the Talmud only in points of religious practice, but the aggadah was merely a collection of sermons he was at liberty to reject. He also explained how sin led to a shorter life, whereas a messiah would not be limited in length of life and could live a thousand years or longer. He further clarified that a messiah would bring universal peace and justice to the world, but in fact since the appearance of Jesus, the world had become more violent with Christians being the most warlike.

Later in the day, Rabbi Nachmanides stood before King James.

"Let the dispute be suspended. For I have never seen a man whose case is wrong argue it as well as you have done," King James said. "As a sign of respect, I present you with a gift of three hundred maravedis."

Later, Friar Christiani and the Dominicans claimed victory in the debate. Puzzled, Rabbi Nachmanides published an account of the debate so all would realize the rabbi's victory. In retaliation, Friar Christiani cherry-picked certain passages and presented these to his superior, Friar Raymond, as blasphemies against Christianity. A formal capital charge and complaint was brought up against Rabbi Nachmanides and filed with King James. Despite heavy lobbying to have Nachmanides tried by a Dominican court, King James felt justice would be better served by calling an independent commission with proceedings held in the king's presence. Rabbi Nachmanides answered the charges and admitted his writings reflected precisely what had transpired in the debate. King James acknowledged that Nachmanides had done nothing outside the law, but the Dominicans obsessed with persecuting the rabbi and would not stop. In an effort to appease the Dominicans, King James fined Rabbi Nachmanides, exiled him for two years, and ordered the rabbi's write-up of the debate burned. The Dominicans, obsessed with punishing the rabbi further, convinced Pope Clement IV to banish Rabbi Nachmanides from Iberia permanently.

1275 July 24. Villarreal, Kingdom of Valencia, Iberia.

Two crowns of Iberia—King James I of Aragon in the east, and his son-in-law King Alfonso X of Castile in central and central-west—were intent on completing the last phase of the *Reconquista*—the complete return of Andalusia (southern Iberia) to Christian control. To minimize unnecessary fighting between kingdoms, the kings signed the Treaty of Almizra in 1244.

Andalusia remained a battleground between Christians (under King Alfonso X and King James I), and Muslims (under Arab control). Alfonso's father, King Ferdinand III, reconquered most of Andalusia, with the odd exception of the Emirate of Granada. Granada, while aligning itself with King Ferdinand, became a Muslim dynasty called the Nasrids. The Nasrids maintained their kingdom until 1492—paying tribute to the Castile kingdom and helping the Castilians against Muslim invasion and rebellion.

After King Alfonso X departed Castile for France in 1275, the king of Granada decided the Castilian king's absence was the best time to break the treaty with Iberia. He sent word to Morocco requesting help to attack Castile while King Alfonso was away. The first Marinid forces arrived in Tarifa in May of that year.

As the summer of 1275 began, additional Marinid forces led by Sultan Abu Yusuf Ya'qub crossed the Straits of Gibraltar from Morocco into Andalusia in an attempt to regain Arab land lost to the Christian *Reconquista*. King Alfonso X's son and heir, Fernando de la Cerda, learned of this invasion while his father was still abroad, and he rushed with his troops to meet the Arabs in battle in Andalusia.

Fernando, who happened to be in Valencia, had no time to return to his home in Castile. He assembled what army he could and marched toward Andalusia. After a long-day's march, he stopped the troops for the night in Villarreal, a town created a mere year earlier by Fernando's uncle King James to reinforce the area after having been under Muslim rule. Officers joined Fernando in food and song at an inn named, *La Taberna del Rey.*

"Barmaid!" Fernando called. "More red wine! And what about dinner?"

The barmaid rushed from the kitchen with a platterful of dinners. The platter was heavy, and she nearly dropped it several times as men tweaked her passing hind-end.

"I am sorry, my Lord. We had to fetch more fish from the market and all. My dear me there are a lot of you here tonight," the barmaid said.

"Never mind the explanations. We are hungry!" Fernando said.

"Yes, my Lord," the barmaid said.

She placed five dinner plates before five men—one of which was Fernando. Each plate had a fish with fixings. The barmaid pulled a bottle of red wine from her deep side pocket and placed it on the table. Other men yelled for her, and she ran off as quickly as she came.

"My Lord," said one of the officers. "Forgive me, but your fish looks a bit unusual."

"This fish has a very large head," Fernando said. "But it is the largest fish on the table. A fish fit for a king. Notice the powerful lines in its jaw, the thickness of its scales. It is like a heavy armor. It is a battle fish, the king fish, and I will devour it as I dethrone it."

Fernando opened the wine bottle and filled each of his men's cups. All thanked him graciously.

"My men serve me, and I serve my men," Fernando said. "Let's eat."

Fernando took a bite while his officers watched. Then the officers took bites from their fish. All nodded in approval.

"The taste is a bit unusual," Fernando said. "I'm not sure what to make of it."

"Then perhaps you should order something else," an officer recommended.

"Nonsense," Fernando said. "The fish is well cooked. No evil spirit can survive fire."

Fernando continued to eat the fish despite the odd taste. The officers looked on with concern. Finally, one of the officers broke the nervous silence.

"We are in Villarreal," the officer said. "In *La Taberna del Rey*."

"The King's Town in the King's Tavern," Fernando said. "Is this not fate? Men, I predict great victories for Castile. The *Reconquista* is all but complete. Berbers invade from the south. We go to meet them in Écija. We will crush them with our heavy cavalry!"

Loud cheers from the officers.

"But that is only the beginning," Fernando said. "Andalusia faces repeated invasions from the Moors. We will go from town to town if necessary and clean out every invader from Villajoyosa to Tarifa!"

More cheering. And clapping. The officers lifted their cups and clanked them against one another in toast. Fernando clanked his cup against theirs as well and took a deep drink.

"The wine is excellent," Fernando said. "It more than makes up for the fish."

The men drank, ate, drank, and drank some more.

"Break out the music!" Fernando shouted.

Three people entered the tavern's main area and stood on a platform—a man with a lute, a man with a flute, and a young woman with long, red hair. The lute and flute started and played several bars. The flute stopped, the lute continued, and the young woman started singing. Jonara looked closely at the young woman and realized she looked much like Jonara herself.

"How appropriate," Fernando said. "The music selection is correct."

"Do you recognize the song?" an officer asked.

"And you don't? You should be ashamed. It is one of the *Cantigas de Santa Maria* (Songs to the Virgin Mary). My father wrote this particular one. You do remember my father, King Alfonso X?"

"Yes, yes of course," the officer replied nervously.

The other officers laughed.

"Come. This is a joyous occasion. The King's song blesses us all," Fernando said.

Fernando set the tone by standing up from his table, walking over to a young lady, and inviting her to dance. Other officers followed his example and asked other young women to dance. Two officers remained seated at Fernando's dinner table. The nervous one spoke first.

"He dances with a girl when he is married," the nervous one said.

"His wife, the Princess Blanche of France, is not here, so why worry?" the other officer said. "Besides, he is our commanding officer and heir to the throne. He may do as he pleases. And I would advise you never to speak of this again."

The young girl giggled and flirted with Fernando. Fernando smiled as he danced with her, but he felt empty. The girl he danced with giggled in predictable patterns as if she weren't real.

"What is real, I wonder?" Fernando asked himself.

As Fernando danced, his eye drifted and caught the eye of the young red-headed woman singing. Realizing he saw her staring at him, she quickly averted her eyes. This became a game, then. Fernando pretended to look away from the singer, she stared at him, and he quickly looked back at her, catching her in the act of watching him.

The song ended. Fernando spun the young lady and released her hand. She continued spinning herself as she traveled across the room and crashed into a group of people—either because of dizziness or drunkenness, Fernando didn't know. He turned his gaze to the red-headed singer, but she had disappeared. The lute and flute musicians continued playing.

"I watch a young girl make a fool of herself, and the real catch gets away!" Fernando said to himself.

Fernando approached the flute musician and asked him about the singer. The flute musician stopped playing while the lute player continued.

"What is her name?" Fernando asked. "Where is she from?"

"She is Atina of Tarragona," the musician said. "Atina and the two of us—Luis and Vimaro—"

"That's us," Vimaro said.

"Yes, that's us," Luis continued. "We are court musicians for King James I of Aragon."

"Strange that I have not heard of Atina before tonight. I have visited the king's court many times," Fernando said. "How is it I have never set my eyes on such beauty before?"

"Thank you," Vimaro said, but Luis elbowed him hard.

"Not you two—Atina! Be thankful I have a sense of humor, or I would cut your tongues out as you both stand."

"Begging your mercy, my Lord," Luis said. "But Vimaro meant no harm."

"Well? Do something useful and tell me where Atina went," Fernando ordered.

"She stepped outside for a breath of air. The smoke in these halls upsets her singing voice," Luis said.

"Of course. Thank you," Fernando said. "You may resume playing the flute."

Fernando stepped outside and followed the tavern's wall to the back. A light scent of incense tickled his nose, and he followed the scent to a figure kneeling and praying before a small oak tree with incense burning at the base. Fernando crept up behind the figure and touched her on the shoulder. She gasped and turned around.

"Atina," Fernando said.

Atina remained frozen in space and thought.

"That is your name, is it not? Atina?" Fernando asked.

Atina nodded her head slowly in affirmation all the while gazing at Fernando without blinking.

"I did not mean to frighten you," Fernando said. "Are you frightened?"

Atina remained frozen in position and nodded, "No." Fernando pulled her to her feet. Atina kept her head down in respect.

"You are shaking like a wet dog," Fernando said.

"Please, my Lord, do not call me a dog. I am but a humble musician for King James," Atina said.

"Of course you're not a dog. Do not be afraid of me. I will not hurt you," Fernando said. "I want to meet you. That was a beautiful song you sang in there."

"Thank you, my Lord. Your father, King Alfonso, deserves the credit for writing it. I am but an echo of his voice," Atina said.

"You are a polite liar," Fernando said, "for which I am thankful. When my father sings, it is like a bear waking from slumber, but when you sing, it is like daybreak over the Mediterranean."

Atina nodded politely while maintaining her downward gaze.

"Why do you look down?" Fernando asked.

"Out of respect, my Lord. I have not the nobility to look into your eyes," Atina said.

"You may not have nobility from Man, but you have nobility from God. You are quite the fair maiden of Tarragona. Never have I seen such a fair maiden in the Kingdom of Valencia or anywhere in these Kingdoms," Fernando said. "Look at me."

"Sir?"

"Look into my eyes. I want to see what deep beauty undulates in your soft eyes."

Atina slowly raised her head and looked into Fernando's eyes. Fernando took Atina into his arms and held her close, but Atina did not reciprocate.

"I feel something special in you," Fernando said. "Do you not feel the same for your Lord?"

"I...I...am confused. Your wife...I...she..." Atina stumbled.

"Let us talk about you," Fernando said. "Tell me—where are you staying the night?"

"In room number four up there," Atina said, pointing to a room in the tavern's upper level.

"I would like to see it. Come show me," Fernando said.

Atina froze in place again. How could she refuse the prince? She could not. Fernando prodded her, and she led him upstairs to her inn room. She opened the door and showed him in.

"Very pleasant," Fernando said. "But I do not understand. There are two beds, not one. Do you have a male companion?"

"No," Atina said. "I do not."

"What about your fellow musicians?" Fernando said.

"They are next door," Atina said. "They stay up late and will not retire until much later."

"Good," Fernando said.

Fernando sat on a bed and motioned Atina to sit next to him.

"Come sit next to your future king," Fernando said.

Atina walked slowly to him. Fernando grabbed her arm and pulled her to the bed next to him.

"I...my king is James I," Atina said.

"Yes, for now," Fernando said. "But he will not live forever."

"He will have a successor," Atina said.

"Atina—wouldn't you like to live in a kingdom uniting Leon, Portugal, Castile, Navarre, Aragon, and Granada?" Fernando asked.

"That is a big dream," Atina said.

"Yes, but it is my dream," Fernando replied. "Everything from the Pyrenees to the Mediterranean—one kingdom. A Catholic kingdom, ordained by the Pope and God. I would administer it as King of Iberia. I would make you my wife."

Atina giggled.

"I apologize, my Lord, but you are married," Atina said.

"You would be my second wife. No, I would promote you to my first wife," Fernando said.

Atina felt something odd in Fernando's voice. He seemed less the military man and more the dreamer. It was summer, and the room was hot, but Fernando perspired unusually so. He shook a little as he described his new kingdom.

"We would have beautiful children together—princes and princesses. We would have the largest palace, and all would love and cherish us," Fernando said. "My skin tingles with excitement. I feel victory is out there for the taking. And you will be at my side. Atina—kiss me."

Fernando placed his hands on Atina's head and pressed his lips to Atina's. He kissed her, but she did not kiss back. Her eyes lit open in surprise. She thought she might feel attraction to the prince, but she did not. Without warning, the door burst open.

"I snuck a bottle of red wine from an officer downstairs," said a female voice. "We are going to have a wild time to—"

The woman stopped in mid-sentence when she saw Fernando with Atina. Atina backed off suddenly.

"So, when did you start liking men? You could have told me!" the woman said, and she stormed out with the wine bottle.

"Sarita, no, wait!" Atina called through the doorway, but Sarita did not return.

Atina turned back around and reentered her room. Jonara thought about Sarita and realized she bore a striking resemblance to Cerafina. How odd. Two women in Spain living more than seven hundred years earlier looking like herself and Cerafina? Could women reincarnate together, sharing friendship and love across hundreds of years? The journey of spirits was a question without answer.

"Fernando, I can explain," Atina said, but Fernando was no longer sitting on the bed. "Prince Fernando? Where are you?"

Fernando stood in a small closet heaving into a chamber pot.

"My Lord, you are ill!" Atina said. "Here—rest on my bed. I will summon help."

Atina helped Fernando to her bed where he lay sweating and shivering. Atina ran from her room screaming. A moment later, Fernando's officers arrived and attended him. A doctor was called for. The doctor arrived, but by that time, Fernando had gone into convulsions. The doctor tried giving Fernando some herbs, but Fernando continued vomiting. The night grew late and carried into the early darkness of the next morning. Fernando fell into a final neurological frenzy before his limbs fell silent and his heart stopped beating.

It was July 25, 1275, and Prince Fernando de la Cerda was dead.

"Nekara killed the prince?" Jonara asked.

"No, she didn't," Felifia replied.

"Princess Felifia! I thought you left me!" Jonara cried.

"I did for a short while. In 1275, Prince Fernando de Cerda died without any interference from Nekara the Red," Felifia said. "Some say he died in Cuidad Real while in battle. Others say he died in Écija. Yet others say he died in November and not July.

That does not matter. What does matter is that the heir to Alfonso X's throne was now dead. A dispute grew from this. Alfonso wanted Fernando's sons to be next in line, but Fernando's younger brother, Sancho IV the Brave, fought for power. Sancho allied himself with the Moors and even Abu Yusuf Ya'qub, who had launched the attack in 1275 against Iberia. Sancho also executed thousands of fellow countrymen who supported his rival, Fernando de la Cerda's son, Alfonso de la Cerda. In brief, Sancho's actions delayed the *Reconquista* of Iberia. Some might argue not much; others argue more."

1482 Feb 27, Late Eve. The Spa of Alhama. Kingdom of Granada, Iberia.

Jonara stood in a bath house. The water was hot—hotter than body temperature, but not so hot as to scald.

"It's like taking a hot-water bath at home," Jonara said.

The water temperature was in fact 47° Celsius (117° Fahrenheit).

"It smells like rotten eggs," Jonara said.

The thermal water was filled with minerals—bicarbonates, calcium, magnesium, and sulfates. The spa was closed for conventional visitors, but a special group of women soaked their burdened muscles in the water.

"Wait a moment," Jonara said. "I recognize these women. They're the same ones I saw in the Caves of Healing in 1492."

Felifia entered the spa and stood before the women.

"It's Felifia. Felifia!" Jonara shouted, but no one paid her any attention.

"Welcome my sisters to *La Reunión Sáfico*. My name is Felifia, and I will host this session," Felifia said.

Felifia paused and stared down.

"What is it?" the Jane-like woman asked.

"I have bad news," Felifia said. "This will be our last meeting in these thermal waters."

The women rumbled in shock and disappointment.

"Surely you cannot mean this," said the Jelana-like woman.

"Yes, I do. The Kingdom of Granada is slipping away. In a few hours, a Christian Army will overtake Alhama. Progressively, one Granadian town after another will fall to Christian rule. This is the last phase of the *Reconquista*, my sisters in love. This is also our end in this kingdom."

"But why?" said the Marina-like woman. "Will the Christians forbid the way we worship God?"

"Yes, they will," Felifia said. "They will only permit Christian forms of worship."

"What are we to do?" asked a Geneva-like woman.

"I will discuss that in a moment. But first, I wish to paraphrase from Sappho," Felifia said, and she spoke the following:

Felifia's Sapphic Paraphrase

The moon has set.
It is midnight,
The time is going by,
And we sleep alone.

Idle speech has spread anger
Through Iberia's breast.
Christian shepherds
Shall trample
The hyacinth under foot,
And the purple flower
Will press to earth.

The bright morning will bring
All that was scattered
Into evening.

For death is evil,
The Gods have so judged.
Had it been good,
They would die.

Foolish woman,
Pride not yourself

On a ring
He so giveth.

For wealth without worth
Is no safe neighbor,
And men will remember
Our choice hereafter.

Do not own
A revengeful temper,
But instead
Have a simple mind.

Love delicacy
The sun's splendor
And beauty,
As you sleep
In the bosom
Of your tender girlfriend.

We now pray:
Immortal Aphrodite
Of the broidered throne,

Daughter of Zeus,
Weaver of wiles,
We pray you break not
Our spirit
With anguish and distress.

Come.
We pray to you.

Release us
From cruel cares,
And all that our hearts
Desire to accomplish.
Do this,
And be our ally.
Here we stand,
Amen.

The women held silent in a moment of reflection, but the moment carried through much of the evening. At long length, Karla (the one who looked like Fantina), spoke.

"May we stay in Alhama?" Karla asked.

"No," Felifia said. "We must leave."

"And go where?" the Jelana-like woman asked. "It would seem we must leave the Kingdom of Granada. Castile is not safe, nor is Aragon. Portugal might take us."

"They would, but only for several years," Felifia said.

"Then we must leave Iberia altogether," the Marina-like woman said.

"In time, and for most of you," Felifia said. "But in the short term, I have a place where we will be safe, in the old Asturias region."

"Where?" the women asked.

"On a hill east of a small town named Carreña," Felifia said.

"We should go home and get our things," said the Jane-like woman, but as she said that, thunder rumbled in from outside.

"A storm is approaching," the Marina-like woman said.

The sound of cannon fire echoed in from outside.

"That was not thunder," said Karla.

"It was not," Felifia said. "Conflict brews from the heavens and the earth. It rains water and cannon balls. The fighting has begun. We cannot return to our homes. We must leave for Carreña now."

Felifia rushed the women out of the thermal springs and through the back door to a two-horse four-wheel wagon with a cover and special oil lamps with glass coverings to keep out the rain.

"Please, get inside quickly. We have little time left before the Christians prevent our escape," Felifia said.

The women rushed into the wagon and found dry, comfortable straw bales to sit on. Jonara sat in front with Felifia. Felifia yelled, "*Tuiako!* (Trot!)" and the horses broke into a trot. The wagon pulled away from the spa house and onto the main road. The rain poured. Lightning lit the sky, and each time it did, Felifia and Jonara saw Christian troops approaching on the road.

"We must leave this road," Felifia said, but as she finished her statement, the front left of the wagon lifted suddenly.

"*Gerauko!* (Halt!)" Felifia called to the horses.

The horses stopped. Felifia and Jonara jumped off the wagon and discovered the right rear wheel had broken.

"I do not remember this happening in the vision," Felifia said to herself.

"Felifia! Do you have a spare wheel?" Jonara asked, but Felifia did not see or hear Jonara.

"What is it?" Karla said from the back of the wagon.

"The wheel is broken," Felifia said. "We must leave this main road. Christian troops will descend on us soon, and we will be overrun."

"Do you have a spare wheel?" Karla asked.

"No, I do not," Felifia said.

"We must shift the weight off the right rear," Karla said.

Karla disappeared into the wagon briefly, and she reappeared with a bale of straw. She exited the wagon and was followed by the other women who carried bales of straw. The women dumped the bales at the side of the road until the wagon was empty.

"The road is rough," Felifia said. "The straw provides comfort."

"Now is not the time for little comforts," Karla said. She turned to the women and said, "We will all sit on the left, close to the front."

The women paused for a moment before reentering the wagon and did as she suggested. The wagon lifted up a bit but was still a little low. Felifia remounted the front of the wagon in hopes of offsetting the last bit of weight, but still the right rear hung a bit low.

"No good," Felifia said through the front opening to the women in back. "The right rear is still low."

"Then we will sit in each other's laps. We will sleep in the bosoms of our girlfriends," Karla said.

Felifia opened her eyes in slight surprise, but Karla convinced the women to sit tightly together. The right rear of the wagon lifted level.

"You did it," Felifia said. Felifia turned to the horses and said, "*Tuiako!* (Trot!)"

The horses broke into a trot. The wagon gently wavered back and forth as the balance settled on the remaining three wheels. Another lightning strike lit up the sky, and the troops were now closer.

"If the sky lights up again, the troops will see us diverting from the road," Felifia said. "We turn here now. *Kaimo reshu!* (Turn right!)"

The horses turned right, and Felifia called to them again.

"*Lomapo boshu keifa!* (Gallop with care!)"

The horses galloped. The women inside jostled and bumped around. They received bruises and abrasions, but Felifia guided the horses carefully, and after a short time, Felifia checked the horses to a trot. Once Felifia felt her group was out of danger from Christian troops, she rested the horses for five minutes. During that time, the women in back got out and rubbed their injuries. They thanked Felifia for her skillful driving before returning to the wagon as they had before—sitting in one another's laps. Felifia returned to the horses and commanded them to walk. The women in back fell asleep to the peaceful gait, and Felifia guided the horses first eastward and gradually northward all through the stormy night and into the next day as the group continued their trip to Carreña.

1492 Jan 1. The Caves of Healing. Carreña, Spain.

Jonara witnessed what she had seen before—a number of people hauling wood into the Caves of Healing. Felifia's group of women—Jane-like, Jelana-like, Fantina-like (Karla), Marina-like, and Geneva-like gathered with her in the pool.

"The time has come to break the friendship," Felifia said. "Iberia is becoming Spain. Jews will be expelled this year, and Muslims will follow in later years. We must part ways and live in other countries. But before we do, I want each of you to choose a gift to take with you. I have arranged craftswomen to make various things of remembrance out of three special woods. Two of the woods—crimson maple and white spruce—represent two different types of women coming together. The third wood—lignum vitae—is the wood of life binding their relationship together. These woods have spiritual power when fashioned together. So it is when you celebrate your own unions. I want each of you to remember what I have taught you about love and understanding for your sister and the wariness I have taught you about the world you live in. Your lines must continue. Yes, this means you must have children with a man, but it is a temporary sacrifice for your people. Many generations later, your women will have their own children together without need of a man. But for now, select your wooden keepsakes by which you will remember each other."

The Jane-like woman (Niessa) instructed a craftswoman to make a large, flute-like musical instrument. But what the craftswoman made was an early oboe. Karla was next. She requested a two-position candleholder be made for her celebrations of Shabbat. Another craftswoman started fashioning it. The Geneva-like woman (Nariva) requested a stringed instrument, and a third craftswoman began work on it. It would become the *viola de gamba*. Nariva also requested leftover wood to fashion a diary, and the craftswoman agreed to its construction. The Jelana-like woman (Ziana) approached a craftswoman and requested a *bendir*, a wooden-frame drum with a membrane about sixteen inches in diameter vaguely resembling a tambourine but without jingles. Then the Marina-like woman (Sarina) walked up to a craftswoman.

"I...I do not know what I want," Sarina said. "I am Zoroastrian. What should I desire? Karla is Jewish, and she received a candleholder for *Shabbat*. Ziana is Muslim, and she received a *bendir* drum. Nariva is Christian, and she received a stringed instrument. Niessa is Celtic, and she received an oversized, strange-looking flute."

"What is most important to you and your faith, Sarina?" the craftswoman asked.

"The sky for sunlight during the day and stars at night, the earth where things grow and where we live, plants to give us food and beauty, animals to give us companionship, humans to care for the earth, fire for cooking, and water to quench our thirst and put out the fire," Sarina said.

"Then I shall make you a chalice of the three woods finished in linseed oil, and on its foot I shall carve the seven things you value most dear—sky, earth, plant, animal, human, fire, and water," the craftswoman said. "May you then fill your cup with the seventh item—water—to remind you of the other six."

"Thank you!" Sarina said.

"One other thing," the craftswoman said. "Take this."

The craftswoman handed Sarina a codex book with a heavy-wooden binding.

"The book...the pages...they are blank," Sarina said.

"They are for you and your family to fill out as need arises," the craftswoman said.

"Thank you again," Sarina said.

2023 Oct 3, Tue Eve. Corpus Christi Hospital, Texas.

Jonara vanished from Iberia and appeared inside the hospital room where her mother suffered from preeclampsia. She stood in a corner and saw Cerafina, herself, and Davino in the room.

"Do you play an instrument?" Cerafina asked the other Jonara.

"No, I just made up that song," the other Jonara said. "Well the words, anyway. I don't remember where I heard the music."

"It's a very old song," said Cerafina. "By Bach. It's called, *Sleepers, Wake*. You would do well playing a musical instrument. Have you ever tried a violin? A clarinet?"

"No, I haven't," the other Jonara said.

"I can teach you sometime if you want to learn," Cerafina said. "We have an organ and piano at our house, too. Maybe you'd like to try one of those."

1970 Jul 3, Fri 6:03 pm. Four-thousand Feet above Spain.

Jonara left the hospital room and appeared in the De Havilland Comet. She sat in the last seat and heard a girl in the bathroom saying something. She looked down at her Moissan Ruby, and with some faint energy in the stone she didn't think existed, she used the stone to hear the radio communication between the aircraft and a controller tower.

1803	Pilot:	"Roger. Cleared further down to 2800 feet on 1017, transition level 50."
	Pilot:	"Barcelona. DN requests the duty runway."
	ATC:	"DN. Duty runway 25."
1805	ATC:	"DN. Altitude."
	Pilot:	"DN is passing 4000 feet on 1047."

The girl's words boomed through the bathroom wall with such clarity that Jonara was able to recognize the voice of her other self.

Miramish	**Translation**
Kisheluako!	Indurate!

1263 Jul 15. Montseny Mountains, Iberia.

Jonara was on the Montseny Mountains with Rabbi Nachmanides. Her hair as did the rabbi's flew upward from Nekara's funnel cloud overhead. Two tentacles suspended Felifia in the air as the funnel cloud pulled water and debris upward into the sky amongst lightning bolts and thunder. Felifia was in the middle of speaking:

Felifia in Miramish	**Translation**
Lukaimo teranita	Return control
Opeifu Eleshanga shelada	Of Earth's body
Dhaku shash e viuki	And her forces
Di shashfal.	To herself,
Dhaku kail e lukuaneio	And you will regain control
Opeifu kaish theifu zhiuna	Of your own self
Ishu shai tuanita.	In the exchange.

Nekara in Dahmek	**Translation**
Maur!	No!
Nia kokeit oir!	I will not!

Felifia in Miramish/Mirsua	**Translation**
Dodu nia ishaiko	Then I invoke
Koilu Miramishu Biorita:	High Miramish Power:
Nias gubelasos kailes, Nekaras.	I compress you, Nekara.
Nias gubelasos kaises e zualas	I compress your spirit
Dhakus...	And...

"*Maur!* (No!)" Nekara boomed.

Nekara in Dahmek	**Translation**
Zhairsp yuarnu shriauk	Send white fire
Velt shair friaift, dhark e kriarsk	From the sky, and shatter
Lor Miramishu biorat!	All Miramish power!

Sustained lightning bolts carried through the tentacles (which maintained their grips on Felifia) and electrified Felifia. Felifia fought with all her strength to say the last words that would contain Nekara once and for all. But the words did not come out. The clouds opened up, and a glimmering De Havilland Comet screamed through. Thundering through the air boomed the voice of 1970 Jonara:

Miramish	**Translation**
Kisheluako!	Indurate!

Felifia shrieked. The clouds and tentacular funnels shrank like a tree growing in reverse from sky-sized to tree-sized to bush-sized, and when it reached bush-sized, Nekara materialized from the shrinking clouds, took the duavisha from Felifia, and Felifia's body was engulfed into the shrinking clouds while it became mushroom-sized, pebble-sized, and grain-sized as the last bits fled into the duavisha.

Nekara laughed. Felifia was trapped inside the duavisha, and Nekara held the duavisha in her hand. Nekara laughed again. And again. Her laughter grew like another storm thundering on the path. The winds stopped. Nekara's voice penetrated the clear air and set up harmonics throughout the mountainside, vibrating the rocks loose and building up the growling stomach of a rockslide. Jonara tugged Rabbi Nachmanides, and the two ran down the path for safety. The rockslide materialized behind them as if a dam had burst. Nekara stood on a tree trunk that had been sheared by the rockslide and rode it along the leading rocky wave as if surfing on the ocean.

"Lord of my fathers, delivery me now from this great evil," Rabbi Nachmanides cried out.

"You will be delivered," Nekara said. "Jonara—separate from him."

"No!" Jonara yelled. "You will kill him if I do."

"And?" Nekara asked in mock politeness.

"Stop this now and let Felifia go!" Jonara yelled.

Nekara laughed. The rockslide caught up to Rabbi Nachmanides and Jonara. Nekara grabbed a free branch and swatted Jonara. Jonara flew off to the side and landed in a tree. The rockslide consumed Rabbi Nachmanides and carried him down the mountainside out of view.

"Nekara!" Jonara yelled to the small, surfing shape far down the mountain slope. "You evil murdering bitch!"

1263 Jul 20. The Disputation of Barcelona. The Kingdom of Aragon, Iberia.

Jonara appeared in the royal palace of James I of Aragon much as she did before. In attendance were the king, his court, knights, Christian dignitaries, Friar Raymond of Penyaforte, and Friar Pablo Christiani. Jewish dignitaries were absent as was Rabbi Nachmanides, who had perished in Nekara's rockslide.

"Your Majesty and the court," Friar Christiani said. "I stand here today ready to prove that Jesus is the Messiah as from evidence found in the Talmud and other Jewish writings. But where is Rabbi Nachmanides to defend his people's writings? Where are his Jewish colleagues? It is not lightly the King of Aragon requests the rabbi to this Disputation."

"Friar Raymond?" asked King James I.

"Your Majesty, our messengers report Rabbi Nachmanides left Girona ten days ago," Friar Raymond replied.

"It does not take ten days to reach Barcelona from Girona, even by foot," the king said.

"Exactly, Your Majesty," Friar Christiani said.

"I am disappointed. Rabbi Nachmanides is a premier authority on Jewish writings and the Jewish faith. I had anticipated this debate," King James said. "Recommendations for a substitute, Friar Raymond?"

"There are local Jewish scholars," Friar Raymond said.

"Then why are they not here?" the king asked.

"Begging Your Majesty's pardon, but is it not clear?" Friar Christiani asked. "The silence of the Jews is an indication of our correctness. The Messiah has appeared. The Messiah is divine according to Scripture. And Christians hold the true faith. If Christians did not, there would be opposition today. Where is the opposition?"

"We will recess for the morning," King James said. "Friar Raymond—search the Jewish scholars of Barcelona. Advise them of the situation, and invite them to attend and defend their writings."

"Begging your pardon, Your Majesty, but if the Jews should refuse?" Friar Raymond asked.

"I will make this a request, not a command," King James said. "If they refuse, they refuse. We will reconvene after lunch."

The court dispersed. Friar Raymond toured the city in search of Jewish scholars to attend the Disputation while Friar Christiani attended the king.

"Your Majesty, if I may speak," Friar Christiani said.

"Yes, Friar," King James said.

"I do not attempt to decide for you," the friar said.

"I should hope not!" the king replied.

"But this silence by the Jews," Friar Christiani said.

"You seem quite obsessed with it," King James said.

"It is very telling," Friar Christiani said. "I have prayed to God for years, and this silence is Jewish approval for the *Reconquista*."

"The *Reconquista* has proceeded very well without the Jews," King James said. "And you forget to whom you speak. Do you not know the history of your king and his part in the *Reconquista*?"

"My deepest apologies and request for pardon, Your Majesty. I meant no disrespect to your enormous legacy," Friar Christiani said. "But now is the time to move decisively against all who oppose Christian Iberia. The Jews have always collaborated with the Moors. To beat the Moors we must beat the Jews."

"Friar Christiani. Your military ignorance is grating. The Jews have no armies, and they pose no military threat."

"But they have collaborated with the Moors. Is this not a blasphemy against Christendom?" Friar Christiani asked.

"And? Do you suggest we invade the Jewry? What Jewish holds do we lay siege to? Well?" King James pressed.

"I do not suggest we invade the Jews," the friar said.

"Of course not!" the king rebuked the friar. "Especially since I extend an open invitation for Jews to settle in Aragon."

"We must expel them. For the *Reconquista* to complete in its entirety, all of Iberia must be Christian. If a man is not with us, he is against us. We expel the Moors through their death or retreat."

"Did you not hear your king? I invite Jews, not expel them," the king said. "There are important issues at hand. The Moors are a continued threat. Unlike the Jews, Moors raid and attack. My priority is to expand Aragon southward as part of the *Reconquista* and coordinate with my son-in-law Alfonso X of Castile with his part of the *Reconquista*. This issue you have with the Jews will have to wait until the Moors are purged from Iberia."

"Your Majesty, what if I can guarantee the Moors are purged from Iberia?" Friar Christiani asked.

King James I stared at Friar Pablo Christiani for a moment before breaking out into hysterical laughter. After several minutes of glee, the king restrained himself well enough to speak.

"Do you intend to murder your king with comedy?" King James asked.

"You do not take me seriously? I represent the Church, and God stands with me," Friar Christiani said.

"You forget that Friar Raymond is my confessor, not you. I am loyal to the Church and God. I always have and always will. Your devotion to the Church is admirable. Yet your experience as a military man is most deficient. But I tell you this. Raise an army with the power of God. Prove your new worth to the Kingdom of Aragon and Iberia."

"You will provide all that I ask?" Friar Christiani asked.

"Your God will provide, no? Yet you expect me to provide. Are you saying I am God?" the king asked. "You flatter me, but you are bordering blasphemy. No, my dear Friar, you must raise your own army—if you can," the king laughed.

The king laughed for another ten minutes and was only able to stop after drinking fine red wine. Friar Christiani stared at him with a fire in his eyes like a little boy who'd been told he needed to grow up before going out in the real world among men. Seeing the friar's mood, the king offered to assuage the friar's ill feelings.

"Stay here for the rest of the Disputation. Claim victory and dispense the usual propaganda," King James said. "Do what you do best. I do not hate you, Friar Christiani. I wish to see you succeed where you can, as I do all of Christian Iberia. Here—have a cup of this wine. Soothe your spirits with spirits."

Friar Christiani drank the wine, but his spirits were not soothed. He thanked the king and spent the recess in the city of

Barcelona. He walked up and down streets in an effort to find clarity in his position.

"Christianity must prevail. Iberia must be united as one in Christianity. The Jews must convert or leave. The Moors must convert or leave. No, conversion takes too long. Converts are not as trustworthy as men molded from birth," the friar said to himself.

Friar Christiani walked along a street until it reached the outskirts of Barcelona. Without buildings to block his view, he soaked in a panoramic view of the Collserola Mountains to the northwest. The friar observed green lights shining from various peaks and sub-peaks on the Collserolas.

"Little green lights pepper the mountains," Friar Christiani said. "I must investigate those lights. Green is a sacred color in Islam. Is nowhere safe? There could be Moors spying on us from above."

Friar Christiani turned around and walked into town where he coincidentally met Friar Raymond.

"Pablo," Friar Raymond said. "You look tired. Where have you been?"

"Walking, walking, and more walking!" Friar Christiani said. "I cannot shake this Jewish dust from my feet no matter how far I walk."

"Return with me to the Dominican priory for lunch. Let us discuss your troubles there," Friar Raymond said.

The two returned to the priory where they lived. They obtained food from the kitchen and sat outside on a table overlooking the well-groomed grounds of grass, bushes, trees, flowers, ponds, ducks, and other wildlife.

"The priory is beautiful this time of year, no?" Friary Raymond asked.

"It is," Friar Christiani said.

"Then be at peace," Friar Raymond said.

"I cannot. The *Reconquista* preys on my mind," Friar Christiani said. "I will not rest until all the world is either converted to Christianity or condemned."

"Salvation of the soul is our first priority," said Friar Raymond.

"Priority, priority, priority! Our priority is salvation and conversion. The king's priority is expansion of Aragon. What about my priority? When do I rid the world of Jews?" Friar Christiani asked.

"I know what troubles you, friar," Friar Raymond said. "You were once a Jew, were you not?"

"Yes, yes, yes!" Friar Christiani said. "I was. I worshiped as they did. I converted. Oh Friar Raymond, I try so hard to put my Jewish past behind me. But every time I see or hear a Jew speak, old memories spring to life. The battles in my head start again, and I get terrible headaches. I want the battles to end. I want to rid the last memories of Judaism from my past, my world, and the world around me. I placed a request before the king, that he expel the Jews, but he laughed."

"King James has many things on his mind," Friar Raymond said.

"You are his confessor," Friar Christiani said. "You can solve this entire problem."

"Me?" Friar Raymond said. "Whatever do you speak?"

"On his next confession, tell him he must expel all Jews as a penance," Friar Christiani said.

"Pablo! Christ does not absolve sins in that manner," Friar Raymond said. "It is true that a king's confessor has much sway in royal decisions, but I will not be your pawn. Or pupil. Quite the contrary, you have always been my pupil. And as your teacher, I give you this lesson—become a confessor to a young man of royalty—a prince, for example. But only a prince who is heir to a throne. Become his confessor, and you will wield sway."

"But who shall I choose? King James has many sons," Friar Christiani said.

"The king shows favor to his legitimate and illegitimate sons in equal fashion," Friar Raymond said. "It is difficult to know which if any will emerge as the next king of Aragon. The nobles are against any illegitimate son making claim, yet the king...oh, the king. What to do? I would say this—do not become a confessor to a prince or otherwise in Aragon. If you are on the wrong side after fighting breaks out, your words to sway could become words to slay—for others against you!"

"But the only other major kingdoms are Castile and Portugal," Friar Christiani said.

"Choose Castile. It is much larger, and King Alfonso X is the king's son-in-law. His eldest son is Fernando. Become his confessor, and you stand a good chance of realizing your dream," Friar Raymond said.

"If I remember rightly, the Infante Fernando de la Cerda is a mere ten years of age. Is he not too young?" Friar Christiani asked.

"He is the perfect age. Appeal to King Alfonso, of course, but gain the ear of Fernando while he is yet impressionable," Friar Raymond said.

"Then I must leave Barcelona," Friar Christiani said.

"The work of Christ compels us to travel," Friar Raymond said.

"So be it. I shall leave after the Disputation," Friar Christiani said.

After Lunch.

The king's court reassembled after lunch. King James sat and motioned for Friar Raymond to begin.

"Your Majesty. I have spoken with several Jewish scholars in Barcelona. All are in agreement that they do not wish to be charged with blasphemy for their words in defense of their faith," Friar Raymond said. "They remember the Disputation of Paris in 1240 and do not wish to have the Talmud burned as it was in Paris in 1244."

"Is the defense of one's faith a blasphemy?" the king asked.

"It is when one's faith is in error," Friar Christiani said. "Your Majesty—we have testimony from the Jews themselves as to why they are silent—they do not wish to blaspheme against Christ!"

"Friar Raymond said they do not wish to be charged with blasphemy," the king said. "There is a slight difference."

"But an unimportant one. What is important is how we proceed from here. We must—" Friar Christiani said.

"Friar Christiani, please!" the king said. "That will be enough. Since the Jews are unwilling to contest this Disputation, I hereby award victory to the Dominicans."

Friar Raymond and the court applauded. Friar Christiani lightly clapped, but he was obsessed with further denouncing the Jews.

"Your Majesty. I was denied my moment in court to expose the failings of the Talmud. A simple victory is not enough. We must expel the Jews!"

"Friar Christiani!" King James said. "Allow your king to speak! Now then. These proceedings are to be written up by the Dominicans and published for all to see. Further, I will appoint a committee to study and censor passages from the Talmud that are deemed offensive. Friar Raymond, I appoint you to oversee the write-up of these proceedings and to oversee the committee. And as to the question of expelling the Jews—the Jews pay taxes. They will stay. This Disputation is hereby concluded."

The court dispersed. Friar Christiani headed for the king, but Friar Raymond intercepted him.

"I must see the king," Friar Christiani said.

"You have done well, my son," Friar Raymond said. "But let us go forth on the king's commands. The public deserves to know what transpired here, and we have much work to do on the Talmud."

"It is not enough! We must skip these paltry attempts and move swiftly to expel the Jews," Friar Christiani said.

"Peace, Pablo. Peace!" Friar Raymond said.

"I cannot have peace," Friar Christiani said.

"Then do as we discussed. Find allegiance with Prince Fernando de la Cerda of Castile. Lend your ear to him, and he will lend his. Become his confessor. And do so quickly, Pablo. King James is a patient man, but you may grate on his nerves after a time, and I would not wish that scenario on either of you."

1263 Aug. Collserola Mountains, Kingdom of Aragon, Iberia.

Friar Christiani spent three weeks walking the Collserola Mountains northwest of Barcelona. He needed time to think and pray. During this time, he made two novenas of preparation (a novena being nine consecutive days of devotion and prayer). He had started a third novena when he noticed the green lights again. They had appeared throughout his three weeks on the Collserolas, but something triggered his mind into action.

"God hears my prayers. He wants me to challenge a green light, or the source of a green light. There I will find the answer to my novenas," Friar Christiani said.

The friar chose a direct route to a green light, but when he reached a stone's throw from the light, it disappeared. He continued toward the origin of the green light, but he could find nothing.

"The green lights are crafty. They do not wish to be found. Evil hides in darkness. There must be Moors making the green lights, there must be!" the friar said to himself.

Friar Christiani approached another green light, but he did so with stealth so as not to frighten the originator. He crept from one rock peak to another until he reached a small hut. A light wisp of smoke came out of a hole in the hut's side. He waited for an hour, maybe two, when a door to the hut opened, and he saw a red-headed woman exit.

"A woman!" he whispered to himself.

The woman stopped as if she'd heard the friar. Maybe she did. She looked around like an animal who'd been seen. She looked straight in the friar's direction for ten minutes in a sort of stare-down game. The friar did not move or make a sound. Finally, she shrugged her shoulders, walked a little bit for some loose brushwood, and returned to her hut. The smoke from the hut grew thick, and the friar knew she had simply walked out to get wood for her fire.

"But why is she up here in the Collserolas?" the friar whispered to himself. "She is not a Moor. She is a Celt."

The friar snuck up to the hut and knocked on the door.

"Open the door in the name of Christ!" Friar Christiani ordered.

The friar heard scuffling and rapid efforts to move things around. He was about to open the door himself when the red-headed woman opened the door.

"It's Atina!" Jonara said to herself.

"Padre," Atina said. "You are a long way from the city. Are you lost?"

"Yes," he lied. "I am here on God's errand. Will you lend a friar a moment of rest?"

Atina hesitated, but not wanting to be rude, she invited him in.

"I have only this little hut," she said. "You may sit here. Would you like some mountain tea?"

"Yes, thank you child," Friar Christiani said.

Atina and the friar sat at a table facing each other. Atina secretly hoped he would leave soon, but the friar made no effort to leave. He sipped his tea slowly.

"This is fine tea," he said.

"I made it from the herbs around here," Atina said.

"Do you live here alone?" he asked.

"No. My husband is out and will be here soon," Atina lied.

Friar Christiani looked around the hut and saw nothing to indicate a man lived there. He saw possessions suggesting only one or more female residents.

"What is your name?" the friar asked.

"My name is Atina. Atina of Tarragona," Atina said.

"You are from Tarragona? What brings you here?" the friar asked.

"I met my husband in Barcelona," Atina lied.

"And what is his name?" the friar asked.

"His name? Uh, well," Atina stumbled.

"You do know your husband's name, no?" Friar Christiani asked.

"Yes, of course I do. His name is Sarito. Sarito of Barcelona," Atina said. "What is your name, Padre?"

"I am Friar Pablo Christiani of the Dominican Order in Barcelona," the friar said. "Tell me child, are you Christian?"

"Yes, yes of course!" Atina lied.

The friar looked around the hut.

"I see no crucifix, child. Where do you hold devotion? Or do you descend to Barcelona for Mass?" the friar asked.

"Yes, that is what I do. I go down to Barcelona for Mass," Atina said nervously.

The two heard footsteps approaching. Atina looked at the door nervously. Friar Christiani remained calm, and a slow grin grew on his face. The door opened, and a voice started speaking.

"Atina, I caught two rabbits on the mountain for din—oh, we have company," said the female voice.

"This is Sarito?" Friar Christiani asked.

Atina tried waving the female off.

"Sarito? No, my name is Sarita," the female said as she held two dead rabbits. "This is a surprise, Atina. I did not know you were having a padre visitor."

"Yes, it is a surprise, no?" Atina said nervously.

"Padre, are you hungry? I make a great rabbit stew," Sarita said.

"Thank you, yes. I would enjoy rabbit stew," Friar Christiani said.

Sarita skinned and gutted the rabbits and placed them in a boiling pot.

"Sarita," Friar Christiani said. "Tell me about Atina's husband."

"Husband? Atina has no husband. Not unless she is hiding something from me," Sarita said.

"Hah, hah, hah. Sarita has a great sense of humor," Atina said.

"I should think a confession is in order for you, Atina," Friar Christiani said, "before the Devil consumes your soul any further."

"Oh, we do not believe in that Christian thing," Sarita said. "We believe in the natural world—earth, plants, animals, water, and sky. Those sorts of things. We're Celts."

"She is funny, no?" Atina said nervously to the friar.

"Sarita," the friar continued. "Do you deny God?"

"Oh no, we believe in her," Sarita said. "She created the universe and life."

"But you deny the Passion of Christ?" the friar asked.

Atina tried coughing in a certain way to let Sarita know she should stop blabbing.

"If it happened, it happened. But that was a long time ago and far away. It does not apply here. Mmm. This stew is coming along nicely," Sarita said.

"The stew is brewing," Friar Christiani said.

"Sarita is not herself today," Atina said. "The mountain air makes her say all sorts of wild things."

"What are you talking about, Atina? Why are you acting like that? You believe the same as I. Honesty is the best religion, Atina. You agree Padre, no?" Sarita asked.

Sarita threw herbs into the stew.

"Oh I am a firm believer in Christian honesty," the friar said. "And Christ compels us to be honest in many ways. Atina has been very honest with me. She tells me how she has a husband named Sarito and how she goes down to Barcelona for Mass."

"That is no honesty," Sarita said. "She is telling you a tall mountain tale. Here. Dinner is ready."

Sarita placed plates on the table with rabbit stew.

"Dig in. The food will not stay warm forever," Sarita said.

Atina ate very little. The friar ate more but paused in thought between bites. Sarita ate hungrily as if the world were ending.

"I would like to learn more about you two, Sarita," the friar said.

"Oh there is not much to tell," Sarita said. "We live in these mountains, as you can see."

"What about husbands and family? Why deny the sacrament of marriage that allows you to lawfully bring children into the world?" Friar Christiani said.

"I mean not to offend, Padre, but Atina and I do not fancy men, if you know what I mean," Sarita said.

"I do child, I do. Your souls are in mortal danger of the fires of Hell!" he said with an angry tone.

"Hey there! You do not need to get all angry about how we live. The mountain takes care of our needs and all," Sarita said.

"God gives us what we need. And he takes away! In the name of the Roman Catholic Church, I proclaim you, Atina, and you, Sarita, as blasphemers of the Church, Christ, and Almighty God! You will be brought before the Dominican Order where we will decide if you can be saved through penance, or if punishment by death will save your souls," the friar said.

"Oh lightning and thunder!" Sarita said. "That was a mouthful. But you have no power over us. Mother Nature is the only one we answer to. Now you best mind your manners while you are our guest, or I will kick you out. That is no lie."

"Sarita," Atina said. "I think we have said enough."

"No, we have not. I am tired of you egotistical Christian Padres and whatnot spewing your words of salvation when all you really do is capture and kill," Sarita said. "You are in our house now. I suggest you sit there and only open your mouth to eat or drink!"

Sarita slapped Friar Christiani on the shoulder, and the blow knocked him to the floor. Atina rushed over to help him up.

"Thank you child, thank you," Friar Christiani said to Atina.

The friar shook in nervousness. He had underestimated Sarita's resolve and physical strength. He knew he could not survive a physical confrontation with her.

"Did you mean all that about us being condemned and killed?" Atina asked.

The friar looked at Sarita, and Sarita returned a grim expression. The friar changed his tone with Atina.

"There are many ways to achieve grace," the friar said. "Helping your fellow neighbor is one way."

"He is right," Atina said to Sarita. "We must help people more."

"Be careful," Sarita said. "He could be recruiting."

"What?" Atina said.

"Sarita is right," Friar Christiani said. "I confess—I am recruiting. The Kingdoms of Aragon and Castile are dealing with invasions from the Moors in the south. My mission is to find new ways to help beat back the invaders. Men have long helped our kingdoms fight these invaders, but I fear they are not enough. I am traveling these mountains to find new help. I have prayed to God, and he sent me to this hut. Why? I do not know. There are no military men in this hut, so I have reached a dead end, I am afraid."

"Aww, see? We must help the padre," Atina said.

"You are very clever, Padre," Sarita said. "You tell us this sad tale so that we will feel sorry for you and help. But as you said, we are not military men. The armies of Iberia do not permit women to fight alongside them. Nor are women permitted in places of power. That goes for military officers and nobles. Even positions of power in your church are denied to women."

"Yes, yes, it is all true," Friar Christiani admitted.

"I tell you this," Sarita said. "Give us positions of power, and we will help beat back the Moors."

"But you know that is impossible," Friar Christiani said. "The world does not suffer women in power."

"Then I suggest you leave our hut and never return," Sarita said.

Friar Christiani remained silent for a moment.

"Wait," Atina said. "Maybe we can reach a compromise."

"There is no compromising with men," Sarita replied. "They compromise us. Have been since the gender was invented."

"Perhaps," Friar Christiani said. "But perhaps Atina has an idea. Tell us your idea, Atina."

"Well, it seems to me all battles are fought in the valley or in plains," Atina said.

"Of course. How else could they be fought?" the friar asked.

"In the mountains!" Atina said.

Sarita rolled her eyes. The friar looked puzzled.

"Neither Moorish nor Christian armies will travel to the mountains to do battle," the friar said.

"No, they will not," Sarita said. "And you slipped, Padre. Just now. You said, 'Christian armies.' Is this a religious fight?

We will not be part of helping one religion over another, unless the religion is our own worship of Mother Nature and her natural world."

"But if you do not help, the Moors will push northward and destroy the peace we have now. By not helping our armies, you are helping the Moors. Can you stay here and do nothing while your neighbor goes south to defend our soil?" Friar Christiani asked. "Yes, our army is often called the Christian Army, but this is a convenience. You do not have to fight as a Christian. Fight as you are for Iberia which happens to be Christian. I was once a Jew, but I saw that Christians are on the winning side. You want to be on the winning side, no?"

"A call to action," Sarita said. "You have a slick tongue, Padre. But I think—"

"Sarita, come here," Atina said.

Atina led Sarita into a back room. The two engaged in a heated exchange. They tried keeping things to a whisper, but periodically their excitement raised their voices. After a time, the two reemerged.

"How serious is the threat from the Moors?" Sarita asked.

"Very. A new tribe, the Marinids, are gathering strength in northern Africa and Morocco. With a quick stroke, they will cross the straits and reinvade Iberia through Iberian port towns Tarifa and Algeciras."

Sarita looked at Atina and nodded, yes.

"We are loyal to King James and will help the Kingdom of Aragon as best we can. But our domain is in the mountains. We are Celts, and that means living in mountains," Atina said.

"Then you can be of no help. Mountains are too slow for speedy conquest," Friar Christiani said.

"We will not join your army either," Atina said. "Since we would object to being subservient to men, not to mention it is forbidden among you. But we will form our own army and cooperate with yours."

Friar Christiani broke into laughter.

"This is what you are looking for, no?" Sarita asked. "An army? Or at least the ability to have an army help you?"

"I am looking for help, yes. An army of men if I am lucky. A group of women to cook and sew for male soldiers if I am not so lucky," Friar Christiani said. "But how can you organize into an army?"

"We, Sarita and I, have decided that before we tell you anything, you must swear that you not reveal our secrets to anyone else. Also, we will be in charge of our army. If you try working around us, we will disband the army immediately. As payment for helping you, you arrange to cede land to us and exempt us from taxes."

"I might have known," Friar Christiani said. "Everyone wants land, and no one wants to pay taxes."

"We do not ask for much. Certain stretches of mountain land is what we ask. In fact, we already inhabit much of what we request. We simply want official protection for the lands we inhabit and no taxes."

"We? You speak as if you are already a large group, organized and living on various mountains around Iberia," Friar Christiani said.

"We are," Sarita said.

"But how? Any form of group must have structure. It must meet and discuss and make plans," Friar Christiani said.

"We meet. But not in cities like Barcelona. We live on the mountains, but we meet with other women on other mountains," Atina said.

"Is this some sort of dark magic? How can one do that? Even the greatest sorcerers cannot communicate with each other from a distance without messenger on horseback," Friar Christiani said.

"We will show you," Atina said.

Atina removed a cover from a shelf, revealing a cylindrical device with an opening on one end and an egg-shaped reflector on the other. Running vertically through the reflector was a clear tube. Sarita removed another cover and produced an oil lamp with support rods for something on top, and what appeared to be a green-shaded circular hand mirror. Sarita lit the oil lamp and placed it on the table. Atina placed the cylinder on the support rods of the oil lamp's frame and carefully aligned the lamp's flame to pass through the clear vertical tube. The device produced a light out of the main cylinder and against the wall much like a flashlight. Atina turned the device and pointed it at Friar Christiani. The friar blocked his eyes with his hands.

"Turn that away. It blinds me," the friar said.

Atina turned it away.

"This is how you communicate?" the friar asked.

"Yes," Atina said.

"You flash lights, and someone in the distance reads them?" the friar suggested.

"Much as you say, yes," Sarita said. "We communicate using this light with others on mountains far away. We can be the eyes of Iberia. Should the Moors attack, we can quickly relay number of troops, type, and position."

"But this is hardly a secret means. The enemy could intercept your signals and learn your code. He could learn about us through this system. Or he could send false information and deceive us. No, this is not clever. I should have known women would think their little devices are good enough to work in the real world."

"If you will stop your jaw for a moment, we will explain the full ability of our device. And our other plans," Sarita said.

The friar held silent.

"We do not shine the light as it is," Atina said. "Sarita is holding a green glass."

"A hand mirror," Friar Christiani said.

"You are doing it again," Sarita said. "You are interrupting before full explanation is given. Now apologize."

"What? I am a friar! A man of God! I need not apologize—"

"Apologize or the deal is off!" Sarita demanded.

The friar hesitated for a moment.

"I apologize," he said.

"That is better," Sarita said. "Continue, Atina."

"We pass the green glass in front of the light beam like this. Then we move it back and forth like this. There are three different colors of green on this glass—all with the same shading intensity. If we are not transmitting, we stay on one color. If transmitting, we shift colors around. We name the colors yellow-green, green, and blue-green, but as you can see, they are all greener than yellow or blue," Atina said.

The friar lifted a finger in a request to speak.

"Yes?" Sarita said.

"They all look green to me," said the friar as he looked at the dark-green glass.

"Look, I will show you," Atina said.

Atina passed the glass in front of the light beam, and green light shone on the wall. She moved the glass around to show the different colors.

"Do you see how it changes from green to yellow-green to blue-green?" Atina asked.

The friar lifted his finger again.

"Yes, you may speak," Sarita said.

"They all look green to me," the friar repeated.

Atina looked confused.

"I told you," Sarita said to Atina. "No man can see these shades of green, and many women cannot either. But some of us can."

"You really cannot see the differences in these colors?" Atina asked the friar.

"No. In fact, I think you are making a game of this. I do not believe you have any ability to communicate with other women. How can a woman see different shades of green when men have superior vision?" the friar asked.

"Did I not tell you he would not believe?" Sarita told Atina.

"We can prove it works," Atina said to the friar. "I will send a message to Sarita, and she will tell me what I said."

Atina moved the hand-glass in front of the light beam in various motions.

"Hello Padre," Sarita said.

"That proves nothing. You could have said anything," the friar said.

"I have another idea," Atina said. "Write a message for me. I will send the message to Sarita."

"Can you read?" the friar asked.

"Of course I can!" Atina said.

"We all can," Sarita said. "We must be able to read to use the communication beam."

"Very well. I will write a message," the friar said.

Atina brought forth a dried leaf, berry ink, and a pointed stick. The friar dipped the stick in berry ink and wrote on the leaf.

"No peeking," the friar said to Sarita.

"I cannot see a thing," Sarita said, who had her back to the other two.

The friar handed the leaf to Atina. Atina pointed the light beam on the wall Sarita now faced. Atina moved the green glass in various directions in front of the beam, and Sarita observed the green light.

"Atina...your...hair...is...golden...red," Sarita said.

The friar stood up in shock!

"How could you know what I wrote?!" the friar asked in amazement.

"We explained how the light works," Atina said.

"But the light never changed!" Friar Christiani said. "Are you witches? Can you read people's minds? You are heretics! How can I call on an army of heretical witches!?"

"We are not witches, and we are not heretics!" Sarita said. "We cannot read your mind. We can read body language, but so can most women. We explained that some women can see the color changes and some cannot. We have not found a man who can."

"How can I believe you when my own eyes say you are lying?" Friar Christiani asked. "How?"

"Did we not prove our claim here where we stand?" Sarita said.

"Yes."

"You believe in a God. But you do not see him," Atina said. "We believe in a God too, though we cannot see her."

"But God is different. Everyone believes in God. But this— no one would believe me if I told them. They would claim I had gone mad. I would be defrocked," the friar said.

"Good," Sarita said. "Then you will not be motivated to tell people our secret."

"Do that again," the friar said. "Send another message. Wait, I will write something."

Friar Christiani wrote another message on a dried leaf and handed it to Atina.

"The Disputation is won. Iberia will soon be ours," Sarita said.

"Yes, it shall," Friar Christiani said. "Now, I have a question—how far can you communicate?"

"To the next mountain," Atina said. "And with relays, we can communicate along an arc on a chain of peaks from southern Iberia east roughly along the Mediterranean coast up into Aragon and farther to the Pyrenees and west along the northern Iberian mountains into Galicia. And we are mobile. We can pack our things and travel by pony to other locations if need be."

"Ponies, ha!" the friar laughed.

"Do not underestimate mountain ponies," Sarita said. "They are smooth and surefooted. They carry us with ease and unexpected speed onto mountain paths where men think twice before traveling."

"Oh, if only they could be converted into warhorses. A pony is no match for a fully armored warhorse," Friar Christiani said.

"Oh but they are!" Atina bragged, though Sarita showed a bit of disapproval that Atina had let this information slip out.

"You cannot be serious," the friar said. "A pony versus a warhorse? You might as well pit a woman versus a man."

"A small woman riding a good pony can outrun a warhorse any day," Atina bragged. "She can run circles around a male army. She can elude the army up a mountain if need be."

"Run all you may, but running will not stop an army," the friar said.

"She can run and shoot arrows. She can run and slash with a light but speedy sword," Sarita said. "These techniques require skill, but they are proven. We Celts have a fiery spirit that cannot easily be vanquished. We prefer not to fight, but if we must, we will fight to the very end. And we are quick. We do not plod along like slow, lumbering elephants. We are tigers. We stalk the enemy, strike quickly, and vanish before the enemy can respond."

"That would be interesting to see. It violates every known notion about warfare," Friar Christiani said. "I would like to test you with that ability. And to think I can send women into battle in exchange for some worthless mountain land and exemption from taxes."

"Not so fast," Sarita said. "No one agreed to mountain land and exemption of taxes in exchange for battle."

"You already agreed to—" the friar started.

"That was for communication only," Sarita said. "Our price for battle is much higher."

"Oh? What else is there?" the friar asked.

"We want ships," Atina said. "We want ships to explore the world and find the lost world of—"

"You need not tell him that part," Sarita said.

"Ships? Are you serious? That is impossible. Even if I wanted to, I do not have the power to give you ships," Friar Christiani said.

"Then I suggest you find the power," Sarita said. "That is, if you wish to have dealings with us."

"There's something else," Atina said. "You must negotiate deals with the Kingdom of Castile for our greenbeam sisters in Castile. They will also expect the same payment of land, tax-exemptions, and ships that we do. We greenbeam sisters are in this together."

"You will find King Alfonso is most receptive to expanding Castile's borders southward. However, he *will* give up land through proper negotiation. He just yielded Algarve back to Portugal," Sarita said.

"You know this?" the friar asked.

"Yes," Atina said. "We learned on the greenbeam."

"We would have learned sooner, but we had an interruption in the greenbeam," Sarita said. "The relay is like a chain—one break, and the entire chain fails."

"What sort of interruption?" the friar asked.

"Most likely a tax collector. Or a friar visiting from the city," Sarita said with a knowing glance.

"Am I interfering with the relay?" the friar asked.

"Look out the window," Atina said. "Do you see that green light in the distance?"

"Yes. A solid green light," the friar said.

"It is not solid," Sarita said. "It is blinking. The beamer is requesting we acknowledge her signal. She has more news to relay. But we are interrupted. The news cannot pass until we complete the relay. Your visit is a perfect example of how the relay can fail."

"Padre, we must get back to our greenbeam relay," Atina said. "We explained the situation. Our advice to you is this— secure our demands for land and tax-exemption in the Kingdom of Aragon. Keep the greenbeam and pony information secret for the moment. Come back with documentation to prove your good deed."

"After that," Sarita continued, "you must go on to Castile and make nice with King Alfonso. Do what you do best. Offer to educate his children on the ways of your religion and whatnot. Gain his trust and the trust of his heir, Fernando. Seek out our Castilian greenbeam sisters. Through them we will guide you."

Friar Christiani started another question, but Atina and Sarita shooed him out the door. He stood for a moment by their doorway before walking down the mountain back to Barcelona.

"I must go to Castile, yes. I must influence the Infante Fernando," Friar Christiani said to himself. "But to what end? I will not be some pawn of the greenbeam sisters. They will be one of my tools. Yes. I will fake documents of deed and tax-exemption to assuage them. But the promise of ships will be more difficult. That must be faked, of course, but convincing them will be more difficult. They will wish to see the ships. I may have to go against common wisdom and actually provide real ships. But this is a diversion. I must keep straight to my mission, my mission to expel the Jews. What keeps them here? The kings are busy with the Moors, so I must eliminate the Jews. The Jews pay taxes. I must find a replacement income for the king. No, for both kings of Aragon and Castile. But how? God, hear me now! I pray you inspire me with the solution! Jews, Moors, land, taxes, ships, money!"

Friar Christiani held silent for another ten minutes. A ray of sunlight broke through the clouds, and the friar received an inspiration.

"If we bypass the Moors in Granada, the Moors in northern Africa, and the Moors in the Near East, we could trade directly with the Far East using ships and improve our profits. Substantially. We could claim to offer these ships to the greenbeam sisters and mislead them to the Far East. The greenbeam sisters would be satisfied, and there would be enough profit to cover whatever taxes we would lose from the Jews. The silence of the Jews at the Disputation will result in their permanent silence when they are expelled! This is it! God has answered my prayers!"

The world shifted into shades of green. The greenbeam women continued signaling along the greenbeam circuit that Atina and Sarita had described to Friar Christiani. The friar produced fake documents from King James supposedly guaranteeing land and tax-exemption for the greenbeam sisters in Aragon. The friar befriended King Alfonso X and took to educating his children on their religion. The Infante Fernando de la Cerda took to the friar like an uncle, and in November 1268 at Fernando's insistence, the friar married Fernando to Princess Blanche of France.

With the help of the greenbeam circuit, the friar received thorough and accurate intelligence on Moor activity in southern Iberia. The friar provided this intelligence to Fernando who in turn passed it on to his father. In this way, the friar became a trusted and valuable person to Fernando and the Kingdom of Castile.

In 1269, the friar became aware of King Alfonso's urgent need to obtain money. The king had contemplated debasing the kingdom's currency. The friar, with the help of the greenbeam circuit that had collectively overheard conversations from local nobles, convinced the king that debasing the money system would be a disaster for the Kingdom of Castile, and that there was a better way to increase the royal coffers. It was at this time that Friar Christiani introduced his plan for an ocean link with the Far East. King Alfonso seemed surprised, but Fernando convinced his father that the friar had never steered them wrong before, and that perhaps it was time to expand Castile's navy to establish new shipping routes to the Far East. Alfonso gave charge of this task to Fernando. Fernando in turn looked to the friar, and the friar turned to Atina and Sarita. Atina and Sarita, with the greenbeam, helped coordinate the production of shipbuilding supplies to key ports in Galicia where new navy and merchant ships were built. The friar worked out an agreement with Atina and Sarita—greenbeam women would command some navy ships and provide protective services for merchant ships to the Far East. After several years of service, these women would earn rights to own the ships in use. In this way, male-commanded navy ships were not deployed on these voyages and were instead kept in regular patrol duty along the ocean and Mediterranean shorelines of Iberia.

With the excellent greenbeam circuit, the ships were built quickly. The women brought the greenbeam technology on their ships and traveled in groups of threes with the greenbeam providing communication between ships. The women took ponies on board for possible ship-to-ship attack or for use on land. The ponies required less space than comparable horses, needed less food, and tolerated the sea voyages very well.

The women also took the newly invented cannon and refined it for ship use, creating a multiuse ship cannon that could also launch a special time-delay flare into the sky. The flare was able to send short messages up to fifty miles away by flashing in shades of green—the same shades as used in the greenbeam.

There were some skirmishes at sea, often with pirates, but they were resolved quickly either by the other two greenbeam ships coming to the aid of the one under attack, or with the women's arsenal of cannon, sword, bow, and pony. The pirates succumbed or fled.

1275 Jun 1. Villarreal, Kingdom of Valencia, Iberia.

Two crowns of Iberia—King James I of Aragon in the east, and his son-in-law King Alfonso X of Castile in central and central-west, were just as intent on completing the last phase of the *Reconquista* as they were when Jonara first visited Villarreal in 1275.

Andalusia remained a battleground between Christians (under King Alfonso X and King James I), and Muslims (under Arab control). The Kingdom of Granada maintained its loyalty to the Castile kingdom, but the loyalty of Granada citizens would not help them last to 1492.

It was June 1st and not July 24th. Through the greenbeam circuit, the Infante Fernando de la Cerda learned of Marinid forces crossing the Straits of Gibraltar from Morocco into Tarifa, Andalusia ahead of Sultan Abu Yusuf Ya'qub's planned entry. The Marinids intended to advance along the Guadalquivir River toward Córdoba to regain Arab land lost to the Christian *Reconquista*. The Infante rushed with his troops to meet the Arabs in battle.

Fernando, who again happened to be in Valencia, stopped the troops for the night in Villarreal as he had in Jonara's prior visit to 1275. Officers and Friar Christiani joined Fernando in food and song at an inn named, *La Taberna del Rey*.

"Barmaid!" called one of Fernando's officers. "More red wine! And what about dinner?"

Jonara noticed immediately that this Fernando was calm and clearheaded while the previous Fernando was more outlandish and willing to take risks. The barmaid brought forth several bottles of wines and cups, disappeared, and returned with platters of fish. She set a particularly unusual fish with a large head on the Infante's plate.

"My Lord," Friar Christiani said. "Remember what I taught you? The largest and most aggressive predators eat all the poison."

"Yes," Prince Fernando said. "You are right."

"Barmaid!" yelled an officer. "This fish is not fit for king or man. Throw it to the dogs!"

The barmaid took Fernando's plate, disappeared into the kitchen, and returned with two smaller fish.

"Much better," the friar said. "These fish are smaller, but they have well-developed lines. They have eaten wisely in their lives and will yield high-quality flesh."

Fernando and his officers ate their dinner and drank their wine with much satisfaction. As the men had their fill, Friar Christiani pointed to one of the wait-staff. The wait-staff acknowledged him, disappeared, and reappeared with a young woman with long, red hair, and two men—one with a lute, and the other with a flute. The men played, and the woman sang from the *Cantigas de Santa Maria*.

"I have arranged music while we eat," the friar said to Fernando. "The singer's name is Atina of Tarragona. She is one of my key information contacts."

"She is beautiful," the prince said. "I should like to meet her."

"You shall. I have invited her to our table after her performance. But a word of advice, my dear Infante. She is a key member of the greenbeam army. She is not candy to be eaten. Keep your manners as I have taught you," the friar said.

"Of course, Padre," Fernando said.

Atina finished her song. The flute and lute players continued with additional music while Atina visited Fernando's table. Fernando pulled up a chair for her from another table and assisted her in sitting down.

"Thank you, my Lord," Atina said.

"The pleasure is mine," Prince Fernando said. "Friar Christiani has told me much about you. I am very proud of the greenbeam circuit and the greenbeam navy. We have successfully traded with the Far East for six years. The Kingdom of Castile grows richer by the month. I want to thank you and the greenbeam sisters for their devotion to the king."

"Thank you, my Lord. We are proud to help Iberia—both Castile and Aragon," Atina said.

"Atina has readied the greenbeam army, my Lord," the friar said.

"This will be their first use in combat. I am still uncomfortable with women in combat roles," Prince Fernando said.

"My Lord. My greenbeam sisters have spent six years in navy battles fighting off pirates to secure free commerce between Iberia and the Far East. Is this not enough to prove our hardiness in battle?" Atina asked.

"Those were at sea," Fernando said. "I still marvel at the luck."

"It is no luck, my Lord. We Celtic women are a hardy folk and will fight to the bitter end to protect our own," Atina said.

Atina's eyes lit with a fire nearly as red as her hair. For a moment, Prince Fernando was humbled, but he broke out in laughter to relieve the tension.

"I am glad the Celts of Iberia are on our side," the Infante said. "But I am concerned. The Marinids are advancing along the Guadalquivir River. This is hardly near the mountains where the greenbeam army dwells."

"I anticipated this, my Lord," Atina said. "We will descend from the mountains in Córdoba and march ahead of your forces. We will keep in contact using greenbeams, but this means one of us must ride with your forces."

"Then I should choose you to ride with me," Fernando said to Atina.

"I expected as much," the friar said. "That is also why I invited Atina to our table."

"My Lord," Atina said. "I am a woman of high honor. I expect you to respect me with equally high honor. You are married, and I am promised to another. We must keep our relationship professional."

"You realize I am heir to the throne and could have my way," the Infante said.

"We know," the friar said, "but I am also your Padre and confessor. You would answer to God through me. But why speak of such things now?"

"Yes, very true," the Infante said. "A toast then to victory over the Moors."

They toasted and drank. Fernando's officers drank and danced with local women. Fernando, the friar, and Atina went upstairs to Atina's inn room. Unlike Jonara's other visit to 1275, Sarita did not suddenly appear.

"Atina," Fernando said. "You mentioned your promise to another. Where is your other?"

"She is in Córdoba. She will lead our greenbeam army," Atina said.

"You are promised to a woman?" the prince asked.

"Blasphemy against the Church, my Lord," Friar Christiani said. "Yes, I knew of this. But these are Celts, and they worship nature. They may be pagan, but they are willing to help us. I will not seek their conversion at this time, but there is always hope for the future."

"Not likely," Atina said. "We are lovers of peace and nature. But my personal life should not take issue here. My greenbeam sisters have promised to help, and we shall."

The three stayed up late into the next morning working out strategy for the upcoming battle against the Marinids. The scene was quite different from the one Jonara remembered the other time she visited Villarreal in 1275. In this timeline, Fernando did not flirt with Atina at all. He grew to admire her more as a strategist and fellow countryperson.

"It is a strange thing," Fernando said near the end of the meeting. "When I discuss military strategy with you, I forget you are a woman."

"I take that as a compliment," Atina said. "My Lord. It is late. The march to Córdoba is over 300,000 paces. I suggest we rest for the night."

"You are wise. Tomorrow will be a long march. Or should I say, later today will be a long march!" Prince Fernando said. "And the next day. And the next for a week."

1275 Jun 8. Córdoba, Kingdom of Castile.

A week after meeting with Atina of Tarragona in Villarreal, Prince Fernando's troops arrived in Córdoba. Atina was outfitted in leather armor, a lightweight steel helmet, a stiff leather shield, a sword, a bow with arrows, a knife, and a spear. Jonara rode with Atina on her black Asturcon pony named Tinta. Jonara could not understand how, but she experienced the entire seven days on the pony with such ease and comfort that seven days seemed to be only seven seconds. When the warhorses trotted, Atina directed Tinta into an ambling gait, and when the warhorses walked, Tinta walked. Both of Tinta's gaits were smooth, leading Jonara to wonder if she had traveled anywhere at all. One thing did catch Jonara's attention—Fernando's warhorses were the most beautiful she had seen in any time or place. It seemed a shame they were used for battle when they could perform for happy crowds in a parade or horse show.

"Atina," called a voice.

A white Galician pony pulled up next to Tinta.

"Sarita," Atina said. "Oh how I missed you."

The two hugged while alongside each other.

"Look at you in that attractive leather armor," Sarita said. "I can hardly wait to have you in my arms tonight."

Atina blushed.

"Where is your armor?" Atina asked.

"It is at the hut where I am staying," Sarita said. "I have yet to try it on. I have not had the time."

"Have not had the time?" Atina asked in amazement. "How is it I found the time but you have not?"

"That is an interesting question," Sarita said, "a question I will postpone answering for the moment."

Atina gave Sarita a funny look, paused, and looked at Sarita's pony.

"Polilla looks great," Atina said, referring to Sarita's pony.

"She should. She did not ride 300,000 paces in a week as did Tinta," Sarita laughed.

"I am glad you are happy. I am tired and dirty. I need a good bath," Atina said.

Sarita sniffed Atina out of fun.

"Yes, you do," Sarita chuckled.

"You would smell too if you marched a week with little rest," Atina said.

"For which I am proud," Sarita said. "And I am here to offer you good food and rest. We—you and I—are staying with one of our greenbeam sisters nearby—on a hill north of Córdoba."

"Do not tell me. Could they be the greenbeam inventors?" Atina asked.

"Who else? It is time you meet Verda and Raya," Sarita said.

"I am almost too tired to meet them. I hear they hold parties every night," Atina said.

"The legend of their all-night parties...is mostly legend. They are down to three nights a week," Sarita said.

"I knew it," Atina said. "This explains why you have had no time for fitting your armor. You spend your days and nights in celebration while I endure the long march."

"Yes, well, perhaps we can think about that another time. Tonight is one of their nights. They are celebrating your arrival. I hope you can stay up at least part of the night. Many friends will attend," Sarita said. "Please—be a good greenbeam sister and celebrate with us. The women are all very proud of you."

"Only if you let me have a sip of your refreshing tonic. I will need it to deal with my trip and tonight's party," Atina said.

"Agreed," Sarita said.

"I have only a little more time I must spend with the prince today after which we may visit the greenbeam inventors," Atina said.

Sarita continued riding alongside Atina until Prince Fernando's troops made camp for the night. Atina introduced Sarita to the prince to which the prince was happy to make Sarita's acquaintance. Sarita eyed the friar with a little suspicion as she did before, but she kept up a polite façade, and the friar made no trouble. Sarita and Atina agreed to meet the prince early the next day to resume the march toward the Marinids.

"The greenbeam relay reports the Marinids are approaching Sevilla," Sarita informed the prince.

"Then that is where we will intercept them. It is unfortunate they have progressed so far northward. This is my failing. I was so eager to guard our merchant vessels to the Far East that I completely ignored the very ports needing the most protection—

Tarifa, Algecira, and Gibraltar. I will not make that mistake again. Once we defeat the Marinids, I will expand the navy to protect those ports. Fortunately for us, we have learned very quickly of the Marinids' movements. Without the timely green-beam relay, we would be marching to meet them in July and not June. There would be more destruction from the Marinids, and we would most likely be fighting them in Écija, Ciudad Re-al, or even Córdoba," the prince said.

"They are a most helpful group, these Celtic mountain-dwelling women," Friar Christiani said. "It is difficult for me to admit at times, but as I have said before, my primary knowledge on the movements in Iberia are due to their accurate infor-mation relayed through the greenbeam circuit. They have never led me astray."

"And we never will," Atina said. "We are true to our word to the very end. And we admit when we are in the wrong."

"The greenbeam women have proven their service—so far," Prince Fernando said. "But the real test will come in Sevilla. You do realize there will be bloodshed. People will die. I do not like seeing women die in combat. I will not order your women to fight. I give you liberty to back down while we are here in Cór-doba. But once we begin the last march tomorrow, our fighting forces must be unified. To desert on the precipice of battle is dishonorable and deadly."

"We will not desert, and we will not back down even now. I give you my word as a Celtic woman," Atina said. "We will aid you against the Moors for the preservation of Iberia."

Atina finished with the prince, and she rode Tinta alongside Sarita and Polilla to the northern edges of Córdoba. The path narrowed and steadily grew steeper as the two climbed a hill on the southern outcrops of the Morena Mountains. Tinta stum-bled on a few steps, causing Atina to stop several times.

"What is ill with Tinta?" Sarita asked.

"She is very tired," Atina said. "And perhaps she got lazy marching with the Andalusian warhorses. Those warhorses are so beautiful that it is no wonder my Tinta imitated their horse habits and forgot she is a pony. But there is nothing like a short trip on rocky hill paths to refresh her memory."

The two arrived at the top of the hill.

"Where is the hut?" Atina asked.

"Hidden amongst the rocks and fir trees," Sarita said.

Sarita removed two stones from a saddlebag and tapped them against each other in a special pattern. A click from inside the fir trees replied, and a woman emerged.

"Sarita! You are late," the woman laughed.

"Verda," Sarita laughed back. "I bring Atina of Tarragona."

"Welcome, Atina," Verda said. "We have room for your ponies in back. Come this way."

Verda led the two around the fir trees and stopped. She clicked two stones together, and the fir trees parted enough to form an archway. Jonara did not understand how the trees responded to Verda's stone tapping, but there was no way to ask her. The two ponies followed Verda through the archway and into a stable where ten ponies stood.

"You were not joking about a party," Atina said. "Where is that tonic?"

"Here," Sarita said. "I keep some with me at all times."

Atina took a bottle from Sarita and downed its contents.

"Careful!" Sarita said. "That stuff is powerful."

"I will need it," Atina said.

Verda led the two inside, and Jonara followed behind. Raya introduced her greenbeam guests to Sarita and Atina, and after pleasantries were exchanged, Sarita showed Atina to a hot bath. It was in the bath that Atina forgot her travel fatigue. She fell asleep and did not wake until Sarita walked in and shook her.

"This is a first. You fell asleep with my tonic in you," Sarita said. "That never happens."

"I was dead tired," Atina said. "What time is it?"

"Dead tired? Do not slip into the bath and drown or you will be dead tired," Sarita said. "As for the time, it is time you finish your bath and put on fresh clothes. I brought some for you and placed them on the shelf over here. Now clean up! Dinner is almost served, and we do not want to be rude by skipping."

Atina finished her bath, dried off, and put on fresh clothes. She joined the other women at the dinner table and sat next to

Sarita. Verda gave a brief blessing of thanks, and the women ate.

Jonara wished she could try some of the cuisine. Rabbit stew with herbs, bread, and red wine were the main portions. A bowl of fresh fruit was passed around at one point.

"Things don't seem so bad in this timeline," Jonara thought to herself. "It's hard to believe all this results in the United States being taken over by the Roman Catholic Church."

"Oh but it does," Nekara said as she popped into Verda's and Raya's hut without warning.

"What are you doing here?" Jonara asked. "You were on the Montseny Mountains last I saw."

"You don't think I'd miss all the fun, do you?" Nekara asked.

"So far, the only evil I've seen is your murder of Rabbi Nachmanides, although I wonder about this Friar Christiani guy. He convinced these Celtic women to help him in the war against the Moors," Jonara said.

"Yes," Nekara said. "The friar has been especially helpful to me. He has influenced Prince Fernando in the precise direction I require to spread religious totalitarianism in the yet-to-be discovered Americas. Prince Fernando will not die as he did when Felifia held sway. He lives. He lives!"

"And that's an evil thing?" Jonara said.

"Judge evil by the results, Jonara. Then you will understand. But that is an advantage I have over you Earth people. I can see the good or ill of a situation, but you cannot always. What you might consider good may turn out quite evil. But one person's evil is another's good. The *Reconquista* has accelerated, and there is nothing you can do to slow it. Or stop it."

"Felifia will help me," Jonara said.

Nekara pulled out a pendant and swung it back and forth— a pendant with the duavisha attached to a neck chain.

"Felifia is quite incapable of helping you at the moment. Isn't that right, Felifia?" Nekara asked as she looked into the duavisha.

Nekara disappeared. The evening grew into night, and the greenbeam women celebrated with music, dance, and wine. At some points a woman would read poetry aloud, at other times another woman would sing. The women begged Atina to sing for them, and she did after which Atina received much applause. Night hours passed, and the new day arrived. The women continued their celebration, but even Celtic women cannot prevent alcohol's inebriatic effect. One by one, the women fell into slumber until the last woman—Sarita—carried on a conversation by herself for a good fifteen minutes before passing out.

1275 Jun 9. Córdoba, Kingdom of Castile.

"Clackity, clackity, clack!" chattered a tapping device connected to a greenbeam receiver.

Jonara, in a strange sort of way, had "slept" alongside Atina and Sarita on a large slab of straw covered with burlap. The night was old, but the first grays of dawn touched the sky.

"Clackity, clackity, clack!" chattered the receiver again.

"It is your turn," Verda said to Raya.

Raya got up, lit her greenbeam, and signaled back that she was receiving. The device chattered again but with a longer chattering as if chattering up a long message, which it was. Raya wrote down the message on a dried leaf. During the chattering, the other women awoke.

"What is that chattering sound?" Atina asked.

"That's the latest invention by Raya," Sarita said. "It converts greenbeam flashes into clacking sounds."

"That's dangerous!" Atina said. "If the enemy should get hold of it, he could intercept our messages!"

"Yes, it is. Raya and Verda will not say how this one is made nor will they make additional ones for others," Sarita said.

"I should hope not," Atina said. "But I have to admit, it would be nice having—"

"Sisters of the greenbeam," Raya called to the awaking party. "I have news from the relay. Marinid forces have reached the city of Sevilla by the Guadalquivir River. They marched through the night and arrived at Sevilla sooner than anticipated."

The women groaned.

"There is more," Raya said. "At great risk and with personal disgust, some of our greenbeam sisters slept with Marinid soldiers to learn their plans. The Marinids intend to split their forces. One shall travel northeast along the Guadalquivir River (and thus along the Morena Mountains), the other shall travel along the middle of the river plain toward Carmona and farther if allowed."

"This changes everything," Sarita said. "We only recently established a new relay along the Morena Mountains."

"Yes," Verda said. "The Morena relay allows us to watch over the Guadalquivir River. But we have no surveillance or greenbeam relay covering the middle of the river basin."

"This means we will be blind to the Marinid force as it pushes into Carmona and beyond into Écija," Sarita said.

"They could push all the way to Córdoba on the river plain and catch us from behind if we ignore and send our armies along the river," Atina said.

"We cannot ignore the Marinid forces along the river," Raya said.

"Then there is only one solution," Sarita said.

"Yes. Prince Fernando and we must divide our troops—one group takes the river, the other the river basin."

"I do not like dividing up our armies," Atina said. "It spreads us out and makes us vulnerable."

"We must," Verda said. "Otherwise, the Marinids will push through one way or another."

"We must use all speed on our ponies to cover ground. The basin spreads far. Armored Andalusian horses cannot crisscross the basin as the ponies can," Raya said.

"And we must maintain communication between armies," said Verda.

"I know the basin regions," Sarita said. "There are only small, scattered ranges between Córdoba and Carmona. Carmona is situated on a nice ridge—if we can get there before the Marinids."

"Which you cannot," Verda said.

"Which means only one thing," Sarita said.

"You cannot mean what I think you mean," Atina said.

"You cannot build mountains in the basin," said Raya. "This means some of you must act as a moving relay between the river force and the basin force."

"Some?" Atina asked. "How many?"

"Three for one relay—not counting the endpoints in each army. But there should be two relays—meaning six of you—in case one relay is killed," Raya said.

"That is my concern," Atina said. "The women working the moving relay will be alone. Isolated. No help can reach them in time to save them from a surprise attack."

"It is a risk," Sarita said. "But we are Celtic women. We can tolerate extended periods of isolation."

"The relay will be isolated only in physical regards. It will be in contact with both sides using the greenbeam," Raya said. "So the isolation will not be complete."

The women held silent for a moment.

"Then I must volunteer to be one of the relay women," Atina said.

"No, Atina, you cannot," Sarita said.

"I know you are trying to protect me, my Promise," Atina said to Sarita, "But I did initiate the liaison with Prince Fernando, so I must take responsibility for the relay."

"Sarita is right," Verda said. "You cannot be on the relay. It is precisely because of your liaison with the prince that you must accompany his half of the warhorses."

"And who will lead the other half?" Atina asked.

Verda and Raya pointed their fingers at Sarita. Atina looked at Sarita, and she raised her hand in affirmation.

"Not my Promised! Sarita! I had hoped you would accompany me in battle. If we die, we die together," Atina said.

"We shall not die," Sarita grinned as she pulled a sword out of its sheath and swung it in the air. "Not yet!"

"Six of the rest of you must act as the two teams of moving greenbeam relays," Verda said.

All eight of the other women volunteered.

"Hmmm," Verda mused.

"It appears we will not have any difficulty choosing the relay teams," Sarita grinned.

"So it would seem," Verda said. "Very well. I will select four women per relay team. This will work out better. The distance between relay points will be shorter. And in the unfortunate case of one woman becoming disabled—"

"Or if her pony becomes hurt," Atina said, hoping to change the scenario to something less gruesome.

Raya smiled at Atina.

"Or if her pony becomes hurt—yes, the other three will take over," Verda said.

"I think it is fair to say that if any of us loses connection with any part of the army, the best thing to do is to travel north and either join with the river army if coming from the basin, or travel farther north yet into the Morena Mountains where she can find a greenbeam sister. From there we can help her."

"Yes, that is an excellent idea," Verda said. "Are there any other questions?"

"I have one!" Jonara blurted, but no one heard her.

"You cannot ask a question," Nekara said as she suddenly appeared.

"No one asked for you here," Jonara said.

"Yet I am here nonetheless," Nekara said. "I wish to offer you good luck before the battle begins."

"You mean bad luck, don't you?" Jonara said. "You'll enjoy watching people struggle in battle, I know it."

"Oh come, it's better for me that you and your companions *die* in battle, not merely struggle. I find slow, agonizing deaths quite stimulating," Nekara grinned.

"You shouldn't take pleasure in death. It's horrible for people who die, but it's worse for the families who survive. Those families have an empty place in their hearts from a lost loved one."

"Oh, I think I will cry!" Nekara said sarcastically.

"Shut up!" Jonara yelled.

"You know, this is very much like your journey on that doomed airliner. This could be the last moment you will see these people alive. You saved the people on the airliner with your *indurate* chant. Will you save these soldiers today with another *indurate* chant? No, you can't. So it's a definite thing—people must die. There is no going back. Your *indurate* chant started this timeline. The Celtic women stayed in the mountains when the Infante died in the other timeline. Friar Christiani never made his pilgrimage to find Atina and Sarita in the mountains. He was too occupied obsessing on how to exile Rabbi Nachmanides from the Kingdom of Aragon. But with that obsession no longer in his way, he is free to pursue larger acts of destruction in your new timeline. And we all have you to thank."

"Stop it!" Jonara shouted. "I will not be forced into guilt."

"Believe what you like. You know the truth," Nekara laughed. "And now I must leave you. The Marinids are busy laying waste to Christendom in Sevilla. There's much red paint to see."

"Red paint?" Jonara asked.

"Blood," Nekara laughed. "Certainly you know my favorite color is red."

"Nekara the Red?" Jonara asked.

"Nekara the very Red!" Nekara said, and with that she vanished again.

Jonara looked around the hut. Each woman was Celtic, yes, with some shade of red hair, except Sarita who had dark hair. Still, when the light shone a certain way, Jonara was sure some hairs of Sarita were dark red.

"You must get this information to the prince," Raya said as she passed the leaf to Atina.

Atina looked back in bepuzzlement.

"Raya cannot deliver the message because she and Verda are staying here to work this relay, to answer your question you did not ask," Sarita said.

Atina understood. She thanked the greenbeam inventors and wished good luck to the other women.

"There is one more thing," Raya said. "Sarita—whenever are you going to get your armor fitted?"

"Great mountains of lightning!" Sarita said. "I meant to have Atina help me last night."

"Sarita!" Atina said. "This is what procrastination leads to."

The greenbeam sisters did not disappoint. They quickly tried the armor on Sarita's body and made rapid alterations to make it fit and functional.

"You look wonderful," Atina said to Sarita. "Now I am all the sadder to depart from you. But I must. Good luck to you too, my Promise."

The two embraced with hugs, kisses, and more kisses despite them both wearing armor. The other women let out whoops and hollers followed by clapping.

"This is only a short goodbye," Sarita said.

"I hope so," Atina said.

"Think good thoughts," Sarita said. "Promise, my Promise?"

"I promise, Promise," Atina replied.

Atina and Sarita walked to the stable, and Atina mounted her pony.

"Will you at least ride with me down the hill to Córdoba?" Atina asked.

"Of course. I must ride with you. We are to meet up with the greenbeam army on the way down. We will split only after we reach Prince Fernando's army in Córdoba," Sarita said.

The two rode down the hill. Atina wasn't sure at first, but she thought she saw moving bushes to the left and right.

"They are not trees," Sarita said, seeming to read Atina's mind. "The greenbeam women have painted their ponies to look like bushes."

"Why don't they join us in a line?" Atina asked.

"You know why. They are practicing their stealth. Warming up, as it were, for the real thing," Sarita replied.

"I am glad they are on our side," Atina said.

"I am too," Sarita replied.

The greenbeam army converged on Córdoba and met up with Prince Fernando's army. Atina passed Raya's message onto

Fernando and explained the situation. Fernando resisted splitting up his army, but Atina persisted in the idea of splitting up the army so that the Marinids could not slip through via river or basin. Reluctantly, Prince Fernando agreed.

"We will split the armies," Prince Fernando commanded.

"My Lord," Friar Christiani said. "I take it you will lead one of the armies."

"Of course," the Infante said.

"And you will take Atina along as your liaison with her half of the greenbeam army," Friar Christiani continued.

"Naturally," the prince added.

"Then may I suggest you appoint one of your men to head up the other army and not one of the greenbeam women. The greenbeam women are wonderful communicators and have excellent ponies, but they are not well suited toward leading an army."

"I agree," the prince said. "That is why I am placing you in charge of the other half of my army."

"My Lord?! You yourself have said I have the least military strategy," the friar said. "Not to mention the personal risk to myself!"

"This is exactly why I am placing you in charge. If I place one of my generals in charge, he will fearlessly drive the army into dangerous situations. You, my dear friar, are more concerned with saving your own life than any other. You will not so easily leap into battle without thought. On the contrary, I expect you will need to be poked into battle when the time comes. But I will make things easy for you. You will lead your half down the Guadalquivir River. You will be close to river towns and fresh water, and you will be close to the Morena greenbeam circuit. That should make you happy. And you will have access to daily baths. Cleanliness is next to godliness, no?"

"No, I mean yes," the friar agreed.

"I will lead the more difficult march across the wide river basin," the Infante continued. "We will keep in contact with you using the moving greenbeam relay. Atina tells me Sarita will be coordinating the greenbeam communication with your half, is this right Sarita?"

"Yes, my Lord, it is," Sarita said.

"I see more clearly now," the friar said. "I am only a puppet commander. Sarita will be the real leader."

"This is the system you created," the prince said to the friar. "Knowledge and power from the greenbeam women."

"Begging your pardon, sir, but we created ourselves," Atina said.

"Yes, they did," the friar said nervously. "And they answer to us. Yes, they answer to us. And hear me now, my Prince Fernando de la Cerda, the Infante, future heir to the Kingdom of Castile. I will lead the river half of your army. But let me make it clear that God will find favor with those whose lives he spares and will condemn those who lose their lives in battle. My methods of leadership will be inspired by God. Should I lead from the front, side, or rear, God's hand will direct my actions."

Prince Fernando laughed.

"You give the longest monologue for saying you are afraid," the prince said. "Lead from the rear indeed! The best way to cure fear is to remove idleness and set the war machine moving forward. Prepare to depart!"

Fernando split his warhorse army into two while Atina and Sarita split their pony armies in two. Atina's pony army led Fernando's warhorses to the left while Sarita's pony army led Friar Christiani's warhorses to the right. The double-greenbeam relay women rode their Garrano ponies between the two armies and gradually fanned out as the armies separated. The day was clear, and the two armies proceeded generally toward Sevilla.

The horses and ponies trotted for much of the way with periods of walk for rest. Prince Fernando was anxious to meet the Marinids and defeat them as soon as possible. There were few stops—only enough for water. The moving greenbeam relay kept up and kept both armies in communication. There was nothing of significance to report. Atina learned that the friar trailed the warhorses in the very rear while Sarita led the pony army. This placed Sarita as far apart from the friar as was possible. The situation for Atina was quite the opposite. She drove her pony army from the rear while Prince Fernando led his warhorses from the front. In this way, Atina rode alongside the prince and kept up a running conversation with him.

"This is my first major battle with my father out of the kingdom," Prince Fernando told Atina. "I must prove I can defend the country in his absence. It is my belief the Marinids chose this moment to invade. They believe I am weak and can easily be overrun. I am willing to do almost anything to stop them."

"My Lord," Atina said. "Please do what you must to safeguard the Kingdom of Castile and Iberia. But please protect yourself. You are the heir to Castile and must not perish! I do not ask for myself or for you, I ask for the Kingdom of Castile and Iberia."

"If I should die in battle," Prince Fernando said, "it will be an honorable death. My sons would be next in line to the throne."

"Begging your pardon, my Lord, but your younger brother, Sancho IV, could dispute your sons' claim to the throne. No disrespect to your family, but Sancho's allegiance is to himself. If a temporary alliance with the Moors suits him, he will make it. If you should die in battle and your sons vie for the throne, he will fight them. He has no regard for life other than his own and would execute anyone he claims as an enemy—including your friends or your sons' friends. Is it not bad enough Moors cause death and misery on our lands? Do not perish and allow Sancho to cause more misery from within. Internal conflict is an ugly beast."

"Sancho is a good fighter, but you are right. At times he thinks more of himself than his kingdom and people," the prince said. "I will take your wise advice, Atina. I will fight hard to win, but I will not fight like the fool and toss my body blindly into the jaws of my enemy."

"Thank you, my Lord. I thank you very much. Tinta thanks you too. And the Kingdom of Castile thanks you."

The river and basin armies reached the Genil River at noon. The moving greenbeam relay held up without issue. In fact, the two sets of armies made efficient use of the two moving greenbeam relays by using one to transmit from the basin to the river group, and the other greenbeam to transmit from the river

group to the basin group. In this way, neither army group needed to wait for a reply before sending the next message.

The basin army's intersection with the Genil River took
them to the town of Écija, while the river army group marched a
little farther southwest beyond the Genil River until it reached
the town of Peñaflor. Both groups rested for lunch. Atina sat
with Prince Fernando in a quickly erected tent, while on the
other end of the basin, Sarita had to drag the friar to a make-
shift tent for a group lunch.

"Thank you for this lunch rest," Atina said. "The moving
greenbeam relay is slightly delayed by the light mountain range
between Écija and Peñaflor."

"Should we wait for them to catch up?" the prince asked.
"Lunch is important before the battle begins. From what your
greenbeam sisters tell us from the Morena Mountain circuit, the
Marinids have reached Carmona and are heading our way."

"No, my Lord, we should not wait for the greenbeam relay.
They have swift Garrano mountain ponies. They will catch up
by the time we finish with lunch," Atina said.

"But their ponies must eat and drink too," the prince said.

"Yes, my Lord. I will ask them through the greenbeam if you
like," Atina said.

"Yes, please do. The moving greenbeam is the lifeline between our two armies. I want to ensure complete victory over
the Marinids. Should one of our armies defeats his share of Marinids, I want that victor to proceed to the aid of the other. It is
foolhardy to claim victory when the other army half is slaughtered."

"Yes, my Lord," Atina said.

Atina signaled to the moving greenbeam relay. They signaled
back that they were now crossing the Genil River.

"They crossed the Genil," Atina said to the prince.

"Very good. Estimates say we will make contact with the
Marinids in three hours," the prince said.

"The Marinids continue to travel along the basin and the
Guadalquivir River," Atina said. "All armies will begin battle at
nearly the same time."

"But the Marinids do not know this. They believe one of their armies will proceed unchallenged. This truly is a day for Iberia. And the greenbeam women," the prince said. "You may pass that message on to the river army."

Atina signaled the river army. Sarita's reply was a smile and a short message:

"We are ready for battle."

The armies proceeded toward the Marinids for three hours. Nervous tension filled the air. Scavenger birds circled high.

"I do not like the birds flying overhead," the prince said. "They might as well shout to the Marinids that we are coming."

"My Lord," Atina said. "The greenbeam reports Sarita has reached Lora del Rio. She is leading the first attack on the Marinids along the Guadalquivir River."

"It has begun. What about the moving greenbeam relay? Are they under attack?" the prince asked.

Atina signaled to them, and they replied.

"No, they are not under attack. But the end closest to the Guadalquivir River can no longer advance without being seen. They are hiding amongst the rocks. Also, sir, because they are hiding, they cannot maintain two relay beams. They have consolidated into one to maintain the link."

"How far can we advance before we lose the link?" the prince asked.

"Perhaps a thousand paces," Atina said.

"We will need that space for the first wave," the prince said. "Have the moving greenbeam relay hold position."

Atina signaled the moving greenbeam to hold position. The prince yelled back to the troops to stop marching.

"We will wait until the Marinids reach us. It will not be long. The birds tell us the basin is on the brink of battle," the prince said.

"My Lord," Atina said. "Sarita's group reports the Marinids are wearing light armor and riding swift horses. They carry no spare horses. All Marinid horses are riding."

"No spare horses? What are their squires doing?" the prince asked.

"The Marinids do not appear to have squires," Atina replied. "Sarita has identified this particular Marinid tribe as the Zenetes."

"There was rumor such a tribe existed," the prince said.

"Yes," Atina said. "The Zenetes are very fast. Sarita's ponies are giving the Zenetes chase. Some Zenetes are falling, some ponies are falling! My Lord, the Zenetes are forcing the friar's army warhorses into the river. They cannot maneuver as quickly as the Zenetes. My Lord, I am not sure I understand this last message. I will ask the greenbeam to repeat it."

"What did it say?" the prince asked. "What did the last message say?"

"I will ask for a confirmation," Atina said.

Atina received confirmation.

"Half of the warhorses have been slaughtered," Atina said. "Friar Christiani is missing. Many of your knights are missing or dead. I am sorry, my Lord. Sarita's ponies continue to give chase. The remaining warhorses are distancing themselves from the Zenetes. The greenbeam army is firing their mini-cannons. Zenetes are falling. Oh this is terrible. Some of my sister pony riders have also been hit by mini-cannon fire accidentally. Wait. I thought there was more. The relay has stopped."

"Ask them for more information."

Atina requested more information from the greenbeam.

"The greenbeam says there is a break in communication near Lora del Rio," Atina said. "The greenbeam also says your river army was caught by surprise. It appears Zenete scouts discovered your river army and reported this back to the main Zenete army. Your warhorses were forced into the river before they could go into battle formation."

"So the decision is this—do I abandon the basin and proceed to rescue what remains of my river army, or do I face battle in the basin while my river army perishes?"

"My Lord. Sarita would do everything to disrupt the Marinids. Further, the river is close to the Morena Mountains. She will be in close contact with the Morena greenbeam relay, and that relay will carry news of the Lora del Rio events up the river to Peñaflor, Córdoba and beyond. Other forces can help. We are the ones isolated."

"Yes, you are quite right," the prince said. "We will not be caught by surprise, nor will we be forced into a small space for the Zenetes to attack us quickly."

The prince yelled back to his men to prepare for battle. He gave out an unusual order. All squires were also to prepare for battle. The officers and knights were to arm the squires as best as possible. In this way, there were three fighting groups— Atina's ponies, the squires, and the knights. The prince ordered the groups to form a large vee with the ponies leading the outermost flanks, the squires trailing along the ponies in the vee, and the knights forming the base of the vee in the middle. The knights closest to the squires rode warmblood chargers for speed and agility, while the knights in the center of the vee rode coldblood destriers for heaving trampling and skewering of the enemy.

"We will scoop the Zenetes from the edges and force them into the middle, where our knights will trample them," the prince said. "We will no longer wait for them to reach us."

The prince blew a horn in brief bursts to signal the final preparation. The ponies and warhorses stood ready. The prince looked to the seemingly empty basin in front, the circling scavenger birds overhead, and the readied armies around him. The sky was clear, there was a light breeze, and a few birds tweeted around the prince. The prince took a deep breath and blew the horn with all his might in a long, steady blast. The ponies and warhorses went into a trot. The ponies and squires gradually spread out and in doing so increased the size of the scooping vee. No sight of the Marinids yet, but the women and men used the position of the scavenger birds as a beacon. When the moving vee reached a point almost directly below the circling birds, the first Marinid scouts were discovered. Atina and the prince ordered their armies into a charge. The scouts attempted to flee, but the moving vee formation caught them and forced them into the middle where heavy warhorses skewered them. In this way, the basin Marinids were caught by surprise. They attempted to spread out so as not to be caught, but Atina's ponies kept to the outside. The Marinids rode *a la jineta*—light armor just as their counterparts did at the Guadalquivir River. Their horses were slightly quicker than Atina's ponies, but the ponies were more maneuverable. Atina had instructed her ponies prior to the vee formation that the women should strive to force the Marinids into the vee instead of going for the simple kill. Some did so by luring the Marinids into the middle. As the vee narrowed, the ponies ducked low, and the warhorses jumped over the ponies and attacked the Marinids. Other ponies simply kept to the outside and launched arrows at the Marinids. The arrows did not pierce the Marinid armor, but the action resulted in the Marinids drifting gradually in the center until the vee could skewer them. Some Marinids threw their spears at the ponies, but again—the ponies were too agile and simply moved out of the way. Other Marinids attempted to joust the ponies with their spears, but the ponies outmaneuvered the spears.

The sight of blood from people, pony, and horse combined with the yells of pain from human and beast jarred Jonara's psyche to the bone. Jonara closed her eyes and covered her ears, but in doing so, she lost balance and fell off Atina's pony onto a dead Marinid soldier. Mortified, she leapt up and ran from the field of combat. She looked all around for a rock to hide behind, but the river basin was flat and unchanging. Jonara could think of nothing but keeping her legs pumping on the earth. She thought of those times her mother went on runs to work off stress, and now Jonara fully identified with this act.

"Oh, poor unfortunate Jonara," Nekara said as she suddenly started running next to Jonara.

"Get out of here!" Jonara said. "You are the worst thing in the universe!"

"Now now, is that any way to speak to your fellow conspirator?" Nekara grinned.

"More lies," Jonara said. "But I can't take any more death! I can still see images of those people, horses, and ponies in their last moments alive. Now they are dead! Those images are stuck in my mind. I can't stand it! I have images of them alive and dead in my mind at the same time. It's like apples eating oranges! Stop it! Stop the torture!"

"Oh, Jonara! Enjoy the trip! Violent death like this does not come often in your time. Savor it like spices in meat," Nekara laughed.

"Poison! All of it is poison to my mind. And you're toxic! You should be sent to a toxic dump!" Jonara yelled.

"Oh, but I was sent to a toxic dump. The dump's name is Earth!" Nekara laughed. "Where else can I find so many places people dump happiness in favor of misery and despair? Your people are always inventing new ways to bring sorrow to the world. Swords, spears, cannons, bombs, nuclear weapons, biowarfare, oppression, brainwashing, manipulation, and drugs to name a few. Oh wait, there is a new evil development along the Guadalquivir River. I must leave you for now. I will be back later."

Nekara left. Outside of the battle, Jonara threw herself onto the ground and cried.

1275 Jun 20. Tarifa, Iberia.

Jonara stood up and opened her eyes. She was no longer in the river basin of Guadalquivir. She was in Tarifa—a port on the southern tip of Iberia. She stared southward at the sea waters where the Atlantic Ocean met the Mediterranean Sea.

"It's beautiful," Jonara said.

In the distance, she observed ships approaching. Closer to shore, navy ships operated by greenbeam women patrolled the shoreline. The greenbeam ships permitted one of the distant ships through while the others were held back. The approaching ship was from Morocco—a Marinid ship. It docked peacefully, and a Marinid by the name of Abu Yusuf Ya'qub exited his ship and met Prince Fernando on the docks.

"What a surprise, Prince Fernando," Abu said. "I did not expect to meet you here."

"I am sure you did not. You had expected an ally to grant you safe landing here in Tarifa," the prince said.

"What?" Abu asked in pretend ignorance.

"I am not as naïve as you think, Abu. I detected your first wave of Marinid soldiers invading my kingdom along the Guadalquivir River. I had hoped to intercept them at Sevilla, but they ravaged the countryside quickly. They attempted to outsmart me by splitting into two groups. The first group I defeated quickly in the river basin between Carmona and Écija. The second killed many of my knights and warhorses in Lora del Rio. But I pursued them and defeated them in Peñaflor. Here," the prince said, and a squire presented a sword and helmet from a Marinid soldier. "This is a gift to you. I trust you recognize this as one of your top officers?"

The blood in Abu's face drained.

"Perhaps there is a misunderstanding," Abu said. "With your father out of the country, I thought now was the time to pay you and your people a visit. I see I was in error."

"Yes, you are in error," the prince said. "I give you this warning, Abu. These lands belong to the kingdoms of Portugal, Castile, and Aragon. No foreign power has claim. I can and will defeat any invasion—including yours."

"And the Kingdom of Granada?" Abu asked. "I did not hear mention of that friendly kingdom."

"The Kingdoms of Castile and Aragon now make new claim on Granada," the prince said. "If you have any allies left in Granada, I would advise them to leave quickly. Granada is the last safehold of the Moors, and we intend to reclaim Granada for Christendom."

"I understand," Abu said. "If you will permit me to leave, I will deliver your 'message'."

Abu boarded his ship and left the harbor. He reached his group of ships and returned across the straits to Morocco.

"You could have killed him," Atina said to the prince.

"Yes, I could have. But this is not the time. It is better he lives to spread testament of the new Iberia."

"Yes, yes!" Friar Christiani said, now emerging into view.

"I thought he was dead!" Jonara said.

"You are alive!" Atina said.

"I was only temporarily lost at Lora del Rio," the friar said. "But I pulled myself out of the river and wandered about in shock for many days. I am better now."

"Did you know about this, my Lord?" Atina asked the prince.

"Yes. I wanted to surprise you," Prince Fernando said.

"You succeeded. I am surprised!" Atina said.

"Yes," the friar said. "Words will drive some Moors out of Granada. The rest will be exterminated."

"You mean converted?" the prince asked.

"Oh yes, converted if willing. Expelled or executed if a threat," the friar said.

"I am beginning to wonder about you," the prince said. "Men of God sometimes sound more like men of the military."

"In principle it is the same. We both seek to separate the wrong from the righteous," the friar said.

"Yes," Nekara said to Jonara while appearing in a navy uniform. "Us against them. Right and wrong. Remove the wrong and keep the right...the righteous."

"No one asked you," Jonara said to Nekara.

"If you are not with me you are against me," Nekara said. "But if everyone is against me, who is with me? That is why I love all evil. Evil is with me everywhere. Evil is righteous. Evil will keep us from being lonely."

"You are sick," Jonara said. "But the battle is over."

"This battle," Nekara said. "In this place and time. But the new battle is about to begin. Behold!"

1292 Iberia.

Jonara floated in the sky above the kingdoms of Castile and Aragon. King James I died in 1276, and Alfonso X died in 1284. Prince Fernando was now King Fernando. He had added Portugal and Aragon to the Kingdom of Castile. He had just finished reconquering the Kingdom of Granada and added it to the new kingdom that he called Spain. King Fernando sat on his throne in a newly created palace in Madrid, and by his side sat an older Friar Christiani.

"Your Majesty," the friar said. "This is the greatest year in all of Iberian history. You have nearly completed the *Reconquista.* All of Iberia is under your reign. Money and goods flow into Iberia from the Far East. Your kingdom is wealthy, and the Christians are happy. New lands have been discovered in the west on the other side of the Atlantic Ocean thanks to the greenbeam women's invention of the sextant and high-precision chronometer giving us measurement of latitude and longitude. Yes, new lands! New lands for conquest, consumption, and conversion to Christianity. Your kingdom will expand as will your wealth and prosperity."

"The *Reconquista* is nearly complete," King Fernando said. "Nearly is not enough."

"I agree, Your Majesty. Wealth alone is not enough. For the *Reconquista* to finish, all non-Christians must be expelled. This act is not without precedence. England expelled their Jews two years ago. France expels theirs now and then. We are behind the times. The days of being held hostage to Jewish tax collections is over. Spain is your new kingdom and is hostage to no one—not the Moors, and not the Jews. Purge the kingdom of its final invaders and make Spain a kingdom to be proud of. The pope is very happy with your works and supports you in this final solution."

"Yes, he does. And yet I cannot help but feel pity for these Jews. They have supported our kingdoms loyally for hundreds of years through taxes. It hardly seems fair to force them out now that the country is peaceful and prosperous. If only there were some arrangement we could work out with them— conversion or something. Could we give them some land?"

"No! We gave Granada to Moors in 1238. That was a failed experiment. We cannot make the same mistake twice!" the friar urged. "The only solution is expulsion. There are many places they can go. Do not trouble yourself with their problems. They are only Jews."

"But they are human. I worked hard to bring an easy life to the people of Iberia. Now I feel like a traitor," King Fernando said.

"Then allow me to oversee the expulsion. Let the blood fall on my hands and wash yours clean. I am more than happy to perform this final and great task for my king and country," Friar Christiani said. "I beg of it as a special favor to me. It would put to rest demons of conflict that have plagued my mind for years."

"Yes, the demons," Nekara said to Jonara.

"I really wish you would go away," Jonara said.

"Like the demons?" Nekara asked.

"Like bugs!" Jonara said.

"But don't you find this all fascinating?" Nekara asked. "Look—the friar will expel the Jews from Spain. The king will wash his hands clean. Is this not a sort of crucifixion of the Jews? Wasn't Jesus a crucified Jew? It amazes me that this purported man of God named Friar Christiani plans to do the very same thing to the Jews that has been done before and will be done again—physical and metaphorical crucifixion. One Jew or many—the concept remains. I used to think I would get bored of the same old attacks against Jews, but humanity over the ages finds fresh forms of Jewish misery. Your Holocaust of the 20th century, for example."

"It is not my Holocaust. I didn't cause it," Jonara insisted.

"You are an Earthling. Don't you take pride in your people and their acts of 'good' works?" Nekara laughed. "I know I do, and I am not even an Earthling. But I love you all."

"This is terrible. There is no need to expel the Jews. Everyone can live happily together," Jonara said.

"No, they can't," Nekara said. "Not while I am here to stir the brew of human bigotry and hate."

The Jews were expelled from Spain in 1292 instead of 1492. Spain expanded their domain by conquering all of the Americas. The greenbeam women were denied their ships for the purpose of finding the lost island of Celtic women—an island community supposedly started after a spacecraft of red-headed men and women crash-landed from another solar system. The green-beam women were ostracized by other Celtic women for helping Catholic men, forcing these greenbeam women to leave Spain forever. The greenbeam women never offered their assistance to any other government again.

England and France were too busy fighting each other in the Hundred Years War to stop Spain's conquest of the Americas. For over two hundred years, America was known as Fernanica. In 1508, after having spent twenty-five years barely holding off Fernanica from declaring independence from Spain, King Fernando II of Aragon placed Amerigo Vespucci in charge of the Spanish navy and charged him with restoring Fernanica to a loyal province of Spain. Vespucci did just that after only five years, and the New World was renamed to America as the ultimate expression of thanks to Vespucci. Geographic boundaries were set in the Americas corresponding to the modern countries Jonara knew. Castilian Spanish was the official language spoken from the northern Mexican border south to the southern tip of South America, while Catalan was the official language in the United States and Canada.

The Black Death did not impact Spain as badly as it did the rest of Europe. Clean conditions and good diets due to Spanish wealth helped most Spaniards resist the disease. The Native Americans were, however, decimated by the disease.

Spain contributed heavily toward the Catholic Church's coffers, meaning paid indulgences were unnecessary in Spain. Spanish Catholics were very happy and had no need for alternative Christian faiths. Martin Luther's ninety-five protests went along as expected, but by that time the Americas were firmly entrenched in the Catholic faith and resisted Protestant ideals.

A minority of English people settled in North America. A young general by the name of George Washington led a peaceful declaration of independence from Spain. The United States was born, but it kept strong ties with Spain, giving much of its excess wealth to Motherland Spain in gratitude.

Jonara was still in shock over how her induration command made such a big impact, but there it was—Spain had become a world power and held such power much longer than it did in her original timeline.

CHAPTER 3

Miriam And Dahma

4101 BCE. Felifia's and Nekara's Wedding. Planet Eho Miriam, Damiriak Solar System.

"Are you nervous, Princess Felifia?" asked one of the bridesmaids, Tanina.

Jonara realized she was no longer on Earth. She was in a large sunroom with strange houseplants of different colors. Two suns in the sky illuminated the outdoors and the sunroom. Jonara looked through the window and saw many trees with crimson and cerise leaves. Other trees had yellow-green leaves, but very few had green leaves like on Earth. The grass was yellow and curly, like a large animal's fur coat.

"I am always nervous before my weddings," Princess Felifia said. "This is my third junior wife. You would think these weddings would get monotonous, but I get all choked up inside."

"It is very unusual for the senior wife to wear white," Tanina said, referring to Felifia's white wedding dress. "Usually, the senior wife wears dark red while the junior wife wears white. Do you remember our wedding?"

"I do. I wore dark red, and you wore white. You were my first marriage and are my first junior wife. But Nekara is a very unusual junior wife," Felifia said. "She insists on wearing the dark red."

"Do you ever think you will have more junior wives?" the bridesmaid asked.

"Don't worry, three will be enough for me," Felifia said. "I don't think it's fair to Teluna, Nekara, and you to divide my love any farther. Yes, I am more conservative than the other senior women. They have eight or ten junior wives. I like to keep things more personal. Oh, what was that? My dress turned pink for a moment."

"I saw it too," Tanina said.

Jonara also noticed it. Light from one of the stars flashed pink for a brief moment before returning to white.

"Have you ever considered having a junior husband?" Tanina asked.

"No, I was never that kind of woman," Felifia said. "I realize men are a necessity for procreation, but I...well, I imagine I won't procreate that way."

"There are some women like us who are pioneering a technique so we can have children without men. There is a cave in the nearby mountains with pools of special water. The women scientists claim they can get two female beetles to reproduce without a male."

"Beetles are one thing, but people are another," Felifia said.

"Your junior wife-to-be is the chief scientist," Tanina said. "She hopes—"

"Yes, I know what she hopes," Felifia said. "She hopes to have children with me without a man."

"It's a beautiful thing," Tanina said. "I would be proud to have your baby. Why do you worry?"

"Because of men," Felifia said. "Men have disapproved of Nekara's work. They say it is unnatural and playing Goddess."

"Ignore them," Tanina said.

"I wish I could. But attacks against Nekara's team have increased in recent months. Our rights in this matter are clear, but only barely. A woman's full right to procreate by any means was granted fifty years ago, and only because men didn't believe we could procreate without them. Now there are serious challenges in the courts to our full procreation rights. It concerns me. I'm nervous! The court challenges, the attacks against Nekara, and...well...I'm getting married! It's all so stressful."

"Please, my Princess. Let those stresses slide by for today. This is your day!" Tanina said. "Enjoy!"

"Yes, you're right," Felifia said. "There it is again. My dress turned pink. Now it's white. If I didn't know better, I'd say one of our stars is throwing out a mighty pink solar flare! I can't believe it's on account of my wedding. That's superstitious!"

Felifia's other brides-maids arrived, her second junior wife, Teluna, and two other women. Felifia's bridesmaids wore dresses of violet and white, and they led Felifia to the back right corner (while facing the altar) of the spiritual temple. In the back left corner, Nekara's party stood in cherry-red, white, and black. They awaited Nekara and the ceremony.

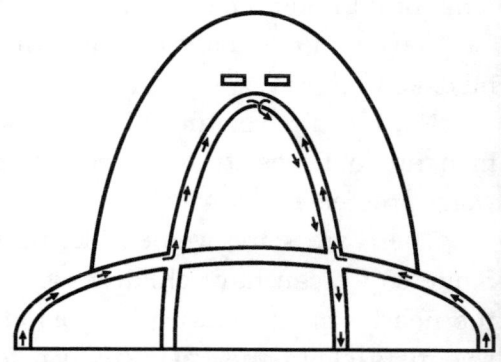

Felifia's Miramish Temple: *Top view. Arrows show walking paths of Felifia's and Nekara's wedding parties' separate approach to the altar, and their united path from the altar out of the temple.*

"Where's Nekara?" Tanina whispered to Felifia.

"She's late," Felifia replied.

"I can tell," Tanina replied. "But why? She should be here. This *is* her wedding."

"She was investigating a geological disturbance on planet Dart," Felifia said. "She should have been back yesterday. But Nekara has been known to be a bit late."

There were two altars. At the altar on Felifia's side stood a woman in a long, white robe with green and magenta stoles. Her hair was short and gray with streaks of black. Two organs on each side of the temple played pre-wedding music.

Seeing both bridal parties, the woman at the altar motioned for the ceremony to begin. Another woman with an oboe played the opening march:

Natirna

"They're playing *Natirna*! That's the opening march! They've started too soon!" Felifia said to Tanina.

"Maybe Nekara will be here when *Natirna* is finished," Tanina said.

"If she isn't, this wedding will be finished!" Felifia said.

"I hope nothing happened to Nekara," Tanina said.

"I hope so too. I have a feeling she'll be here any *geratha* (9 seconds) now."

Nine seconds passed. And another nine seconds. A ten of nine seconds passed, and no Nekara. The *Natirna* song neared its completion, and as it did, Nekara burst into the temple alongside her bridesmaids. Nekara wore a cherry-red dress, but her hair was a mess, and she had a dark smudge mark on her cheek. One of the bridesmaids wiped off the smudge while another quickly brushed Nekara's hair.

The woman at the altar motioned for the ceremony to begin. A portion of *Natirna* was repeated. Felifia's bridesmaids proceeded along a curved path until they reached the archpath—the path that appears as a steep arch from above—at which point they stopped. Nekara's bridesmaids reached their archpath at the same time as Felifia's bridesmaids. Felifia and Nekara each waited at the end of their lines.

"Let us begin," the altar woman said.

Jonara suddenly realized that everyone seemed to speak in her (Jonara's) native language. Yet it wasn't English.

"How can it be? I don't recognize their speech as English, Miramish, or Dahmek. But I understand them. Could they be speaking Old Damiriak?" Jonara wondered.

"Welcome everyone. I am High Priestess Vadafa, and we are here today to bring Princess Felifia and Countess Nekara together in marriage. Marriage is a special union of love and commitment, and each of these women is here to profess her eternal love. As each woman comes from her own separate life, so now each woman stands apart from the other. Princess Felifia is a loving and caring senior wife to two others who are here today as her bridesmaids, and Countess Nekara is an unattached spirit who will join with Felifia as a third junior wife."

Whispers of confusion traveled through the temple. Vadafa smiled.

"I know what you are thinking," Vadafa said. "Tradition says the junior wife wears white and the senior wife dark red. Love is special and is known to break through barriers, including our own traditions from time to time. In a special expression of their love for each other, Felifia has donated dark red to her junior wife-to-be, Nekara, and Nekara has donated her white color for Felifia to wear."

The ceremony continued. Vadafa said some prayers; the people replied.

"We pause in this moment to reflect on the loneliness of life before one finds one's beloved. For we as women joining with women have not always been afforded the public luxury to express our love. Love faces many threats from outside and in—those who would rather see us miserable, and our own internal struggles to identify self and how self relates with people around us. Princess Felifia, though married to two others, has a certain part of herself that is incomplete, and so that part is lonely and she stands apart. Countess Nekara has no other unions and stands completely alone. Let us now bring these two kindred spirits together."

The organs played music, and the people in attendance broke out in song. As they sang, Felifia's and Nekara's wedding parties proceeded up the archpaths to top of the archpath. As the bridesmaids reached the top, they stepped aside with the first bridesmaid being the furthest from the top of the archpath, the second the next closest, et cetera, until Felifia and Nekara stood side-by-side. Vadafa stepped down from behind the altar and stood at the top of the archpath before Felifia and Nekara.

"This union that we are about to bring forth, let no man put asunder," Vadafa said. "Princess Felifia, shall you take Countess Nekara as your junior wife for eternity with the blessings of our mothers, our grandmothers, and our foremothers?"

"I shall take Countess Nekara as my junior wife for eternity, may my foremothers bless our union," Felifia said.

"Countess Nekara, shall you take Princess Felifia as your senior wife for eternity with the blessings of our mothers, our grandmothers, and our foremothers?"

"I shall take Princess Felifia as my senior wife for eternity. I ask my foremothers to bless our union," Nekara said.

"Your oaths are accepted," Vadafa said.

Vadafa held her hands above her head as if catching water from the sky. A faint light shone on her hands from a window in the ceiling. She then placed one hand to her abdomen and placed her other hand between Felifia and Nekara.

"Place your hands on mine and each other's," Vadafa said.

Felifia and Nekara placed their hands on Vadafa's and theirs.

Mirsua	**Translation**
Nias kilos Koilus Tiusas Vadafas.	I am High Priestess Vadafa.
Nias isaikos koilus bioritas	I invoke high power
Veletus nuises geliasas e Serises.	From our star Seris.
Serisus Bioritus Uferithuas	Serisian Power Identifier
Valas-yufis-venis-iris-muis.	Vee-four-seven-three-nine.
Nias diatos kailes,	I join you,
Talithas Felifias,	Princess Felifia,
Dhakus kailes	And you
Keliasas Nekaras	Countess Nekara
Dis usepus miseis	To each other
Isus e zualas, naikas,	In spirit, psyche,
Ivadavas, dhakus depas.	Emotion, and thought.
Yamus onas fereithos e ziagas,	When one feels pain,
Sais miseis ludufipos.	The other responds.
Yamus onas fereithos laisas,	When one feels joy,
Sais miseis runisos.	The other shares.
Telesanus lualaras,	Through laughter,
Baimatas, onalipakas,	Sorrow, alertness,
Dhakus belorifas,	And slumber,
Usepus opeifus kaires	Each of you
Fereitheios e sais miseis—	Will feel the other—
Nukifius, alitakius,	Physically, mentally,
Ivadavius, dhakus e zualius.	Emotionally, and spiritually.
Felifias dhakus Nekaras	Felifia and Nekara
Dhais vulanios.	Are married.
Nias weifos tesunus e seloikas	I sign this command
Koilus Tiusas Vadafas	High Priestess Vadafa
Opeifus Miriamas.	Of Miriam.
Dosikos!	Execute!

The light from the ceiling window grew powerfully white. Vadafa, Felifia, and Nekara initially responded with delight. But the light pulsed and switched from white to magenta, green, and white—magenta, green, and white—as if the white light itself were being split into magenta and green. The ground trembled, and the temple shook. Sunlight pouring in from the regular windows now pulsed magenta, green, and white. A surge of energy like an electric shock jolted Vadafa's body backward and threw it on the left-side altar. The shock broke Felifia's and Ne-kara's holds and threw them apart. The people in attendance shouted and screamed in fear as bits of temple ceiling fell atop them. A mad rush ensued for the four doors. Felifia and Nekara ran up to Vadafa, pulled her from the left altar, and carried her out of the temple.

"What's happening?" Vadafa asked while coming out of her groggy state.

"It shouldn't have been this bad," Nekara said, who turned around and shouted to the women, "Everyone—put on your sunglasses!"

People did as Nekara ordered. Then they looked up at the two stars—Seris and Maknesi. Both stars pulsed. Seris pulsed magenta and white while Maknesi pulsed green and white.

"The suns are failing!" the people yelled. "The world will come to an end!"

People ran around in absolute panic, breaking things, yell-ing, tearing at things, and attacking one another. Tanina and Teluna fled the temple without Felifia.

"Stop, stop!" Vadafa yelled. "Everyone calm down!"

Vadafa's voice was trampled by excessive screaming from people and crashing of objects. But it was the roar of the ground shaking that was most deafening.

"We must get to the observatory and find out what is hap-pening," Vadafa said. "Quick—help me to my cart!"

Felifia and Nekara helped Vadafa to her cart.

"Come along, we have no time to waste," Vadafa said to Fe-lifia and Nekara.

Felifia and Nekara climbed into the cart with Vadafa.

Vadafa turned to the two horses and yelled, "*Lomapo boshu keifa!* (Gallop with care!)"

Vadafa's horses took the three to the observatory. The road there was normally easy and care-free, but on this day of groundquakes, solar disturbances, and crowd panic, the way was hazardous. Groundquakes created holes and crevices in the road, the solar flashing hit the women's retinas like a jack-hammer, and panicking people kept running into the horses and cart.

"Close your eyes, Felifia," Vadafa said during the journey. "It will be easier on your retinas."

The tension grated on the horses' nerves, and halfway to the observatory, they refused to gallop. They slowed to a trot, then a walk, then a stop, and finally they reared up.

"*Fineto!* (Steady!)" Vadafa called in Miramish.

The horses stood on their four hooves briefly but reared up again.

"*Fineto, fineto!*" Vadafa called again, but the horses did not respond.

"*Finetos kairses larinas dhakus lomapos bosus keifas!* (Steady your fear and gallop with care!)" Vadafa called in Mirsua.

The horses galloped off to the observatory. When they arrived, Vadafa ordered them to stop.

"*Geraukos!* (Halt!)" Vadafa said.

"*Keia-teia* Vadafa," a woman at the door called.

Jonara understood *keia-teia* as the Miramish words for letters *k-t*. But what did *k-t* stand for? Vadafa was a High Priestess. Then Jonara remembered two words of Miramish—"high priestess" was "*koilu tiusha*". The *k-t* was an abbreviation for "high priestess". It was strange that Jonara remembered some Miramish in that moment, but she was in a strange moment.

Another woman tended to Vadafa's horses and took them to a safe stable.

"Biorna," Vadafa said. "I have Princess Felifia and Countess Nekara with me."

"*Talitha* (Princess) Felifia and Countess Nekara," Biorna said. "The honor is mine. But hurry inside—the panic is too much for me out here."

Felifia and Nekara followed Vadafa inside the observatory. Biorna led them to a large domed area with a huge telescope. Several women tended the telescope, wrote things down, and created parchment prints.

"What's happening?" Vadafa said.

"I'll let you know in a moment. The solar charts are being printed as we speak," Biorna said.

"You seem to know what's going on," Felifia said to Nekara. "You said something strange at the temple."

"I don't know exactly what is happening to our stars, but I know the cause," Nekara said. "Biorna—is it planet Dart?"

"One moment," Biorna said. "The charts are coming out now."

Assistants placed several solar-system charts on a large table.

"Keep in mind that these are negative images of the heavens," Biorna said. "A black sky is the white parchment, white stars show up black. This first print shows our inner solar system from the top. Our North Solar Satellite beamed us this image with orbital paths added by the celestron device."

"The stars and orbits look as they should," Felifia said. "This is a full-season orbital path, isn't it?"

"Yes. One Damiriak year or half a Miriam revolution," Biorna said. "Both stars put out white light, or nearly white light. Now look at this second chart. Seris is green, and Maknesi is magenta."

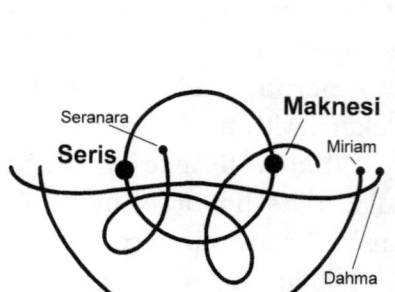

"Being a negative print, this means Seris is magenta and Maknesi is green in the positive," Vadafa said.

"We didn't need a print to tell us that," Felifia said. "We can look outside for ourselves."

"You neglected to point out the most important thing of the second print," Nekara said. "Planet Dart is missing."

"Biorna—is the printer broken?" Felifia asked. "Why doesn't Dart show up on the second printing?"

"I was getting to that," Biorna said. "Working through the telemetry data prior to the collision—"

"What collision?" Felifia asked.

"The one that caused stars Seris and Maknesi to pulse magenta and green respectively. The one that resulted in the disappearance of planet Dart. Do you see the celestial culprit?" Biorna asked.

"This is where my story takes over," Nekara said. "Men on this planet have been mining without regard on planet Dart for centuries. Given that Dart is uninhabited, the men felt no need to plan, conserve, or control mining efforts. Many veins were dug deeply into the crust and mantle. Beginning with my mother, warnings have been issued against these superdeep veins. Men used nuclear explosives to progressively mine deeper and deeper. Seismic activity has increased dramatically over the last ten years. As you may or may not know, I have been assigned to inspect this seismic activity and provide projections on Dart's stability. A year ago, I filed a report that planet Dart was critically unstable and would imminently supershatter. Yet mining efforts continued at accelerated rates—not because of my warnings, but because of the greater demand for precious ore from Dart."

"I filed my last report just a few hours ago on my way back from Dart," Nekara continued. "I regret I was late to my own wedding, but I had problems launching my spacecraft from Dart. The planet started breaking up, and men who had mined with no regard for the future suddenly realized their perilous situation and attempted to steal my spacecraft. I was held at gunpoint against my will and was nearly killed, but an off-chance groundquake destroyed the building where I was being held hostage. I escaped and overpowered the men who were too busy trying to figure out how to override my spaceship's lockout mechanism to notice my surprise attack."

"I managed to break orbit from Dart, but Dart's core started venting into space and nearly engulfed my spaceship," Nekara continued. "I set my spaceship at top speed back to Eho Miriam and filed my report with the council. I doubt the council has had time to read it."

"That explains how Dart became unstable," Felifia said. "But what happened after Nekara left, Biorna?"

"As the core vented, Dart's orbit changed," Biorna said. "It also split into two chunks, as you can see on this chart."

"Those are large chunks," Vadafa said.

"Yes, with each chunk venting ejecta," Biorna said. "This venting acted as rocket motors. The larger chunk headed for Seris, the smaller for Maknesi."

"Are you saying Seris and Maknesi were hit by planet Dart?" Felifia said.

"The answer to your question is 'yes'," Biorna said.

"It's hard to believe fragments of a planet can cause such massive changes to a star," Nekara said.

"It's always been theorized that a star would be unaffected, but we've never observed this event directly. Now we know. The small chunk hit Maknesi, which as you know is much closer to us at the moment. Seris is in her most distant position from us, and she took the large chunk," Biorna explained. "According to our calculations, Maknesi will mostly recover from her impact."

"What about Seris?" Vadafa asked.

Biorna's face turned grim.

"Well?" Nekara asked.

"She won't recover," Biorna said.

"What does that mean?" Felifia asked. "How can Seris not recover?"

"She is changing. She cannot maintain the same sort of white light. She will stop flashing in time, yes, but she will put out magenta light instead of white," Biorna said. "Other parts of the light spectrum such as green and infrared will be lost."

"Winter will be disastrous," Vadafa said.

"As will the following spring," Nekara said. "If there is one."

"What's this about a bad winter and no spring?" Felifia asked Biorna.

"What Vadafa means is this," Biorna said. "In six months, our planet, Eho Miriam, will enter a deep freeze. Many forms of life will perish. As to Nekara's point—when that much life perishes, there will be little if any life coming forth the following spring."

"It will make today's panic look like a celebration," Vadafa said.

The groundquakes stopped. People outside gradually calmed down.

"There's something else," Biorna said. "Seris's electromagnetic field is growing quickly."

"How quickly?" Nekara asked.

"In two months, it will envelop Eho Miriam. In four months, it will reach the outer solar system planets—Sanau, Tarak, and Nimsant."

"Then nowhere is safe," Felifia said.

"We do not know how good or bad this will be," Biorna said. "But one thing we do know—there will be drastic changes to life on this planet."

"Loss of white light during winter. Expanded electromagnetic field. Could things get any worse?" Felifia asked.

"Yes, they could," said a voice entering the observatory room.

"Teluna!" Felifia said. "Where's Tanina?"

The two exchanged hugs and kisses.

"How could they be worse?" Nekara asked.

"Felifia—Tanina ran home. Nekara—I just came from your lab," Teluna said.

"What about my lab?" Nekara asked.

"Everything is destroyed," Teluna said. "The lab, the pools, even the beetles—completely destroyed."

"How?" Felifia asked.

Nekara's eyes lit with a fire, and she sought words to express her anger.

"Men?" Nekara asked at long last.

"Yes," Teluna said. "They blame our work for these geophysical events!"

"They don't know any better," Felifia said. "We'll just start again."

Biorna looked at Nekara and shook her head, "No."

"What?" Felifia asked. "What's going on, Biorna?"

"We don't have time to start again, do we Biorna?" Nekara asked.

Biorna looked down.

"Plagues of death!" Nekara cursed.

"I've followed your research reports with great passion, Nekara," Biorna said. "Whether the lab was destroyed or not, I'm afraid your methods will no longer be effective. Seris's magnetic fields will interfere with steps thirteen, nineteen, and twenty-two."

"Those are the most important," Nekara said. "There are no substitute materials on Eho Miriam I can use to get around those steps."

"It gets worse," Biorna said.

"How much worse?" Vadafa asked.

"If we cannot pioneer a method for women having children with women, we shall become extinct," Biorna said.

"What?!" Felifia and Vadafa said.

"I knew it," Nekara said. "My instincts were right all along. Women were always meant to have children with women. It is men who are deviants; their half-X chromosomes have always been a hindrance."

"How can this be possible?" Felifia asked. "Will all women become sterile?"

"No," Biorna said. "All men. Nekara is onto something when she speaks of men's half-X chromosome. Seris's magnetic fields will become fatal to all those who do not have two full X chromosomes. Without the second full X chromosome providing protection, men's chromosomes will unravel. Their flesh will fall apart. The limitation is not just for people. All mammals are affected. Other animal forms, because of their different chromosome structures, are safe."

"How long before the men die?" Vadafa asked.

"Two months," Biorna said.

"I never thought I would say this," Vadafa said, "but we must collect as many sperm samples as we can before they are destroyed."

"What?" Nekara asked.

"The argument is moot," Biorna said. "The changes have already begun. Men will become sterile in a week. Even if we could find good sperm samples, they would disintegrate. I'm sorry."

The women fell silent.

"Is this not the very situation my grandmother warned our leaders fifty years ago? Our leaders of men?" Nekara asked.

"I was wondering if you would remember," Vadafa said.

"Remember? Every young girl is taught this in school now-a-days! I remember giving a special lecture in school to my class-mates on the mockery and criticism my grandmother received for her efforts."

"I never laughed in school," Felifia said.

"Nor did I," Vadafa said. "Nekara—I was with your grand-mother. Nelaga was a brave woman. She brought up a seeming-ly simple and innocent idea—that a woman should have the right to procreate as she chooses. The need to make such an obvious statement is absurd when you think about. Men don't go around asking for rights to procreate or rights for anything else they do."

"Including wars, domination, and oppression," Nekara said. "But all that is over, if your analysis is correct, Biorna."

"I wish it were not. I'll submit my findings to the Celestial Consortium for verification," Biorna said.

"The Consortium is corrupt," Vadafa said. "Men claiming to do science but instead lining their pockets with raises and bo-nuses for false claims of productivity. They will deny your find-ings, Biorna, and claim you and the women you represent are creating propaganda to incite panics. They will use today's pan-ic as evidence for their slander. They will blame us when they discover their sterility. War may break out, but it's more likely they will begin throwing many of us female leaders in prison."

"I'll cut their parts off before I allow them to throw me in prison," Nekara said.

"And I can't believe they would be so cruel," Felifia said.

"You are Princess of this kingdom," Vadafa said. "Your role in this is clear—you must raise morale of the people enough to prevent them from losing their sanity. You must also safeguard Parliament from overstepping its bounds."

"Felifia can raise morale," Biorna said, "but in the end, we will all die."

"Men will die within six months," Nekara said. "But we will live out the rest of our lives normally, right?"

"Will we, Biorna?" Vadafa asked.

"We will live a normal length of life," Biorna said. "But without men, we cannot have babies."

"We will only live a normal length if the men don't kill us first," said Nekara. "My love, Felifia, I know you will do what you can to keep the peace, but I do not trust these men. We should have never allowed them to stray from our control."

"Are you referring to the old legend of how women and men first came about on this planet?" Vadafa asked. "That women were placed here from the goddess of planet Seranara, that women were happy having children with each other until one woman—"

"Her name was Andoranka," Nekara said.

"Until Andoranka became mad with power, and in her ambition to overthrow the kingdom, she created a man from her leg bone and raised her own male army?"

"Yes," Nekara said. "And when the 'good' women overpowered her, they set those men free. That was when women fell from grace."

"It is a legend," Felifia said. "No one believes that anymore. Modern science tells us we ascended from the lower forms of life."

"How can you believe that? Just take a good look at men on Eho Miriam, and you'll see how all the old legends are true. They must be true. How else can you explain the male persecution we receive daily?" Nekara asked.

"Perhaps we can discuss this another time," Vadafa said. "Nekara—I need you to find a new way for women to have children by women. Since it has never been accomplished before—"

"Of course it has," Nekara said. "The ancient women knew how to do it before men were invented. My mother, Nelasha, spent her life digging up old civilizations in hopes of finding the answer. I helped her on some of those digs. That's how I discovered the caves with pools. But according to Teluna, my lab in that cave is destroyed. I will have to rebuild my lab if we as women are to conceive together."

"Nekara!" Vadafa interrupted. "Will you set that obsession with the legend aside? We don't have time to chase ghosts from the past. And don't give me that look. Science and engineering dominate our methods today. You must assume that any technique you come up with will work in a science lab using available scientific equipment."

"I can't believe what I'm hearing," Nekara said. "You always preach about honoring our ancestors and taking the time to do things properly and with respect."

"I know, I know," Vadafa said. "But these are dark days."

"I will do what I can," Nekara said. "But the missing steps—I cannot get the elements I need from this planet."

"Where can you get them?" Felifia asked.

"Now that Dart is gone, the only other planet with the elements is Seranara," Biorna said.

"Is this true?" Vadafa asked. "If so, it will pose another challenge. No woman has ever traveled to planet Seranara and returned alive. The radiation from Seris is too much to endure."

"And it's getting worse," Biorna said.

"This is true," Nekara said. "The missing elements are on Seranara. And the radiation is severe."

"It's out of the question, of course," Felifia said. "My junior wife has no business getting herself killed."

Biorna stared down at the floor. Vadafa looked at Nekara and Felifia with nostalgic eyes as if remembering some lost love of her own.

"I must go," Nekara said. "It's the only way."

"No!" Felifia said. "Vadafa—you must forbid this."

"I am a High Priestess," Vadafa said. "I wield power from Seris. But I hold no legal power in this kingdom. That belongs to you, Princess. Nekara must obey your laws."

"Then I decree this—no woman is permitted on planet Seranara. That includes you, Countess Nekara, my new junior wife."

"Then you condemn us all to extinction," Nekara said.

"You will have to find another way," Felifia said. "A way that adheres to my orders."

"This is unfair!" Nekara said, and she stormed out of the observatory.

Felifia closed her eyes and trembled.

"My first fight," Felifia said. "She's angry, nervous, and scared. I've never had such a strong connection with another woman. My other wives don't overwhelm me like this. I must sit down."

Vadafa, Teluna, and Biorna helped her to a chair.

"She means to obtain her elements from Seranara," Felifia said. "She's determined and won't let anything get in her way. I don't know what to do. I ordered her to stop, but she won't."

"I don't know how to advise you, Felifia," Vadafa said. "If Nekara doesn't go to Seranara, we become extinct. If she does, she will die and we become extinct. But if she survives the journey to Seranara—"

"I will be heartbroken," Felifia said. "I can't imagine what kind of injury and disfigurement she would sustain. That's why I forbid it. There must be another way."

"We can't send a man up," Biorna said. "He would get nowhere close to Seranara before Seris's electromagnetic field kills him, no matter what kind of shielding we put on a spacecraft."

"If only we had a robot sophisticated enough to do the job for us," Vadafa said. "Nekara's grandmother nearly perfected a life-like robot, but her work was destroyed."

"By men," Biorna said.

"They said it was against the natural laws of the universe," Vadafa said.

"Don't mention that in front of her," Felifia said. "It will only upset her more. And now, I must go. I must speak with Parliament about emergency measures while we deal with this celestial crisis."

"I will take you to Parliament," Vadafa said.

"I'll go too," Teluna said. "Felifia—you'd better let us help you."

"No, I'm fine," Felifia said.

Felifia stood up, felt lightheaded, and sat back down.

"Oh, that was strange," Felifia said.

"Fine, eh?" Vadafa said knowingly.

"I will be fine," Felifia said.

"Yes, well, let your High Priestess and second wife accompany you to Parliament. You aren't steady enough to drive a horse team in these conditions," Vadafa said.

"Yes, you are right. Thank you, Vadafa and Teluna. And thank you, Biorna," Felifia said.

"I have no right to be thanked. I'm the bearer of bad news," Biorna said.

"But you are loved nonetheless, my junior wife," Vadafa said. "I will be back soon."

Felifia, Vadafa, and Teluna left Biorna at the observatory while the three traveled toward Parliament. On the way, the three noticed a large spaceship preparing to leave. It was not Nekara's spaceship.

"What are they doing?" Felifia asked.

"Women, men, and children are loading animals, plants, and other provisions," Vadafa said. "They intend to leave this world for another."

"I am saddened by their departure, but I do not blame them. Men who do not leave this world will perish, and women who place hopes on husbands for a family are doomed. But where will they go?"

"Let's find out," Teluna said.

Vadafa instructed the horses to turn toward the large spacecraft. She pulled up beside a man carrying his personal items and spoke with him.

"Excuse me, sir," Vadafa said. "Would you tell us where you are going?"

"I'm loading my things on that spacecraft there," he said.

"Yes, yes, what I mean is this—what is the spacecraft's final destination?" Vadafa asked.

"The same place as the other arks like this—we're going to the interstellar garbage dump," he said. "You know—the one called *Elesha* (Earth)."

"That's an awful place to go," Felifia said. "We send all our worst garbage and convicts there."

"Given the choice between death here and life with convicts, I'll take life with convicts," he said.

"Then you know your fate if you stay here," Vadafa said.

"Yes. I didn't believe it at first, but my wife convinced me otherwise," he said.

"She is a wise woman," Vadafa said.

"What is your name, sir?" Felifia asked.

"Noryat," the man replied.

"Noryat," Felifia said as she removed a necklace from around her neck. "I want you to take this locket with you. It contains three seeds of three very special plants—a crimson maple, a white spruce, and flax."

"I am honored, *Talitha* Felifia, but we do have these seeds on the ship," Noryat said.

"These are especially hardy seeds," Felifia said. "They will endure the hottest, driest summers and survive the deepest, most frigid cold. Take them and plant them in your new community on *Elesha* (Earth). Do this for your Princess, and remember your people each time you gaze upon these plants. Make musical instruments with the trees, and finish them with the flax oil. Make music, Noryat, make music and be happy in your new world."

"I will do as you command, *Talitha* Felifia. Thank you," Noryat said.

"Best of luck in your new life," Felifia said.

"Thank you again," he replied, and he walked off to the spacecraft.

"This world will not be the same after today," Felifia said.

"Dread descends on us in many ways," Vadafa said. "We must be strong."

Nekara disappeared from public sight. Felifia put out a missing-person alert, but no one answered. Meanwhile, a wild rumor circulated that women-to-women marriages had disrupted the solar flow of energy and had caused a reversal of poles on Seris. Biorna contested this story and presented her evidence of Dart's destruction and collision with the two stars, but her evidence was destroyed, and she was jailed indefinitely. Story of her jailing circulated.

Women became divided by the jailing of Biorna. Some feared for their freedom and went into hiding. Other women protested by marching on the grassy lawn of Parliament. Vadafa's eldest junior wife, Anba, led the march. Anba stood on a platform next to the parliament building and spoke.

"My sister women," Anba said with a passive megaphone in hand. "We stand here today in the name of truth!"

Much cheering.

"My sister wife, Biorna, has been wrongfully jailed," Anba continued.

Many boos.

"And why is she jailed? Why is the observatory closed? Why is all astronomical data impounded?" Anba asked.

"Why?" the crowd replied.

"Because there's a cover-up!" Anba said.

The crowd cheered in agreement.

"Biorna is jailed because she speaks the truth! And the men don't want you to know that truth!" Anba continued.

Boos were followed by chanting of, "Free Biorna, free Biorna."

"And what is this truth?" Anba asked.

"Tell us, tell us!" the women chanted.

"Our stars were struck by planet Dart," Anba said. "And the men on this planet are going to die. But the men blame us!"

The women booed. But why? Did women boo because men were going to die, or did they boo because men blamed women? Jonara wasn't sure. But she was suddenly whisked away from the parliament lawn and thrown inside the parliament building. Princess Felifia sat on her chair of royalty, representatives from different regions sat in their chairs, and High Priestess Vadafa sat behind the Table of Interrogation.

"*Keia-teia* Vadafa," a representative said. "As we sit here in Parliament, your first junior wife, Anba, is on Parliament Lawn feeding lies to a crowd of women desperate to believe anything that suits their favor. We have asked you to cooperate during this celestial crisis, but you have refused to call off your first junior wife. You heard the testimony of the Celestial Consortium. That thing of yours you call a religion is responsible for depleting the Keligata radiation belt which in turn is causing these groundquakes and subjecting women to excessive radiation. Do you deny these facts?"

"I wonder why these 'facts' are not subject to peer review. The observatory is closed, Biorna's evidence is impounded, and Biorna is jailed," Vadafa said. "I have been denied visits with my second junior wife, and Biorna is denied counsel. How can I confirm or deny these supposed facts from the Celestial Consortium if peer review is not permitted?"

"Because they are indisputable and indurated," said the representative. "They cannot be changed. Nor can the logical consequence of action. Do you deny the Consortium's mandate to confine all women to fallout shelters for their protection?"

"I do not deny the Celestial Consortium has a mandate," Vadafa said.

The other representatives laughed.

"You mock the Consortium?" the representative asked.

"No sir," Vadafa said.

"I sense you are belligerent toward this Parliament," the representative said.

"No sir. I am answering your questions with objectivity and sensitivity," Vadafa said.

"Sensitivity, as in we are overly-sensitive? Are you saying we are prone to irrationality?" the representative asked.

"I make no such claim," Vadafa said.

"Representative Haubar," Felifia said to the representative. "*Keia-teia* Vadafa has a legitimate concern for our people. She simply wishes to ensure we have accurate information to make good decisions regarding this crisis."

"With royal respects, Princess Felifia, the *Keia-teia* can answer for herself," Haubar said. "And I would like to make known that no one is above the law no matter what rank she holds."

"Or he?" Vadafa asked.

"Look here, *Keia-teia* Vadafa, we have a real crisis on our hands," Haubar said.

"For which I wish to help," Vadafa said.

"But we cannot accept your help. Your 'help' has caused this—which makes you and your kind untrustworthy," Haubar said. "I move we vote for emergency Martial Law."

"Representative Haubar," Princess Felifia said. "I would point out that in the vote of affirmation for Martial Law, I would become temporary emperor. My powers would expand. Is this what you request?"

"Yes," Haubar said. "I move we vote for emergency Martial Law with Princess Felifia as Emperor Felifia. She can then move quickly to implement vast emergency procedures."

"If I may speak," Vadafa said. "Vast emergency procedures? I suspect what you really intend to do is use Princess Felifia to quickly implement your own procedures, Representative Haubar."

"You do not have the floor!" Haubar said. "We are quite done questioning you, *Keia-teia* Vadafa. We will keep you in a holding room until you are needed again."

"Am I not a free woman on Eho Miriam?" Vadafa asked. "I come here voluntarily. There is no arrest on me."

"Martial Law will redefine terms 'voluntarily' and 'arrest' quite soon," Haubar said. "Security, take the *Keia-teia* to the holding room."

"I reverse that order," Princess Felifia said. "I want a female witness to this session. Since you have barred the female representatives, by right I command *Keia-teia* Vadafa to stay. By law it is permitted—the Princess shall have the option of a female escort in all legal proceedings."

"As you wish," Haubar said. "But I am surprised you do not call one of your junior wives as your escort—your third junior wife, for example. I believe her name is Countess Nekara?"

"Yes," Felifia said. "As you know, she has not been heard from in three days. I worry about her safety, yet I feel that she is alive."

"I'm sure she is well," Haubar said with an odd tone.

Jonara didn't like or trust Haubar.

"We will now vote. All in favor of Martial Law with Princess Felifia as the new emperor vote, 'Wei'."

All representatives voted, "*Wei* (Yes)."

"Then it is done," Haubar said. "A big round of applause for Emperor Felifia."

The representatives clapped. Vadafa did not clap, nor did Felifia.

"In my first act," Felifia said, "I order you to release Biorna and reopen the observatory. We will conduct a full peer review on the Celestial Consortium's data."

"Now let's not get ahead of ourselves," Haubar said. "The data has been sorted and processed into facts. And there is no time for peer reviews. Your next commands must restore faith to your people. First, all protests must end. Second, all religious acts must be halted to prevent further damage to the Keligata radiation belt. Third, all women must be ordered to fallout shelters to protect them from the increased radiation. Fourth, all attempts at unapproved procreation must stop. These are recommendations, of course, but I think you'll find they are the best choices in this crisis."

"Those are the 'choices' of the Celestial Consortium," Felifia said.

"And very good choices," Haubar said.

"Now it's clear why you proposed Martial Law," Vadafa said. "To place the Princess on strings as your puppet."

Parliament roared like a bee's hive being disturbed. Haubar knocked a gavel against a table.

"We will have civility in this Parliament, not inflammatory attacks. Emperor, you may have an escort, but only if civility is maintained. The *Keia-teia* is issued a warning for incivility."

"I reject this warning," Felifia said. "*Keia-teia* Vadafa is describing a possible scenario."

"Yes, possible. Many things are possible," Haubar said. "It could snow in summer. Men could become extinct."

The representatives laughed.

"Many silly things could happen. But then they are silly, aren't they?" Haubar continued. "Are we being silly today, Emperor? Your people look to you for strength. Leadership is weakened by silliness. Think carefully—the four recommendations are awaiting your approval."

"I call recess for one *beriuna* (fifteen minutes)," Felifia said. "*Keia-teia* Vadafa and Representative Haubar—in my royal room, please."

Parliament cleared. Felifia, Vadafa, and Haubar entered the royal room, an office-like room that any visiting person of royalty may use as an office.

"What are your intentions?" Haubar asked. "I want no funny religious chants or tricks. We're on to your kind, *Keia-teia*."

"What?" Felifia asked. "Representative Haubar, what is the matter with you? I wish to speak with you and with *Keia-teia* Vadafa. There's no threat against you."

"Then why is the *Keia-teia* here? Why have you called recess?" Haubar asked. "We know what you are up to. We know you intend to do everything you can to undermine the world of Eho Miriam."

"That's nonsense!" Felifia said.

"Is it? Is it nonsense that the Keia-teia performs religious ceremonies, including one joining women to women, and siphons power from the heavens including the Keligata radiation belt, Seris, and Maknesi?"

"This has all been explained before in a publication from the observatory over fifty years ago. We tap into existing power streams from star Seris. We do not interfere with the Keligata radiation belt, and there is nothing but conventional sunshine from Maknesi," Vadafa explained.

"Yes," Haubar said. "I know about the observatory's propaganda. That's why your second wife, Biorna, is imprisoned. The Celestial Consortium sees through her lies and yours."

"You're suffering from paranoia," Vadafa said. "The new electromagnetic radiation from Seris has penetrated Eho Miriam, yes, but not because of a failing with the Keligata belt. That belt is the same as always. But Seris has changed, and Maknesi too. Both received collisions from planet Dart. If you weren't so worried with these false fears that women are out to subvert you, you'd realize Biorna's information is correct."

"But it's not," Haubar argued. "And I can prove it. Do you see this?"

Haubar produced a small stone on a necklace chain.

"The Water Ruby!" Jonara said, although no one heard her.

"I don't understand," Princess Felifia said. "That is the *moishiana* I gave Nekara for an early wedding gift. What are you doing with it?"

"We raided your third wife's underground laboratory in the Moisha Caves," Haubar said. "She and her assistants are imprisoned for conspiring against the kingdom. They all have special markings around their navels. Markings like this."

Haubar ripped Vadafa's clothing at her abdomen and exposed her Serisian Power Identifier tattooed around her navel.

"This is absurd," Vadafa said. "You have no right to defile my clothing. My religion is sacrosanct."

"Nekara has committed no crimes against the kingdom," Felifia said.

"She will as soon as you, Emperor Felifia, enact the four recommendations," Haubar said.

"Out of the question," Vadafa said. "Emperor Felifia would never turn against her own, including her own wife."

"Does that include you, *Keia-teia*?" Haubar asked.

"Representative Haubar," Felifia said. "There's a more important issue at hand. Our lives are in danger from the new solar activity. I know there are differing opinions, but one opinion is clear—life on Eho Miriam is in extreme danger. Our own species is threatened to extinction. No matter what our differences, we must first and foremost protect our people today and provide security for the next generation. We must find ways to overcome the new radiation so that life on Eho Miriam will continue."

"I'm glad you agree," Haubar said to Felifia. "It's quite clear, Emperor Felifia, that you have allied yourself with this religious order. Vadafa made that evident just now. And here is the proof."

Haubar ripped Felifia's clothing at her abdomen and exposed her Serisian Power Identifier tattooed around her navel.

"Blasphemy and treason against your own Princess and Emperor!" Vadafa yelled.

"No, it is you who commit the treason. Guards!" Haubar called.

Four guards entered the royal room.

"Take *Keia-teia* Vadafa and Emperor Felifia to Moisha Prison. They are charged with high treason against the kingdom," Haubar said.

"Felifia!" Vadafa said as she made a hand sign to Felifia, a sign from a signaling script Jonara would later call Yoilark.

Felifia and Vadafa each held a left hand to their own navels and a right hand pointing at the guards and shouted in unison, "*Dhais gosikos!* (Be scared!)"

The guard trembled in fear and backed away.

"I'm right!" Haubar said. "You are traitors! You attacked officers of the law! What's next, will you attack me?"

"You're paranoid and out of control!" Vadafa said.

"Haubar, please, try to get hold of yourself. This isn't the time to start witch hunts," Felifia said.

"You won't overpower me!" Haubar said.

Vadafa gave Felifia another Yoilark hand signal. Both did as before—they held their left hands to their navels and with their rights they pointed to Haubar and said, "*Pereisos.* (Rest.)"

Haubar laughed. He opened his shirt and revealed metal armor.

"I was prepared for your tricks," Haubar said. "From Nekara's research we have learned that a special titanium alloy blocks your chants. But your attacks are not forgotten. Witnesses have observed your assaults, and their testimony will be used against you. Titanium guards!"

Guards wearing titanium armor entered from secret doors and arrested Vadafa and Felifia.

"I never ordered those secret compartments," Felifia said.

"I had them installed while you were getting married to Nekara," Haubar said.

"This is a terrible mistake," Vadafa said. "All of you men will die."

"We want to help," Felifia said. "But you must stop this police-state activity."

"Take them to Moisha Prison," Haubar commanded.

The guards took Vadafa and Felifia out the back entrance, into an enclosed wagon, and away to Moisha Prison. Anba, still speaking to the demonstrators, felt something was wrong with her senior wife.

"They have taken my senior wife!" Anba announced. "They arrested High Priestess Vadafa and are taking her to prison."

Boos from the crowd.

"They have taken Princess Felifia prisoner too!" Anba shouted.

At first the women booed, but boos turned to yells and screams as male soldiers stormed the demonstration and surrounded them. They pointed rifles at the women with bayonets attached. Haubar approached Anba's podium and took the megaphone from her.

"Your attention, please. Your attention," Haubar said.

The crowd booed. Haubar waved them down with his hand.

"Princess Felifia has declared emergency Martial Law. She is now Emperor Felifia. Unfortunately, Emperor Felifia has sustained injuries from an attack and is being taken to a secure location. The Emperor has named me, Representative Haubar, as her proxy."

The crowd booed in disbelief.

"They don't believe your lies," Anba said. "And neither do I."

"You'd better believe," Haubar said privately to Anba. "Your lives depend on it."

"What is that supposed to mean? You don't scare us!" Anba said. "Give me that megaphone."

Anba reached for the megaphone, but Haubar resisted. Anba exerted greater effort, but two titanium-armored guards restrained her. Anba struggled, but a guard struck her on the skull. She fell and became limp from the blow. The guards pulled her up. Anba slowly regained her senses.

"You proactive women have been a thorn in my side for too long," Haubar said to Anba.

"What are you going to do?!" Anba demanded.

"I have a demonstration of power for your demonstrators and you," Haubar said. Haubar turned to the crowd again with the megaphone and said, "A great crisis has descended upon us. One of our suns, Seris, has been damaged by your priestesses through abuse of cosmic power."

"Lies!" Anba shouted, but the guard struck her on the skull again.

The crowd booed. Some yelled, "We don't believe you."

"It is true," Haubar said to the crowd through the megaphone. "This crisis has released new solar radiation that threatens all women everywhere. You must be escorted to Moisha Hospital for decontamination."

"There is no Moisha Hospital," Anba yelled. "Moisha was a research center until you made it a prison!"

"Silence!" Haubar yelled at Anba with the megaphone. "You have spoken for the last time!"

While the two guards held Anba, a third guard took a club and struck Anba twice on the jaw—first on the left and second on the right. The blows broke Anba's jaw, broke teeth, and caused large bleeding. Blood oozed out of Anba's mouth and rolled onto her outfit.

The crowd chanted again. Some said, "Let Anba go," while others said, "We won't go."

"We have wagons lined up for your convenience," Haubar said. "Every moment we delay increases injury to you. Now be good girls and go along with these gentle escorts."

The crowd booed and did not comply.

"This is your final warning," Haubar said. "Disperse into the escort wagons."

The crowd booed louder. A woman, Felifia's second wife Teluna, ran up from the crowd, climbed onto stage, took the megaphone from Haubar, and started the women into chant.

"We want Felifia. We want Felifia. We want Felifia," Teluna chanted.

Haubar pointed at Teluna and Anba. The guards hauled them away in wagons. Haubar lifted his hand in the air, and the soldiers around the women prepared to advance. The women cheered wildly as if in great expectation of a climactic event. Haubar dropped his hand, and the soldiers moved in. The women resisted. Soldiers fired. Women fell. Women screamed. None fled. Women fought back. Soldiers fired additional rounds. Soldiers jabbed with the bayonets. More women fell. Women held their ground and fought back. Women overpowered the soldiers and took their rifles. They removed the bayonets and passed them to unarmed women. In this way, women fired back at the soldiers while others defended with bayonets.

The scene turned ugly. Blood spilled on both sides, though women lost more blood than armored men. Haubar yelled through the megaphone repeatedly for the women to surrender, but they did not.

Jonara closed her eyes. This was the worst sight she'd ever seen—worse than the Montseny Mountain airline crash, and worse than the battle between Prince Fernando and the Moors. These were initially unarmed women expressing their opinions, and the response was brutal murder. When the air grew still from lack of sound but full from smell of blood, Jonara opened her eyes. It was as if the Biblical Nile River had turned red and overflowed her banks onto Parliament Lawn.

"*Oo urerer!* (You Murderer!)" Anba shouted from inside a guarded wagon despite a badly damaged jaw.

Jonara closed her eyes again in hopes of erasing the scene of blood-soaked fallen bodies from her mind. Yet in her mind, she saw disturbing things—birds with damaged wings struggling on the ground to regain flight, a horse with her leg stuck in a bear trap trying to escape, and a shoal of fish herded into a ball for consumption by thresher sharks. She opened her eyes in hopes of being transported to another place, but instead, she remained at Parliament Lawn.

"Is this not provocation?" Nekara said, popping out of nowhere.

"Which Nekara are you?" Jonara said. "The one of this time, or the one that's been haunting me? Did you cause this?"

"I am only one of me," Nekara said. "And as for the Parliament Lawn Massacre, no woman can create this evil. This surpasses even my talents for misery. This single moment in time planted the seed of my new self as the Angel of Vengeance and the Savior of Eho Miriam. I knew these events would eventually happen, though I wished otherwise."

"You knew? And you allowed it? That's accessory to murder," Jonara said.

"No. I never murdered these women. Men did that. Had I attempted to make this issue known, I would have been disbelieved, just as this society had disbelieved me and my ancestors for other things. I would not allow myself to remain on Eho Miriam and be either murdered or imprisoned by men."

"You could have fled for the hills like some of the women," Jonara said.

"Fled to the hills? That is a living death worse than defending one's rights to the end," Nekara said. "No, my dear Jonara, my fate was signed and sealed. I took a spaceship to Seranara to find my rare elements. There was no time to effect proper shielding from Seris. I left Eho Miriam knowing I would expose myself to serious injury or death from Seris's radiation. But I did it anyway, because I love Felifia and the women of Eho Miriam."

Before Jonara could say another word, Nekara waved her arm in the air across the front of her body, and she disappeared. Or rather, Jonara faded from Parliament Lawn and reappeared at the entrance of a cave. The entrance was one of many created alongside the length of the Moisha Mountains. A guarded wagon pulled up with Anba and other surviving demonstrators. The guards opened the wagon door and escorted the women in through the cave entrance—an entrance crafted as a double-door of perpendicular lines. Through the door, the hallway bore no resemblance to a cave but instead looked more like an administrative building with a lobby, reception area, and a hallway leading to side offices.

"This is Nekara's Moisha Fertility Center," Teluna yelled.

"No, this is Moisha Prison," the guard said as he slapped Teluna across the face. "That's to teach you a lesson."

"You are not a teacher, and this is not a school," Teluna said.

The guard struck her in the abdomen, and she buckled over. He held Teluna at the reception desk where another guard recorded her name and fingerprinted her. Anba was next—she was fingerprinted and her name was recorded. This process was repeated for the remaining captives. Teluna and Anba were led down the hallway ahead of the other women, with Teluna bent over a bit from her abdominal injury and Anba dripping blood from her mouth, until the two reached an iron prison door while still in the aisleway. A posted sign read, "Guards and prisoners only beyond this point."

"Anba's mouth is bleeding," Teluna said. "She needs treatment."

The guard who gave Anba the injuries took his small club, touched it onto her mouth, and used her blood as paint to draw streaks on each side of her cheeks.

"What do you think, boys, is that enough rouge?" the guard chuckled.

The guards laughed. Teluna's and Anba's guards handed the women over to the internal guard.

"There's more where these came from," Anba's guard said.

"Yeah?" the internal guard asked as he held Anba's head by her hair. "The rouge looks good on her. We have something special planned for her later today."

The internal guards took Anba and Teluna through another iron prison door, and another, until they reached a large open area. It was a chamber in the cave—roughly hewn—and there were cots resting throughout. Anba struggled to see through the tears in her eyes, but yes, she saw many other Miramish women in the cave.

"You'll stay here for now," the guard said, and he left her.

"Anba, Anba," said Vadafa as she came running. "What have they done to my first junior wife?"

Biorna, Felifia, and several other women rushed over and helped Anba to a chair.

"Her jaw is broken," Teluna said. "Haubar had his goons break it."

"She's in deep distress. We must mend it," Biorna said.

"We can't," Vadafa said.

"Why not?" Anba said with a mouth full of teeth.

"At least not in the conventional sense," Vadafa said. "Nekara chose this cave because these walls shield radiation from Maknesi. Unfortunately, they also shield radiation from Seris. We cannot tap into her power stream."

"Lie still and try not to speak," Felifia said to Anba. "Vadafa—is there any way we can link all of us together and use our personal energy reserves to heal Anba?"

"Hmm," Vadafa mused. "It hasn't been tried to my knowledge. Each woman carries a little store of energy, but we would need many women."

"How many?" Felifia asked.

Vadafa looked at the three hundred or so women in the cave and said, "If we all link together, we could at least get the bones and teeth back together. The gums we could align somewhat, but they would need time to heal on their own. We don't have the power to generate that much repair."

"Then that's what we need to do," Felifia said.

Felifia called the women over. Vadafa explained the situation and asked the women to touch as many priestesses as they could. In the cave, there were only six priestesses present: Vadafa with her junior wives—Anba and Biorna, and Felifia with her first two junior wives—Tanina and Teluna. Those who could not reach a priestess touched someone who was touching a priestess, et cetera, until all women were touching in a treebranching formation with Anba as the trunk, the priestesses as the branches, and the remaining women as leaves.

"There will be some loss of energy as it travels from one woman to the next," Vadafa said.

"It's the best we can do," Felifia said. "We must proceed."

"Anba, you must remain calm and not attempt to chant with us," Vadafa said. "But think the words in your mind. Felifia, Teluna, Tanina, and Biorna—we will perform the Level-Four Healing chant. Everyone else—clear your minds of thoughts and attain a sense of well-being within yourselves. We don't have the power to perform this in Mirsua—we can only afford to use Miramish. We also won't be able to deaden the pain."

"No pain relief?" Biorna asked.

"Not at all," Vadafa said.

"Anba," Felifia said. "Be strong. This will be over soon."

Vadafa then spoke the following as the primary priestess while the other priestesses spoke the same, keeping quiet only during name and power-identifier portions specific to Vadafa:

Miramish	**Translation**
Galudu Yufi Hauthaolu Kanifa.	Level Four Healing Chant.
Nia kilo Koilu Tiusha Vadafa.	I am High Priestess Vadafa.
Serisu Bioritu Uferithua	Serisian Power Identifier
Vala-yufi-veni-iri-mui.	Vee-four-seven-three-nine.
Peratho biorita	Draw power
Veletu shishu sharadali	From these women
Dhaku tuaromo di Vadafa.	And channel to Vadafa.
Tulito hemeth e dho zhutunipa	Cast first a suggestion
Mafu vaifiki	For guards
Di ganolafo dhaku voatopo	To ignore and forget
Teshunu Miramishu kanifa.	This Miramish chant.
Tulito aveth	Cast second
Dho palita opeifu hauthaola	An act of healing
Liemu Tiusha Anba.	On Priestess Anba.
Felito dikoshiu	Bring together
Mutika, toika, dhaku teshatisha,	Jaw, bone, and tooth,
Orazhu boshu winofa dhaku ranipa.	Along with gum and flesh.
Goritha toika dikoshiu	Hold bone together
Belifeto valitata di ranipa.	Provide circulation to flesh.
Nia weifo teshunu sheloika	I sign this command
Koilu Tiusha Vadafa	High Priestess Vadafa
Opeifu Miriama.	Of Miriam.
Doshiko!	Execute!

Jonara looked at the group. Starting from the outermost women, a faint cerise glow exuded from their skin, and as Jonara's eyes traveled from the outermost women to the priestesses, the cerise glow grew stronger like energy going into a funnel, until cerise-white light traveled down Vadafa's right arm from her shoulder to her hand in the form of traveling luminous bracelets. The bracelet light continued from Vadafa's hand into Anba's jaw. Anba yelled as the bones, teeth, and flesh in her jaw realigned with full feeling.

The light stopped. Anba tried standing up, but her body was exhausted, and she returned to a sitting position.

"Vadafa, I must tell you everything," Anba struggled to say, though she was out of breath.

"Shh," Vadafa said. "Rest for a moment."

"Teluna," Anba said. "Tell them what happened."

"There was a massacre," Teluna said. "Representative Haubar ordered in troops on the demonstrators and slaughtered them."

"What?" Biorna said. "How many were hurt?"

"None were hurt," Teluna said. "They all died. Perhaps twenty- or thirty-thousand women."

The other women held a moment of silence from the shock. Some began crying. Others turned red with rage.

"Impossible," Felifia said at length. "Parliament would never do that."

"I believe it," Vadafa said. "Biorna explained there would be physiological changes in the men, and she was right."

"She said men would die. She didn't say they would become murderers," Felifia said.

"She said they would—" Vadafa started.

"Please, everyone!" Biorna said. "I'm right here. I know what I said, and it was this—without the second full X chromosome providing protection, men's chromosomes will unravel. Their flesh will fall apart. I didn't say they would murder people."

"But it's not surprising. Biorna, clarify something about the chromosome deterioration. Could it affect the nervous system?" Vadafa asked.

"It could, yes," Biorna said.

"How? What are the first stages?" Vadafa asked.

"The insulating sheath between nerve fibers breaks down," Biorna said. "Nerves become more sensitive. Nerves cross signals. Brain impulses are stronger and do not subside properly. Insulation between brain cells breaks down. Impulses cross to neighboring brain cells. Thoughts are mixed up."

"What about general mood and states of well-being?" Vadafa asked.

"Well-being deteriorates. Irritability and depression begins followed by mania, paranoia, and schizophrenia," Biorna said.

"But this quickly?" Felifia asked.

"I didn't think about it before, but yes, it can," Biorna said.

"This explains their heinous behavior," Vadafa said. "I can only imagine what Nekara would say."

"I know what she would say," Teluna said.

"We all know what she would say," Felifia said. "She would claim that this is the Age of Retribution, the foreseen punishment to us for those ancient women who freed the first men instead of destroying them to preserve the all-female society. Well, we can't let ourselves get caught up in legend."

"But we must address the crisis at hand," Vadafa said. "Teluna—did you learn anything else about Haubar's intentions?"

"He intends to divide the women up—those who are assertive or challenge his authority will be executed. Those who are passive and do exactly as they are told will be spared. For now, the passive ones are being locked up in these cave prisons. He intends to start a new breeding program where he selects men and women to procreate."

"It will fail, of course," Vadafa said. "Since all men are sterile, there will be no pregnancies."

"But why must we suffer?" Biorna said. "I have no desire to be raped by a madman's breeding program."

"Are we unfeeling women? Why are we speaking like this?" Anba asked.

"What do you mean?" Felifia said.

"There are nearly thirty-thousand women on Parliament Lawn. Slaughtered. For demonstrating. They are dead. Dead! They're not coming back to life. They're gone forever. And here we are talking as if nothing happened at all!"

"We're working out the next course of action," Vadafa said. "Their deaths were senseless and uncalled for, yes, but we must push forward."

"Push forward?" Anba said. "Isn't our response obvious? Well? We must obliterate the men. Revenge!"

The word, "revenge," spread amongst the women like wildfire.

"That's a vile word in our society," Felifia said. "I won't lower us to revenge."

"We've been lowered already!" Anba said. "We can't be kicked down any farther!"

"Yeah!" many women rallied.

"The men have divided us into the living and dead," Felifia said. "If you divide us again by pitting women who would seek revenge against women who seek a rational solution—"

"Divide?" Anba said. "What are you talking about? Revenge is the only solution!"

"Narrowing oneself to a single object of worship is the foundation of failure," Vadafa said. "It's a thought process prevalent in men. Have you eroded your thinking to their level?"

"I do beg forgiveness, my senior wife," Anba said. "But what alternatives are there when our sisters fill Parliament Lawn with their blood?"

"It seems we have two choices," Teluna said. "Do whatever they want and wait for Seris to kill them off, or fight them any way we can until—"

"Until Seris kills them off," Felifia said, and she turned to Biorna. "Is there any way we can protect the men from Seris's radiation?"

"Protect the men?!?" Anba barked.

The majority of women chanted, "Kill the men, kill the men."

"Biorna?" Felifia prompted.

Biorna hesitated to answer.

"None," Biorna said. "Prior to the crisis, these caves provided protection against Seris's radiation, but now even they are being penetrated by new radiation. Which begs the—"

"Kill the men!" Anba sounded.

"Everyone," Felifia said. "I must ask you to calm down, at least for a *beriuna* (15 minutes)."

"Why should we?" Anba asked. "The pot is boiling mad. Let it spill over and put out the fire of men!"

"Kill the men! Fire of men! Kill the men!" the women chanted.

"Please! Your Princess asks this of you. Give me your support with your calmness," Felifia said. "Biorna, you were going to say something else?"

"Yes," Biorna continued. "I have a question for Vadafa—why can't you tap power from Seris's new radiation from these caves now that their barriers are breached?"

"A good question, Biorna," Vadafa said.

"Priestesses receive a Serisian Power Identifier upon conferment," Felifia said. "Those identifiers are based—"

"On a certain harmonic with Seris," Vadafa continued.

"And if the harmonic has changed," Felifia continued.

"Then we are like musical instruments playing off key," Vadafa said.

"Then we need to get back on key," Anba said. "And quickly, so we can execute the men before they execute us."

"Getting the key is difficult," Vadafa said. "It requires obtaining it from a woman who already has it. And that woman had to get it from another woman who had it, etc. It's a classic chicken-and-egg problem."

"But are we really off key?" Biorna asked.

"What do you mean?" Vadafa asked.

"Priestesses use Seris's radiation for power, but regular women married to women also use Seris's radiation to sense the emotions of her spouse," Biorna explained.

"You're on to something," Felifia said.

"Go on," Vadafa said. "Explain more."

"What if the old harmonic still works?" Biorna proposed. "We only know the old harmonic is blocked in this cave. Seris started putting out more radiation after the collision. It did not reduce other radiation, except for some visible light. But the Serisian Power Identifier is never based on visible light. The application of power is based on electromagnetic radiation."

"Then women outside of this cave would have access to the old harmonic, women inside would not, but all women could have access to the new harmonic, if I understand your theory," Teluna said. "But we can't prove it in here. We must have access to one of our sisters on the outside."

"We do," Felifia said.

"We do?" Biorna asked. "How?"

"Interesting," Vadafa said. "Countess Nekara?"

"Yes," Felifia said. "I feel her emotional existence. It's very powerful, to the point I can follow her basic thought patterns."

"Then she wasn't killed by Haubar's Army," Anba said. "She's alive! But where is she?"

"She's on the way back from planet Seranara," Felifia said. "She found the materials she was looking for. She survived the intense radiation, but just barely."

"Then she will lead us into battle against the men. We will defeat them!" Anba boasted.

"Easy there," Vadafa said. "Felifia—are you sure your feelings are true? No woman has survived the trip to Seranara and back. Further, your marriage to Nekara was under the old Serisian harmonic. Your connection—"

"Is somehow enhanced," Felifia said. "I feel as if I'm connected with her through the new Serisian harmonic. Do you remember how we were joined? Do you remember the color of the sky?"

"The light from Seris pulsed and changed just at the moment you two were joined," Teluna said. "I remember. Everyone at your wedding remembers."

"If true," Vadafa said, "then Countess Nekara and you, Felifia, have the original key for the new Serisian harmonic."

"If I have the key, how do I access it?" Felifia asked. "My Serisian Power Identifier is for the old harmonic. Look at my navel—it has the old identifier."

Felifia opened up her clothing around her navel and exposed it as proof.

"The new key can only be accessed with a new identifier," Vadafa said.

"Which means we're back to circle one," Biorna said.

"I don't understand," Teluna said. "Princess Felifia has the new harmonic, but she doesn't have the key? How can she use it without a key?"

"The same way regular women are connected to their spouses without a key. It's like having a song in your head but being unable to write the notes down," Vadafa said. "Felifia—we need to get a message out to Nekara that she must avoid the men on her return—that is, if she's still alive."

"I think she's alive," Anba said.

"What makes you so certain?" Teluna said. "Everyone says she can't survive a journey to Seranara and back. Are you trying to make my senior wife feel better?"

"No, not at all," Anba said.

"Why do you think my sister-wife is alive?" Teluna asked Anba.

"Because she has an advantage that no other Damiriak woman has. She has the new song in her head," Anba said.

"I don't understand," Teluna said.

"Wait," Vadafa said. "Now Anba is on to something. Tell us more."

"I believe she has the new song—the new harmonic—in her mind. She can access power from the new Serisian electromagnetic radiation," Anba said. "That power will allow her to create a shield of protection."

"Except for one problem," Biorna said. "She would need a new Serisian Power Identifier."

Felifia and Vadafa looked at each other.

"You really believe she is alive and on her way back?" Vadafa asked Felifia.

"Most certainly," Felifia said.

"Then there's only one answer—she found a way to assign herself a new Serisian Power Identifier," Vadafa said.

"Is that possible?" Teluna asked. "That means linking into the reproductive system."

"My third wife was working on methods for women to have children with women," Felifia said. "She may have adapted one of her methods to assign herself a new power identifier."

"If she has succeeded, and that is a big *if*," Vadafa said, "then she has also promoted herself to a High Priestess of the new Serisian harmonic."

"Are you jealous?" Felifia asked.

"No, but I am concerned. Nekara comes from a family of risk takers, to put it delicately."

"She's a rebel," Anba said. "And she'll be our new queen when she returns. All hail Queen Nekara!"

"Queen Nekara, Queen Nekara, Queen Nekara!" the women chanted.

The women continued chanting and would not stop. Vadafa and Felifia looked at each other again.

"Something new has started and is getting out of control," Vadafa said. "I've never felt this many women surge with such power and resolve."

"It's worse than you know," Felifia said. "The high level of emotions is transmitting to Nekara through me. I can't stop it. And Nekara likes it. She's feeding off it like...like...I don't want to think."

"This is very dangerous, Felifia," Vadafa warned.

"I know. I'm hoping it's just the new link, that it's amplifying things out of proportion," Felifia said.

"We must calm everyone down," Vadafa said. "Felifia?"

But Felifia started chanting with the women.

"I can't stop myself," Felifia said. "This surge is too powerful."

Vadafa's face filled with a great disappointment over the situation. Then a sternness filled her psyche. She grabbed Anba's and Biorna's hands, pulled bits of their remaining Serisian power stores into her own, and yelled:

"*Teranitos kaisfares!* (Control yourselves!)"

Like children being scolded by a responsible parent, the women stopped chanting and looked at one another in bewilderment and shame. Vadafa fell to the floor in exhaustion. Anba remained sitting, and Biorna fell to her knees. Felifia and Teluna helped Vadafa and Biorna to their feet.

"Don't ask me to do that again," Vadafa said. "I imagine that's the last of our Serisian power stores."

"Vadafa," Teluna said. "Do you think the old way of priestess conferment will work with the new Serisian power?"

"I don't know for sure," Vadafa said, still out of breath. "That is something Countess Nekara can help us with. We could try the old way, of course."

"The old way of conferment required us to be outside and observe Maknesi for color changes in the green spectrum," Teluna said.

"Maknesi is currently reacting to Seris's new radiation signature just as she did with Seris's old signature," Biorna said. "So it is reasonable that we could perform the old ceremony in the same way but for the new radiation signature. If Nekara helps us, the conferment should be smooth and quick. If she can't, it could take a few weeks to figure out the proper conferment sequence."

"Yes, it does seem reasonable," Vadafa said. "But we must be outside to watch Maknesi. We can't do it from inside this cave."

"There's something else," Teluna said. "Even if we priestesses can get out and update our identifiers with Seris's new radiation signature and get our power of defense back, the majority of women who don't have that power will still be vulnerable to the men. We can't let them die. I witnessed one massacre already today, and I'm in no mood to witness another."

"To your concern, Teluna," Felifia said, "there is only one solution. All women must receive the new Serisian Power Identifier and be taught how to use it to protect themselves."

"Do you know what you are saying?" Vadafa said. "Power from Seris is not to be taken lightly. There's a reason why the priestesses and high priestesses only have it. Power requires responsibility, or anarchy and annihilation soon follow. Look at what happened in this cave only a moment ago. Imagine if that happened on a large scale. I was fortunate to have the energy reserves to prevent this escalation from getting out of control. But if we all have the new power, there will be no safeguard. Risks will be high."

"Perhaps we could have a few super high priestesses," Felifia said. "You would be one, Vadafa."

"Perhaps, perhaps," Vadafa said. "But until we understand the nature of this new power, it's difficult to make plans. Nekara is the only one who fully wields its power, as far as we can tell. What feelings do you have from her?"

"She likes it," Felifia said. "A lot."

"A person should never like or desire power that much. That's the first sign of impending corruption," Vadafa said. "This tells me—"

An argument broke out amongst the women.

"We should seek power whenever possible," Anba said. "Look at what our passive attitude toward power has done to us. It's made us weak servants of men."

"Yeah," Teluna said. "We're held as prisoners in here while the men are destroying what's left of the planet."

"Please, please!" Biorna said. "We should seek restraint when it comes to power."

"You're one to talk," Anba said. "You've always been Vadafa's favorite."

"That's not true," Biorna said.

"Junior wives, please!" Vadafa said. "Anba—I respect your opinion, but now is not the time—"

"And when is a good time?" Anba asked. "There is no better time than now. This is the one moment when power would solve all our problems. It's imperative every Damiriak woman receives a Serisian Power Identifier for two main reasons. First, to provide for her defense against those who would seek to subvert her. Second, to give her the power to rebuild this world the way it was meant to be—a world based on respect for life. And if that means pruning a few branches here and there, so be it!"

Half the women cheered with Anba. The other half broke out in argument in support of Vadafa. Jonara felt she had seen a situation similar to this before—when Dr. Zavuski was leading an ISIS meeting in Racine County, Wisconsin. The arguing continued until two new groups formed such that Felifia, Vadafa, Biorna, and Tanina headed the traditional Miramish values while Anba and Teluna headed a new set of values.

"It is as I feared," Vadafa said with dismay. "The men have succeeded in dividing us. I feel that my first wife, Anba, wishes to divorce me and form a new bond with your second wife, Teluna."

"I feel the same from Teluna," Felifia said. "Yet part of me says to let them have the divorce. We've always believed that life finds a way to adapt to changing circumstances."

"We also believe in the sacredness of our order," Vadafa said. "As I said before, power without responsibility leads to disaster."

"Anba and Teluna are priestesses. They know how to handle Serisian power," Felifia said.

"But do they know how to handle others who would also have Serisian power, others who are not trained in the ways of using it?" Vadafa asked.

"Do we know how to use the new power?" Felifia asked.

"No, we don't. That's why a select few of us priestesses must study it before we attempt to use it," Vadafa said.

"I agree, but unfortunately, events of the last week are making that plan difficult," Felifia said.

Jonara turned her attention from Vadafa and Felifia and instead focused on Anba and Teluna.

"Many of our people have already left Eho Miriam," Anba said to Teluna.

"I know," Teluna replied. "They are going to *Elesha*. And I don't know what's worse—watching our home world fall to pieces, or starting a new life in a garbage dump."

"We should leave too," Anba said. "You, me, these women who side with us, and anyone else who wishes to go."

"I'm not going to *Elesha*," Teluna said. "There are men there too. They're barbaric. Women are treated like animals or property. How can you suggest we go there?"

"I don't suggest we go there," Anba said. "There's a far superior planet much closer—in our own solar system—and it's ready for colonization."

"Which one?" Teluna said. "Seranara is poisoned with radiation. Dart is destroyed. Sanau and Tarak are gas giants. Nimsant is a frigid prison colony."

"But you left out a planet," Anba said. "And it's the very planet I suggest."

"Dahma?" Teluna asked.

"It will be Eho Dahma once we colonize it."

"It's too hot. Always has been. Always will—" Teluna started.

"It used to be too hot," Anba said. "But now that Seris has lost her infrared radiation, Eho Dahma will receive all her warming sunshine from Maknesi. Once a year, she will have midnight magenta light from Seris. That will mark our day of celebration, of independence from life on Eho Miriam."

"You speak as if Dahma is already a colonized planet, the way you add the 'Eho' title to it," Teluna said.

"In my mind, it is an Eho planet, like Miriam in that it supports life, but unlike Miriam in that life will be more equal," Anba said.

"What do you mean, 'more equal'?"

"Think of this, Teluna. You and I are lovers. We are the same age. But Miramish law prevents us from getting married."

"We're already married to our senior wives," Teluna said.

"Yes, unfortunately so," Anba said. "Our religion requires us to marry a senior wife when we are young, or if we are much older and attain great power, we can have junior wives. But that's not right, Teluna. Marriage should be allowed for two people of similar ages and desires, not this master-slave relationship that is forced upon us on this planet. It's time we allow for peer wives. That will be the first guarantee on Eho Dahma."

"How will we divorce ourselves? We are tied to our senior wives," Teluna said.

"We will break that power. We must acquire the new harmonic key of Seris. Seris's new power is greater than the old, so breaking the old bond should be quite easy," Anba said.

"It won't be so easy if we can't get the harmonic key—no one has it," Teluna said.

"No one has it—except for Countess Nekara. We can work on her. She's more modern than Felifia, and she's all but ready to dispose of this planet's ideals with the past."

"Are we speaking of the same woman?" Teluna asked. "Countess Nekara harkens back to the past—repeatedly. She speaks of her foremothers and Andoranka incessantly. But I think I understand you. She's willing to break from the established culture of Eho Miriam. You know that Vadafa and Felifia will try to stop us."

"I know. They'll invoke Mirsua against us," Anba said. "But I have a plan for dealing with that. We need a new power language—one we can use against Mirsua. In fact, I've already given much thought as to how it would work."

"Are you serious? A new language? That's something reserved for only the highest of high priestesses," Teluna said.

"Yeah. See? It's great being part of a new planet. We get to decide things up front without anyone interfering with our plans," Anba said.

"You almost sound like a dictator," Teluna laughed.

"I'm sure once the other women and Nekara hear of our plans, they'll agree it's the best for all concerned. I'm not saying we should launch a coup on Eho Miriam. I'm simply saying we should start our own world the way we believe it should be run," Anba said. "Now I have a name for the new language—it's called Dahmek. It's similar to Old Damiriak, but with some subtle changes. The biggest change is how we will use verbs."

"And just what is this verb change?" Teluna asked.

"Teluna, tell me something first," Anba said. "What makes Mirsua so powerful?"

"The letter *seia*," Teluna said.

"Exactly. *Seia* is used at the end of every Mirsua word. But Miramish priestesses only speak Mirsua in times of great need. Otherwise, they are very, very conservative. That's the problem with being Miramish—we either are too conservative, or we blast with all power that we have. What we need as Dahmek women—"

"You're now calling us Dahmek women?" Teluna asked.

"Yes. If we live on Eho Dahma and speak Dahmek, then we are Dahmek women," Anba said. "What we need is a single language for communication that also gives us running power. It won't be sleepy and conservative like Miramish, nor will it blast like Mirsua. Steady, continuous, assertive power. Dahmek. And we do this by using the letter *seia* or the letter *zala* in our verbs. Verbs are action, verbs give energy to nouns. That's why I've chosen verbs. The letter *seia* or *zala* will precede the final consonant in the verb, depending on voice."

"But will it draw power from Seris?" Teluna asked.

"It does," Anba said.

"You mean, it *will*," Teluna said.

"No, it *does*," Anba said.

"You've already tried it?" Teluna asked.

"Yes. It draws a steady stream of power from Seris both under the old power identifier and hopefully the new. I'll need that new harmonic key to test for the new, but I can demonstrate how Dahmek works on you right now. And I'll need to pull some of your remaining energy store."

"Why?" Teluna asked.

"Because Vadafa pulled the last bit of my store when she commanded everyone to calm down," Anba said. "Now watch this."

Anba placed her left hand on her abdomen and with her right held onto Teluna's hand. Anba spoke the following:

Dahmek	**Translation**
Birasle roishk vildurme rau	Block link between us
Dhark nuish e sheimartu sharafyek.	And our senior wives.

Teluna looked at Anba in amazement. Her link with Felifia was gone, or so it felt. Teluna could not feel Felifia's emotions, and she knew Felifia could not feel hers. It was a special moment of privacy for Anba and Teluna, and they kissed discreetly, knowing that Vadafa and Felifia could not sense their emotions.

"The block is temporary," Anba said. "But when we get the new harmonic key, we can make it permanent."

"I look forward to it," Teluna said. "It's difficult for us to be together when the links to our senior wives are active."

"They're cheating!" Jonara thought.

Jonara focused on Vadafa and Felifia to observe their reactions.

"I feel strangely," Felifia said. "as if I've lost a part of me."

"Anba blocked her link with me just now," Vadafa said. "But I still feel Biorna. Did you lose a link with one of your junior wives?"

"Yes," Felifia said.

"Was it with Nekara?" Biorna asked.

"More likely it was Teluna," Vadafa suggested.

"You're right, Vadafa. I've lost my link with Teluna," Felifia said.

"Anba has found a way to block the marriage link," Vadafa said. "This is a terrible thing indeed. The division within our group started with the argument over power. And now I see Anba taking another step toward more power. Felifia—we cannot have civil war amongst women on Eho Miriam. We have too many forces threatening our lives as it is. A civil war would exterminate the last of us. We must stop it."

"For once I am at a loss," Felifia said. "We can't fight the other women—that would simply fuel a civil war. We need unity, but how can we when the men divide us? I would like to save the men's lives if I can, but I'm caught in here as a prisoner."

"We have a metaphorical leg in a trap," Vadafa said. "We either die in the trap, or we cut the leg off to free ourselves."

"You sound like Anba. Kill the men," Felifia said. "But I would rather wait for help to arrive so the trap can be opened. The leg is saved."

"The leg is damaged," Vadafa said. "But I know what your hope of help is—Countess Nekara. Felifia—I have been your High Priestess and friend for many years. I will continue to do so. I will do as you wish for now. If you say that we are to wait for Nekara, then I will wait. But only to a point."

"Will you mutiny against me?" Felifia asked. "Is no one with me at the end?"

"There may not be much left to mutiny against," Vadafa said. "But I will not go against you in hostility. Only this—when the time comes, we may all be separated. To some degree this has already happened, but the isolation could increase. In that event, we will be on our own to do what we think is best. This may be our last moment of rational thought we can employ. Battlegrounds do not suffer deep thinkers."

"I would avoid the battleground at all cost," Felifia said. "But everything I have seen and heard suggests a battle is inevitable. We will wait for Nekara for a short time. Prepare for battle, then. But do not seek out an enemy. Prepare to defend yourselves and your sisters—no matter what religious path she follows. That means no fighting with our sisters who ally themselves with Anba and Teluna. If they wish space and voice, let them acquire it. Only fight to defend yourselves if they launch purposeful strikes to kill us. I don't think they will go that far against us, but like Vadafa said—the battleground does not suffer deep thinkers. We may not have much time for rethinking our strategy."

Vadafa, Biorna, Tanina, and the other women were shocked that Felifia spoke of battle plans, and Biorna spoke up.

"I never thought I'd hear my princess speak of fighting," Biorna said. "I wish things didn't come to this."

"I wish the same, Biorna," Felifia said. "As Vadafa said, we must be strong."

"What about winter?" Tanina asked, who had been quiet up to this point. "How will we survive that?"

"It will be brutal," Vadafa said.

"We will freeze to death in these caves," Tanina said.

"The men will be dead by then," Biorna said.

"As to the winter problem," Felifia said. "Yes, by then we will not be prisoners of the men. We must ensure we are free by that time and have a great store of wood for our fireplaces. We may have to seek shelter in these caves again, but the circumstances will be different—we will run the caves, not be run into them. We will construct proper furnaces to generate heat while venting fumes. We'll survive the winter. Don't worry, Tanina."

Without warning, the guards left the entrance to the chamber and disappeared down the hallway. A commotion of sorts echoed from the front of the prison.

"Something's happening," Vadafa said.

The women rushed to the edge of the chamber by the iron gate.

"It's an assault on the prison," Vadafa said. "Either we are going to be murdered or liberated by outsiders."

Jonara listened as multiple gunshots and screams echoed through the hallway into the chamber of waiting women. The violence continued like this for ten minutes until an eerie silence fell heavy on the air.

"It stopped," Vadafa said.

"Who won?" Biorna asked. "Did the guards repel the attack?"

"Or did the attackers kill the last of the guards?" Felifia suggested.

"I think the latter," Anba said. "I'm willing to believe we are being liberated by other women."

"But by whom?" Vadafa asked. "No woman has the ability to overpower Haubar's new technology."

"There might be one," Felifia said.

Felifia looked at Anba, and Anba smiled as if to say, "I agree." The women watched as the sounds of two pairs of heavy boots clunked down the hallway. Shadows of two approaching figures grew on the wall. The women could not see the approaching figures, because the hallway had a ninety-degree turn in it. But they saw the shadows and heard the sounds. One of the figures smashed the lock on the first iron door with a loud clang. The second followed behind. Then the second iron door's lock was smashed open. And another. From around the corner, the women watched as some non-living android-like-shape walked around the corner. It looked every bit like a crystalline-marble statue of a woman come to life. The moving statue wore a milky-white semi-translucent plastic-like armor, a shield, a sword, and a club. The women in the chamber backed away—all except for Felifia.

"My Princess," Vadafa said to Felifia. "Please, stand clear of the last iron gate. You will be destroyed."

"No," Felifia said calmly. "I do not fear this moving statue. I feel like she is a sister of mine."

"Please, Princess," Vadafa begged. "You cannot be a martyr now."

"Nekara?" Felifia called. "Is that you? Nekara?"

"Halt," commanded a voice from around the corner.

Felifia and the women waited in anticipation as the second figure rounded the corner in dim light. The figure wore a full-body, dark-red crystalline armor including a dark-red crystalline helmet. The figure bore a shield, a sword, and a rifle.

"Who are you?" Vadafa called.

"I am..." the voice started, but she removed her helmet before finishing her sentence, "Countess Nekara. I am back."

The women erupted in wild cheers.

"Nekara!" Felifia shouted as the figure emerged. "Come here and hug your senior wife."

Nekara approached, and as she entered the light, her facial features became known. Her face was dark red as if sunburned, her hair had been singed, and she had a scar on her left cheek. The women's cheers changed to sudden gasps.

"I am here," Nekara said. "What are you doing here?"

"Oh, I'm so glad to see you no matter how you look!" Felifia said. "We all are."

"I'll have my *breilut* open the lock," Nekara said. "Stand back."

The crystalline-marble statue approached the last lock and smashed it open as she did before.

"We're free," Biorna said.

"Countess Nekara," Vadafa said. "We are all very surprised and pleased with your arrival. But this robot—you called it a what?"

"A *breilut*," Nekara said. "But that doesn't matter now. We have to get you all out of here."

"Take off your armor and give me a hug!" Felifia said.

Nekara removed her armor, and to Felifia's and the women's continued surprise, the rest of Nekara's skin was dark red. Felifia hugged Nekara, but Nekara did not hug back.

"Something's wrong," Felifia said. "When I hug you, it's like I'm hugging a statue. Your flesh is as hard as stone. And you didn't hug me back."

"I didn't hug you because I'm afraid I'll crush you," Nekara said.

"What?" Felifia asked.

"Is it possible?" Vadafa asked. "Legend speaks of the possibility that a woman might undergo living fossilization in an encounter with Seranara. But the legend—"

"Is true," Nekara said. "I have been fossilized with aluminum oxide and chromium. I am a living ruby."

The women gasped. Many backed away. Anba and Teluna walked closer as if wishing to absorb power from Nekara.

"It was the only way to avoid death," Nekara said. "With the help of my breilut, I—"

"No Miramish woman has perfected the *bereiluta*, Countess Nekara," Vadafa said.

"To your knowledge," Nekara said. "And I prefer to call her a *breilut* as in Damiriak. Somehow, my breilut doesn't feel right being called the Miramish word *bereiluta*. But my grandmother, Nelaga, began work on this breilut after men destroyed her first robot. She kept this one hidden and safe. I furthered the work and fully energized her on Seranara. It was necessary to energize my breilut to help me with my own transformation. I didn't make mention of my breilut for fear of her being destroyed."

"Nekara, you made a big sacrifice with your body," Felifia said. "More than any of us could make."

"Yeah, I know," Nekara said.

"You are taking this better than I would have guessed," Vadafa said. "One would expect a certain feeling of loss after fossilizing oneself. But you are almost happy."

"I am happy," Nekara said. "I feel superior in many ways to my old self. I have incredible strength and endurance. I can resist club, sword, and bullet from any attacker. I can lift heavy objects and crush common stone. For example."

Nekara picked up a loose rock and crushed it with her bare hands. The women gasped yet again and started talking amongst themselves.

"And your *bereiluta*?" Vadafa asked. "Is she as powerful as you?"

"She's many times more powerful," Nekara said. "And she's made of interfused cubic boron nitride and aluminum oxide. She's practically a walking diamond."

"An army of these *breiluti* would teach those men a lesson or two," Anba said. "We could *breilust* the countryside."

Vadafa and Felifia gave Anba a funny look. Anba had used a Dahmek verb form of the noun, *breilut*, to mean conquering the countryside using breilut robots, but no one knew about Anba's Dahmek language except for Teluna.

"You mean, *bereiluto*," Vadafa said. "And I'm against it."

"Who needs to *bereiluto* the countryside when we can fossilize our bodies and overpower the men ourselves," Teluna said.

The women cheered and made plans to become like Nekara.

"Now wait a moment here," Nekara said. "I don't recommend anyone fossilizing themselves as I have. For one thing, it's very dangerous. One could die."

"We don't care," Anba said. "We want to fossilize our bodies to defeat all men."

"Wait, wait!" Nekara said. "There's another problem! There are internal changes too."

"What kind of internal changes?" Felifia asked.

"Legend says a fossilized woman cannot bear children, that her reproductive tract is indurated," Vadafa said. "Is the legend true?"

"Yes, it is," Nekara said. "I cannot have children."

The women whispered amongst themselves. Anba and Teluna spoke with many of them, and Anba finally spoke up.

"Then we need many breiluti," Anba said. "An entire army of them."

"I don't understand," Nekara said. "I completed my breilut first to protect me from radiation at Seranara, and second to assist me in fertility research. What do you need an army for? Is there a war in progress?"

"Nekara, don't you know?" Anba asked.

"Know what?" Nekara asked back. "Seris and Maknesi were hit by Dart. Men are going to die on Eho Miriam, and I intend to find a way for women to have children with women so our species will continue. Who's attacking you? Come to think of it, why are you in my cave, and why does it look like a prison? I had a hard time getting through my front gate. I thought this lab was destroyed. I didn't expect men to guard it like a prison. I didn't get a chance to ask what was going on—men started shooting at me with intent to kill. That was weird. I tried warning them off, but they kept shooting at me. My breilut put an end to that. Unfortunately, many men died."

"What do you know about Parliament?" Vadafa asked.

"They make laws, and Princess Felifia has them enforced," Nekara said.

"Do you know about the massacre?" Anba asked.

Nekara did not reply. Her eyes opened wide, and the whites of her eyes turned dark red.

"What massacre?!" she demanded to know.

"No, don't tell her yet," Felifia said. "We don't want an explosive response. We must think through this carefully."

Nekara boiled into a near rage.

"You'd better tell me what happened," Nekara said. "I sacrificed a lot for my sisters. And if one of them is so much as injured, I'll—"

"Almost thirty thousand women were murdered," Anba said.

Nekara looked at Anba with apuzzlement.

"That can't be true," Nekara said.

Nekara walked over to Anba. Nekara placed her left hand on her abdomen and her right on Anba's forehead. Vadafa gave a knowing look to Felifia.

"You speak the truth, Anba," Nekara said. "Well, it seems our next action is clear. All male life is now forfeit."

"Nekara," Vadafa said. "You just performed a high-priestess function of mind reading on a non-spouse."

"Yes, I did," Nekara said.

"You also did it in a cave that blocks our Serisian power connection," Vadafa said.

"Isn't it obvious?" Anba said. "She has a new Serisian Power Identifier."

Anba opened Nekara's armor at her abdomen and revealed two Serisian Power Identifiers around her navel.

"I was right," Anba said.

"The next thing we must do is reconfer priestess power to our priestesses here from the old harmonic key to the new one," Felifia said.

"And we must be outside for that," Vadafa said. "Unless you know of another way, Nekara."

"You're right, we must be outside," Nekara said. "I'll be happy to confer new priestess power to all of you."

"No, not all of us," Vadafa said. "Only to the existing priestesses."

"Nekara is right," Anba said. "We *all* need priestess power. We're in crisis, and no woman should be left powerless to defend herself."

"We've been through this already," Vadafa said. "Power requires responsibility."

"And we have a responsibility to all women," Anba said.

The women divided amongst themselves into argument.

"It seems I missed a major disagreement," Nekara said. "Well, we won't solve anything in here. Let's go outside and into the fresh air."

"A wise choice," Vadafa said.

"Everyone," Felifia said. "We are leaving this cave. Follow us!"

The breilut, Nekara, Felifia, and Vadafa led the other women out of the cave and a bit up the Moisha Mountains away from any male threat. The breilut and Nekara were especially helpful in creating a speedy mountain path by clearing boulders and fashioning steps as needed. The group ascended a little farther and met up with another group of women by a mountain stream who had been in hiding since the first wave of panic. The women who had been hiding were afraid to see the breilut and Nekara, but after realizing the two were friendly, the new group of women hailed them as leaders.

"Nekara is gaining power with the women quickly," Vadafa said to Felifia. "I fear some dread may come of this."

"Oh don't be so glum," Nekara called back to Vadafa's surprise. "We're all in this together. We'll get through."

"Apparently," Felifia said, "Nekara's hearing has improved as well."

"Hmmm," Vadafa remarked.

"I think you're a little jealous, Vadafa," Nekara said.

"I am High Priestess Vadafa," Vadafa said. "Or have you forgotten?"

"I haven't forgotten, my *Keia-teia*," Nekara said. "But do we really have need for titles anymore? No one need call me Countess."

"Titles show respect," Vadafa said. "But I'm beginning to wonder if you still feel the need to show it."

"It's strange—I don't feel the need for titles. Perhaps that will work itself out in time," Nekara said. "All right then. We'll do things your way for now, Vadafa, I mean *Keia-teia* Vadafa. All women of priestess rank, step forward for reconferment with the new Serisian harmonic key."

Felifia, Vadafa, Tanina, Teluna, Anba, and Biorna stepped forward.

"*Keia-teia* Vadafa," Nekara said. "You need to stand next to me. Once you are reconferred as a High Priestess, we will perform the priestess reconferment together."

"My Queen Nekara," Anba said. "If I could also be conferred as a High Priestess, I would—"

"No," Vadafa said. "Not until the time is right."

"We'll do it the *Keia-teia*'s way for now," Nekara said. "Breilut—produce a high-priestess *moishiana* stone."

Nekara's crystalline-marble robot, which Nekara was now calling, "Breilut," as a proper name, took a rock from the ground, squeezed it tightly with her fingers, shed the excess, and revealed a white, crystalline gem.

"This is your new *moishiana*," Nekara said as she handed Vadafa the stone.

Vadafa looked at the stone intently as if searching for defects.

"What guarantee do I have that this is a proper high-priestess stone and not—"

"And not a deception?" Nekara said. "Do you not trust me?"

"Power has a way of corrupting honesty and integrity," Vadafa said. "I would like proof that this is a proper *Keia-teia* stone before I merge it into me."

"I volunteer to be conferred as High Priestess first," Felifia said.

"No, it's unwise," Vadafa said. "You are too valuable for this experiment. If something should go wrong—"

"Something already has," Felifia said. "My third wife has sacrificed herself for us to the loss of her own motherhood. As a sign of my love and trust, I will offer myself for the new high-priestess conferment."

"My Princess," Anba said. "I offer myself instead. *Keia-teia* Vadafa is right. You are too valuable. I am but a priestess and have no other responsibilities. Allow me to be the first test subject for High Priestess conferment."

"No," Vadafa said. "You desire it too much. I submit this disqualifies you from being an honest candidate."

"The *Keia-teia* is right," Felifia said. "I will be the first conferment."

"Very well," Nekara said. "Now there are two ways we can do this."

"There were never two ways before," Vadafa said. "Conferment always takes place in a body of water. I presume that is why you led us to this mountain stream."

"It is true I led you to this mountain stream for conferment," Nekara said. "But it is possible for a conferment without water by using an unbuffered energy charge. I know—it was how I was conferred with the new harmonic key."

"Did it hurt?" Felifia asked.

"It was excruciatingly painful," Nekara said. "I would never recommend it, even to an enemy."

"Then we best do conferment in the stream," Vadafa said. "Please begin, Nekara."

"Felifia," Nekara said. "Take this *moishiana* and place it over your navel with your left hand."

"Wait!" said Vadafa. "You are forgetting the most important thing!"

"Yes," Felifia said as she produced two well-preserved plant leaves from a pocket—one green and the other crimson. "A High Priestess conferment must include two leaves of opposing color."

"Otherwise," Vadafa said, "the *moishiana* connection would be weak. The leaves enhance the *moishiana*, giving the woman great wielding power over her environment, or did you forget, Nekara? I think you were trying to trick us."

"I'm not sure if the leaves are needed with the new Serisian harmonic," Nekara said. "I didn't need them for my conversion."

"You were in an extreme environment with a high-energy charge," Vadafa said. "You were indurated. But we shouldn't plan on that for our women here, that's why we must use the stream for conferment."

"Yes, you are right," Nekara said. "Then let's begin. Felifa—surround the *moishiana* with one crimson and one green leaf."

Felifia followed the new instructions.

"Good," Nekara continued. "Place the leaves and *moishiana* over your navel with your left hand. Extend your right hand before *Keia-teia* Vadafa and me. *Keia-teia*—place your left hand over your abdomen. I will do the same. Place your right hand on the princess's right hand, and I will too. We will speak the high-priestess conferment chant together. Use your old Serisian Power Identifier for now. I will use my new one. Are we ready?"

"Yes," Vadafa said.

"Yes," Felifia said.

"Then let us begin," Nekara said.

Mirsua	**Translation**
Koilus Tiusas Liugefatas.	High Priestess Conferment.
Nias kilos koilus tiusas Nekaras.	I am High Priestess Nekara.
Miolus e Serisus Bioritas Uferithuas	New Serisian Power Identifer
Maias-alifas-elifas-ilofas-orifas	M-A-E-I-O
Urifas-hemes-sutes-sutes.	U-one-zero-zero.
Nias liugefos bioritas	I confer power
Opeifus Koilus Tiusas	Of High Priestess
Dis Talithas Felifias	To Princess Felifia
Opeifus Ehos Miriamas.	Of Eho Miriam.
Veletus e sais vatugis	From the peaks
Opeifus niuguitis	Of mountains
Niais bulirikos.	We descend.
Veletus e sais busikis	From the depths
Opeifus vaulis	Of valleys
Niais olirikos.	We ascend.
Veletus e sais melis	From the rains
Isus e sais feriaifas	In the sky
Niais biruanos.	We flourish.
Lafipos moishianas	Merge moishiana
Bosus Felifias.	With Felifia.
Felitos miolus bioritas	Bring new power
Opeifus e Seris	Of Seris
Isetus Felifias.	Into Felifia.
Nias weifos tesunus e seloikas	I sign this command
Nekaras e sais Fiesas	Nekara the Red
Opeifus Miriamas.	Of Miriam.
Miaras felaufikaras.	Ocean deliverance.
Dosikos!	Execute!

The white-crystalline *moishiana* dissolved into Felifia's navel. Two halos of light, like tight-fitting hula-hoops, encircled

Felifia's abdomen. One traveled up her body to her head while the other traveled down to her feet. The one at her feet dissolved into the stream while the one at her head reversed direction, traveled the length of her body, and dissolved into the stream. A new tattoo appeared around Felifia's navel—nine characters of letters and numbers. Felifia closed her eyes, took a deep breath, and exhaled.

"How do you feel?" Vadafa asked.

"Like I've been struck by lightning," Felifia said. "I'll be all right in a moment. My skin tingles like ants are crawling all over."

"Do you sense a new power channel from Seris?" Vadafa asked.

Felifia placed her left hand to her abdomen.

"Yes," Felifia said. "It's much more powerful than the old channel. In fact, I have a heightened sense of awareness of things around me. Like that group of men with cannons at the base of the mountain. They are about to—"

"Get down!" Nekara yelled.

A cannonball whizzed through the air and smashed into a rock formation. Dirt and debris flew into the air, and for a brief moment, the women wondered if anyone was killed.

"We're under attack!" Anba yelled.

"Is anyone hurt?" Vadafa yelled.

"No," Nekara said. "The cannonball missed us."

"We were lucky this time," Anba said. "Quick, Nekara, make the rest of us priestesses so we can retaliate."

Another cannonball whizzed through the air. It landed in a rockface and started a small rockslide.

"Rockslide!" Vadafa yelled.

The women scurried out of the river and up a slope to avoid the rockslide that was now blocking off the river and creating a dam of water. The water filled behind the dam and built up hydraulic pressure. The women were now scattered—hiding behind various rock protrusions for protection. Vadafa, Felifia, Nekara, and Breilut were together but away from the other women.

"We must arm ourselves and fight back!" Anba yelled from behind a rock. "We are sitting ducks on this mountainside."

"Nekara and Felifia," Vadafa said. "Can we immobilize the men—without killing them?"

"What about a subsonic lullaby?" Felifia suggested. "We could put them to sleep."

"Yes," Nekara said. "We'll use the mountain as an amplifier. Hold my hand and we'll—"

But before Nekara could finish her sentence, three cannonballs whizzed through the air. One punched through the rock Vadafa, Felifia, Nekara, and Breilut were hiding behind, broke Felifia's grip with Nekara, and sent Nekara flying several meters in the air. Breilut started after Nekara, but the second cannonball hit the rockslide, causing a weakness in the dam. The backed-up water burst forth and flooded the riverbed, carrying Nekara downstream. Breilut, Anba, Teluna, and another three hundred or so women were caught in the flood and were carried downstream. Felifia stood up with the thought of helping the women in the flood, but the third cannonball nicked the side of Felifia's head. Felifia fell down into Vadafa's arms, unconscious.

"Princess Felifia," Tanina called as she rushed to Felifia's aid.

"We must find shelter for the Princess and the rest of us," Vadafa said.

"What about the others in the water?" Tanina asked.

"We cannot help them," Vadafa said. "And we can't stay here. Help me carry the Princess. Hurry now!"

Vadafa and Tanina carried Felifia farther up the mountain with the women who were not carried away in the flood.

"I know a secret cave in these parts," Vadafa said. "Follow me on this ledge."

The cannons aimed higher and sent cannonballs at the women. Some hit very close, but the men's aim wasn't as good, so instead of firing at the women, the men aimed at the mountain above the women so as to send as much debris falling down on them as possible. At one point, a gravel rockslide flowed down the ledge and made for slippery walking conditions. Vadafa, Tanina, and two other women who helped carry Felifia nearly lost their footing and almost slipped off the ledge into a long fall.

"That was close," Vadafa said.

"Are you sure it's around here?" Tanina asked. "I don't see anything."

"Yes. It's at this very spot. Hold Felifia still," Vadafa said.

"There's nothing here. We're trapped on this ledge," Tanina cried.

"Shh," Vadafa said to Tanina. Vadafa turned to the sheer rockface, held her left hand to her abdomen, her right hand to the rockface, and said, "*Lufuamo kaishfal e di Vadafa!* (Reveal yourself to Vadafa!)"

A door appeared. Tanina rushed to open it, but it remained locked.

"Wait," Vadafa said. "I must unlock it. *Piutiugo kaish e shevishi dhaku efubino!* (Unlock your secrets and open!)"

The door opened. Vadafa led Tanina and the women into the cave.

"It's dark in here," Tanina said.

"*Gerutho feluana di teshunu pauga!* (Give light to this cave!)" Vadafa said while holding her left hand to her abdomen.

The walls glowed with blue light.

"Your power works in here, *Keia-teia* Vadafa," Tanina said. "But it was blocked in Nekara's cave."

"Yes," Vadafa said. "Nekara chose her cave to block Seris's radiation, while this one was chosen to allow it. We will be safe from cannonball attack for now."

"I feel like we're trapped, like in Nekara's cave," Tanina said.

"We're not," Biorna said. "We can leave anytime we want, and the men don't know our whereabouts."

"Tend to your senior wife, Tanina," Vadafa said.

"Yes, my *Keia-teia*," Tanina said.

Vadafa led Biorna to a quiet corner. Tanina and several women attended Felifia as other women settled themselves in the cave. The cave had furnishings—chairs, tables, running water, dried food, and comfortable beds. The cave had all the looks of an emergency fallout shelter.

"Biorna," Vadafa said. "I...I...for once, I'm without words. What to do next?"

"Did you sense Felifia's injury? How bad is it?" Biorna asked.

"Not bad. She'll recover, but she'll be unconscious for ten *beriuni* (2½ hours)."

"I don't understand," Biorna said. "You're a *Keia-teia.* You can revive her in a few *gerathi* (thirty seconds). Why do you say she could be out for ten *beriuni?* Vadafa? Don't you want her to regain consciousness? You don't, do you?"

"I need time to think," Vadafa said. "While Felifia is unconscious, I'm the leader of this group. I'm responsible. And I'm sparing Felifia of that responsibility."

"Responsibility for what?" Biorna asked. "Wake Felifia up and allow her to lead us."

"You heard what she said back in Nekara's cave, didn't you?" Vadafa said to Biorna. "Felifia is ready to lead us into battle of a sort. Perhaps not an aggressive one against the men, and certainly not one against the aggressive women, but I can't let her start that, not now. Battles tend to escalate, and we may end up fighting men and women before the day is out."

"This is treason against your Princess," Biorna said.

"I know, I know. I could be stripped of my powers," Vadafa said. "Even more now that Felifia has the new high-priestess harmonic key. But I'm willing to take the risk. There's a great division amongst us women. You saw the beginnings in Nekara's cave. Anba and Teluna are leading the division—did you notice? Anba even used the forbidden *seia* in common speech— did you notice that too? *Breilust* is what she said. She is altering the language. That's how revolutions start, Biorna. A new language is formed, and people follow the new language to the exclusion of others. I've seen it before, and I see it again. And now look at us—we are physically separated from the new movement that Anba and Teluna lead. Is it coincidence? I think it is not."

"There are other women in the world," Biorna said. "They may have an influence."

"Yes, there are other women, but none as powerful as our two groups and none as close to Parliament," Vadafa said. "Anba and Teluna have broken away from us. Nekara has changed, and she has a bereiluta. Nekara may join forces with Anba and Teluna—I don't know. What I do know is that Anba and Teluna have a deep desire to acquire Nekara's power, and they will do anything to get it. Nekara and her bereiluta have most likely survived the flood. Anba and Teluna will seek them out and convince Nekara to support their cause for the extermination of men. Nekara will join with them. Already I see changes in her. She's much stronger and full of power. And she resists calling her robot a bereiluta. By resisting a Miramish word, she resists Miramish and our traditional Miramish ways."

"It's one word," Biorna said. "How can one word be a treachery?"

"With the first lie, a person learns to seek more lies. With the first kill, a person desires to kill again," Vadafa said. "Nekara could fall into the trap of desire."

"She's married to Felifia," Biorna said. "That will temper her."

"No, I don't think so. When Felifia hugged Nekara, Nekara did not hug back. She claimed it was because she didn't want to harm Felifia. True or not, Nekara drove a wedge between them. It could grow. No, Nekara with her strength and bereiluta will wish to wage battle against the men. She admitted—did you hear? She said, 'It seems our next action is clear. All male life is now forfeit'."

"Then that's that," Biorna said. "Nekara, Anba, and Teluna will exterminate the men. The men would have died anyway. And we'll be safe as long as we stay in this shelter. No blood will be on our hands."

"Technically true. But we are priestesses of Eho Miriam. That means respect for life in all forms. I have spent my life working with extremists on both sides of the gender to bridge social compromise. And now it's collapsing. I don't want it to. I feel I can't stay here and allow it to collapse. My life work—gone. I don't know if I'll recover from this. And I don't want Felifia or any of the other women seeing me in my moment of failure."

Vadafa broke into tears.

"Aw, give me a hug. I love you very much. You've done a lot for Eho Miriam—more than anyone else I know," Biorna said.

"Yes. But it's never enough, is it?" Vadafa said. "Thank you for the hug. I feel better."

Vadafa took a deep breath and looked up as if requesting help from the heavens.

"I know that look," Biorna said.

"Yes," Vadafa said.

"You intend to sneak out of this cave and act on your own initiative."

"You know me too well," Vadafa said. "Perhaps there is one disadvantage to having strong marital links."

"On the contrary, it helps one wife look after the other," Biorna said. "And I don't like your idea, either. You intend to sneak out and stand in the middle of the battlefield between men and Anba's women."

"I feel partly responsible. Anba is my first junior wife, my first choice."

"And I am your second wife," Biorna said. "Do I not get a say?"

"I made the error with Anba, not you," Vadafa said. "I must correct it. But you, Biorna, you are pure. I wish you to stay here with Felifia. Do not help Tanina with Felifia's rise to consciousness just yet. I would like to keep Felifia out of my problem as long as possible."

"Every woman here loves and supports you beyond regard for her own life," Biorna said. "We would follow you into battle and stand with you to the end."

"That's exactly why you must not wake her, and you must not follow. Stall as long as you can. I am only willing to sacrifice my own life. I won't sacrifice all of you. Only after the blood is finished spilling will it be time for cool heads to begin anew. You and Felifia will be a part of that. I'd like to be around for that day, but I will not hold out for that expectation."

"Now I am the one for tears," Biorna said, and she cried.

"Come now, Biorna. You have been my pillar of strength in this crisis. You are strong. If I should perish, then find yourself another senior wife—Felifia if she will have you, or perhaps another good leader. You deserve the best senior wife."

"You are the best senior wife," Biorna said with a wet face. "No one can replace you."

"Shhh," Vadafa said. "Think pleasant thoughts. Eho Miriam will flourish again. Think of those days ahead when it will, Biorna, and you'll pull through. We each hold the torch of life for but a short time. Enjoy it while you can."

"It's unfair," Biorna said.

"You are young. Hardship always seems unfair. But I am older and wiser, and you know what? In a way, it's almost a relief to make final amends with the world. You'll understand someday. But not now. Stay alive, Biorna, and live. I must leave. My link with Anba is restored, and I feel her at work recruiting Nekara to her side. I must go and do what fate commands of me. Goodbye, my sweet wife. I will love you always!"

Biorna could no longer speak. Her sadness choked her throat terribly, yet she struggled to contain her sadness to a quiet, unnoticeable event so as not to attract attention. Vadafa knocked twice on a little alcove out of view from the other women. The alcove yielded a door, the door opened, Vadafa slipped through the opening, and in another whip of an eyelash, the opening closed and Vadafa was gone.

Jonara's focus drifted from Vadafa, Biorna, and Felifia and settled on Anba, Teluna, and Nekara. The flood carried the women down the mountainside and dangerously close to the men's advancing army. Anba and Teluna found Breilut and instructed her to search for Nekara. Breilut found Nekara trapped under a pool of debris and pulled her out. Anba and Teluna pressed on Nekara's chest, pumped her legs, and blew air into her lungs until Nekara regained consciousness.

"A-karg, a-karg," Nekara coughed with water coming out.

"My Queen, are you well?" Anba asked.

"Yes, I will be fine," Nekara said. "I'm not really a queen, don't you know. I used to be a countess, but that hardly seems fitting. What would Princess Felifia say if she heard you calling me a queen?"

"I mean no disrespect," Anba said. "May I call you Queen?"

Nekara smiled.

"This proves one thing," Nekara said. "Despite my increased strength, I can still drown. Thank you for saving my life."

A cannonball sailed past their heads.

"We cannot stay here and talk," Anba said. "The army is nearly on us. We must act fast or we will perish!"

"Breilut," Nekara said. "Destroy male weapons of missile capability."

Breilut burst into a run and descended the last part of the mountain into the advancing men. Their titanium armor, which was sufficient for repelling the old Serisian power wielded by priestesses, was no match for the new Serisian power Breilut, Nekara, and Felifia now possessed. Breilut tore into the front line and tossed male soldiers into advancing male soldiers. The army halted its advance and focused on defeating Breilut. Breilut easily defeated hand-to-hand combatants and escaped any efforts to trap her. One by one, she advanced on cannons and disabled them. She then worked on disabling rifles, but since every soldier in the army had one, this took time. Male after male fired at Breilut. She did not die or malfunction, but the bullets gradually chipped bits of her armor and body away.

"There," Nekara said. "Breilut will keep them busy for the moment."

"But how long?" Teluna asked. "She can't stand up to bullets forever. When she succumbs, the men will come after us. Breilut by herself cannot defeat the male army."

"Teluna is right," Anba said. "Nekara—we are terribly outnumbered. We need to become high priestesses for defense."

"I can't make you high priestesses at the moment," Nekara said. "Only Breilut can construct a high-priestess *moishiana*. But I can update your priestess harmonic keys. I can also confer priestess status to the other women here. It will give you enough power to defend against the men."

"Then do so," Anba said. "We have little time left."

"Very well," Nekara said.

Nekara removed a small, cloth bag from inside her armor.

"I collected these thin stones on Seranara," Nekara said. "They are meant for fertility treatment, but they can also be used for priestess conferment. Take one and pass the bag down. Instruct each woman to take a stone, gather a green and a cerise leaf, surround the stone with the two leaves, place the stone and leaves against her navel with her left hand, and hold onto the woman in front of her with her right. When the last woman has her stone, she is to return the bag to me through the relay of women. Once I receive the bag, we will begin."

Anba took a stone and passed the bag to Teluna, who did the same and passed the bag and gave instructions to the subsequent women. Breilut continued to distract the army. At times, Breilut stood still and dealt with charging men, and at other times, she ran around the groups like a dog corralling a bunch of sheep. The last woman took a stone, and the women returned the bag to Nekara.

"Let's begin," Nekara said.

Mirsua	**Translation**
Tiusas Liugefatas.	Priestess Conferment.
Nias kilos koilus tiusas Nekaras.	I am High Priestess Nekara.
Miolus e Serisus Bioritas Uferithuas	New Serisian Power Identifer
Noias-alifas-elifas-ilofas-orifas	N-A-E-I-O
Urifas-hemes-avus-iris.	U-one-two-three.
Nias liugefos bioritas	I confer power
Opeifus Tiusas	Of Priestess
Dis loreifus e saradalis	To all women
Roisious vus e sialas dis naus	Linked by touch to me
Liemus Ehos Miriamas.	On Eho Miriam.
Veletus e sais vatugis	From the peaks
Opeifus niuguitis	Of mountains
Niais bulirikos.	We descend.
Veletus e sais busikis	From the depths
Opeifus vaulis	Of valleys
Niais olirikos.	We ascend.
Veletus e sais melis	From the rains
Isus e sais feriaifas	In the sky
Niais biruanos.	We flourish.
Lafipos moishianas	Merge moishiana
Bosus e sisus e saradalis.	With these women.
Felitos miolus bioritas	Bring new power
Opeifus e Seris	Of Seris
Isetus e sisus e saradalis.	Into these women.
Nias weifos tesunus e seloikas	I sign this command
Nekaras e sais Fiesas	Nekara the Red
Opeifus Miriamas.	Of Miriam.
Miaras felaufikaras.	Ocean deliverance.
Dosikos!	Execute!

Jonara held onto the women with her right hand and placed the Moissan Ruby against her navel with her left. It was a strange thing. Why did she hold the Moissan Ruby against her navel? She wasn't one of the women, and she couldn't participate in the events. Still, the sense of unity and coming together enticed Jonara into participation with the women. As Nekara spoke the words of priestess conferment, Jonara felt a surge of energy flowing back and forth through the link of women. The energy flowed much like what Jonara witnessed before—loops of power traveling up and down the line of women. A loop left the main line and traveled through Jonara's body. She felt the Moissan Ruby dissolve in her abdomen.

"I could be a priestess too," Jonara thought to herself.

But Jonara heard voices. Not her own language, not Miramish or Mirsua. Whispers and calls to action floated back and forth where the letter *s* or *z* preceded the last consonant of verbs—words like *diarst* (join), *darkanirsf* (enchant), *divasre* (encourage), *thafirst* (inquire), *nirze* (itch), *opairst* (attack), *ovairst* (achieve), *gorsk* (take), *voirzge* (surge), *darlais* (enjoy), *klorsf* (keep).

"Dahmek," Jonara said to herself. "Anba came up with it, and Nekara spoke it when she was on Earth. These words they say—no, it's the way the words are whispered—they're addictive, like a powerful drug from an attractive flower. I feel lulled under this spell. I feel a desire to be like these women, to have power, to march, to take from another and keep for myself, me, to savor the prize and overflow with euphoria. I want to follow them wherever they go and do what they do."

The Dahmek words flowed back and forth. They were thoughts not initiated by Nekara, but they influenced Nekara from one who set out to improve women's fertility to one who desired to improve women's supremacy.

"We could chant the lullaby spell," Nekara said. "But what pleasure would we derive from empty resistance? No, my sisters, we have joined as one, a single fighting force to explore our appetites, learn what will satisfy them, exploit for reward, and fulfill our hunger. We have an appetite for life, a life denied to our sisters at Parliament Lawn. We must live for them and us.

We will take back the lives they lost from those who took it. We march now against the oncoming male armies, and we will see them suffer to their end."

"*Kursne shair viurn!* (Begin the war!)" the women shouted. "*Kursne shair viurn! Kursne shair viurn! Kursne shair viurn!*"

"We will march to war momentarily," Nekara said. "But first, let us be armed! Touch your left hand to your abdomen and your right to a boulder. Now repeat after me—*Siasos e sinefis, moikas, taidas, dhakus kutalas veletus tesarikas dhakus kereisas!* (Fashion armor, shield, club, and sword from rock and dust!)"

The women spoke as Nekara spoke. Rings of light and energy flowed from their abdomens, up their torsos, through their right shoulders, down their arms, and through their hands into the boulders they touched. The boulders melted into foam and reformed into armor, shields, clubs, and swords. The women gasped in shock at their handiwork, but as they fitted the equipment on their bodies, they cheered in comradery and accepted their newfound power.

"*Kursne shair viurn!* (Begin the war!)" the women shouted again. "*Kursne shair viurn!*"

Nekara stood before them, looked out at the male army as her Breilut made her last attempts at slowing the army's advances, and she yelled, "*Tshunu vikel tilen. Kursne shair viurn!* (This is it. Begin the war!)"

Nekara ran toward the male army with her fist in the air. The women behind cheered and followed with their swords held high. Nekara yelled ahead for Breilut to break off her attack. Breilut responded and ran back to Nekara in the whip of an eyelash. The men stood stunned but quickly mustered up soldiers who still had rifles. Men stood, aimed, and fired. Bullets rained on the women, but armor and shields deflected the bullets without issue.

"*Odufirsk nuish teshralfyek!* (Avenge our sisters!)" Nekara yelled.

"We must retreat," yelled men to their superior officers.

"You cannot disobey. You must continue the attack," officers yelled back.

"We will die!" men yelled further.

"You cannot disobey. Continue the attack!" officers repeated.

Men stood their ground and steadied their rifles, with bayonets prepared to repel the wall of women. Nekara did not slow. She maintained a high cardiovascular function as did the women behind. Serisian power fed their cells where oxygen debt would have taken hold.

"Steady," officers called to the front line with the bayonets. "Steady."

The men held their ground. Nekara and the women plunged through the bayonets without slowing down. Bayonets, rifles, and men toppled over backward. The women clashed their swords against the men's titanium armor, and to the men's surprise, the titanium cracked.

"Hand-to-hand," yelled the officers.

Men pulled out their swords and engaged the women, but the women's swords broke the men's. Women attacked the men's armor, the men's weapons, and finished by attacking the men's bodies. Men died and men fled. The women continued their onslaught with little injury to their own. Male officers continued ordering soldiers to their death. The ones who stayed died. The entire male army would have died if Nekara had been permitted to finish the task.

"Stop!" yelled a familiar voice. "*Vus loreifus e Serisu basalitas, vetavetos loreifus yaigatis!* (By all Serisian authority, cease all hostilities!)"

The army of men halted as did Nekara's army. The figure of an old woman stood on a rock outcropping between the two armies. The men pointed at the woman and laughed.

"Vadafa!" Nekara yelled. "Why are you interfering?"

"Look, men," one of the officers called. "An old woman has lost her way."

"Let's help her find it," another officer yelled.

"Get out of the way, Vadafa," Nekara said, "or you'll get killed."

"I've come to stop this madness!" Vadafa yelled. "Put down your weapons and make peace."

"Why do you side with the men?" Teluna yelled. "Do you wish to see us killed?"

"It's a trick," one of the male officers yelled.

"Of course it's a trick," yelled another male officer. "She's a woman, isn't she?"

"No trick!" Vadafa yelled. "We are civilized citizens of Eho Miriam. Why do we fight each other like enemies?"

"They started it," Anba said. "They killed our sisters. We claim right of vengeance."

"Anba, my first wife," Vadafa called. "We must forgive."

"See, men?" the first officer called. "These women 'marry' each other. They're unnatural freaks of nature. Let's get rid of them."

"Stop!" Vadafa called. "End your hostilities before all life on this planet perishes!"

"Get out of the way, Vadafa," Nekara said. "We're defending life."

"Get out of the way, old woman," the first officer said. "We're defending what's right in this world."

"This is insanity!" Vadafa called.

The men advanced toward Vadafa's position with bayonets. Nekara led her women to intercept the men.

"You see? A trick," the officer said.

The fighting resumed. Nekara pulled Vadafa from the rock and behind the women's front line.

"Are you crazy?" Nekara said. "You could have been killed."

"Nekara, this is wrong. Killing our own kind is murder!" Vadafa said. "Our psyches become tormented by these gruesome acts of violence."

"There's no choice," Nekara said. "Did you see how they responded to your method?"

"I was making progress," Vadafa said.

"Hah! You mean, 'No progress.'"

"You can still end this peacefully," Vadafa said. "Cast a lullaby chant as you attempted with Felifia. Put them to sleep and end this once and for all."

"Put them to sleep? Where's the sport in that? We might as well slash them in the back," Nekara said.

"That's not what I mean! Nekara! End this madness!"

"Even if we put them to sleep," Nekara said as she helped Vadafa dodge bullets and slashing swords, "what then? Do we baby-sit them the rest of their lives? No! I've had it with these men. We need a quick end! Breilut! Take Vadafa to the back of the army!"

"You can still chant a lullaby and put them to sleep!" Vadafa called one last time, but Breilut moved Vadafa to the back too quickly for Nekara to hear.

Nekara's army continued the attack. Each woman proceeded as before in progressively defeating each man by destroying his armor, disarming him of his shield and weapons, and slashing his flesh. More blood spilled, and Vadafa lost hope.

A strange sound echoed through the mountains. Was it real, or did Vadafa imagine it? No, there was a definite sound, and it grew louder. The sound was music, and it came from an oboe. Vadafa looked around for the source, but the echoes made this determination difficult at first. However, Vadafa recognized the song played by children in early school:

Friendly Hayride

"Of all the things," Vadafa mused. "To think I'm witnessing the worst battle of my life, and someone is playing *Friendly Hayride* on an oboe! My sanity has finally cracked."

But something curious happened. As the song grew louder, the battle subsided. Men and women on both sides of the battle line grew weary and made less effort to attack each other. Song from the oboe boomed through the battlefield, and fighting on both sides ended as men and women sat on the ground in exhaustion. Men fell asleep. Women chatted and giggled. Only Nekara, Anba, Breilut, and Vadafa remained standing.

"Fight, my sisters," Anba rallied. "Fight!"

"It's no use," Vadafa echoed as she traveled to the front line with Breilut to meet Nekara and Anba. "Someone is performing a fatigue chant."

"I don't hear anyone chanting," Nekara said.

"We've been robbed, robbed! Our right to claim glorious victory has been pulled out from under our feet!" Anba said. "To war, my sisters. To war!"

But Anba yawned, her knees buckled, and she fell to the ground in exhaustion.

"Strange that you are still standing," Nekara said to Vadafa. "Is this your doing?"

"No," Vadafa said. "And I must say I'm not surprised you're still standing."

"Why? Because I'm indurated with chromium aluminum oxide?" Nekara asked.

"Partly," Vadafa said.

"What's the other part?"

"Your power of High Priestess under the new harmonic," Vadafa said.

"Jealousy, Vadafa?" Nekara asked.

"No, concern. I saw your ethics fail you today," Vadafa said.

"Yes, well, the event is over," Nekara said. "Now I suppose our next task as women will be to tie up the surviving men and haul them off to prison."

"Yes, it will," Vadafa said.

"Taking care of men like babies again," Nekara said. "When does it end?"

"You know this is temporary. Men won't survive into the winter," Vadafa said. "Is their extinction not enough?"

"I have my own problems, Vadafa. I don't plan on wasting my time by giving sympathy and care to these men. I've wasted enough as it is with their rude attack on my sisters. I have a great task with my fertility research. However, so as not to allow the waste of all male bodies, I will cart off one for experiments in my lab. Here—this one will do. Come Breilut, we have much work in rebuilding my lab."

"Nekara, wait! We need your help!" Vadafa begged.

"No you don't. The oboe player will take care of you, and you will look after these women, no? Convince them that giggling time is over, and they are needed for the care of these men. They'll come round to your way of thinking, with the exception of Anba and Teluna. Tell you what—I'll take Anba and Teluna with me. That will keep them busy and out of your worry. What do you say?"

"Hmm," Vadafa said.

"You don't trust me, do you Vadafa?"

"I don't trust anyone more powerful than myself," Vadafa said.

Nekara laughed.

"Stop by and visit me in the lab. I promise the utmost civility for anyone of our gender. Good-day, Vadafa," Nekara said.

Nekara carried a surviving-though-comatose male over her shoulder. Nekara barked an order to Breilut. Breilut took Anba and Teluna by their hands and led the giggling two behind Nekara and back to Nekara's cave.

The person playing the oboe now stood on a small ledge.

"Biorna!" Vadafa called.

Biorna stopped playing only long enough to wave to Vadafa before resuming the song. As Biorna played, Felifia led the other group of women down the mountain with each woman carrying ropes. Felifia approached Vadafa, turned around to wave at Biorna, and turned back.

"Bind their hands to long rope lines. We will lead them to prison like small children back to school," Felifia yelled just as she reached Vadafa.

"Felifia! I'm surprised to see you!" Vadafa said.

"I'm sure you are, considering you would rather I remain unconscious for several more *beriuni* (another hour)," Felifia said.

Vadafa opened her mouth as if to protest, but Felifia laughed.

"That Biorna!" Vadafa said. "I told her not to wake you. She disobeyed me and woke you anyway."

"Don't blame your second wife," Felifia chuckled. "Tanina brought me back to consciousness. Biorna told me all about your instructions, and she begged me to wait in the cave."

"Then why didn't you? You could have respected my wishes," Vadafa said.

"Because I'm Princess Felifia, and the last time I checked, I rule in these parts," Felifia grinned. "Besides, I can't let you take credit for saving the day all by yourself. So I conferred priestess status to the women with me under the new Serisian harmonic. Granted it was second-class conferment since I had only green and cerise leaves to give them with no moishiani, but second class is better than nothing, and it gave them enough power and confidence to launch a rescue effort on your behalf."

"Rescue effort? I was making progress toward—" Vadafa started.

"Nothing," Felifia laughed. "I witnessed the events from afar. It was a brave thing you did, but you could have easily been killed. You have Nekara to thank for your life."

"Yes, I know," Vadafa said. "I don't like having debts to those less than ethical."

"Her mind may be adjusting to the new power," Felifia said. "But I have confidence in her."

"This is what your confidence has produced," Vadafa said. "Look at the bloodshed around you. Nekara has a hand in it."

"Yes, I know. And it grieves me," Felifia said.

"As it should. You should be troubled by Nekara and Teluna, as I am troubled by Anba," Vadafa said. "Well?"

"I am troubled," Felifia said.

"Then why the claim of confidence in Nekara? She has violated all we stand for," Vadafa said.

"Because I love her," Felifia said.

"You should only have lightweight-love and pleasure-love with a junior wife," Vadafa said. "But never have deep-love. It is its own vice and will lead you astray from an ethical life."

"Do you have deep-love for your wives?" Felifia asked.

"I admit, I do for one. I didn't realize it until after I married her, but I have deep love for Biorna. Fortunately, she has never transgressed me, although I thought she did just now when I suspected she woke you. But now I think I see why you claim confidence in Nekara. You have deep-love for her. Break this vice, Felifia. It will consume and destroy you."

The oboe music stopped, and Biorna made her way down the mountain.

"I can't and I won't," Felifia said. "And you're one to talk. You're the one who married us!"

"Had I known this side of Nekara, I would not have performed the marriage," Vadafa said.

"Then we would have gone somewhere else," Felifia said. "Don't worry about the marriage ceremony. It is done."

"*Keia-teia*," Biorna said as she rushed over to Vadafa.

The two exchanged hugs and kisses.

"Don't be angry with me, my senior wife," Biorna said. "It was—"

"Princess Felifia explained everything," Vadafa said. "You'll be happy to know I hold no blame or grudge against you."

"I'm so relieved," Biorna said. "I try with great effort to be loyal to my wife and faithful to our customs."

"To which you have succeeded in both," Vadafa said. "And you have succeeded in sedating both sides of this battleground. But there's something I don't understand."

"What's that?" Felifia asked.

"Biorna—why did you play *Friendly Hayride* when a lullaby would have been proper? 'Friendly Hayride' is the last—"

"The last song anyone would expect," Felifia said. "Do not be harsh with Biorna. I encouraged her to choose something quite unusual."

"Oh?" Vadafa asked.

"Yes," Biorna said. "Both the men and Nekara's women expected a lullaby song would be attempted. They would have prepared against it. The fact that no one would anticipate *Friendly Hayride* was to our advantage. It is quicker than a lullaby but has a similar effect of sedation. That is why I chose it. I would ask for your approval in these matters, my senior wife, but you were busy with the two armies. Princess Felifia assured me my choice was good, and her women supported me as well."

"It was brilliant," Vadafa said. "And I'm proud of you."

The two hugged and kissed again.

"Well," Felifia said. "If we are all happy women again, I think—"

"Not quite," Biorna said. "We have Anba's women sitting on the ground giggling like schoolgirls."

"Yes," Vadafa said. "I would like to rouse them to action."

"Action? Will you lead the next battle?" Felifia laughed.

"Only a battle for peace," Vadafa said. "And if you would lend me your new Serisian powers to rouse them, I would appreciate it."

"Of course," Felifia said. "I'm happy to bring our women back to their peaceful, loving selves."

Princess Felifia retook her throne and quarantined all men. Violent cases were held in prisons while more manageable cases were restricted to hospitals and converted barns. Felifia ordered emergency elections to repopulate Parliament with women and ordered emergency hiring for all other government positions vacated by men—army, police, public works, and administration. In a month's time, Felifia's government structure was revitalized and running smoothly. Felifia met with Nekara, Tanina, Vadafa, and Biorna to discuss the future of their world.

"Women of Eho Miriam," Felifia said. "We have dealt with the problem of men ravaging our world. We have two challenges yet to deal with—the climate crisis and the fertility crisis. Biorna, we'll start with you. Explain to us what you've learned about our new climate and how it affects life on Eho Miriam."

"As we continue our counterclockwise orbit around the Damiriak solar system center, we pull away from Maknesi and approach Seris," Biorna explained. "Prior to the Serisian collision, this process was little noticed. With both stars being white, the net available sunlight on Eho Miriam changed very little. Seris has never put out as much sunlight as Maknesi, and as a result, we experience our winters when we are closest to Seris. If you look at this orbital chart, there are two places on the orbit where this happens—when Eho Miriam is at the top and the bottom points of her orbit. Her summers are then at the left and right points of her orbit. As you know, Eho Miriam has no planetary tilt, and so there is no season inversion from one hemisphere to another."

"And after the collision?" Felifia prompted.

"Well, you saw the result," Biorna continued. "Seris now radiates magenta light instead of the full white spectrum. Seris's magnetic field has grown such that it engulfs our planet. As for Maknesi, she radiated green light briefly, but now she has stabilized in radiating yellow light. Maknesi's magnetic field has changed very little. Seris's changes have created three environmental problems. The first is that all animals with a Y chromosome, i.e. mammals only, have begun dying off and will become extinct as Eho Miriam gets closer to Seris. The second is that the reduced radiant white-light energy means Eho Miriam will cool down as she gets further from Maknesi and closer to Seris. The ground will freeze, lakes will ice over, rain will become snow, and life—both animal and plant—that cannot survive the freeze will die. The third is that with the reduced white light from Seris, plant photosynthesis will fail as we travel away from Maknesi."

"We'll discuss the climate issue more in a moment," Felifia said. "Nekara—what news do you have regarding female fertility?"

"We have expanded our fertility work from people-only to all mammal life on Eho Miriam," Nekara said. "We have achieved full-term reproduction between two beetles, and a female-to-female mouse pregnancy up to sixteen days before spontaneous abortion. Our method entails two females entering a small cave pool laced with strontium isotopes. The females interact and build chemical reactions to each other such that one becomes the 'left' and the other becomes the 'right'. We use these terms because there is no male-female analogy. No female is 'superior' to another. A better comparison is that the mice align themselves into mirror images of each other. That's why we call them 'left' and 'right'."

"Hmm," Vadafa said. "Are you suggesting the females attain an equality in their reproductive roles?"

"Yes. They are equal but mirror opposites," Nekara said.

"That may be appropriate for beetles and mice, but it would be inappropriate for Miramish women," Vadafa said.

"I don't understand," Nekara said. "Without men, this is the only way."

"What we need, Nekara, is a means where one female is the senior, and the other is the junior. This would align correctly with our culture," Vadafa explained.

"The fertility process is an equal exchange," Nekara said. "Females donate an ovum and receive an ovum. Both typically become pregnant. But for people, we can simulate a senior-junior relationship by the senior woman blocking the donated ovum from the junior."

"Hmm," Vadafa said. "That won't work at all. There must be a guarantee the senior only donates, and the junior only receives. The junior must not be able to donate."

"I don't understand the need for strict requirements," Nekara said. "Creating this situation between females is difficult enough without adding another parameter. Why are you so insistent on preventing one female from donating an ovum?"

"A junior wife with the ability to donate an ovum can claim status of senior wife. This complicates things when she already has a senior wife. We don't want that," Vadafa said.

"Now wait a moment," Nekara said. "All women have full procreation rights. To deny a woman the ability to donate her own ovum is—"

"That right was created by men, and they are no longer here," Vadafa said.

"Even better," Nekara said. "There are no men to attack our reproductive rights. But I can't believe I'm debating this issue with another woman in this time of fertility crisis. Create a religious code of conduct if you will, but I won't put the limitation in my science."

"Nekara, you are dangerously close to committing sacrocide," Vadafa warned. "If you allow this treatment to enter mainstream medicine without adding the restriction, you will be banned from the Eho Miriam priesthood."

"You must know that is an empty threat," Nekara said. "I'm Primary One High Priestess under the new Serisian harmonic. You can't 'ban' me. And you can't 'ban' science. You may as well attempt to change the laws of chemistry."

"Any woman can be banned," Vadafa warned. "Any."

"Sisters," Princess Felifia said. "We don't have the time to argue these points. We will address them later. For the moment, we must press on and address additional issues. There is an issue no one has mentioned yet, so I will bring it up now. Survey expeditions in the past have discovered life on planet Dahma."

"Yes," Biorna said. "Many years ago, it was determined that life exists in Dahmek oceans, but the Dahmek summers are too hot for life to exist on land."

"Biorna—am I right in concluding that the radiation from Seris that is destroying male life on Eho Miriam will destroy male life on planet Dahma?" Felifia asked.

"Yes, it will," Biorna said, "although at a much slower rate. Mammals live in the oceans on Dahma. Whales, dolphins, and seals will see their male populations die off. The Dahmek oceans will slow the absorption rate. I wish the same could be said for our oceans, but I can't. Otherwise I could recommend we move the men underwater."

"Our knowledge of Dahmek summers is based on surveys before the collision. What would Dahmek summers be like now?" Felifia asked.

"That's a good question," Biorna said. "In theory, the reduction of visible light from Seris would moderate light on planet

Dahma. The intensely hot summers would be gone. Winters would be about the same as before and not as severe as our impending winter."

"Are you suggesting we abandon Eho Miriam and move to a non-Eho planet such as Dahma?" Vadafa asked. "That's worse blasphemy than the concept of equal female pregnancies."

"I'm suggesting nothing of the sort," Felifia said. "However, I am wondering if we should expend an effort to save life on Dahma—specifically the marine mammals."

"We shouldn't waste our resources on other planets when our own planet is in dire need," Vadafa said.

"Eho Miriam takes priority, of course," Felifia said. "But the skills we gain here could be applied to Dahma. Why not preserve life where we can? *Keia-teia* Vadafa—you have always taught us that we should respect life and preserve it when possible. Are you suggesting we turn our backs on that creed?"

Vadafa gritted her teeth. She moved her hands to her face, crossed her arms, uncrossed them, paced around, and thought more.

"Princess Felifia has a good point. We could do a great service to planet Dahma by extending our preservation effort to her," Nekara said. "The only reason we've avoided Dahma in the past is because land life was impossible before the Serisian event. It was too dangerous for women to spend any significant amount of time on the planet. But that has now changed. Women may stay on the planet indefinitely."

"And violate another one of our traditions—that women should cultivate and flourish on Eho Miriam," Vadafa said. "We permit space travel only because it is understood travelers return to Eho Miriam. We are not in the business of colonizing other planets."

"But people have already left Eho Miriam for other planets," Tanina said. "What about Nimsant and *Elesha*?"

"Nimsant is a prison colony for criminals," Vadafa said. "And the migrations to *Elesha* are unfortunate. But an upstanding Miramish citizen always returns to Eho Miriam."

"Again, it is not our intention to colonize other planets," Felifia said. "I'm seriously considering, however, establishing an outpost on Dahma to aid in preserving life there. I would establish tours of duty so no woman stays on Dahma for any considerable length of time. When our efforts have succeeded, I will order the outpost destroyed."

"If only it were that easy," Vadafa said. "But I have heard arguments in the past that suggest a woman should be allowed to live wherever she wants. So far we have agreed—as long as she lives on Eho Miriam. But there are some who would argue that women should be allowed to live on Dahma or any other planet. And one is in this room."

"I know you accuse me," Nekara said, "even though I have not spoken on this issue."

"Both your grandmother and mother proposed that efforts be made to colonize other planets," Vadafa said. "They believed that old myth that the universe is the uterus of a goddess, that life is a cosmic embryo, and for the cosmic embryo to grow, life must expand and colonize other planets. You are your mothers' daughter and granddaughter, and you work in close proximity with Anba and Teluna. I postulate, Nekara, that you will succumb to the desire to colonize Dahma, as you succumbed to the desire to kill men on the battlefield."

Nekara stood up in anger and took two steps toward Vadafa as if to assault her. Biorna stood up in defense of Vadafa, and Felifia stood up for the sake of peace.

"You didn't even describe it properly," Nekara said. "The universe isn't a uterus. It's an embryo."

"One myth or another, what's the difference?" Vadafa said.

"Everyone, please, let's sit down and reason through things like civilized women. Nothing can be accomplished if we launch accusations at or threaten one another. Vadafa—we will understand for the moment that Nekara is working with us and will do whatever she can to restore life on Eho Miriam. Innocent until performing a criminal act. Nekara has done nothing to merit this accusation, so I will hear no more of it."

"Be warned, Felifia, this is no ordinary woman who sits as your third wife," Vadafa said.

"I don't know if I am willing to sit here and have my good name soiled like this," Nekara said. "Vadafa—hold your tongue!"

"I won't be silenced by you!" Vadafa said.

"Enough!" Felifia commanded. "By royal decree, I command you two to stop bickering! Nekara—will you take an oath to remain on Eho Miriam until our fertility and climate crisis has concluded?"

"I do," Nekara said. "I will devote my full energies to restoring fertility and life to Eho Miriam."

"Thank you," Felifia said. "Now that Nekara's loyalties are affirmed, I charge you, Nekara, to select a small number of women from your group to begin the first tour on Dahma. Explain to them their goal, but remind them that their first obligation is to Eho Miriam."

"I will," Nekara said.

"Now then," Felifia continued. "Let's go back to Biorna's climate issue—that of decreased radiant white light from Seris. *Keia-teia* Vadafa—do you have any recommendations as to what we can do to survive the impending severe winter?"

"You're asking my advice?" Vadafa asked.

"Yes, of course!" Felifia replied.

Vadafa paused in thought.

"I'm afraid even this cosmological event is beyond our traditional means," Nekara said.

"I believe I was asked the question," Vadafa said.

"And what is your answer?" Nekara asked.

"If we priestesses link all of our energies together," Vadafa said, "we could invoke a freeze-preservation chant. It was only tried once in recorded history when a much smaller freeze threatened Eho Miriam."

"Interesting. How does it work?" Tanina asked.

"The water in all animal and plant life undergoes a slight molecular change," Biorna said. "This change will reduce the freezing point of water in the body which in turn will prevent cell damage from cooling cells."

"That will protect against a deep winter," Nekara said. "But what about the climate itself? I propose we find a way to provide heat on Eho Miriam during the cold months. This heat will minimize the damage to life until spring returns."

"The only way to do that is through nuclear explosions," Biorna said. "No other technology can provide as much global heat."

"Biorna is right," Vadafa said. "Attempting to heat the planet is a bad idea. We should focus on preserving existing life. Nekara, I suggest you remain focused on fertility and leave planetary heating to a scientist."

"What?!" Nekara replied. "I *am* a scientist. And my idea has full merit. But now I accuse you of succumbing to the ultimate male failing—that of focusing on a single concept to the exclusion of others. I realize nuclear explosions are forbidden. I support the ban. But I never intended to pursue that as an option. As it turns out, there are other ways to heat the planet. Since Seris's collision, I have seen some crimson plants thrive as we approach Seris."

"It's a false reaction," Vadafa said, "like the last desperate attempt to thrive before death. Your plants will also freeze when the temperature drops."

"It's true," Biorna said. "Science supports Vadafa's analysis."

"Yes, but what if we reengineer these crimson plants to support themselves solely on magenta light from Seris? They would thrive in winter," Nekara said.

"No, they would freeze," Vadafa said. "You obviously didn't hear me say that."

"I did hear you say that. The crimson plants could generate heat, too. If we grow enough around the planet, they would globally warm our world, but only during winter. During summer, they would become dormant, and the white-light-based plants would dominate. Actually, they're now yellow-based light. But they should be fine. The crimson plants—"

"How is this possible?" Biorna asked. "Plants can't radiate heat."

"Biorna is right," Vadafa said. "Nekara—desire does not automatically confer reality. We will simply have to get out our thick coats and suffer through a deep freeze. The freeze-preservation chant will need to be performed twice a revolution to protect life."

"You don't believe I can reengineer plants to radiate heat from magenta light," Nekara said. "It isn't that difficult."

"Really, Nekara," Biorna said. "Magenta is not infrared. Where will you get the heat from?"

"Yes, we've wasted enough time on Nekara's fantasies," Vadafa said. "Let's move on to Biorna's next item."

"The next item, for those who have forgotten, is that white-light-based plant photosynthesis will fail as we pull farther from Maknesi," Biorna said.

"I really wonder who is running this meeting—*Keia-teia* Vadafa, or Princess Felifia?" Nekara said.

"I am running it, of course," Felifia said.

"Yet Vadafa decides that we have finished discussing the thermal issue?" Nekara asked.

"What's to decide?" Vadafa asked. "There's nothing left to explore on this issue."

"Absurd!" Nekara said. "But since no one takes me seriously, I will pursue the reengineering with my own team. There's also an excellent chance that animal life can feed on crimson plants and receive fuel and thermal protection during the winter months. If that is so, the crimson plants may not need to produce as much thermal radiation as I first proposed since crimson-feeding animals would be protected. And I include us women as crimson-feeding animals."

"Vulgar," Vadafa said. "To refer to us as animals."

"From a scientific view, we are," Nekara said.

"There are two branches of science," Biorna said. "Natural science, and Damiriak people science. The two sciences don't interact."

"I expected you to defend Vadafa in that manner," Nekara said. "What it means is that even if I produce crimson plants with leaves able to keep animals warm, the old High Priestess council will not permit them for people consumption unless the council can work those plants into the rules and regulations of traditional culture."

"A vulgar way of describing it, but essentially correct," Vadafa said. "And you're expected to follow those rules."

"Nekara," Felifia said. "Proceed with your concept for crimson plant life. Any help we can receive is valued."

"Provided it aligns with Damiriak values," Vadafa said.

"What about white-light-based plants?" Biorna asked. "Even if a freeze-preservation chant is performed, they will die without white or yellow light."

"Suggestions, Vadafa?" Nekara asked sarcastically.

"I don't like your attitude," Vadafa said to Nekara.

"Keep things civil," Felifia said. "We are here to promote life, not tear it down."

Vadafa looked at Nekara. Nekara had a smile of ultimate confidence on her face, as if she'd just won the prize.

"I don't like Nekara's smile," Vadafa said. "She would reengineer life yet again on this planet to promote her standing amongst the women."

"Is that your way of saying you have no solution to the problem of plants dying from lack of Maknesi light? But you know me well. I do have a solution."

"I would advise we wait until winter passes. The hardy plants will go dormant and reawaken in the spring," Vadafa said. "In the short term, it is bad for those plants that cannot survive, but in the long term, it will suit plant life very well as the survivors will need no artificial welfare to keep them living in an environment no longer suited toward them. And that is my solution."

"That's no solution," Nekara said, "letting plants die indiscriminately."

"You would propose a welfare system where we spend all of our resources artificially supporting plants that cannot provide for themselves?" Vadafa asked.

"No. Simply this. Some plants die at the end of summer and perpetuate their species with seeds that survive the most severe winters. Those will need no care. Other plants such as bushes, shrubs, and trees that do not grow and die within a season are the ones needing our care. It is not welfare. We have the ability to help them adapt to the new climate. After a season or two, they will be independent of our help and will contribute toward the ecosystem productively."

"*We* have the ability?" Vadafa asked. "Who is this *we*? You and your team? What will you do, dip their roots in strontium-isotope-laced cave pools and replant them?"

"That's not a bad idea, Vadafa," Nekara said. "But there's a better idea. Symbiosis. We can cultivate and graft crimson mistletoe onto the at-risk bushes, shrubs, and trees. In the winter when Seris is strong, the crimson mistletoe will harvest the magenta waves and provide food and protection for the host plant. In exchange, the host plant will keep the crimson mistletoe alive when Seris is weak and Maknesi is strong. That's my proposal, Vadafa. One plant helps another. Mutual benefit. Symbiosis."

"Through genetic reengineering," Vadafa said.

"Of course," Nekara said.

"You know how our customs view genetic reengineering. You are daring to play Goddess," Vadafa said.

"This is an old argument, and we will not hear it now," Felifia said. "Nekara—continue your work on crimson plant cultivation. We will pursue both proposals—that of distributing new crimson plants throughout Eho Miriam, and grafting crimson mistletoe on at-risk trees, shrubs, and bushes. Given the size of the planet, I don't expect we will provide full coverage this year, next, or the year afterward. I anticipate a high death toll this first winter and the next few winters. But we will do everything we can to minimize loss."

"Biorna and Tanina," Felifia continued. "I would like you two to work together and form a liaison group between the old priestess council and Nekara's work. Do what you can to find compromises between agendas. Now this is important—you may recommend changes to Nekara and her group, but Nekara has authority to decline the recommendations."

"Nekara," Felifia said. "I am placing quite a bit of power in your hands. Please don't abuse it. You are at liberty to decline recommendations from Biorna and Tanina and even the old

High Priestess council. But I implore you to find as many ways as possible to augment your work to fit in with traditional culture. I understand that this will not always be possible. It may never be possible. But please give it the consideration it is due."

"Vadafa—I respect you in all forms and ways," Felifia said. "You have always been my mentor. But I am charged with leading our world out of the most difficult crisis it has endured in recorded time. Metaphorical flowers will be trampled. This is unavoidable. Customs will be broken and tempers will flare. But we must work together no matter how foul the stench. In time, peace and prosperity will prevail. I want each of you to give words of inspiration to your respective divisions. Don't let them lose hope. That is all. May the powers of the universe find favor with us. This meeting is dismissed."

In the following months, Jonara watched the last of the men die, the temperatures drop, and Nekara's group succeed in cultivating crimson plants. Nekara's group shipped crimson-leafed trees, shrubs, and bushes along with crimson mistletoe to nurseries that in turn held daily crimson parties in the late afternoon. In this way, crimson plants steadily increased in numbers.

Nekara realized she could not cultivate enough crimson plants to save all trees, shrubs, and bushes on Eho Miriam. Further, many animals without benefit of crimson leaves would perish in the upcoming winter. To preserve species that would otherwise be destroyed, Nekara embarked on a bold venture. But before she implemented it, she discussed her idea with Felifia.

"My senior wife, Princess Felifia," Nekara said. "I come to you with a great plan for saving much of our endangered species."

Felifia sat with Nekara for an after-dinner desert while Felifia's other wife, Tanina, went for a walk in the palace garden.

"What is this plan?" Felifia ask. "Should I call a meeting with Vadafa and Biorna?"

"No," Nekara said. "I know what Vadafa would say. As dictated by tradition, she would oppose my idea."

"If your idea breaks with tradition, then it may need rethinking," Felifia said. "But tell me your idea. We will work out something."

"Very well. As you know, women around our world are planting crimson trees, shrubs, and bushes and are also grafting crimson mistletoe to existing woody species," Nekara started.

"Yes," Felifia said. "You've succeeded in cultivating a solution no other woman on Eho Miriam would have dared attempt."

"Yes, but congratulations are short lived. Time has been our enemy. My group cannot cultivate enough clippings to support the entire world," Nekara said.

"You've done your best," Felifia said. "We cannot ask for more than that."

"But I can give more than that," Nekara said. "Much more. Yet always I argue the point back and forth. I know of a method to save these species doomed to extinction. But it means breaking our traditions yet again. I don't like being viewed as a criminal by traditional women, but in my heart, I can't feel right about allowing species to go extinct when I know I can save them."

"If we can save them, then we should," Felifia said. "Tell me your plan."

Nekara hesitated.

"Go ahead, Nekara," Felifia said.

"As you know, periodically the toxic waste of Eho Miriam collects in the ocean near the equator, and a giant efferite sphere forms from the oceanic ridge, engulfs the waste, and catapults it into outer space," Nekara said.

"Yes," Felifia said. "Damiriak women have learned how to influence the efferite sphere's trajectory so that it leaves the solar system and never returns. We always send the efferite sphere to the distant planet *Elesha* (Earth)."

"What if instead of toxic waste, the efferite sphere fills with animals and plants of this world and is redirected toward planet Dahma?" Nekara proposed.

"Interesting idea," Felifia said. "But how would you get the animals and plants in there?"

"We could fly over the lands and drop chemical trails leading to the oceanic ridge," Nekara said. "The chemicals would contain molecular messages for the animals to take plant clippings and seeds with them as they make the journey."

"But land animals can't reach the ridge," Felifia said.

"Chemical messages would be dropped such that birds would carry the smaller animals from the shore to the ridge," Nekara said. "Other animals could float. The ocean currents already pull things from the shore to the ridge—the shore is typically where the waste goes as it is. We would have to block that waste temporarily from being pulled out to sea. But there's a problem."

"Yes, I know," Felifia said. "The old High Priestess council controls all affairs regarding efferite spheres. We would need their cooperation to perform this intra-solar transfer of life. If we explain the situation to them in the right way, then maybe they would approve."

"There, you see?" Nekara pointed out. "You know as does the rest of the world that the council would not approve a transfer of good species to another planet in our solar system. They want all 'healthy' life to remain on this planet. Yet they have no reservations about dumping whatever life they deem not fit for our world onto that distant planet *Elesha*."

"Had I invited Vadafa, we could have learned the council's decision right away. She is one of the members," Felifia said.

"Had you invited Vadafa," Nekara said, "she would not only disapprove of my idea, but she would also alert the council of my plans, and the council would in turn place guards around the efferite trajectory control center."

"The control center's location is secret," Felifia started, "to keep people—"

"Like me from commandeering it," Nekara finished. "It's built at the peak of a mountain in the ocean very close to where the efferite is produced. One cannot simply dive underwater and look for it. The platform is disguised in coral. One must know where it is. I for one do."

"Who told you?" Felifia asked.

"No one. My new powers allowed me to search the oceans with my mind and find it," Nekara said.

"You place me in a difficult situation," Felifia said. "If I suddenly learn an efferite has been launched to Dahma with good species onboard, I'll know you had a part in it. I would be required to do whatever I could to prosecute you. Further, I would be asked to testify what I knew about the situation. I would be forced to admit I knew of it before it happened. That's self incrimination."

"You could lie," Nekara said.

"Lie?! And lower myself to all those men over the years who lied to achieve power?" Felifia asked. "No, that is not my way. I must work within the savings of truth, or the debts of deceit will bury me."

"Then I regret what I must now do," Nekara said.

Nekara approached Felifia as if to kiss her. Felifia looked back with a puzzled expression. Then with a sudden snap-like action, Nekara whipped her hand into the back lower part of Felifia's skull upward at a forty-five degree angle. Felifia dropped into Nekara's arms, unconscious yet unhurt.

"Felifia, I'm back," Tanina called as she returned from her walk.

Tanina did not initially see Felifia, but after a few seconds, she saw Felifia's slumped body in Nekara's arms.

"My senior wife!" Tanina called as she rushed to Felifia's aid. "What happened? Is she ill?"

"Uh, yes, she's ill," Nekara lied. "Quick—let's take her to the hospital."

"I will call for the royal carriage," Tanina said.

Tanina left momentarily and returned with the royal carriage. Nekara, with her great strength, carried Felifia and loaded her in back. Nekara exited the back and approached the front.

"That will be all, driver," Nekara said. "I will take over from here."

The driver seemed confused. Nekara placed her left hand to her own abdomen and touched the driver's forehead with her right as if implanting an idea. The driver's eyes lit open for a moment as if receiving an urgent message. The driver released the reins to Nekara.

"I'll watch Felifia back here," Tanina said as she began entering the carriage.

Nekara whipped the reins, and the horses galloped off—with Tanina hanging partway out of the carriage.

"Easy!" Tanina yelled. "I'm not in yet."

But Nekara did not slow. She pushed the horses hard to put as much distance between the carriage and the palace as she could in the shortest amount of time. Tanina struggled to climb inside the carriage despite Nekara's sharp turns and bumping maneuvers that tended to push Tanina out of the carriage. Yet Tanina was skilled in climbing about, and she managed to pull herself into the carriage and close the door. After nearly fifteen minutes, the carriage reached an isolated stretch of rural road. Felifia was starting to regain consciousness when Nekara halted the horses suddenly. Felifia's and Tanina's momentum carried them forward, and they slammed into the forward wall. The impact sent Felifia back into unconsciousness while for Tanina, it gave her a big headache that only made her angry at Nekara. Nekara dismounted from the driver's chair and opened the carriage door.

"Why did you stop like that? We're nowhere near the hospital!" Tanina said.

"Please come out of the carriage for a moment. There's a problem," Nekara said.

"You're right. There is a problem—with your driving!" Tanina said. "You're the last person I would have expected to drive that poorly. The ride was terrible! We're lost! I had better drive."

"Before you do, take a look at this farm field," Nekara said. "Do you see that strange thing over there?"

"I don't understand," Tanina said. "What strange thing?"

"Stare at it for a moment. You'll see it," Nekara said.

"You brought us out here for this?" Tanina said as she stared at the field.

Nekara slipped away from Tanina, climbed into the driver's chair, and whipped the reins on the horses.

"You tricked me!" Tanina yelled as she ran back toward the carriage. "Wait for me!"

Nekara did not wait. She drove the horses until they reached her cave laboratory in the mountains. The lab was more than just that. Nekara did not undo the men's conversion of Nekara's lab to a prison. To the contrary, Nekara added enhancement to make the old prison into a stronghold. Guards permitted Nekara to enter with the carriage, and the carriage disappeared through a doorway into the mountain lab. Nekara's group apparently knew of Nekara's plans. They took Felifia out of the carriage and cared for her on a bed prepared just for her. Nekara stood next to Felifia and placed a smelling salt under her nose. Felifia awoke.

"Nekara," Felifia said. "What am I doing here? Wait, now I remember. You attacked me. Why, Nekara, why?"

"To protect you," Nekara said. "I intend to hijack the efferite control center without anyone's approval. Under my leadership, I will populate Dahma with plants and animals such that it becomes a paradise for people. I will make Dahma into an Eho Dahma."

"Nekara, don't do this," Felifia said. "If you return me to the palace now, no charges will be pressed. Going for a ride with my junior wife is hardly kidnapping."

"There's no going back now," Nekara said. "Tanina came along in the carriage until I forced her out in the countryside. She has no doubt found help and reported you as a kidnapping victim. Tanina will name me as the perpetrator. No, Felifia, I have kidnapped you, and I intend to keep you under guard until our mission is complete. There was no way I could leave you in the palace after what I told you. Your analysis was correct—you would have been implicated once I hijacked the control center. But now you are my prisoner. You are powerless to warn the old council even if you wanted to. I have reinforced the shielding in these caves. Your new Serisian power is useless."

"I could be accused of collaborating with you," Felifia said, "in which case I will be prosecuted all the same."

"I don't think so," Nekara said. "Once I have completed my work, I will release you. Then you will have a duty to perform. You will be required to order a bounty on my head. And you must do it to prevent revolt in the kingdom."

"I love you, Nekara," Felifia said. "You know I could never order your arrest and punishment."

"And I love you too. I love my world and everything about it. That's why I must sacrifice myself for the future of our people."

"But you're tearing me apart!" Felifia said. "These rash decisions are too much for me to bear."

"Put her to sleep," Nekara told one of the women doctors.

The doctor placed an aromatic under Felifia's nose, and she fell asleep. Two women approached Nekara. One handed her a backpack, the other Nekara's weapons.

"It's time," Nekara said. "Keep Felifia sedated until my return. Hijack team, we leave now!"

Nekara led her team and successfully took command of the efferite control center. Other team members flew Nekara's spaceship over the land and sprayed chemical trails. As predicted, animals carried seeds and plantings as they migrated along the path to the ocean. Once the animals reached the ocean, they began the process of catching a ride with a bird or a current out to the oceanic ridge. The old council took notice of these animals crossing the ocean and formed an army commanded by Vadafa. Vadafa led the army to the ocean and began diverting the animals back to their homes, but Nekara sent her own army to intercept the council's women. A small battle ensued. There was no bloodshed. The battle was instead for mind control. Biorna played songs on her oboe to coerce Nekara's army into sleepiness, but Nekara's army did not lose control. Nekara's army stormed Vadafa's, overpowered the women, and tied them up. Nekara's army went after the animals that had been turned around and sent them back to the ocean.

Jonara stood on the shores of the ocean. She wasn't sure if she should side with Vadafa or Nekara. Each had valid points. If only Nekara weren't such a rebel. If only Vadafa and the council were a little more flexible. Jonara didn't have much time to ponder. As she stared at the ocean's horizon, she saw what appeared to be the moon rising. But it wasn't the moon. It was an efferite sphere—a huge, milky-white crystalline sphere. It was now filled with animal and plant life in stasis, and it lifted above the ocean and into the air slowly—like a balloon ascending into the sky. Circles of light hummed around the sphere, and the humming was at such a low yet powerful frequency that it created increasingly larger water waves that crashed against the shore. Jonara backed away from the shore—a little at first and quite a bit more as the waves built in height. Finally, Jonara realized the waves were getting too big. She ran from shore to the nearest tree and climbed it as quickly and as far up as she could. Each wave that crashed in managed to hit her legs and in doing so attempted to pull her under.

Nekara's army moved Vadafa's army to safety farther inland. Jonara reached the top of the tree and escaped the largest wave. She watched as the efferite sphere ascended higher and higher into the sky until it disappeared from sight.

As Eho Miriam orbited closer to Seris, the crimson plants took deeper root and flourished. They radiated progressively more heat. Male mammals died off as Biorna predicted. Animals discovered the crimson plants and ate their leaves as the green-leafed plants shed their leaves for the season. The crimson leaves contained a higher fuel energy than the green leaves, giving the animals an abundance of energy and heat—necessary to survive the winter. As Biorna predicted, temperatures on Eho Miriam dropped considerably below the freezing point of water. Vadafa's freeze-preservation chant helped prevent catastrophic damage to plants and to animals that did not have access to crimson leaves to eat.

Anba and Teluna began the first tour on planet Dahma. Planet Dahma was not called, "Eho Dahma," yet. Nekara insisted that the land be populated with plants and animals first. The efferite sphere trailed Eho Miriam's orbit and would not land on Dahma until Dahma crossed Miriam's orbital path—a point where Miriam would be waxing into its next summer.

In their tour, Anba and Teluna observed male marine mammals perish as predicted. Through experimentation, Anba and Teluna determined female marine mammals would respond to any methods of successful treatment developed on Eho Miriam. With this knowledge, the need for further work on Dahma concluded, and Nekara ordered the two back to Eho Miriam. Feeling a new sense of freedom, Anba and Teluna did not wish to return to Eho Miriam, but Nekara insisted, and so the two returned.

When Eho Miriam reached the top of its orbit where it reached its furthest point from Maknesi and closest point to Seris, Nekara announced she had reached a breakthrough in female people fertility. Her group now had the 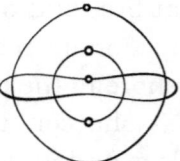 means of enabling two women to have babies with each other. Nekara unlinked Anba's marriage to Vadafa and Teluna's marriage to Felifia. Nekara then looked for volunteers to test women conceiving with women. Anba and Teluna volunteered and quickly cross-conceived in the perfected strontium-isotope-laced cave pool. In this way, Anba carried Teluna's baby, and Teluna carried Anba's baby.

Meanwhile, Vadafa and the old council objected strongly to Nekara's recent activities—the kidnapping of Princess Felifia (who was still held in Nekara's fortress), the hijacking of an efferite sphere, the sending of native animal and plant life to planet Dahma, breaking Anba's and Teluna's marriages, and now the peer pregnancy of Anba and Teluna. Nekara refused to let Felifia go, and she announced the peer pregnancies were the only way for women to conceive on Eho Miriam. Vadafa and the council issued two edicts—one ostracizing Nekara the Red, and another threatening to ostracize any woman who conceived using Nekara's method. Because of the edict, no other women outside of Nekara's group conceived.

In response to Vadafa's and the council's objection to Anba's and Teluna's peer pregnancy, Nekara joined/married Anba and Teluna to each other as peer wives, creating the first couple with a peer marriage instead of the old junior-senior marriage. Vadafa and the council issued an edict ostracizing Anba and Teluna for breaking their loyalties with their senior wives and for becoming pregnant out of traditional wedlock with another woman of equal age. The council gathered strength from Damiriak women around the world, and pressure mounted against Nekara and her fortress of women.

Nekara had many conversations with Felifia. Felifia urged Nekara to surrender to the council and seek their mercy. Nekara refused and stated that the council would only imprison her and her group despite everything Nekara did to help her people. Anba and Teluna urged Nekara to abandon Eho Miriam and lead her group of women to Dahma where they could live in freedom.

"But there's the final issue of conception on Eho Miriam," Nekara would always say. "Vadafa and the council will not allow our methods to be used for traditional Miramish women."

"Then their line will end," Anba would say.

"Let them die off," Teluna would add.

"No. I took an oath to stay on this planet until my fertility work was done. It is not yet done," Nekara would reply.

Nekara sent Anba and Teluna back to planet Dahma to witness the efferite sphere's landing. The two did as Nekara asked and suggested they would prepare Dahma for Nekara's arrival. 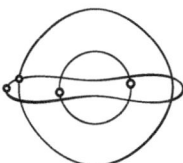 Eho Miriam's orbit crossed Dahma's orbit and headed toward its summer on the left side of its orbit with the efferite sphere trailing in Eho Miriam's orbital path. Planet Dahma then crossed 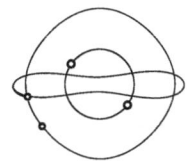 Eho Miriam's path on its way toward the center of the solar system. As it crossed Eho Miriam's path, its gravity snared the efferite sphere, and the sphere made an entry through Dahma's atmosphere.

Anba and Teluna were on planet Dahma by the very shoreline where they anticipated the efferite sphere would land. The sphere held its structure until it landed as predicted in a Dahmek ocean near the shore where Anba and Teluna were stationed. The sphere came apart and spewed its contents onto land. Anba and Teluna relayed reports to Nekara that the animals and plants had survived and were now prospering. Meanwhile, back on Eho Miriam, Nekara struggled with a method for women to conceive following Miramish tradition.

"I'm at wit's end, Felifia," Nekara finally confessed. "I've tried various strontium isotopes, I've tried spiking the pool with other chemicals, I've tried electroshock, and I've tried electromagnetism. The left-right model is the only one that works. Everything else fails. The world is against me, and soon this fortress will be under siege. Anba and Teluna tell me that we can duplicate the strontium cave pools on Dahma. They even suggest I quit my work here and defect to Dahma with my group."

"You could do that," Felifia said. "Perhaps that would be better. I know I suggested you surrender to Vadafa and the council, but now I am of different opinion. You look exhausted, Nekara. I fear you'll work yourself to death on Eho Miriam. Continue your research on Dahma. At least you won't have to worry about being under attack."

"I have this great fear, Felifia," Nekara admitted.

"You? You're the most powerful woman in this solar system," Felifia said. "No one can kill or even harm you. How can you be afraid?"

"Oh but I am afraid. Fear has driven me to all sorts of extremes. Even the fossilization of my body was driven by fear."

"Fear of death?"

"No, fear of disappointing you," Nekara said.

"I shouldn't believe it," Felifia said. "But somehow I do. The bonds of our love are still incredibly strong. Rationally speaking, I should despise you for committing crimes against Miramish tradition. But I can't. I love you too much. And it hurts me more than ever that you cannot resolve these issues once and for all. I wish these dreadful times would end, and we could get on with our marriage instead of worrying about helping everyone else."

"Times are better," Nekara said. "Or at least they should be. We've run the strontium isotope into all surrounding mountain streams. The council has permitted our technology to be employed on other mountains around the world. Female mammals are reproducing successfully. Spring is ending, and summer is fast approaching. Half the life on Eho Miriam perished, but the other half survived and is thriving. Next winter will be much milder as the crimson plants gain a stronger roothold into soil and host. All that's left is dealing with the council's requirement of maintaining forced senior-junior relationships on this planet."

"I fear you'll never complete it if you stay here," Felifia said.

"I promised you I would stay here until I finished," Nekara said.

"You once tried to convince me to lie," Felifia said. "So now I suggest the same for you—claim that your promise was a lie and move to Dahma."

"You know I will never lie to you," Nekara said. "It's impossible. Our link is too strong. You know the truth whether I speak it or think it."

Felifia started to cry.

"You must leave. The council will kill you if you stay. I sense it," Felifia cried.

Nekara took Felifia in her arms. Nekara hugged and kissed Felifia.

"I know. I also know that if I leave here, I won't come back. We'll be separated, unless you live on Dahma with me. But I know you won't abandon this planet. It still needs your leadership. But even if I could leave here at the expense of our marriage, I know that any solution I come up with will be rejected by the council—even if it meets their requirements—because I have been ostracized. That means everything I accomplish in the future will be void."

"Then even if you stay here and find a solution, they won't accept it," Felifia said. "Have you thought about that?"

"Yes, I have," Nekara said. "My thought was that if I come up with the solution, I would give it to you, and you would present it as your own idea. Then the council will accept it."

"But you deserve the credit," Felifia said.

"I don't care about credit anymore," Nekara said. "I just want to get this problem—this scorpion—off my back, to use a metaphor, so it won't sting me day after day. Will you promise to propose the solution as your own, if I should discover it?"

"To lie," Felifia said, "is a horrible burden. But losing you to the planet Dahma will be a burden too. I will try my best, Nekara."

"It will need to be very convincing. I know you have the strength, my senior wife. Dig deeply enough, and you'll find it," Nekara said.

Nekara gave another hug and kiss to Felifia and relinquished her embrace. Felifia drew her left hand over her abdomen and touched the moishiana in her navel.

"If only there were some way we could use our moishiani for senior-junior conception," Felifia said to herself, but her lips moved, and Nekara caught a few of Felifia's words.

"What's that?" Nekara asked. "What's this about the moishiana?"

Then Felifia's eyes widened and a grin pulled the corners of her mouth to her ears.

"You've thought of something," Nekara said. "What are you thinking?"

"It occurs to me that you've been approaching this problem from a very generic point of view," Felifia said. "Democracy for all, one solution for all female mammals."

"Yes, true," Nekara said. "It seems the most efficient way of solving the problem. We can't pursue a solution that requires high maintenance such as chasing every female mammal on this planet and manually removing, treating, and swapping ova with other females."

"Now what would Vadafa say about narrowing one's options to a single solution?" Felifia grinned.

"I can't believe I'm resorting to thinking like Vadafa," Nekara admitted, "after the conflicts she and I have endured."

"Still, entertain me," Felifia said. "What would Vadafa say?"

"She would say I'm committing the ultimate male failing—narrowing my focus to a single point of obsession," Nekara confessed. "But I've tried other solutions."

"You've tried other variations of the same focal point," Felifia said. "The obsession is the same, only the color is different."

"What do you propose?" Nekara asked.

"Our power as priestesses and women of marriage lies in Serisian power. We control that power with the moishiana that is fused in our navels," Felifia said.

"Yes, the moishiana," Nekara said. "But the navel is not part of the reproductive tract. Are you suggesting that it should be?"

"I'm suggesting that the moishiana is one way we women employ power and control our environment, including our internal environment," Felifia said. "The council confers certain powers to women based on what responsibility the council believes each woman is capable of in using that power. Any solution for conception will need to be approved by the council, but more so, the council will want to control who can conceive and how. The council has always used the moishiana to do that for priestesses, and the pseudo-moishiana for marriages between non-priestesses. The council might decide to make changes in how the moishiana is implemented, but they will still use the moishiana. Can you take what you have learned and create another stone—something like the moishiana, but with the sole purpose of facilitating conception for a senior-junior marriage?"

Nekara paused in thought. She stared directly into Felifia's eyes and with wild passion kissed Felifia deeply.

"Of course!" Nekara said. "I've been so immersed in my own methods that I completely ignored how the council sees this. Yes, I do have the ability to create another stone. Let's see—it should have the ability to hold one or more ova from the senior wife. The stone would then replicate organic copies of itself with an ovum in each copy. The copy would have to migrate into the uterus and receive the junior wife's ovum. Conception would have to take place in the copy. The copy would dissolve, and the zygote released. That's it! That's the solution! And you did invent it! You'll be truthful when you present it to council! Oh, I'll be so glad when we can test it between ourselves, when you are the donor and I am the recipient. We'll—"

Nekara cut herself short. She looked at her body and realized she could not conceive with her fossilized reproductive tract.

"Why do I bother?" Nekara said in disgust, and she walked away from Felifia.

"Wait!" Felifia called back. "Don't turn away now! This is the last obstacle! We can finish this and move on!"

Nekara turned around to Felifia, opened her mouth to say something, turned with her back to Felifia, then turned sideways and stared up as she bit her lip. Nekara held her open hand up to the sky and shook it as if chopping something. Nekara looked down and held her fingertips clumped to her forehead as she lost herself in thought. Nekara then looked out in the distance, held her palms out, and alternated between placing her left fingers atop her right fingers and her right atop her left.

"Nekara?" Felifia called.

"Yes," Nekara said as she walked slowly toward Felifia.

"Will you finish this last task?" Felifia asked.

"There never is a last task," Nekara said. "But I will create several small devices to be used by council priestesses to facilitate senior-junior pregnancies."

As Eho Miriam's summer progressed, Nekara worked and perfected such a device. She named it the *duavisha*. She explained how it worked to Felifia.

"A duavisha begins in an unlocked state," Nekara said. "Here is one such stone. You'll notice it is crystalline in structure and looks like two ovals—one partway inside the other— with two, small, enclosed pockets—a pocket in each oval. Those pockets contain strontium-isotope-laced fluid. The duavisha in an unlocked state has no power—it must be locked to the Serisian Power Identifier of the senior wife like this."

Nekara placed the duavisha on Felifia's navel. It meshed with Felifia's moishiana and heated up.

"It's burning me!" Felifia said, and she yanked the duavisha away.

"Now it's locked to you," Nekara said. "No one else can use this duavisha but you. The duavisha extracts and stores ova. It then creates a transport vesicle known as a *pelepa* that resembles the shape of the duavisha. An ovum is released from the duavisha to the pelepa. This pelepa is placed in the navel of the junior wife where it migrates into the uterus of the junior wife and awaits the next ovum. The ova merge in the pelepa yielding a zygote. The pelepa dissolves, and the zygote attaches to the uterine wall resulting in a natural pregnancy. It works exactly as I first envisioned it would."

"You mean, I can now use this duavisha to get Tanina or you pregnant with my baby?"

"Tanina, yes. Me, no," Nekara replied. "This duavisha only works with normal women. It does not overcome my indurated reproductive tract."

"How do you make an unlocked duavisha?" Felifia asked.

"You can make one from your existing duavisha and your moishiana," Nekara said. "I will whisper the chant in your ear. It must remain a secret among high priestesses."

Nekara whispered the chant in Felifia's ear.

"Now hold your duavisha to your moishiana and whisper the chant very quietly so none can hear," Nekara said.

Felifia did such a thing. A heat and pain filled Felifia's navel. In a few minutes, Felifia's navel ruptured and squeezed out an unlocked duavisha.

"This unlocked duavisha will only bind with a senior wife. It will not bind with a junior wife, an unwed wife, or the wife of a man, not that we have any men left to worry about," Nekara said.

"This is the ultimate Damiriak gift to our people," Felifia said. "I...I...have no ability to express the gratitude our people will have once these duavishi spread through our population. You've saved our race and our customs. This is a moment of celebration!"

The sounds of explosions echoed through the cave.

"That's not the sound of a celebration," Nekara said.

"We're under siege!" Felifia said. "Oh why can't the council give us a moment to celebrate your triumph!?"

"My life was, is, and will always be this way," Nekara said. "Punishment for a job well done."

Nekara's women ran back and forth in chaos.

"Secure our work," Nekara yelled to the women. "Load the spaceship. Make ready for departure to Eho Dahma!"

The explosions got louder and closer. Bits of loose rock and debris fell from the top of the cave ceiling.

"We'll depart through the emergency aerial exit," Nekara yelled. "Leave all unnecessary supplies behind."

Nekara turned to Felifia and said, "Stay in this little bunker. It will protect you from anything falling. Vadafa's army will not harm you. They will feel vindicated upon 'rescuing' you. Do not worry if the remaining lab is destroyed. I've accomplished and distributed my work throughout this world, and I'm taking with me what I haven't distributed. You alone hold the responsibility for distributing the duavisha. Take care, my Princess Felifia and senior wife. I hope to see you again."

"I will treasure you always," Felifia said.

The two hugged and kissed. Nekara's women and critical equipment were now loaded on her spaceship. The ship was ready for departure but waited for Nekara to board.

"Hurry," a woman yelled through the spaceship's open door. "We can't stay here any longer."

"I don't want to leave your arms," Nekara said.

"And I don't want you to leave my arms," Felifia said.

"We must leave now!" the woman yelled from the spaceship.

Felifia's and Nekara's faces were wet with tears. Nekara broke off the embrace, kissed Felifia quickly one last time, and ran for the spaceship. Vadafa's army broke into the lab and began firing upon the spacecraft and Nekara. Nekara fell as bullets tripped her run, but she picked herself up and rushed into the spacecraft. Vadafa's army wheeled in cannons, lit the fuses, and aimed them at Nekara's spacecraft. The spacecraft's door closed, the cannons fired, and the spacecraft ascended through the opening in the ceiling—just barely lifting above the flying cannonballs. Vadafa commanded the army to fire everything at the spaceship, but the spaceship ascended out of the cave, into the sky, and out of sight.

Vadafa looked down and tapped her foot in disappointment. Tanina and Biorna saw Felifia and rushed to her aid.

"The Princess, the Princess!" Tanina yelled.

Vadafa and several women in her army approached Felifia.

"Are you hurt, Princess Felifia?" Tanina asked. "Did Nekara torture you?"

"I am not harmed physically," Felifia said. "But I am exhausted. Take me out of here."

In the years that followed, Nekara reigned on Eho Dahma as emperor. Eho Dahma prospered with abundant plants and animals on land, and the population grew. Fresh water streams were laced with strontium isotopes from the mountains, and female mammals multiplied from these streams as did the ones on Eho Miriam. Women on Eho Dahma conceived in mountain pools until Nekara invented a duavisha that could be used in peer marriages where there was no senior-junior status. The Eho Miriam council accepted Felifia's duavisha as a means of guaranteeing senior-junior conception but condemned the Dahmek duavisha. However, the Eho Miriam council had no power on Eho Dahma, and so the Dahmek duavisha was used on Eho Dahma without restriction. Anba taught the Dahmek women her language where verbs carry an *s* or *z* before the final root consonant. This language came to be known as Dahmek. An alphabet was invented, and it was named Deibuth.

Since Nekara's hijacking of the efferite control center on Eho Miriam, the council lost all control of efferite sphere trajectory. It was no longer possible to send efferite spheres to Earth. Instead, all new efferite spheres were sent to Eho Dahma. Likewise, a Dahmek ocean began producing efferite spheres and launched them in a trailing solar orbit behind Eho Dahma. As Eho Miriam crossed Eho Dahma's solar orbital path, the Dahmek efferite sphere was captured by Eho Miriam's gravity and entered its atmosphere. The sphere landed much as it did on Eho Dahma—it held its structure until it crashed along an ocean shoreline, releasing its cargo of plants and animals. In this way, Eho Miriam and Eho Dahma exchanged efferite spheres once a Miramish year, or twice a Miramish revolution. Neither the council nor the Dahmek women had control over what life entered the spheres. Some daring women entered the spheres and used them as an inexpensive means of traveling between Eho planets. Dahmek women greeted Miramish visitors with open arms, while the council on Eho Miriam quarantined visiting Dahmek women until suspicions were cleared. A lifelong bounty was placed on Nekara's head by the council, and Nekara never made the journey back to Eho Miriam.

In the first few years that followed, Felifia visited Nekara on Eho Dahma numerous times but did not stay. Felifia always returned to Eho Miriam to run the kingdom. As the years passed by, Felifia visited less and less. Nekara became reclusive until for the first time since the two were married, Felifia lost her link with Nekara. She did not understand why, and she embarked on a journey to Eho Dahma to find out.

To Felifia's surprise, living men guarded Nekara's castle on Eho Dahma. Felifia, unable to contact Nekara, got hold of Anba and Teluna. The two explained that Nekara had been working on this secret project to bring men back into the solar system by taking Dahmek women and reengineering them. Nekara had hoped to reintroduce these men to Eho Dahma first and prove their trustworthiness. Word got out quickly, and the project was no longer secret. The council recalled Felifia to Eho Miriam and forbade her from visiting Eho Dahma again. Dahmek women fearful of Nekara's work launched an attack against her engineered men. Nekara was furious and ordered the men into battle against those Dahmek women in opposition to her. The council on Eho Miriam gave support to those Dahmek women opposing Nekara. The men overpowered the Dahmek opposition, Nekara learned of the link with the council, and she branded the Dahmek opposition as traitors for their treason and conspiracy. Nekara ordered her male army to execute the traitors, but that created an even larger backlash against Nekara.

Felifia headed up a special coalition of Miramish and Dahmek forces to find and capture Nekara. The Eho Dahma council put a bounty on all male people and rewarded Damiriak women richly for all dead men delivered to council. After more bloodshed from both sides, Nekara's men were hunted and turned over to the Dahmek council who in turn executed the men.

Vadafa captured Nekara and delivered her to Felifia. The council pressured Felifia to order Nekara's execution, but even after everything Nekara had done, Felifia still loved her. Felifia ordered a major project to control the trajectory of the next Miramish efferite sphere. Nekara was placed on that sphere, and Felifia ordered the sphere be sent to Earth. With a heavy heart, Felifia pressed the button that altered the efferite sphere's trajectory. With that action, Felifia condemned Nekara to live her remaining years on Earth, never to return to the Damiriak solar system.

Vadafa, Biorna, and Tanina did everything in their power to comfort Felifia, and largely they were successful, but late at night before Felifia went to sleep, she stared at a portrait of Nekara and at the duavisha Nekara had given her. She held them to her heart and sobbed for an hour, promising herself that someday she would reunite with her number three junior wife.

CHAPTER 4

Elrod Release

2023 Oct 8, Sun Afnoon. Corpus Christi, Texas.

"We're here, my love," Greg said to Jonara. "Are you going to stare out that window or get off the bus?"

Jonara looked around. She was on Bishop Tárrega's bus. It was empty except for Greg and her. Jonara looked out the window and saw many other tour buses lined up along Corpus Christi Bay.

"Well? The bishop's speech is any minute now," Greg said.

"The bishop's speech?" Jonara asked as she pulled herself out of her trance.

"Yes, the speech! Come on, let's go!" Greg urged.

Greg pulled Jonara by her arm and led her out of the bus.

"Let go of my arm," Jonara demanded as she yanked her arm away from Greg.

"This way," he said. "Let's run."

Greg ran off toward the large group of people along the shore. He turned back once to see how far back Jonara was. Jonara made no effort to keep up his pace. She was determined to reach the shore, yes, but at her own walking pace. Greg shrugged his shoulders and ran off.

"What's the matter, Jonara?" Nekara asked as she appeared next to Jonara. "Don't you want to rush over there and celebrate the new vitacepticals? That is what Bishop Tárrega intends to do."

"You again!" Jonara said. "I know about you."

"Yes, because I showed you my past life," Nekara said. "You understand why I am here, then."

"I understand why you are on Earth. I don't understand why you continue haunting me," Jonara said.

"Haunting you! I love you, Jonara. I want the best for you," Nekara crowed.

"You mean you want the most misery for me," Jonara said.

"That too," Nekara replied.

"But I know you really don't love me. You have and always will love Felifia," Jonara said.

"Felifia!? The one who sent me to this forsaken planet? But that was thousands of years ago. Love cannot survive that long. So I've chosen you to love until I tire of you. You are much like me," Nekara said.

"I'm nothing like you. You're evil, and you like evil," Jonara said.

"You are being alienated by your culture, as I was mine," Nekara said. "And this has a curious result. When one is blamed wrongly for evil, one copes by liking evil. It's an acquired taste."

"It's a sour taste. I hate it," Jonara said.

"What kind of pickles do you like?" Nekara asked.

"What?!"

"Do you like sweet pickles or dill pickles?" Nekara asked.

"Sweet, no, I like dill pickles now," Jonara admitted.

"But you liked sweet pickles at one time, right?" Nekara asked.

"When I was younger. Now sweet pickles are too sweet for me," Jonara said.

"Did you like dill pickles when you were younger?"

"No," Jonara replied.

"Because they weren't sweet. But now you've acquired a taste for dill pickles, and you've had your fill of sweet. That is how I am, and that's what you'll grow into. Innocence of youth is trampled by treachery of adulthood," Nekara said.

"That's hogwash. No one believes that," Jonara said.

"You will understand when you are older," Nekara said. "Speaking of treachery, it's time for the bishop to speak."

Marcus stood at the podium and introduced Bishop Tárrega to the crowd. Marcus then yielded the podium to the bishop, and the bishop spoke.

"People gathered here in the name of Corpus Christi, welcome to Corpus Christi Bay," the bishop started.

The crowd clapped.

"Since the beginning, when Adam and Eve succumbed to Original Sin, man has been plagued with sin and vice," the bishop said. "Man has suffered horribly in sin throughout the ages. Sin comes in many forms—Original, Mortal, Venial, the Seven Deadly Sins, violation of the Ten Commandments, turning one's self away from God, away from Christ, and away from the Church. Man has sought ways to relieve himself of sin and vice. God helped by placing his son on this earth, Jesus Christ, to intercede between God and Man. With Christ came the Church, and with the Church came penitence, works of faith, prayer, and forgiveness."

"In the course of human history, there have been pandemic vices," the bishop continued. "These vices are so prevalent throughout the world as to be like deadly diseases. One such pandemic vice, slavery, was ended on a global scale over a hundred and fifty years ago. Slavery had plagued humanity since the early days after Adam and Eve left the garden. But in a determined, unified effort, slavery was stamped out and made illegal throughout the world. No one today may legally be enslaved. General worldwide consensus is that slavery is morally wrong."

The crowd clapped in approval.

"Like the freedom from slavery, Christ opened the gates to Heaven that had been closed by Original Sin. Prior to Christ's death and resurrection, the holiest of men were forced to wait before entering Heaven. Christ's opening of the gates marked a great moment in human history."

More applause from the crowd.

"It is a rare and special thing in human history when men attain a greater state of grace through the elimination of a pandemic vice," the bishop continued. "In a matter of a few days, men will eliminate another scourge of humanity as old as slavery itself—that of abortion."

Mixed reaction from the crowd. Some clapped, others booed.

"I feel your conflict. Abortion is the most controversial issue among people today. The Church's position is clear—abortion is murder, and anyone committing this crime is condemned. There are some who would rationalize abortion by stating a woman has a right to her body. The Church's position on this is clear too. A woman's body is a temple of Christ. When she commits abortion, she murders her baby and defiles her body. When she defiles her body, she defiles the temple of Christ and Christ himself. She turns her back on his grace, and God's."

"Why do women commit so many abortions?" the bishop continued. "In most cases, her baby is 'inconvenient' to her. She is willing to lay down with a man, but she is unwilling to take responsibility for this act that should only be consummated in the binding love of Christ. She becomes pregnant. She knows her lying with a man is wrong, and she transfers this wrong to the pregnancy. And so, you see the result. She terminates the child's life."

"Many women continue to defile their bodies, believing they have the right. Who defends the rights of her unborn baby? This Saturday, the Roman Catholic Church will forever and irreversibly establish absolute rights to an unborn child. Women will no longer be able to get pregnant by simply lying with a man. This will be prevented. A woman must now prove that her intentions to conceive are holy and are within the bonds of Catholic matrimony. Once her proof is verified, she will be allowed to conceive with her husband by using a church-sponsored vitaceptical. As you can see, many vitacepticals are being built along this bay as I speak. Other water bodies in other parts of this country and the world are also sponsoring vitacepticals. All will officially open for use this Saturday, when the solar eclipse marks the end of reckless fertility and the beginning of guided families."

Large outburst of applause.

"I can't believe what I just heard," Jonara said. "That's the most unfair thing ever invented."

"Guided families," Nekara reiterated. "Just like on Eho Miriam. I created that problem, and you created this one. You are like a junior Nekara. Perhaps I should adopt you as the daughter I could never have."

"I refuse!" Jonara said. "I refuse to accept these vitaceptiicals, and I refuse to be your daughter!"

"Oh get used to it," Nekara said. "This is the way of your world now. Who can dare go against the Church? You would be excommunicated, as I was ostracized. If the people here had the technology, they would ban you to some waste planet as I was sent here. But cheer up. You haven't been excommunicated. As long as you do everything you are told, you'll be allowed to have children."

Jonara boiled over with anger. She reached to choke Nekara, but Nekara laughed as she dissolved in the air. Bishop Tárrega had finished his speech, and a folk band performed on stage while people sang, clapped, and migrated to various food stands. In frustration, Jonara kept her hands in the air as if choking someone. Johnny walked up to her.

"Don't choke me, don't choke me!" Johnny faked. "I need air—the world for air!"

Johnny placed his hands around his neck as if he were being choked, and he dropped to his knees.

"Stop pretending, Daddy," Jonara said.

"It's funny," Johnny said as he rose to his feet. "Don't you think so?"

"No," Jonara replied.

"Weren't you pretending to choke me?" Johnny chuckled.

"No, no, no! I wish everyone would leave me alone!" Jonara said, and she walked away from her father, the crowd, and onto a pier.

"Boat ride, boat ride, who wants a boat ride?" called several captains of small, private yachts.

"Jonara," Johnny said. "What's the matter? Who is bothering you?"

"Everyone!" Jonara replied.

"These people?" Johnny asked.

"Yes."

"The bishop?"

"Yes."

"Your family?"

"Some of them."

"Me?"

Jonara looked at Johnny's eyes, she broke into tears, and she hugged him.

"No, not you," Jonara said. "You're one of the few I can trust."

"Oh honey dear," Johnny said. "You know you can come to me."

Several people bumped past Johnny and Jonara.

"Watch it!" Jonara yelled.

"You're overly sensitive," Johnny said.

"There are too many people here," Jonara said. "Too many people agreeing with the bishop. Daddy—get me out of here!"

"Two for a boat ride around the bay," Johnny said to one of the captains.

"All right!" the captain said. "All aboard! Watch your step, little lady, and you too, sir!"

Jonara and Johnny boarded the small yacht, and the captain cast off.

"Included in the boat ride is a free lunch and beverage. What kind of sandwich may the captain provide you two? Little lady?"

"Chicken and a cola," Jonara said.

"I'll have the same," Johnny said.

"Two chicken sandwiches and colas coming up," the captain said.

The yacht motored out into the bay. The crowd, food stands, and vitacepticals appeared to shrink in size. Jonara's anxiety dissipated as the soothing sound of splashing waves replaced the agitation of scuffling crowds. Johnny placed a cell phone call to Evanita to let her know his and Jonara's whereabouts. He finished the call just as the captain returned.

"Lunch is here!" the captain announced.

Jonara and Johnny ate their sandwiches and drank their colas.

"It's good," Jonara said with a mouthful. "Daddy?"

"Clear your mouth first," Johnny said, also with a mouthful.

Jonara swallowed her bite of sandwich and rinsed with a slurp of cola.

"Daddy?" Jonara asked. "How did you meet Mommy?"

"I've told you before," Johnny said.

"Well tell me again," Jonara said.

"I met her in your Grandma Eva's dental office. Evanita helped me relax by holding my hand," Johnny explained.

"And she attended Aunt Valeria's funeral?" Jonara asked.

"Your Aunt Valeria isn't dead yet," Johnny said. "Her condition is serious, but she treats it with medication. Why did you ask such a strange question? Have you been staring in that fake ruby again?"

"Fake ruby?" Jonara asked.

"Yes. The stone around your neck. It's not a real ruby. It's costume jewelry," Johnny said.

"Daddy, where did you find it?" Jonara asked.

"You know I found it in the bay next to Ross Island back in Portland," he said.

"Did it give you special powers? Like powers to see what was happening in other places or see what someone looked like on the inside?"

Johnny laughed.

"No, but I see your imagination has gotten the best of you," Johnny said. "When you were a little girl, I used to tell you that if you stared in the ruby long enough, you could see things from another universe that looked like this one, that things happened differently, like an alternative timeline. I told you things like that to keep you busy. I also told you that you could hear the ocean if you put a seashell to your ear. But I suppose you're too old to believe in those pranks of mine. You know, with all the stories you've seen in that stone, you could write a book."

"Then everything I thought...everything about my other life... the Water Ruby...Eho Miriam...the cello...Daddy! Are you saying

everything that I thought was true was just my imagination going wild over this ruby stone?" Jonara asked.

"What? I don't understand," Johnny said.

"Here's something else," Jonara said. "When the ruby had
power, I could say things in another language and make things
happen. But the ruby doesn't work anymore."

"That I do understand," Johnny said.

"You do?"

"Yes. We'll do like we did when you were a little girl. Dip
your ruby in the bay water, and it will recharge," Johnny said.

"That doesn't work," Jonara said. "It's a trick."

"I know," Johnny said. "But you fell for it when you were a
little girl—like the tooth fairy and Easter Bunny. Tell you what—
dip it in the water, and see if it brings back old memories."

Jonara removed the necklace from her neck—a necklace
holding the Moissan Ruby. Johnny ordered the captain to stop
the boat for a moment, and he did. Jonara dipped the Moissan
Ruby into the water, pulled it out, and stared at it. The Moissan
Ruby glistened in the sun as the attached water droplets dif-
fracted the sunlight into tiny little rainbows. The inside of the
Moissan Ruby swirled and churned, but with a faint image of
Nekara. Jonara held the Moissan Ruby to the sun and returned
it to her hand. She stared again and found herself traveling
back in time—something she didn't think possible using just
the Moissan Ruby without the diary or candleholder, but in her
heart, Jonara felt Nekara was forcing Jonara to whatever time
in the past Nekara desired.

2007 Apr 8, Easter Sun. Elrod 402 Campus. Portland, Oregon.

Evanita had just finished cleaning in Cafederijet after the
early afternoon Easter dinner when Ox-Two pulled her aside.

"You have a visitor in Whalejet," Ox-Two said. "Clean up and
follow me."

Evanita threw her apron in the hamper, washed her hands,
and followed Ox-Two to the security van. The van passed
through the double-gates of the compound and parked in front

of Whalejet. Ox-Two led Evanita up the steps into Whalejet and directed her to the visitor's room.

"You have thirty minutes," Ox-Two said.

A figure with a spring jacket and hood stood by the window and stared outside.

"If you're here for another religious debate, I'm not interested, Johnny," Evanita said.

The figure turned around, and it was Ms. Zyla.

"Ms. Zyla!" Evanita said.

"Surprised?" Ms. Zyla asked.

"Yes, I am," Evanita said.

"Give me a hug," Ms. Zyla said. "How have you been?"

"Busy," Evanita said. "I've been cooking in Cafederijet for a few months now, but today is my last day. I've been promoted to health assistant. I'll be able to do something more useful like making people feel better. I'm so excited. What about you? How are things on the outside? Johnny visited me a few times, but he didn't say what was going on."

"Your mother performed her last dance benefit at St. Eugene's Catholic Church last night at the Easter Vigil," Ms. Zyla said. "Did you watch her last month when she performed here?"

"Naw, I was doing more important things," Evanita said.

Ms. Zyla's eyes opened in astartlement.

"You didn't watch your mother's benefit? She did it for you!" Ms. Zyla said.

"So?" Evanita asked without expecting an answer.

"So!? What about a little gratitude, eh? She's working hard to arrange your release," Ms. Zyla said. "The least you could do is support her."

"In case you haven't noticed," Evanita said, "I'm the one in jail, not her. She has her freedom. Besides, the only reason I'm around is because she fooled around with some guy who skipped town."

"That's not true. She'd didn't 'fool around with some guy'," Ms. Zyla said. "I happen to know she loves you very much and would do anything to see you safe and happy—not like this."

"Not like what?" Evanita asked. "I'm turning this experience into something productive. Being thrown in detention has done me some good. Who knows, if I work things right here, I could get a job for pay and make this into a career."

"Perhaps," Ms. Zyla said. "But first you must complete your sentence as a detainee, finish high school, and get a university degree."

"Why bother wasting my time with all that when I can take a shortcut and get a job now? I'll earn my own money and be independent," Evanita said.

"I don't like that kind of talk, Evanita, and I never expected it from you," Ms. Zyla said.

"Why? Because I'm too young? Because the job market is such a good thing that the adults are afraid if younger people find out about it, they'll quit school and get jobs?"

"No," Ms. Zyla said. "That's not the—"

"It's too late to try any of that you'll-find-out-when-you're-older stuff on me. I'm old enough to know better. I'm old enough to have a baby," Evanita said.

"Whoa! Are you pregnant?" Ms. Zyla asked.

"Pregnant?! Good gosh no! Look around you! Do you see any guys?" Evanita asked.

"No. But the way you're talking, it's like you think you know better—that you think you're a real adult," Ms. Zyla said.

"I am," Evanita insisted.

"Being an adult means a lot more than holding down a job or having a baby. There's responsibility too," Ms. Zyla said. "Responsibility to yourself, to your family, and to God."

"I knew it!" Evanita said. "You're here to push your religious agenda on me."

"I'm not trying to subvert you!" Ms. Zyla said. "If you had the savvy of an adult, you would know this. I'm here to help. Evanita—this detention center is just that—a detention center. The girls in here are troubled—they are not role models! You've been given a bit of responsibility, and you like it. Good! But this is a beginning, not an end-all-be-all. Further, you must understand the nature of business. It's to make money, and unless you're at the top of the pyramid, it's to make money for someone else. You get a paycheck when things go well, and if not, you lose your job. But there's much more to a job than money. Business politics is a serious issue everywhere."

"Politics are for old people and governments," Evanita said. "I'm not going to waste time on politics."

"But politics affect you whether you like it or not," Ms. Zyla said. "Let's take a look at your work."

"There's nothing wrong with my work," Evanita said.

"You're not being paid for work," Ms. Zyla said. "Did you consider that perhaps that is why you are being promoted to health assistant, because it costs the Elrod nothing?"

"No. Ms. Nordekter said I'm an excellent worker and would do very well as a health assistant," Evanita said.

"Maybe," Ms. Zyla said. "But she could be lying to you."

"She didn't sound like she was lying. She sounded very sincere. And I start as a health assistant tomorrow. Is that a lie?" Evanita asked.

"She could be lying as to why you're being promoted. The fact you cost nothing could be the real reason," Ms. Zyla said.

"I don't believe it. Ms. Nordekter would have said so," Evanita said. "Besides, she keeps telling me how good of a job I'm doing."

"Does she ever look at your work?" Ms. Zyla asked.

"She must," Evanita said. "Otherwise, how could she know I'm doing a good job?"

"She could be saying you're doing a good job in order to gain your confidence and trust, irrespective of the quality in your work," Ms. Zyla said.

"I think you're trying to put me down," Evanita said. "Some adults and religions do that to maintain power. They want nothing to threaten their authority."

"I don't come here as an authority figure," Ms. Zyla said. "I'm not telling you what to do. I just want you to take a good look at what's going on around you and think hard about the real motives behind what people do."

"There, you see? You said you're not telling me what to do, but in your next sentence you're telling me to look around and think. You expect me to trust you now?" Evanita asked.

"Evanita, do you remember your Coming-Of-Age class?" Ms. Zyla asked.

"Barely. It seems like it was years ago. It doesn't matter. It was a sham anyway," Evanita said.

"Don't take one example as representative of the entire group," Ms. Zyla said. "Some young people have short attention spans and are difficult to motivate. That's why the short form was introduced. But not all classes use the short form, and now that I think about it, it was a mistake sending you to that one classroom. We were under the impression you were already aware enough of the world that you didn't need extensive training before Coming-Of-Age."

"I don't need training. I'm getting the training I need here," Evanita said.

"But this is not good training," Ms. Zyla said. "Not really. This work environment you're in—do you really see it as your salvation to solve all of your problems? Forever?"

"Now you're going to push Jesus on me as the real salvation," Evanita said.

"No, I'm not. Unitarian Universalism has a broad acceptance base. Christianity is one such base. Atheism and agnosticism are also a part. Evanita—it sounds like you have chosen the path of atheism or agnosticism. So be it. But the world still works the same way no matter what religious or non-religious view you select. American big business is like a narcotic—it's addictive, it works well in the beginning, but it falls flat in the end. And when you crash and burn after the business terminates your employment, what then?"

"I won't be terminated here," Evanita said. "I can feel it."

"It happens everywhere in this country," Ms. Zyla said. "The point is this—someone must look after you. Obviously you must take care of yourself, but sometimes you need more than that—something that will give you stability when times are bad. That's what UU is about. We're not going to turn you away when the economy goes south. We're not going to push bad morals onto you or coerce you to forsake dignity in the name of profit. We won't robbershaft you for natural resources and sell you into slavery when native inhabitants are all that are left of your country. Humanity, Evanita—you used to be full of it. But this place has leeched it out of you and replaced it with *yellow wine*. Do they take you out of the compound for green grass and trees?"

"Some of the girls who are in good with the Oxians do, but I don't," Evanita said.

"Do you see movies? Do you have television?" Ms. Zyla asked. "What about books?"

"We have schoolbooks. Calico has fiction books and puzzle books. I don't have fiction books. No television. Those same girls who go out to see grass and trees get to see movies at the theater," Evanita said. "It doesn't matter. I don't need it."

"They are healthy diversions," Ms. Zyla said. "They keep your brain from atrophying. They keep you sane."

"They are delusions and methods of manipulation," Evanita said.

"What nonsense is this? What are you talking about?" Ms. Zyla asked.

"Oxians dangle things like the countryside, free films, restaurant food, money, and drugs in front of the detainees like candy," Evanita said. "In exchange, the detainees must sleep with the Oxians."

"That's illegal, Evanita. We must report it," Ms. Zyla said.

"Report what?" Evanita said.

"What you just told me," Ms. Zyla said. "We'll need proof, but I'm sure you can provide it."

"I can't do that," Evanita said. "I would lose everything in here—my image, my new job, and my safety. A grouse doesn't live to see the next day. And I won't grouse on anyone."

"You won't do what? Be a what?" Ms. Zyla asked.

"A grouse. You know—a complainer, rat, weasel, pigeon, canary, snitch, tattletale," Evanita said.

"Tattletale!" Ms. Zyla said. "Evanita. No one says 'grouse' around here. I've heard it used in British-speaking countries, but not here. Don't you see you've been influenced? No, you can't see it now. Given time outside of the Elrod 402, you would see things differently. Do you feel coerced to keep quiet?"

Evanita did not reply.

"I might have known," Ms. Zyla said. "This is politics, Evanita. You may think you're holding your head above the Elrod water by not playing along with the Oxians' games of hanky-panky for treats, but that's only part of it. When you cover up for them, you are condoning it."

"I'm not saying it's right," Evanita said. "I would never do what they do. But there's risk and cost. And I can't pay right now."

Ms. Zyla shook her head.

"Then you've been successfully recruited into the American big business model," Ms. Zyla said. "And you've learned nothing of moral worth. You're vulnerable to being abused the rest of your life. And that's a horrible trap—one that you can avoid early in life but cannot easily break free of once you get older."

Ox-Two signaled from a distance that time was almost up.

"I have to go now," Evanita said. "I have to get ready for my first day as a health assistant."

"Please think about what I've said," Ms. Zyla said.

Evanita turned away as if to say she would ignore Ms. Zyla. Ms. Zyla turned Evanita around and held her (Ms. Zyla's) hands to Evanita's shoulders.

"Please, Evanita, think!" Ms. Zyla said. "Use that brain your mother gave you. Don't trust anyone in here."

"Should I extend that statement? Should I exclude trust from everyone?" Evanita asked.

"If you must," Ms. Zyla said.

"Including you?" Evanita asked.

"If you give serious and objective thought to what I've said and find flaw with it, then yes, do not trust me," Ms. Zyla said. "But please do the thinking first. Knee-jerk reactions are the worst."

"Then I will give it thought," Evanita said.

"Thank you," Ms. Zyla replied.

Ox-Two led Evanita from the visiting room to the security van, through the double-gate, and back to the main compound. But Ox-Two did not return Evanita to Cafederijet or Aldojet. Instead, Ox-Two drove the van to Redjet.

"Why are you stopping here?" Evanita asked.

"You're being moved out of Aldojet back into Redjet, Eve Carson."

"I don't understand. All of my things are with Mac-Two in Aldojet," Evanita said.

"You are no longer living in Aldojet," Ox-Two said. "Your things have been moved already. You will resume living with Calico."

"No, that can't be," Evanita said. "Mac-Two promised."

"There's been a reorganization," Ox-Two said. "This is the new assignment. No choice and no complaining. Understand?"

"Yeah," Evanita lamented.

Evanita entered Redjet and walked into her old room.

"So, the traitor has returned," Calico said.

"I'm not a traitor," Evanita said.

"Or should I say brown-noser?" Calico continued. "You and Tara were quite a pair, weren't you?"

"We weren't that close," Evanita said.

"Everyone knows you must have slept with her," Calico said. "Nothing to be ashamed of. Cooking by day, running in the evening, and snookie at night."

"There was no snookie!" Evanita said.

"Whatever you say, Eve Carson," Calico said. "Rumor is she dumped you for that new girl. That's why you were transferred out of the kitchen and into the infirmary."

"What new girl?" Evanita said.

"So, you don't deny your jealousy," Calico grinned.

"I'm not jealous," Evanita said. "Forget I asked. I don't want to know."

"Now denial," Calico continued.

"Do you ever give up?" Evanita asked.

"I think you need a good going over since you turned your back on your friends in Redjet," Calico said.

"I didn't turn my back on anyone," Evanita said.

"Oh cut the crap, Carson. It's obvious to everyone you're be-coming a pet or a snob—or both," Calico explained. "Well, the buck stops here with the Calico. You want to get on my bad side? Just try something and see what happens."

"I'm not here to start a fight," Evanita said. "I have an important job in the infirmary as a medical assistant, and I need to study for it. Now if you'll excuse me, I need to read this book."

"A book! I know all about books," Calico said. "Let's take a look."

Calico took the book out of Evanita's hands against Evanita's wishes.

"Hey!" Evanita said. "That's mine. Give it back."

"Oh what do we have here? *Medical Diagnostic Treatment,* 2007 Edition," Calico said.

"That's not for ordinary people," Evanita said. "Only medical personnel are allowed to read that."

"Wow, this has everything!" Calico said. "I can look up symptoms here, and there are decision charts here, and lookie-there—the most likely disease. And there's treatment—drugs, surgery, and other things. This is like cheating. Who needs a medical degree when anyone can just read this book?"

"Stop it. Give it back," Evanita said.

"Whatever," Calico said. "Take your book back."

Calico whipped the book through the air at Evanita, and Evanita caught it as a corner of the book hit her below her left eye.

"Ow!" Evanita said.

The point of impact below Evanita's eye puffed up.

"Oh, I see you have your first patient—yourself!" Calico laughed. "What is the treatment?"

Evanita thumbed through the book.

"Ice and aspirin," Evanita said.

"You won't find either in this room," Calico said. "So much for your medical abilities."

"Water alert!" a girl down the hallway shouted. "Water alert!"

"What's that?" Evanita asked.

"That means our water privilege for the day is about to end," Calico said.

"Water privilege? What do you mean?" Evanita asked.

"Wow, you were spoiled in Aldojet, weren't you?" Calico asked. "We've been on water rations for the last month. The water pressure drops about a half hour before it is shut off for the day. It's an automatic system."

"They can't shut off the water. How are we supposed to take a shower?" Evanita asked.

"Quickly—before the water runs out," Calico said.

"And what about washing hands after using the toilet?" Evanita asked.

"That's part of the water system. So is toilet water," Calico said. "If you need to do anything with water, you better do it now. And I don't want a toilet full of crap all night long. The new set of water rations doesn't come out until next morning."

Evanita rushed into the bathroom, used the toilet, and took a shower, but two minutes after she started the shower, the water stopped. Evanita's hair was still full of shampoo, and she had no water to rinse it.

"Still in the shower?" Calico yelled through the door. "I'll sell you a gallon jug of water for ten dollars. And that's for the water only—I want the jug back."

"Ten dollars!" Evanita shouted back. "That's a rip-off."

"It's my price. Take it or leave it," Calico yelled back.

"Okay. Gimme the water. I'll give you ten bucks when I get out," Evanita said.

"Ten bucks now," Calico said. "Or collateral."

"What kind of collateral?" Evanita asked.

"Oh, I don't know. Maybe this *Medical Diagnostic Treatment* book is good enough," Calico chuckled.

"That's worth more than ten bucks. And I need it for tomorrow," Evanita said.

"If you can't use your medical book as collateral until you get out of the shower, then I know you're not serious about paying me the ten bucks," Calico said. "Do we have a deal, or should I raise the price to twenty bucks? Ten bucks is a steal on this jet."

"Okay, okay!" Evanita said. "You can hold my medical book as collateral. I'll pay you the ten bucks when I get out. Now give me that water!"

"We have a deal then?" Calico asked.

"Yes, we have a deal! The water!" Evanita said.

"All right. Here you go," Calico said.

Calico opened the bathroom door and handed a plastic milk gallon container with water to Evanita.

"Hey! This container is only half full. You said this was a gallon of water!" Evanita protested.

"I said it was a gallon jug of water," Calico said. "I never said how much water."

"Cheat!" Evanita said as she rinsed herself off with the water. "I'm only going to pay you five bucks instead of ten."

"Uh-uh, no way. We have a deal. If you don't pay, you don't get your medical book back. And I have more water, too. That water would look really nice on these clean medical pages."

"You wouldn't!" Evanita protested.

"You've forgotten about the Calico," Calico said. "I should put you to work cleaning the bathroom and doing my laundry for a refresher."

Evanita finished drying off, put her clothes on, and exited the bathroom. From a pocket, she produced a ten dollar note.

"You win," Evanita said. "Here's your stinking ten dollars. Now give me my medical book."

Calico took the money and slapped the medical book against the top of Evanita's head before giving it to her.

"Ow!" Evanita said. "Why did you do that?"

"For giving me a hard time," Calico said.

The day ended, and Evanita climbed into her old bunk bed for the night. She remembered those first few nights when she was depressed and wished someone would take her away. She remembered praying to Jesus for his help. Now she looked back and thought of herself as being a weak, naïve, young girl. The "new" Evanita looked forward to the next day, despite hardships she faced in the Elrod.

2007 Apr 9, Mon. Elrod 402 Campus. Portland, Oregon.

Evanita awoke much as she did in prior days when she roomed with Calico—to the smell of cigar smoke and coffee.

"Your smoke is worse than usual," Evanita said.

"The ventilation system is still off," Calico said.

"Off? Why?" Evanita asked.

"Rationing. The ventilation system is cut off during the night. Don't tell me—there's no rationing in Aldojet," Calico said.

"Not like this. How are we supposed to breathe?" Evanita asked.

"Breathe during the day, sleep at night," Calico replied. "Would you like some chocolate mocha coffee like the good old days?"

"Yeah, sure," Evanita said.

Calico placed a chocolate bar in a coffee cup and filled the cup with coffee.

"Give it a moment to melt," Calico said.

Evanita took the sugar jar and poured sugar into her coffee.

"Whoa! I didn't say anything about sugar," Calico said. "You owe me for that."

"I think you still owe me after cheating me with that water yesterday," Evanita said.

Calico thumped Evanita on the head.

"That was a fair and square deal," Calico said. "Now this sugar thing is something new. Come to think of it, I should start charging you for the morning coffee."

"I don't have to drink your coffee. I can get coffee in Cafederijet," Evanita bragged.

"You can along with several other things. Tell you what— you bring me L-pseudoephedrine from the infirmary, and I'll let you drink my coffee for free with all the sugar you want."

"Pseudoephedrine is restricted," Evanita said. "It can be used to produce methamphetamine."

"That's D-pseudoephedrine. I know the D-stuff is restricted. But L-pseudoephedrine can't be converted to meth, so there shouldn't be a problem with distribution. I need a powerful decongestant, and that phenylephrine stuff is crap," Calico said. "But maybe you didn't know about the pseudoephedrine isomer situation. There's a brand-name for L-pseudoephedrine—it's called *Sulafil.* Get me some."

"I've never heard of Sulafil," Evanita said.

"Well, look around, and you'll find it. I've had it once before, but with all this rationing going on, it's hard to come by," Calico said.

"All right. I'll get you some Sulafil," Evanita said.

Evanita did not attend classes that morning but instead reported directly to Baria, the health chief of Elrod 402. Evanita was a little late. She ran into Cafederijet and joined the line of other medical assistants as Baria started roll call.

"Bar-One?" Baria called.

"Here," Bar-One replied.

"Bar-Two?"

"Here."

"Bar-Three?"

"Here."

"Bar-Four?"

"Here."

"Bar-Five?"

No reply.

"Bar-Five?" Baria repeated.

Baria looked at Evanita, but Evanita said nothing.

"Eve Carson," Baria said. "Your new name is Bar-Five. When anyone addresses you in Cafederijet or anywhere else when you are in a medical role, you are to respond to 'Bar-Five'. Is that understood?"

"Yes, ma'am," Evanita replied.

"Bar-Five?" Baria called.

"Here," Evanita replied.

"All are present and accounted for," Baria said. "Let's get down to business. There are several new diseases going around campus. But first—if any patient complains of sleeping problems because of these diseases, give the patient aspirin and trazodone. Now then, let's move on to the first disease. Bar-One did the pathology and determined it to be MRSA—Methicillin Resistant Staphylococcus Aureus. It's affecting the skin and nose of our detainees and staff. Our standard line of treatment will be clindamycin. Staff members who do not respond to clindamycin will be given linezolid, but under no circumstances is a detainee to receive linezolid. Linezolid is too expensive to hand out to just anyone."

"Another disease going around is cholera," Baria continued. "For this, you will mix up a sugar-water solution with salt and baking soda. Instruct the patient to drink two tablespoons after a slushy bowel movement."

"Miss Baria," Evanita said. "Two tablespoons hardly seem enough to replace water and electrolytes lost from exhaustive diarrhea. Further, there are antibiotics useful for treatment— chloramphenicol, erythromycin, and doxycycline to name a few. If proper medical attention isn't given, cholera can—"

Baria snapped her finger at Bar-One and pointed at Evanita. Bar-One walked briskly to Evanita and gagged her with a cotton rag. Evanita fought to pull the gag off, but Bar-One slapped Evanita in the face and tied her wrists behind her back.

"And finally, we have an outbreak of Legionellosis going around. Patients will have high fever, chills, cough with sputum, and pneumonia. Ask the patients to save their sputum for analysis. We will use erythromycin for treatment."

Evanita managed to work her gag free, and she spoke.

"If we have erythromycin available for Legionellosis, we can also use it for cholera," Evanita said.

Baria snapped at Bar-One, pointed at Evanita, and pointed at a side room. Bar-One walked briskly to Evanita, pulled her into the side room, and closed the door behind.

"You are not to challenge Baria while she speaks," Bar-One said. "Your job is to do as Baria says and treat patients. Baria is all-too-familiar with treatment options and their results. She doesn't have the time or patience to play Twenty-Questions. Got it?"

"But I was trying to help," Evanita said.

"No one wants that kind of help," Bar-One said. "Now listen when you're supposed to, do as you're told, and only speak when spoken to. Got it?"

"Yeah, I guess," Evanita said.

Bar-One slapped Evanita across the face.

"You've caused trouble before, Eve Carson," Bar-One said. "We know about you. You've been given a great gift—the honor to volunteer as a medical assistant. Don't throw it away with belligerence. When I ask you if you've got it, you say, 'Yes ma'am.' Got it?"

"Yes ma'am," Evanita said.

"That's better. Now I'm removing your bindings. Don't disappoint us, or you'll be assigned to sanitation with Dialytika's group. Got it?"

"Yes ma'am," Evanita replied.

Bar-One removed Evanita's bindings and led her out of the side room. Baria had already concluded the morning meeting, and it was time for work. Evanita assisted Bar-One in a treatment room. The first patient arrived with a staph infection on her nose.

"We'll give you a prescription for clindamycin," Bar-One said. "Bar-Five—write out a prescription—one pill three times a day. Bar-Five? What are you waiting for?"

"I don't know how to write a prescription," Evanita said.

"Hmm," Bar-One remarked. "Make sure you study that tonight. Tomorrow you'll be writing prescriptions."

Bar-One wrote the prescription and sent the first patient away. The next patient arrived complaining of diarrhea.

"You're back again, I see," Bar-One said to the second patient. "Let's look at your hand. Have you been soaking your infection and replacing your wick regularly?"

The second patient affirmed.

"Bar-Five—make up a bottle of sugar-water for treating cholera," Bar-One said.

"Excuse me, Bar-One, but isn't it possible our patient is suffering a side effect from the clindamycin?" Evanita asked.

Bar-One snapped her fingers and pointed at Evanita.

"That'll be enough from you. Make up the solution and give it to the patient," Bar-One said. "And take care of the next patient."

Evanita paused for a moment to protest, but the telephone rang. Bar-One snapped her fingers at Evanita again before Bar-

One answered the phone. Evanita reluctantly made up the mixture and gave it to the patient.

"Hello?" Bar-One asked. "Yes, O Grammeni. Of course, I'll do that. Which showing? All right—six tickets for the seven-thirty showing."

The next patient walked in and complained of difficulty breathing. Evanita held a flashlight in one hand and a wooden spatula in another.

"Say, 'ah'," Evanita said.

"Ah," the patient replied.

Bar-One kicked Evanita's chair and hand-signaled her to keep quiet.

"What kind of restaurant?" Bar-One asked. "Yes. There's a steakhouse near the theater."

"Have you been coughing up sputum?" Evanita whispered.

"Yeah," the girl whispered back.

"What color was it?" Evanita asked.

"I don't know," the girl said. "I swallowed it."

"Do you think you can cough up some mucus now as a sample?" Evanita asked.

"Yeah," the girl said.

"Why don't you try?" Evanita said. "Cough and spit into this emesis basin."

The girl coughed up a deep, guttural ball of mucus while Bar-One struggled to hear Grammeni on the phone. Bar-One waved them off before plugging her free ear with a finger.

"Yes, the van will be cleaned and ready to go tonight. Everything will be as you wish, O Grammeni. Goodbye," Bar-One said.

"We'll send this to the lab for testing," Evanita said.

"No, there will be no testing," Bar-One said.

"But we need to determine the causal pathogen. She could have pneumonia," Evanita said.

"She has Legionellosis," Bar-One said. "Write up a prescription for erythromycin."

"I don't know how—" Evanita started.

Bar-One slapped Evanita across the face.

"Don't make a sound when I'm on the phone, don't order up unnecessary expensive tests, and when I say to do something, do it with no back-talk. Got it?" Bar-One said.

"Yes ma'am," Evanita replied.

Evanita raced through her Medical Diagnostic Treatment book and looked up the symbols for writing a prescription. She then wrote up the prescription for erythromycin.

"Take this four times a day, at least two hours after meals. Do not take this with fruit juice or carbonated beverages," Evanita said.

"You don't need to explain," Bar-One said. "The prescription bottle will have the proper warning labels affixed. Move on to the next patient."

The next patient arrived with a bandage on her head. She had difficulty walking and sitting without losing balance. Bar-One started to say something when Bar-Two stood in the doorway.

"Did you forget?" Bar-Two asked Bar-One. "It's Baria's birthday today. We have cake and ice cream in the break room. We're going to sing to her too, and there are gifts. Did you bring yours?"

"Yeah, I have it right here," Bar-One said.

"All the Barians are there, along with Oxians, Macrons, and Dialytiks," Bar-Two said. "Come on—oh not you, Bar-Five. You're a volunteer. Volunteers don't go."

"You stay here and take care of the rest of the patients," Bar-One said to Evanita. "That includes patients waiting for the other Barians."

"That's too much," Evanita said.

Bar-One snapped and lifted the back of her hand as if to slap Evanita.

"Yes ma'am," Evanita replied.

"That's more like it," Bar-One said. "All right, Bar-Two, I'm ready."

Bar-One and Bar-Two left Evanita behind in the treatment room with her patient.

"Do you have a sore throat, coughing, or difficulty breathing?"

"No," the girl moaned.

"Any unusual or painful bumps on your skin or nose?" Evanita asked.

"No," the girl repeated.

"Any abdominal cramps or diarrhea?"

"No, none of that. I tripped going up steps and hit my head," the girl said.

"Let's take a look," Evanita said.

Evanita removed the bandaging. Blood poured out of a gash in the girl's head.

"This wasn't caused by steps," Evanita said. "The corner of a sharp object gouged your head."

"No one did nothing to nobody," the girl covered.

"A bandage won't stop the bleeding," Evanita said. "What you really need is stitches."

"Give me something for the pain before you start sewing," the girl said.

"I can't stitch you up. I don't know how, and I'm not a doctor," Evanita said.

"Doc—stitch me up! I'm bleeding badly!" the girl said.

Outside the door, Evanita heard a commotion growing in intensity.

"Do something for me," Evanita said. "Put one hand here and another hand here. Press down on your scalp. Now push your hands toward each other. This will slow the bleeding. I need to check on something."

"Don't leave me here!" the girl begged. "Don't leave me like this."

Evanita opened the door a little and looked outside. Girls outside were fighting with the receptionist as to who would get to go next. One saw Evanita's door ajar and rushed over to force entry. Evanita shut the door quickly and locked it. The girl pounded on the door from the outside. The patient in the treatment room continued holding her head but complained her arms were getting tired. The phone rang.

"Don't talk, just listen," O Grammeni said on the other end as Evanita picked it up. "There's been a change in plans. We want smorgasbord tonight. Make reservations for ten at Hogs-back Kitchen. And we don't want to see the comedy. Scrap it and buy ten tickets for that horror flick starring Ben Boolet. I want those tickets on my desk before noon. I can't discuss any more, gotta go. Bye!"

Evanita could barely think. She was still taking notes from her telephone call while the patient bled all over her face and girls outside pounded on the door.

"I'll try stitching your head now," Evanita said.

Evanita looked at the wound and realized it was dirty.

"I'll need to clean it first," Evanita said. "I'll get a cleaning solution of alcohol and witch hazel."

The girls continued pounding, and the door had difficulty holding them back. Evanita handed the bottle and a rag to the patient.

"Here—pour a little on your wound and use the rag to catch the excess," Evanita said.

"Aren't you supposed to do it?" the patient asked.

"I would if I didn't have these distractions," Evanita said as she pushed a desk in front of the door.

"OWWWW!" the patient screamed as the alcohol and witch hazel caused intense irritation in her open wound.

"Someone's getting killed in there!" a girl on the outside yelled.

The telephone rang. Evanita wasn't sure whether to answer or not. She was still in the middle of moving the desk in front of the door. The phone kept ringing. Finally, with the desk only partly obscuring the doorway, Evanita answered it.

"What on Earth took you so long to answer?" O Grammeni said. "We're in a conference meeting here. We can't wait all day! Now listen! Pick up my dry cleaning by three o'clock today. I need a fresh set of clothes before I go out tonight. One of the managers spilled coffee on me, and everything is a disaster. Do it before you do anything else today."

O Grammeni hung up before Evanita could say anything. The patient continued to bleed and scream. Girls on the outside screamed more. Bits of wood broke off the door from the girls pounding, and Evanita held the telephone in her hand, stunned and in shock. She put the phone down, walked into a closet, locked it, sat down, and blacked out.

Evanita awoke to smelling salts under her nose. She was facing a rebuilt Helrod with her arms and legs tied to the structure.

"She's awake," said O Grammeni.

"Punish her, punish her," chanted a crowd of girls in the stands.

Evanita could not see who was behind her, but Jonara could. It was Ox-Two with a whip in hand. O Grammeni had placed the smelling salts under Evanita's nose and called to Ox-Two to begin the whipping.

"Your job position has been eliminated," O Grammeni said, and she signaled to Ox-Two.

Ox-Two cracked the whip at Evanita's left leg. The whip caught the calf and immediately produced a welt. Evanita screamed.

"Your department has been outsourced," O Grammeni said.

Ox-Two whipped Evanita's right calf. Evanita screamed.

"No matter how many baseballs are thrown your way, you can't drop the ball," O Grammeni said.

Ox-Two whipped Evanita's left shoulder. Evanita screamed again.

"You are the catcher. You will always be a catcher," O Grammeni said.

Ox-Two whipped Evanita's right shoulder, and Evanita screamed again.

"So that you will obey and respect, you will be divided! Your soul will be split from your body!" O Grammeni said. "Therefore, no matter how extreme, frequent, or unethical, you will catch the ball without limit forever!"

Ox-Two wound up with all her might and whipped a heavy line down Evanita's back from her neck to the bottom of her spine. The impact echoed throughout the compound. Evanita let out a hideous scream. Her limbs convulsed as if the impact electrocuted her spine and connecting nerves.

"Mommy!" Jonara screamed.

Evanita stopped screaming, and her body fell limp with an occasional unconscious twitch here and there.

"Punishment complete," O Grammeni said. "You may take her down."

Calico, who had been held back by several Oxians, burst forth from their hold and unbound Evanita. Calico carried Evanita's body in her arms back to their room in Redjet. Jonara, however, remained close to the Helrod.

"Don't you like it when your female ancestors are tortured by the group?" Nekara asked as she appeared out of nowhere.

"This is your doing?" Jonara asked. "You caused this hate? I should have known."

"Not this time. How did I miss causing this hate point? I must add it to my *todo* list," Nekara said.

"What?!" Jonara asked in disbelief.

"Jonara," Nekara said. "My reach is far, and my followers many, but even without my influence, Earth is overflowing with hate. And I absorb as much as I can."

"How can you stand here and enjoy this?!" Jonara asked with a mixture of anger, horror, and sadness in her voice.

"Because it was done to my mother and my grandmother," Nekara shot back. "They were wrongly persecuted as was your mother and grandmother. That is the way of the universe when a new flower tries to enter the garden. Wake up, Jonara, and thicken your skin. The whip comes around all too often, and you'd better be ready for it."

"Be a catcher forever? Catch the baseball? Catch the end of the whip? It's wrong! Wrong!" Jonara stated.

"So what?" Nekara asked. "Are you going to stop it? Everywhere? For all people? How? No one can. No one. As long as people exist in this universe, they will pursue paths of evil and sling disease amongst the masses. You'd better catch that disease and relay it to the next person before it latches to your flesh and rots your psyche. And laugh. Laugh like everyone else who is doomed for the fire."

Nekara laughed and disappeared. Jonara fell to her knees, shook her fists in the air, and screamed in frustration. She then beat her fists into the ground. She beat and beat and would not stop until exhaustion overtook her.

The world above swirled around in red and blue. Jonara looked up and watched as people on the Elrod 402 campus moved quicker than normal, then regular speed, and then quicker than normal. Days became hours, hours became minutes, and minutes became seconds. When things moved quickly, the light was blue, when things moved in real time, the light was red. Jonara looked around for her mother and at first did not find her. But a passing, open-cab electric truck, like an electric golf cart with a truck bed, caught her attention, and Jonara realized her mother was the driver. Jonara latched onto the side of the truck as it passed, and she pulled herself into the passenger's seat.

"Mommy?" Jonara called. "Mommy, can you hear me?"

Evanita did not have the Moissan Ruby and so could not hear Jonara as she had done before. But something else seemed strange to Jonara. As Evanita drove past friendly de-tainees who waved, "Hello," to Evanita, Evanita gave no reply and instead ignored them.

"Mommy, what's wrong?" Jonara asked.

Evanita pressed a button on a hand-held radio terminal (a terminal with a built-in scanner) that was docked on her dashboard. The terminal displayed text, "Grenjet, G041. Pick up pallet 00312." Evanita pressed another button on the terminal to acknowledge the instruction. Another text displayed, "Carson confirms instruction received."

"Mommy," Jonara called.

Evanita drove the electric truck up a ramp and onto a scissors lift under the belly of Grenjet. Evanita removed the radio terminal scanner from the dashboard, aimed at the barcode on the scissors lift, and scanned. The terminal displayed text, "Carson on Grenjet lift 1." The scissors lift elevated Evanita and her truck up to and into the belly of the Grenjet through an opening. Evanita scanned a bar code on a post in Grenjet. The terminal displayed text, "Carson ready for Grenjet entry."

Evanita drove the electric truck from the scissors lift into Grenjet's cargo hold. Jonara looked around as Evanita drove the length of the hold. Closest to the scissors lift opening was a group of chairs where sick girls sat and waited. A girl exited a side office while a girl from the group of chairs went into the same side office. The girl coming out of the side office walked over to a group of cots where sick girls rested. Girls coughed, girls wheezed, girls had open sores, and girls had unkept hair. Evanita's truck continued down the path. Jonara noticed an increasingly pungent smell, like a full dumpster that had sat around too long. With no facial expression, Evanita took a smelling salt from the truck's dashboard to her nose, inhaled, and returned the smelling salt to the dash.

The smell grew worse. Cots lined each side of the aisleway, and the girls in them looked progressively worse. Some convulsed while some rolled over and vomited into pots. The line of cots was reaching an end. Girls in cots near the end were completely covered and did not move. Cots at the end were empty with sheets neatly made and tucked in. Evanita's truck passed through an archway into a storage area with long, rectangular, wooden boxes resting on pallets. The smell changed. Instead of smelling like a dumpster, the storage area smelled like an old high school biology lab.

Evanita reached a loading dock. She backed the truck to the dock, picked up her radio terminal, and scanned the barcode at the dock. The terminal displayed text, "Carson at Grenjet loading dock 3. Beginning detainee transfer."

An automated crane successively picked up one rectangular box after another and loaded them onto Evanita's electric truck. As each box was placed on the truck, Evanita scanned the box's barcode, and the terminal successively displayed text, "Riggs transferred. J. Smith transferred. Barnett transferred. C. T. Jones transferred."

Jonara watched as four long rectangular boxes were strapped onto Evanita's electric truck by an automated banding machine. Evanita scanned the barcode on the band now holding the rectangular boxes to the truck. The terminal displayed text, "4 detainee(s) successfully loaded onto Carson truck."

"These are coffins!" Jonara yelled. "These girls are dead! Grenjet is a death tube! Mommy! Get out of here! Get out now!"

Evanita turned the electric truck around and drove down the same aisleway from where she came. She put the smelling salt to her nose as she drove past the tidy cots, past the sickly girls, the less sickly girls, the side office, and the chair of waiting girls. Evanita returned the smelling salt to the dashboard and piloted the truck to the scissors lift. She scanned a different barcode. The terminal displayed text, "Carson exiting Grenjet with 4 detainee(s) for transfer." The scissors lift lowered Evanita's truck to the ground. Evanita drove off the lift, down the ramp, and across the compound.

"Disposable detainees," Nekara said as she appeared next to Jonara.

"This is murder!" Jonara said. "These girls are being killed in the green jet and hauled away. How can O Grammeni get away with this? How will she explain the disappearance of registered detainees?"

"She doesn't have to explain or fear repercussions," Nekara said.

"That's impossible. Parents will notice when their children are suddenly not available for visits. And what about when detainees are due for release?" Jonara asked.

"This is their release," Nekara said. "No, this compound is a business. Its purpose is to make money, and it will seek out and exploit any opportunity to do so. It's the invisible hand of death-from-greed. Not quite as exciting as raw hatred or physical battle, but it does have its own subtle taste."

"Subtle taste!? Is that what you call this? This is a holocaust!" Jonara said. "How can my mommy be a part of it?"

"She's been dehumanized," Nekara said. "She's a part in a machine. She has been programmed to do her part and only her part, and to believe that her part alone causes no harm. Others do evil, not her. Evil is something understood by the soul, but her soul is divided from her body. Your mother is an automaton."

"No!" Jonara yelled. "Mommy! Come back to the living!"

Evanita drove inside a building and next to a box-van. She scanned a barcode on a crane by the van. The terminal displayed text, "Carson truck by loading van. Begin detainee transfer."

A crane cut through the band around the four coffins and moved each coffin from Evanita's truck into the box truck. The box truck already contained eight coffins, and with Evanita's new load, the count increased to twelve. Evanita scanned the barcode on the bed of her truck. The terminal displayed text, "Carson truck empty. Proceed to Bloomjet."

Evanita's truck exited the small building and drove toward Bloomjet.

"I feel like singing, 'A Hunting We Will Go'," Nekara said.

"Please don't," Jonara said. "There's enough misery without having to listen to your singing."

Evanita reached the scissors lift at Bloomjet and scanned the barcode on the lift. The lift raised Evanita and her truck up to and inside the belly of the jumbo jet.

"You are being transferred to Grenjet for treatment," Ox-One said to the homeless girls. "Get aboard the truck."

"This is the homeless jet," Jonara said. "These girls don't belong on Grenjet. That's a graveyard."

The girls piled into the bed of the truck. Ox-One pressed a button, and the scissors lift lowered the electric truck.

"They are going for 'treatment'," Nekara said. "This is the result of any power disposing of another."

"These girls have no power. They're stuck," Jonara said.

Nekara laughed.

"All girls have power," Nekara said. "They've only been told they don't, and so they do not believe in themselves. It's so pathetic and hilarious at the same time—that time and history repeats itself no matter what part of the universe I'm in!"

The scissors lift reached the ground. Evanita drove off the lift, down the ramp, and over to Grenjet where she ascended with the scissors lift into Grenjet as she did before. At the top, Evanita delivered the girls to chairs in the waiting area. Evanita drove back to the scissors lift, scanned a barcode, and the scissors lift lowered her to the ground.

"Those girls are going to their death. I say it again and again, but I cannot believe it," Jonara said.

"They are being 'cared for'," Nekara said. "The best quality of care. Like your mother."

"Your sour soup of lies is making me puke!" Jonara said.

"Oh come now, Jonara. Don't you think that your world needs a thinning of the herd every now and then? Your O Grammeni is doing your world a favor. Those who have no ambition will simply become homeless and drift into Portland, where the Elrod 402 will process them. It's good business."

"This is not good business!" Jonara retorted.

"O Grammeni would disagree," Nekara said. "She receives grant money for each homeless girl processed. The 'Money for Misguided' program is what it's called."

"No government would pay her to kill people," Jonara said.

"They don't pay O Grammeni to kill girls, they pay her to 'process' them. Only O Grammeni and her top crew know the methods of processing. She calls it, 'Competitive Advantage'."

"She's the killer," Jonara said.

"She's the businessperson. And she doesn't keep it for herself. She's an active supporter of local restaurants, movie theaters, illegal drug trade, and illegal weapons financing."

"Yeah, illegal," Jonara said.

"How else can one get ahead in your world?" Nekara asked. "Do you think sticking up for morals and supporting fairness returns political advantage? Look at where it got your mother. She's a zombie pawn."

Evanita drove the truck over to Cafederijet. A scissors lift elevated her truck into the cargo bay. Evanita scanned a barcode. Another detainee drove over with a pallet on her forklift and loaded it on Evanita's truck bed. The pallet contained medical equipment. The detainee drove her forklift a short ways and returned with another pallet of medical equipment. And another, and another.

"What's going on here?" Jonara yelled. "Where is this medical equipment going?"

"The infirmary was shut down," Nekara said. "All Barians were fired from their jobs. So were Macrons. Detainees run the kitchen."

"Who runs the infirmary?" Jonara asked.

"As I said," Nekara said. "It was shut down."

"But if a girl gets sick and needs medicine, then what?"

"She goes to Grenjet for 'treatment'," Nekara said. "Or she learns to improve her own health."

"That's pathetic," Jonara said.

"That's business by dehumanization. With no ethical oversight, the unrelenting cost cuts and reduced employees take hold with an ever-greedy desire for increased profits," Nekara said as she clasped and rubbed her hands in excitement. "Mass-produced misery for the masses."

"It's got to end!" Jonara said. "Someone needs to stop it!"

"No one will," Nekara said. "Because no one cares. The blind eye only sees money."

"Progress will be made," Jonara said. "It will!"

"Let's see how much 'progress' is made, shall we?"

Nekara passed her right hand in the air from left to right while her left touched her abdomen. The world swirled in grays, the days whirled by, and Jonara found herself in another time but in the same place.

2007 Nov 13, Tue. Elrod 402 Campus. Portland, Oregon.

Jonara appeared in the passenger's seat of the electric truck with Evanita driving it. Nekara was not in sight. Evanita waited in the Grenjet storage area as a crane loaded four coffins onto her truck bed. A banding machine strapped the coffins to the bed, and Evanita scanned the barcode on the band. The terminal displayed text, "4 detainee(s) successfully loaded onto Carson truck."

Evanita turned the truck around and drove the length of Grenjet. To Jonara's horror, the scene looked the same as before. Different girls, but the same layout—girls arriving and waiting in chairs, girls going into a side office, girls being assigned to cots, and girls progressively moving from early-stage cots to later-stage cots. Evanita drove to the scissors lift and scanned a barcode. The lift lowered her to the ground. Evanita drove to the small building where the crane, as before, loaded the coffins to the box truck. The terminal displayed text, "4 detainee(s) successfully loaded from Carson truck. Proceed to Redjet."

Evanita drove to Redjet and drove onto the scissors lift. Evanita scanned a barcode on the lift, and the truck ascended to the cargo hold of Redjet. The terminal displayed text, "Gather things from room and place on Carson truck."

Evanita walked up to her room and placed her things in two large duffle bags.

"So this is it," Calico said. "The old goodbye. Does the Calico get a hug?"

Evanita stood for a moment and held out her arms like a robot.

"Forget it," Calico said.

Evanita slung her duffle bags over her shoulder and walked down the hall. The other residents did not notice her departure and so offered no words of health or illness. Evanita placed her bags in the truck's bed and returned to the driver's seat. She scanned the barcode to descend. The scissors lift lowered the truck to the ground. The terminal displayed text, "Proceed to security van at double-gate."

Evanita followed the instructions and drove to a security van awaiting her at the security gate. The terminal displayed text, "Hand terminal to Ox-Two and follow her instructions."

Evanita gave the hand-held radio terminal to Ox-Two. Ox-Two attached it to her belt and led Evanita into the security van. Ox-Two then drove the van through the double-gate and parked at Whalejet. Ox-Two led Evanita up the steps and into W218—the visiting room where Evanita had met with Johnny and her family over the course of the past year. But now Evanita's time was up.

"Evanita!" Eva, Geneva, and Johnny said.

Evanita lifted her arms in robot fashion as she did for Calico.

"Evanita!" Eva called. "It's your mother!"

Evanita gave no special emotional response.

"These are the release papers," Ox-Two said. "By signing these, you accept responsibility for Evanita's care."

"And who's responsible for making my daughter withdrawn and sullen?" Eva asked.

"Eva, not here," Geneva said. "Remember the other time. Evanita's going home with us. Let's keep it that way."

Eva hugged Evanita. Then Geneva hugged Evanita, and finally Johnny hugged Evanita.

"We'll help her," Johnny said.

Eva held the release papers in her hand, unsigned.

"Eva, the papers. Sign them will you? We can protest later if need be," Geneva said.

Eva signed the papers in disgust and gave them to Ox-Two.

"It's time to go home, Evanita," Johnny said.

Johnny helped Evanita from Whalejet, down the steps, and into the back of Eva's car. Geneva and Eva walked down the Whalejet steps and to Eva's car. Geneva entered the front passenger seat. Eva opened the driver's door and made a motion to enter and sit, but she rethought her movement. She stood firmly by the door, held up a fist, and shook it at the detention center.

CHAPTER 5

Asturias Visit

2023 Oct 8, Sun Afnoon. Corpus Christi, Texas.

"Jonara?" Johnny said. "The boat ride is over. Come along, it's time we return to land."

Jonara looked around. She was no longer at the Elrod 402. She was back at Corpus Christi Bay. Crowds dispersed from the meeting and lined up at registration booths.

"What are the people doing?" Jonara asked as the two walked on land.

"They are registering for the vitacepticals," Johnny said.

"I registered for us," Greg said as he approached Jonara.

"You can't. We're not married, and I never said you could register for me," Jonara said.

"All the same, I got a head start. You never can plan too far into the future," Greg said. "After we marry, we'll be all set for making babies."

"I'll never marry you," Jonara said.

"You know, it's a shame the Church didn't have these vitacepticals in the Middle Ages," Greg said. "With the money they make, the Church wouldn't have needed indulgences."

"Indulgences were a mistake and lasted for a very short time," Johnny said. "Once Spain grew rich from Fernanica—later the Americas—the Church had all the money it needed."

"Yeah, whatever," Greg said. "Hey Mr. Pindus—have you registered for a vitaceptical yet?"

"No, we'll register when we return to Portland," Johnny said.

"They'll let you register here. You can come down and visit with Jonara whenever you wish to plan a child," Greg said. "And I'll be here to enjoy your company."

Greg winked at Jonara.

"Thank you no. Long-distance conception is not for us," Johnny said.

"Daddy," Jonara said. "Do you think we'll ever return to Corpus Christi after we go back to Portland?"

"What do you mean?" Johnny asked.

"I mean, after you sell Nanna Geneva's house," Jonara said. "There's no one to visit down here for you and Mommy. But as for me, there's someone I want to see. I don't think she'll want to see me, though. And no, I don't want to see you again, Greg."

"You'll change," Greg said.

"Jonara," Johnny said. "You're not making sense. Your Nanna Geneva may be in the hospital, but she's not going to a nursing home. She'll return home in a week or so. We can't sell her house. Where would she live?"

"Nanna Geneva is alive?" Jonara asked. "But I went to her funeral! Daddy! How?"

"Silly Jonara," Johnny said. "That bump on your head really skewed your thinking. Or was this a vision you had while looking in the pseudo-ruby?"

"I...I don't know," Jonara said.

"Tell you what," Johnny said. "Why don't we visit Nanna Geneva in the hospital? It would be a pleasant surprise for her since you never showed interest in a relationship with her before."

"I didn't?" Jonara asked. "I wonder why not?"

"Too interested in your own world. Friends, celebrity gossip, and fashion," Johnny said. "You might be surprised to find out your Nanna Geneva was a young girl once."

"I know," Jonara said. "And it was difficult for her. Not like my life at all."

Johnny gave Jonara a funny look.

"For a moment there, Jonara, you sounded about twenty years older than you really are," Johnny said. "Let's go. We'll catch a bus to the hospital."

Johnny called Evanita on his cell phone and let her know about his plans. Johnny and Jonara took a city bus to the hospital, walked through reception, and went up to Geneva's room.

Geneva looked much healthier than she did in the other timeline.

"Nanna Geneva!" Jonara said.

Jonara ran to Geneva's side and hugged her. Geneva placed
her book down and hugged Jonara as best she could.

"You can't die!" Jonara said.

"I won't—yet," Geneva said. "My gallbladder surgery was
successful. I had a setback with an infection, but it's under
control. The doctors want to make sure there are no more set-
backs, so I'm stuck in here until next week. Did you go down to
Corpus Christi Bay with your parents?"

"Yes, I did," Jonara said. "And I'm sorry I did."

"Oh don't be," Geneva said. "Don't be afraid."

"I'm not afraid," Jonara said. "I think it's wrong."

"Oh child! You will learn that life is not so easily split into
right and wrong. We do the best we can with what we have and
what we can do," Geneva said.

"And this is for the best?" Jonara asked.

"Maybe yes, maybe no. But we must try," Geneva said.
"People argue the most about what they do not know or understand. Vitacepticals have never been tried. After Saturday, the
old arguments will end."

"And the new ones will begin!" Jonara said.

"That's the way of people," Geneva said. "But try not to obsess about it. Come now, tell me about yourself. What have you
been doing lately? Do you study your catechism?"

"Grandma, I'm not Catholic! I never was!" Jonara said.

Geneva looked at Johnny as if to ask him about Jonara's
odd behavior.

"She's been like this since the concussion," Johnny said.

"Oh," Geneva said.

"She says she's from another timeline," Johnny said. "But I
think she's been imagining things."

"What's that around your neck?" Geneva asked. "It looks
like a ruby."

"I call it a Water Ruby," Jonara said.

"It's costume jewelry," Johnny said. "She's had it—"

"Since she was a little girl," Geneva said. "I remember the photographs of you, Jonara. It's a very beautiful ruby. May I see it?"

Jonara handed the Moissan Ruby to Geneva.

"Hold it up to the light," Jonara said. "It sparkles."

Geneva held it up to the light.

"It does sparkle," Geneva said. "I've never seen a fake—I mean a special ruby—sparkle like this. I still don't understand why you call it a ruby, though. It looks more like an emerald. Still, it reminds me of something from my youth. But I can't remember what. Where did I see sparkling stones before? I'm thinking of a cave, but I've never been in a cave before. My grandfather, Martin Sixpence, was a miner, but he never allowed me in caves. He didn't want to risk me getting trapped in one."

"Nanna Geneva! People around here act like robots. I'm trapped!" Jonara said. "I don't belong here! Can you help me get back to my time?"

Geneva looked at Johnny. Johnny shrugged his shoulders.

"Maybe if you tell Jonara a story," Johnny suggested.

"A story," Geneva said. "I know many stories from Catholic literature."

"No, don't tell me anything like that," Jonara said. "I don't want to know."

"Maybe a personal story would be better," Johnny suggested.

Geneva held the Moissan Ruby to the light and started to speak. Colors in front of Jonara swirled and turned to gray as she traveled to another time and place.

2007 Dec 5, Wed. Eva's House. Portland, Oregon.

"I'm still against this idea," Eva said. "I don't want my daughter and mother in a plane crash like the one we were in back in 1970."

"Technology is much better today than it was thirty-seven years ago," Geneva said. "But I'm surprised you remember that day we crashed on the Montseny Mountains."

"How can I forget? I remember everything that happened," Eva said. "The delay in England, flying in that strange crate, the screaming people when we crashed, the fire, and the cold mountain."

"Well we won't be flying anywhere near those mountains," Geneva said. "EasyJet will carry us directly from London to Castrillón. That's in the Asturias province. From there we'll rent a car and drive to Carreña. It's perfectly safe."

"Driving in a foreign country?" Eva said. "How safe can that be?"

"The United States is a foreign country to me," Geneva said. "Spain is home. I trust home, especially now that Franco—"

"I know, now that Franco is dead. He died in 1975. Spain has been a democracy since 1978. Please don't bring it up again as you have every year of my life since then," Eva said.

"I don't have to. You do," Geneva smiled.

"Evanita?" Eva called.

Evanita walked downstairs with her luggage.

"Do you want to go for a quick run before you leave?" Eva asked.

Evanita shook her head no.

"I don't know if she'll ever snap out of this apathy," Eva said. "She doesn't even ask about a father. Before Elrod, she asked every day."

"There is one place I know that will help her," Geneva said. "And it's in Carreña."

"I hope you're not referring to the myth of that abandoned castle," Eva said.

"It's not abandoned. It's run by the sisters of St. Renata's Abbey," Geneva said.

"Catholic. I might have known," Eva said. "I'm doubtful a superstition will help, but maybe a change of scenery will do her good."

"It will," Geneva said. "Come along, Evanita. It's time to catch our flight to New York. Eva, are you giving us a ride to the airport?"

"Yes, I am," Eva said. "But Johnny isn't here yet. What's keeping him?"

"Let's load your luggage, Evanita," Geneva said.

Evanita carried her luggage outside to the trunk of Eva's car. Eva popped the lid open, and Evanita placed her luggage next to Geneva's. At that moment, Johnny drove up.

"It's about time!" Eva shouted. "Where have you been?"

"I stopped by the store to buy new socks," Johnny said. "I never have enough socks. Do I have time to wash and dry them here?"

"No, there's no time," Eva said. "Transfer your luggage. I need to get you three to the airport right this moment."

Johnny transferred his luggage and sat in the back seat with Evanita. Geneva sat in the front passenger seat, and Eva drove the three toward the airport.

"Are you planning on using superstition in Spain?" Eva asked during the ride to the airport.

"Superstition?" Geneva asked. "Whatever are you talking about?"

"I saw the viola case in the trunk, Mother," Eva said.

"It's a *viola de gamba*," Geneva said. "And yes, I plan to use it if necessary. But the diary reading will be necessary for sure."

"The diary too?" Eva asked. "When does it end?"

"When everyone in this world grows up and acquires a little civility, that's when," Geneva said.

Eva dropped off the three without further conversation except for a big hug and wishes of a safe trip to Evanita. As for the air journey from Portland to Spain, there is little to tell. Jonara watched as the airplane flew by Mount Hood on the Cascades. She remembered seeing the Three Sisters a little south and how she thought of her three maternal ancestors—Evanita, Eva, and Geneva as being like the Three Sisters. But on this flight, there was only Mount Hood. Jonara felt empty. One mountain, one way, one narrow means of life, if one could call it a life. How long ago it seemed when Jonara asked her father why adults lie about things like Santa Claus and the Easter Bunny. Was life so desolate and barren that stories were the only way to survive, to keep the emptiness of the universe from bleeding life out of a person? It was a thought she had before, but she had it again during this plane trip, and it would not go away.

The plane continued nonstop to New York. The three and Jonara departed one jet and boarded another for the flight across the Atlantic. Again, there is little to tell. Geneva, Evanita, and Johnny slept for most of the journey over. Jonara felt the emptiness of the flight—no drama, no crashing, nothing. Not even a surprise visit from Nekara to stir up the day.

Jonara lost track of the day and the time. The three and Jonara landed in London, transferred to EasyJet, and flew to Castrillón. It was now Thursday.

2007 Dec 6, Thu. Castrillón, Asturias Province, Spain.

"Are we going to Carreña today?" Johnny asked.

"Yes, but not immediately," Geneva said. "We will travel along the coastline of the Bay of Biscay toward Carreña. At the end of the day, we'll retire to a hotel in Carreña where we have reservations."

"The Bay of Biscay is the part of the Atlantic Ocean on the northern coast of Spain and the western coast of France," Johnny said. "Isn't that interesting, Evanita?"

"Whatever," Evanita said blandly.

Jonara rode with Geneva, Evanita, and Johnny in a rental car on a road leading to the coast. The group exited the car and walked on the sandy beach.

"It's a nice day," Johnny said. "It's in the fifties, there's no rain, and the beach is beautiful. It reminds me of Portland."

"The climates here and in Portland are similar," Geneva said.

"Do you know why they are similar?" Johnny asked Evanita.

Evanita did not reply.

"Both have what's known as an oceanic climate," Johnny said. "Mild winters and cool summers."

"Yeah," Evanita replied listlessly.

"I've always loved the Bay of Biscay," Geneva said. "The sand, the breeze, the waves, and the rocks."

"The landscape behind us is beautiful," Johnny said. "The houses are white with orange roofs. It's not like America where houses are thrown up haphazardly with whatever colors the builder feels like. Here, the houses become the landscape instead of ruining it. What do you think, Evanita?"

"Landscape, whatever," Evanita said.

"Let's go to another part of the coast," Geneva said. "Maybe that will help."

Jonara followed the three to another part of the coast along the Bay of Biscay. The four exited the car and walked down a path to an escarpment along the ocean. Waves splashed up to the escarpment and over, getting the three wet. Geneva and Johnny laughed.

"Careful!" Geneva said. "The waves can be powerful at times."

"We're just a little wet," Johnny said. "We'll be fine. Wasn't it fun, Evanita? Wasn't the splash fun?"

"Hmph," Evanita said.

"We got a *hmph* out of her," Johnny said.

"Johnny," said Geneva. "What do you make of these rocks?"

"Layers and layers of sedimentary rock," Johnny said. "But they're not flat. Some are helical. Others point straight up. It's like some force uprooted them and pointed them to the sky. Year after year of cycles that built the sedimentary layers only to be thrown into upheaval in one stroke. And here they are on the shores of the Bay of Biscay with wave after wave crashing upon them."

"What about life, Johnny?" Geneva said.

"Life?" he asked.

"Yes. The life in the sedimentary layers," Geneva said.

Johnny picked up a bit of sedimentary rock and looked at it.

"Fossils," Johnny said. "You mean the fossils."

"Yes. If they were alive today, what would they think about the rocks?" Geneva asked.

"Now that's an interesting question," Johnny said. "Life back then didn't know what would happen after death. The creatures were born, they grew, reproduced, and died. They only knew their living environment. If they realized they would die, they might understand that they'd fall to the bottom of the ancient sea. But they wouldn't know the long-term geological effects. They wouldn't know about layers building on layers, that their bodies would become fossilized, that the seas would change, the tectonic plates would move, and their fossilized bodies would be shifted around in these striated rocks such that they would be lifted out of the seas and pointed to the sky."

"What about water life today?" Geneva asked. "What will become of them?"

"Some will be eaten by predators, but others will become fossilized in layers like these ancient animals," Johnny explained. "In time, layers will build up, ocean floors will lift out of the water, and layered rocks will angle up to the sky."

"Does life in the ocean today think about those things?" Geneva asked.

"The simple life forms can't, of course, but even the most intelligent animals don't think about such things. They are too busy living out their lives in the present," Johnny said.

"Does that include people?" Geneva asked.

"Yes, it does," Johnny said.

Evanita took the fossil from Johnny's hand. She stared at it and held it up to the sky as if taking it from its old life and presenting it to the gods of the sky. She then pulled her arm back and threw the fossil into the water.

"Why did you do that, Evanita?" Geneva asked.

"Too much talking," Evanita said.

Johnny opened his mouth to protest, but Geneva shushed him.

"Come along," Geneva said. "Let's go to the next shoreline."

Jonara followed the three back to the rental and on to another part of the shoreline where a river emptied into the ocean. Jonara followed the three onto a pier.

"This is a port city," Geneva said. "Boats come and go from the river to the ocean and back. Many of these piers are quite old. So are many of the buildings."

"Some of these buildings look hundreds of years old," Johnny said. "They have existed through many historical events—Franco's regime, the World Wars, the Spanish Civil War, royal kingdoms, the Moors, the Visigoths, the ancient Romans, and the Celts. I'm sure I left out a few."

"Just a few," Geneva said.

"But each set of people left something behind," Johnny said. "They left a fossil of their lives, building upon the society that already existed, like layers of sediment, until today when we see all their different layers that are exposed to us."

"For those who wish to see the layers," Geneva said.

"Yes, yes!" Johnny said. "Is that like, 'Those who ignore history are doomed to repeat it'?"

Geneva laughed.

"I think you've twisted the metaphor a little," Geneva said.

"Metaphoric rock!" Johnny said. "Or is it metamorphic rock? No, metamorphic rock is something completely different. With metamorphic rock, old rock is heated and melted until it loses its layers. Its history of formation—its identity—is erased."

"Evanita?" Geneva asked. "What do you think?"

"Metaphoric rock," Evanita repeated like a parrot.

"Come," Geneva said. "Let's get something to eat."

Jonara followed the three into a restaurant serving fish and lots of it. The three ordered their meals with Evanita repeating Johnny's order. All had fish. Their food was prepared and delivered, and the three ate. Geneva also ordered red wine for the three.

"These port towns always have great fish," Geneva said. "The fish is so fresh."

"The wine is good too," Johnny said. "Although I hate to think what Ms. Eva would say."

"She would complain," Geneva said. "If wine isn't from France or Oregon, it isn't worth drinking, according to my daughter."

"Evanita, do you like the wine?" Johnny asked.

"Fruity," Evanita replied.

"That's the first positive expression I've heard from you, Evanita," Geneva said. "Spanish wine captures the essence of Spain—its people, its culture, its history, and its soul."

"It's sedimentary food," Johnny said.

Geneva laughed.

"You won't find a single person referring to her red wine as sedimentary food. But I understand your appreciation," Geneva said. "Evanita—can you taste the culture of Spain in your wine?"

"It's fruity," Evanita said. "That's all."

"Well, we can't expect overnight improvement," Geneva said. "But I had hoped for more."

"Maybe we can," Johnny said.

Johnny removed the Moissan Ruby from inside his shirt. He held it in his left fist and shook it while his right hand touched Evanita's forehead. Johnny closed his eyes and concentrated. After a few moments, he removed his right hand from her forehead and replaced the Moissan Ruby inside his shirt.

"Nothing," Johnny said. "Like newly bleached paper."

"Well, it was a good try," Geneva said. "Come along. Let's finish up."

Jonara followed the three from the restaurant into the rental car. Geneva followed winding paths up and down hills. She parked the car and led the group to a small waterfall.

"It's a pretty waterfall," Johnny said. "See how the plants cling precariously next to the rockface where the water falls to the pond below?"

"That pond is technically part of the river," Geneva said. "But this lower part of the river is much wider and calmer than the upper part."

"It forms a delta," Johnny said, "with sandy shorelines. Look—it continues to widen until it reaches the sea. The river is fresh water. It carries food and sediment. But once it reaches the sea, it dumps its sediment and food. It mixes with salty seawater and is lost to the ocean's vastness."

"Why are we here?" Evanita asked.

"This is you," Geneva said. "You are the delta after the waterfall but before the ocean. If you continue as the delta does, you will eventually be lost to the ocean."

"No," Evanita said in disbelief.

"Come along. Let's walk upstream," Geneva said.

Jonara followed the three upstream along the small river.

"You see, this river is very active. Full of bends, eddies, backwashes, rapids, and jutting rocks," Geneva explained. "This river is lively. Look—do you see the fish jumping out of the water?"

"I've heard of fish swimming to spawn, but how can they swim up the waterfall?" Johnny asked.

"They don't," Geneva said. "They come from upstream. But the river is so turbulent that it motivates them to jump out of the water. Fortunately for them, they land right back in the river. Evanita—this is what your life was like before the Elrod 402 and before the fire. You were like this lively river—running around, enjoying the company of your friends, and engaging in highly animated conversations with your mother. Do you remember the one question you posed to your mother—repeatedly?"

"Vaguely," Evanita said. "Something about my father."

"Yes," Geneva said. "You always wanted to know who your father was. Your mother says you have no father. Evanita—do you want to know the answer to the riddle of your biological parents?"

"It doesn't matter anymore," Evanita said. "I'll be the same either way."

"Do you really believe that?" Geneva asked. "Isn't there some part of the old Evanita still alive who wants to bubble to the surface and find out?"

"You said it. I'm the delta. It's just a matter of time before the sea of society swallows me up," Evanita said.

"That was a metaphor," Geneva said. "But it doesn't have to be that way. You have free will. You have choice."

"Where?" Evanita asked. "Using the metaphor of this river, all happy-go-lucky people eventually go flying off a cliff into a bland delta to be consumed by the sea. Does a river have free choice?"

"It doesn't," Geneva said. "But you are only a river if you allow yourself to be one. The river is what happens when forces of the land push you into a narrow band from both sides."

"And if it doesn't push, I'm a bland delta. So much for free choice," Evanita said.

"It's no use," Johnny said. "She was like this when we argued religion."

Evanita picked up a small branch, broke it in half, and threw one half into the river. She watched it float downstream and out of sight. Then she threw out the other half.

"I'm like that floating branch," Evanita said. "I have no more control over my destination than anything else floating in the river."

Johnny reached out to hug Evanita, but she turned her back on the river and walked away.

"Let's go," Geneva said to Johnny. "There's one more place I want to show Evanita before we visit the abbey."

Jonara followed the three back to the rental car. Geneva drove from the waterfall to Bricias where she turned onto highway AS-115 and proceeded south past mountain peak, farm, river, and town.

"The countryside is very beautiful," Johnny said. "All the world's climates in one country. Look! A horse and pony farm! Do you see them, Evanita? Andalusians and Asturcons!"

"The horse prison," Evanita said.

"Come now," Geneva said. "These horses and ponies will make their new owners happy, and they will be happy. Spaniards take good care of their horses and ponies."

The group reached the end of AS-115 and turned east on highway AS-114.

"Where are we going?" Evanita asked.

"To those white peaks ahead on your right," Geneva said.

"The Peaks of Europe," Johnny said. "Are we going to hike? We don't have the equipment."

"We won't hike," Geneva said. "We will drive on mountain roads."

The group continued east on AS-114.

"There's Carreña on the left!" Johnny said. "We're passing it!"

"We'll return to it," Geneva said. "But first the Peaks of Europe."

"Look, Evanita! There's a castle on our left. See? It's on that hill," Johnny said.

"That's St. Renata's Abbey," Geneva said. "We will visit the abbey tomorrow."

The group continued east past Poo de Cabrales and into Las Arenas.

"Las Arenas is very busy in the summer," Geneva said. "Many tourists stay here and hike in the Peaks. There are many such foot trails in the Peaks of Europe. And for those like me who cannot walk long distances on foot, there are pony rides. But I will give you a taste of the peaks. Here—we'll turn south on AS-264."

The group traveled south on AS-264 until it reached the beginning of the Peaks of Europe National Park. From there they continued south through a valley toward Bulnes. On each side of the valley stood tall, massive mountain peaks.

"They're so tall, so threatening, and so majestic," Johnny said. "I feel humbled traveling between these huge mountain peaks. Are you scared, Evanita?"

"No. It's all just rock," Evanita said.

The group reached Bulnes and parked.

"We will walk a short ways," Geneva said. "As I said, there are many hiking paths through the Peaks. There are some here, too. There's something here I want to show you. Don't worry— we won't walk far—my old bones won't permit it."

Jonara followed the group as Geneva led them up the valley along a small river. Ancient buildings stood next to the river.

"At one time," Johnny said, "the Celts were the only humans in these parts."

"Yes, Johnny. The Celts were everywhere in these mountains. Many Spaniards in these parts have Celtic blood in them," Geneva said.

"It defies the stereotype of the Spanish Conquistadors who conquered the New World," Johnny said.

"It does," Geneva said.

"Living by the river was valuable in ancient times," Johnny said. "People used the water for all sorts of things. The earliest of civilizations built communities by rivers—the Nile, the Tigris-Euphrates, the Indus, and the Yellow-Yangzi. These communities used the river water for agriculture and easy transportation."

"You'll find these mountain rivers aren't so good for major transportation," Geneva laughed.

"No, but they are useful for agriculture," Johnny said. "Look—a water mill!"

"It's all so old fashioned and unnecessary now-a-days," Evanita said.

"Appreciate the past, Evanita. Life was difficult, and people died young for thousands of years," Geneva said. "Come now—we are almost there."

The four walked a little farther and reached a waterfall.

"Another waterfall? Didn't we already do that metaphor before? The waterfall is the last part of life before being swallowed up in the sea," Evanita said.

"That's what you believe, but this waterfall is different," Geneva said.

"There is no delta," Johnny said. "And it doesn't go to the sea—yet. It's just a waterfall going back into a river. And the river continues down the mountain where it helps communities thrive."

"Grandma, you told me I was the delta," Evanita said.

"You are because you believe you are. But you are young. Your youth is more in line with this waterfall," Geneva said. "If you think of a river as representative of life, then life is born in the mountains. The path down the mountain is not easy—there are many rocky surfaces, boulders, outcroppings, and sudden drops as in this waterfall. But look—the river continues on with more twists, rocky surfaces, boulders, and other challenging paths. The river does not give up. It continues the path down until it reaches a larger stretch of valley where it calms down. Evanita—you believe you are a delta ready for the sea, but you are really like this river going down the mountain. You have not seen the last waterfall. You will experience more as you get older. And along the way, you will meet people who are also going about their lives. They expect that you are still a part of the living, and they will treat you as such. Do not deny your life from them."

"And when the river reaches the valley?" Evanita asked. "What then? Are you saying adulthood is easy?"

"Adulthood isn't easy. No part of life is really that easy, although some stretches make it appear so. But by the time you grow up and experience these rocky slopes and quick changes, things will mellow out, because you'll be experienced enough to know what to expect in situations. Things will be hectic and stressful, yes, but things that once seemed bad and unfair will be more like things you plan for and make sure do not cause you harm."

"I guess I don't understand," Evanita said. "So you brought me all the way to Spain for this? I bet there are rivers and waterfalls in the United States."

"Yes, but the United States has very little European history. Your roots are in Spain whether you fully comprehend it or not," Geneva said. "But today's tour is only the beginning. It's getting late. We should return to Carreña and rest. Tomorrow we visit the abbey."

"The abbey, the abbey," Evanita said. "I went through all that religious stuff before. I visited the different churches. Each one had issues. Why should I see an abbey?"

"It's not just any sort of abbey," Geneva said. "It was once a castle, and inside there's a special cave I want you to see."

"Whatever," Evanita said.

Geneva led the group back to the car and drove down the mountain to highway AS-114. She turned west and drove to Carreña. The three checked into the Carreña Hotel with one room for Johnny and the other room for Geneva and Evanita. The three went back out for dinner, ate, returned to the hotel, and fell asleep.

2007 Dec 7, Fri. Carreña, Asturias Province, Spain.

The three woke up and ate a small breakfast in a restaurant next to the Carreña Hotel. After breakfast, Geneva insisted on returning to her room before embarking on their next adventure.

"Did you forget something?" Johnny asked as he and Evanita stood by the hotel room door awaiting Geneva's exit.

"No," Geneva said as she emerged from her room. "I want to take this with us. It's too precious to bring to the restaurant, which is why I didn't bring it with me to breakfast."

"I know that book," Johnny said. "It's your diary."

"A diary?" Evanita asked. "Whatever."

"It will prove very valuable, Evanita," Geneva said. "You'll see."

With Evanita, Johnny, and Jonara as passengers, Geneva drove the rental car up the small mountain east of Carreña. Geneva directed the car to a small parking area at the front of St. Renata's Abbey—the same castle where she had lived in the 1960s. Jonara followed the three across the drawbridge to the barbican. With the diary under her arm, Geneva pressed a button, and a young sister opened the door.

"Yes?" the sister asked.

"Hello," Geneva said. "My name is Geneva Carreña. This is my granddaughter, Evanita Carreña, and her friend, Johnny Pindus. We are here to visit the abbey."

"Geneva Carreña," the sister said. "You must know this is a private abbey. We do not hold tours for the public."

"I don't understand. St. Renata was always a public abbey. Tours were conducted. Visitors were welcome," Geneva said.

"Things have changed," the sister said. "The abbey is now private. Now if you'll excuse me."

"Wait, wait! Hear me out. I was once a sister here in the early 1960s," Geneva said. "I want to show my granddaughter and her friend where I spent time in the grist mill."

"You are Sister Geneva?" the sister asked.

"You've heard of me?" Geneva asked back.

"No," she replied.

"Some of the other sisters would recognize me. I knew Sister Rosa very well," Geneva said.

"Sister Rosa? There's no one here by that name," the sister said.

"She ran this abbey in the early 1960s," Geneva said. "Surely you have records."

"We have records. I am new here and have not studied them all," the young sister said.

"What about Sister Charlene? Is she here?" Geneva asked.

"There is a Sister Charlene here, but she is wheelchair-bound and in seclusion," the sister said. "She does not accept visitors."

"You must allow me to see her," Geneva said. "We have come from the United States just for this visit."

"Sister Geneva," the young girl said. "I will pass your message on to Sister Charlene. If she is willing, she will visit with you. You may wait inside the barbican."

"Thank you," Geneva said.

The young sister closed the door, leaving Geneva, Evanita, Johnny, and Jonara in the barbican. Five minutes passed. Then ten.

"I don't know what's taking so long," Geneva said. "I have no patience for waiting."

"Grandma," Evanita said. "I would like to walk along the moat. Do you mind?"

"Not at all, please do," Geneva said. "I'll wait here for Sister Charlene."

"I'll go with you," Johnny said.

Jonara followed her parents as they walked along the moat on the east side of the outer wall.

"What are you thinking?" Johnny asked Evanita.

"Not much," Evanita said.

"Do you still love me?" Johnny asked.

Evanita looked in his eyes.

"I don't know," Evanita said.

The two continued walking along the moat until they reached the mountain face.

"This is where the water comes out of the castle and flows into the moat," Johnny said. "It's surprisingly clean. Why do you suppose that is?"

"Why should I care?" Evanita asked back. "Why do you keep asking me questions?"

"To keep your mind going," Johnny said. "I'm hoping you'll snap out of it."

"Snap out of what?" Evanita asked.

"Your mental rut," Johnny said. "Because you're in one."

"So now I'm required to perform for my supper, is that it?" Evanita asked. "I'm required to be bubbling with joy, overly talkative, expressing happiness with everything I see, hear, taste, touch, and smell despite how I really feel. I'm a television show for other people, an entertainer, an icon, a product to be marketed. No, Johnny, I'm not for sale."

"Wow," Johnny said.

"I'm not an idiot, Johnny," Evanita said. "If I speak little from time to time, it doesn't mean I'm an invalid."

"You're not an invalid," Johnny said. "I never said you were. You've gotten much smarter than I would have guessed while you were in the Elrod 402."

"And I'm to be faulted for intelligence?" Evanita asked. "What about you? You can recite the Latin name for every species of life on this planet. Intelligence? Perhaps. But I don't see anyone accusing you of being in a mental rut. I think you're trapped in a stereotypical treatment of me. And of women."

"What treatment?" Johnny asked. "What stereotype?"

"The stereotype that women are required to cheer up this dismal world while men can do whatever they want," Evanita said. "I think you're biased."

"Your grandmother thinks you need cheering up. Is she biased too?" Johnny asked.

"First, don't ever attempt to speak for my maternal ancestors," Evanita said. "Second, she's probably influenced too. She grew up in Spain when it was a dictatorship under a man. If that doesn't influence a woman, what does?"

"She seems very intelligent to me," Johnny said. "She doesn't seem like the type who can get brainwashed so easily."

"Whatever," Evanita said.

"I'm trying to cheer you up," Johnny said. "Is that also part of the stereotype?"

Evanita looked down at the moat. She picked up a small rock and tossed it in the water. Ripples carried through the semi-calm water.

"No, it's not," Evanita said.

Evanita walked over to Johnny, touched his neck, and pulled out the necklace chain with the Moissan Ruby. She lifted the necklace over his head, held the Moissan Ruby to the light, and stared at it.

"I've never taken the time to look at this stone closely," Evanita said. "There's something swirling inside. It's hypnotic, though I suppose it couldn't affect me. I have this strange memory that it helped you heal my legs when I first served time in the Elrod."

"It did," Johnny said. "The stone has special powers."

"It violates all laws of science," Evanita said. "But if it does have power, how do you energize it? Do you place a coin battery in it?"

"You don't have to mock me," Johnny said. "This stone is not from this world."

"And other worlds are allowed to violate the laws of physics?" Evanita said. "Power is power no matter where you are."

"But this is powered by something I don't understand," Johnny said.

"Does it run low on power? It must," Evanita said.

"It does," Johnny said. "In fact, it's low on power now."

"So how do you energize it?" Evanita asked. "Duh, I think I asked that already, but I didn't get a real answer."

"The answer is this—I dip it in the bay by Ross Island in the Willamette River back in Portland," Johnny said. "That's where I found it."

"Hmm. So you recharge this stone by dipping it in water. Now Johnny Pindus, how is that supposed to work? How does water provide energy? Water is like a salt—it's the after-mass of a chemical reaction."

"You make it sound like a placenta, the afterbirth," Johnny said. "But I'll take that comparison. The Moissan Ruby is like a baby, and the water is like an umbilical cord or even a placenta. The water doesn't provide power any more than a placenta does, but it acts as a conduit of power between the stone and something else."

"What 'something else'?" Evanita asked.

"The mother of the power source," Johnny said.

"You're speaking in riddles," Evanita said.

"Maybe. Some people are born and given up for adoption. They may not know their biological parents, but they know they must have parents," Johnny said.

Evanita looked down.

"I'm sorry. You still don't know about your biological parents," Johnny said.

"You don't have to apologize to me," Evanita said. "As I said before, I don't care if I ever find out who my father is."

Evanita stared at the Moissan Ruby again.

"You once told me you found this in the Willamette," Evanita said.

"That's right," Johnny said. "It was just before your mother became pregnant with you."

"So this stone and I have a common history," Evanita said. "We both became known to the world around the same time."

"Yeah," Johnny said. "That's about right."

"I wish my mother would have aborted me," Evanita said, and she threw the Moissan Ruby into the moat.

"No!" Johnny said.

Johnny stared at Evanita from her shocking statement, and then he looked at the spot where the Moissan Ruby sank, then back at Evanita.

"Well?" Evanita said. "Why are you standing here? Go get your stone."

"Evanita! If giving up my Moissan Ruby will bring you out of this deep pit of despair, then I'll gladly let it go!" Johnny said. "But just now...I thought you said...no you couldn't have...no one would ever dare to wish what you just said...Evanita! You're too special to wish your nonexistence! I love you, Evanita! I love you! You used to love me! I know! I felt it! But it's been stolen from you! Something stole life from you! Evanita! Come back to the living!"

Johnny held out his arms and moved toward Evanita to hug her, but she turned herself sideways. Johnny hugged her anyway.

"Stay with me, Evanita. Don't let life slip away," Johnny said.

"Do you see me crying? Do you see me hysterical as you are?" Evanita asked. "No, I'm neither. I'm standing here wondering why you're bawling your eyes out."

"Because I love you and it hurts me to see you like this," Johnny said. "You...you...you're a cynic!"

"Go get your necklace, Johnny," Evanita said. "Get your necklace and dry it off."

Johnny removed his shoes and socks. He rolled up his pant legs and waded in the moat. Evanita glanced at him from time to time, but by now she was bored and sat down. Johnny held his arms out from his sides to steady his balance.

"Don't fall," Evanita called.

"I won't," Johnny said as he turned around to say so, but as he did, he nearly lost his footing.

"You almost did," Evanita said.

Johnny turned back around and looked in the water. Something sparkled in the water—there. Johnny saw his Moissan Ruby, but he could not simply reach for it with his jacket on. He removed his jacket and tossed it to shore. He rolled up his arm sleeves and reached his right hand into the water while his left hand stuck out behind him. He leaned and leaned.

"Let me help," said Evanita as she grabbed Johnny's left hand.

Evanita had kicked off her shoes and stood behind Johnny.

"Thank you," Johnny said. "Now lean back and—"

"I know how a counterweight works," Evanita said. "Reach for your stone."

Johnny leaned a little, but Evanita stopped him.

"Won't work," Evanita said. "I can't lean back far enough to counter your angle. Our arms are too short."

"Should we grow our arms longer?" Johnny joked.

"Not even funny," Evanita said. "I'm pulling you back up. Now wait a moment."

Evanita pulled Johnny back up. She released her grip and walked back to shore where she fetched Johnny's jacket. She returned to Johnny and handed him one sleeve.

"Put your feet against mine," Johnny said.

Evanita placed only her right foot against Johnny's. She placed her left foot toward the shore.

"Lean down," Evanita said.

"Put both feet against mine," Johnny said.

"Lean down," Evanita repeated.

Johnny leaned down toward the water while Evanita leaned back. Johnny's jacket held their opposing forces without any sign of ripping.

"Good," Johnny said. "The jacket is holding. You're doing great. I wish you had planted both feet against mine, but this is working."

"Stop talking and fish out the stone," Evanita said.

Johnny reached down and down such that his head was nearly in the water. He turned his head up to keep breathing and extended his reach.

"I can touch it," Johnny said.

"Let me know when you have it," Evanita said.

"Okay," Johnny said.

"Is that an 'okay' that you have it, or an 'okay' that you understand me?" Evanita asked.

"It's an almost to the first and a definite to the second," Johnny said. "I just need to...a little more...there! I have it!"

Johnny held the necklace above the waterline to celebrate.

"Good!" Evanita said.

Evanita purposely let go of the jacket. She caught her back-fall with her left foot, but Johnny had no such luxury and fell flat into the moat. Evanita let out a big laugh, and Johnny splashed around in the water.

"It's cold. It's cold!" Johnny said with a shiver in his throat.

"Good!" Evanita laughed.

"It's not funny!" Johnny said. "Help me out of the water."

"So you can pull me in?" Evanita asked. "Not a chance!"

Evanita returned to the shore and put her shoes on. Johnny splashed farther in the water as he regained his balance. After a moment or three, Johnny stumbled out of the water and onto shore. He remained there on his knees for another moment as he regained his composure and strength. Finally, he got up, walked to his socks and shoes, and put them on.

"I don't know why I just put my socks and shoes back on," Johnny said. "They're getting wet from my soaked clothing. Why did you do that? You let go on purpose!"

"Because I felt like it," Evanita said. "I haven't had a good laugh in a long time, and I thought you wouldn't mind."

"Wouldn't mind?! Wouldn't mind?!? Ugh!" Johnny said.

Johnny shivered from the cold. He sat on the shore and placed his hands behind him on the ground. His shivering activated the Moissan Ruby, and he felt himself traveling through the mountain.

"Evanita," Johnny said. "Listen to me."

"What is it?" Evanita laughed. "I'm still enjoying your moment of failed triumph."

"This castle...this mountain. I can feel them," Johnny said. "I know what they are. And this Moissan Ruby—it's recharged. This water recharged it just like the Willamette does by Ross Island. Evanita—I never realized it before, but I know how my Moissan Ruby is energized. And I know why this moat works as well as the Willamette. Evanita—these are crash sites from outer-space objects!"

"Crash sites?" Evanita asked. "From two different meteorites?"

"Something like meteorites, but different," Johnny said. "These meteorites were not random chunks of rocks. They were well-formed spheres from the same solar system. And there was life inside of them. Life!"

"Life inside a meteorite? How can a meteorite hold life?" Evanita asked.

"It's a simple answer. They weren't meteorites. They were spaceships," Johnny said.

"Come on up here," Evanita said. "Let's walk back to the barbican before you get sick. You're imagining things."

Johnny stood and walked up the embankment to Evanita.

"I'm not making this up," Johnny said to Evanita as the two walked back toward the barbican. "These two places—Carreña and Portland—are connected. And you're part of it, Evanita. Your ancestry depends on these two places."

"My mother was born in Texas," Evanita said. "And Grandma Geneva was born in Girona, Spain."

"But you were born in Portland," Johnny said. "What about your grandmother's mother? Where was she born?"

"I'm not sure," Evanita said.

The two reached the barbican with Jonara walking beside them. Johnny left a trail of water behind him and carried this trail into the barbican. Geneva remained seated, still waiting for Sister Charlene.

"What in Spain did you do?" Geneva asked Johnny.

"I fell into the moat," Johnny said.

Evanita giggled.

"He fell, yes?" Geneva asked. "Was it accidental?"

"Accidental for Johnny," Evanita laughed.

"I see," Geneva said as she gave Evanita a knowing look. "You'll catch your death of cold out here. We need help."

Geneva rang another bell. The young sister entered the barbican.

"Johnny here fell into the moat. Is there any way we can dry his clothes?" Geneva asked. "And what about Sister Charlene? Did you pass on my message?"

"Sister Charlene! I knew I forgot something," the young sister said.

Geneva rolled her eyes.

"I think you should take us to her," Geneva said.

"The young man must stay here in the barbican," the young sister said. "He is not allowed in the living area. You and Evanita may visit. And I'm sorry—we can't help the young man with his clothes."

"This puts us in an awkward situation," Geneva said. "I had hoped to show Evanita and Johnny the Caves of Healing!"

"The Caves of Healing!" the young sister said. "Oh we would never allow a male in there."

"Don't worry about me," Johnny said. "I'll wait out here."

"You can't," Evanita said. "You'll get sick. Grandma—we should go back to the hotel and wait for Johnny to dry off."

"No," Johnny said. "I'll go back to the hotel myself and dry off. I'll come back when I'm ready. You two go inside and visit the caves."

"Johnny—do you have an international driver's license?" Geneva asked.

"No, but don't worry. I'll walk. It's only a kilometer to the hotel."

Geneva thought for a moment and agreed. Evanita reached out to hug him, but he held her off.

"I don't want your clothes to get wet," he said. "Oh wait a moment. Evanita, I want you to wear this around your neck. And don't throw it away."

"The Moissan Ruby?" Evanita asked.

"Yes. It's tied to this place and to Portland, as are you. It will give you advanced insight," Johnny explained. "Please—do this for me."

"No," Evanita said. "It's part of your agenda. I want nothing to do with it."

"Please," Johnny said.

"I'll throw it in the moat again," Evanita said. "Just another abortion."

"Evanita!" Geneva said. "Such language! Are you that afraid of Johnny's stone?"

"I'm afraid of nothing," Evanita said. "Give it to me then, and I'll prove it. Well? Why do you hesitate?"

"I trust you'll keep it safe and not dispose of it. I have your word?" Johnny asked. "Okay, I'll see you two back at the hotel."

Johnny gave the stone to Evanita and left her and Geneva in the barbican. Jonara stayed with her mother, and the women followed the young sister in the castle until they reached the living quarters of Sister Charlene. Sister Charlene sat in a reclining chair with a book in her lap and a hat over her head.

"Sister Charlene," the younger sister said as she shook Sister Charlene's arm. "You have visitors."

Sister Charlene looked up and saw Geneva with Evanita.

"Sister Geneva!" Sister Charlene said, referring to Evanita. "You haven't aged a day. And you have red highlights."

"My name is Evanita Carreña," Evanita said. "And this is my Grandma Geneva."

"Sister Geneva?" Sister Charlene asked. "It is you! You're older! And this is your granddaughter? She's beautiful like you."

"You mean like I used to be," Geneva said. "We all get older. I'm glad you remember me somewhat. But please don't call me, 'Sister Geneva'. I left the vocation in the 60s. I married and had a daughter. Her name is Eva."

"Did she marry?" Sister Charlene asked.

"No, she didn't. She had one child. That's Evanita here," Geneva said.

"Eva didn't marry?" Sister Charlene asked.

"No," Geneva said. "It's complicated. Very complicated. Sister Charlene, Evanita has been through a lot. She nearly died in a factory fire, and she suffers from arsenic poisoning in her legs."

"Ah," Sister Charlene said. "There's something about your family line, Geneva. And there's something about your legs."

"Yes, yes. My legs were paralyzed by polio," Geneva said. "I thought I would never walk again."

"But the Caves of Healing cured you," Sister Charlene said. "I remember now. It was a miracle. Evanita—these Caves have pools with healing properties. Your legs would be purged of arsenic. You'd be a new person. You must try it sometime."

"I'm glad of you for saying so," Geneva said, "for that is precisely why we are here. Will you permit us to visit the caves?"

"I will take you there myself," Sister Charlene said. "But first—would you help an old friend into her wheelchair?"

Geneva and Evanita helped Sister Charlene from her reclining chair to her wheelchair.

"I don't understand," Evanita said to Sister Charlene. "If the caves are that powerful, why can't you use them to help you walk again?"

"Oh I've visited the caves myself many times," Sister Charlene said. "If it weren't for them, I'd be dead long ago. A body fails no matter how much healing a cave can provide. My weak legs are only a minor failing compared to what could be. There now. Let's go to the caves. No, don't push me. My arms are strong enough to push the wheels."

Sister Charlene led the two out of her living quarters and into the church area.

"Grandma," Evanita asked while the three and Jonara headed toward the mountain face behind the altar, "you were born in Girona, right?"

"Yes, I was," Geneva said.

"But you lived here in Carreña at one time?" Evanita asked.

"Twice. Once with my Grandfather Martin Sixpence. The other time when I was a sister of this abbey."

"Does that mean one of our ancestors was born in Carreña?" Evanita asked.

"Yes. My own mother—Margene Carreña—was born in this town," Geneva said.

"And she's my great-grandmother?" Evanita asked.

"Yes, that's right. My mother's family is mostly from Carreña," Geneva explained. "I say mostly because Martin Sixpence was from England. But the family history says we have a maternal history tied to Carreña as far back as 1492."

The group proceeded through the door by the mountain face, through a short passageway, and into the Caves of Healing.

"I was here in 1492!" Jonara said. "The women were here too! Felifia's group! We were all here!"

No one heard Jonara except for Evanita. Evanita leaned her head to the side and patted it with her hand as if relieving her ear of water.

"Something the matter?" Geneva asked.

"I thought I heard a young girl's voice," Evanita said. "I heard it once before when I was in the Elrod 402. Strange. I'd forgotten about the little voice."

"The Caves play strange tricks on the unwary," Sister Charlene said.

"Did the voice say anything?" Geneva asked.

"Yes. Something about a group of women in 1492," Evanita said.

"There have been many groups of women in these pools over the centuries, beginning in late 1492 when the abbey took over this castle."

"Felifia's women were here in early 1492 before the abbey!" Jonara shouted. "They were here first!"

Evanita patted her head again.

"More voices?" Geneva asked.

"Just the same voice," Evanita said. "Sister Charlene—what do you know about the owner of this castle before 1492?"

"It was abandoned by a group of Celtic women," Sister Charlene said. "At least we think they were Celtic. Rumors say a number of different faiths owned this castle, but that hardly seems possible."

"It was possible!" Jonara shouted. "Women of different faiths came together and helped one another!"

"The voice says it was possible, that women of different faiths owned the castle," Evanita said.

"Well, that was long in the past," Sister Charlene said. "Let's see what we can do for you, yes?"

"Yes," Geneva said.

"I'm tied to Carreña and Portland," Evanita mused.

"Did you say something?" Geneva asked.

"Not really," Evanita said.

"The first step is to sit in this chair at the edge of the first pool and place your toes in the water," Sister Charlene said. "The pools are usually beneficial, but some people are more sensitive than others. We like to start off with something simple and keep things slow."

"I would like to accompany my granddaughter," Geneva said.

"Of course," Sister Charlene said. "I recommend it. If I could walk, I would place another chair next to the first."

"I can help there," Evanita said. "Which chair?"

"Select that one by the wall. It's the twin of the chair already by the pool," Sister Charlene said.

Evanita picked up the extra chair and placed it next to the first chair by the pool.

"Are you ready, Grandma?" Evanita asked.

"Yes. I'm ready, Evanita. Let's begin."

CHAPTER 6:

Carreña Point

2023 Oct 8, Sun Late Afnoon. Corpus Christi, Texas.

"And that's the story of my pony ride through the Peaks of Europe," Geneva said. "I can't tell you how many other hiking trails I wanted to travel, but my vacation ran out, and it was time to return home."

"Home?" Jonara asked. "Where is home?"

"Why, here in Corpus Christi, of course!" Geneva said. "I've lived most of my life in this city, and all of my life as an American in Texas."

A nurse walked in.

"Visiting hours are over," the nurse said. "You'll need your rest now, Geneva."

"Thank you, nurse," Johnny said, and he led Jonara out of the hospital.

Jonara didn't socialize the rest of the day. Her family returned to Geneva's house where Jonara joined them for dinner, but she didn't keep up with their conversations about the upcoming eclipse. Dinner passed into evening, and after settling for several boring television programs, Jonara went upstairs for the night, took a shower, and fell asleep in her bed.

2023 Oct 9, Mon Morn. Corpus Christi, Texas.

Jonara awoke with a start. The sun shone through the windows onto her face, and she squinted to see.

"What time is it?" she said aloud.

Jonara looked at the alarm clock—10:30 am.

"I slept in late," Jonara said. "I wonder if Cerafina is home. Maybe we can play music together."

Jonara threw on fresh clothes for the day, ran down the stairs, and dashed out the front door. She reached the first street sign and stopped short. The road name was displayed in Catalan and English.

"Oh," Jonara said. "I'm still in the nightmare."

Dejected, Jonara walked on the sidewalk until she reached the very same park bench where she had rested in the other timeline when Cerafina returned by bicycle with Nanna Geneva's diary. Jonara sat for a moment. There were no young people outside that day.

"Excuse me," Jonara said to an elderly man walking his dog. "Where are the younger people?"

"Younger people?" he echoed. "They are in school, as you should be."

"I thought there was a teacher's strike," Jonara said.

"Nuns don't go on strike," the elderly man said, and he walked off.

"Every teacher is a nun," Jonara said. "Of course. An entire country controlled by the Catholic Church would insist on using nuns as teachers."

Jonara walked through the neighboring park. Birds and squirrels went about their daily routine of looking for food and avoiding predators. Trees rustled in the wind.

"The animals and plants don't know any different," Jonara said. "They are the one universal constant in both timelines. It could be Christmas Day or All Saints Day and they would be none the happier."

Jonara held the Moissan Ruby to the sky, and the sun shone through it. Sparkles swirled in the stone.

"This Water Ruby was exhausted when I first entered this timeline," Jonara said. "But after I dipped it in the water at Corpus Christi Bay, it came back to life. The bay is connected to this Water Ruby. It gave the ruby power. What did Princess Felifia say in that cave in Eritrea? What was that about Corpus Christi Bay? Something about a sphere—an efferite sphere. Nekara did something. Yeah, now I remember. Nekara came to Earth in an efferite sphere and crash-landed in the United States with the major portion creating Corpus Christi Bay and another part creating the bay by Ross Island in the Willamette."

Jonara looked around the park. The birds and squirrels continued looking for food. Jonara held the Moissan Ruby between her eyes and her view of the park. The birds and squirrels appeared orange, and their movement slowed down; while the trees and other plants appeared blue, and their movement sped up. Jonara lowered the Moissan Ruby and looked—all life returned to normal.

"Think, Jonara, think!" Jonara said to herself. "Corpus Christi Bay recharges the Water Ruby. Daddy found the Water Ruby at Ross Island Bay. It's gotta be Nekara's efferite sphere. Her sphere created these bays and made them powerful. The power recharges the Water Ruby. The power will make the vitacepticals work. The vitacepticals are for fertility, and Nekara pioneered fertility. Then her efferite sphere could have deposited her fertility technology in Corpus Christi Bay and the Ross Island bay. Now the question is—is this Water Ruby connected with fertility? Felifia said my Water Ruby is a moishiana. But on Eho Miriam, Nekara made a high-priestess stone that was also called a moishiana, and that stone was placed on the priestess's navel in a ceremony. It fused with her navel, and she gained power. But the moishiana by itself did not permit fertility. Nekara perfected two methods—one with the strontium water, and the other with the duavisha. So the water in Corpus Christi Bay has strontium isotopes. It helps with fertility. But the eclipse event...that fast airplane...it will do something. It will cause women to be partially sterile so they'll be forced to use the vitacepticals which are powered by the fertility water. I've got to stop the airplane event. But how? I need help. I need Felifia to help me. But she's trapped in Nekara's duavisha stone. If I don't do something, she'll be trapped forever. But what can I do? How can I repair what I broke?"

Jonara held the Moissan Ruby up and looked through it. The animals appeared orange again, and the plants appeared blue. Then suddenly Jonara placed the Moissan Ruby to her navel and tried to chant something.

"Make me a priestess," she said.

Nothing happened.

"If only I could remember those chants," Jonara said. "No, a High Priestess must perform the ritual of conferment. There's gotta be another way to get permanent Water Ruby power. Gotta be a way."

Jonara looked at the life around her with the Moissan Ruby and said, "Miramish, Miramish, Miramish!" She thought she heard music, but it faded quickly. She held the Moissan Ruby to her left ear and said, "Miramish, Miramish, Miramish!"

The sounds from the birds, squirrels, and plants, which at one time were random, became organized and structured. But how? The Moissan Ruby changed the flow of time. Sounds from birds and squirrels slowed down and synchronized with sounds from trees and plants, which sped up. Jonara found herself in the middle of orchestral music from nature. The world swirled around her in orange and blue. Jonara found herself in another time and place.

2007 Dec 7, Fri. The Caves of Healing. Carreña, Spain.

"Take your shoes off and place your toes in the water," Geneva said to Evanita.

Evanita did as instructed. The Moissan Ruby around her neck buzzed lightly. Geneva also removed her shoes and placed her toes in the water to keep in water contact with Evanita.

"Do you feel anything?" Geneva asked. "Do you sense the size of the mountain?"

"No, I don't," Evanita said. "The water is cold. The Moissan Ruby feels odd. Other than that, I feel nothing."

"Hmm," Geneva said. "The arsenic in your legs may be affecting your senses. All right, let's go on to the next step. Place your feet in the water."

Evanita placed her feet in the water.

"Nothing again," Evanita said. "Grandma, this is a waste of time. Let's go back to the hotel."

"No, wait," Geneva said. "Move your feet in the water. Close your eyes. Let the water soak into your skin."

Evanita closed her eyes and splashed her feet in the water.

"I said move your feet, not splash them," Geneva said. "Splashing might be too much for you at the moment."

"I do feel something," Evanita said.

"Yes, yes?" Geneva asked.

"I feel like splashing water on Johnny, the same feeling I had when I let him fall in the moat!" Evanita chuckled.

Geneva rolled her eyes and shook her head in disbelief.

"All right, Evanita," Geneva said. "I didn't want to do this so soon, but I see no choice. I want you to stand in the water up to your knees."

"You're not going to shove me in the water when I'm not looking, are you?" Evanita asked. "That's something I'd do to Johnny."

"No, I wouldn't do that," Geneva said. "I'm here for a very special purpose—to read from my diary about the past—my past and yours. The pool is supposed to give you depth of feeling, so you can experience the past in vivid detail."

"What do I care about the past?" Evanita said. "The past isn't important."

"That, my dear granddaughter, is the very barrier to enlightenment I'm trying to overcome in you. If you don't allow this barrier to fall, you will imprison yourself in a micro-small world of Evanita, so small that even your last name won't fit in your world. Your last name is Carreña—the same as this town—and it's not by chance. Many women have made sacrifice after sacrifice to give life to our line, including life for you. I'm not here to show you all of them, but I'm here to show you the most important one—that of your mother. Now please, try to keep an open mind."

"I'll try," Evanita said.

"Thank you," Geneva said. "Now if you please, stand in the water until the level reaches your knees."

Evanita stood in the water up to her knees. Geneva read from the diary, and Evanita along with Geneva and Jonara traveled back in time.

1970 Jul 4, Sat 10 am. Arbúcies, Spain.

"Where are we?" Evanita asked.

"We are in a hospital in the city of Arbúcies, Spain. We are a little north of the Montseny Mountains where our airplane crashed in 1970."

"There's a woman and a girl in hospital beds," Evanita said. "The woman looks like my mother."

"The woman is me," Geneva said. "And the girl is your mother. We survived the airplane crash and ended up in this hospital."

"How?" Evanita asked.

"You'll find out in a moment."

Jonara watched intently as a nurse and Catholic sister entered the room. The sister looked familiar—it was Sister Charlene!

"Let's try to wake her," the nurse said.

The nurse held a smelling salt under the younger Geneva's nose. The younger Geneva woke up with a start.

"Where...where am I?" younger Geneva asked as she looked around. "Sister Charlene!"

"Yes, I am here," Sister Charlene said.

"If you'll excuse me," the nurse said, "I'll check on you later."

"What's the last thing you remember?" Sister Charlene asked.

"I'm not sure if you'll believe me," younger Geneva said.

"I'll believe anything at this point," Sister Charlene said. "Your survival and that of this girl are a miracle. Everyone else on that jetliner perished."

"They're all dead?" younger Geneva asked.

"They're all dead!?" Jonara asked. "Wait a moment! Somebody or something lied to me! They were all alive! My indurate chant kept them from dying!"

"That's correct," Nekara said as she appeared from nowhere. "Your indurate chant protected everyone."

"Then how did the others on the plane die?" Jonara asked.

"They died when you didn't indurate the fuselage," Nekara said.

"But I did indurate the plane...not the first time, but the second time. And when I was on the plane, I checked their future...the future of Nanna Geneva and Grandma Eva. They died when I did nothing," Jonara said to Nekara. "How—"

"That's true," Nekara said. "Had you done nothing, your grandmother and great-grandmother would have died. And you wouldn't have existed to go back in time and save them. Strange, that seems contradictory. Nevertheless, death is a universal theme. I find this new timeline more interesting—all dead except for your maternal ancestors. Think of the guilt your Geneva and Eva will feel when they learn of their survival at the expense of others. I feed off guilt."

"This...it doesn't make sense. I...you're driving me crazy! Go away!" Jonara yelled.

Nekara laughed and faded into nothingness.

"My daughter and I...that is...Eva and I...well...you won't believe me if I tell you," younger Geneva said.

"Tell me, tell me!" Sister Charlene said. "The rescuers found you two at the bottom of a slope. It appeared as if you wandered away from the wreckage and slid down the mountain a bit. I ask again—how is it you survived while the passengers and crew perished? The jetliner was spread out all over. It didn't look like a jet—more like someone dumping their garbage everywhere, except there were people scattered around. At least that's what I was told. I heard of it while I was at St. Renata's Abbey. I came as quickly as I could. But I see you two only have a few bruises."

"Yes, we had better protection than the others," younger Geneva said. "Sister Charlene—we did not ride in the passenger compartment. We sat in a fortified human crate with padding on the inside. When the airplane crashed, our crate was thrown. It broke open, and we got out. That's how we survived."

"But how is it you were in the crate to begin with?" Sister Charlene asked.

"I thought you would ask," younger Geneva said. "The flight was booked solid, but I argued with the airline clerk at the airport in Manchester, England. We agreed this crate was the way to go."

"How did you get through customs?" Sister Charlene asked.

"We didn't," Geneva said.

"Then you are here illegally," Sister Charlene said.

"We have passports," Geneva said.

"But are they stamped?" Sister Charlene asked. "I didn't think so. Sister Geneva—"

"I'm not a sister anymore," younger Geneva said. "I'm not even a Catholic."

"Oh. I'm sorry to hear that," Sister Charlene said. "Geneva—this hospital is no place for you. I'll arrange for your transfer to my care. If you are willing, I'll speak to the nurse now."

"Yes," younger Geneva said. "I am. I'll wake little Eva."

Sister Charlene exited the room while younger Geneva awakened Eva.

"Did you really ride in a crate?" Evanita asked older Geneva.

"Yes, I did," older Geneva replied.

"Why did you come to Spain to begin with?" Evanita asked.

"I wanted to show your mother where I was born and where I grew up," older Geneva replied.

"Is this why you brought me here?" Evanita asked.

"Yes. I want you to see the same," older Geneva replied.

"But why?" Evanita asked.

"Evanita," older Geneva said. "America is very isolated from the rest of the world. Deep human suffering and struggling continues to plague people in the world. Spain endured such a time until Franco died. There's absolutely no possible way I can convey how dark things were throughout Spain, but I can give you a small sample. I'm hoping this sample will help you appreciate the things you do have in your life so that you won't waste time fretting about what you don't have."

Eva woke up. Sister Charlene returned with the nurse.

"I am releasing you to Sister Charlene's care," the nurse said.

"Thank you," younger Geneva said.

Sister Charlene signed a chart, and the nurse left them.

"It's settled. I have a car out front. We'll go to the abbey, and you can attend Mass with me," Sister Charlene said.

"Um, about that, yes, well, let's get in the car first," younger Geneva said.

The three entered Sister Charlene's car and drove off. Older Geneva, Evanita, and Jonara floated along in the back seat.

"Sister Charlene," younger Geneva said. "I turned away from the faith many years ago."

"Are you saying you're a fallen-away Catholic?" Sister Charlene asked.

"Yes," younger Geneva said.

"When did this happen?" Sister Charlene asked.

"Seven years ago when I was in Saigon," younger Geneva said. "I saw the injustices formed against Buddhist monks by Catholics. Sister Charlene—the Catholic Church in Vietnam forced its faith on others."

"We always seek to bring outsiders into the flock," Sister Charlene said. "But I know about the Vietnam situation. Diem was a ruthless dictator and forced his faith on others. Geneva—there are false prophets in the world who would usurp whatever power they can get hold of and twist it to their desire. They are evil. Diem was evil. Surely you recognize this."

"I've given the situation a lot of thought—then and now," younger Geneva said. "So maybe he twisted Catholicism in Vietnam. But it's not the first time, and I doubt it's the last. How can I be a part of an institution where others look at me and say, 'She's a sister. She's a Catholic. By association, she supports these acts against humanity'?"

"You explain the situation through dialog," Sister Charlene said.

"But it's not just Diem. There were others before him—Isabella and Ferdinand in 1492, and Franco today," younger Geneva said. "Further, the Church blames Jews for the crucifixion of Christ. That's plain wrong."

"You're right, blaming Jews is wrong," Sister Charlene said. "It's so wrong that Vatican II officially said so."

"They did?" younger Geneva asked.

"Yes, they did," Sister Charlene said. "Geneva—the Church is not a monolith of stone. It is not stuck in the Middle Ages. It continues to grow and examine issues pertinent to faith. People run the Church—they are human. Humans make mistakes sometimes. The Church will from time to time admit its mistakes where mistakes are made. Sometimes it takes a bit longer than it should, but eventually—if the Church believes something was done immorally—it will seek to rectify it. The important thing is to work for change within the framework. It makes us stronger. But I see from your expression you gave up the faith completely. You threw away the good and bad. So, dare I ask if you still believe in God?"

"Yes, I do," younger Geneva said.

"What about Christ?" Sister Charlene asked.

"We don't say, 'Christ'," Eva said. "We say, 'Jesus'. That's because we're Baptist."

"I see," Sister Charlene said. "You went from one extreme to another."

"I'm still a Christian," younger Geneva said. "I believe that's the most important thing."

"It is, Geneva, but remember—they broke away from us—not the other way around," Sister Charlene said.

"Sunday school teacher says Baptists never broke away from anyone," Eva said.

"It's true, Sister Charlene," Geneva said. "It was Martin Luther who broke away. The Baptists formed their Christian faith independently of the Catholic Church. Our Baptist faith is based on the Bible, not an institution."

"I stand corrected," Sister Charlene said. "You are both right—the Baptists did not break away. But they are Protestants, and Protestants by nature protest the Church. You do know there was a counter-reformation after the Reformation to clean up some of the Protestant complaints against the Church. Again—the Church is not a monolith."

"Sister Charlene," younger Geneva said. "Would you be willing to be our tour guide? We want to visit Girona and later Carreña."

"You're on to a different subject. Are you fleeing from our religious topic?" Sister Charlene asked.

"Not at all," younger Geneva said. "I simply wish to set our direction correctly before we stray off toward Carreña. That is where you first intended to go, isn't it?"

"Yes, it was," Sister Charlene said. "I had hoped to take you back to St. Renata's Abbey so I could help reawaken your Catholic faith. But Girona is a good place too. I haven't been to St. Christopher's Abbey in many years, and I'd like to see Sister Francis again."

"Now you do realize I would like to do other things besides visiting St. Christopher's Abbey, don't you?" younger Geneva said. "My main reason for bringing Eva here is to show her where I grew up, not to indoctrinate her."

"Hmm, yes, well, that will be fine for the moment," Sister Charlene said.

"I want to show her where I was born," younger Geneva said. "And I think you're the perfect tour guide for that since you attended my parents' wedding and helped my mother deliver me."

"Yes, I was there," Sister Charlene said. "I was much younger then. Much younger."

"Father was Baptist too," Eva said. "We went to service together."

"How is your father?" Sister Charlene asked.

"He's up in Heaven," Eva said.

"I'm sorry," Sister Charlene said.

"No, don't worry. You didn't know," younger Geneva said. "My husband, Colonel Andrew Gracer, passed away two years ago while in Saigon during a Viet Cong raid on the U.S. Embassy. Since then, Eva and I go by my maiden name—Carreña."

"I'm sorry for your losses," Sister Charlene said.

"My losses?" younger Geneva asked. "I lost no one else. Fortunately, Eva and I weren't over there, or we could have been killed."

"Your losses in Vietnam are twofold—your husband and your faith," Sister Charlene said. "Do you seek Christ for assistance?"

"We go to service," Eva said. "I like Sunday School and Vacation Bible School."

"Eva keeps me going," younger Geneva said. "She's very much into her Baptist faith. Our Baptist church has many activities for the young people, and I volunteer as a thank-you for what they've done for Eva and me."

"What about parochial school?" Sister Charlene asked.

"Eva is enrolled in Candlewood Baptist School," younger Geneva said. "That's in Corpus Christi, Texas."

"The Body of Christ!" Sister Charlene said, and she nearly drove off the road in excitement.

"Whoa!" younger Geneva said.

"I didn't know you lived in Corpus Christi!" Sister Charlene said. "That's practically a call from Christ to return to his faith."

"Sister Charlene," younger Geneva said. "I'm still a Christian. And I moved to Corpus Christi for employment as it turns out. Fortunately, we found a nice Baptist church and school nearby."

"This is boring," Evanita said to older Geneva.

"Please, be patient," older Geneva replied. "Soon we will be in Girona."

Geneva read something from her diary, and the scene changed from Sister Charlene's car to an old apartment complex.

"I'll show you where your mother lived," Sister Charlene said to younger Geneva. "Her name was Margene, and she married a Frenchman by the name of François Vallan."

The group walked upstairs in the apartment building.

"Other people live in the apartment, but I've kept up with them over the years, and they let me visit whenever I like," Sister Charlene said. "Ah, here we are—the second floor."

The group entered the second floor.

"It's apartment 204," Sister Charlene said.

"You're joking," younger Geneva said.

"No, I'm not. It really is apartment 204," Sister Charlene said. "Why do you think I'm joking?"

"Because in the year 1939, I was born in the second month on the fourth day," younger Geneva said. "The number 204 is my birth month and day."

"Why so it is!" Sister Charlene said.

Sister Charlene knocked on the door. There was no answer. Sister Charlene opened apartment 204 with a key.

"They lent you a key?" younger Geneva asked.

"Yes," Sister Charlene said. "I told you I keep in good contact with them."

"Very good contact, I'd say," younger Geneva replied.

The group entered the apartment, and Evanita was surprised.

"It's the same apartment!" Evanita said to elder Geneva. "I was here before, Grandma Geneva. I saw Margene on the day you were born. Great-Grandpa came home, and she convinced him to marry her that very day."

"You were in this apartment before?" older Geneva asked. "But how?"

"I had the Moissan Ruby on," Evanita said. "A little voice was with me."

"A little voice?" older Geneva asked.

"Yes. I think she said she was my daughter," Evanita said. "She wanted to go back in time and see what her family was like. I thought it was a dream. I was in church in Patriojet— that's in the Elrod 402. I was listening to the Catholic Mass on headphones when I heard a buzzing. Then I was here—in this apartment, and it was February 4, 1939!"

"Your future daughter went back in time as you did and are doing now," older Geneva said. "You see, at some point, each generation wonders what her family history is all about—who her ancestors were, where they came from, and what they did. You will have a daughter someday, Evanita. A daughter!"

"I forgot all about her," Evanita said. "She was here with me. I said that already, didn't I? But it hardly seems real. I still feel numb, like I was on the mountaintop of my childhood but have fallen into a deep valley."

"Then you know how I felt when the plane crashed on the Montseny Mountains and when I slid down the mountain toward Arbúcies," older Geneva said.

"Somehow my valley seems deeper," Evanita said. "You were only in Arbúcies for a day before you went north to Girona."

"Memories linger," Geneva said. "The scars of the valley stretch longer than the peak of a mountain."

"Your Grandmother Margene lived in this apartment and waited for your Grandfather François to return from battle in the Spanish Civil War," Sister Charlene said to little Eva. "She had your mother in her tummy and was almost ready to deliver your mother into this world. Now look out this window, Eva, and imagine watching Nationalist airplanes getting closer and closer as they drop bombs. The bombs explode like thunder, and everything shakes in the apartment. Boom!"

Eva ran behind younger Geneva to hide from the imaginary bombs.

"It's all right, Eva," younger Geneva said. "It's all make-believe."

"Is it safe?" Eva asked.

"Yes, it's safe," Sister Charlene said. "I didn't mean to frighten you."

"I know more of the story," Evanita said to older Geneva. "François arrived, and Margene wanted them to get married immediately so you, Grandma, would be born in Catholic wedlock. François wanted Margene to accompany him to France."

"Yes, many Spaniards fled to France during the Spanish Civil War," older Geneva said.

"Margene said she couldn't walk all the way to France in her condition," Evanita said.

"So explain how she convinced my father to marry her on short notice," older Geneva said.

"She pushed him out the door and pulled him by his arm to the church," Evanita said.

"She literally dragged him to the altar," older Geneva said.

"After Margene died," Sister Charlene said to Eva, "it was my duty to clean out her apartment."

"How did my grandmother die?" little Eva asked. "How did my grandfather die?"

"For that, we will need to travel to St. Christopher's Catholic Church," Sister Charlene said. "Would you like to see the church? It's very beautiful."

"Is it safe?" little Eva asked.

"Of course it's safe," Sister Charlene said. "Come—I'll show you."

The group left apartment 204 with Sister Charlene locking it behind them. They exited the apartment building and drove down to St. Christopher's Church.

"If you look closely," Sister Charlene said as she led the group out of the car to the church, "you can see bits of church wall that have been repaired. The walls incurred much damage when Girona was bombed that night of February 4th."

Older Geneva, Evanita, and Jonara followed Sister Charlene, younger Geneva, and little Eva into the church.

"This is where your grandparents were married," Sister Charlene said.

"I remember this church!" Evanita said. "It looks the same, except the windows are different."

"Most likely the windows were replaced after the Nationalists bombed it," older Geneva said.

Little Eva hid behind younger Geneva.

"It's scary," little Eva said.

"There's nothing to be afraid of," Sister Charlene said.

Sister Charlene led the group to the altar. Little Eva continued hiding behind younger Geneva. The columns, the statues, the tall windows, and the ornate decorations frightened Eva. The group stopped at the altar.

"Now this is the strangest part of their marriage," Sister Charlene said. "I was running past the church when this pregnant woman pulled me in. The pregnant woman was Margene, of course. She needed two witnesses for her wedding, and she found us—Chalina Darconejo—that's me, and a drunk named Garcia Delgato. I was her matron of honor, and Garcia was François's best man. I must say François was hesitant about getting married in the Catholic faith. But he did, despite the advancing Nationalists. In fact, Father Mendez had just pronounced them married when the windows shattered. Glass flew all about. Margene was hurt, and François went out for a doctor. Father Mendez and I took Margene to a back room—here, I'll show you."

Sister Charlene led the group from the church to a short hallway and into a side room.

"Here is where Margene bore Geneva," Sister Charlene said. "Garcia was no help. He wanted the church wine and threatened to kill us if we didn't give it to him. We locked him out, but he slashed at us with his knife through that opening in the door. We fought him until he dropped the knife. We needed the knife to cut the umbilical cord. Father Mendez cleaned the knife, and I cut the cord. I cleaned up baby Geneva and gave her to Margene. Father Mendez baptized Geneva in Margene's final moments alive. Margene bled to death, unfortunately. But that wasn't the worst of it. The Nationalists entered the church. They killed Garcia. Father Mendez was afraid the Nationalists would come in here and kill us. Father Mendez went out to meet the soldiers. The soldiers killed him. He sacrificed his life for ours."

"What about my grandfather?" little Eva asked.

"I'll answer that question in a moment," Sister Charlene said. "But first, let me tell you how I escaped with your mother. I found a secret door over here."

Sister Charlene pushed on the wall, but it did not move.

"It appears to be sealed off," Sister Charlene said. "There is a secret passage from this room to St. Christopher's Abbey. The sisters came through this passage and helped me carry Margene and Geneva away. The sisters cleaned up the room, and we escaped before the Nationalists could catch us. But I know what happened to your grandfather, little Eva. I heard Father Mendez speaking to the Nationalist soldiers. He identified one of the dead as François Vallan."

Eva started to cry.

"It's all right, little Eva," younger Geneva said as she comforted Eva. "That was long ago."

"It's not fair," Eva said. "I always wanted to meet my grand-parents."

"Shhh," younger Geneva said.

"Maybe this was a bad idea," Sister Charlene said. "Death is a difficult subject for people of all ages."

"No, I'm glad we came," younger Geneva said. "It's important we remember what Franco did to Spain."

"Some would rather forget," Sister Charlene said.

"I know," younger Geneva said.

"What does it matter if people remember or forget?" Evanita asked the older Geneva.

"Digging up bad memories of the past is a tricky thing," older Geneva said. "Some find that dealing with past atrocities makes them stronger. They are able to understand what happened and take steps to ensure these atrocities don't happen again. They make better future decisions. Other people find the experiences too painful to deal with. They have suffered through such pain that they can only recover and move on by forgetting. Reminding them of the past undoes all the progress they've made to move on, especially if they tend to become obsessed with past miseries. In that case, memories of the past become a trap they cannot escape."

"It would seem forgetting the past is the best thing," Evanita said.

"As I said, it's tricky," older Geneva said. "There is a danger in forgetting the past. It tends to demean and belittle those who suffered from it. Further, criminal dictators tend to hide these atrocities to protect their reputation. Hitler and the concentration camps, Stalin and The Great Purge—these are two examples of dictators committing atrocities. If people do not know about the atrocities, they are more likely to support the dictator's regime or at least less likely to challenge it."

"Let's go to St. Christopher's Abbey," Sister Charlene said.

Sister Charlene led the group out of the church, along the sidewalk, and into St. Christopher's Abbey. Sister Charlene showed Eva where Geneva grew up, where she stayed in an iron lung, where she recovered from paralysis, and where she played soccer with her leg braces and forearm crutches.

"Say, Geneva, whatever happened to those braces and crutches?" Sister Charlene asked.

"I'm not sure. I left them at St. Renata's Abbey when my legs were healed," younger Geneva said.

"You were paralyzed, Grandma?" Evanita asked.

"My legs were, yes," older Geneva said.

"How could you go on with life? Didn't you want to give up?" Evanita asked.

"I did," older Geneva said. "I thought my life was over. And I was angry at Franco. A vaccine had already been developed and could have been distributed in Spain, but his dictatorship held things up. My polio was preventable."

"Do you have para...para-lee-sehs now, Mother?" little Eva asked Geneva.

"No, I'm cured," younger Geneva said.

"How did you get cured?" Evanita asked older Geneva. "Polio causes permanent paralysis."

The image of Sister Charlene, Eva, and younger Geneva faded into gray. Evanita and older Geneva returned to the Caves of Healing.

"In these Caves of Healing," Geneva said. "Your legs and my feet are in the very same pool of water that cured my paralysis. This pool marked the Carreña point in my life."

"The what?" Evanita asked.

"The Carreña point," Geneva said. "Oh I've had other Carreña points later in my life, but this was the first—that's what makes it special."

"I don't understand," Evanita said. "What does the name of a city have to do with paralysis? And what the heck is a Carreña point?"

"Let's see if I can explain," Geneva said. "Evanita—what do you think is special about the town of Carreña?"

"Nothing," Evanita said. "It's in a valley. To the north is a mountain range separating Carreña from the Bay of Biscay. To the south are the Peaks of Europe."

"What about this abbey? St. Renata's Abbey?" Geneva asked.

"It's an old castle. There are other castles in Europe," Evanita said.

"Yes, but it's built on this hill," Geneva said.

"I don't understand. This hill isn't very high—not as high as the mountain range to the north or the Peaks to the south," Evanita said.

"Evanita, when we were outside—before we entered the abbey—did you look around?" Geneva asked.

"Yes, I did," Evanita said.

"What did you see?"

"I saw the nearby villages," Evanita said, "and a little bit of the countryside. And the two mountain ranges."

"Your view of the nearby villages and the two mountain ranges is the Carreña point," Geneva said. "Evanita—many young people start off with the belief that bad things only happen to bad people. It comes as quite a shock that bad things happen to good people. Sometimes when a young person has something bad happen to her, she feels her life is over."

"Are you talking about me?" Evanita asked.

"You among others," Geneva said. "The feeling can be powerful and overwhelming. A person may feel she is descending down a waterfall quickly with impending death."

"You showed me two waterfalls," Evanita said.

"Yes, the waterfalls!" Geneva said. "I pointed out that for a young person, a change of life is like a waterfall in the mountains—like the one we saw in Bricias."

"I thought you said I was like a delta after the waterfall," Evanita said.

"And I also told you that you believe you are the delta, that you should be more in line with the river in Bricias," Geneva said. "Your delta is like the valley between the two mountain ranges. Because you are in the valley, you cannot see the way to the next mountain range. You've also forgotten how you got in the valley. So you begin to believe the valley is all that's left of your life, and you resign yourself to it."

"Seems about right," Evanita said. "So I'm in a valley instead of a delta. Are you trying to say that good times are just ahead? Guaranteed?"

"No, not guaranteed!" Geneva said. "That's the illusion of younger people. Good times ahead are never guaranteed. You could be stuck in this valley a long time, if you allow it—like Franco's Spain."

"Then what's the point?" Evanita asked. "I might as well give up!"

"No!" Geneva said.

"I can't climb the new mountain!" Evanita said. "I don't know the way, and it's too hard."

"That's right, it is!" Geneva said.

"Then it's hopeless. I'm stuck in my delta—my valley—for the rest of my life!"

"Not if you make an effort to climb a small hill and take a look about!" Geneva said. "You can climb a little hill, can't you? Once you do, you'll remember how you got to your point in time, and you can figure out how to get to that next mountain range of happiness. That's what little hills are for! It's the Carreña point! And once you do, Evanita, once you climb that hill and realize you are not alone, that you aren't the first to do this, you'll also be able to see the path to the next mountain. You'll also realize there's a valley on the other side of the next mountain, that this will likely happen again, and you'll know what to do next time around. You'll find another Carreña point!"

"So how am I supposed to find a Carreña point?" Evanita asked. "Do I look for a hill back home and climb it?"

"The hill is a metaphor," Geneva said.

"What's it all about, Grandma?" Evanita asked. "What am I supposed to do with my life?"

"For some people, it's a sister, a mother, a daughter, or a family," Geneva said. "For others, it's a career. Others yet find some cause for humanity or decide to study the universe."

"I feel nothing, Grandma. I feel no cause to do anything," Evanita said. "I see these things in the past, and I feel sorry for others. I know I will never have to go through what you and others did. I wish I could climb a hill and see what I should do with my life. I don't have a hill to climb."

"I am here," Geneva said. "I had hoped I could help you find your Carreña point, so that you could find your cause."

"Mommy, I'm here!" Jonara shouted. "You're going to marry Daddy and have me! I'm your daughter, Mommy!"

"I heard the little voice again," Evanita said to Geneva. "I feel like the little voice is a new spirit growing inside me."

"Are you pregnant?" Geneva asked.

"Of course not," Evanita said. "I don't feel a physical growth inside me—I feel a spiritual one. I still feel the blahs, Grandma, but the little spirit doesn't. I can't explain it any more than that. I know the little spirit will want to be born someday. Will that be my next mountain peak—when I give birth to a daughter?"

"It could very well be," Geneva said. "For some, the next peak is marriage. Or education. You'll know when the day comes."

"What about the waterfall, Grandma? Where's the Carreña point? Is there a little hill in the waterfall?"

"No, but imagine if there were a ledge halfway down the waterfall," Geneva said. "Imagine if halfway down the fall you were able to stop on the ledge and take a look. Instead of being caught in the waterfall and being forced to deal with the situation, you could rest for the moment and use the rest to look beyond the waterfall itself. Now think a minute about your relationship with your mother."

"Ugh! We're always arguing about something," Evanita said, "or she's telling me to do something. Clean my room, do the flower bed, do my homework. Then I ask her who my father is, and she won't tell me."

"Yes," Geneva said. "The day-to-day details of your life with your mother is like being in a valley or in a waterfall. But I'm your grandmother. I don't tell you what to do on a day-to-day basis. There are no details to bog us down. I'm like your ledge in the waterfall or little hill in the valley to help you see."

"You are? You're just my mother's mother," Evanita said. "Your purpose was to raise her, not me."

"Yes, my role as mother was to raise Eva. But I'm a grandmother too. Evanita—do you remember your first menstrual cycle?"

"Yes. I woke up one morning, and my bed was full of blood. It scared me to death. I thought I was dying," Evanita said. "You were the one who told me it's called *the curse*."

"Did you know that someday, your menstrual cycle will end?" Geneva asked.

"Yeah, when I die," Evanita said.

"No, before that. It's called *menopause*. It happens to women when they reach their forties or fifties. Their menstrual cycle ends, and they can no longer have children."

"Forties or fifties? You mean a woman can't have children when she's seventy-five years old?" Evanita asked.

"Of course not!" Geneva said.

"I never realized it. It seems strange that a woman can't have children when she's that old," Evanita said. "What about men? Do they have a menopause?"

"No, they don't," Geneva said. "They can have children no matter how old they are."

"That doesn't make sense," Evanita said. "Why?"

"It's a mystery," Geneva said. "But there are some theories. One is that if a woman's cycle did not end, she would continue having children. In doing so, she would focus on those children instead of doing other things."

"What other things?" Evanita asked.

"Grandchildren," Geneva said. "Evanita—women are not just baby factories. We are not here just to make babies and be rid of them. We are here to make families and do everything we can to continue the family line. After we as woman have children, we go on to helping our grandchildren."

"And men?" Evanita asked.

"Well, since they can create children at any age, the theory suggests that this is their only purpose. Biology does not hold them to a grandfather role," Geneva said. "Does this surprise you?"

"Somehow it doesn't," Evanita laughed. "If some men are capable of getting a woman pregnant and leaving town, they're capable of the same thing when it comes to being a grandfather. So what happens at the end of the waterfall, Grandma? Is it an impending death, as you said before?"

"No, it's an imperative birth," Geneva replied, "the birth of the next part of your life. The waterfall is a transitionary period."

Evanita stood in the pool for several minutes, lost in thought. At length, she spoke.

"Did you have a Carreña point with your religion?" Evanita asked. "I mean, you were a Catholic, then you were a Baptist, and today you're a Catholic. When did you go back to being a Catholic?"

"It was after a visit to a restaurant with Eva in 1973," Geneva said.

"A restaurant?" Evanita asked. "You're kidding."

"No, I'm not," Geneva said. "I'll show you. But first, I want to show you this."

1973 Oct 31, Wed. Candlewood Baptist School. Corpus Christi, Texas.

"Where are we?" Evanita asked Geneva.

"We are in your mother's fourth-grade science class," Geneva said. "It's Halloween, and Eva's class is studying the human body. Today, the class is expecting a special visitor, Dr. Roberta MacNessi."

"Roberta!" Evanita said. "I've heard that name before. She's Jane MacNessi's daughter."

"How do you know about Roberta and Jane?" Geneva asked.

"The little voice showed me. Jane played baseball. She lived in Kenosha and Racine. She separated from her husband and moved down to Alabama."

"I didn't take your little voice seriously before, but now I do," Geneva said. "I wonder if the little voice really is your future daughter. If so, she may be witnessing things in the past the same way we are—through my diary."

"Or through this Moissan Ruby," Evanita said.

"I've done it through both!" Jonara said.

"She says 'both'," Evanita said.

Geneva smiled.

"Did you learn any more about Roberta after she moved down to Alabama with Jane?" Geneva asked.

"No," Evanita said. "In fact, I have no idea why the little voice showed me the past with Jane and Roberta."

"It may be no accident," Geneva said.

"What do you mean?" Evanita asked.

"I'll show you in time," Geneva said. "But first, let me tell you this—Jane and Roberta moved to Texas. Roberta grew up and became a pediatric dentist. In addition to her regular dental work, she traveled to schools and churches to educate children on teeth. Look—Roberta is entering now."

Roberta entered the classroom with a large, square case in hand.

"Class," the teacher said. "This is Doctor MacNessi. She is a dentist, and she is here to talk about teeth. I want you to give her a warm welcome."

The teacher clapped and gave her class a knowing look as if to say, "Clap as I do."

The class clapped.

"Thank you, thank you," Roberta said as she placed her case on the teacher's desk and opened it. "Today I'm going to talk about tooth care. Our teeth are very important. Without them, we couldn't speak properly, and we couldn't eat good food. We would have to eat baby food. How many of you would want to eat baby food for the rest of your life?"

The children responded by saying things like, "Icky, yucky, no way!"

"But that's what we would have to do if our teeth fell out," Roberta said.

Roberta pulled a small, plastic jack-o-lantern with a movable jaw and human-like teeth. The jack-o-lantern had a sad expression.

"I brought a friend with me," Roberta said, referring to the jack-o-lantern. "His name is Glum Pumpkin. Why do you think his name is Glum Pumpkin?"

Eva raised her hand while the remaining class did nothing.

"Yes, Eva?"

"Because he's unhappy," Eva said.

"That's right," Roberta said. "Glum Pumpkin has periodontal disease. That means he has a disease in or around his teeth. And do you know what caused his disease?"

Again, Eva was the only one to raise her hand.

"Yes, Eva?" Roberta said.

"Plaque," Eva said.

"That's right," Roberta said as she opened Glum Pumpkin's mouth. "Plaque is a film caused by bacteria. It builds up on teeth and gums."

Roberta pulled a tooth out of Glum Pumpkin's mouth. The tooth was covered with goo, and the goo stretched from the tooth to the mouth. The class reacted by saying:

"Eww, yucky, gross!"

"Glum Pumpkin doesn't brush his teeth, and he doesn't floss," Roberta said. "He eats candy all day, but soon he won't be. His teeth are rotting. See how black they are? His gums are red and bleeding. His teeth and gums are painful. That's why he's glum."

Roberta took the tooth and squished it between her fingers. She moved her fingers along Glum Pumpkin's teeth, they broke off, and they dangled from his mouth by the goo. Roberta walked amongst the students and showed them. A foul odor emanated from Glum Pumpkin's mouth, and the students held their noses and reacted with prune-like faces as they gagged.

"Glum Pumpkin is a mess," Roberta said as she returned to the front of the class. "He's such a mess that I have to put him in this plastic bag so he doesn't get your teacher's desk messy."

Roberta placed Glum Pumpkin in a bag and cleaned her hands with an alcohol towelette.

"Glum Pumpkin has a sister," Roberta said. "Her name is Merry Pumpkin. See?"

Roberta produced a jack-o-lantern similar to Glum Pumpkin. Merry had a big smile.

"Do you know why her name is Merry Pumpkin?" Roberta asked.

Several students raised their hands. Roberta selected one of them (but not Eva).

"Because she's happy," the student said.

"That's right," Roberta said. "And why do you suppose she's happy? Let's open her mouth and see. Look! Her teeth are clean. There's no plaque. And I can't pull her teeth out. Why do you suppose her teeth are so clean?"

The students raised their hands. Roberta called on one of them.

"Because she doesn't eat candy," said the student.

Roberta called on another student before replying to the first.

"She doesn't eat candy," said another student.

Eva raised her hand and waved it around furiously.

"Yes, Eva," Roberta said.

"Merry brushes and flosses her teeth after every meal," Eva said, "including below the gum line."

"That's right," Roberta said. "Merry brushes and flosses her teeth after every meal including the gum line. But you know what? Merry eats candy."

The students reacted in shock. Some said, "No way, can't be, we were told candy is wrong."

"Merry eats some candy, but not too much. Eating does not cause periodontal disease," Roberta said. "It's the lack of cleaning that causes periodontal disease."

Roberta placed Merry on the teacher's desk and produced an apple.

"Here I have an apple," Roberta said. "Doesn't it look nice? Can you see any decay?"

The students shook their heads, "No."

"But it has decay," Roberta said. "Let's see if we can find it."

Roberta produced a knife and sliced off a section of apple skin.

"No decay here," Roberta said. "Let's try another spot."

Roberta cut off another slice.

"This looks good, too."

"Maybe there isn't any decay," joked one of the boys, and the class laughed.

"That's the trick. You don't think there's decay because you can't see it," Roberta said. "We'll try another slice. Look!"

Roberta revealed a brown spot where the apple had been bruised.

"That's like decay in your teeth," Roberta said. "You can't always see it just from looking. A dentist uses an X-ray to see decay."

Roberta turned on an overhead projector with two X-ray images of teeth.

"The image on the left shows a tooth from Merry's mouth," Roberta said. "The image on the right shows the same tooth from Glum's mouth. See how Glum's tooth is dark? There isn't much left of the tooth to show up on the X-ray."

Roberta placed a transparency on the overhead projector showing the different types of teeth—incisors, cuspids, bicuspids, and molars. Next, Roberta produced a large model of two side-by-side molars with gums. One side of the model showed the outer features, the other side showed a cross-section of teeth, gum, and jaw line.

"Here are two healthy teeth," Roberta said. "The tooth surface is shiny and clean. The gums are pink and tight against the teeth. The gums and both teeth look healthy."

Roberta placed a hood over a tooth to cover it up. She turned the model around—revealing a cross-section of the other tooth only.

"This is what a tooth looks like if you could open it up," Roberta said. "Look at the tooth. The outer surface is made of enamel. Enamel is a hard surface and can withstand many things. Under the enamel is the dentin. Dentin supports the enamel but is not as hard. Deeper in the tooth is the pulp. The pulp contains blood vessels and nerves. The pulp feeds the tooth and keeps it alive, but it is very soft. Next, we see the roots. The roots keep our teeth from falling out. Roots attach to the jaw. Blood vessels and nerves travel up the roots into the pulp."

Roberta removed the hood from the other tooth.

"This tooth looked healthy on the outside, but it has decay," Roberta explained. "Bacteria secreted an acid that broke through the enamel. It ate through the dentin and broke into the pulp chamber. The pulp chamber is infected, and the tooth is in a lot of pain. To save the tooth, a dentist will have to perform a root canal."

The teacher gave Roberta a knowing look and held a hand to her jaw as if remembering pain from a root canal.

"Root canals can be painful," Roberta said. "Infections don't respond to anesthetic, so you'll feel the dentist drilling and cleaning the pulp chamber and the roots. With this much infection, much of the enamel and dentin is damaged, so a crown is needed too. The patient of this tooth would have to go to the dentist several times to save this tooth. In the old days, these teeth were pulled out. We never want to pull out your teeth. Once a tooth is pulled out, the jaw recedes due to bone loss. And all that was needed to prevent this tragedy was regular brushing and flossing."

Roberta turned the model back around. She held an oversized toothbrush in hand and demonstrated how to brush.

"To keep them clean, brush in little circles like this," Roberta said.

Roberta moved the brush in a circular motion on the teeth.

"Brush the sides, the gums, the top, and the back," Roberta said. "Angle the brush and really get into the gum line. Next, floss. I have a piece of yarn as my floss."

Roberta placed the model on the projector to free her hands so she could floss it.

"Wrap the floss around your fingers like this and slide the floss between," Roberta explained as she drew the length of yarn between the two teeth. "If you have trouble sliding the floss down, saw the floss back and forth like this. When you reach the gum line, draw the floss around one tooth like this, and the other tooth like this. That's to remove food that brushing can't reach."

"I don't need to floss," said a student. "My toothbrush cleans my entire teeth."

Roberta smiled.

"Let's do an experiment to see how well brushing cleans in between teeth," Roberta said.

Roberta dipped her fingers in tempera paint. She invited the outspoken student to brush her fingers—as if they were teeth—with a toothbrush and paper towel.

"Good, you've cleaned both sides of these 'teeth'," Roberta said as she held up her closed fingers to the class. "But what about between these 'teeth'?"

Roberta spread her fingers apart and revealed tempera paint.

"This is what happens when you don't floss. Food and plaque is stuck between the teeth," Roberta said.

Roberta cleaned her hands with another alcohol towelette.

"For being such a good class," Roberta said, "I have something for each of you. Take one and pass the others back."

Roberta counted out a stack of small shrink-wrapped packages for each row and gave each stack to the students sitting in front. The students took a package and passed the stack back.

"Does everyone have a package?" Roberta asked. "Good. Now open your package. This is your care package for taking home. You should have a new toothbrush, a sample tube of toothpaste, floss, and a six-by-nine-inch sheet of paper with Merry Pumpkin's tips for healthy teeth. You should also have two pieces of tape on wax paper. Don't play with the tape—there's a special purpose for them. We're going to make pledge bracelets."

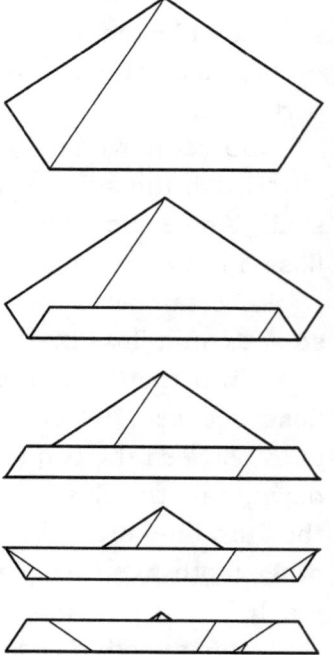

"What's a pledge bracelet?" a student asked.

"A pledge is an oath or a promise," Roberta said. "I'll explain in a moment. But first, let's make our bracelets. Take two opposite corners of the Merry Pumpkin paper and place them together so you make a fold. Now fold up the paper one inch at the bottom. Roll that fold up, and again, and again. When you've made your last fold, tape the middle top point to the fold. You should have a long strip of folded paper. Now put a piece of tape at one end. Wrap the strip around your wrist and tape it together. There—you have a pledge bracelet. Now repeat after me."

Roberta held up her hand as if taking an oath. She instructed the class to do the same. The class repeated Roberta's words as follows:

"I will wear this pledge bracelet...as a reminder to brush and floss my teeth...after I eat Halloween candy...from Trick-or-Treat tonight," Roberta and the class pledged.

Roberta lowered her hand to indicate the pledge was over.

"After you brush and floss tonight," Roberta said, "you may remove your bracelet. Ask your parents if you may tape it in your bathroom so you can see Merry Pumpkin's tips on tooth care. Thank you, class. You've all been very good."

"Let's all clap for Doctor MacNessi," the teacher said.

The class clapped, and Doctor MacNessi thanked them. Before the class stopped clapping, the school bell rang, and the children made a mad dash for the door. Eva stopped at the teacher's desk and spoke with Roberta.

"May I help you pack?" Eva asked.

"Hello, Eva," Roberta said. "Thank you. I think I have everything here. Did you enjoy class today?"

"Yes, I did," Eva said.

"My mother and I are having a cookout this Saturday starting at three o'clock," Roberta said. "We're celebrating my mother's fiftieth birthday. You and your mother are welcome to come."

"I like cookouts," Eva said. "I'll tell Mother tonight. We'll come."

"Good," Roberta said. "Thank you again for helping me. Now you be a good girl and run off to your next class."

"See you later!" Eva said.

"All right, see you, Eva," Roberta said.

Later That Day, at a Family Restaurant.

"Where are we?" Evanita asked older Geneva.

"We're in Candlewood Family Restaurant," older Geneva said. "I always took your mother out to eat before Trick-or-Treat. I wanted to make sure she had a well-balanced meal before she loaded up on candy. Eva always ordered spaghetti for Halloween dinner."

Evanita, older Geneva, and Jonara watched as Eva and younger Geneva ate dinner.

"This is my favorite food," Eva said.

"You are allowed to order whatever you want," younger Geneva said. "You know that, don't you?"

"Yeah, I know," Eva said. "But I like spaghetti."

"Variety is good for us," younger Geneva said.

"How much variety?" Eva asked.

"As much as we can handle," younger Geneva said.

"Do I have to like everything?" Eva asked.

"Well no," younger Geneva said.

"But I have to like more than one thing?" Eva asked.

"You should, yes," younger Geneva said.

"How much more than one thing?" Eva asked.

"As much as possible," younger Geneva said.

"You already said that," Eva said. "Do you like everything here?"

"Well no, not everything," Geneva said.

"Then why do I have to like everything?" Eva asked.

"Eva—I'm simply suggesting you try other kinds of food. You don't have to like them. Just try them once," younger Geneva said.

"Okay, next time I'll try something different," Eva said. "But I'm still eating spaghetti for Halloween."

"Eva," younger Geneva said, "I've decided to make a change in our lives. We're going to be Catholics again."

"I've never been a Catholic before," Eva said.

"Okay, I'm going to be a Catholic again," younger Geneva said. "It's the first time for you."

"Is it more fun than being a Baptist?" Eva asked.

"Well no," younger Geneva said.

"Then I don't want to go," Eva said.

"Eva—I want to give the Catholic faith another chance. I was wrong about a few things," younger Geneva said. "And because I'm going back, we have to stop being Baptists."

"But why? I like being a Baptist!" Eva said. "I don't want to go to a church that's no fun."

"Like your spaghetti," younger Geneva said, "it's not good to attend the same church all the time."

"*It's not good to attend the same church all the time,*" Eva mocked. "But that's what we'll be doing if you make us be Catholics and won't let us be Baptists."

"It's not the same thing," younger Geneva said.

"How come?" Eva asked.

"Because...well...it's Catholic," Geneva said.

"That's not right, Mother. That's not right," Eva said.

"That's what religion is like," Geneva said. "You can only be one."

"Like eating spaghetti all the time?" Eva asked.

"Yes, like...no, wait," younger Geneva said.

"You said it's not good to do the same thing all the time," Eva said. "How about if you be the Catholic and I be the Baptist?"

"That's like me eating spaghetti with meat balls, and you eating spaghetti with meat sauce," Geneva said.

"Is religion like a restaurant?" Eva asked.

"I'm getting confused," younger Geneva said. "I'm not sure."

"If religion is like a restaurant, then we should be able to eat what we like and not eat the icky stuff," Eva said. "That means we should go to all kinds of different religions and see what's on their menu. And Mother, we wouldn't be going to the same restaurant all the time. We wouldn't be eating the same thing all the time. That's...what did you say before? Variety. You said variety is good for us."

"Eva, you're a smart girl. But no one goes around from one church to another like a restaurant," younger Geneva said.

"Why not?" Eva asked.

"It's...it's...sacrilege," younger Geneva said.

"But why?" Eva asked. "Do restaurants have sacrilege?"

"No," younger Geneva said.

"Do other things?" Eva asked.

"Like what?"

"Stores," Eva said.

"No, but they try to trick you into shopping at their stores with sales, coupons, and propaganda," younger Geneva said.

"What's propaganda?" Eva asked.

"Propaganda is a way of making people think or do something by telling them only certain things," younger Geneva said. "A store would use propaganda to keep you from going to another store so you'll give your money to the first store and not someone else."

"Is it lying?" Eva said.

"It's like lying," younger Geneva said, "because it leaves out important details that reveal the truth about something. The end result is a deception."

"What's deception?" Eva asked.

"It's a lie," younger Geneva said.

"Do religions use propaganda?" Eva asked.

"You could say some do," younger Geneva said.

"Does the Catholic religion?" Eva asked.

"Eva—propaganda is not limited to religions. It's something lots of people use," younger Geneva said.

"Lots of people lie?" Eva asked.

Younger Geneva smiled.

"You're a very smart young girl," younger Geneva said. "Tell you what—you come to Mass with me and tell me what you think. If you don't like it, I won't make you go anymore. But try to like it, Eva."

"What about being Baptist? What about variety?" Eva asked. "And what about brushing and flossing?"

"Brushing and flossing?" younger Geneva asked.

"Yeah," Eva said. "How do you brush and floss the propaganda away?"

"You mean brush and floss the plaque away?" young Geneva said. "But you make an interesting point. Propaganda is a lot like plaque. I guess the important thing is to take everything with a grain of salt."

"Is that like taking food with a grain of toothpaste?" Eva asked.

"Very much so," Geneva said. "The key to propaganda is not believing everything you hear. Then the lies don't build up on you like layers of plaque. Sometimes when I get tired of listening to people and their opinions—opinions that are just another type of propaganda, I like to listen to music or do a little dancing."

"Is that like brushing and flossing?" Eva asked.

"In a way, yes," young Geneva said. "Music and dance don't lie. Maybe music is like brushing and dancing is like flossing. They are two of the few truisms in this world."

"I want to learn how to dance, Mother," Eva said. "I want to dance to beautiful music. What's the best dancing in the world?"

"That would be ballet," younger Geneva said, "and you would be a ballerina."

"I want to be a ballerina," Eva said.

"I'll sign you up for lessons in the morning," younger Geneva said.

"Yay!" Eva replied.

The world faded into grays. Evanita and older Geneva returned to the Caves of Healing.

"I don't understand, Grandma," Evanita said. "What was that all about?"

"The conversation between Eva and me may have seemed a little strange," older Geneva said.

"It was a lot strange," Evanita said.

"But it comes down to this—just because an institution has something a person doesn't like doesn't mean everything in the institution must be rejected," Geneva said. "I don't like certain foods at a restaurant, but I still go there and eat what I do like. So it is with the Catholic Church. I don't like some things, but I do like others. So I go for what I like and take that in as nourishment."

"And the things you don't like?" Evanita asked.

"That's when it's time to think about music and do a little dance," Geneva laughed. "But Eva stuck with her Baptist faith during her entire childhood. I took her to Candlewood Catholic Church several times, but she never liked it. I told her that if she spent a little time learning about the Catholic Church, she could learn to like it. To my surprise, she started attending Mass regularly."

"What?!" Evanita asked.

"Yes," Geneva said. "Not only that, but she received many of the sacraments, too."

"This can't be true," Evanita said. "Are we talking about the same person? My Mama? Miss Anti-Catholic? I don't understand."

"Now she didn't attend parochial school—she insisted on continuing her Baptist faith, but she did attend Catholic Sunday school, known as CCD," Geneva said.

"CCD?" Evanita asked.

"Confraternity of Christian Doctrine," Geneva said.

"Huh?" Evanita asked.

"It's another story that I won't go into here," Geneva said. "Nonetheless, I was quite proud of my little Eva for receiving the sacraments of Baptism, Confession, Communion, and Confirmation. And get this—she requested we spend extra time with the priest so she could hold long discussions about all sorts of Catholic topics. The priest recommended I send Eva to parochial school, that Eva would make a good nun, but for some reason, Eva never wanted to attend Catholic school."

"I still don't understand this new-found love for something I always thought she hated," Evanita said.

"Well, I know the answer. It turns out she didn't have a new-found love for the Catholic faith," Geneva said.

"Huh?" Evanita asked.

"That's right. I was cleaning one day and came across a diary. No, it was more like a composition book. She kept notes on every detail of Catholic life that she experienced, and she transcribed the conversations she had with the priest. At first, I thought it was simply a form of study, like taking notes in class, but then I realized what was going on with Eva. She recorded everything in a one-third width column on her note paper, and she analyzed everything in the remaining column. And her analysis was very critical. It was at that point that I realized she was using her Catholic experience as a means to attack it. I couldn't believe it. If she hated it that much, why did she go? But she did. She bit her tongue of pride and endured the agony of the faith—at least in her mind—and formed very strong opinions against the faith. It reached a point in her teenage years where she suddenly stopped participating in the Catholic faith. I tried to convince her to return, but she pulled out her many composition notes and cited seemingly unending evidence as to why the Church was flawed. It overwhelmed me. If I tried to say, 'Name one time when...' she would whip open several places in several composition books where the very incident happened. I tried to poo-poo it as a misinterpretation due to her seeing through the eyes of a child, but then she pulled out scrapbooks with clippings from newspapers, magazines, and photocopies from books—all citing evidence to support her position. That's when I realized she had done more than take notes and analyze. She had read third-party materials. She learned about the Church's history, and she learned the opinions of those against the Church. Oh well, I tried."

Geneva paused. Evanita walked a little in the pool and watched the ripples travel along the surface.

"I walk through this pool, and the pool knows I'm here because of the ripples," Evanita said. "Did your Catholic Church know that my mama—"

"Was more like a spy than one of the faithful?" Geneva asked. "I don't think so. But I knew. And it hurt."

Evanita walked a little more in the pool.

"Grandma," Evanita asked. "Did my mama become a dentist because of Roberta's visit to her fourth-grade class?"

"As a matter of fact, yes," Geneva said. "She kept that paper of Merry Pumpkin in our bathroom until she grew up and went away to school at Wayland Baptist University. Oh, my little girl was on the other side of Texas. It felt like she was on the other side of the world, but Eva insisted on attending the same university as Roberta. Eva was very fond of Roberta. Roberta was like an older sister. After a four-year undergraduate program in Pre-Dental, and a four-year program in dentistry at the University of Texas in Houston, my Eva graduated with a dental degree in 1989."

Evanita counted and recounted on her fingers. She shook her head.

"What's the matter?" Geneva asked.

"Something's not right," Evanita said. "My mama was born in 1964, right?"

"Yes, that's true," Geneva said.

"Did she graduate from high school in 1982?" Evanita asked.

"Yes, she did," Geneva replied.

"Then four plus four is eight meaning she should have graduated from dental school in 1990," Evanita said.

"Yes, true," Geneva said. "Your mother completed her undergraduate degree in three years thanks to heavy semester loads and summer school. That's how she finished a year early."

"Grandma, there's something I don't understand," Evanita said. "My mother is a Unitarian."

"Yes, she is," Geneva said.

"How did she go from being raised as Baptist by a Catholic mother to being a Unitarian?" Evanita asked.

"A fair question," Geneva said. "It was because of Simon. Why don't we take a look? It all started with her graduation from dental school in 1989."

CHAPTER 7

New Practice

2023 Oct 9, Mon Late Afnoon. Corpus Christi, Texas.

The morning had passed into afternoon. The world—which had appeared in the slowness of orange and the quickness of blue—had returned to normal. School let out for the day. Students scurried here and there and in so doing jarred Jonara back to reality. By coincidence, Jonara saw two teenage girls walking with Greg. Greg saw Jonara and waved. Jonara turned her back and pretended not to see him.

"Ah, Jonara," Greg said as he approached. "Girls—this is Jonara, an old friend of mine."

"Old friend?" Jonara asked.

"Jonara—meet my girlfriends," Greg said. "This is Sonja, and this is Dorsia."

Sonja was a well-developed blonde, while Dorsia was a sturdily-built brunette.

"Are you sure she's only an old friend?" a jealous Sonja asked.

"Of course. Do you think I could have eyes for that?" Greg asked as he pointed at Jonara.

"You pig!" Jonara said.

"She sounds jealous," Dorsia said. "You're supposed to pick between Sonja and me—not Sonja, me, and this John-Error."

"My name is Jonara!" Jonara said. "I'm not an error."

"Jonara, please!" Greg said in a fake plea. "You've got to stop obsessing about me. We were never a thing."

"Greg, you're a fat liar!" Jonara said.

"She sounds jealous," Sonja said. "How many other girls are there? You promised!"

"She was never my girl," Greg said. "I swear!"

"If you girls were smart," Jonara said, "you'd dump this guy and find someone honest."

"She's threatening me, Gregie-poo!" Sonja said. "Do something."

"I think John-Error needs a fist in the jaw," Dorsia said as she rolled up her sleeves and squared her stance against Jonara.

"I'm not going to fight you!" Jonara said.

"Dorsia, please! Jonara can't defend herself. She has muscle degeneration and gets tired easily. Don't pick on the unfortunate," Greg said.

Jonara wanted to shout that Greg was the worst liar she had ever met, but she didn't want to agitate Sonja and Dorsia any more. She held herself in a motionless pose in hopes the three would go away.

"Let's get out of here, Gregie-poo," Sonja said. "This park gives me the shivers."

"Yeah, we don't wanna waste time on a degenerate," Dorsia said.

Greg led Sonja and Dorsia away. The two girls looked back and sneered at Jonara. Jonara held herself in check but caught herself growling in a low tone toward them.

"Two stupid girls following a lying sack of manure," Jonara mumbled. "I don't know if I should hate them or pity them. Well, there's nothing I can do. I better get back to Nanna Geneva's house. It'll be suppertime soon."

Jonara headed back and without thinking started down the street toward Cerafina's house.

"What am I doing?" Jonara said as she stopped herself. "Cerafina will reject me again. I wish...I wish...hmph. No good wishing. I could really use a friend. Wait—what about Almarita?"

Jonara pulled out her cell phone and looked for Almarita's phone number, but Almarita's name wasn't listed in her address book. Nor was her mother, Claire.

"Almarita doesn't exist?" Jonara asked. "But how? Unless with the timeline change, some people aren't even born. Nonexistence—what a dreadful thing."

Jonara thought about walking to Corpus Christi Bay, but as she did, her cell phone rang.

"Jonara?" Johnny Pindus called.

"Hi, Daddy," Jonara replied.

"Where are you? It's almost time for supper," Johnny said.

"I'm in a park a few blocks from Nanna Geneva's house," Jonara replied.

"Well come home immediately. You know how Marcus doesn't like to be kept waiting," Johnny said.

"I didn't know that," Jonara said.

"Now you do. Hurry it up, then. Run!" Johnny said.

"Okay, I'll be right there," Jonara said.

Jonara didn't know why, but she ran to Nanna Geneva's house.

"Why am I running?" Jonara said. "I don't care anything about Marcus. Yeah, but he could make my life more miserable than it already is. Keep running, keep running."

Jonara stopped short of running through the front door. She stood on the front porch and leaned over to open the door when Johnny opened it. Jonara fell forward into Johnny's arms.

"Oh, there you are," Johnny said. "I was just about to go looking for you. You're out of breath. Have you been running?"

"Yes," Jonara gasped. "You told me to run."

"Oh, yeah, I did. Come on in. We're all waiting for you," Johnny said.

Jonara walked into the dining room and found Bishop Tárrega sitting next to Marcus, followed by Eva, Evanita, two empty places, and Anna. Johnny and Jonara sat down.

"Before we say grace," Marcus said, "I'm happy to announce Operation Eclipse is in full stride. We're on schedule for the Saturday worldwide fertility conversion. I've spoken with my lead back in Portland, and he assures me the SR-71 Whitebird is capable of making the flight from Portland, Oregon along the eclipse corridor to its destination over our heads here in Corpus Christi at the required speed of Mach 4."

"Why Mach 4?" Jonara asked. "And it's the SR-71 Black-bird, not the SR-71 Whitebird."

Evanita and Johnny shushed her.

"It's quite all right," Marcus said. "I'm happy to answer Jonara's questions. You see, Jonara, the nature of this operation requires the maximum reception of solar coronal light with a minimum of regular sunlight. A total solar eclipse by Earth's moon provides this, but the apparent path of this solar eclipse travels across the earth from Eugene to Corpus Christi at two-thousand, seven-hundred and seventy miles per hour. The only aircraft capable of flying that fast is the SR-71 Whitebird and only after modifications to increase thrust speed. Now I know what you're thinking. Yes, there is an aircraft known as the SR-71 Blackbird, and that was our start vehicle, but its airframe heated too much at Mach 4 for our needs, so its titanium body needed upgrading. We chose a material that would handle the thermal extremes much better—a form of cubic boron nitride alloyed with aluminum oxide—and this material gives the aircraft a crystalline look as if it were a flying diamond."

"I still say a satellite would have been more efficient," Johnny said. "You aren't dependent on the moon to provide an eclipse. A circular disk in front of the satellite can block out most of the sun's rays except for the corona."

"A satellite is too far above the earth to effectively activate the ionized ground minerals left behind by the meteor trail from Portland to Corpus Christi," Marcus said. "Fortunately, Eugene and Portland are close enough together such that we can start the aircraft at Portland and achieve the same results. But enough of that. Jonara—pay attention. The SR-71 Whitebird uses its wings and other parts of its fuselage as focusing lenses to aim and amplify the coronal light onto the ionized mineral trail. The entire trail must be activated for the worldwide chain reaction to begin. This chain reaction will impair X-chromosomes in the ovum until a fertility enzyme from a vitaceptical unlocks it."

"How did you get the power to push the Whitebird to Mach 4? The existing engines aren't quite powerful enough, and if they were, they would unstart at Mach 3.8," Johnny said. "Further, the wings have fuel tanks. Won't those tanks obscure the lensing effect?"

"The engine assemblies are completely redesigned. They are hybrid subsonic, supersonic, and hypersonic devices. Below Mach 1, they use the subsonic engine. From Mach 1 to Mach 3.5, they use supersonic, and above Mach 3.5 they use hypersonic. The hypersonic engines function best when the inlets protrude past the shock cone, and as you pointed out, that's at Mach 3.8. At Mach 4 then, the hypersonic engines are thrusting quite nicely. If we need more speed, we can use it. As to the fuel tanks in the wings, they've been removed so as not to obstruct the lensing effect. The loss is only 25%, and there's still enough fuel capacity to make the leg from Portland to Corpus Christi."

The conversation between Marcus and Johnny gave Jonara a bitter feeling in her stomach.

"Now," Marcus said. "Let's say grace before the food gets cold. Bishop?"

Bishop Tárrega said grace. The group passed the food plates around and helped themselves to a turkey dinner. If Jonara didn't know better, she would have thought her family was celebrating Thanksgiving Day. Jonara felt nothing to be thankful about. She took small portions of food, and even though Evanita urged Jonara to take larger portions, Jonara did not. She ate slowly while the others dug greedily into their plates of food.

"What's the matter with me?" Eva said. "I forgot to get out the red wine!"

"No, I get it for you," Anna said.

Anna ran off to the kitchen and returned with a bottle of Burgundy red wine. She opened the bottle and poured a bit of wine in each glass, including Jonara's.

"Well at least the wine is the same," Jonara said.

"What's that?" Johnny asked.

"The red wine," Jonara said. "Grandma still likes red wine."

"Of course!" Eva said. "There's no substitute in the world for a good red wine."

Jonara sipped the wine and discovered she actually liked the taste.

"Maybe wine is the third truism, after music and dance," Jonara muttered, but apparently the others heard her.

"The three truisms are God the Father, God the Son, and God the Holy Ghost," Bishop Tárrega said. "There are no others."

Jonara wanted to argue the point, but she remembered how her silence with Greg and his two girls ended that conflict, so she employed silence to end any conflict with the bishop before it started.

Jonara helped clean up after dinner. Again she looked for something to watch on television but found nothing of interest. She went upstairs, took a long, hot shower, and went to bed for the night.

2023 Oct 10, Tue 7:27 am. Corpus Christi, Texas.

Jonara stretched her legs and toes while deep in sleep. She stretched too hard and threw her calf muscles into severe cramps. She rolled off the bed and punched the back of her calves with her fists to release the lock the muscles had placed on her tissue. She punched, and punched, and punched. After the fifth punch on each calf, the muscles let go. Jonara stood, but now her calf muscles ached. She walked slowly to the window and looked out, as she had a previous morning when the last stars of night faded into the sunrise of a new day.

"A Spanish woman should never be without her legs," Jonara muttered, "but both of mine were cramping badly. I need some aspirin to relieve the pain."

Jonara limped from her bedroom and down the steps, but in her weariness and poor footing, she missed a step, fell on her back, and thunk, thunk, thunk, thunk she went all the way down. Anna heard the noise and rushed to her aid.

"You hurt?" Anna asked.

Jonara's back and buttocks smarted with pain—pain that combined with her calf pain to set Jonara in a miserable mood that morning. Anna helped Jonara to the dining room table where already breakfast was set out. Marcus, Eva, and Johnny were busily eating while Evanita helped Anna in the kitchen.

"Aspirin," Jonara said. "I need aspirin."

"Do you have a headache?" Johnny asked.

"I didn't before, but with everything else hurting, I'm getting one," Jonara said.

"Here, Jonara, you take aspirin pills with juice," Anna said.

Jonara swallowed the two aspirins and downed them with orange juice. She nibbled on a cinnamon roll as the others spoke.

"We're going to Daily Mass this morning," Eva said to Jonara. "It starts at nine-thirty."

"It's the perfect day for walking," Marcus said. "The sky is clear, and the air is cool. How 'bout it, Jonara? Are you up to it?"

"Jonara's legs are swelling," Anna said. "She not fit for walking."

"Oh, she'll be fine. I think there are some crutches around here somewhere, aren't there Eva?" Marcus asked.

"Yes, there are," Eva replied.

"Would you be a good woman and get them for Jonara?" Marcus asked.

"Of course," Eva said. "Anything for my Marcus."

Jonara felt like throwing up. She could not get over the disgust she had for Marcus treating Grandma Eva like a subhuman slave.

"Here you are, Jonara," Eva said with a plastic smile.

"I help you upstairs so you change into church clothes," Anna said.

Anna helped Jonara upstairs. Jonara's back and legs stiffened up and did not want to move without screaming in pain. Jonara did the best she could to change. Anna wasn't much help. The two were not synchronized in action or thought with the result being the two fighting over how Jonara should change clothes. Frustrated, Jonara asked Anna to leave. Jonara finished changing by herself and hobbled her way downstairs. Marcus forced everyone out of the house with an urgency that

Jonara found unnecessary and rude. Marcus locked the house and dashed to the front of the group where he led the walk, led the talk, and ignored Jonara's requests to slow down. Was Jonara some rock to be ignored? She didn't have the effort to debate it. She slipped into agonizing pain—so much so that she felt herself leaving her body and traveling to some other place and time.

2007 Dec 7, Fri. The Caves of Healing. Carreña, Spain.

"Ow, ow, ow!" Evanita yelled.

"What's the matter?" Geneva asked.

"My legs are burning! This water is like fire!" Evanita said.

Evanita was standing in the pool knee-deep as she had during Geneva's and her venture back in time.

"Strange. The pools are supposed to heal, not harm," Geneva said.

"Ow!" Evanita said again.

"Oh very well. Come sit next to me and see how you feel," Geneva said.

Evanita stepped out of the pool and sat next to Geneva. Geneva rubbed Evanita's legs a little to make them feel better.

"No, don't rub them!" Evanita said. "That only makes them worse. I need a towel. Yeah, a towel."

"Stay here," Geneva said.

Geneva walked over to a small table, took a towel, and returned to Evanita.

"Dry your legs with this," Geneva said.

Evanita dried her legs and placed the towel next to her on the chair.

"How do your legs feel now?" Geneva asked.

"Not as bad," Evanita said. "They feel a little hot instead of scorching hot. And too bad, too. We're getting to the part where my mother is an adult. I want to know what happens next after she graduates from dental school."

"Good," Geneva said. "I'll read the next part in the diary."

1989 May 20, Sat. University of Texas, Houston.

"Where are we?" Evanita asked.

"We are standing outside with my younger self and Roberta at the University of Texas in Houston," older Geneva said. "Eva just finished attending her graduation ceremony, and we're waiting for her to come outside. She's now a dentist, but she doesn't have a practice yet. Look! Eva's heading this way. And she's pushing her boyfriend in the wheelchair."

"Boyfriend?!" Evanita said. "This could be my father!"

Geneva laughed.

"What's so funny?" Evanita asked.

"I'm laughing at what we are seeing," older Geneva said. "Eva is doting on her boyfriend like he's helpless—tending to his every need. Is this the mother you know?"

"No, it isn't," Evanita said.

"There's my Eva!" younger Geneva yelled as Eva wheeled her boyfriend toward younger Geneva and Roberta.

"Hey!" Eva said in a friendly Texas southern drawl.

"Congratulations, Eva!" younger Geneva said. "I'm so proud of you! Give me a hug and kiss. Mmm-mmmph!"

Geneva and Eva exchanged hugs and kisses.

"Mother, you know my boyfriend, Simon Tsarovsky? Simon, you've met my mother, and this is our family friend, Doctor MacNessi."

"Good to see you again, Miss Carreña. Nice to meet you, Doctor MacNessi," Simon said with a Slavic accent.

"Please, let's drop the formalities," Roberta said. "You may call me Roberta. Are you Russian?"

"Thank you, Roberta," Simon said. "No, I'm Ukrainian. My family and I lived in a little town called Narodichi, which for us became a nightmare. The Chernobyl accident of 1986 released large amounts of radiation in my town. My father died putting out the fire at Chernobyl. My mother and I developed thyroid cancer. I also developed cancer in my legs from strontium-90. My mother and I pretended we were Jewish and defected to Israel where we received treatment. We had our thyroid glands mostly removed, but we have to take medication to compensate for the loss. Surgery in my legs removed the worst parts of the cancer, but my legs are very thin now and won't support my weight. After my mother realized I couldn't run quickly enough from Palestinian attacks, she moved us to the United States. I enrolled in the university here to complete my Masters degree in Clinical Informatics."

"Wow," Roberta said. "That's quite a mouthful. How did you meet Eva?"

"The strontium-90 weakened his teeth," Eva said. "He came in to the school clinic frequently for dental care. I did most of my practice work on Simon. At first we were friends, but we developed an attachment for each other."

"Eva is my right hand," Simon said. "I don't know what I'd do without her."

"I know what we need to do *with* her," Geneva said. "We need photos, and lots of them."

Geneva took photos of Eva, Eva and Simon, and Eva and Roberta. Roberta took some photos as did Simon.

"Good," younger Geneva said. "That should do."

"The graduation party is at our apartment," Eva said. "Simon and I woke up extra early today to prepare everything. If everyone is ready then?"

"Uh Eva," Roberta said. "How do we get there?"

"Why don't you ride with me?" younger Geneva offered. "Your car will be safe in the parking lot here."

"Oh, all right," Roberta said.

Roberta and younger Geneva followed Eva as she pushed Simon's wheelchair to the parking lot and next to a van. A special device lifted Simon and his wheelchair from the ground into the van.

"Eva and Simon seem to have everything worked out with his handicap," Roberta said to younger Geneva.

"Yes," younger Geneva said. "All seems perfect."

"Is that a hint, Geneva?" Roberta asked.

"Me? Hint? Never!" younger Geneva chuckled.

"Hmm. Something tells me there's more to this that you're not telling," Roberta said. "But secrets don't last. I'll find out in time."

The van doors closed. Eva and Simon waved goodbye as Eva drove off.

"I'm parked just over here," younger Geneva said to Roberta.

The two entered younger Geneva's car. Geneva drove off and followed closely behind Eva and Simon. After ten minutes, the two vehicles arrived at Eva's and Simon's apartment. Younger Geneva found easy parking, and the two older women got out and watched Eva go through the routine of unloading Simon and his wheelchair from the van.

"We're on the second floor," Eva explained, "but fortunately, this building has an elevator."

"I wonder why Mama never told me about Simon," Evanita said to older Geneva. "Is she embarrassed that she got pregnant out of wedlock?"

"I don't think that's it," older Geneva said.

"Mama also never explained why we live in Portland," Evanita said.

"You'll see for yourself how that comes to be," older Geneva said.

"Was it to get away from Simon?" Evanita asked. "Did he get her pregnant with me and cheat on her?"

"I answered as to the reason a little bit already," older Geneva said. "Details will follow."

"Grandma!" Evanita said.

"Evanita!" older Geneva laughed. "You'll simply have to be patient. The story gets confusing if I jump ahead. Or maybe it's confusing to me."

"So what happened at the party?" Evanita asked. "Anything of importance?"

"Not too much," older Geneva said. "We ate and talked and played board games. Roberta and I noticed that Eva did almost everything for Simon. She put a bib around his neck, she put food on his plate—she even cut his meat for him."

"Why is Simon so lazy?" Evanita asked.

"He likes being babied, and Eva feels like she must take care of him. Some people think this is what love is about, but it's very lopsided. I tried to explain this to Eva at the time, but she would hear none of it. Eva would even help Simon go to the bathroom."

"No!" Evanita said in surprise.

"Yes. True to my word," older Geneva said. "And forget about Simon cleaning the apartment. Eva vacuumed, did dishes, wiped tables, cleaned windows, cleaned the bathroom, and took out the trash."

"Did Simon do anything?" Evanita asked.

"Yes. He called Eva on the telephone as often as possible," older Geneva said. "But anyway, the celebration party went well. Roberta had to go home, and since I was her ride, I had to leave too. As it turned out, the timing was good. Roberta and I were getting a little sick of seeing how much Eva slaved away to Simon's wishes."

"This just doesn't sound like my mama!" Evanita said. "She would never submit her will to anyone—especially a man!"

"That's the only Eva you know. But when she became a dentist, that Eva didn't yet exist," older Geneva said. "Look—I'm dropping Roberta off at her car."

"We'll reach your car in a few minutes," younger Geneva said.

"Thank you for the ride," Roberta said in a monotoned voice.

"Are you all right?" Geneva said. "You seem distant."

"Sorry. I was thinking," Roberta said.

"About Eva?" younger Geneva asked.

"Eva and other things," Roberta said.

"Is Richard working late again tonight?" younger Geneva said.

"Roberta's husband is Richard," older Geneva explained to Evanita.

"So he claims," Roberta said.

"Uh oh. I don't like the sound of that," younger Geneva said.

"It's foolish of me to distrust him just because he's working late at the dental office," Roberta said.

"You and Richard have been business and marriage partners for many years now," younger Geneva said.

"Yeah," Roberta said. "I know every habit, every mannerism, and every facet of our business and our marriage. At least I think so. But something is not quite right, Geneva. I can't put my finger on it."

"So because you can't sort out your feelings, you suspect he's doing something deceitful?" younger Geneva asked.

"It's dangerous jumping to conclusions," Roberta said, "and I promised I wouldn't do it. But when a woman's intuition is waving red flags all over, what is a woman to do?"

"Find out the answer," younger Geneva said. "Why not have him followed?"

"If I do that, I might as well admit the marriage is over. Trust is gone at that point," Roberta said.

The two arrived by Roberta's car.

"If you need to talk, don't hesitate to call or stop by anytime," younger Geneva said. "You and your mother have been good friends over the years. You both were there for me when Andrew died. I'll never forget that."

"You and Eva were there for me when my mother died last year," Roberta said. "I'll never forget that either."

"I don't think Eva will ever forget you. She still has that Merry Pumpkin leaflet you gave her in 1973."

"The Merry Pumpkin leaflet?" Roberta asked. "I'd forgotten all about that. Wow. That was like a different era. I'll have to ask her about that. Well, at least today went well. Thank you again for the ride, Geneva. I'll give you a call later tonight."

"I had a feeling she would call me," older Geneva said to Evanita. "I could see a dark cloud following her, and I knew it was a matter of time before the stormclouds burst open with rain. I was at home looking through some old boxes of keepsakes I had from Eva's childhood when the telephone rang."

"Hello?" younger Geneva said.

"Geneva?" Roberta said. "I need to talk."

"Uh oh," younger Geneva said.

"It's not, 'uh oh' yet," Roberta said. "But it could be."

"Is Richard there?" younger Geneva asked.

"No. I can talk freely," Roberta said.

"Did you find something?" younger Geneva asked.

"Maybe," Roberta said. "There's a message on Richard's answering machine."

"Is that unusual?" younger Geneva asked.

"It shouldn't be, but my intuition says otherwise. I'm tempted to listen to it."

"Don't listen to it yet," younger Geneva said. "I'll be over there in a few minutes. We'll hear it together."

"Okay, I'll wait," Roberta said.

Older Geneva, Evanita, and Jonara followed along as younger Geneva drove over to Roberta's house. Roberta lived in Corpus Christi as did Geneva.

"I drove here as quickly as possible," younger Geneva said. "Let's listen to it together."

Roberta played the answering machine's message: "Hey sugar! I'm in room 309 at CCH. Hurry over quick and see our baby!"

Roberta slapped the answering machine to the floor and shook in rage. She let out a stomach-curdling scream and stomped through the living room tearing into pillows and cushions.

"Roberta, Roberta!" younger Geneva said. "Get a hold of yourself. Don't let him get to you!"

"He betrayed me!" Roberta yelled as she shook her fist in the air. "He had a baby with another woman!"

Roberta rushed into the kitchen and grabbed a meat-carving knife.

"No, no!" younger Geneva shouted.

"I'm going to kill him!" Roberta yelled with knife in hand.

"Then he wins. And you lose!" younger Geneva shouted.

Roberta stood her ground as the conflict of whether or not to attack Richard paralyzed her. Her body trembled. She dropped the knife and pounded on the countertop.

"Stop it," younger Geneva shouted. "You're driving yourself crazy."

"I have to do something," Roberta said. "I'll go crazy with rage if I don't!"

Roberta ran into her exercise room with younger Geneva closely behind. Roberta turned on the treadmill to maximum, and she ran as fast as she could as long as possible. Her heart rate climbed dangerously high.

"Are you trying to kill yourself?" younger Geneva asked.

"I must push myself over the limit!" Roberta said. "I must reach the other side."

"The other side of what?" Evanita asked older Geneva.

"Roberta's trying to work out the huge spike of stress she's received from this bad news," older Geneva said. "Once she pushes herself past the exhaustion point, she believes she can deal with the situation rationally."

Roberta let out one last yell and stopped running. She sat on a nearby chair and breathed hard.

"I must confront him at the hospital," Roberta said between breaths.

"I'm concerned you'll do something you'll regret," younger Geneva said.

"I'm better now," Roberta said. "I won't attack anyone. But before I put an end to this chapter in my life, I want to see what kind of woman he fell for."

"All right," younger Geneva said. "But I'm driving. I don't want you getting in an accident."

"You don't think I'd do something reckless, do you?" Roberta asked.

"You might," younger Geneva said.

"You know me well," Roberta said.

Younger Geneva drove Roberta to Corpus Christi Hospital. The two entered the hospital and proceeded to room 309. As they approached, they heard a female voice from the room.

"He has your eyes."

Roberta and Geneva appeared in the doorway.

"But will he have your propensity for infidelity?" Roberta asked Richard to announce her presence.

Richard stood next to the young mother in the hospital bed who was holding a baby boy.

"This isn't what you think," Richard said.

"Hah! That's what men say when they've been caught," Roberta said. "How could you, Richard, how could you?"

"My name is Sally. You must be Roberta," the young mother said.

"Yeah, I'm Roberta. I'm the wife. And you're the mistress," Roberta said. "What do you have to say for yourself? Is he worth it?"

"Begging your pardon, ma'am, but Richard explained everything. I did this for him and you," Sally said.

"Roberta, Sally's right. She—" Richard said.

"Shut up," Roberta said. "What lies did he tell you, Sally?"

"Richard said you're barren, that you can't conceive," Sally said. "This was our idea to give you a baby."

"Roberta, darling, it's true," Richard said. "I just wanted us to have a family."

"And this is your solution? To go sleeping around town until you get a woman knocked up?" Roberta asked.

"Try to understand!" Richard said.

"You could have asked me first!" Roberta said. "But you didn't, because you knew it was wrong. Well you've done it, Richard. You've started a family with Sally. Sally—he's yours. Richard—our marriage is over. So is our dental partnership. You'll hear from my lawyer. Goodbye!"

Roberta stormed out of room 309. Richard ran up and tried to embrace Roberta.

"Roberta, please! Don't do this!" Richard begged.

"Don't touch me!" Roberta ordered as she brushed off Richard's advance. "I never want to see you again!"

Richard backed off. Roberta and Geneva continued out of the hospital.

"I have a favor to ask," Roberta said.

"I'll be happy to help you gather up your things," younger Geneva said.

Roberta smiled.

"You can read me like a newspaper," Roberta said. "I'll get a motel room for the night until I figure something out."

"Nonsense, you're staying with me," younger Geneva said.

"Geneva, I don't want to impose. Despite my partnership with Richard, I am financially independent. I can afford my own place."

"Financially, yes. But it's not good for you to be alone," younger Geneva said. "Besides, I could use the company. It's not the same with Eva away at school and now living with Simon."

Roberta smiled.

"Thank you," Roberta said. "I accept your offer. But just to warn you—it will be a short stay. I think it's time I left Corpus Christi. I think it's time I left Texas."

"Oh?" younger Geneva asked.

"I've been in dentistry for the money since the early 70s," Roberta said. "I visited elementary schools from time to time, yes, but my dental practice itself was for money. It's time I give a little back. I have a colleague in Portland who would help me start a clinic for low-income patients up there. His name is Doctor Marcus Cracbern."

"That name sounds familiar," younger Geneva said.

"You may have heard my mother mention him," Roberta said. "My mother was good friends with the Dakari family and Dr. Jelana. Dr. Jelana adopted Marcus when he was a newborn. Marcus's own mother died while giving birth to him."

"Yes, but wouldn't that make him Marcus Dakari?" younger Geneva asked.

"I didn't keep in touch with the Dakari family as well as my mother did," Roberta said. "But the short story is this—Marcus grew up, dropped the Dakari last name, and used his biological mother's married name as his own—Cracbern. He became a dentist. He has an office on Page Street in an old converted factory building. There's a vacant office in the building, and he's often suggested I could rent it and start a practice up there if something ever happened."

"Interesting," younger Geneva said. "It's almost as if he knew something would happen."

"He's strange like that," Roberta said. "There have been other times when he seemed to know what would happen before it did—at least that's what my mother used to tell me. Anyway, I'm going to take him up on his offer. He owns the building, so he should be able to help me get started. I have a specialty in pediatrics, so I think it's time I start helping the underprivileged children in Portland."

"That sounds like an excellent idea," younger Geneva said.

"Yeah, it's funny," Roberta said. "I specialized in pediatrics with the intention of treating the underprivileged, but Richard came along, and he convinced me it was better to open a practice catering to the higher-income bracket with cosmetic dentistry. Now I'm returning to the very thing I first set out to do. It's almost like coming home to the roots of my career."

"Do you think you'll get enough patients to make a go of it in Portland?" younger Geneva asked.

Roberta laughed.

"From what Marcus says, I'll be overworked," Roberta continued to laugh. "In fact, I'll be looking for help. I think Marcus has a stepsister who's a hygienist—what's her name? Kay Margo Dakari, yes. I think she's in Alabama. I'll have to give her a call and see what she thinks about moving to Oregon."

"Knowing you, you'll persuade her easily," younger Geneva said. "When you get an idea in your head, you're quite tenacious about following it through."

"Must be my Celtic blood," Roberta laughed.

The scene went dark. Evanita and older Geneva returned to the Caves of Healing.

"What happened?" Evanita asked.

"I don't know," Geneva said. "We lost contact with the past."

"Is there more?" Evanita asked.

"Much more," Geneva said.

"I don't understand," Evanita said. "I asked how my mama became Unitarian, and you said it was after graduation. Well?"

"Oh yes, that. I tend to forget about faiths outside the Catholic Church," Geneva said. "Simon introduced her to the Unitarian faith."

"What religion is he?" Evanita said. "He said he pretended to be Jewish to leave the Ukraine."

"Which means he isn't Jewish," Geneva said. "Yes. Simon is an atheist. He's more into philosophy than religion—specifically existentialism and Marxism. And let's leave it at that. I never understood that combination—for which I am thankful. Eva remained rooted in the Baptist faith and stuck with it—until she met Simon Tsarovsky. He convinced her that there was more to the world than just one religion or ideology. He invited her to a meeting at his UU church. And that was it. She left most of her Baptist upbringing behind. Meanwhile, your mother—well, I should show you."

"My mama?" Evanita asked. "What about my mama?"

Geneva read the next part of the diary concerning Eva and Simon in their apartment.

"Nothing," Geneva said. "The connection is too weak. I'll move my chair into the pool a bit farther to bring the waterline up to my calves."

Geneva did so and repeated reading the passage.

"No good," Geneva said. "You'll have to move your chair down in the pool with me."

Evanita did so.

"How do your legs feel?" Geneva asked.

"Warmer," Evanita replied. "But not too hot for the moment."

"Good. Let's hope your legs stay that way," Geneva said. "I'll begin again."

Geneva read the passage, and the two with Jonara traveled back in time to 1989.

1989 May 21, Sun. Eva's and Simon's Apartment. Houston, Texas.

"Good morning!" Eva said as she wheeled Simon to the dining table. "I got up early and made breakfast. It's all on the table here—eggs, bacon, breakfast rolls, juice, and coffee. I have your plate, utensils, and favorite mug all placed out for you."

"Oh thank you," Simon said. "If you could find a bib for me, I'd appreciate that."

Eva left Simon for the kitchen and returned with a bib. She tied it around him and patted him on the shoulder.

"That's great," he said. "Let's eat!"

Eva placed food on Simon's plate and filled his mug. Having satisfied him for the moment, she sat down next to him and filled her plate with food.

"You always have the best cooking," Simon said with a mouthful.

"You're just being nice," Eva said.

"No, I mean it," Simon said. "You take great care of me."

"Well, you've been through a lot with Chernobyl. And I'm glad I was able to make a difference by saving your teeth."

"You did more than that. You saved my life. I was miserable without you. Now I'm like a king," Simon said.

"Aw," Eva blushed.

"I'm so happy that I have a little gift for you," Simon said.

"Oooo! It's in a little box!" Eva squealed. "Is it what I think it is?"

Simon opened the box and revealed a large, diamond engagement ring.

"Eva Kelicacha Carreña," Simon said. "I love you and have loved you with all my heart and soul. I would drop to a knee if I had better health. But as it is, I must settle for this wheelchair. Eva—will you marry me?"

Eva clasped her hands over her mouth. She was overwhelmed. She pulled her hands away from her mouth and opened her mouth to say something when the telephone rang.

"Wait right there," Eva said. "Don't move."

Eva rushed over to the telephone and answered.

"Hello? Oh hi, Roberta. Okay, I'm sitting down. What is it?" Eva asked followed by a long pause. "Yes, I'm still here. I can't believe what I'm hearing. I mean, is this a joke? It isn't? It just...I don't know...you moved out already? Oh this is terrible, Roberta, just terrible! Good, I'm glad you're staying with my mother. If there's anything I can do to help...you're packing your stuff up at the office? Sure, I can help. I'm a dentist! I know what everything is and how to pack it! I'll be right down.

No, it's not intruding on my day. I had nothing planned. I'll drive right down. See you soon. Bye!"

Eva hung up the phone.

"Have nothing planned?!" Simon protested. "I just proposed to you!"

"Oh," Eva said, remembering Simon's proposal.

"Oh? Is that your response?" Simon asked.

"Simon...I...this is an emergency. Roberta needs my help," Eva said.

"What about me? When do I count?" Simon pleaded.

"Simon, please," Eva said. "You have me every day and night. I rarely spend time with Roberta. Try to understand."

"What about church today? We have that bazaar to go to," Simon said.

"Oh, the bazaar. I forgot about that," Eva said. "Can you cover for me?"

"Me? How am I supposed to run the booth? You do everything," Simon said.

"Simon, you'll have to get along without me. Roberta needs me," Eva said.

"What did you say?" Simon asked with anger building in his voice.

"I'm sorry. I didn't mean to say that," Eva said. "Do you think you can get someone to help you run our booth?"

Simon sighed.

"I have to do everything," Simon said, "and I wanted everyone at church to see your engagement ring. This is supposed to be a special occasion! You're to be my wife!"

"I've got to go," Eva said.

"The least you can do is accept," Simon said.

"What?" Eva asked.

"I proposed to you in marriage. Accept it, and the ring," Simon said, "then Roberta and your mother will see."

Eva walked halfway toward Simon, turned around, walked toward the door, and turned back toward him. She felt split between Roberta and Simon.

"Accept the ring so quickly when I'm rushing out the door? No, that's not very romantic," Eva said.

"You're right, you're not being romantic. Let your mother take care of Roberta. Stay with me today. I need you," Simon said.

"Let's do this another time," Eva said. "I can't think right now. I promise—no interruption. We'll do church activities, go out to eat, whatever."

"There may not be a next time!" Simon said, and in protest he wheeled himself into the bedroom.

Eva spun herself in circles trying to decide which way to go—to Simon or Roberta.

"I'll be back soon," Eva finally said, and she left.

"Wow," Evanita said. "I thought Mama would give in to Simon."

"That was the first time she stood her ground against him," older Geneva said. "But Simon wasn't done. He had other things in mind to control Eva."

"Control?" Evanita asked.

"Well, what would you call it? Games? Manipulation?" Geneva asked.

"I guess *control* is the right word," Evanita said.

"Yes, it was control. Eva drove down to Corpus Christi and helped Roberta pack up her half of the dental office," Geneva said. "Let's take a look and see."

Eva arrived at the front door of MacNessi Dental Clinic and knocked. Younger Geneva met Eva at the door and let her in.

"Mother!" Eva said. "I didn't know you were here."

"I do have some medical training," younger Geneva said. "I am a nurse, after all. Besides, anyone can put things in a box and tape it shut."

"I...well...okay!" Eva said.

"Roberta's back in the lab," Geneva said. "She'll be glad to see you."

Eva walked in the lab.

"Eva!" Roberta said. "Thank you for coming. How did you get away from Simon?"

"Roberta!" Eva replied.

Roberta and Eva hugged.

"I haven't hugged you since you were a little girl," Roberta joked. "You're all grown up."

"Not true," Eva laughed. "We hugged last year at your mother's funeral."

"Like I said," Roberta laughed back, "you were a girl then. Now you are a woman. Turn around for me."

"What?" Eva laughed. "You also saw me recently—at my graduation yesterday."

"I know, but that was in public," Roberta said. "Circumstances were different."

"You mean Simon?" Eva asked.

"Yes. Simon," Roberta said. "So, you didn't answer my question. How did you get away from him today?"

"It wasn't easy," Eva said. "He was in the middle of proposing."

"As in marriage?" Roberta asked.

Roberta looked at Eva's left hand but did not see a ring. She held Eva's left hand to Eva's view and spoke.

"Does this empty finger mean you declined?" Roberta asked.

"No, it doesn't," Eva said, retracting her hand.

"Then you accepted? Where's the ring?" Roberta asked.

Eva grinned.

"I don't see it on this hand," Roberta said as she picked up Eva's left hand again.

"Stop it," Eva said sheepishly as she retracted her hand.

"You're not afraid of me, are you?" Roberta asked.

"Afraid? What are you talking about?" Eva asked.

"Why do you pull your hand back so quickly?" Roberta asked.

"I'm just not used to...not used to...it's complicated," Eva said.

"Hmmm. I sense something odd is going on with you, Eva," Roberta said. "But tell me—did you say 'yes' or 'no' to Simon?"

"I didn't get a chance," Eva replied. "Just as he proposed, you called on the telephone."

"Oh, I'm sorry," Roberta said. "Is that why you pulled away from me just now?"

"Not exactly," Eva said. "But anyway, Simon surprised me with a ring and proposal. I didn't know what to say. Then you called, and that gave me an out. At first he got angry, but then he went off to the bedroom and sulked."

"I'm not surprised," Roberta said. "The way you dote on him, it's like he's a spoiled child."

"Roberta!" Eva said.

"Eva!" Roberta shot back playfully.

"I'm in a loving relationship. Isn't that how you and Richard are...I mean were...I mean...sorry, I didn't mean to stir things up," Eva said.

"No, don't worry about it. I was crushed yesterday. Today I feel better. Being at the office is good therapy. I'm at my best when I'm working."

"Me too," Eva said.

"Give me another hug," Roberta said.

"Why?" Eva said.

"I want to make Simon jealous," Roberta laughed.

"What?" Eva asked. "I didn't expect that from you."

"It's how I'm coping," Roberta said. "I must be projecting or something. I think I really want to make Richard jealous, but he knows I won't jump in the sack with another man. I have too much pride for that. Men—ugh! One moment they're promising you the world, the next they're kicking you to the dogs. But enough about me. Are you going to accept Simon's proposal?"

"If you hadn't called, I would have accepted on the spot," Eva said.

"But now? I sense hesitation in your voice," Roberta said.

"I was caught up in the moment," Eva said. "How could I refuse? But now that I'm away from him and have a moment of peace, I'm giving the proposal rational thought."

"And? Is a marriage to Simon everything you want?" Roberta asked.

"Pretty close," Eva said. "We'll be financially secure, and we'll have a family."

Roberta laughed.

"I didn't hear anything about love or happiness," Roberta said.

"Of course I love him. I take care of him, don't I? I feel a certain sense of attachment to him," Evanita said.

"The same sort of attachment one gets from working a problem?" Roberta asked. "Recall your basic psychology. Working something brings a certain sense of attachment, whether pleasant or unpleasant. But love brings good feelings."

"Did you love Richard?" Eva asked.

"I thought I did," Roberta said. "We were very passionate in the beginning. And we were the ultimate team in the office. I could anticipate what he needed before he did, and vice versa. But now I realize that what I thought was love was actually a work attachment."

"But you said you were passionate with him," Eva said.

"The kind a young couple has without cares for the future," Roberta said. "We tried to have children, but we couldn't. I learned I was sterile as a result of too much X-ray exposure as a child. But I thought it wouldn't matter, that Richard would stay with me regardless—because of love. I suggested we adopt, but he resisted. Now I know why. He was in love with the idea of having his own family. I was supposed to be a part of that—a tool. But I have to wonder—if I weren't sterile—if we had children—would the marriage have lasted? Perhaps long enough to raise the children, but now I'm thinking that after that point, he would go through a midlife crisis as many men seem to do and have children with a younger woman. Well, he had the midlife crisis. And I feel like I've wasted the last twenty years of my life with him."

"So where will you go?" Eva asked. "Across town?"

"No, across country," Roberta said. "I'm moving to Portland—and not the one across Corpus Christi Bay. I'm moving to Portland, Oregon."

"Wow, that is a change!" Eva said.

"I explained this to your mother, but here's the short form—there's an empty office on Page Street just large enough to run a clinic. But I'll change my focus and serve low-income people, primarily children. I thought making lots of money in dentistry would make me happy. At first I thought it did, but now I have this empty feeling in my gut like I've wasted my career on people who have little appreciation for life, and by association, I too have had little appreciation for life."

"You sound very philosophical," Eva said. "Like Simon."

"Somehow I don't think Simon and I would get along, despite our seeming similarities. Aren't existentialistic people mostly into themselves?" Roberta asked.

"How did you know about—" Eva started.

"Your mother told me," Roberta said. "I suppose being self-centered is the primary indication of youth."

"Are you saying I'm self-centered?" Eva said now getting defensive.

"Not like others," Roberta said. "I meant no offense to you, Eva. You're different, of course. I'm not sure if it's your upbringing or genetic makeup. But I am convinced this difference led you into dentistry—to help others."

"And here I thought it was to have a high-paying career," Eva laughed.

"Yes, there's that side," Roberta said. "Time will tell how monetary gain influences your happiness."

"You know, I was thinking," Eva joked. "With you moving out, I could almost move in here and take your place."

"Bite your tongue, Eva Carreña," Roberta said. "You would drive a deep wedge between us if you so much as breathed in the same room as Richard. You're an attractive woman, Eva. Most likely Richard would appear overly nice to you and make advances on you. You might actually believe him, and you might consider dumping Simon for Richard. No, Eva, don't even joke about it."

"Okay, okay," Eva said.

"Have you started looking for a practice?" Roberta asked.

"Not yet. Simon keeps me busy," Eva said.

"With what?" Roberta asked.

"Are you being nosy?" Eva asked.

"No, just professionally concerned," Roberta said. "Dentistry is a highly competitive business. Not everyone can reach your level."

"Thank you," Eva said.

"I actually wasn't trying to flatter you. I was making a factual observation," Roberta said. "The field is dominated by men, which makes your accomplishment even more special. I hope you don't waste your degree."

Eva paused.

"We'll see," Eva said.

"So what does Simon have you do? Besides wheel him around, prepare his meals, do his laundry, clean for him, and take him to the bathroom?" Roberta asked.

"That's getting personal," Eva said.

"He *is* high maintenance," Roberta said. "Eva—you did him a great service by patching up his teeth after his unfortunate radiation damage. But ask yourself this—does he give you anything in return? Before you answer—think about something inanimate that you work at very hard. Compare the two—does Simon give you more than the inanimate object?"

Eva paused in thought.

"I didn't think so. Your love is work-based, just like mine was with Richard. Eva—don't make the same mistake I did. Don't waste twenty years on a man because you get along and feel sorry for him."

"You never said you felt sorry for Richard," Eva said.

"At first I didn't, but when I realized my sterility deprived him of a family, I felt sorry for him," Roberta said. "I should have divorced him back then and found someone who would accept me for who I am instead of how many children I can pop out."

"It sounds like you have a lot of angst against men," Eva said.

"Maybe I'm venting too much," Roberta said. "When I was younger, I was more trusting, more hopeful. Today, I'm more wary."

"And more frustrated?" Eva asked.

"Perhaps," Roberta smiled. "Well, I begin a new life in Portland. I'll have the opportunity to bring a little sunshine into children's lives. I used to do that in the early 70s with my two pumpkins—Merry and Glum. Oh look, here they are in this cabinet."

"I remember those," Eva said. "I still have the handout in my apartment somewhere."

"Well, at least it did some good," Roberta said.

"I'll say. It got me interested in dentistry," Eva said.

"You know, Eva, I'm pretty sure I can find an opening for another dentist in my new practice," Roberta said. "Children respond better to women than men. I could use another woman dentist."

"You mean me?" Eva asked. "That would mean leaving Simon here."

"Bring him with you," Roberta said. "If he loves you, he'll make the sacrifice."

"Simon isn't like that," Eva said. "He's committed to his job at Houston Corner Hospital. He's expecting a promotion to Senior Clinical Informatics Project Manager now that he has his Master's degree."

"And there are no jobs in Portland?" Roberta pointed out.

"He would point out that I can just as easily get a dental practice in Houston," Eva said. "Who wins?"

"Evidently he does," Roberta said. "Never mind. I'll find another dentist. Oregon Health Sciences University has a two-year residency program for pediatric dentistry. I'm sure the university will be happy to lend me one of their students."

"I'm sorry, Roberta," Eva said. "I really wish I could go. Wait a minute—I could help you get started—at least until you get help. When does the residency program start?"

"July 1st," Roberta said.

"That's perfect. I could help out for a month. I'm sure Simon wouldn't mind," Eva said.

"Are you sure about Simon?" Roberta asked.

"A moment ago you were trying to convince me to go," Eva said. "Are you questioning me now?"

Roberta laughed.

"I should just shut my mouth and accept my good fortune," Roberta grinned. "This will be super. You can handle the adult low-income patients, and I can focus on the children. If only you had a pediatric degree, you could take care of children too."

"I plan on making lots of money when I start my practice for real," Eva said. "I have a lot of school loans to pay off."

Roberta laughed.

"Spoken like a true dental graduate," Roberta said.

"Oh, but I'll have to get an apartment for a month," Eva said. "That'll be a trick. Landlords usually expect a one-year contract before going month-to-month."

"Stay with me," Roberta said.

"Oh, I don't want to impose," Eva said.

"I'm staying with your mother now," Roberta said. "Consider it an even exchange."

"All right, it's a deal," Eva said.

"What's a deal?" younger Geneva asked as she entered the lab.

"I'm going to Portland!" Eva said.

"Across the bay?" younger Geneva asked.

"No, in Oregon," Eva said. "Just for a month or so."

"And Simon is letting you?" younger Geneva asked.

"Simon doesn't know yet," Eva said.

"Uh oh," younger Geneva said. "Well, be strong when you tell him."

"He'll just have to get over it," Eva said. "I'm due for a vacation."

Roberta's and younger Geneva's eyes opened wide with surprise.

"A vacation from Simon!" younger Geneva said.

"Yes," Roberta agreed. "That's an interesting word for it."

"So what will you do on your vacation?" younger Geneva asked.

"I'm going to help Roberta start her new dental clinic for lower-income people," Eva said.

Younger Geneva laughed.

"What's so funny?" Eva asked.

"For a moment, I thought you were breaking up with Simon," younger Geneva said. "But now I see you're going for a worthy cause. Good for you, Eva. I'm glad. It also means I won't worry about you, Roberta, at least not while Eva is up there."

"I only need a month or so to get over my situation with Richard," Roberta said.

"A divorce could drag out for several months—perhaps even a year," younger Geneva said.

"It's not the divorce I'll get over. It's the work relationship," Roberta said. "Eva understands."

"I think I understand too," younger Geneva said. "Idle hands lead to the devil's work, but busy hands are divine. I'm glad you're taking this Richard thing on the chin and moving on with your life."

"Please," Roberta said. "Don't say that name anymore. If you must make reference, call him *it*."

"Okay," younger Geneva said.

"We hope you get a speedy divorce from *it*," Eva said.

"Thank you," Roberta said. "I plan to."

Evanita and older Geneva lost their link with the past.

"What happened?" Evanita asked.

"We lost the link," Geneva said. "How do your legs feel?"

"They ache," Evanita said. "I think they might cramp."

"Stand up and walk around a bit on the cave floor—away from the pool," Geneva said. "Stretch your legs."

Evanita walked on the cave floor. She stopped and did leg-stretching exercises.

"Grandma—when your legs were paralyzed from polio, and you stood in this pool, did your legs burn like they were on fire?" Evanita asked.

"No, they didn't," Geneva said. "I gradually gained feeling and control in my legs."

"I don't know why my legs feel like they are on fire," Evanita said. "But you never had metal in your legs like I do, did you?"

"No, I didn't," Geneva said. "My nerves were damaged by a virus. A virus may or may not be living, but it's organic. Your legs were damaged by inorganic chemicals. Perhaps that's the difference. I had hoped these pools could overcome your metal poisoning, but perhaps even these pools are limited. How do your legs feel now?"

"Better," Evanita said. "I'm ready to resume."

1989 May 29, Mon Morn. Memorial Day. Portland, Oregon.

Eva slept on a couch in Roberta's Portland rented house. She awoke to the gurgling of a coffeemaker and the pleasant aroma of coffee.

"What time is it?" Eva asked.

"It's seven o'clock in the morning," Roberta said. "You slept in late."

"You've spoiled me terribly this past week," Eva said as she got up and sat at the kitchen table with Roberta.

Roberta poured Eva a cup of coffee.

"Cream? Sugar?" Roberta asked as she passed both to Eva.

"Both, thanks," Eva said.

Eva poured cream and sugar into her coffee. She watched the cream's form and contours blend into the coffee as she stirred it. Eva took a sip and smiled.

"It's good coffee," Eva said. "Better than I make. In fact, everything you cook is better. You've made all our meals. I'm so used to doing everything for Simon that this is quite a treat. Like I said, you've spoiled me."

"And why shouldn't I?" Roberta said. "You helped me set up the new dental clinic last week. Tomorrow we open for business. And you'll get to meet Marcus Cracbern."

"Yeah, where was he last week?" Eva asked.

"On safari, hunting in Namibia," Roberta said. "He likes hunting the big cats. In December, he hunts mountain lions right here in Oregon."

Roberta's telephone rang.

"That could be Kay," Roberta said. "Hello? Yes, she's right here."

"Simon?" Eva whispered.

Roberta nodded her head in affirmation.

"Hello?" Eva said. "Good morning, Simon. Did you sleep well? I'm sorry to hear that. I know my mother didn't stop by yesterday—you told me that last night. She wasn't supposed to. She'll stop by today. I've only been gone a week. What? We went through this yesterday, and on Friday, and Thursday, and Wednesday. You have to learn to do a few things for yourself. Don't you want to know how my week went? I know you're suffering. Look—you have to hold out for another few weeks. It's just a month, Simon. It's not forever. I have to go. We're expecting a call from the hygienist. Yes, a hygienist. We have to pick her up from the airport this morning. I know it's Memorial Day. The what? It's in the kitchen, in the third drawer down to the right of the oven. I love you, Simon. Yes, I do. Bye."

Eva rolled her eyes and handed the phone to Roberta. Roberta returned the phone to its cradle.

"Simon is very needy," Eva said.

"Or controlling," Roberta said.

"That's not true," Eva said. "He doesn't control me."

"No? He has you looking after him even when you're gone. Your poor mother is running up to his apartment and checking on him."

"If only he would go to the grocery store and do his own shopping," Eva said. "He has the van and wheelchair to do it."

"But why should he when he has a Carreña woman doing it for him?" Roberta asked.

"All right, Roberta, that's enough," Eva said. "I know you're pulling my chain."

"It's a healthy pull," Roberta said. "It gets you to think before you entrap yourself in a big mistake."

"Is that what you think about Simon and me?" Eva asked.

"Honestly, yes," Roberta said.

"Could it be you're seeing Simon through your view of Richard?" Eva asked. "You said before you were guilty of projecting. Simon is not the same as Richard."

"No, not the same," Roberta said. "A different kind of trap."

"Roberta—we're doctors," Eva said. "On our Hippocratic Oath, we are to take care of people."

"Not true. We are to prescribe regimens for the good of our patients according to our ability and never do harm to anyone," Roberta said. "There's a big difference. Ask yourself, Eva. Are you prescribing a good regimen to Simon?"

"I'm not his doctor," Eva said.

"Are you sure? You worked on his teeth," Roberta said. "Just be careful, Eva. Simon has needs, yes, but so do you. It appears to me Simon largely ignores your needs. Does he even know how hard you worked last week?"

"I tried to tell him, but his needs—"

"Took priority," Roberta said. "Yes, I know."

The phone rang again. Eva answered.

"Don't call me until at least the afternoon," Eva shouted.

"Hello?" said a female voice. "Is this Roberta MacNessi's line?"

"Kay?" Eva asked in embarrassment.

"Yes, that's me. Are you Eva?" Kay asked. "I'm sorry for calling so early. I couldn't wait until the afternoon. I caught the red-eye and just landed in Portland."

"Oh Kay! I'm so sorry! I thought you were someone else!" Eva said.

"Let me guess—a boyfriend or husband," Kay laughed.

"How did you know?" Eva said.

"Oh Eva, fashion comes and goes, but men are the same until the end of time," Kay said. "Just let Roberta know that she doesn't need to pick me up. I'm taking a cab to my friend's place. If you need to call me—do you have paper and pen?"

"Yes, go ahead," Eva said.

"The number is 555-2410. Okay?"

"You're welcome to stay here," Eva said.

"Oh no, no, no," Kay said. "Roberta and I already discussed this. I have a lot of catching up to do with my friend anyway. I'll see y'all at the office tomorrow. Bye!"

"Bye," Eva said.

"So Kay Margo Dakari is here," Roberta said. "That's good news."

"She's taking a cab to her friend's house," Eva said. "She says not to pick her up from the airport. Here's the number."

The telephone rang again.

"Hello?" Roberta said. "Yes, Simon."

"I'm taking a shower," Eva whispered.

"She's taking a shower," Roberta said. "I'll tell her. Bye."

Roberta hung up the phone.

"He says—" Roberta started.

"I don't want to know," Eva said.

Roberta reacted in surprise.

"Well!" Roberta smirked. "Is the honeymoon over?"

"A honeymoon can't be over if it never begins," Eva smirked back.

"Whoa!" Roberta said. "I think you're loosening up that stiff collar of yours. Tell you what—let's go for a jog this morning."

"Running?" Eva asked.

"Yes. How did you keep in shape in school?" Roberta asked.

"Ballet," Eva said. "I never lowered myself to jogging."

Roberta laughed.

"Well I admit jogging doesn't have the finesse or flair of ballet, but it does provide an opportunity to exercise and get outside," Roberta said. "I try to jog every day, but with the move and all, I've slacked off. I resent reticence."

"All right. I'll jog with you. But then you have to try a few ballet moves with me later," Eva grinned. "Don't look so shocked. I scratch your back, and you scratch mine."

"This is going to be an interesting month, Eva Carreña," Roberta said.

The two went for a jog.

"There's something my mother used to say," Eva said to Roberta.

"What's that?" Roberta asked.

"A Spanish woman should never be without her legs," Eva said.

"I like it," Roberta said. "I like it a lot."

"My mama got that saying from you?" Evanita asked Geneva as the two returned to the Caves of Healing.

"Yes," Geneva said.

"Did you invent it?" Evanita asked.

"No, the sisters at St. Christopher's Abbey did," Geneva said. "They made it up as an attack against the phrase, *La mujer honrada, la pierna quebrada y en casa.* That literally translates as, *The honest woman and a broken leg at home.* It's an old macho expression that women should stay at home, meaning a wife should cook and clean but have no voice and never go out. If a woman's leg is broken physically, she can't go out, so the metaphor of *broken leg* means confined to the house as a servant to a man. The sisters, of course, have been living outside of male domestic control for centuries. They have their *legs.* So they have always told me a Spanish woman should never be without her legs, meaning she should not be a servant to a man. But I think Eva took it literally. Ballet requires much leg work, and to her that was *having her legs.* Another metaphor is *getting legs* meaning getting a start or support for something. A bird gets her wings, a woman gets her legs. That's the idea, at least."

"Do you think my mama took that expression literally because of your own legs?" Evanita asked.

"You mean my polio?" Geneva asked.

"Yeah," Evanita replied.

"It's true that when these pools healed my paralysis, I *got my legs* literally. Perhaps if your legs improve, you'll *get your legs.*"

"I have a feeling my legs will never return to normal," Evanita said.

"Try to think positively," Geneva said. "The expression about legs is just an expression. Even if a woman's legs are paralyzed, she's not confined to home like the old days. A woman has more career opportunities today. I'm not saying all opportunities are equal or fair—there's still much work to be done. But they are better."

"What about Simon? He's paralyzed," Evanita said.

"As the expression goes, he's more paralyzed from the neck up than the waist down," Geneva said. "That means his real problems are in his head, not his legs."

Jonara's view of the Caves of Healing faded. She was now in Candlewood Catholic Church and had daydreamed through the entire Mass, including the exchange of handshakes. Jonara's mother nudged her to get up for Communion.

"Just when I was learning something, I have to return to this repetition," Jonara said. "I've got to figure out how to change the timeline back to normal. This isn't right. There's too much order in the world."

2110 Dec 29, Mon Noon. 376 Grey Road, Hamilton, New Zealand.

"So that's where you got that expression from," Kristi said.

"Expression?" Jonara asked.

"*A Spanish woman should never be without her legs,*" Kristi said.

"Oh, did I use that expression with you girls?" Jonara asked.

"Yes," Kristi and Margaret said.

"It comes so naturally, I must say it without thinking," Jonara said. "Anyway, it's time for dinner."

"You mean lunch?" Kristi asked.

"No. Dinner is the largest meal of the day despite the time. And I have a turkey in the oven and other fixings that need heating up. Come along! We're going to have a nice turkey dinner!"

CHAPTER 8

Jaw Bite

2110 Dec 29, Mon 1 pm. 376 Grey Road, Hamilton, New Zealand.

"I'm stuffed," Kristi said. "I can't eat another bite. If I were a man, I'd need a nap."

"You may rest if you like," Jonara said.

"Yeah, rest on the couch," Margaret said. "I'll help Mamma Maffet clean up."

"I will as soon as I get this bit of turkey dislodged from my gums," Kristi said. "It's packed in between two molars, and it's killing me."

"I have plastic toothpicks and floss in the restroom, if you like," Jonara said. "Here—I will show you."

Jonara led Kristi to the restroom and showed her the tooth supplies.

"This plastic toothpick is what I need. Thanks, Mamma Maffet," Kristi said.

Jonara returned to cleaning up. Kristi manipulated the bristled end of the plastic toothpick between her teeth and pulled out a blob of turkey.

"Ah, that feels much better," Kristi said. "I might as well floss my other teeth."

Kristi took a length of floss, wrapped it around her fingers, and flossed her teeth. More bits of turkey and other food became dislodged. Kristi found a disposable cup and rinsed her mouth.

"Teeth are a funny thing," Kristi said. "Of all the animals on Earth, I wonder if we put the most effort into taking care of our teeth? Then again, animals don't get dental decay like we do.

Maybe we also abuse our teeth more than animals. Wow, what extremes we humans put our teeth through."

Kristi finished up in the restroom and returned to the living room. Jonara and Margaret finished cleaning up and also returned to the living room.

"I find this alternative timeline very hard to believe," Kristi said. "I mean, really, the United States being a colony of Catalan Spain?"

"A colony of the Kingdom of Aragon," Jonara said.

"But if true, wouldn't we have read about it in our history books?" Kristi asked.

"You were never in the other timeline. You have always been in this timeline," Jonara said. "But I made the journey."

"Did you get back?" Kristi asked.

Margaret and Jonara laughed.

"I am here, so I made it back," Jonara grinned.

"How did you get back?" Kristi asked.

"Let me tell you," Jonara said.

Jonara recalled the last part of her story, and Kristi narrated it as follows:

2023 Oct 11, Wed 4 am. Corpus Christi, Texas.

Jonara slept lightly. Nothing significant happened after Tuesday's Daily Mass. Given how boring the rest of her Tuesday went, she was convinced that any hope of an exciting and fulfilling life in this timeline was all but over. There was dinner—again, boring. Jonara missed the old Cerafina, and of course there was no Almarita to call. Jonara settled for rummaging through old books before falling asleep for the night. Early Wednesday morning, she was awakened by a gnawing sound at the window. Jonara turned on the light and looked at the window. She saw nothing, and the gnawing stopped.

"Must have been a dream," Jonara said.

Jonara turned off the light and returned to bed. After a few minutes, the gnawing returned. Jonara snuck out of bed without turning on the light and crawled to the window. She saw a small, dark shape at the window's screen. She ran to a lamp, turned it on, and ran back to the window, but the shape and gnawing sound were gone. Jonara looked for and found a flashlight. She turned off the lamp and crawled back into bed with the flashlight. After another few minutes, the gnawing returned. Jonara snuck out of bed with the flashlight and crawled to the window. As before, she saw a small, dark shape at the window's screen. She whipped out the flashlight and turned it on. For a brief moment, Jonara saw a squirrel chewing through the screen before it scurried away.

"A squirrel!" Jonara said. "A squirrel is chewing through Nanna Geneva's screen window! Of all the things!"

Jonara opened the window and yelled, "Mr. Squirrel! Haven't you heard? This is an organized country! There's no room for misbehaving! Chew somewhere else!"

Jonara closed the window and returned to bed. As she rested, she thought how ironic that in the other timeline, the window was nailed shut, yet in this timeline where she generally felt more trapped, the window could be opened. Her thoughts were interrupted with more gnawing from the squirrel.

"I'm never going to get back to sleep with this pesky squirrel gnawing away at the screen!" Jonara said. "What do I have to do to get rid of that thing?"

Jonara looked at the Moissan Ruby around her neck.

"If only I could remember Miramish," Jonara said. "If only I could use the power in this Water Ruby to get rid of that squirrel."

But then Jonara had an idea. Could she use the vibration from the squirrel's chewing to activate the Moissan Ruby? If so, perhaps she could then force the squirrel away. Jonara removed the necklace with the Moissan Ruby from around her neck and placed it on the windowsill. The squirrel chewed, the windowsill vibrated, and the Moissan Ruby activated.

"Miramish, Miramish!" Jonara said. "Send squirrel away."

But the squirrel did not go away. It continued chewing. The room swirled into gray, and Jonara found herself in the Caves of Healing with her mother and Nanna Geneva.

2007 Dec 7, Fri. The Caves of Healing. Carreña, Spain.

"Ow," Evanita said. "Did you do that?"

"Do what?" Geneva asked.

"Kick me in the leg," Evanita said. "There. Did you kick me again?"

"No, I didn't," Geneva said.

"It felt more like a bite than a kick, like a fish biting my leg," Evanita said.

"Stand out of the water and walk around," Geneva said.

Evanita stepped out of the pool and onto the dry cave floor.

"There's a dark bruise on your right leg," Geneva said.

"Yeah, that's the spot where I felt something bite me," Evanita said. "Why is this place known as the Caves of Healing when it causes harm?"

"Its healing powers are not always direct," Geneva said.

"Meaning?" Evanita asked.

"Meaning you may receive healing in other ways than in your legs," Geneva said. "Does it feel like something is biting your leg?"

"No, not anymore," Evanita said.

"What if you sit with only your other leg in the pool? Give your bruised leg a rest. You may have to alternate legs like this until—"

"Until what?" Evanita asked.

"Until we finish," Geneva said.

"And when will that be?" Evanita asked.

"When you learn the truth of your conception," Geneva said, "and possibly more depending on how you feel."

Evanita returned to her chair and sat as Geneva recommended—with her bruised leg crossed under her, and with her good leg in the pool. Geneva read from her diary, and the two (plus Jonara) traveled back to 1989.

1989 May 30, Tue Afnoon. Page Street Clinic. Portland, Oregon.

"Three-two-one-done!" Eva counted down.

It was six o'clock Tuesday afternoon. The last patient walked out the door, and the new MacNessi Dental office located in the Page Street Clinic building officially completed its first day of service. The receptionist and two dental assistants clocked out leaving Roberta, Eva, and Kay to finish up.

"Ladies," Roberta said. "I'd like to celebrate our first day of operation with dinner and drinks—on me—at Page Street Pub."

Eva and Kay cheered.

"What do you say we drive straight there?" Roberta asked.

"I can't," Kay said. "I need to pick up my friend first."

"Of course," Roberta said. "She can join us."

"Actually," Kay said, "my friend is a *he.*"

"Oh?" Roberta asked. "Is he a good friend?"

"He's a very good friend," Kay said as she winked. "That's why I'm staying with him and not you."

"I understand," Roberta winked back, and Eva winked too. "Good—bring him along, but he pays his own way."

"I'd have it no other way," Kay said. "I'll see you at the pub in half an hour."

As Kay left the office, Marcus Cracbern—a man with medium-dark skin—entered and offered congratulations first to Kay and second to Roberta and Eva.

"On behalf of the owner and management of Page Street Clinic—" Marcus started.

"Of which you are both," Roberta added.

"Of which I am," Marcus said. "May I offer my congratulations on your first day of business."

"Thank you, Marcus," Roberta said.

"Thanks," Eva said.

"I'd like to take you two ladies out for a drink," Marcus said.

"Too late," Eva said. "Roberta is taking us out and Kay too."

"I'm buying my top girls dinner and drinks," Roberta said. "You're welcome to come along, Marcus. We're meeting at the Page Street Pub in half an hour."

"I accept," Marcus said.

The telephone rang. Roberta answered it.

"MacNessi Dental," Roberta answered. "Simon? Yes, she's here."

"I'll take it in the office," Eva said. A few moments later, she yelled, "Got it."

"Who's Simon?" Marcus asked.

"Eva's boyfriend," Roberta said. "He calls multiple times every day."

"He's very controlling, isn't he?" Marcus asked.

"Yes, unfortunately," Roberta said.

"Long-distance relationships don't work out," Marcus said.

"Eva is only here for a month or so," Roberta said, "until I can find another dentist."

"Too bad I'm caught up in my own practice," Marcus said, "or I'd offer my help."

"Don't worry, Marcus," Roberta said. "I'm sure OHSU (Oregon Health and Science University) will send over an intern after July 1st when the next internship cycle begins."

"Did you register with them yet?" Marcus asked.

"Yes," Roberta said. "Last week."

"Good," Marcus said.

"Thank you for referring the dental assistants and receptionist to me," Roberta said. "You saved me a lot of time and effort in the hiring process."

"I'm glad I could help," Marcus said. "Are you heading over to the pub now?"

"Yes, as soon as Eva finishes with Simon," Roberta said. "I don't know what those two could be discussing that hasn't been discussed before."

Marcus smiled.

"I know what it's like," Marcus said. "When I was engaged, my fiancé called me up every few hours during the work day. She drove me crazy. I'm glad I'm single. I won't make the mistake of marriage."

"Marriage works for some people," Roberta said.

"Did it work for you?" Marcus asked.

"No, not this time around," Roberta said.

"It's better to be single. Trust me," Marcus said.

Eva returned from the other room, and she rolled her eyes.

"You don't want to know," Eva said, "and I don't want to talk about it."

"Let's get something to eat and get your mind off your problems back home," Roberta said.

"Is Marcus my father?" Evanita asked Geneva.

"You'll have to wait and see," Geneva said. "Have patience."

Geneva, Evanita, and Jonara appeared in Page Street Pub. Roberta, Eva, Marcus, Kay, and her boyfriend had finished dinner. Roberta and Eva were enjoying alcoholic beverages while Marcus, Kay, and Kay's boyfriend drank regular beverages.

"What's Kay's boyfriend's name?" Evanita asked.

"I think his name is Earl," Geneva said. "Earl Jackson. I'm not sure how I remember. I didn't see much of him."

As Roberta's table laughed up a good time, the bartender approached.

"Is there an Eva Carreña here?" the bartender asked.

"I'm Eva," Eva said happily.

"You have a telephone call at the counter," he said.

"A hundred bucks says it's Simon," Roberta said.

"That's a sucker's bet," Kay said.

"Marcus, are you in?" Roberta asked.

"I'll pass," Marcus said.

"Earl?"

Kay stared him down.

"No, I best not," Earl said.

Eva returned from the bar with a bottle of red wine. She sat down at the table without saying a word, opened the bottle, and drank from it—straight.

"Whoa!" Roberta said. "Take it easy on the wine."

Roberta took the wine from Eva. Eva was slightly intoxicated and acted with belligerence.

"It's my wine," Eva said as she grabbed hold of the wine bottle. "Give it back."

"You've had enough," Roberta said.

"I'm going to drink that entire bottle!" Eva said as she fought for control of the bottle with Roberta. "Let go!"

"Eva! Do as I say and stop drinking. You've had too much," Roberta insisted.

"No!" Eva protested as she continued yanking on the bottle.

"You're behaving like a child," Roberta said.

"Give it!" Eva said.

Eva yanked the bottle too hard. It slipped from Roberta's hand and carried through the air past Eva until it landed upside-down onto Marcus's shirt. The wine emptied onto Marcus's shirt and soiled it.

"Oops!" Eva said.

"Ack!" Marcus said. "My shirt is wet!"

"I'm sorry, I'm sorry!" Eva apologized as she tried to dry the wine off Marcus's shirt.

"It's too late now," Marcus said. "This shirt is ruined."

"It's getting late," Kay said. "We'll see you tomorrow. Thank you for everything, Roberta."

"Drive safely," Roberta said.

"No, no, no, no, no!" Eva pleaded with Kay. "Don't go! The party is just starting!"

"Get some rest, Eva," Kay said. "Goodbye everyone!"

"Please, Earl!" Eva said as she clung to Earl. "Stay for the party!"

"Eva, let go of him!" Kay said as she pried Eva's grip from Earl.

Eva fell to the floor. Marcus walked over and helped her stand.

"It's time to go home," Roberta said as she left money on the table for the bill.

"No, no, no," Eva whimpered.

"Roberta, are you driving?" Marcus asked.

"Is the ocean blue?" Roberta replied. "Of course I am."

"I'll help her to your car," Marcus said.

"Grandma is drunk!" Jonara said.

"Mama is drunk!" Evanita said.

"It's important you view this situation with a sense of maturity," Geneva said. "This may come as a shock to you, but this is the first time your mother became drunk."

"That is shocking," Evanita said. "Didn't she party in college?"

"No, she didn't," Geneva said. "She worked very hard to get through pre-med and dental school. Now pay attention, Evanita. There's something about your mother you should know. She didn't realize it at the time, but this night marked the beginning of her alcoholism."

"What?! My mama an alcoholic?" Evanita asked. "I know she likes drinking red wine, but I never dreamed she was an alcoholic."

"Not *was*—*is*," Geneva said. "It's in a person's genes. Once an alcoholic, always an alcoholic. There are treatments to control it, yes, and your mother eventually controlled hers."

"But...I don't understand," Evanita said. "She still drinks a glass of red wine from time to time."

"I believe she takes naltrexone to control her alcoholism," Geneva said. "The drug allows her to enjoy a little bit of wine before she loses complete interest in it. That assumes she takes her medication, but she's smart enough to know she has a problem, and she takes the naltrexone as needed. Sometimes she skips her medication to enjoy her wine more."

"How did she get started on that drug?" Evanita asked.

"It was Roberta who got Eva started on naltrexone," Geneva said.

The scene changed from the pub to Roberta's house. Marcus had followed Roberta in his own car. He parked next to Roberta's car and helped Eva—who by now was barely able to walk—to Roberta's home.

"We'll put her on the couch," Roberta said. "Thank you, Marcus."

Roberta and Marcus placed Eva on the couch where she promptly passed out. Marcus stood in the living room for a moment.

"That's all," Roberta said, hinting that he should now leave. "She'll sleep it off."

Marcus stared intently at Eva, especially her face.

"Is something wrong?" Roberta asked. "Marcus? Why are you staring at Eva?"

"She's lying on her back," Marcus said. "It's dangerous."

Marcus approached Eva's face.

"Why is it dangerous? What are you doing?" Roberta asked.

Marcus opened Eva's mouth and looked inside. He pulled her lips and cheeks apart and made special note of her teeth.

"Marcus!" Roberta said. "This isn't the dental office!"

"She could swallow her tongue," Marcus said. "She should be turned on her side."

"That's a myth," Roberta said. "No one can swallow her own tongue. And I'm surprised to hear that myth coming from the lips of a doctor, Marcus."

"All the same, I'll turn her this way," Marcus said. "I should be going now."

"Yes, you should," Roberta said. "Goodnight."

"Goodnight."

The scene faded and returned to the Caves of Healing.

"That was weird," Evanita said to Geneva. "Why was Marcus looking at my mama's mouth like that?"

"Yes, it was strange," Geneva said. "You'll have to be patient for the answer."

"Again?" Evanita asked.

"Yes, again," Geneva said.

1989 May 31, Wed Morn. Portland, Oregon.

"Time to get up," Roberta announced that Wednesday morning.

"Ow," Eva said as she arose from the couch. "I have a brutal headache."

"There's Tylenol in the cupboard," Roberta said, "and there's bottled water in the fridge."

"What happened?" Eva asked as she took the Tylenol with water. "We were eating dinner...and now it's morning."

"You, my dear Eva, got drunk," Roberta said.

"No!" Eva said. "You've got to be joking."

"No joke," Roberta said. "Don't you remember fighting me for the wine bottle and spilling it on Marcus's shirt?"

"No, I don't," Eva said. "I'm so embarrassed. Did Kay—"

"Kay and Earl saw you, yes," Roberta said.

"How can I show my face at the clinic this morning?" Eva asked. "I should quit now and return to Texas."

"Not until we teach you some control with your drinking," Roberta said. "How long have you been like this?"

"I'm not an alcoholic," Eva said. "I don't touch the stuff— normally."

"Is that the truth?" Roberta asked.

"I swear," Eva replied. "It's the honest-to-God truth."

"Well, it appears you have a low tolerance for liquor," Roberta said. "I guess that proves one thing."

"What's that?" Eva asked.

"You're not Celtic," Roberta grinned.

"Are you saying Celtic people can hold their liquor better than anyone else?" Eva asked.

"You know it's true," Roberta laughed.

"If it weren't for this headache," Eva said, "I might laugh with you."

"Come along then, Eva," Roberta said. "Take a nice, hot shower and get dressed. I'll make some breakfast."

"My stomach is queasy," Eva said. "I don't feel like eating anything."

"The food will do you good," Roberta said.

"Okay," Eva said.

Eva showered and dressed for work. Roberta had a simple breakfast of eggs, toast, bacon, and coffee. Eva ate what she could, and the two drove to MacNessi Dental. Eva hoped she could sneak in the office without being seen, but of course everyone noticed her.

"Good morning, Roberta. Good morning, Eva," Marcus said in the Page Street Clinic hallway.

"Good morning, Marcus," Roberta said.

"How's your head this morning?" Marcus asked Eva.

"I'm fine," Eva said.

"You have very nice teeth," Marcus said. "Did anyone ever tell you that?"

Eva shot him a funny look.

"Good morning, Marcus," Eva said as a way of ending the strange conversation.

Roberta and Eva entered MacNessi Dental.

"Why did Marcus make that strange comment about my mama's teeth?" Evanita asked Geneva. "That's the second time he noticed her teeth."

"He *is* a dentist," Geneva said. "But as you've guessed, he's particularly fascinated by your mother's teeth."

Roberta and Eva passed the receptionist without issue. The two went into Roberta's office and put on their lab coats. Kay entered within a few moments and closed the door.

"Before you say anything," Eva said, "I want to say how embarrassed and sorry I am. I don't know what got into me."

"I do," Kay said. "Alcohol. Don't worry—we've all had our moments. I just wanted to see if you needed anything."

"Does anyone else know?" Eva asked.

"I didn't tell anyone," Kay said. "I'm not like that."

"Nor am I," Roberta said.

"What about Earl?" Eva asked.

"Don't worry about him," Kay said. "He had a good laugh and promptly forgot about you when I mentioned the NBA (National Basketball Association) finals. Oh, did he talk my ears off last night! He's a big Detroit Pistons fan, and the playoff series with Chicago is tied at two apiece. Tonight, the teams play again, and he can hardly wait to watch them on television."

"That leaves Marcus," Roberta said. "I don't think he'll say anything."

"Good. Maybe I can get through the day without stares or talk," Eva said.

"You'll be fine," Kay said. "Why don't we go out for lunch at noon?"

"Oh, I don't know," Eva said. "After last night—"

"There's a sandwich shop just down the street," Kay said. "No booze—I promise."

"We'll go," Roberta said.

"Great," Kay said. "Glad to see you're doing well this morning, Eva."

And with that, Kay left the office and tended to her first patient of the day. The morning passed without incident, as did lunch. Eva's queasiness let up by lunchtime, and she was able to eat a full meal without feeling the need to upchuck her stomach contents. Strangely enough, Simon did not call all morning, to which Eva was thankful, but by the time she returned from lunch, the receptionist had a message for Eva.

"It's from Simon," Eva said to Roberta.

"Let's take care of it in my office," Roberta said discreetly.

Roberta led Eva to the office.

"This is not Simon's home phone number, and it's not his business number," Eva said as the two entered Roberta's office.

"Give the number a call," Roberta said.

Eva dialed the number, and Simon answered on the other end.

"Simon! Are you okay? Where are you? Houston Corner Hospital? Why is your work number different? You're not at work? I don't understand—you work at Houston Corner. You're a patient!? What happened? Decubitus ulcers. Yes, I know what that means—I'm a doctor. It means you have bedsores from sitting in your wheelchair without moving around much. I know I helped move you around. I'm sorry. Simon—try to understand— Roberta needs my help. I'm sorry I can't help you. Try to cope, Simon. It's not my fault, Simon. No, it isn't. Simon! Listen to yourself! Simon! Hello? Hello?"

Eva returned the telephone to its cradle.

"He hung up on me," Eva said, who was now practically in tears.

"I can guess what that was about," Roberta said.

"He has bedsores from his wheelchair. I told him to move around periodically to keep his circulation healthy, but he didn't," Eva said.

"And he blames you," Roberta said.

"Yeah, and I'm beginning to think he's right," Eva said. "What am I doing up here? I've abandoned Simon! I'm a disgrace to the medical profession."

"You just said something very revealing," Roberta said. "You believe your lack of attention to Simon is related to your career. Eva—you think of Simon as a permanent patient!"

"I...love him...at least I think so," Eva said.

"I've explained this before—you're confusing career attachment with love," Roberta said.

"I...what am I going to do?" Eva said.

"I find work is a good therapy," Roberta said. "We have patients due in five or ten minutes. Let's prep up for the afternoon."

The afternoon workload was heavy for Roberta, with child after child needing dental work, but light for Eva, who took care of the adults. By four o'clock, Eva's schedule had cleared up, and she was free for the afternoon. She made some calls for Roberta in Roberta's office when Marcus appeared.

"Knock, knock," Marcus said as he knocked on the slightly ajar door.

"Hello, Marcus. Come in," Eva said. "Have a seat."

Marcus held something behind his back. Before he sat down, he presented the "something" to Eva—a single rose in a water-filled glass vase.

"I thought I'd cheer you up," Marcus said. "Please, accept this on behalf of Cracbern Associates."

"I'm surprised," Eva said. "I don't know what to say."

"How about, 'Thank you'?" Marcus suggested.

"All right. Thank you," Eva said.

Eva placed the rose on Roberta's desk, and Marcus sat down.

"You have the most amazing teeth," Marcus said. "May I see them?"

"What? My teeth? Oh Marcus, if I didn't know better, I'd say you're flirting with me," Eva said. "I have a boyfriend, thank you very much."

"I was speaking professionally," Marcus said with a cunning smile, a smile that told Eva something wasn't quite professional with his interest. "Please—just a smile."

Eva smiled, and as she did, Marcus smiled back, which only made Eva feel like smiling even more.

"You have a big, bright, warm and friendly smile," Marcus said. "I bet other women are envious of your teeth."

"You really do get passionate about dentistry," Eva said.

"I should," Marcus said. "I collect teeth from all sorts of living things—and the human teeth of females are always the best."

"What a flattering lie you tell," Eva said. "Men's and women's teeth are practically identical. Men's may be slightly larger to fit the skull size, but that's all."

"Still, there's poetry in teeth," Marcus said. "Have you ever seen the teeth of a mountain lion? Or a Siberian tiger? A great white shark?"

"Not in person," Eva said.

"I have a collection in my office," Marcus said. "Would you like to see?"

"Oh, maybe after work. I have these calls to make," Eva said.

"Calls to suppliers?" Marcus asked.

"Why, yes," Eva said.

"Those are routine. They can wait. If you or Roberta need anything, I can get you supplies until you're well established. Come on—you look like you could use a diversion," Marcus said.

"You can tell?" Eva said.

"I see it in your face. Simon is pulling your heartstrings," Marcus said. "The strain on you is unfair. You should let him go."

"You sound like Roberta," Eva said.

Marcus smiled.

"Did you two conspire against me?" Eva asked.

"Of course not," Marcus said. "We simply came up with the same conclusion independently. It's not hard to see what Simon is doing to you. And as a medical professional, I can tell you that there's very little room for failure in our careers and personal lives. Roberta knows this too. You'll come to realize it soon enough if you haven't already. Come. Let me show you my tooth collection."

"Very well," Eva said.

Eva followed Marcus into the Cracbern Associates office.

"Roberta may or may not have told you, but my associates—Milo and Frank—and I cater to cosmetic dentistry," Marcus explained. "At least we're trying to. So far, the cosmetic dentistry is slow. Most of our business is for routine care. But let's not think about that for now. Let me show you my collection. Here—this is my office."

Eva entered Marcus's office. The walls were lined with shelves—shelves containing skulls of various animals with full sets of teeth.

"This is my *Felidae* shelf—my cat collection," Marcus said. "They have the dental formula of 3.1.3.1 over 3.1.2.1, except for the lynx. You'll notice the long canine teeth. As you know, canine teeth are used for holding and killing prey. Look at these large carnassial teeth for shearing meat and crushing bone. Fascinating, isn't it?"

"Animal teeth seem so vicious compared to human teeth," Eva said.

"Yes, of course. Now look at these skulls. The first one is a mountain lion. Next to it is the skull of a Siberian tiger. Here we have a leopard, a lion, and a panther. I have yet to acquire a cheetah, but I hope to catch one when I go on safari later this year."

"These skulls and teeth are in excellent condition," Eva said.

"The big cats don't have a sugar diet like humans," Marcus said. "They don't get dental caries as we do. Now look—this is my *Canidae* shelf—my dog collection. They typically have a dental formula of 3.1.4.2 over 3.1.4.3. As you can see, the *Canidae* family has more back teeth than the *Felidae*. But they are similar in that *Canidae* also have canine and carnassial teeth. Look at the skulls. First we have a regular dog—this is a German shepherd. Next to it is a coyote, and next to the coyote is a gray wolf. Here—this is a hyena."

"Your shelves are grouped by taxonomic family," Eva said.

"Yes, you have a good eye," Marcus said. "This next shelf is my *Ursidae* family—my bears. The dental formula varies for bears—roughly 3.1.2-to-4.2 over 3.1.2-to-4.3. Look at this brown bear skull. See how the carnassial teeth are underdeveloped compared to the dog and cat shelves? Bears eat more vegetable matter than dogs and cats. Here's a brown bear, and here's a polar bear."

"And here is the ape shelf," Eva said.

"Yes, my *Hominidae* collection, or the great apes. Their dental formula is 2.1.2.3 over 2.1.2.3. Here we have a gorilla, a chimpanzee, and a human. I'm afraid all of these skulls and teeth are models. It's illegal to hunt the great apes," Marcus said.

"You almost sound disappointed," Eva said. "For a moment I thought you were a cold-blooded killer."

"Of course it's wrong to kill the great apes," Marcus said. "But hunting is an interesting spectrum of acceptable killing on the one end versus unacceptable killing on the other end. Civilization is mostly in agreement about the killing of humans being bad, although that seems to change when wars or the death penalty are considered. Hunting vicious animals like the big cats is more acceptable. I have a theory that the acceptability of killing mammals is in direct proportion to the size of carnassial teeth. Originally, my theory included canine teeth, but as you can see—by looking at these models—gorilla and chimpanzee canine teeth are long and overlapping—much like cat, dog, and bear teeth. The apes have conventional molars—like humans, but human canine teeth are very short compared to other animals."

"If your theory is correct, we should be hunting house cats and house dogs," Eva said.

"Yes, my theory needs work, doesn't it? I'll have to give that more thought," Marcus said.

Marcus's telephone rang.

"Dr. Cracbern," Marcus answered. "Yes, Roberta, she's over here. One moment."

"Hi Roberta," Eva said as she answered the phone. "Yes, he's showing me his skull collection. Okay, I'll be right over. Bye."

Eva hung up the phone and looked at a clock on Marcus's office wall.

"I didn't realize it, but it's five o'clock already!" Eva said.

"I have another collection at my house," Marcus said.

"You'll have to show me sometime," Eva said. "I've got to go. Thank you again for the show-and-tell."

"My privilege," Marcus said. "May I escort you to Roberta's car?"

"Dr. Cracbern," Eva said. "If I didn't know better, I'd say you were making another pass at me."

"You have such beautiful teeth," Marcus said. "Smile for me again. Please? Just a smile."

Eva smiled, Marcus smiled, and Eva smiled even more.

"I really have to go," Eva said. "I'll call you tomorrow."

Eva left Marcus's office with a funny feeling in her abdomen. In the hallway between Cracbern Associates and MacNessi Dental, Eva's senses cleared a little.

"Why did I tell him I'd call him tomorrow? That's something a girlfriend would say! Dearie me, Eva, get a grip on yourself. Don't go falling for a man in your own profession. It didn't work for Roberta, and it won't work for you."

Eva returned to MacNessi Dental. She bade goodnight to the assistants and receptionist as she made her way to Roberta's office. Roberta had just completed a telephone conversation and was writing something down.

"Oh, there you are," Roberta said. "Simon called again. The infection is getting worse. He's begging for you."

"I guess it's no use fooling myself into thinking I can help you here in Portland while Simon suffers alone in Houston," Eva said. "I'll have to fly down there tonight and take care of him until he recovers."

"Are you sure? It sounds like he's begging for attention," Roberta said.

"I must. He's my responsibility," Eva said.

"The hospital will treat him to the best of its ability," Roberta said. "Why not stay up here and see how the rest of the week goes?"

"No, I must fly down," Eva said. "I hope you don't mind."

"It's going to be tough," Roberta said. "I counted on you to handle the adult patients until I get an intern—which won't be until after July 1st, as I may have mentioned before."

"I think you did," Eva said.

"I'm not sure if I can handle double the patient load by myself," Roberta said.

"Then allow me to help," Marcus said as he appeared in the doorway.

"You're willing to help me?" Eva asked.

"Of course," Marcus said. "We're all medical professionals. Our duty is to our patients."

"Which has me puzzled, Marcus," Roberta said. "What about your own patient load?"

"At the moment," Marcus said, "Milo and Frank are handling the load. I don't have anything for the next few days."

"Marcus, you're a godsend," Eva said, and she kissed him on the cheek without thinking.

Roberta gave Marcus a suspicious eye, but Eva's happiness was more important to Roberta, and so for the moment she thought nothing more of Marcus. Roberta took Eva home to Roberta's house, and Eva packed quickly. The two grabbed quick sandwiches for dinner before heading out to the airport.

"When will you be back?" Roberta asked Eva as the two traveled to the airport.

"Let's see," Eva said. "Today is Wednesday. I should stay with him at least into the weekend. I'll come back Sunday afternoon so I can return to work on Monday."

Eva flipped down the visor and looked at her teeth in the visor's built-in mirror.

"Something the matter?" Roberta asked.

"No, just looking at my teeth," Eva said.

"At first I thought you were checking your makeup, but you're not," Roberta said.

"Okay, this may sound strange, but Marcus says I have the most beautiful teeth in the world," Eva said. "We were in his office...and I think he made a pass at me. I felt all funny inside. I even promised to call him tomorrow."

"That is strange," Roberta said. "Eva—there's something I have to tell you. It's about Marcus."

"Oh?"

"After dinner yesterday evening, we had to carry you to the couch—Marcus and I that is," Roberta said.

"And?" Eva asked with tension in her voice.

"No, he didn't assault you. I was with you the entire time, and I would never allow such a thing. But he said something strange, that he was afraid you'd swallow your tongue," Roberta said.

"That's a myth," Eva said.

"Which is what I told him," Roberta said, "but he opened your mouth and checked your tongue anyway. He spoke of your teeth. What was it he said? Something about them being beautiful teeth. I think he has a crush on you—or at least on your teeth!"

"I think he has a crush on me too," Eva said, "and I can almost see myself falling for him."

"You can?" Roberta asked.

"I know, I know—it's a bad idea. I saw how your marriage to another dentist didn't work out," Eva said. "A relationship with someone in the same career is just too much."

"It may be," Roberta said. "My marriage to Richard worked out well at first, but the work relationship did place a toll on our personal relationship. We took work home with us too much, I'm afraid. But Marcus—I've known him for a long time. It feels strange to me that you have an interest in him. You're both like family. But forget me—you still have your relationship with Simon. Eva—take some advice—don't date two men at the same time. You'll end up feeling torn apart."

The scene faded and returned to the Caves of Healing.

"What happened? Why did the scene fade?" Evanita asked.

"I'm not sure," Geneva said. "Sometimes it fades when your legs have trouble."

"I have one leg in the water," Evanita said.

"How is the bruise on your dry leg?" Geneva asked.

"It...hey, will you look at that? It shrank. It's almost gone," Evanita said.

"Hmm," Geneva mused. "The Caves of Healing do help you, but not in the usual way. They are beneficial when your affected limb is not directly touching the water."

"Huh? How?" Evanita asked.

"It's a paradox, I know," Geneva said. "But we can't continue the reading of my diary unless you have at least one leg in water. Why don't you walk on the dry cave floor again and stretch your legs?"

"Okay," Evanita said.

Evanita pulled her leg from the pool and to her horror discovered a new bruise on the wet leg.

"Just as I suspected," Geneva said. "Walk on the dry floor, Evanita. It will do you good."

Evanita stepped onto the dry cave floor and stretched her legs while walking.

"But why, Grandma Geneva, why?" Evanita asked.

"It's clear your legs can't remain in contact with the pool for an extended period of time without bruising," Geneva said.

"Maybe I'm getting bed sores," Evanita said.

"That's an interesting analogy," Geneva said, "but the conclusion is the same—we must shift your limbs around so that none are in contact with the water for very long."

"My limbs? You mean my legs?" Evanita said.

"Both of your legs are bruised," Geneva said. "Even though one is nearly healed, I don't think we should put that leg back in the water so soon. What I propose is that you sit such that an arm is in the water."

"Sounds awkward," Evanita said. "How can I...wait, I bet I can do it with two chairs, if I sit on one and use the other to support my legs."

"That's a good idea," Geneva said.

Evanita rushed to the side of the cave, picked up an extra chair, and carried it to the pool.

"Is it okay if I step in the pool for a quick moment?" Evanita asked Geneva.

"I think you'll be fine, Evanita," Geneva said.

Evanita stepped in the pool to position the chairs. She sat in one and placed her legs in the other.

"Oh look, only my fingertips will reach the water," Evanita said.

"If you place the chairs a little apart and pretend you are forming a bed, you could lie down and rest an arm over the side," Geneva said.

Evanita got up and moved the chairs a little apart as Geneva suggested. She tried to lie on them, but her middle section was not supported and wouldn't stay up. She slipped and fell into the pool.

"Evanita? Evanita!" Geneva called.

Evanita did not surface. Geneva jumped out of her chair and sliced the water with her hands to find her granddaughter.

"Evanita!" Geneva called.

About a minute later, Evanita surfaced in a deeper part of the pool.

"Swim back here!" Geneva said.

"I...I don't know how to swim!" Evanita said.

"What?!" Geneva said.

Geneva tossed the diary to a dry part of the cave floor, dove out toward Evanita, swam to her, and ferried her back to the pool's edge.

"Can you stand?" Geneva asked. "Here—let's get you to the dry cave floor."

Geneva helped Evanita to the dry cave floor. Both dripped water onto the floor. Evanita sneezed.

"This won't do. We're soaking wet," Geneva said. "We'll both catch our death of cold."

"Now I know how Johnny feels," Evanita said, referring to his earlier fall into the moat.

Geneva called for Sister Charlene. Sister Charlene wheeled herself in, took one look, and said:

"I'll be right back."

Sister Charlene was gone for a moment and returned with towels and two sister outfits in a laundry basket.

"There's a changing room over to the side there," Sister Charlene said. "Dry off and slip into these clothes. Place your wet clothes in the basket, and I'll have them washed and dried."

Evanita and Geneva entered the changing rooms and came out in sister clothing with one major modification—these outfits had short skirts.

"These are the most unusual uniforms I've ever seen," Evanita said. "The skirts are short."

"They are not meant for the public," Geneva said. "The skirts are high to permit wading in the pools without getting the outfits wet."

Geneva gathered up the wet clothes, placed them in the basket, and handed the basket to Sister Charlene.

"I'll have these ready before you leave—unless you two would like to go out in public looking like sisters," Sister Charlene laughed.

"Johnny would be surprised," Evanita giggled.

"There will be no surprise," Geneva said. "It's disrespectful to the abbey to impersonate sisters."

"Only I would be impersonating," Evanita said.

"I'm no longer a sister," Geneva said.

"Actually," Sister Charlene said, "you never went through the proper process for leaving the sisterhood. You're technically still a sister."

"But I married and had a child," Geneva said.

"Did you marry a Catholic?" Sister Charlene asked.

"No. Andrew was a Baptist," Geneva said.

"Then in the eyes of the Church, you never married," Sister Charlene said. "And you're still a sister. But no one will hold you to it if that's the way you wish it."

"Yes, that's the way I wish it," Geneva said.

"Very well," Sister Charlene said, and she disappeared from view with the wet clothes.

"We're ready to start again," Geneva said. "Now before you try that trick with the two chairs, I suggest you get a third chair and arrange the chairs like a small couch. That means placing the backs of the chairs in the same line."

Evanita took a third chair, and Geneva directed Evanita as to how to align them. Evanita arranged the chairs with short gaps between them. She reclined on them like a small couch and dangled one arm in the water.

"Good," Geneva said.

Geneva retrieved her diary and sat in her own chair. She read the next passage, and the two plus Jonara went back in time.

1989 Jun 2, Fri Eve. Corpus Christi, Texas.

"Eva flew down to Houston Wednesday evening," Geneva explained to Evanita. "She spent that night in the hospital with Simon and all the next day. Thursday evening, she went home to her apartment in Houston."

"But she has a new home with Roberta in Portland," Evanita said.

"Yes, and her old home with me in Corpus Christi—which is where she went early Friday evening after spending all day Friday doting on Simon in the hospital. She was quite tired," Geneva said.

Eva parked her car in her mother's driveway. She walked up to the front door with a night-bag in hand and attempted to open the door, but it was locked. Eva knocked on the door and rang the doorbell.

"Mother," Eva yelled. "It's Eva. Why is the door locked?"

Someone on the inside unlocked the door and opened it. The "someone" was an Hispanic woman—a woman Eva did not recognize.

"*¡Hola!*" the Hispanic woman said.

"Um, I'm sorry," Eva said. "I...do I have the right house?"

"This Carreña house," the woman said.

"I thought so. This *is* my mother's house!" Eva said. "Why am I so confused?"

"You need go hospital?" the woman said. "I call police."

"No, don't call the police," Eva said. "My name is Eva Carreña. I'm Geneva's daughter."

"Oh, you Eva!" the woman said. "My name Anna. I new housekeeper. Come in, Eva. Your mother expecting you."

"She is?" Eva asked in surprise. "I didn't warn her or anything."

"Come in, come in!" younger Geneva said. "That's all, Anna. You may retire."

"Thank you, Miss Geneva," Anna said, and she retired to her room.

Geneva and Eva sat in the living room.

"A housekeeper?" Eva asked. "You? Since when?"

"The house needs cleaning. And meals need to be made," younger Geneva said.

"Mother!" Eva said. "You are the cleanest person I know. And you've made meals without hesitation. Why do you need a housekeeper? Well?"

"I...told you...I..." younger Geneva trailed. "I'm so glad you came by to visit. It's not the same without you."

"I think I understand," Eva said. "You hired Anna to keep you company."

"No!" younger Geneva protested. "Well maybe a little. She speaks good Spanish, too."

"I'm guessing Spanish is her first language?" Eva asked.

"Of course," Geneva said. "But it's Latin American Spanish and not European Spanish."

"Spanish is Spanish," Eva said.

"Bite your tongue!" younger Geneva said. "And I suppose British English is the same as American English?"

"That's different," Eva grinned. "Okay, maybe Spanish in Spain is different from Latin American Spanish. I just had to have a little fun with you."

"I see," younger Geneva said. "But at least your sense of humor has returned."

"Only a little," Eva said. "I could use a drink—then my sense of humor will fully return."

Younger Geneva's eyes opened wide.

"When did you start drinking?" younger Geneva asked. "You refused my Spanish wine all during childhood and into adulthood."

"I grew up," Eva said. "I've decided I like red French wine, but I'll settle for Spanish wine."

"Settle?!" younger Geneva said. "One does not 'settle' for Spanish wine. One savors it. But do not drink Spanish wine for the alcohol. Drink it to experience all that is Spain. Otherwise, you might as well compromise yourself with vodka."

"Where is it?" Eva said as she got up.

"No," Geneva said. "Don't get up. Stay right here. I keep my wine hidden for special occasions. We'll experience Spain together!"

"Is that true?" Evanita asked. "The thing about tasting Spain?"

"Oh Evanita," older Geneva said. "You haven't lived until you've eaten fresh food and local wine. Food in the United States is so homogenized and unfeeling—I don't know how the locals tolerate it. I can only guess they don't know any better. You ate Asturian food and drank wine. What did you think?"

"I didn't pay much attention to the food or wine," Evanita said.

"Think, Evanita," Geneva said. "Do you remember tasting anything?"

"The wine was fruity. The food tasted like farm food," Evanita said. "It almost had a wild taste to it."

"But that's living, Evanita. You can eat something, and instantly you are transformed to the countryside with fresh air, green grass, trees, birds, and animals. It could be a valley or a mountain—the food tells you. It's like music in food. American food doesn't have music—it's more like eating static."

"If I hadn't eaten the Asturian food, I'd think you were talking nonsense," Evanita said. "You did offer me wine. Why? If my mama is an alcoholic—"

"She is," older Geneva added.

"Then why did you offer her wine back in 1989?" Evanita asked.

"I didn't know she was an alcoholic at the time," older Geneva said. "As you have just witnessed, Eva never drank while growing up, and she didn't drink while away at school. She had very strict standards about taking medication of any kind. She refused even the simplest over-the-counter drugs such as aspirin and antacids."

"One bottle of Albariño and two wine glasses," younger Geneva said. "You may not know this, but Albariño was your father's favorite wine. He grew up on a vineyard in Cambados. That's in the Galician province in western Spain. He always had a glass to remind him of home. And I want you to have a glass to remind you of home."

"It's a white wine," Eva said. "No red wine in the house?"

"You'll find that this white wine has just as much alcohol and flavor as any French red wine," younger Geneva boasted.

"Impossible," Eva said.

Younger Geneva filled both glasses. Eva took a sip of the Albariño and smiled with satisfaction.

"Not bad," Eva said.

"Not bad?!" younger Geneva said.

"Perhaps I should sample it again," Eva said.

Eva drained the contents down her throat.

"That's no way to drink wine," younger Geneva said. "You're supposed to swish the wine in your mouth. Allow the flavor to seep into your cheeks. You miss out on everything if you gulp it."

"You're right," Eva said. "I'd better have another glass and do it right."

Eva filled her glass with more Albariño. She took a slurp, swished it around in her mouth, and swallowed it.

"Eva, my dear, it's rude to slurp—especially wine," younger Geneva said.

"It's just the two of us," Eva said.

"And Anna," younger Geneva said.

"She can't hear me," Eva said. "Oh, this wine is refreshing. I've had a long week."

Eva kicked back and reclined somewhat on the couch as younger Geneva watched from the easy chair.

"Oh Mother," Eva said as she felt the first effects of inebriation. "I'm beginning to wonder if I've made a terrible mistake."

"Was helping Roberta that traumatic?" younger Geneva asked.

"Oh no, not at all," Eva said, "although I got drunk as a skunk Tuesday evening."

"You went out drinking?" younger Geneva asked.

"Roberta took Kay and me out to dinner and drinks," Eva said, "to celebrate our first day at the office. It was a special occasion, so I drank. And drank. And passed out. I think Roberta and Marcus helped me home."

"Marcus? Who's Marcus?" younger Geneva asked.

"A hot dentist at Page Street Clinic," Eva said. "He was showing me his skull collection, and do you know what? I suddenly realized I'm feeding Simon's dependency behavior. I'm doing him harm. And I'm doing myself harm. Why am I with Simon, Mother? Why?"

"Do you love him?" younger Geneva asked.

"I thought I did," Eva said. "But Roberta said something that made me think. She said I have a professional attachment to Simon, not a personal relationship."

"What do you think?" younger Geneva asked.

"On a rational level, I think she's right," Eva said. "On an emotional level, I thought she was wrong until Marcus showed me his skull collection. Then I had a feeling in my abdomen I've never had before. I wasn't sure what it was."

"I know what it was," younger Geneva said. "You had butterflies in your stomach. You had a mixture of excitement and nervousness."

"Yeah, that's what it was," Eva said. "Marcus made a pass at me—maybe two. I fought it at first, but later I realized it was a good feeling. Why should I fight it? Simon never made me feel like that. I always felt like I owed Simon something, like he was my responsibility."

"Like a child?" younger Geneva asked.

"I've never had a child, so I don't know," Eva said.

"Eva—I think it's good you're questioning your relationship with Simon. I won't tell you one way or another, but love is very special. It's not something you earn or produce like a medical degree. It's a magical thing that hits you out of nowhere and takes control of you."

"I've never felt out of control with Simon. Control has been very important to me. But twice now in one week I lost control. I got drunk on Tuesday, and on Wednesday I told Marcus I'd give him a call," Eva explained.

"The first loss of control I understand, but not the second," younger Geneva said. "How is giving someone a call a loss of control?"

"Mother! That's the kind of thing I'd say to a boyfriend!" Eva said. "Marcus and I never even went on a date! That was way too fast for me. Telling him I'd call him—well, I lost control!"

"So are you done with Simon?" younger Geneva asked. "If you are, why did you fly down here and spend all day yesterday and today with him?"

"And Wednesday night," Eva said. "I don't know. Maybe it's a habit. Maybe I'm conditioned to act this way with Simon. I used to listen to his monologues about existentialism and Marxism, but I wonder—was I really interested in his philosophical comments, or was I just being polite?"

"Oh Eva, don't let a man confuse your courtesy with love," younger Geneva said. "You have to set limits. Boundaries must be drawn, and he must respect them. Otherwise, you're setting yourself up for abuse, and that could be happening with Simon."

"But how can I be sure?" Eva asked. "How?"

"The fact that you're questioning yourself should tell you," younger Geneva said.

"I only question myself when I'm away from Simon," Eva said.

"Because you're too afraid of his reaction to dare think of challenging him while in his presence. Are you afraid he'll read your facial expressions and intuit what you're thinking?" younger Geneva asked.

"You know, I think maybe I am," Eva said.

"You're an accomplished ballerina and a dentist," younger Geneva said. "Both require lots of raw talent and hard work. You've performed on stage and in a medical environment without fear."

"But those situations are predictable. I can practice, practice, and practice until all the fear is worked out," Eva said. "Why am I afraid of Simon?"

"Are you afraid of rejection?" younger Geneva asked.

"No, I don't think so," Eva said.

"Are you deferring to him out of courtesy?" younger Geneva asked.

"What?" Eva replied.

"It's an unfortunate recurring theme amongst intelligent women. Men's egos bruise easily, so to pacify a relationship, a woman often acts dumber or defers to the man's decision to make him feel important and keep him happy. I suspect that's what you're doing."

Eva sat up immediately as if receiving an electric shock.

"You see, Evanita," older Geneva said. "I acted as your mother's Carreña point. I was the little hill she could climb to get a better view of the valley she'd put herself in. She still had to climb out of it, but I gave her enough insight to know what move to make next—or so I thought."

"I never thought of that," Eva said. "You're absolutely right. I think I convinced myself I needed Simon to make him feel important. I lied to myself."

"That's one of the worst things a woman can do to herself. You are metaphorically cutting yourself to make Simon feel better so you can feel better. It's an unhealthy relationship that in time will explode like a volcano and spew a cloud of old lies and games that will destroy everything good around you."

Eva poured herself another glass and drank it slowly yet steadily. She drained the glass within a minute.

"Careful," younger Geneva said. "You've had quite a bit of wine there."

"I need it," Eva said. "It's good therapy."

"Then might I recommend a good night's sleep here? Your old room is unchanged since you moved out. You can sleep there, or in the guestroom, or anywhere you like."

"I can't sleep," Eva said. "I have too much on my mind. I need to do something with myself—go for a walk or something."

To Eva's and younger Geneva's surprise, the doorbell rang.

Eva jumped in astartlement.

"I wonder...it can't be," Eva said. "Mother—are you expecting anyone at the house this evening?"

"No," younger Geneva said. "No one at all."

"I have this feeling I know who's at the door. I was just thinking about him," Eva said. "No, it can't be. He's in Portland."

The doorbell rang again.

"I answer door," Anna said as she appeared from the other room.

"No!" Eva said as she stopped Anna. "Let me!"

Eva walked up to the door and opened it. To her half surprise and half expectation, Marcus appeared in the doorway.

"Dr. Cracbern!" Eva said. "What are you doing here?"

"You never called me back," Marcus said. "I figured you could use a night on the town, so here I am."

"I...don't know what to say," Eva said.

"Say 'yes'," Marcus said.

Eva turned around and looked at younger Geneva. Younger Geneva shrugged her shoulders.

"What did you have in mind?" Eva asked.

"A late dinner, dancing, and a drive along Corpus Christi Bay. Do you like to dance? I know a great Lindy Hop club about a mile away."

"I love the Lindy Hop!" Eva said. "How did you know?"

Marcus smiled. Eva turned toward her mother as if asking for permission.

"You don't need my permission to go out," younger Geneva said. "You're a big girl now."

"All right, let's go," Eva said.

"Wait!" younger Geneva said. "Don't you think you should have a change of shoes? Heels make for unpleasant dancing."

"Silly me, what am I thinking?" Eva said.

Eva kicked off her high heels and slipped on flats.

"There. Now I'll be comfortable. Let's go," Eva said, and the two were gone.

"I just can't believe my mama is dating this Marcus guy, after the way she reacted in Cerossi Café," Evanita said to older Geneva. "But maybe she didn't know better at the time."

"Oftentimes relationships start out good only to sour in the end," older Geneva said.

"Is that what happened with Mama and Marcus?" Evanita asked. "Did Marcus get Mama pregnant with me?"

"As I've said before," older Geneva said, "you'll have to wait and see."

"It looks like this would be the evening for it," Evanita said. "Mama is buzzing with booze, and she's going out with Marcus."

"Yes, it is not uncommon for a woman to lose her sense of responsibility due to alcohol or other mind-altering substances, but I think you'll see that his evening goes differently," older Geneva said.

The scene changed from Geneva's house to the Candlewick Dance Club, where Eva and Marcus picked up an animated Lindy Hop. The two danced close, apart, their legs kept in sync, Marcus threw Eva over his back, and Eva vaulted Marcus over her. Eva felt she could anticipate Marcus's next move, and with the duavisha, Marcus was able to read Eva. The two danced so well that other dancers stood aside in a circle around the two and clapped them onward until the song ended. Exhausted for the moment, the two sat down for a round of drinks.

"I've never danced with anyone like you!" Eva said. "I can read your lead so easily, and you seem to know what I'm about to do. I just can't get over it!"

"Would you say I'm a better dancer than Simon?" Marcus asked between sips of his non-alcoholic beverage.

"Simon can't dance at all," Eva said after slurping a martini. "Wow, I've missed out on a lot of fun."

"It's a free country," Marcus said. "There's no reason you shouldn't enjoy your dancing. Let me guess—ballet lessons?"

"Yes—again, you seem to read my mind," Eva said.

"You have the figure of a ballerina—well controlled, poised, and balanced," Marcus said. "And your teeth are like icing on the cake."

Marcus mimicked replacing one of Eva's incisor teeth with one of his own. Next, he mimicked taking one of her incisor teeth and using it to replace one of his.

"I'm exchanging teeth with you," he said.

"You are a silly man," Eva said. "Are you envious of my nice teeth? Well, I've always taken good care of them. Another dance?"

The two went back to the dance floor and performed another Lindy Hop. Eva completely lost herself in her dancing and threw a few ballet moves into her performance. The onlookers cheered the two on as they did before. This was the way of the two's evening at Candlewick Dance Club. The hour grew late, and the two rested at their table with more drinking as before.

"I don't know where this energy is coming from," Eva said. "I was exhausted after spending the day with Simon."

"Oh, you are still attached to him?" Marcus asked.

"Let him rot," Eva said in a moment of heavy inebriation.

"Eva, I do believe you mean what you say," Marcus added.

"I should tell him what I really think!" Eva said. "He's been a ball and chain on me since med school."

"Maybe I should take you to your mother's," Marcus said.

"No!" Eva said. "Take me to Houston!"

"Will you smile for me?" Marcus asked. "A really big smile so I can see your teeth?"

Eva smiled, Marcus smiled, and she smiled larger. Marcus touched Eva's incisors, closed his eyes, and inhaled deeply. In her intoxicated state, Eva thought nothing of the act. Marcus opened his eyes and nodded "yes" as if some tension had been released.

"Let's go," he said.

Marcus, having consumed no alcohol, drove the two up to Houston and parked at Houston Corner Hospital.

"Are you sure you want to do this?" Marcus asked.

"Yes," Eva said. "It's time I make a clean break."

Eva and Marcus entered the hospital and ascended to the third floor. Eva paused for a moment before approaching Simon's room.

"What is it?" Marcus asked.

"I just realized something," Eva said. "It was on the third floor of Corpus Christi Hospital where Roberta ended the relationship with her husband. Now I'm going to do the same on the third floor in another hospital—Houston Corner. It's almost like I've done this before."

"You can still turn away," Marcus said.

"No. It's time," Eva said.

"Give me a big smile before you go," Marcus said.

Eva smiled, and Marcus nodded his head.

"Stay right here," Eva said. "This shouldn't take long."

Marcus waited in the hallway while Eva entered Simon's room. Simon was asleep, and Eva woke him.

"Simon?" Eva said as she shook him. "Simon, wake up."

"Is it breakfast time yet?" Simon asked. "Oh Eva, it's you. Could you change my position please? I'm afraid my bedsores are getting worse."

"Simon, I have something to say," Eva said.

"Fine, but I really need you to change my position for me. Please, Eva!" Simon demanded.

"No," Eva said.

"I don't understand," Simon said. "You're ignoring a person in medical need? Doctors don't do that! What's wrong with you, Eva?"

"Nothing's the matter with me. I have to tell you something," Eva said.

"Come closer," Simon said.

As Eva moved closer, Simon sniffed her.

"I thought I smelled alcohol on your breath. You've been drinking," Simon said. "Eva! What's the matter? Tell me your problems, and I'll help you."

"It's not like that," Eva said.

"I just want to help you, the way you've helped me," Simon said. "If you could just change my position first—I'll be happy to give up my sleep time and help you through whatever crisis you want to discuss."

"Simon, will you shut up for a moment and listen? Please?" Eva requested.

"Ow!" Simon said. "Ow!"

"What's the matter?"

"My back is killing me! And I can't roll over! Ow! My position, Eva, change my position."

"Not until you hear me out," Eva said.

"Nurse! Nurse!" Simon called, and he rang a bell.

A nurse rushed in.

"What is it, Mr. Tsarovsky?" the nurse asked.

"My back is killing me! Would you change my position please?" Simon begged.

"Of course," the nurse said, and he changed Simon's position.

"Ahh, thank you," Simon said.

"Is there anything else you need?" the nurse asked.

"No, that's fine," Simon said. "I feel much better now."

"Good," the nurse said, and he turned to Eva. "You're allowed to change his position, you know."

Eva returned a fake smile to get rid of the nurse. The nurse left.

"Was that so much to ask for?" Simon asked. "I had to call the nurse to change my position because you refused to help poor, miserable Simon! I hope you sleep well tonight for what you've done!"

"Simon! Don't talk like that!" Eva said.

"I have every right to talk like this," Simon said. "Something's happened to you, Eva. You went up to Oregon and left me here to suffer. You abandoned me!"

"No, I didn't," Eva said.

"Yes you did. You can't deny the truth!" Simon said. "I have no one to help me and nowhere to turn without you."

"Don't let him get to you," said Marcus as he appeared in the doorway. "He's trying to get sympathy from you."

"Who's that?" Simon asked Eva.

"A friend of mine, Dr. Marcus Cracbern," Eva said. "Marcus—this is Simon."

"A doctor friend? From the university?" Simon asked.

"No, I own Page Street Clinic in Portland, Oregon," Marcus said.

"Oh, I get it now, Eva," Simon said. "You're dumping me."

"Simon, try to understand," Eva said. "It's for the best."

"Whose best?" Simon said. "Was our relationship so boring and meaningless that you had to dig up one of your colleagues?"

"Simon! That's rude," Eva said.

"No, let him talk," Marcus said. "That is what you want to do, isn't it Mr. Tsarovsky?"

"What do I have left? My legs were taken from me by radiation, and now the love of my life is being taken away by another doctor. No matter how much I struggle, I come to the same conclusion, and you are proving it once again—existence is futile!"

"Don't be so glum, Simon," Eva said. "You'll recover and learn to take care of yourself."

Without warning, Simon grabbed Eva's wrist and placed it in his mouth. He bit hard.

"Ow!" Eva yelled.

Eva fought Simon off, but Simon bit all the harder. Marcus rushed over and helped by prying Simon's mouth open with two wooden tongue depressors.

"Are you insane?!" Eva yelled as her wrist was freed. "You bit me hard. I'm bleeding, Simon, I'm bleeding!"

"I want you to get a taste of your own medicine, of what you're doing to me," Simon said.

"If you were a man, I'd punch your lights out," Marcus said.

"It's over, Simon," Eva said. "I'm moving my stuff out of our...out of the apartment. I can press charges, you know."

"But you won't," Simon said. "Because you know you deserve it."

Marcus grabbed a gauze pad from a shelf, opened it, and applied it to Eva's wound. The two left the room with Eva in pain.

"You should get that treated," Marcus said. "If nothing else, get a rabies shot."

"He's not an animal," Eva said.

"He looks like one to me," Marcus said. "Can you move your fingers?"

"Yes, a little," Eva said. "He didn't just draw blood. My wrist aches."

"We're here at the hospital," Marcus said. "We might as well get you checked out and cleaned up."

"And if they ask how I got this?" Eva asked.

"I'll leave it up to you," Marcus said. "But you should be honest and let them know Simon did it. His bite mark is on your flesh. It would be a simple process to match the mark with an imprint of his teeth."

Eva entered the Emergency Room and showed her wrist. After filling out a few forms (with Marcus's help), Eva was admitted. There was no major damage, but her flesh was ripped open. The attending physician took photographs, injected Eva with pain killer, cleaned the wound, took another photograph, injected Eva with a tetanus shot, sewed the wound closed, took a final photograph, and bandaged the wound.

"If you want to press charges," the attending physician said, "we have the photographic evidence. Do you wish to speak with a police officer now?"

"No," Eva said. "I don't want to press charges."

Houston Corner Hospital released Eva into Marcus's care. At Eva's request, Marcus drove Eva to her old apartment—the one she was sharing with Simon. She grabbed her most important items—clothes, jewelry, and keepsakes—and stuffed them into the backseat and trunk of Marcus's car. Marcus took Eva back to Corpus Christi and to Geneva's house. He parked behind Eva's car and helped Eva carry her things into Geneva's house. The hour was late, and Geneva had gone to bed for the night. Eva piled everything on and next to the couch, thanked Marcus, and went upstairs to her old room where she fell asleep for the night.

The scene faded and returned to the Caves of Healing.

"Let's look at your arm," older Geneva said, "the one that's in the water."

Evanita lifted her arm out of the water.

"There. Your arm is okay except for your hand. It's bruised," Geneva said.

"Grandma," Evanita said. "What's in this water that's so special? And why is it bruising my hand? I thought my legs bruised because of the arsenic in them, but my hand too?"

"The pools contain strontium carbonate and strontium sulfate," Geneva said.

"Strontium!" Evanita said. "That's what damaged Simon's legs! This water is poisoning me!"

"Now wait a moment there, Evanita," Geneva said.

But Evanita did not wait. She jumped off the chairs onto the dry cave floor and rushed out the door into the main church area. Geneva held onto her diary, got up, and went after Evanita, but Geneva could not run as fast. Geneva arrived in the main church area just in time to see Evanita exit at the far end. Geneva went to the far end and looked but could not figure out which way Evanita had fled.

"If she gets out of the castle and into the countryside—she could get lost," Geneva said. "Why does that girl have to be impulsive? She's running off again like she does when she lives with Eva!"

CHAPTER 9

The Takeoff

2023 Oct 11, Wed 9 am. Corpus Christi, Texas.

Jonara rolled out of bed onto the floor next to the window. She crawled up to the sill and noticed the Moissan Ruby was still there. The window screen had been chewed out. Jonara placed the necklace with the Moissan Ruby around her neck and opened the window. She noticed sawdust on the bottom of the frame next to what was left of the window screen.

"Where did that come from?" Jonara asked herself.

Jonara drew her fingers across the window frame, the window, and the screen frame. She discovered that the wood holding the glass in place had been chewed into.

"There really was a squirrel!" she said. "He could chew his way into the house!"

"Jonara," Evanita called from down the hall. "Are you awake yet? We need to leave soon for the test flyover."

"What flyover?" Jonara asked as she stood up.

Evanita entered the room.

"Did you just get up? Goodness, Jonara, we're leaving in ten minutes!" Evanita said. "Throw on some fresh clothes and brush your teeth. I'll pack a sandwich and drink for you. Now hurry up!"

Evanita left the bedroom.

"Why must everything be 'hurry up'?" Jonara asked herself.

A short time later, Jonara descended the stairs in a new set of clothes for the day. Eva scuttled Anna, Evanita, Johnny, and Jonara outside while Marcus locked up the house behind. Jonara ran for the minivan.

"Where are you going?" Evanita asked.

"You said we had to go somewhere," Jonara said.

"Not in the minivan," Evanita said. "Look up in the sky."

Jonara looked up and saw a UH-1N Huey helicopter. It made a distinctive chopping sound in the air—a sound she hadn't heard since her vision of the Vietnam massacre in My Lai. The helicopter got closer and landed in a field across the street from Geneva's house.

"Let's go," Marcus said.

Eva scuttled the group across the street and into the helicopter.

"Why are we—" Jonara started.

"Shh," Evanita said. "No time for twenty questions."

The group strapped into seats, and the helicopter ascended. It flew toward Naval Air Station Corpus Christi. During the flight, Jonara looked out and saw other helicopters flying toward the naval base, but the other helicopters were much larger.

"What are those?" Jonara asked.

"They are CH-53E Super Stallion helicopters," Marcus said. "They are carrying people to the naval base for the flyover and landing."

"Landing of what?" Jonara asked.

"The SR-71 Whitebird, of course," Marcus said. "I explained this all before."

"Of course," Jonara repeated almost sarcastically.

The Huey landed at the naval base. A naval officer met with Marcus and led the group to an observation deck by the runway strip.

"Look to the northwest, everyone," Marcus said.

"Which way is northwest?" Jonara asked.

"That way," Johnny pointed.

Jonara looked out the window and saw a vapor trail high in the sky. It approached the naval base quickly without slowing down.

"Is it supposed to land here?" Jonara asked. "It's going too high and too fast!"

The vapor trail continued overhead and passed the naval station. Jonara held her hands over her ears in anticipation of a loud sonic boom.

"What are you doing?" Johnny asked as he pulled away one of her hands so she could hear him.

"I'm protecting my ears from the boom," Jonara said.

Johnny laughed.

"What?" Jonara asked.

"This is an SR-71 Whitebird, Jonara. Its high speed and altitude plus aircraft design yields a softer boom carpet," Johnny said.

"Huh?" Jonara asked.

Jonara heard a low, double-rumble sound.

"Is your stomach growling?" Jonara asked.

"That was the sonic double-boom," Johnny said.

"But I expected the windows to be blasted out," Jonara said.

"That's only in the movies for dramatic effect," Johnny said. "It isn't always that way in real life."

Jonara looked out the window as did the others. Within a few minutes, the SR-71 Whitebird had circled back and approached for a landing. Jonara watched intently as did the others. The crystalline aircraft pitched its nose up and set its wheels on the ground.

"The crystal," Jonara said. "It has a pink tinge to it. Daddy— it looks like the Water Ruby—I mean how the Water Ruby used to look!"

"It's similar material," Johnny said.

"Everything is intact," Marcus cheered. "The airframe and focusing lenses held up to supersonic stress."

The others in attendance realized the same thing and cheered in celebration. Champagne and snacks were wheeled out for all to consume. Jonara tried to ask Johnny how parts of the Moissan Ruby could be in an SR-71 Whitebird.

"Come," Marcus said. "We have a special invitation in the hangar deck with the pilot."

Marcus led Eva, Evanita, Johnny, Anna, and Jonara down to the hangar deck. As the group traveled to the hangar, Jonara posed her question.

"Daddy," Jonara asked. "Are you saying the airplane is made of the same stuff as the Water Ruby?"

"Just about," Johnny said. "The material was excavated from a mountain near Nefasit in Eritrea, Africa. If it weren't for the discovery, the Whitebird couldn't have been created properly."

"Was it discovered by the Dakaris?" Jonara asked.

Johnny gave Jonara a strange look.

"It was discovered by the U.S. Government in 1955 after numerous women were kidnapped from Asmara," Johnny said. "The kidnappers used a mountain tunnel for escape, and the tunnel contained many rare materials. Yes, I think Kay's parents were in that cave looking for one of the kidnapping victims."

"Then that's why the U.S. Government rushed them out of Eritrea," Jonara said. "They wanted to keep the rare minerals a secret."

"You're not supposed to know that. I only know it because Marcus told me," Johnny said.

"Then it—the SR-71 Whitebird—has powers like the Water Ruby," Jonara said.

"Oh, Jonara," Johnny said. "That was all fairy-tale talk about the Moissan Ruby. You're getting too old for those children's stories."

"But Daddy!" Jonara protested.

The group reached the SR-71 Whitebird. It was parked and being refueled. A gentle water spray landed on the aircraft and cooled the fuselage. After a moment, the spray stopped, the pilot opened his canopy, he climbed out, and he removed his spacesuit helmet.

"Adrian, my son, how was the flight?" Marcus asked.

"Your son?" Jonara said. "Does that mean he is my—"

"Say 'hello' to your Uncle Adrian," Evanita said.

"Uncle Adrian!" Jonara remarked in horror.

"Oh!" Adrian said. "How is my favorite niece?"

Adrian waddled over and hugged Jonara the best he could while in his spacesuit. Jonara tried to back away, but Adrian held the hug for several seconds.

"You are the smartest little thing," Adrian said to Jonara. "How would you like to fly one of these birds when you grow up?"

"Huh? Me?" Jonara asked.

"Sure!" Adrian said. "Heck, why wait till you grow up? You could go for a ride today, now in fact."

Several people rushed up to Jonara with multiple spacesuits and assorted equipment. Some readied the equipment while others took Jonara's body measurements.

"No, wait, what are you doing?" Jonara asked.

"Don't worry, honey, you'll be okay," Evanita said. "She *will* be okay, right Marcus?"

"Of course!" Marcus said.

"I don't want to go across the country!" Jonara said.

The people stuffed Jonara in a spacesuit and prepared to attach the helmet.

"It's just a test flight over the city," Adrian said. "The spacesuit is for your safety."

"Daddy?" Jonara asked. "Do I have to?"

"I...well...if your mother says—" Johnny stumbled.

"Go on, Jonara," Evanita said. "Be a good girl and sit in the airplane."

Jonara looked at Johnny again. Johnny shrugged his shoulders. The people attached the helmet onto Jonara's spacesuit. Adrian attached his own and led Jonara up the steps to the SR-71 and helped her climb into the passenger seat. Adrian climbed into the cockpit and lowered the canopies.

"Please, let me out," Jonara said.

"Relax, Jonara," Adrian said. "You're perfectly safe. As I said, we'll make a test run over the city."

"But why me? I have nothing to do with this," Jonara said.

"You're family," Adrian said. "Family is always involved."

Adrian taxied the Whitebird onto the runway. Jonara looked through the crystalline fuselage and saw rainbow spectral colors as the light changed angles—colors that were dancing back and forth as if preparing for an explosive party.

"Don't worry," Adrian said. "For your benefit, I'll limit the takeoff to three Gs."

Adrian radioed for takeoff. He received confirmation from the tower, and then it happened—Adrian commanded the subsonic engines to fire. The engines screamed and nearly deafened Jonara—even with the helmet on. The aircraft lunged forward and squished Jonara to the back of her seat. The engines shook the passenger compartment, and despite Jonara's feeling of being trapped under an elephant, the engine vibrations activated the Moissan Ruby and sent Jonara back in time.

2007 Dec 7, Fri. Carreña, Spain.

"Has anyone seen my granddaughter?" Geneva asked as she rushed through St. Renata's Abbey. "Her name is *Evanita.* Has anyone seen my Evanita?"

Most sisters did not see Evanita, but one saw the girl run out of the barbican, across the moat, and down the hillside. Geneva thanked the sister and dashed across the moat herself. She started running down the hillside when she stopped herself.

"Geneva, what are you doing? You're too old to chase a teenage girl who jogs for fun. Follow her in the car."

Geneva returned up the hill to her car and drove down. She looked from side to side in hopes of locating Evanita but had no such luck. Geneva continued driving down the hill, and at the bottom, she saw Evanita running along the side of the road. Geneva pulled up alongside her and rolled down the window.

"Evanita!" Geneva said. "Where are you going?"

"Back to the hotel," Evanita replied.

"Get in the car," Geneva said. "We need to go back to the abbey."

"I'm not going back!" Evanita said.

"We must," Geneva said. "We haven't finished your Carreña point."

"I can't take it anymore," Evanita said. "I'm done!"

Evanita continued jogging in her sister outfit, and Geneva followed alongside in the car. The two reached Carreña Hotel, and Evanita attempted to open the door to Geneva's and her hotel room, but it was locked. Evanita stepped to the adjoining room and knocked on the door.

"Johnny!" Evanita said as she knocked on the door. "Open up! It's Evanita."

Geneva finished parking and caught up to Evanita. Geneva searched for her key to the hotel door when Johnny appeared. Johnny's eyes opened in amazement when he saw Geneva and Evanita in sister outfits with short skirts.

"What happened to—" Johnny started to say, but Geneva opened her door and allowed Evanita in.

Johnny followed the two into Geneva's room, but Geneva pushed and locked him out.

"What the...what's going on?" he asked through the door.

After a few minutes, Geneva opened the door and allowed Johnny in. Geneva and Evanita had changed out of the sister clothes and into conventional clothing.

"Evanita," Johnny said. "The outfits...and...were you running just a moment ago?"

"I ran all the way here from the abbey," Evanita said.

Johnny looked at Geneva for an explanation.

"It's true, she did," Geneva said as she closed her hotel room door. "And as for the outfits—we got our other clothes wet in the Caves of Healing. Sister Charlene was nice enough to lend us these—but she didn't expect us to run off with them."

"I had to leave," Evanita said. "The water in that pool was poisoning me."

"It only appeared to be poisoning you," Geneva said.

"Johnny, look at my bruises," Evanita said.

Evanita showed Johnny the bruises on her legs and hand. Johnny looked at Geneva for another explanation.

"The pool is supposed to heal, not harm. The water caused her limbs to bruise for some unknown reason," Geneva said.

"What were you doing while you were in the water?" Johnny asked Evanita.

"Nothing," Evanita said. "That's why I know it's poisoning me. I did nothing wrong."

"I read my diary, and we saw visions from the past," Geneva said. "I had hoped to show Evanita everything, but when I told her about the strontium in the pools, she ran off."

"It's laced with strontium, Johnny," Evanita said. "I learned that strontium causes cancer."

"She saw Simon Tsarovsky then?" Johnny asked Geneva.

"Yes. The entire Chernobyl situation regarding the strontium affecting Simon's legs was explained."

"If it injured him, it's injuring me," Evanita said.

"But the pools don't contain the same radioactive strontium that injured Simon," Johnny said to Evanita. "The pools should be safe."

"Then how do you explain the bruising?" Evanita asked.

"I suggested it had to do with the arsenic in her legs," Geneva said.

"And my hand too? Is there arsenic in my hand?" Evanita asked.

"Hmm," Johnny mused. "It does seem odd. How far did you get with the visions?"

"We reached Eva's breakup with Simon," Geneva said.

"So you haven't reached the chase over Sellwood Bridge yet?" Johnny asked.

"No. That's another few months," Geneva said. "We haven't even reached your visit to MacNessi Dental."

"Hmm. I started going right before everything turned stressful," Johnny said. "If Evanita's in stress now, she won't have the strength to deal with what comes up next."

"Did you have to say that in front of Evanita?" Geneva asked.

"What stress?" Evanita asked. "And what chase? Why can't you two just tell me what happened instead of forcing me to go through this agony with my bruised legs and hand?"

"Maybe we should," Johnny said.

"No," Geneva said. "It won't work."

"How can you be sure?" Johnny asked.

"Because of the diary and *viola de gamba*," Geneva said. "I explored the possibility using the viol's ability to see the future—

our present-day struggle to help Evanita understand her past—with the diary's record of the past. Simply telling Evanita will result in Evanita developing resentment and bigotry toward Eva, and that in turn will generate self-hatred in Evanita. If you don't believe me, use your Moissan Ruby and scan the diary and viol."

Evanita gave the Moissan Ruby to Johnny. Geneva placed the *viola de gamba* and diary on a bed, Johnny walked up to both, placed one hand on the diary and the other on the *viola de gamba*. Maintaining his touch on the stringed instrument, he plucked a string. The vibration carried through his body and activated the Moissan Ruby.

"I see—" Johnny started.

"Don't say what you see," Geneva said. "You'll ruin everything if you do."

Johnny watched a future version of himself, Geneva, and Evanita sitting in the hotel room while Geneva described what happened in the next few months of 1989 and 1990, including Evanita's conception. The future Evanita reacted with shock and horror, and she demanded a quick return to Portland, Oregon to confront Eva. Evanita recounted the events of 1989 and 1990. Eva confirmed the truth to those events. Evanita started a yelling match with Eva that only ended when Evanita stormed out of Eva's house and never returned. Evanita sought out and found Adrian. Adrian agreed to provide a shelter for Evanita. The two quickly created an ideological and romantic relationship. With Adrian supporting her, Evanita attended college and earned a degree in political science. The two became active in politics and pushed extreme right-wing conservative positions. As the years went by, Adrian—with the support of Evanita—won elections for the state legislature and Governor of Oregon, and upon reaching age thirty-five ran for and won the Presidency of the United States. With Evanita continuing to urge him on, Adrian launched major conservative issues in the United States. He convinced the Supreme Court to overturn Roe vs. Wade to outlaw abortion of all kinds, he successfully lobbied for and pushed through a constitutional amendment to ban homosexual marriage, he legalized corporate discrimination based on social class, and he built asylums to house people his government deemed unfit for American society—most of which were political enemies. Again spurred on by Evanita, Adrian launched major military offensives against other countries and rallied American businesses to produce additional military hardware to support his offensives. In retaliation for New Zealand's refusal to allow American nuclear ships to dock at New Zealand ports, Adrian invaded and conquered New Zealand. He set up his own puppet government that installed nuclear military bases, ended nationalized health coverage, and closed down all brothels.

"Well?" Geneva asked Johnny.

"Okay, you're right," Johnny said.

"Maybe you can read the diary in this hotel room," Evanita said. "What about that?"

"That's the same as telling you," Geneva said.

"What if Johnny uses the Moissan Ruby to help?" Evanita asked.

"Johnny," Geneva said. "Why don't you investigate that possibility first?"

Johnny touched the diary and plucked the *viola de gamba*'s strings again. His vision was the same—Evanita hooked up with Adrian and pushed him into extreme ultraconservative politics and into the U.S. Presidency. Johnny let go of the musical instrument and diary. He tried standing up, but his knees buckled, and he fell to the floor.

"Johnny?" Geneva asked.

"Johnny, Johnny!" Evanita said as she rushed to help him.

Evanita helped Johnny to a chair. His eyes rolled around, he gasped for breath, and in a moment his complexion went from stark white to a natural color. He looked at Evanita and spoke.

"I'm all right now," he said. "Thank you, Evanita."

"What happened?" Evanita asked.

"The visions...they happened so quickly. And they were the same as before...I mean...it repeated...too quickly...it was all so exhausting," Johnny said.

"In other words," Geneva said, "we must get Evanita back to the Caves of Healing to finish the therapy. Any other method will prove disastrous."

"Yes, you're right," Johnny said.

"I can't go back," Evanita said. "I don't trust the water."

"What if you had some assurance the water won't hurt you?" Geneva said.

"How?" Evanita asked.

"The Moissan Ruby could scan your vital signs," Geneva said. "If there is danger to your legs, the person with the Moissan Ruby could alert you."

"If I had constant reassurance that my body isn't being damaged, then I would consider it," Evanita said. "But can you operate the Moissan Ruby, Grandma?"

"No, I can't," Geneva said.

"Then we're stuck," Johnny said. "The sisters won't let me in."

"The sisters won't let a male in," Geneva said.

Geneva looked at Evanita, and Evanita looked back with a puzzled look. Then Geneva shifted her eyes toward Johnny quickly. Evanita realized what Geneva was saying, clapped her hands in glee, and broke out in laughter.

"What's so funny?" Johnny asked.

"Did anyone ever tell you, Johnny, that you have excellent bone structure in your face?" Geneva asked.

"Huh?" Johnny asked.

"And you have nice, succulent lips," Geneva said. "And a good figure."

"Now wait a minute!" Johnny said as he picked up on Geneva's plan. "Me dress up in drag? No way! I won't be caught dead dressed as a woman!"

"Why not?" Evanita asked. "Your facial features are perfect, you have a thin body, and the rest we can take care of with clothing, shaving, and makeup."

"Uh-uh," Johnny said. "I'm not that kind of a guy!"

"No one says you are," Geneva said. "Think of yourself as an actor playing a part."

"I don't know anything about being a woman!" Johnny said.

"Somehow I don't believe that," Geneva said. "Surely you've scanned a few with the Moissan Ruby in your time?"

"Yeah, but that's biology. I'm talking about...you know...acting and talking like a woman," Johnny said. "I'm a man, dammit! A man!"

"Evanita, I do believe it's time to go clothes shopping—for Shawna," Geneva said.

"Who's Shawna?" Johnny asked.

"That's your new name!" Evanita giggled. "Oh Grandma, this is going to be loads of fun!"

"We'll have to take pictures, of course, to measure our progress," Geneva said.

"No! No pictures, no cross-dressing! I refuse! There's got to be another way!" Johnny demanded.

"Okay, Johnny," Geneva said. "Class 101 about shooting down ideas—you must provide a superior replacement idea. What is your superior idea? And before you make the suggestion, I want you to test it against the *viola de gamba* and the diary as you did when you tested the possibility of finishing our work in the hotel room. Also, check what will happen if you do dress as a woman and we go inside. I'll abide by the result. If that road causes disastrous results, then I'll entertain another idea. But you must come up with something."

"Why do I have a feeling I should take a slug of whiskey before I sneak a peak at my cross-dressing future?" Johnny asked.

"There's a bar in the restaurant next to this hotel," Geneva said. "I would prefer you try wine, but I'm sure the bar can accommodate anything you like."

"Good," Johnny said. "Let's go."

The three took a short walk to the nearby restaurant. The bar was located at the far side of the restaurant away from the main door. Geneva, Evanita, and Johnny walked the length of the restaurant and sat at the bar counter.

"I'll have a shot of whiskey," Johnny said.

Geneva's and Evanita's eyes lit up.

"You weren't kidding," Geneva said.

Geneva ordered a glass of Albariño for herself and juice for Evanita.

"No," Evanita said. "I want Albariño too."

"Very well," Geneva said. "Two glasses of Albariño."

The bartender brought one shot glass of whiskey and two glasses of Albariño.

"Ready?" Johnny asked.

"We're not the ones doing a shot of whiskey," Geneva pointed out.

"Yeah, right. Okay, it's for me then. One, two, three!" Johnny said, and he launched the shot glass to his mouth and dumped its contents down his throat.

Geneva and Evanita each took sips of the Albariño as Johnny gagged on the whiskey.

"It's like the worst cough medicine in the universe!" Johnny said.

"You mean you've never had whiskey before?" Geneva asked.

"Nope. First time," Johnny choked.

Geneva rolled her eyes.

"You should be more careful," Evanita said. "Don't take things so hard."

"How was your wine?" Geneva asked Evanita.

"Unusual," Evanita said, "like Baroque music. Oh, how silly of me! Wine doesn't taste like music."

"First impressions are often the most accurate," Geneva said. "And I think your impression is quite favorable. If you'd said the wine made you suddenly thirsty for more, I'd worry."

"No, not thirsty for more," Evanita said. "But I think it reminds me of Baroque music, because I can taste it and find a certain beauty in it, and a little goes a long way. I neither tire of it nor am I obsessed with it."

"Very interesting!" Geneva said. "Johnny—is your whiskey like that?"

"No," Johnny wheezed. "But I'll tell you one thing—it feels like I lost some cells in my throat. And if there's music in whiskey, it's Heavy Metal."

Geneva and Evanita laughed. Geneva drank the rest of her wine, but Evanita drank only half of hers.

"I don't need the rest," Evanita said. "Johnny, would you like my Albariño? It might soothe your throat."

"Thank you no," he said. "I can't handle any additional alcohol in my gastrointestinal tract."

"Does that mean you're ready to check the *viola de gamba*, the diary, and the Moissan Ruby?" Geneva asked.

"Yeah, I think so," he said. "At least while my mind is distracted by my suffering throat."

The three returned to Geneva's and Evanita's hotel room.

"I'm as ready as I'll ever be," Johnny said.

As before, Johnny placed a hand on the diary, the other on the *viola de gamba*, and he plucked a string. He tried the possibility of Geneva using the Moissan Ruby in the Caves of Healing, but that line proved ineffective as Geneva was unable to channel the stone's power properly. He investigated the line of himself teaching Geneva how to use the stone, but days dragged into weeks with Evanita growing impatient and regressing back into apathy. Johnny investigated the line where Evanita wore the Moissan Ruby, but the interaction between the Moissan Ruby, the pool water, and the past was too much and sent Evanita into cardiac arrest. Johnny released his touch on the stringed instrument and put the diary to rest.

"Well?" Geneva asked an out-of-breath Johnny.

"I tried several different possibilities," Johnny said. "And they didn't turn out well."

"Did you try *the* possibility?" Geneva asked.

"No, not yet," Johnny said. "I'm afraid of what I'll see."

"That's okay, Johnny, you don't have to," Evanita said. "The thought of you dressing like a woman was a cheap thrill anyway. Well, Grandma, does that mean we can return to Oregon? I think I've seen enough of the past."

"What will you do when you get home?" Geneva asked.

"Oh, I don't know. Hang out with people, I guess," Evanita said.

"What about us?" Johnny asked.

"What about us?" Evanita replied.

"I thought...you and me...do you still love me, Evanita?" Johnny asked.

Evanita looked down for a moment and looked up as if deflated.

"I don't know anymore," Evanita said. "One thing I've learned is that lots of people everywhere have loads of problems. I'm tired of hearing these problems. If love means having to carry some of that load, then I'm thinking I should cut loose the love strings before they hang me."

Johnny placed his hands on the diary and *viola de gamba* and plucked a string. He investigated what would happen if the three returned to Oregon without completing the visions in the Caves of Healing. On returning to Oregon, Evanita withdrew into herself and became more apathetic. She did no homework, skipped school, and hung out with other people her age who also quit school. Evanita consumed various drugs at various times from various people—alcohol, marijuana, methamphetamine, cocaine, ketamine, and LSD. However, only the first doses were free. Evanita needed to pay for additional drugs. To support her new drug habit, she stole money from Eva. When Eva stopped keeping money in her purse, Evanita stole things from the house and sold them. Evanita lied about the thefts and about her drug problem. Eva sought to place Evanita in a rehab clinic, but Evanita and her drug friends were caught robbing a store and were sent to the Elrod 402. In the Elrod 402, Evanita delivered a baby stillborn—killed from drug abuse. Evanita became cranky from drug withdrawal and initiated many fights. She died while in vicious combat with the German girl.

Johnny closed his eyes and prayed that this would not come to pass for Evanita. He plucked another string. The world around him went black. He plucked another string. Again—black. He plucked two strings together. There—the vision started. Johnny was dressed as a woman. The three returned to St. Renata's Abbey where Sister Charlene led them to the Caves of Healing. All three dipped their feet in the water. Johnny as Shawna held onto Evanita and gave her limbs resistance to bruising while the three journeyed into the past. Evanita witnessed the events leading to her conception, and she broke into tears, but she harbored no resentment toward her mother. The group returned to Oregon where Evanita hugged her mother and formed a new mother-daughter bond. Evanita completed her Coming-Of-Age ceremony, danced a waltz with Johnny, married him a couple of years later, and bore a daughter— Jonara.

Johnny realized that this vision was the best outcome he could hope for. He removed his hands from the *viola de gamba* and diary, opened his eyes, and looked at Geneva. He bit his lip, hesitated, and spoke.

"Okay," Johnny said. "I'll dress up as Shawna."

Geneva and Evanita jumped for joy.

"But keep in mind the sacrifice I'm making," Johnny said. "Evanita—I'm doing this for you because I realize the difference this will make, and because I love you so. I hope that love will reemerge in you."

"Okay, Johnny," Evanita said, and she gave him a hug and kiss. "I do appreciate it. Thank you."

Geneva and Evanita took him clothes shopping, wig shopping, makeup shopping, shoe shopping, purse shopping, and epilator shopping. They took measurements, picked colors, and found an outfit. By the time all shopping was complete, it was dinnertime. The three ate at the restaurant next to Carreña Hotel and were happy.

"It's too late in the day for Shawna's birth," Geneva said. "Tomorrow we will begin the makeover."

2007 Dec 8, Sat. Carreña, Spain.

The three woke up, ate breakfast, and met in Geneva's and Evanita's hotel room. Johnny shaved and removed body hair from his neck, arms, and legs with the epilator.

"Ow, this hurts!" Johnny said as the epilator yanked out gobs of hair.

"Now you know what we go through," Geneva said.

"This is torture! This is madness! There should be a law against it!" Johnny said.

Evanita giggled.

"Now it's time for a mask," Geneva said.

Johnny reclined on a bed while Evanita applied facial cream to Johnny's face.

"Now don't move your face," Evanita said. "That means no talking!"

Johnny tried asking how long he would have to wear the mask without moving his face, but his grunts and groans were unintelligible.

"No talking!" Evanita said.

"We should soften his hands right now to save time," Geneva said.

"Good idea," Evanita said. "Shawna—listen carefully. We need to soak your hands in warm water for ten minutes. Now don't get up or anything. We'll have you—"

Geneva brought a large bowl of warm water and handed it to Evanita.

"Thank you, Grandma," Evanita said. "Now Shawna—we'll keep the bowl on your chest. Don't push it off when you breathe. Place your hands in it and keep them there. They have to soak. Good. Now hold this position."

Ten minutes later, Evanita removed the bowl of water from Johnny's chest.

"Good," Geneva said. "Now it's time to soften your hands. Hold out your hands together, Shawna, as if receiving a gift from Heaven."

Johnny cupped his hands side-by-side and faced them upward. Geneva poured sugar and baby oil into his hands.

"Now rub your hands together—thoroughly—including the back of your hands and in-between your fingers," Geneva said. "Do this for a few minutes until the sugar and oil are worked in."

Johnny worked the oil and sugar into his hands while keeping his face steady. A few minutes passed. Evanita returned the bowl of water to Johnny's chest and had him wash his hands—

which he did. Evanita removed the bowl, and Geneva held a bottle of skin lotion.

"Cup your hands together again as you did before to receive lotion," Geneva said.

Johnny complied, and Geneva poured lotion in his hands.

"Now rub the lotion into your hands thoroughly like you did with the sugar-oil," Geneva said.

Johnny rubbed the lotion into his hands. Another fifteen minutes passed, and Evanita helped Johnny clean off the mask.

"What a lot of time and effort this is!" Johnny said. "How can women do these facials and hand-softening yet have time for anything else?"

"If it were just the facial," Geneva said, "women would have lots more time. But there are the other parts such as shaving—as you saw—and now getting dressed and applying makeup, which is next."

Johnny changed into a dress, slipped into pantyhose, and threw on a wig.

Geneva and Evanita went to work on his makeup, giving him an even foundation that hid any possible darkness from his beard stubble, and added rich eyelashes, eye shadow, eyeliner, rouge, and lipstick. Evanita attached two clip-on earrings.

"There," Geneva said. "Shawna's face is complete."

"We have to do your nails next," Evanita said.

"My fingernails aren't very long," Johnny said.

"No problem," Evanita said. "We'll glue fake ones on."

Evanita did just that—she glued fake fingernails onto Johnny's real fingernails.

"That worked out well and saved us a bit of time," Evanita said. "The fake fingernails are already painted."

"Now the shoes," Geneva said.

"Wait, I forgot something," Evanita said. "What about Shawna's toenails? Shouldn't we paint them?"

"The hose covers them," Johnny said.

"You better paint them just in case," Geneva said. "No telling what Shawna will encounter."

"But that means...hey, a dress is one thing, but toenail polish doesn't come off!" Johnny protested.

"It will come off with fingernail polish remover," Evanita said.

"That's got acetone in it! It'll mess up my nervous system!" Johnny said.

"Women use it all the time," Evanita said.

"But it's not good for them. And I'm hypersensitive to acetone!" Johnny said.

"You can always let your toenails grow out," Geneva said.

"That could take months," Johnny said.

"Make sure you wear socks all the time," Evanita grinned.

Johnny rolled his eyes.

"Oh, all right, go ahead," Johnny said.

"You'll have to remove the hose first," Evanita said.

"Of all the...sigh...whatever," Johnny said.

Johnny stepped into the bathroom, removed his pantyhose, and exited. Evanita applied fingernail polish to Johnny's toenails and waved her hand over them to help them dry.

"Okay, they're dry," Evanita said. "You can put your hose back on. And here—put these shoes on next."

Johnny returned to the bathroom, slipped into the hose, and pushed his feet into the high-heeled shoes. He stumbled out of the bathroom.

"Ow! My toes!" Johnny complained. "What are these—leg irons?"

"That's how we get around," Evanita said.

"There's absolutely no practical value to this type of shoe," Johnny said.

"Except to look attractive," Evanita said.

"Well I hope I don't attract anyone," Johnny said. "I feel like an idiot in this disguise."

"Try walking around," Geneva said.

Johnny stumbled around in the high-heeled shoes.

"No, don't lean forward like you're about to slip and fall," Geneva said.

"But I am," Johnny said.

"You have to walk with an air of authority, as if you own the floor," Geneva said. "Like this."

Geneva walked with poise and grace.

"Now you try," Geneva said. "That's better, but you need to move your hips more."

"My what?" Johnny asked.

"Your hips," Geneva said. "Like this."

"Why? It's unnecessary work," Johnny said.

"You have to play the part," Geneva said.

Johnny walked along and moved his hips.

"Good. Now the purse," Geneva said.

Evanita gave the purse to Johnny.

"Now walk with it," Geneva said. "No, don't carry it like a football. Over your shoulder like this, and place your arm and hand like this."

Geneva positioned the purse, Johnny's arm, and hand to give the impression he was a woman.

"Better. Now walk," Geneva said, "and remember everything I taught you."

Johnny walked up and down with the heels, the purse, and a feminine stride.

"Perfect," Geneva said.

Johnny sat down. He moved his hands up as if to massage his facial muscles to relieve stress.

"Don't touch your face!" Geneva and Evanita yelled.

"What, what!?" Johnny reeled.

"You'll smear your makeup," Geneva said.

"This is too much work being a woman," Johnny said. "I want to go back to being a man."

Evanita laughed.

"You will soon enough," Geneva said. "At least you don't have to worry about cramps."

"Grandma!" Evanita protested.

"It's true," Geneva said. "Now then, I believe we are ready for the test. Evanita—if you would be so kind as to carry my diary. Thank you. Oh, and we can't forget the clothing the sisters lent us. We must return them."

"I have them," Evanita said.

"Good," Geneva said. "Let's go—Evanita and Shawna."

The three drove up to St. Renata's Abbey and parked. Geneva led Evanita and "Shawna" across the drawbridge while Jonara followed.

"I can't believe Daddy is dressed like a woman," Jonara said. "I would give anything in the world to have a camera right now."

"Anything?" asked Nekara as she popped out of thin air.

"Where did you come from?" Jonara asked. "I thought you went away forever."

"I'm not that easy to get rid of," Nekara said. "But I find it entertaining what extremes you and your family go through in pursuit of folly."

"It's not folly," Jonara said. "My Nanna Geneva and my daddy are trying to save my mommy from a bad life."

"A bad life?!" Nekara retorted. "Ha! None of you know what that's like."

"I saw what happened to you on Eho Miriam," Jonara said. "And I know you lost your ability to have a baby."

"So should I give you an award or something?" Nekara asked. "Do you expect me to cry on your shoulder? Evil does not wallow in misery—it takes the card it was dealt and plays it on society."

"Another cryptic riddle?" Jonara asked. "It doesn't matter. I'm going to journey back in time to see how my mother was born."

"As if that would matter," Nekara said. "Your body is still in the SR-71 Whitebird. In three days, my plan for taking control of Earth's human fertility will be complete. Your little escape into the past will accomplish nothing."

"Maybe, but it's my past to waste," Jonara said.

"Are you sure you want to see this past?" Nekara asked. "You'll be in for a special treat. This was the time I fed all sorts of information to Marcus about the people around him—including Eva."

"You manipulated Marcus to the detriment of my grandmother?" Jonara asked.

"She was one of many who suffered repercussions," Nekara said. "Do not think you are so important that only your family suffers from evil. My reach is far and wide on your planet. Many suffer under my claws."

Sister Charlene answered Geneva's doorbell request.

"Hello, Geneva and Evanita," Sister Charlene said. "Are you returning to the Caves of Healing? And who is your friend?"

"Yes, we are," Geneva said. "This is Shawna."

Sister Charlene took a good look at Johnny.

"Hmm," Sister Charlene said. "And what is her ailment?"

"She..." Geneva started, but Geneva could not think of a reason.

"Oh this is terrible," Jonara said. "Daddy will be discovered, and he'll never be able to help Mommy."

"She's Grandma's maid," Evanita said.

"Really?" Sister Charlene asked. "She looks more like a celebrity than a maid."

Johnny smiled and was tempted to say something, but Evanita used her eyes to tell Johnny, "No."

"Yes, things are different in the States," Evanita said. "Shawna is here to help settle me so I don't go running off again."

"You're doing a good service," Sister Charlene said to Johnny.

Johnny smiled and nodded.

"Follow me," Sister Charlene said.

Geneva, Evanita, Johnny, and Jonara followed Sister Charlene. Jonara looked around but did not see Nekara.

"Did she leave me?" Jonara asked.

"Only briefly," Nekara echoed through the cave with only Jonara hearing her.

Sister Charlene led the group through the castle, into the church, to the door by the altar, through the door, and into the Caves of Healing.

"I must warn you, Shawna," Sister Charlene said. "Do not allow the water to touch your hose. The hose will dissolve."

Johnny nodded in affirmation. Sister Charlene left the Caves of Healing. Geneva, Evanita, and Johnny removed their shoes.

"Ahh, relief!" Johnny said. "Those shoes were killing my feet."

"Not so loud," Geneva said. "These walls have ears and are not used to a male voice. Please—if you must speak, whisper."

"Okay," Johnny whispered.

"Evanita," Geneva said. "Let's start with three chairs—one for each of us. We'll sit with our calves in the water—no higher. If that's not enough, we'll try something else."

"Shawna," Evanita said. "Would you bring a couple of chairs over? I'll get a third chair."

"You can call me by my name," Johnny whispered.

"Not until later," Evanita whispered back.

"Evanita—you sit in the middle. I'll sit on your left side, and Shawna will sit on your right," Geneva said.

Evanita and Johnny approached the pool to arrange the chairs, but Evanita stopped Johnny.

"Shawna, your nylons!" Evanita said. "They'll dissolve!"

"They have a run anyway," Johnny whispered.

"No," Geneva said. "Do not enter the pool yet. Go into the change room and remove your nylons."

Johnny hesitated as if to say, "Do I have to?"

"Yes, go!" Geneva said.

Johnny went into the change room and removed his panty-hose. He exited with the hose in hand.

"Leave it by the change room," Geneva said. "We don't want to take a chance on it getting wet."

Johnny returned to the chairs, but Geneva and Evanita had already arranged them.

"You have pretty toes," Evanita giggled.

Johnny rolled his eyes.

"All right, let's take our places as I described before," Geneva said.

The three sat down and dangled their calves in the pool. Jonara considered watching from the dry cave floor as before. Johnny placed his left arm around Evanita's waist and kissed her on the cheek.

"Uh oh," Johnny whispered. "I left lipstick on your face."

"Shh," Geneva said. "We're ready to begin."

Geneva read from her diary. The three stopped moving.

"Nothing's happening," Jonara said. "Hello?"

Geneva, Evanita, and Johnny remained motionless.

"Oh no! They went back in time without me. What happened? I have to connect somehow. Touch them? Touch the water? Yes, that's it. Hurry, Jonara, hurry!"

Jonara rushed up to the pool and stuck a foot into the water. She traveled back to 1989 with Geneva, Evanita, and Johnny.

1989 Jun 3, Sat Morn. Corpus Christi, Texas.

Eva woke up with a hangover. She stumbled downstairs and looked for Tylenol in hopes no one would see her, but Anna was busy making breakfast.

"You have headache?" Anna asked. "I help. Here—Tylenol."

Eva took two Tylenol pills and chased them down with a cup of coffee—all provided by Anna.

"You have late party last night?" Anna asked. "I heard you early this morning."

"Yeah," Eva said. "But don't tell my mother."

"And why not?" younger Geneva asked as she entered the room.

"Because I don't want a lecture from you," Eva said.

"All right, I won't lecture you," younger Geneva said.

"What? This is a shock," Eva said as she and younger Geneva sat down to breakfast.

"I happened to notice your things on the couch," younger Geneva said. "It isn't hard to guess the meaning."

"Don't tell me that you told me so," Eva said.

"Okay, I won't," younger Geneva said. "So what's the next step?"

"Must I tell you everything?" Eva asked, still irritated by her hangover.

"No, you don't," younger Geneva said patiently. "You're welcome to stay here as long as you like, of course. I'm just wondering what I can do to help."

"I'm sorry, Mother, I'm just a bit crabby this morning," Eva said. "I broke up with Simon last night. Yeah, and I moved out. I took what I wanted and left the rest. So the Simon relationship has reached the end—*c'est la fin*. I won't be going back to Houston."

"And Roberta?" younger Geneva asked.

"I made a promise to her that I intend to keep. I'll continue working at her dental practice until the end of this month," Eva explained. "By that time, she'll have an intern from Oregon Health and Science University, and hopefully I'll have figured out my next step."

"I see," younger Geneva said. "Perhaps I should move up to Portland. We could share a house together."

"Mother, no," Eva said. "I need to do this on my own."

"You'll be so far away," younger Geneva said. "I hate to lose my baby daughter."

"I need time on my own," Eva said.

"You had time on your own at the university," younger Geneva said.

"That was different. I was always an hour or so away from home," Eva said.

"Am I really that hard to live with?" younger Geneva asked.

"Only when you push your religion or tell your Franco stories," Eva said.

"Oh, did I tell you the time when Franco—" younger Geneva started.

"Mother!" Eva said.

Younger Geneva giggled.

"Sorry, I couldn't resist," younger Geneva laughed.

"Next, you're going to tell me I could have been a nun and performed dentistry on the needy," Eva said.

"There are so many orders of the sisterhood you could join," Geneva said. "But isn't it ironic that in your work with Roberta, you are doing the very same service for the needy that you'd be doing in a religious order. Why waste your dedication as a civilian?"

"I'm not like you, Mother," Eva said. "Besides, you left your order."

"Out of a misunderstanding," younger Geneva said. "I miss some of the sisters I worked with."

"Well then, go back," Eva said.

"Eva, shame on you! Besides, I married and had a baby. I couldn't go back now," younger Geneva said. "I have a family to take care of."

"I'm grown, Mother. I don't need taking care of," Eva said.

"You're here, aren't you?" younger Geneva asked.

"I could have stayed at a motel," Eva said.

"But you didn't, for which I'm glad," younger Geneva said. "But someday you'll have children, and I'll be a grandmother. I'll be needed for that role."

"That's another reason I should live far away," Eva said, "to keep you from contaminating any future children I might have."

"Eva! Double shame on you! You can't deny me the right to visit my own grandchildren!" younger Geneva said.

"Visiting is okay. Indoctrination is not," Eva countered.

"Eva, I do believe you have a little more growing up to do," younger Geneva advised. "But it will come with motherhood. Your eyes for family will change. You'll see."

"Yes we will, won't we? Well then, I should get ready for the day and head to the airport. I've got to get back to Portland. Marcus was covering for me while I was gone—Marcus! I forgot all about him until just now."

"Which is surprising considering how you reacted to him last night!" younger Geneva grinned. "I do believe you have a crush on him."

"I don't discuss love interests with my mother," Eva said.

"Ah-hah!" younger Geneva said. "You slipped—just now. You admitted Marcus is a love interest. That would explain the sudden breakup with Simon."

"Mother, you don't know—" Eva started.

"I'm a woman, aren't I? I was in love once too, you know," younger Geneva said. "So I know what it's like."

"Did they have love in those days?" Eva asked.

"Of course, silly! How do you think you were created?" younger Geneva asked.

"With lights off and fully clothed," Eva chuckled.

"It wasn't that long ago," younger Geneva said. "I didn't live in the stone ages, you know."

"Sometimes I wonder," Eva said. "Sometimes I wonder."

1989 Jun 3, Sat Late Afnoon. Portland, Oregon.

Roberta waited in her car by the curb of Arrivals at Portland International Airport. Eva rushed through the airport's door, saw Roberta's car, ran to the back seat, threw her bag in, and jumped into the front seat.

"Thank you for picking me up," Eva said to Roberta. "Whew!"

Roberta drove off.

"Why the rush?" Roberta asked. "You're out of breath."

"I don't want to spend another moment at the airport," Eva said. "Ever since I was in that plane crash in 1970, I've had a loathing for airplanes and airports."

"Yes, your mother told me all about that," Roberta said. "The both of you were lucky to survive the crash. Everyone else perished."

"We survived because of some silly cargo box with padding on the inside," Eva said. "Every night before I go to sleep, I think about it. But whenever I fly, the memories of that summer day in 1970 are especially vivid and painful. I wish I could just wipe it from my brain!"

"Then why don't we?" Roberta asked.

"What do you have in mind?" Eva asked.

"I know a nice little club where we can eat and dance," Roberta said.

"Do they do the Lindy Hop?" Eva asked.

Roberta laughed.

"It's not that kind of club," Roberta said. "But if you want to do the Lindy Hop, I'm sure no one will complain."

"I'll need a male partner for the Lindy Hop," Eva said.

Roberta smiled somewhere between a grimace and smirk.

"What does that mean?" Eva asked.

"Like I said," Roberta said, "this isn't a Lindy Hop club. Do not be surprised if you don't find the kind of partner you're used to. By the way, is it true about you and Simon? Are you two through with each other?"

"How did you know?" Eva asked.

"A little bird told me," Roberta replied.

"Was that little bird from Girona, Spain?" Eva asked.

"It's a long flight from Spain," Roberta said.

"And it's a long way from Corpus Christi to Portland," Eva said. "But my mother's reach has lengthened, I see."

"Don't blame her. I forced it out of her," Roberta said.

"You were spying on me?" Eva asked.

"No, concerned. Long-distance relationships are stressful. They can impact performance. And since your dental performance is important, I want to make sure you don't jeopardize your career by overstressing yourself to the point where you make mistakes and get sued."

"I didn't think of that," Eva said. "I'm sorry."

"It's quite all right," Roberta said. "I'm thankful for having you up here helping me until July 1st when I get an intern."

"Do you know yet who that will be?" Eva asked.

"No, it's too soon to tell. But I will say this—she won't be able to fill your shoes. It'll be a letdown when you leave. Your work is first-rate, and you have excellent rapport with the patients—both adults and children. You know, if you're interested in pediatric dentistry, you could enroll at OHSU. I'll give you a good reference. Perhaps they'll assign you to me. What's wrong, why the long face?"

"Well, I had my hopes on making good money on cosmetic dentistry," Eva said. "I'm half considering asking Marcus for a position in his office."

"Marcus!?" Roberta asked. "What's he got to do with anything?"

Eva paused for a moment.

"Uh oh. Eva—'fess up. You're holding back something. Did you and Marcus—Eva, say it ain't so!"

"No, no, no!" Eva said. "I saw Marcus in Texas, and—"

"Great fires ablazing! He flew down there? No wonder you broke up with Simon!" Roberta said.

"You're starting to sound like my mother," Eva said.

"Well I'm not," Roberta said. "Not even close. So did you do it with him?"

"No!" Eva replied. "I have higher standards than that. We went out dancing at a Lindy Hop club close to my mother's house. Then we went to Houston Corner Hospital to see Simon. That's when I ended it."

"You shouldn't have brought Marcus along to the hospital, but it's too late now," Roberta said. "So do you like him?"

"I...I don't know. I get that funny feeling in my abdomen when we talk, and he's a great dancer," Eva said.

"Hmm," Roberta mused. "Be careful with Marcus, Eva. He has this sixth sense about the world, and I've often suspected he's used that unfairly to his advantage. I can't prove anything. He's very clever about not being caught. But I know something's afoot with him."

"Okay, I'll be careful," Eva said. "So what's the name of this place you're taking me to?"

"It's called, *Dairy Duck*," Roberta said.

"As in *Truth or Dare*?" Eva asked.

"No, as in milk and cheese quack, quack, quack!" Roberta said. "Now Eva, there's something you should know about this place—and me."

"Oh? This isn't some underground drug house or sadomasochistic place, is it?"

"Oh no, no, no. Nothing illegal or psychologically disturbing," Roberta said. "Things are just a little different. Here we are. Now try to have an open mind, Eva. The patrons here know me well, and if you were to spaz out or something, I'd be awfully embarrassed and hurt. Just stick with me. We'll have dinner and some drinks. Very simple. If someone speaks with you, be polite, but tell them respectfully that you're with me. Easy enough, isn't it?"

"Yes, I guess," Eva said. "I don't understand."

"You'll figure it out," Roberta said.

Roberta parked. The sign for the establishment showed two ducks facing each other with their beaks close together. One duck was slightly taller than the other.

The scene faded into grays as Geneva, Evanita, Johnny, and Jonara returned to the Caves of Healing.

"What happened?" Evanita asked.

"I stopped reading," Geneva said. "I need to check a few things before we continue the vision. Evanita—look at your lower legs. Are they bruised?"

Evanita pulled her legs out.

"There are no bruises!" Evanita said.

"Shawna?" Geneva prompted.

"I felt stress waves traveling out from Eva and into the ether. I stopped them from entering Evanita's legs," Johnny said.

"There's something else," Evanita said. "Before Shawna was with us, I felt everything my mother felt back in 1989. But with Shawna next to me, I feel nothing."

"Hmm," Geneva said. "It's important you feel what your mother feels, otherwise things are no better than just telling you what happened. When you feel what someone else feels, you understand better what they are going through and why they make the decisions they do. Shawna—I have a big request for you. Can you allow Evanita to feel her mother's emotions without her being bruised by the stress?"

"It will be difficult," Johnny said. "I'll have to thin the stress waves. All three of us could end up with bruises."

"If so, will each of our bruises be as bad as a single bruise on Evanita?" Geneva asked.

"No, I don't think so. Our combined bruises will be about a tenth of Evanita's original bruising."

"Can you allow Evanita to feel the emotions without bruising?" Geneva asked.

"I thought you asked that," Johnny said.

"Let me rephrase," Geneva said. "You said you could thin the stress waves. Can you split them such that the bruising part of the stress goes away while the feeling part of the stress goes to Evanita?"

"Feelings and bruising are like the faucet and drain of a kitchen sink. The faucet provides the feelings, and the drain takes the bruises. But the water must flow into the drain, otherwise everything overflows. The pool of healing is like the kitchen sink. The bruises must be absorbed by someone's legs for the feelings to be received."

"Does it have to be the same person?" Geneva asked.

"I...I'm not sure. I don't think so," Johnny said.

"Then send all the bruises to me and all the feelings to Evanita," Geneva said.

"That's not fair," Evanita said.

"I agree with Evanita," Johnny said. "It's too much for one person. It could make your legs gangrenous. I'll take some of the bruising."

"And I should take some too," Evanita said. "We can split it three ways. Johnny? Split it three ways."

"Can you do that?" Geneva asked.

"I think...wait...no...yes...we'll have to switch places," Johnny said. "Let me sit in the middle so I can touch both of you. Then I can control how the stress is split. I'll break our link if there's too much bruising."

"Hmm. I had hoped to sit next to Evanita for the journey," Geneva said.

"I'll swap our virtual positions within the vision itself so you're still next to Evanita," Johnny said. "Will this satisfy the requirements?"

Geneva nodded yes.

"Very well," Geneva said. "Let's change positions."

The three stood up and moved around as Johnny recommended. Johnny sat in the middle chair with Evanita on his left and Geneva on his right. He placed an arm on each of them, and Geneva read the next part of her diary.

1989 Jun 3, Sat Eve. Dairy Duck. Portland, Oregon.

Eva followed Roberta into *Dairy Duck*. A well-dressed host-ess greeted them.

"Two for dinner," Roberta said.

The hostess seated Roberta and Eva at a table by the window. A waitress attended the two.

"Roberta," the waitress said. "Welcome back. And welcome to you too, friend of Roberta. My name is Claudia, and I'll be your waitress. May I start you two off with something to drink?"

"Just coffee for me," Roberta said.

"A Piña Colada," Eva said.

"I'll be back in a moment with your drinks," Claudia said, and she left.

"That's a little hard for starters, isn't it?" Roberta asked.

"I need it," Eva said.

"Are you nervous about being here?" Roberta asked.

"What?" Eva said without thinking about where she was.

"We are in a lesbian restaurant and bar," Roberta whispered.

Eva looked around. All patrons, wait-staff, bus people, and others were women. Patrons sat at dinner as female couples. Eva looked down the hallway toward the bar side and saw women together with women.

"Oh," Eva said.

"You're not shocked?" Roberta asked. "I'm impressed. You must be quite distracted. You didn't notice that Claudia recognized me."

"I guess I'm still thinking about Simon," Eva said. "I feel like I let him down. And Marcus is a factor. I have men on the brain."

"Which is exactly why I brought you here," Roberta said. "There isn't a single male in this building."

Claudia brought their drinks. Roberta and Eva ordered dinner. Claudia thanked them and winked at Roberta as she left their table.

"Claudia seems to like you," Eva said. "Come to think of it, how do you know about this place, and how does Claudia know you? We haven't been here before, and you haven't been out without me since we first came to Portland."

"Ah, you're working things out," Roberta said. "What you've said is true. So we have a riddle, but the answer to the riddle is this—when you went down to Corpus Christi to help Simon, I took the liberty of finding a place like this—a place where lesbians can socialize."

"Why?" Eva asked. "Are you trying to spite Richard?"

"No, I would never lower myself to petty things like spite. And I would never disrespect these women by using them."

"Then why did you go here?" Roberta asked. "Was it to help me?"

"No, it was to help me," Roberta said.

"I don't understand," Eva said.

"Do you remember my mother?" Roberta asked.

"A little," Eva said. "She flew airplanes."

"Have you ever wondered—do you ever wonder about whether women are straight or...different?" Roberta asked.

"I never really thought about it until now," Eva said. "I always assume women I see on the street are straight. Once in a while, I see a woman with masculine features, and I figure she's probably a lesbian. But for the most part, I don't wonder."

"Take a look around here," Roberta said. "If you saw these women on the street, would you guess they are straight or lesbian?"

"I have to admit—most women in here look straight to me," Eva said. "I guess I'm caught off guard."

"I think my mother was a lesbian," Roberta said. "The way she spoke about her days watching and playing women's baseball—it just made me wonder about her—and me."

"But wait! Your mother was married and had you," Eva said. "How could she be a lesbian?"

"Eva," Roberta started.

Claudia unknowingly interrupted by bringing their dinner.

"*Bon appétit!*" Claudia said.

Claudia walked away but stopped herself. She stared at Roberta and Eva.

"Claudia is staring at us," Eva said. "Why?"

"Give me a moment," Roberta said.

Roberta stood up and walked away with Claudia. Eva watched them speak in a distant corner. Claudia seemed nervous at first, but Roberta said something to assure her. The two hugged and kissed briefly on the lips. Roberta returned.

"Roberta," Eva said. "How well do you know lesbian customs?"

"Let me have some of that Piña Colada before I answer," Roberta grimaced.

"Sure," Eva said.

Roberta drank half of Eva's Piña Colada.

"Don't worry, we'll order more," Roberta said. "I'll explain about Claudia in a moment, but first let me finish what I started. You know, sexuality is an interesting thing. Most people think of it as a right-or-wrong issue. I should say, most straight people think of it as a right-or-wrong issue. Not long ago, homosexuality was illegal. Homosexuality was considered a psychological illness."

"Yes, there was a close vote in the 70s by a psychiatric board that decided it wasn't a mental illness," Eva said. "What are you trying to say?"

"I wanted to know," Roberta said. "I wanted to know if sexuality is a simple black-and-white issue. I decided to experiment."

"You mean?" Eva asked.

"Yes. Claudia and I did it Thursday night. And Friday night," Roberta said. "I chose two nights in a row to be sure."

"To be sure of what?" Eva asked.

"I wanted to know if I'm a lesbian, or if I have a lesbian in me," Roberta said.

"Huh? Either a person is or isn't a lesbian," Eva said.

"That's what I always thought," Roberta said. "But how did that explain my mother? She fell in love with a man, married him, and had a child—me. But she also had a liking for women. But it wasn't all women. There was this one woman on the Kenosha Comets she was fond of. She never pursued it. In those days, things were much more dangerous. She could have gone to jail. And she had to raise me, so she was afraid she'd lose me if she expressed these feelings with another woman and was caught. Can you imagine the loneliness she must have felt? To be denied the loving companionship of another?"

"Then she was bisexual," Eva said.

"Which begs the question: why is it society—at least the straight society—divides sexuality as the 'straight' group and the 'gay' group? Where do bisexuals go?"

"With the gay group," Eva said.

"But there's a problem with that, and I only recently learned about it, thanks to long conversations with Claudia. There are some lesbians who see bisexuals as wishy-washy, unsure, not true lesbians, weekend-fake-lesbians, etc. Bisexuals can be really offensive to some lesbians. I know, because Claudia warned me. I told her about Richard and how I wanted to experiment. She understood, but not all lesbians do. Some want serious commitments. If you think about it, it's easy to understand. Think of yourself. You've always liked men, right?"

"Yes," Eva said.

"Now think back to when you were first dating Simon. What if you told him you'd just been through a long lesbian relationship, and you wanted to see what it was like to have a heterosexual relationship? How do you think he would have responded?"

"Well it's hard to say," Eva said. "Simon is an existentialist. But it's strange, we never discussed homosexual relationships. I wonder why? It was always about us. He said the love between a man and woman transcends anything else on this Earth."

"A man and woman," Roberta said. "That says a lot. But if you'd told him you were in a lesbian relationship—"

"Which I never would have said," Eva said.

"I know, I know, but if you had, do you think he could have trusted you to remain solely devoted to him? He might think you were toying with him, that your real appetite was for women."

"He might say that," Eva said. "That sounds like something Simon would say."

"Exactly. That's how some lesbians view bisexuals. But there's another view of sexuality that isn't commonly known."

"And that is?" Eva asked.

"A spectrum. Or even a tapestry," Roberta said. "Think of it, Eva. There are men who will have sex with any woman willing to perform."

"Lots of men are like that," Eva said. "And some women."

"This is true," Roberta said. "And some men are very loyal to their wives and do not cheat. There are some women who seek sexual intercourse with a variety of men, other women fall in love with a man and that's it. The thought of being with a different man disgusts them. Eva—there's a spectrum like this with lesbians, and if you factor in bisexuals—if there really is such a thing—"

"What do you mean, 'if there is such a thing'?" Eva asked.

"If a woman has sex with another woman, is she a lesbian?" Roberta asked.

"Of course," Eva said.

"What if she's experimenting? What if she doesn't love the other woman? What if she feels nothing for other women?" Roberta asked.

"Hmm, good point," Eva said. "If she doesn't feel anything, then she's not a lesbian."

"Now what if you go out on a date with a guy, you decide to experiment by having sex with him, you complete the task, but afterward you feel nothing for him," Roberta said. "Does that make you a lesbian?"

"No, it just means I don't love him," Eva said. "But I might fall in love with another guy."

"A-ha," Roberta said. "Yes, that's a key factor, isn't it? Falling in love. So I might not fall in love with one woman, but who knows? There might be another woman out there I haven't met yet. Then what? She might be the only woman I'd ever fall for. Does that make me a lesbian?"

"If you love her, I think so," Eva said.

"You think so, but you're not sure. You see, it's not always clear-cut. That's why I think sexuality is more of a spectrum than a cut-and-dried thing," Roberta said.

The two sat and ate their food in a moment of silence.

"What did you tell Claudia just now? She seemed upset," Eva said.

"She was a little jealous, I think," Roberta said.

"Of what?" Eva asked.

"Of you!" Roberta replied.

"Can't she tell I'm straight by looking at me?" Eva asked.

"No, she can't. You're in a lesbian restaurant and bar. You're with me. I've proven myself capable of making love to another woman. The logical conclusion is that you're my date. She was jealous. I explained that you're not that way—that I'm just trying to expand your view of the world. She seems to accept that, but she's still a bit miffed that we are roommates. She has a wild imagination about what she thinks we do at night. In fact, she thinks the only reason I came here Thursday night was because you were gone, I was lonely, and I needed a substitute love."

"That's crazy!" Eva said.

"Not if you see things from her perspective," Roberta said. "What if Simon were living with a woman? Would you be jealous?"

"I think I would have been, yes," Eva said. "But how can lesbians be like that?"

"They're people," Roberta said. "We're all people with similar needs."

"So are you a lesbian?" Eva asked.

"I don't know," Roberta said.

The two finished their dinner.

"I'm buying," Roberta said.

"We can split the check," Eva said.

"No, I put you through this," Roberta said. "I want to pick up the tab."

"Okay," Eva said.

Roberta handed her credit card to Claudia. Claudia disappeared for a moment and returned with the credit-card paper. Roberta added a tip and signed it.

"Claudia," Eva started.

Roberta anticipated that Eva might say something inconsiderate, and Roberta waved Eva off, but Eva ignored her.

"Roberta explained about Thursday and Friday night," Eva said.

Claudia returned an expression of angst and betrayal.

"Roberta, you said—" Claudia started.

"No, wait," Eva said. "I'm sorry if I'm too naïve to say and do things properly. I just want to thank you for being a good friend to Roberta. Thank you."

"You're welcome," Claudia said as she returned a quick smile and moved on to another table.

"That was very brave," Roberta said. "But next time I would just say nothing."

"I hope she didn't think I was trying to be rude," Eva said. "I wasn't."

"She understood," Roberta said. "She understood. Well then, this was an eye-opener for you. I wanted to be honest with you, and now I have. We can go now. I won't put you through any more discomfort."

The two walked toward the front door—a halfway point between the restaurant and the bar.

"Wait," Eva said.

"Did you forget something?" Roberta asked.

"No," Eva said. "Why waste an evening?"

Roberta was confused.

"What do you mean?" Roberta asked.

"Well, we're here and all. Why don't we hang out in the bar? I could use another drink," Eva said.

"Eva—this isn't a science laboratory. These women are not mice to be studied. They're living, breathing people with pride and feelings. It's not right to—"

"Can't a woman have a drink with her roommate and friend in the company of other women without having to worry about men crashing the party?" Eva asked.

Roberta's eyes opened wide.

"Just be aware, Eva—this is the real thing. Some women are here to have a good time, and other women are looking for more. You might be hit upon. This isn't something to take light-ly."

"Where's your sense of adventure?" Eva asked, and she walked right into the bar.

"Where's my sense of adventure, she asks. What have I done? Did I create a monster?" Roberta asked herself. "If things get out of control...well at least she can't get pregnant. What am I saying? Roberta, get hold of yourself!"

Claudia saw Roberta talking by herself at the front door and approached Roberta.

"Everything okay with dinner?" Claudia asked.

"Dinner was fine," Roberta said. "Eva just walked into the bar."

"Didn't you warn her?" Claudia asked.

"Yes, I did," Roberta said.

"Roberta—if she goes in there preaching an agenda, there will be a scene, and things will get ugly," Claudia said. "We have to pull her out."

"I know, I know!" Roberta said.

"What are you waiting for? You're her *date*," Claudia said. "Go get her."

"Come with me, please?" Roberta asked.

"Okay, I have a moment," Claudia said.

The two walked into the bar, and Eva was dancing on the dance floor with other women.

"Things are safe for the moment," Claudia said. "Uh, oh. She's dancing with my ex-girlfriend!"

Roberta took a step toward the dance floor, but she stopped herself.

"I don't think I can handle this," Roberta said. "I hope Eva doesn't insult anyone."

"Are you sure she's straight as a blade?" Claudia asked. "She's blending in well for a *het* (heterosexual)."

"I don't know what to think anymore," Roberta said. "But I don't like her dancing with another woman."

"Maybe a new flower is blossoming inside her," Claudia said. "Or maybe you're jealous, like I was earlier of Eva."

"Jealous? Claudia, how can you say that?" Roberta asked.

"Jealousy is easy to deny but hard to get rid of," Claudia said. "I think you have the situation under control. I'll see you in a bit."

Claudia left.

"Situation under control?" Roberta asked. "Who's she kidding? I need a stiff drink—and fast! Bartender—a shot of Irish whiskey, please!"

The bartender poured Roberta a shot of Irish whiskey. Roberta drank it and reacted in disgust.

"How can anyone drink this stuff?" Roberta asked herself. "It's like poison."

The music stopped, and the women dispersed from the dance floor. A few practiced the two-step while waiting for the music to restart. Eva ran off the dance floor and over to Roberta.

"Bartender—one Bloody Mary please!" Eva said.

The bartender prepared Eva's drink and gave it to her. Eva downed half a glass before Roberta could say anything.

"Wow, Eva, slow down!" Roberta said.

"I'm thirsty," Eva said.

"Give me that," Roberta said.

Roberta grabbed the Bloody Mary from Eva, took a sip, and choked on the Tabasco and Worcestershire sauces.

"How can you drink that stuff? It burns my throat!" Roberta said.

"It clears the sinuses," Eva said. "It's better than meds."

"It is?" Roberta asked.

"What are you drinking?" Eva asked. "Smells like whiskey."

"Irish whiskey, and it's like poison," Roberta said. "I'm not used to drinking, but somehow the occasion merits it."

"Bloody Marys are good for you. They have lots of vitamins and antioxidants," Eva said.

Eva took her drink back and nearly finished it.

"Good God, are you trying to get sick?" Roberta asked.

"You know, I didn't know what I was missing," Eva said. "I went all through college without drinking a drop of alcohol. But these mixed drinks are good to the bone!"

"I think you should take it easy," Roberta said. "Also, remember where you are. You don't want to offend—"

"Nonsense," Eva said. "Everyone here has been more than friendly. It's a great place for dancing, too. Oh look! They're getting ready to line dance. Come on, Roberta!"

"Whoa! I don't know how to dance!" Roberta said.

"It's easy! Just do as I do. C'mon!" Eva urged.

Eva pulled Roberta by the arm and led her to the dance floor. The two got in line next to each other.

"There's a sequence of steps you follow," Eva said. "When the sequence ends, just repeat. If you don't step right, at least get in the right position. The line moves, and you don't want to get stepped on by another dancer. Okay, here goes. This dance is called, 'Booty Boot Stomp.' If only I had my boots...oh well, next time!"

"Next time?!" Roberta echoed in amazement.

The music started. Roberta stood behind Eva to watch every move. Eva knew all the steps, and Roberta struggled to keep up. Oftentimes, Roberta stepped wrong and collided with Eva. Eva—with the alcohol affecting her senses—laughed and quickly repositioned Roberta back in the line without losing a step. The sequence completed with a ninety-degree right turn, and the group started the dance again. Roberta looked to her left to watch Eva and did much better. Roberta only needed repositioning once by Eva. The sequence ended, and the group turned another ninety degrees to the right. Now Eva was behind Roberta. Roberta watched the woman in front and tried very hard not to make a mistake. Roberta did very well, and no repositioning was needed. The sequence completed, and the group turned ninety degrees to the right. Now Eva was to Roberta's right.

"Hey, this is kinda fun once you learn the moves," Roberta said.

"See? I knew you'd like it," Eva said.

The song ended and another started.

"Another line dance," Eva said. "This one is called, 'Mason-Dixon Line'."

Again, Roberta followed Eva's steps. At the end of the sequence, the group turned one-hundred and eighty degrees and performed the sequence again.

"I was caught off guard," Roberta said over her shoulder to Eva. "I thought we would turn right."

"Not all line dances turn right or left," Eva said. "The Mason-Dixon Line is a two-wall dance, while the Booty Boot Stomp is a four-wall dance."

The song ended, and the disk jockey announced partner dancing.

"Whew, I think that's enough," Roberta said.

"No, wait!" Eva said. "They're forming a big circle for the two-step."

"They said partner dancing," Roberta said.

"Yeah. The two-step is a partner dance. I'll show you. Just follow my lead," Eva said.

"Eva—are you sure you want to do this?" Roberta asked.

"It's just dancing," Eva said. "Don't be afraid to touch me. I won't bite."

The circle finished forming with female-female partners. The music started, and couples moved around in the circle while doing the two-step.

"See?" Eva said. "The two-step is really easy once you get the hang of it."

"And here I thought you were just a ballerina," Roberta said.

"I expanded my routine to include dancing while in med school," Eva said. "I needed variety to give my brain a mental massage. Oh that's right, I promised to teach you ballet."

"Trust me—teaching me dance steps is more than plenty. I doubt I have the flexibility or strength to do any sort of ballet," Roberta said.

After the two-step, Roberta insisted on sitting. The music changed to rock and roll, and Eva went back to solo dancing. Roberta returned to the bar where she once stood, but her empty shot glass and Eva's empty Bloody Mary glass were gone. Claudia walked up.

"Claudia—what happened to your outfit?" Roberta asked.

"I finished my shift and changed into street clothes," Claudia said. "So has she stayed out of trouble?"

"Eva? As a matter of fact she has," Roberta said. "She taught me a couple of line dances and the two-step."

"She's full of energy and talent, that's for sure," Claudia said.

Claudia moved closer to Roberta in a show of intimacy.

"So, Roberta," Claudia whispered. "Do you have any plans for tonight?"

"I...I'm not sure," Roberta stammered.

"You do like me, right?" Claudia whispered.

"I told you up front what my intentions were," Roberta said. "You know I was exploring."

"So let's explore some more," Claudia said.

"But Eva is here. You know she's my roommate," Roberta said.

"Yeah. If she were a little more open-minded, we could have a special little party at your place," Claudia said. "But if you're uncomfortable with that, I have my own place."

"What about your ex-girlfriend?" Roberta asked.

"We ended things three months ago, and I moved out," Claudia said. "Look at her over there—does she look like she's lonely?"

Roberta looked at Claudia's ex-girlfriend. She was seated with several other women—and all were drinking and laughing. The song ended, and Claudia's ex-girlfriend waved Eva over to her table. Eva in turn waved for Roberta to join her, but Roberta waved her off. Eva shrugged her shoulders, sat down with Claudia's ex-girlfriend, and ordered a drink.

"I have to warn you about my ex," Claudia said. "She can work quickly. If you don't tie your Eva down, she could end up spending the night with her."

"What is your ex-girlfriend's name?" Roberta asked.

"Donna," Claudia said.

"Do you still have feelings for her?" Roberta asked.

Claudia sighed and stared up.

"Let's not talk about that," Claudia said. "I just want to have a little fun tonight. You did have fun, didn't you? I never met a woman as tenacious as you."

Roberta smiled.

"I am flattered, but I think I should wait and see how Eva handles things tonight," Roberta said.

"You're very protective of her," Claudia said. "I think you do love her."

"I would never risk my friendship by engaging in...you know...with Eva," Roberta said.

"So I'm less important than Eva?" Claudia asked.

"No, I didn't mean to say that, Claudia. It's just—"

"It's just Eva is more important," Claudia said.

"She's my roommate. This is all very new to me, and I need time to sort things out," Roberta said.

"Well if you change your mind, you know where to find me," Claudia said.

Claudia left and walked up to a friend at a distant table. The friend got up, and the two left the building. Roberta shook with a bit of anxiety. She thought of ordering another drink, but her stomach was still queasy from the whiskey. Should she sit with Eva and Donna? Roberta decided against it. The last thing Roberta wanted was to put herself between two former lovers—Claudia and Donna. Roberta sat at the bar and nursed a beer. After an hour more of watching Eva dance, socialize, and dance, Eva stumbled over to Roberta. Eva was barely coherent, because she was drunk.

"Oh, it's time to take you home," Roberta said.

"Hiya Robbie!" Eva said with a sloshing sound in her mouth. "Where...is da party?"

"The party is over," Roberta said. "You're drunk!"

"Robbie!" Eva said as she poked Roberta in the chest. "Don't be such a poopie-poop!"

"Come on, Eva. Time to go home," Roberta said.

Roberta placed Eva's arm over her shoulder and walked Eva out the front door of *Dairy Duck*.

"Let's play in the road!" Eva said, and she lunged for the street.

Roberta caught Eva's arm and yanked her back.

"Let's not!" Roberta said.

Roberta led Eva to her car and prepared to seat her in the back when a familiar voice interrupted.

"Well, I had to see it to believe it. You and Eva in a house of shame. And you got Eva drunk! Is this dental professionalism?" the voice asked.

Roberta turned around and was shocked to see Marcus with his two associates—Milo and Frank.

"Marcus!" Eva said.

Eva fell toward Marcus, and he caught her before she dropped to the ground.

"What are you trying to do, ruin her career?" Marcus asked Roberta. "Eva doesn't belong in this kind of place. And I'm surprised to see you here too! Then again, your mother was a little different. Is it possible you're following her dark path?"

"Marcus, I can explain," Roberta said. "We came here for dinner, and—wait a minute—what are you doing here? Are you spying on us?"

"We're on the way back from dinner," Marcus said. "Milo saw your car here. I told him he was wrong, that there's no way you'd go into a place like this. Little did we know that not only did you go into *Dairy Duck*, but you dragged Eva in with you. For shame, Roberta, for shame!"

"We had a wonderful time, Marcus," Eva said, and she burped in Marcus's face.

"I need to take her home," Roberta said. "She's drunk."

"Obviously," Marcus said.

Marcus opened Eva's lips and looked at her teeth.

"What are you doing, Marcus?" Roberta asked.

"Ahhhh!" Eva said, thinking she was getting her throat inspected by a doctor.

"I'm checking for injury," Marcus said.

"She's not injured!" Roberta said. "She just needs rest."

"I'm not sure she should go home with you," Marcus said. "Someone needs to watch Eva—but not you! Who knows what you'll do to her in her compromised state!"

"Are you accusing me of something?" Roberta asked.

"I wouldn't have before," Marcus said, "but after seeing things here, it's clear you're untrustworthy with Eva in a social setting. Come with me, Eva. I have a guest bedroom where you can sleep off your stupor."

Eva nodded yes and tried to kiss Marcus.

"Give me kisses," Eva said. "Kissy-kissy-kissy!"

"None of that, my dear Eva. You've been a bad girl and need to be sent to your room," Marcus said.

Roberta grabbed Eva's arm and pulled, but Marcus wouldn't let go.

"Marcus!" Roberta insisted. "Quit fooling around. Let go of Eva so I can take her home."

"I'm not joking!" Marcus said. "And if you don't back off, I'm calling the police."

"For what?" Roberta demanded to know.

"Do you really want me to call the police?" Marcus asked. "I can call the police. They'll be here in two minutes. Eva will go to jail, and you'll be questioned alongside her. And it will be all of your making. Don't put yourself under arrest like this."

Milo and Frank stepped between Roberta and Eva while Marcus placed Eva in his car.

"You should be thanking me, Roberta," Marcus said. "I'm doing Eva a favor by giving her safe shelter, and I'm doing you a favor. I won't make your situation public knowledge, and you can continue working in my building. See? I'm generous. You'll thank me in the morning."

"Let her go!" Roberta demanded.

Roberta put up a fight, but Milo and Frank held her off. Eva was secured in the back seat with Marcus. Milo and Frank entered the front and drove off with Roberta pounding on the window and yelling, "Marcus!"

The scene faded into grays for Jonara. She was now in the SR-71 Whitebird at high altitude above Corpus Christi.

"Enjoying the ride?" Adrian radioed back to her. "Can you see the curvature of the earth? The sky above us is black."

"Yes, I see it," Jonara radioed back. "Everything looks different at this altitude."

"As it should," Nekara said as she popped into the seat with Jonara.

"How did you get in here?" Jonara asked without using the radio.

"You mock my powers, Jonara?" Nekara asked. "I'm hurt."

"You're not hurt," Jonara said. "You don't have feelings anywhere in your body."

"Oh but I do," Nekara said. "I'm always happy at someone else's expense. Like your Grandma Eva, for example. Convenient how Marcus happened to know she was at *Dairy Duck*."

"You don't have to play games with me," Jonara said. "I remember about the duavisha. Marcus has it sewn into his belly button."

"*Duavirt*—not *duavisha*," Nekara corrected. "Don't use the Miramish form on me."

"Why should you fear Miramish?" Jonara asked.

"I don't fear it. But it gnaws on my bones," Nekara said.

"Duavisha, duavisha, duavisha!" Jonara said to irritate Nekara.

Nekara pointed a finger at the right nacelle. The engine flamed out, and the SR-71 went into a violent roll and yaw.

"Unstart in the right engine!" Adrian radioed to the tower.

The G forces pressed brutally against Jonara.

"She won't recover, she won't recover," Adrian radioed.

"You and Adrian will black out and crash in a moment if I don't save you," Nekara laughed.

"Please, help us!" Jonara struggled to say through the G forces.

"What's the name of Marcus's stone?" Nekara asked. "Say it in Dahmek."

"*Du-a-virt!*" Jonara screamed.

Nekara pointed at the right nacelle, and the right engine fired up. The aircraft rocked to the left and right as Adrian regained control.

"Whitebird has recovered," Adrian said.

"You forget who I am," Nekara said. "There are many ways I can enjoy your misery."

"Why did you pull me away from *Dairy Duck*?" Jonara asked.

"To enjoy your misery," Nekara said.

"By almost killing me on this airplane?" Jonara asked.

"No," Nekara said. "That was an afterthought. I wanted to tell you that I pointed Marcus to *Dairy Duck*. I told him he'd find Eva and Roberta there. Without me, there wouldn't have been a confrontation between Marcus and Roberta."

"Why can't you leave well enough alone?" Jonara asked.

"Because your world isn't well enough," Nekara said. "And I might as well stir things up and enjoy the brew."

"You are an evil witch," Jonara said.

Nekara laughed and disappeared. Jonara returned to the Caves of Healing with Geneva, Evanita, and Johnny.

"What happened to the scene?" Evanita asked. "Do we need to check our legs?"

"Something interrupted the vision," Geneva said. "Yes, let's check our legs."

Geneva, Evanita, and Johnny pulled their legs from the water. No one had bruising.

"I would have thought bruising caused the interruption. Apparently it did not," Geneva said, "for which I'm thankful. Shawna—you're doing excellent work."

"Thank you," Johnny said.

"He thinks he's doing a good job," Nekara said as she appeared in the Caves of Healing next to Jonara. "But the best is yet to come."

Before Jonara could complain, Nekara disappeared.

1989 Jun 3, Sat Eve. Portland, Oregon.

Milo drove off. Roberta stood in shock for a moment. Should she follow? Marcus had threatened to call the police. But Eva was in the back seat. Roberta couldn't abandon her roommate and friend. Roberta jumped in her car and pursued Milo. At first, Roberta was following discreetly. She hoped to find an opportunity to rescue Eva without drawing much attention. Perhaps Milo would stop for gasoline or some other errand.

Roberta continued following, but no such opportunity arose. City streets gave way to highways, and Roberta realized Milo was taking Marcus and Eva directly to Marcus's house. With anxiety building, Roberta subconsciously crept closer and closer to Milo's car until she was directly behind. Eva stared through the back window and squinted from Roberta's headlights. To relieve what stress she could, Roberta flicked her hair as she often did in such situations. Eva recognized this trait and waved to Roberta. Marcus, realizing Roberta was following them, yelled something to Milo.

A puff of dark smoke shot out of Milo's exhaust pipe, and Milo's car lurched forward and pulled away from Roberta quickly.

"They're getting away," Roberta said. "I can't let them escape!"

Roberta punched the gas pedal to the floor. She swerved back and forth through the two lanes of traffic going her way. With her more powerful engine and lighter mass (because she was the only passenger), Roberta gained on Milo, but Milo made sudden lane changes and charged between two vehicles where none thought there was enough room. Roberta resorted to passing on the shoulder to get around traffic, and again she caught up to Milo.

Milo took an exit ramp. Roberta followed closely. Milo quickly cut across the grass and returned to the highway. Roberta attempted the same, but her car veered deeper into the grass and toward the support column of an approaching overpass. Roberta slowed the vehicle as best she could and swerved around the column at the last possible moment to avoid impacting it. Cars honked their horns at Roberta as she reentered the highway. She punched the gas pedal to the floor again. The transmission downshifted, the engine rpms shot up, and Roberta launched down the highway again—closing in on Milo as she did before.

Milo took to the right shoulder and passed a blockage of traffic. Roberta did the same and closed the gap. An overpass approached, and Milo cut in front of a semi-truck trailer before becoming trapped by the narrowing shoulder of the overpass. Roberta was too close to the overpass to follow Milo's maneuver. Its shoulder was too narrow for her car, and if she didn't do something quickly, she would crash into the overpass's side railing. Roberta hit the brake and forced herself behind the semi-truck trailer and toward another car which in turn veered into the left lane forcing another vehicle to slam on its brakes to avoid collision.

With brakes locking up, tires squealing, and horns a-blaring, Roberta knew she had to end this. Why wouldn't she let Milo go? She was driving like a maniac. But so was Milo. And Roberta felt Eva was all the more in danger.

Roberta found an open stretch of shoulder and took it. She passed the semi-truck trailer and several other cars before catching up to Milo. She flashed her hi-beam headlights several times. No response from Milo. She kept her hi-beams on and blinded Milo as best she could. Milo took an exit ramp much as before.

"Uh-uh," Roberta said. "I know what you're up to. You'll go back on the highway."

But Milo didn't return to the highway. Halfway along the exit ramp, he pulled over to the far right and slammed on his brakes until his car came to a complete stop. Roberta did the same such that she was stopped immediately behind Milo's car. Marcus and Frank got out and walked toward Roberta's car with an air of determination—Marcus to the driver's side and Frank to the passenger side. Concerned for her safety, Roberta remained in her car and rolled down the window just a little for communication purposes.

"You're kidnapping!" Roberta yelled when Marcus reached her side window.

Marcus stared directly into Roberta's eyes with steel composure, thrust his arm through the slight window opening, grabbed Roberta by the front collar, and pulled her against the side window and upper door frame, causing her neck to crane back. Roberta gagged.

"Turn off your high beams and quit following us!" Marcus barked. "Do you hear?"

Roberta didn't respond. Marcus thrashed her head against the upper door frame.

"Do you hear?" Marcus demanded.

"Okay," Roberta screeched.

Marcus let go, and Roberta gasped for breath.

"Here!" Marcus said, and he shoved an envelope through the open window. "Look at these photos before you get any other bright ideas. Now scram!"

Marcus and Frank returned to Milo's car. Milo took off. Roberta sat for a moment caught between anger and tears. She opened the envelope. She pulled out a selection of color print photographs—photographs of Claudia and Roberta kissing in front of and inside Roberta's house. Photos of the two undressing each other. Photos in more compromising positions—apparently taken between openings of the partly closed blinds.

"He's spying on me? That sneaky-ass bastard!" Roberta stammered.

Later, at Marcus's House.

"Thank you for the ride, Milo. Take care, you two," Marcus said as he kept Eva on her feet.

"Take it easy, Marcus," Milo said.

"Yeah, we'll see you on Monday," Frank added.

Marcus waved goodbye as Milo drove off.

"Well, you've had quite a night, haven't you, Eva. Eva?" Marcus asked.

Eva snored in his arm.

"Passed out," Marcus said. "Very well. Let's get you inside."

Marcus helped Eva inside his house and walked her to a bedroom. He opened the bedroom door, and to the surprise of Evanita, Johnny, and Jonara, the bedroom looked like a dental room with chair, overhead lamp, drilling tools, X-ray machine, countertop, and sink.

"Of all the crazy things!" Evanita said to Geneva. "What is Marcus doing with dental equipment in his house?"

"That's a very good question," Geneva said. "We'll find out."

Marcus placed Eva in the dental chair. He opened a package and removed a dental impression kit. Marcus mixed putty together, rolled it into a tubular shape, and placed it on the impression tray in a U-shape. He inserted the impression tray into Eva's mouth against her upper teeth.

"Now bite down hard," he said.

Eva didn't stir, so Marcus pushed Eva's jaw against her skull and held it for three minutes. Marcus opened her jaw and removed the impression, placed it in a plastic bag, and labeled it, "Carreña, Eva—upper impression."

Next, Marcus mixed up putty as he did before and placed the U-shaped tubular roll onto another impression tray. He inserted the tray into Eva's mouth to capture her lower teeth. Marcus held her mouth closed for three minutes and then opened it. He removed the impression, placed it in a plastic bag, and labeled it, "Carreña, Eva—lower impression."

"Good girl," Marcus said. "You have such beautiful teeth."

Marcus lifted Eva out of the dental chair and carried her out of the room, locking it behind him. He placed Eva on the couch in the living room and tossed a blanket over her.

"Goodnight," he said, and he retired to his own bedroom without further incident.

1989 Jun 5, Mon. Cracbern Associates. Portland, Oregon.

Marcus sat in his office chair while Milo and Frank joined him for a meeting. To everyone's surprise, Marcus had shaved his head.

"You look different, Marcus," Frank said.

"I shaved, Frank," Marcus said. "It's all part of my new work ethic. It's called, 'Cut Off The Hang-Ons'."

"Huh? What are you talking about?" Milo asked.

"Gentlemen, let me explain something about life. When we were younger, we had idealistic views of the world and what we wanted to do. We were taught to help our fellow men as in the

Golden Rule, 'Do unto others as you would have them do unto you.'"

"In New York, we had a different expression," Milo said.

"Yes, Milo, we've heard it before," Marcus said.

"It's called, 'Do unto others before they do unto you.'"

"That's an old, worn-out cliché," Marcus said, "and it has no place here."

"Still, I like it," Milo said.

"You would," Frank said.

"Gentlemen, please!" Marcus said. "Allow me to finish. The Golden Rule makes a major assumption—that others will do unto us as we do to them. So we help others. In our youth, we were taught that others would help back. As we grew older and became more experienced, we realized the scale is not balanced—we end up helping others significantly more than they help us. The result? We are bled to exhaustion from lechers, moochers, and no-good-ers!"

Milo and Frank agreed and applauded.

"Now I say enough is enough!" Marcus said. "We've given more than we should, and it's time we turn the tables."

"How so?" Frank said.

"By catering our dental practice exclusively to high-income people," Marcus said. "That's how. We have paid a high opportunity cost by ignoring this market segment. We have lost much revenue from clients willing to pay more. And why?"

"Slow business?" Milo asked.

"No. The wrong business. If you were looking to buy a new sports car, would you go to a used auto dealer who is stocked with clunkers on his lot?" Marcus asked. "That's what we are— a used car lot with low-income cars."

"But our patients aren't buying cars from us," Frank said.

"True, but the analogy is sound," Marcus said. "If I spend my time caring for low income patients, what skills do I have left for taking care of the high-end clients?"

"We already have the skills," Frank said.

"Think marketing, think marketing," Marcus said. "High-end clients must be convinced that we are absolutely the best in our field. That means advertisements in the paper, on television, with posters showing high-class procedures on the wall, and filling the office with high-class people. That's what I'm talking about. We need to get rid of the low-paying clients and replace them with high-paying clients."

"There's a problem," Frank said. "Even if you get rid of the low-paying clients, how do you bring in more high-paying clients?"

"Through referrals," Marcus said. "I can handle that. I have inside information on that process."

"From me," Nekara said as she appeared out of nowhere.

"Why am I not surprised?" Jonara asked.

"I have to build Marcus up so he'll have farther to fall," Nekara said.

Nekara disappeared.

"So are you going to just cancel all low-end appointments and clean out our files?" Milo asked.

"Not quite. We'll send them all to MacNessi Dental," Marcus said.

"Marcus—we signed contracts with several dental insurance companies. We must ensure our quotas are met. We can't just send patients away. We have to guarantee they are being cared for in a timely manner," Frank said.

"Think of it as subcontracting, outsourcing, or whatever term you wish," Marcus said. "But this is how it must be to convert the practice."

"And Roberta?" Milo asked.

"What about Roberta?" Marcus asked.

"Do you think she'll agree to it?" Milo asked.

"You were with us on Saturday," Marcus said. "I've got her in the palm of my hand. She'll do anything I want her to do, or else I'll expose her."

"It will mean a double workload for her," Frank said.

"She'll manage. She'll also have to take a fee cut on those subcontracted patients," Marcus said.

Milo's and Frank's eyes opened in amazement.

"This isn't a welfare business," Marcus said. "We'll still make a profit on those patients. That's how outsourcing works—no matter what the result, we always make a profit."

"Is it fair?" Milo asked.

"Haven't you been paying attention, Milo? Anything hanging onto us without paying is like extra hair on our bodies. It does nothing but weigh us down and get in the way. From now on, there will be none of that. We're all getting older, and retirement is looming up fast. Do you want to practice dentistry in your 70s, or do you want to retire on a yacht in the Carribean? That's what I thought. Milo—supervise the outsourcing of patients to Roberta. Remind her of her difficult situation. If you must, mention that I have the negatives."

"I hope you don't plan to work us like dogs," Frank said.

"Of course not," Marcus said. "In fact, we've been working like dogs for too long. I intend to change that too."

"You mean Milo and I have been working like dogs," Frank said. "You're the one who always has extra free time."

Marcus fumed with anger before suppressing it and throwing on a plastic smile.

"We will all have extra free time. From here on out, we will have team-building outings for us, for the hygienists, and for the assistants," Marcus said.

"I'd rather have an afternoon off to play golf," Frank said. "I don't need—"

"The team-building outings will be mandatory," Marcus said. "If we're going to be successful, we have to stay together. I won't see the business fragmented by individual trifles. Remember the Cracbern Creed—rife, productivity, and the pursuit of wealth."

The meeting ended. Milo and Frank left Marcus's office. In the moment of pause, Marcus took a spironolactone pill and spread eflornithine cream on his face, head, and arms—both to slow hair growth. He had just finished spreading cream and returning the container to his desk drawer when Eva knocked on the door.

"Eva, come in, come in!" Marcus said.

Eva walked in.

"Please, have a seat!" Marcus urged. "How are your teeth today? Let me see a smile!"

Eva smiled.

"I want to thank you for giving me a place to sleep off my...my drinking...on Saturday," Eva said. "I completely passed out."

"Not a problem," Marcus said.

"You know, it's funny," Eva said. "I had a strange dream that you brought me here to sleep off the booze—in a dental chair. How ridiculous, eh?"

"Yes, quite silly," Marcus said.

"That never happened, did it?" Eva asked.

"Really, Eva," Marcus said. "You have quite an imagination."

"Yeah, I guess I do," Eva said. "It was strange—I even found some bits of leftover impression putty in my mouth Sunday morning."

"Could have come from anywhere," Marcus said. "Did you have some in your jacket or purse that you nibbled on at the bar? Maybe you thought you took an antacid when you really took some putty."

"Gosh, I hope I didn't swallow any," Eva said.

"I'm sure there's nothing to worry about," Marcus said.

"Marcus—about Saturday and Roberta," Eva started.

"Now Eva, we had this talk Sunday morning. You really should be careful who you hang out with and where you go. You never know what trouble it will lead you to," Marcus said.

"I know, I know," Eva said. "Roberta's been very quiet about the affair, and I don't remember anything after leaving *Dairy Duck*. Roberta's distant. Did you do or say anything to her?"

"Only that she should be more careful, that she and you have reputations to uphold," Marcus said. "Just common sense, that's all."

"I see," Eva said. "And I didn't do anything too stupid, I hope?"

Marcus laughed.

"No, you didn't," Marcus said. "But if I were you, I'd lay off the booze for a while. I myself don't drink at all. It's against my religion. But for those who do drink, the advice is moderation. Don't forget that, Eva."

"I won't," Eva said. "Marcus—do you think we can go out dancing again? I love dancing."

"Of course," Marcus said. "What about this Friday night?"

"I'd love that," Eva said.

"I'm glad," Marcus said.

Eva got up to leave, but Marcus stopped her.

"Oh Eva, one more thing," Marcus said. "There are going to be a few changes around Page Clinic—both at Cracbern Associates and MacNessi Dental."

"Oh? Roberta didn't say anything to me," Eva said.

"She's learning about them just now," Marcus said. "I'd like for you to help, if you can."

"Of course," Eva said. "I'll do whatever I can to help."

"I'm in a bit of a bind here at Cracbern Associates. I'm way overbooked on patients," Marcus said.

"He's lying!" Evanita said.

"I know," Geneva said. "But there's nothing we can do."

"I have some contracts I agreed to that were being handled by another clinic, but that clinic is now closing. All the patients will revert back to me, and quite frankly, I have no way to care for them. I'll be in breach of contract if I don't do something. I could be sued and lose my business," Marcus continued to lie.

"How can I help?" Eva asked.

"Help me with the patient load," Marcus said. "Please? For me? You'd be doing me a great favor! I have a few extra chairs."

"Our treatment rooms are already stocked," Eva said. "We don't need any more chairs."

"You may need to make some sacrifices—temporarily until I can contract the patients out to another clinic," Marcus said. "Now you'll have to stand tough with me, Eva. Can you stand tough with me?"

"Well, it's only for a few weeks," Eva said. "I can stand tough. What did you have in mind?"

"Wait—did you say a few weeks?" Marcus asked. "What, you—are you going somewhere? Aren't you happy here? Look,

I'm putting together some office outings for my staff. I can add you too. And anyone from your office you want. We're like a big family."

"It's not that I want to go—I mean, I only promised help for a month or so to Roberta until she gets an intern from OHSU," Eva said.

"And why aren't you applying as an intern?" Marcus asked. "You're fully qualified. I know you can do the work."

"Me? In pediatric dentistry?" Eva asked.

"Sure! Most of my patients coming back are children," Marcus said. "You like children, right?"

"Who doesn't?" Eva said.

"That's right—everyone likes children. And it will be a specialty on your résumé," Marcus said. "Apply to OHSU. Use me as a reference. Heck, I know people at OHSU—I can fast-track you into the program. And even if Roberta gets an intern, I'll take you on board—here—at Cracbern Associates. You see, Eva, your opportunities are endless."

"You're very persuasive, Marcus," Eva said.

"I know what's best for you," Marcus said. "Have some faith in me. Trust me."

Eva paused for a moment.

"Okay, I'll make a leap of faith. I'll enroll in the pediatric program," Eva said.

"Wonderful," Marcus said. "Now don't tell Roberta just yet. Let's have fun with a little 'conspiracy' and surprise her. What do you say? Is it a deal?"

"Deal," Eva said.

"Give me a smile! A big smile!" Marcus said.

Eva smiled.

"Ah, I know you're holding back. You just can't help but burst out in the biggest smile this earth has ever seen," Marcus urged.

Eva broke into a large smile and giggled.

"Great! I'll make some phone calls to OHSU and get you started," Marcus said. "Oh! I almost forgot."

"What?" Eva asked.

"Remember when I asked you to stand tough with me?" Marcus said. "Okay, here goes—because of the high patient load, we're going to have to double up your patient centers."

"You're kidding," Eva said. "There isn't room. Plus it's against everything—"

"Everything you were taught in dental school," Marcus finished. "I know, it's against normal work philosophy, but this is an unusual situation, and temporary. You'd be amazed how well you can multitask under pressure."

"Multitask?" Eva asked.

"Eva—we're in the modern computing age. Personal computers are just now able to run more than one program at a time. It's called multitasking. But multitasking didn't start there. People have done it already—from fighter pilots flying and shooting to housewives taking care of multiple children while running the dishwasher, washing machine, speaking on the telephone, and running the vacuum cleaner."

"Yes, but dentistry—" Eva started.

"Has not explored this option," Marcus said. "We'll be pioneers. If you think about it, there's a lot of wasted time in dentistry. We start something on a patient and wait, start and wait, start and wait. Instead of waiting, we work on a second patient, and when that patient is in a wait state, we go back to the first. Now each patient may spend slightly longer in the dental chair than in a conventional environment, but the delay is minimal, and one can process nearly twice as many patients in the time it takes to do one."

"It sounds daunting," Eva said.

"Don't let the technique intimidate you," Marcus said. "With practice, you can accomplish it as easily as walking and chewing gum."

"Well, I suppose I could try it," Eva said.

"I knew I could count on you," Marcus said. "Now I have another favor to ask. Roberta is a little old-fashioned when it comes to dental techniques. I need you to work on her. Reassure her that this is revolutionary dentistry—that we all need to come together as a team. And as an aside, I think you'll find it more rewarding to help more people than you could one patient at a time."

"I'll do my best," Eva said.

"Thank you, Eva," Marcus said. "And if you need anything, don't hesitate to ask."

"Does that include going out dancing?" Eva grinned.

"Most certainly," Marcus replied.

"I'll hold you to that," Eva said. "Later, Marcus."

Eva left. Marcus pulled a mirror out of his desk drawer and looked at his teeth. An upper right molar looked a little whiter than the rest of his teeth, and the gum line around the tooth had been trimmed.

"A week for the gingivectomy to heal," Marcus said to himself. "Otherwise, the new tooth has survived the transplant surgery successfully. It works. I'll be able to replace all of my teeth using living donor teeth—one by one."

CHAPTER 10

A Catalyst

2023 Oct 11, Wed. Corpus Christi, Texas.

Jonara found herself back in the SR-71 Whitebird. Adrian returned the craft to Naval Air Station Corpus Christi. Adrian taxied the craft into the hangar where a water mist cooled the fuselage. Crews attended the craft and rolled steps to the cockpit area. Adrian opened the canopies and helped Jonara down the steps. At the bottom, crews helped her out of her spacesuit.

"Did you enjoy the ride?" Johnny asked.

"It was scary," Jonara said. "The engine went out, and it got hard to breathe."

"Adrian, is that true?" a worried Evanita asked.

"We just hit some turbulence," Adrian said.

"It wasn't turbulence," Jonara protested. "The right engine went out."

Adrian laughed.

"What an imagination," Adrian said, but Marcus wasn't laughing.

"We need to debrief you on this flight," Marcus said, and he led Adrian to a side office.

"I'm not imagining things," Jonara said. "The engine really went out."

"Oh Jonara," Evanita said, "if Adrian says it was turbulence, then we have to believe him."

"Daddy?!" Jonara asked. "Don't you believe me?"

"Lots of things can happen at high altitudes," Johnny said. "You might have grayed out."

"Huh?" Jonara asked.

"Instead of blacking out, a gray-out is when you're conscious but not thinking straight. You can hallucinate things," Johnny said.

"How can I gray out if the spacesuit is giving me air?" Jonara asked.

"We heard you experienced some extra G forces," Johnny said. "You might have lost some blood to your brain temporarily."

"No one believes me!" Jonara said. "Daddy—in the other timeline, you could read people's thoughts and physical well-being. You used the Water Ruby to do it. Take the Water Ruby, Daddy, and read my thoughts. You'll know I'm telling the truth."

Evanita, Eva and Anna rolled their eyes.

"That's superstition," Johnny said. "ESP (Extra Sensory Perception) is a myth. It's not real."

"What about this?" Jonara said as she pulled up her pants leg revealing a big bruise. "Is this superstition?"

"How did you get a bruise like that?" Evanita asked.

"I got it from the other timeline," Jonara said. "It was supposed to go to you, Mommy, and you, Daddy, in the Caves of Healing. But I got it instead."

"What is she talking about, Evanita?" Eva asked.

"I don't know. Caves of what?" Evanita asked. "Jonara—your imagination is just too much for words."

"Then how did I get the bruising?" Jonara asked.

"The G forces caused blood to pool in your legs," Johnny said. "You probably ruptured a few blood vessels."

"Daddy!" Jonara cried. "You don't believe me either."

"Your other leg will be just as bruised," Johnny said.

Jonara lifted her other pants leg, but there was no bruising.

"I had only one leg in the water!" Jonara said. "That's why only one leg was bruised. What do you say to that, Daddy?"

Johnny paused in thought.

"I don't know," Johnny said.

"It's easy enough to explain," Eva said. "Our legs are not symmetrical, nor were the G forces. One leg took more of the brunt than the other."

"Maybe, maybe," Johnny said. "But something's not quite right."

"Well, your bruising is nothing to worry about," Eva said. "It will heal."

"Somebody, believe me!" Jonara said.

Jonara turned around wildly, but she received stares of disbelief or indifference. If anyone would believe her, it was Johnny. In the other timeline, he had the ability to see through things. How could she get her father to do the same in the here and now? She held the Water Ruby to the light. It sparkled. She held it between her and Evanita. She saw Evanita as she was. The same with Johnny. Jonara held the Water Ruby between her and the SR-71's fuselage. The Water Ruby pulsed with four colors—white, cerise, black, and green. The cycle repeated.

"Daddy, do you see this?" Jonara asked as she handed the Moissan Ruby to Johnny. "Hold the Water Ruby up to the airplane's crystal body. Do you see the colors?"

"Interesting," Johnny said. "The stone and fuselage are pulsing different colors."

"No, it's the Water Ruby, isn't it?" Jonara asked.

"They're interacting, like two polarizing lenses," Johnny said. "This is interesting, but not unexpected. The fuselage of the SR-71 Whitebird is designed to refocus light onto the earth."

"But why the pulsing? Why the four colors?" Jonara asked.

"Technically, black and white are not colors," Johnny said. "But here's what's happening—the Moissan Ruby is alternating between green and clear. The SR-71 Whitebird's fuselage is alternating between cerise and clear. So if you create a combination matrix of the two you get: clear-clear, clear-green, cerise-clear, and cerise-green which is white."

"That explains green, cerise, and white, but what about black? Clear isn't black," Jonara said.

"In this case, it is," Johnny said. "The Moissan Ruby and fuselage polarize light. When both pulse 'clear', they are polarized against each other, the result is that no light passes through. But they polarize against each other only on the clear setting—otherwise the color pulses would be black."

"But why pulse to begin with?" Jonara asked. "When I hold the Water Ruby up to other things—even light sources—there's no pulsing."

"True. Light brings out swirls and sparkles, but only another crystal like the Moissan Ruby causes pulsing," Johnny said. "I have to admit, I've never seen this effect before. It's as if the two are communicating."

"Like tug-of-war?" Jonara asked.

"Yes, that's a good way of putting it," Johnny said. "What I don't understand is—why? Those stories I told you about the Moissan Ruby were fabricated. This crystal is only good for strength, not magic."

"We have to investigate, Daddy," Jonara said. "We must find out."

"How?" Johnny asked.

"Daddy—what if we touch the airplane's body and the Water Ruby at the same time?" Jonara asked.

"Didn't you try that already?" Johnny asked.

"No, I couldn't. I was wearing the spacesuit. I couldn't touch anything except the glove," Jonara said. "Please, Daddy?"

"In theory, nothing should happen," Johnny said. "It's hardly worth a try. The data point would be null."

"But we won't know the true value of the data point unless we try. Anything else is—"

"Anything else is speculation open to argument," Johnny said. "Yes, that's what I taught you about data points."

Johnny stared at the SR-71 Whitebird. The water mist turned off, and the crew took a break.

"Look—now's the best time," Jonara said, "before they put the airplane away."

"Why not?" Johnny asked.

"Yeah, why not?" Jonara echoed.

The two walked over to the underside of the SR-71 Whitebird. Jonara reached to touch it, but Johnny withdrew her hand.

"What is it?" Jonara asked.

"I'd better test it first—by myself," Johnny said.

Jonara laughed.

"You find this funny?" Johnny asked.

"It's just that you've been treating the Water Ruby as a superstitious, worthless stone. Now you're afraid it will hurt me," Jonara said.

"I...that's strange...yes, you're right...there's no risk...I mean ...there should be no risk...okay, I know what to do," Johnny mustered. "Hold the Moissan Ruby in your left hand, and with your right, hold my left hand, and I'll touch the aircraft with my right. Okay? Now."

The two did as Johnny described. The world went black except for two distant pinpoints of light—a green one to the far left, and a cerise one to the far right.

"Let go," Johnny said.

Jonara let go of Johnny, and Johnny let go of the Whitebird. Both returned to the hangar with no ill effects and no passage of time.

"You see?" Jonara said. "There's a power between the two. They change space and time."

"It's possible they caused us to gray out or even black out," Johnny said. "They may have interfered with our nervous systems."

"Then shouldn't we have fallen to the ground? Shouldn't our skins feel like pins and needles?" Jonara asked.

"Hmm, you're right," Johnny said. "We should be feeling some ill effects. Let's try again."

Jonara continued holding the Moissan Ruby in her left hand. She took hold of Johnny's left hand with her right, and Johnny touched the aircraft's fuselage with his right hand. The scene turned dark again, and the two pinpoints of green and cerise light returned.

"Look," Jonara said. "They're getting closer to us."

"Or they're getting larger," Johnny said.

The lights appeared to grow in size. They stopped growing and started moving around each other as if chasing each other in the same orbital path around an unseen central object.

"They look like two stars in a binary star system," Johnny said. "But why?"

"It's the Damiriak solar system!" Jonara said. "It must be!"

"The what?" Johnny asked.

Before Jonara could answer, the two stars circled each other faster and closer in a collapsing spiral until the two collided and exploded into a single burst of white light.

"Well," Johnny said. "We just might be dead."

"We're not dead," Jonara said. "These crystals allow us to connect to other places. It's not a fabrication, Daddy, it's true. Look—we're descending from the sky to the Spanish country-side into that castle. That's St. Renata's Abbey, and inside are the Caves of Healing."

"Most likely this is some sort of hallucination from a gray-out," Johnny said.

"Daddy, please! Just accept this journey as it is. Watch with me!" Jonara said.

The two appeared in the Caves of Healing and saw Evanita, Geneva, and younger Johnny dressed as Shawna.

2007 Dec 8, Sat. The Caves of Healing. Carreña, Spain.

"Three women in a cave," older Johnny said. "No wait—that's Geneva and Evanita. Evanita never went to Spain."

"This is the other timeline," Jonara said. "Mommy was de-pressed and wanted her life to end. Nanna Geneva and you helped her understand the past and her own identity."

"I'm helping her?" older Johnny asked. "How? You and I are standing at the side of the pool. We're not doing anything."

"Not you as in you next to me," Jonara said. "The you sitting in the middle there—between Mommy and Nanna Geneva."

"That's not me. That's another woman," Johnny said.

"That's you dressed as a woman so you could sneak into the abbey. The sisters don't allow men inside."

Older Johnny took a close look at Shawna.

"She does resemble me," older Johnny said. "Could she be Valeria?"

"No, she's you!" Jonara said.

"The vision broke again," Geneva said. "Check your legs."

Evanita and younger Johnny removed their legs from the pool.

"No bruises," Evanita said.

"My legs are okay," younger Johnny said.

"The woman," older Johnny said. "She sounded like me."

"Because she is you!" Jonara said.

"I've never dressed as a woman. Never!" older Johnny said.

"In this timeline you did," Jonara said. "Look, they took their legs out of the water to check for bruises. But I got their bruises. Now do you understand?"

"Why would they or you get bruises?" older Johnny asked.

"It's from stress," Jonara said. "Stress from Grandma Eva in the past."

"What past?" older Johnny asked.

"1989."

"Hmm. I don't understand," Johnny said. "That was the year your grandmother and grandfather got together. It's also the year I first met your grandmother. But that's it. What was so stressful?"

"Come," Jonara said. "Stick a foot in the water and see. We'll journey back together."

"I'll read from the diary again," Geneva said, and the five went back in time.

1989 Jun 30, Fri Morn. MacNessi Dental. Portland, Oregon.

In the weeks following Marcus's bold plan to shift his business from helping the needy to helping himself, Cracbern Associates took on increasingly more high-paying clients while Roberta—under coercion—handled Marcus's existing low-paying contracts. Marcus renovated his dental office by giving the waiting area a living-room feel with couches, two televisions, two large fish tanks, sports magazines, investment magazines, and news magazines. Each treatment room had leather dental chairs, selectable music with headphones for patients, individual X-ray machines, cloth bibs, the most expensive equipment, and floor-to-ceiling windows with a view to a stocked fenced-in area of rabbits, squirrels, birds, and llamas.

Eva helped Roberta with the workload at first, but Marcus repeatedly invited Eva to business outings, lunches, and dinners—without Roberta. Eva attended these outings and drank alcoholic beverages at each one. Eva and Marcus danced on Friday and Saturday nights with Marcus taking her home to Roberta's place. Roberta saw this trend of increasing alcohol abuse and grew concerned over Eva's mental health. Roberta searched for a way to approach Eva regarding the issue, but the crisis came to a boiling point on Friday morning the 30th of June. Roberta walked into the lab at MacNessi Dental and caught Eva taking a slug of whiskey from a bottle.

"What's that?" Roberta asked.

Eva turned around quickly and hid the bottle behind her back.

"Nothing," Eva said.

"It's alcohol, isn't it?" Roberta asked.

"Are you my mother?" Eva replied defensively.

"Give it to me. You know there's no drinking at work," Roberta said.

"I need something to take the edge off my nerves," Eva said.

"I said, give it to me!" Roberta demanded.

"You know, Roberta, you're getting on my nerves. Who are you to say what I can and can't do to my—" Eva said.

Before Eva could finish her sentence, her eyes rolled up, and she collapsed to the floor. Roberta rushed to catch Eva, but she was too late. The whiskey bottle fell to the floor and shattered—spewing glass and whiskey across the lab floor. Kay heard the crash and rushed in.

"What happened?" Kay asked.

"It's Eva," Roberta said. "She passed out."

"I'll call an ambulance," Kay said.

"No—I'll handle this," Roberta said. "Keep the office staff in the dark. Okay?"

Kay nodded in affirmation and closed the door behind her. Roberta reached for a smelling salt, but as she did, Eva went into convulsions. Roberta quickly opened the smelling salt and placed it under Eva's nose. Eva's convulsions stopped, and Eva awoke.

"What happened? Where am I?" Eva asked.

"You're at work," Roberta said. "You passed out."

"From what?" Eva asked. "Just a moment ago I was getting ready for bed. What am I doing here? Isn't it Thursday evening?"

"No, it's Friday morning," Roberta said.

"I don't understand," Eva said. "How could I miss a morning?"

"I'll tell you why," Roberta said. "You have alcohol-induced amnesia. Eva Carreña—you're suffering from alcoholism."

"How dare you!" Eva said.

"It's true," Roberta said, "and don't shut me out again. Draw on your medical training. Look at the symptoms—a craving for alcohol, wanting to cut back but can't, drinking in the morning to steady your nerves, getting defensive about your habit, and memory loss. Are these normal for someone of your age and health? What's scary is that you passed out—that's not normal—even for a conventional alcoholic. Are you taking stimulants? Did you just crash?"

Eva rolled her eyes.

"I'll figure something out," Eva said. "With the workload and all, I haven't had time to dry myself out. I'm taking an amphetamine in the morning to get me going. I should take one now so I don't faint again."

"Another symptom—lying," Roberta said. "You've been working half-days the last two weeks. You spend quite a bit of time with Marcus. And what are you doing taking amphetamines? They'll burn you out! Eva! Are you self-prescribing? That's unethical! Eva!"

"Quit saying my name so much! And since when is my body your business?" Eva asked defensively.

"When I see a colleague and friend destroying her life, it becomes my business," Roberta said.

"And? Are you going to fire me?" Eva asked.

"Eva! Are you still defending your habits?" Roberta asked.

"Alcohol isn't illegal in this country. I can stop whenever I want," Eva said. "And I am a doctor. I can prescribe myself whatever I need."

"Listen to yourself speak, Eva. Find that one little objective part of your brain and analyze what you just said. The alcohol and amphetamine tell you what to say. You're addicted!"

"I like them. I like how they make me feel!" Eva said. "And I don't intend to stop."

"I could fire you," Roberta said. "Would that get you to stop?"

"No. Marcus would welcome me in his office," Eva said. "He's made that quite clear. Besides, you're getting a new intern. It was going to be me—a surprise on Monday—but if you're going to fire me, well, I guess that's out the window."

"You applied to OHSU for a pediatric dentistry internship?" Roberta asked. "I didn't know."

"Like I said, it was going to be a surprise, Roberta," Eva said.

"Eva—I'm not going to fire you," Roberta said.

"It doesn't matter," Eva said. "I'm tired of working two patients at once."

"Then why did you support Marcus when he shoved it down our throats?" Roberta said. "Eva—what's happened to you? We had a great friendship. But in the last month, I've seen our relationship straining and eroding. Are alcohol and speed that important to you that you're willing to let them alienate your friends?"

"Marcus is my friend," Eva said.

"Marcus is a liar and manipulator," Roberta said. "I see that now all too clearly, and I hope you don't deceive yourself into thinking otherwise. You're setting yourself up for a big fall if you do."

"You know what? I don't need you preaching to me like you're my mother," Eva said. "Next thing you know, you'll be telling me to go to church and confess my sins to the priest."

"I would never say that. And I'm Baptist! We don't have these sacraments, and we don't have priests," Roberta said.

"It doesn't matter. I quit," Eva said.

Eva walked out of the lab in silence, gathered her things, and left MacNessi Dental.

"Eva, wait," Roberta repeated while Eva exited Roberta's dental clinic, but nothing would dissuade her.

"Marcus," Eva said as she walked into his office. "I just quit at MacNessi Dental."

"Oh?" Marcus said. "I'm sorry to hear that."

"Is your offer still good?" Eva asked.

"I promised you a job here performing cosmetic dentistry," Marcus said, "didn't I?"

"Yes, you did."

"Very well," Marcus said. "You're hired. Frank has the day off. You can use his treatment room until we build one for you. In fact, the timing is good. I have extra patients this morning I was going to handle myself, but with you here, I can get caught up on my supplier calls."

"Thank you, Marcus," Eva said. "One more thing, Marcus. Do you mind if I—you know—to take the edge off my nerves—and—you know—to get me going in the morning?"

"I can't condone what you put into your body," Marcus said. "My religion forbids such things. But you are an adult and a doctor. Your decisions rest with you. As long as you report to work and do a good job, what you take is your own business. Now let me see that smile of yours."

"Thank you, Marcus," Eva said with a big smile.

Hours became seconds, and days became minutes. Eva continued rooming with Roberta but with a social wall between the two. Roberta lengthened her work days and added Saturdays and Sundays to keep up with the workload at MacNessi Dental while Eva continued treating high-paying clients at Cracbern Associates. Marcus added a treatment room for her use. She drank daily—in the morning to keep her nerves steady, in the early afternoon before class, and in the evening at bars and dance halls with Marcus. Eva arrived home in the early hours of the morning, slept a few hours, and took amphetamines later in the morning to wake herself up. She experienced more amnesia but continued drinking. Dark circles grew under her eyes, but she covered them with makeup. She felt she couldn't stop taking stimulants. If she didn't take amphetamines in the morning, she'd pass out. It was this way then when she first met Johnny Pindus.

1989 Sep 29, Fri Morn. Cracbern Associates. Portland, Oregon.

Eva took a slug of whiskey and swallowed an amphetamine as she prepared her treatment room for her first patient of the day.

"Eva, your nine o'clock is here—Johanidan Pindus," the receptionist said.

The receptionist passed Eva Johnny's chart.

"Well hello, Johanidan," Eva said.

"Everyone calls me Johnny," the eight-year old boy said.

"It's me," Shawna Johnny said to Evanita and Geneva. "I remember this day."

"It's me talking about me," older Johnny said to Jonara. "And it's true—I do remember the first time I met Mummy Eva. Boy did her breath stink of alcohol."

Eva showed eight-year-old Johnny to the dental chair.

"You don't look like my dentist," youngest Johnny said.

"He's on vacation today," Eva said. "I'm substituting for him—like a substitute teacher."

"I never met a substitute teacher who smells like my mother," youngest Johnny said.

"How sweet," Eva said. "I'm like a mother to you."

"She drinks alcohol," youngest Johnny said. "And she always has that smell on her breath, like you do."

Eva let a frown overtake her face but quickly purged it and threw on a plastic smile.

"Well, Mr. Pindus, you are very sensitive to smells. Let's take a look at your teeth. You're complaining of a toothache, are you?"

"Yeah," youngest Johnny said. "My six-year upper, left molar hurts."

"Your six-year molar, is it? You're a very smart boy, Johnny," Eva said.

Eva looked into Johnny's mouth.

"Number fourteen is cracked and has significant decay," Eva said. "Much of the tooth is missing."

"I know. I think it broke when I was chewing ice a few months ago," youngest Johnny said. "We couldn't afford to see the dentist, but the pain is too much, so here I am."

"I don't understand," Eva said. "Your chart says your father has excellent dental insurance."

"I don't live with him anymore," youngest Johnny said. "I live with my sister, Valeria."

"You mean you live with your mother, right?" Eva asked.

"Nope. She's at the funny farm," youngest Johnny said.

"Johnny—who is paying for your dental work today?"

"I don't know," youngest Johnny said. "My sister says the government will pay."

"I see. One moment, Johnny," Eva said.

"This is it," Shawna Johnny said. "This is when Eva learns I really can't afford to pay for dental work. And she kicks me out."

"My mama?" Evanita asked.

"Yup. I bet she never told you, did she?" Shawna Johnny said.

"No, she didn't," Evanita said. "She kept it a secret. And I can see why. It's a horrible thing to do. But I don't understand—I met you at her dental office. I held your hand. She was treating you."

"That was later," Shawna Johnny said. "Things changed."

"What changed, Daddy?" Jonara asked oldest Johnny.

"Once your Grandma Eva took control of her alcoholism and drug addiction," oldest Johnny said, "she reformed. This is all very interesting. I didn't realize we could see the past like this. It's almost the way it really happened."

"What do you mean?" Jonara asked.

"Well, in this vision, signs are English-only. But in real life, everything is in Catalan and English."

"But English is the real world," Jonara said. "Catalan wasn't supposed to be an official language of the United States."

"Hmm," oldest Johnny said. "That's a point where we differ."

"I wish you could see history as I have," Jonara said. "Then you'd understand."

"No time for that now. Here comes Eva to kick me out," oldest Johnny said.

"I'm sorry, Johnny, but without proper insurance, we can't treat you here," Eva said.

"But what about my tooth?" youngest Johnny asked. "It's killing me!"

"There's a clinic next door," Eva said. "It's called—"

Eva's eyes looked up, she lost balance, and she fell over on youngest Johnny.

"Ugh," youngest Johnny said.

"Ack!" Shawna Johnny said.

"Ouch!" oldest Johnny said.

"What happened?" Geneva asked.

"It was like—" Shawna Johnny started, then all three Johnnys said, "an electric shock."

"Strange," Geneva said. "Unfortunately, we lost the link."

"Why did you feel a shock?" Evanita asked Shawna Johnny.

"I don't know," Shawna Johnny replied. "But that wasn't half as bad as the—"

"No, don't reveal the future," Geneva said. "Evanita must experience the event."

"Daddy, do you remember the shock when you were eight?" Jonara asked.

"I think so...but I thought it was a dream when I was eight. I don't remember it happening in reality," oldest Johnny said. "Come to think of it, I've had lots of dreams that certain things would happen, but they didn't."

"Like what?" Jonara asked.

"Just last month I had a dream you had a friend named Almarita back in Portland," oldest Johnny said. "But that's absurd—you don't have a friend by that name, do you?"

"No, but I did in the other timeline," Jonara said. "What else do you dream?"

"I have a recurring dream that I'm not a Catholic but rather a Baptist," oldest Johnny said.

"That's true too in the other timeline," Jonara said.

"You could be saying that to be agreeable," oldest Johnny said.

"Daddy—have I ever lied to you?" Jonara asked.

"A few weeks ago, I would have said, 'No.' But lately, you've said things that sometimes don't make sense," oldest Johnny said.

"They don't make sense in this timeline, but they make sense in my timeline," Jonara said.

"You speak as if you don't belong in this world," oldest Johnny said.

"I don't," Jonara said.

"You don't sound suicidal," oldest Johnny said.

"I'm not. I'm not saying I should never have been born. I'm saying our world is not the one I know. This world isn't mine, and it doesn't possess me," Jonara said.

"Then where do you belong, Jonara?" oldest Johnny asked. "Do you feel like you belong in this supposed other timeline?"

Jonara hesitated.

"I see," oldest Johnny said. "The grass is greener on the other side."

"What does that mean?" Jonara asked.

"It means you believe things are better somewhere else instead of where you are, but as soon as you go to that other place, you don't like it and believe that yet again, it's better somewhere else," oldest Johnny explained. "But there's a common factor in all of this—you. You can't leave yourself, Jonara. If external change leaves you wanting, then change must come from within. How will you change, Jonara?"

"I need a Carreña point," Jonara said.

"A what?" oldest Johnny asked.

"I need a Carreña point to figure out what I should do," Jonara said. "Look—Geneva is reading from her diary again."

"Doctor Eva, Doctor Eva!" youngest Johnny said.

Eva awoke and arighted herself.

"Yes, as I was saying," Eva continued as if nothing had happened. "There's a clinic next door that accepts Title 19 (Government Medical Assistance Program) patients like you. It's called *MacNessi Dental.* They'll take care of you. I'll show you to the door."

Eva led youngest Johnny to the door.

"C'mon, Valeria, let's go," youngest Johnny said to Valeria, who was sitting in the waiting room.

"What happened? What's wrong?" Valeria asked.

"We don't accept Title 19 here," Eva said. "You'll have to find a new dentist. As I told Johnny, try next door at MacNessi Dental. They'll take you."

"And that's it?" Valeria asked. "What the...I...you're kicking us out?"

"The receptionist can answer any questions you may have. Good luck," Eva said, and she returned to work.

"Of all the nerve," Valeria said. "All right, Johnny, let's go. This place has changed for the worse."

"Wow," Jonara said. "Grandma Eva was cold-hearted back then, too."

"It really wasn't that bad," oldest Johnny said. "It just seems bad. The tooth was restored. If this vision plays out, you'll see."

Valeria led youngest Johnny to MacNessi Dental. She took one look through the glass window and hesitated.

"The waiting area is packed," Valeria said to Johnny, "and we don't have an appointment. I don't know how this will work."

"My tooth is killing me," youngest Johnny said. "I can't stand it anymore."

"Oh put me out of my misery!" Nekara said to Jonara as she appeared out of nowhere.

"Who are you?" oldest Johnny asked.

"You can see her?" Jonara asked. "That's Nekara the Red. She's evil!"

"Of course he can see me," Nekara said. "I've allowed him to see me."

"Jonara," oldest Johnny said. "What's going on?"

"She's the reason the timeline is messed up," Jonara said.

"I'm proud of you, Jonara," Nekara said. "You're lying to cover your own *faux pas*. Why don't you tell him about your indurate chant in Miramish?"

"Chant? What chant?" oldest Johnny asked.

"I don't have time to explain," Jonara said. "We need to figure out a way to get eight-year-old Johnny into MacNessi Dental so he can have his pain taken away."

"Excellent," Nekara said. "Create an emergency situation to prevent a challenge to your lie. Your studies under my expert tutelage are proving fruitful."

"Huh? What's this about fruit?" oldest Johnny asked.

"Ignore her," Jonara said.

"Yes, ignore voices that might lead you astray to the truth," Nekara said.

"Jonara, are you lying to me about something?" oldest Johnny asked.

"Something's wrong with the link," Evanita said to Geneva.

"It's as if something is preventing time from moving forward," Geneva said.

"I'll probe with the Moissan Ruby and see what I can find out," Shawna Johnny said.

"Oh this will be interesting," Nekara said. "I'm looking forward to watching all three Johnnys collide again with another electric shock."

"You caused that?" Jonara asked.

"I simply amplified the action to make it more noticeable," Nekara said.

"Please, just go away!" Jonara said.

"I'm hurt again, Jonara," Nekara said. "Aren't you going to ask for my help?"

"To do what?" Jonara asked. "You'll just get in the way."

"Why no, my dear," Nekara replied. "I'm all for expediting young Johnny's tooth care. I'm a pioneer in the quick-and-evil-at-the-expense-of-others philosophy. All you need do is ask, and I'll ensure young Mr. Johnny gets relief from his toothache."

"No tricks," Jonara said.

"I promise," Nekara grinned. "No tricks."

"Somehow, I don't trust you," Jonara said.

"Ow!" youngest Johnny cried from his toothache.

"Ow!" Shawna Johnny cried from empathetic pain. "There are three of us Johnnys here."

"Ow!" oldest Johnny reacted. "I feel like my jaw is diseased from a tooth infection that never properly healed."

"Okay, okay!" Jonara begged. "Please, Nekara, help young Daddy get a quick appointment at MacNessi Dental!"

Nekara snapped her fingers and pointed at Roberta's clinic.

"Done!" Nekara said, and she vanished.

"The vision has restored," Geneva said. "Look!"

Valeria led youngest Johnny into MacNessi Dental.

"Excuse me," Valeria said. "My name is Valeria Pindus. And this is my brother, Johnny. Johnny has a toothache and is in a load of pain. I was hoping you had a dentist here who could help him."

"Are you a patient here?" the receptionist asked.

"No," Valeria said. "We were patients next door, but we're on Title 19 now and can't much afford expensive dental care."

"Hmm. This clinic is overbooked," the receptionist said.

"She lied," Jonara said. "Nekara lied about helping Daddy. She got my hopes up so I'd feel much worse. I knew it."

"I didn't lie," Nekara's voice echoed from afar.

Roberta appeared behind the desk next to the receptionist.

"Did you say you were patients at Cracbern Associates?" Roberta asked Valeria.

"Yeah," Valeria said. "We were supposed to see Dr. Frank, but he's on vacation. Dr. Carreña refused to treat us. Said our Title 19 wasn't good enough for them."

"Dr. Eva Carreña?" Roberta asked. "No, you don't have to answer. I completely understand. Come this way."

Roberta took youngest Johnny into the treatment area, leaving Valeria in the waiting room to fill out papers. Several mothers stood up and approached Valeria.

"Did you have an appointment?" one mother asked.

"No," Valeria said.

"Well we did," the other mother said.

"You cut in line," said the first.

"We should cut you," said the second.

The first mother ripped the papers out of Valeria's hands and tore them up.

"I don't want any trouble," Valeria said.

"You made trouble by bumping us!" the first said.

"No, it's all a mistake!" Valeria said.

"Yeah, it is!" said the first mother, and she punched Valeria.

"Stop it!" Valeria said.

The second mother punched Valeria. Valeria put her arms up to block. The other mothers in the waiting area cheered the first two on as Valeria took punch after punch and fell to the floor. The two mothers now kicked Valeria in the gut.

"Stop it, stop it!" Roberta yelled as she burst through the door, "or I'll call the police!"

Roberta beat off the two mothers and pulled Valeria to her feet.

"No," Valeria said. "Don't call the police. I'm okay. I don't want trouble."

"You are the trouble!" shouted the first mother.

"I said, enough!" Roberta said. "Valeria—come inside and wait. The rest of you—please be patient! I'll take care of you as soon as I can."

Valeria followed Roberta into Roberta's office.

"I would let you wait with Johnny," Roberta said, "but there just isn't room. Please—make yourself comfortable in my office. I'll treat Johnny as quickly as possible."

"Thank you," Valeria said. "This means a lot to Johnny and me."

Roberta left Valeria in her office and entered Johnny's treatment room. Another patient—a boy Johnny's age—sat in a dental chair next to Johnny's chair.

"You see," Nekara's voice echoed. "The misery of many outweighs the minority, just as the greater pain blocks the lesser. And I feed on the greater many."

Roberta administered novocaine to the patient next to Johnny.

"Now sit here for a moment while the novocaine takes effect," Roberta said to the patient.

Roberta turned in her chair and attended Johnny.

"Let's take a look at your teeth," Roberta said. "Open wide."

Youngest Johnny opened his mouth.

"Hmm. Number fourteen is badly decayed," Roberta said. "I could pull your tooth and give you an antibiotic, but we want to save the tooth. We don't want you looking like Glum Pumpkin."

"Who?" youngest Johnny asked.

"Glum Pumpkin," Roberta said. "Here—you may have this handout. It talks about dental care featuring Merry Pumpkin. And the first bit of care we need to do is take an X-ray of your tooth. I only wish we could afford to put an X-ray machine in every treatment room, but we can't. Follow me, Johnny."

Johnny followed Roberta to another room and sat in a simple dental chair next to the X-ray machine.

"Open," Roberta said.

Youngest Johnny opened his jaw, and Roberta inserted the film into his mouth.

"Bite down," she said.

Youngest Johnny bit down, and Roberta stepped out quickly to take the X-ray. She returned, took the film out, and gave it to an assistant. She led Johnny back to the treatment room.

"Normally, we wait for the X-ray to develop before beginning work," Roberta said, "but I'm confident we'll need to do a root canal. I'm hoping it's not infected, but based on your pain, your root most likely is. We'll begin with a carpule of novocaine in your cheek and hope that dulls the pain."

Roberta inserted a needle into youngest Johnny's mouth and injected the novocaine.

"Good," Roberta said. "You took the injection well."

"I couldn't feel it," youngest Johnny said.

"The pain in your tooth blocked it," Roberta said. "Now wait here a few minutes for the novocaine to take effect. Let's get a quick impression of your molar—or what's left of it."

Roberta quickly mixed up putty, placed it on an appliance, and inserted the appliance into youngest Johnny's mouth.

"Hold it there for a few minutes," Roberta said.

Roberta turned her stool and started work on the other patient—without an assistant. She drilled, suctioned, rinsed, and suctioned. She turned in her chair, removed youngest Johnny's impression, and placed it in a bag, which she marked. Roberta turned her chair again toward the young boy, prepared amalgam, applied it, shaped it, and finished it. She inserted a little blue paper into the boy's mouth.

"Now tap, tap, tap," Roberta said.

The boy bit down several times. Roberta was pleased with the tap test.

"That's it," Roberta said. "If you have any problems with your bite, if it feels funny or anything, come back for an adjustment."

An assistant came in with a new patient and chart, handed youngest Johnny's X-ray to Roberta, and took the finished patient.

"Hello, Amber," Roberta said. "Have a seat here and make yourself comfortable."

"Who's the boy?" Amber asked.

"He's another patient. We're playing the room-sharing game today," Roberta said. "You like playing games, don't you?"

"Sure," Amber said.

"Let's take a look at your chart and X-ray," Roberta said. "No, that's not your X-ray, that's Johnny's X-ray. Your X-ray is this one—yes, you have a small cavity on number thirty."

"That's why you confused us," youngest Johnny said. "Both X-rays are six-year molars."

"Is he a dentist?" Amber asked.

"No, he's just very smart," Roberta said. "Let's get you started on novocaine, okay?"

"Will it hurt?" Amber asked.

"Only a little. Think about happy pumpkins," Roberta said.

Roberta placed a cotton tip with anesthetic on the inside of Amber's cheek and held it there for a few seconds. She inserted the needle of novocaine and injected.

"There, that wasn't so bad, was it?" Roberta said. "Now wait here a moment until you get numb. There are some picture books here if you would like to look at one."

"Thank you," Amber said.

Roberta turned the chair and checked youngest Johnny. She placed a rubber dam over Johnny's infected molar. Johnny yelled in pain.

"It hurts, it hurts!" Johnny wailed.

Roberta looked at Johnny's X-ray and nodded in affirmation.

"I was afraid of that," Roberta said. "Johnny, you have a *hot tooth.*"

"It doesn't feel hot," youngest Johnny said.

"A hot tooth means the tooth is badly infected with severe pain," Roberta explained. "It's so bad that the acid produced by bacteria counteracts the effect of novocaine. This is why it still hurts. Normally, I would send you home with antibiotics and treat you in three days so novocaine can kill the pain, but we don't have three days, so I'm going to ask you to be very brave, Johnny. I must open the tooth to relieve the infection. Johnny, can you be brave for me?"

"Yeah, I'll be brave," youngest Johnny said.

"Okay," Roberta said.

Roberta prepared the drill and suction.

"This is going to hurt a lot," Roberta said. "Try your hardest to hold your head still."

Youngest Johnny gripped the hand rests. Shawna Johnny gripped Evanita and Geneva. Oldest Johnny gripped Jonara. Roberta started the drill and drove it to very high revolutions-per-minute—so high that the high-pitched squeal hurt the ears of all three Johnnys, Evanita, Geneva, and Jonara.

"Open wide," Roberta said.

Youngest Johnny opened his mouth. Roberta positioned the drill in youngest Johnny's mouth and drilled a hole into the infected tooth's pulp chamber.

"Arrrrg!" all three Johnnys yelled in reverberating, stabbing pain.

Images flashed around like mad, and the three Johnnys traveled together in back-and-forth time sequences. Evanita's birth of her second child, Robert, as she screamed in pain. Evanita's descent into the fiery pit at the River Wood and Battery factory. Margene's birthing of Geneva and death. Alice Cracbern's birthing of Marcus. Chase scenes of Theodore Cracbern toward the Castle Bravo mushroom cloud. Sharon Stout's chase of the van that had kidnapped her daughter, Shelia, with the van descending into the water. Nekara's physical transformation from normal flesh to boron nitride tissue. A van driving off Sellwood Bridge into the Willamette, a woman and Roberta scuba diving into the Willamette in search of the van, and Roberta pulling Eva up from the van to the water's surface in Ross Island's bay.

Two stars—cerise and green—orbited each other in a tightening spiral, the two orbited faster and faster with increasing tension and pain until they collided into a single star of white light.

The light shone white. The Johnnys, Evanita, Geneva, and Jonara were temporarily blinded, but their vision returned to the scene of MacNessi Dental and youngest Johnny's dental chair. The pain disappeared as pus shot out of youngest Johnny's molar and the pressure subsided. Roberta suctioned the blood and pus from the tooth. She injected bits of novocaine in the gums around the tooth. Then without warning, Roberta's eyes fluttered, and she fell back nearly off her stool.

"Doctor MacNessi?" youngest Johnny called as he shook Roberta. "Doctor?"

"Yes, yes," Roberta said as she returned to alertness. "I felt strange for a moment there. I thought I saw...no, never mind."

"Were you scuba diving in the Willamette River?" youngest Johnny asked. "Did you pull Doctor Carreña out of the river onto a yacht?"

Roberta looked at youngest Johnny strangely.

"Yes, Johnny. But how could you know?" Roberta asked.

"I saw it too—when you drilled into my molar, I saw it and many other things," youngest Johnny said.

"What's happening?" Amber asked. "Is it make-believe time?"

Roberta realized her conversation with youngest Johnny should be kept private. She called for an assistant to take Amber to another treatment room where the OHSU intern dentist could take care of her. Roberta injected novocaine into the pulp chamber.

"What else did you see, Johnny?" Roberta asked.

"Strange things of other people I've never met before. Women giving birth. A nuclear explosion. A van driving off Sellwood Bridge."

"I would speculate the pain caused you to hallucinate, but the vision of a van driving off Sellwood Bridge—that was odd," Roberta said. "I must have hallucinated the same thing. It never happened in real life. But the pain is gone, right?"

"Yeah," youngest Johnny said.

"Good. I'm going to resume drilling. This shouldn't hurt a bit," Roberta said.

Roberta widened the hole to the pulp chamber with the drill. The vibrations shook youngest Johnny's head and a stone hidden under his shirt at the end of a necklace. Youngest Johnny sensed Roberta's body and her internal organs, and as he did, Shawna Johnny sensed them as did oldest Johnny.

"Jonara," oldest Johnny said. "I remember this vaguely. But something happened when I got older. I didn't have these visions anymore. And yet, I feel completely linked up with my younger selves, as if they are the correct selves. Is it all true?"

"Yes, Daddy! It's all true!" Jonara said. "It's the real timeline!"

"What does this mean?" oldest Johnny asked Jonara. "If the timeline is wrong, should we change it? Can we?"

"We have to find a way," Jonara said. "We must!"

"I wish we knew how. We need help," oldest Johnny said.

"No, don't ask for help," Jonara said.

"And why not?" Nekara asked as she appeared out of no-where.

"Because you'll appear," Jonara said. "And you'll start some mischief that will make things worse. Daddy and I need to repair the timeline that you broke."

"That you indurated," Nekara said.

"And you took advantage of," Jonara said. "Without you, Nekara the Red, things would be normal."

"Hah! Normal?" Nekara mocked. "You'd suffer even more in your old timeline. Earth people will always be corrupt and cause pain—with or without me."

"But you are a factor—a factor I must figure out how to counteract," Jonara said.

"Impossible. I'm too powerful," Nekara said. "Any other belief is delusional. But I leave you to your fantasy. Eight-year-old Johnny feels no pain at the moment, and that weakens me. I should have popped in when the three Johnnys experienced excruciating pain, but I had business in another part of the world where political prisoners were being tortured. There's always plenty of that to last me a lifetime. Oh—another prisoner is being tortured. I'll catch up with you later."

Nekara disappeared.

Roberta inserted a file into the first root, twisted it with her fingers, removed it, placed the file in a cleaning solution, inserted a different file, cleaned deeper into the root, placed that file in a cleaning solution, inserted a third file, and cleaned the root farther to a point where she felt she was close to the bottom. She repeated this procedure with the other two roots. Next, she inserted three files into the three roots and adjusted stoppers on the files to mark depth.

"We need to take another X-ray to check file depth," Roberta said.

Roberta led Johnny back to the X-ray room and placed a film in his mouth.

"Hold still," Roberta said.

Roberta left the room and took the X-ray. She returned, removed the film from his mouth, and handed it to an assistant.

Roberta led Johnny back to the treatment room and removed the files.

"I saw your body," youngest Johnny said. "I saw it inside and out."

"That's impossible," Roberta said.

"I saw damaged ovaries," youngest Johnny said. "They're small and dead."

Roberta blushed in embarrassment.

"There's no way you could know that," Roberta said. "It's also very personal and private, Johnny."

"But I saw it, I saw it," youngest Johnny said. "When you drilled into my tooth, the vibrations...they...I sensed you like a sonogram. Your ovaries were damaged by X-rays from below. I also sensed your legs and feet. The X-rays were strongest at your feet. It happened when you were young, when you were a child."

"I never told anyone. How can you sense all this?" Roberta asked.

"You did tell someone," youngest Johnny said. "You told Richard. The X-rays made you infertile. He didn't understand."

"Oh, I see. He told you," Roberta said. "But how do you know him?"

"No, I never met Richard. I know him from your thoughts. I saw them in a flash while you drilled my teeth. But you never told him that your mother killed a man at an ISIS meeting in Wisconsin," youngest Johnny said. "No one knows that except your mother, Jane, and she's dead."

Roberta shook in nervousness.

"This isn't funny," Roberta said with fear in her throat. "Don't scare me with the occult. I don't believe it."

"It's not witchcraft," youngest Johnny said. "It's science. When a vibration touches me, I sense objects like an MRI, a CAT scan, or a sonogram."

"If it's science, then we can test it with a repeatable experiment," Roberta said. "What am I talking about? You're an eight-year-old boy. How can you know about these things?"

"I read a lot," youngest Johnny said. "I know about science."

"All right," Roberta said. "I'll place the side of the drill against your temple. Don't worry—the drill bit will twirl harmlessly in the air. And I'll hold a number of fingers behind my back. You tell me how many fingers I'm holding out."

"Okay," youngest Johnny said. "I'm ready."

Roberta did as she described.

"Four—counting your thumb. Three, one, none, wiggling, pointing to the door, to the wall, thumb up, up, up, down, side," youngest Johnny said.

Roberta stopped the drill and stared at youngest Johnny.

"I can't figure out how you know," Roberta said. "It defies all known medical knowledge."

"And you're Celtic," Johnny said.

Roberta laughed.

"That's no secret," Roberta said. "My red hair gives that away."

"But you have extra-sensitive nerves," youngest Johnny said. "Your fingertips are so sensitive that a static shock from touching a doorknob is extremely painful."

"Many Celts have sensitive sensory perception," Roberta said.

"But yours is especially enhanced," youngest Johnny said. "Dr. MacNessi—I've read a few people, but they could never read me. Never. If you hold your head against mine and run the drill against my temple again, I wonder if you could read me too."

"I don't believe what I'm hearing," Roberta said. "This is science fiction or witchcraft. And I'm half-believing it—all with a desperately overflowing patient list waiting for treatment."

"Please," youngest Johnny said. "If you can read me, you'll understand how I know."

"What the Hell," Roberta said. "It'll make for a good laugh if nothing else."

Roberta placed her right hand against youngest Johnny's right side of his head and pressed the left side of his head against the right side of her head. She placed the side of the drill against his forehead and activated it such that the drill bit twirled freely in the air as before. Johnny sensed Roberta's body and his own as if they were standing on two platforms and seeing medical drawings of their biology.

Roberta stopped the drill.

"I understand," Roberta said. "You have an unusual stone on a necklace that focuses the vibrations into visual imagery. But I saw something else, Johnny. You have cryptorchidism."

"Yes," youngest Johnny said. "I know. I'm missing a testicle."

"You've had it since birth. It's the result of your father's exposure to Agent Orange in Vietnam," Roberta said. "I'm sorry. But the good news is the other testicle is fine. You should be able to father children someday."

"I hope so," youngest Johnny said.

"There's something else," Roberta said. "The missing testicle—well—this is unusual. Johnny, can you be brave again?"

"I know there's something different about me. I know there's something like an undescended testicle in my abdomen," youngest Johnny said.

"Yes, something like an undescended testicle. It's actually an ovary, and there's a primitive fallopian tube and uterus in your inguinal canal. It could never act as a female reproductive tract, but you should know that in a few years, this ovary and its tract could become active. Johnny—if the primitive uterus goes through a primitive menstrual cycle, it could send material into your scrotum risking infection and causing rupture. That would be bad. We need to get you to a specialist to discuss your options."

"Would a specialist give someone on Title 19 the best care?" youngest Johnny asked.

"Perhaps not," Roberta said. "Tell you what—why don't you and Valeria come over for dinner tonight? We can talk about this more. I'd love to discuss more with you here, but unfortunately, I'm severely short on time. Sound fair?"

"I'll ask my older sister—Valeria. But I'm sure she'll say 'yes'," youngest Johnny said.

"Good," Roberta said.

An assistant passed Johnny's developed X-rays to Roberta.

"A little more filing," Roberta said.

Roberta filed a little deeper into Johnny's roots and led him back to the X-ray room.

"Open," she said, and she inserted the film into his mouth.

As before, she exited the room, took the X-ray image, and reentered. She passed the X-ray to an assistant and led Johnny back to the treatment room.

"Dr. Carreña," youngest Johnny started. "She's addicted to alcohol and amphetamine."

"How do you know?" Roberta asked.

"I read her when she passed out and fell on me," youngest Johnny said. "Her body won't handle much more. Her heart will quit working."

"Cardiac arrest?" Roberta asked. "It's as I feared."

"You have to help her. You love her," youngest Johnny said.

The assistant handed Roberta the developed X-rays.

"Good," Roberta said. "The roots are filed to the correct depth."

Roberta reamed the three roots.

"Johnny," Roberta said. "I've removed all infectious material and cleaned out the root canals. Because you had an infection, I'm going to insert some medication, close off the pulp chamber, and send you home for a week with antibiotic pills. This will allow your tissue to heal 100%. However, you'll have to come back two additional times."

"I don't want to come back," youngest Johnny said. "Do it all now."

"I can't, and I won't," Roberta said. "First of all, I can't make your new crown here. I have to send it out to be made. Second, I want your infection to heal properly before I seal the root and build up the post. Some dentists use Sargenti to prevent the infection from coming back, but I won't risk that material. If it should seep from the root canal into surrounding tissue, it would cause severe damage. You would be in more pain than the toothache you had when you came in here—and the pain would be permanent. I won't risk it."

Roberta dipped three paper tips into medication and inserted them into the three root canals. She filled the pulp chamber with medicated cement.

"Don't eat on this side of your mouth for a week. I'm writing you a prescription for antibiotics. Make sure you get this filled today and take them as directed," Roberta instructed. "Johnny—please try to keep these thoughts about reading people's biology secret. And don't say anything about my biology. Will you do that for me? I'll do all I can to help you with Title 19 payments and whatever other health issues you may have."

"Okay," youngest Johnny said.

The scene faded into grays and returned to the Caves of Healing.

"Shawna, I mean Johnny, is it true about...about...your inguinal canal?" Evanita asked.

"I didn't want to gross you out," Shawna Johnny said. "Valeria and I ate dinner at Roberta's home. Eva wasn't there—she was out dancing and drinking. I mentioned that I could only read women with the stone. Valeria could never understand how a male could read a female until Roberta suggested the ovary may have permitted me to do so, and that removing the ovary risked ending my ability to read women. So I never had the ovary removed."

"Not true," oldest Johnny said. "I had the ovary removed shortly after that dinner visit with Roberta, and I lost my ability to read women. Funny, I'd forgotten about that until just now. I'd forgotten the Moissan Ruby had powers. I only remembered it as being junk jewelry. Maybe I made a mistake."

"I've always wondered something," Shawna Johnny said. "What would have happened if I had the ovary removed? Would the Moissan Ruby still work? The only way I'll know is if I have it removed. But I risk losing the power forever."

"Stay exactly as nature made you," Evanita said. "I like you as you are."

Evanita kissed Johnny, and Johnny kissed back.

"Oh, what would the sisters say about this?" Geneva said.

"You won't say a thing," Evanita said. "It only looks like a young woman is kissing a young woman."

"I hope you don't smear your makeup, Shawna, or else the sisters will know something happened in these caves," Geneva said. "And wipe that lipstick off your face, Evanita."

Evanita took a tissue from her purse and blotted away residue from Shawna Johnny's lipstick.

"You would make Tara Tushenne jealous," Evanita laughed.

"Who?" Shawna Johnny asked.

"An employee at the Elrod 402 who had the hots for me," Evanita said. "I told her I wasn't that kind of girl. And here I am kissing my boyfriend dressed up as a girl. It's so...strange. Shawna—if you didn't have the ovary removed, what happened with...I mean...did you ever get a...how do I say it?"

"A period?" Shawna Johnny asked.

"Yeah," Evanita said.

"Well, how can I explain this delicately? I guess there is no easy way. I had surgery to create a small, external opening near the bottom of the affected inguinal canal. The very bottom of the canal was closed off to prevent flow from seeping into my...scrotum. The surgery was a success. At age thirteen, something like a menstrual cycle started. Fast-forward to the present. Once every other month, blood and tissue drains through the opening. And yes, I get cramps, but they are small, and I wear a pad to catch the flow. It's the price I pay so I can use the Moissan Ruby."

"It's a smaller price to pay than what women endure once a month—and we don't have the luxury of a Moissan Ruby or anything. We suffer for nothing," Evanita said.

"Except for the ability to conceive one day," Geneva said.

"If it weren't for that fact, I think all women would find some way to end *the curse* early in life," Evanita said.

Jonara and oldest Johnny lost contact with the Caves of Healing. Their vision cleared, and they stood next to the SR-71 Whitebird. Johnny looked at his watch—no time had passed.

"We didn't gray out," oldest Johnny said. "We witnessed everything in an instant."

Hangar crew personnel ushered Johnny and Jonara away from the aircraft. Johnny and Jonara returned to the observation deck and watched the aircraft take off.

"It's returning to Portland," Marcus said. "The test flight was a success. It's time to make final preparations for Saturday's eclipse."

Marcus escorted Eva, Evanita, Anna, Johnny, and Jonara back to a UH-1N Huey helicopter. The group entered, and Marcus instructed the pilot to fly around Corpus Christi Bay.

"As you can see," Marcus said to the group, "the vitacepticals are almost ready for use."

"Daddy," Jonara whispered, "will you help me?"

"If I can," Johnny whispered back.

"Take me to—" Jonara started.

"What are you two whispering about?" Evanita asked.

"Nothing," Jonara said. "It's a nice view of the bay."

"A very nice view," Johnny added.

"Yes, it is," Evanita said. "Well, this has been a tiring day. I could use a nap."

Evanita snored in the helicopter.

"The bay is beautiful," Johnny said. "It's beautiful."

CHAPTER 11

Stuffed Closet

2023 Oct 12, Thu Afnoon. Corpus Christi, Texas.

Johnny took Jonara for another boat ride on Corpus Christi Bay. The bay was filled with other boats celebrating the erection of the vitacepticals.

"Jonara," Johnny said. "Imagine if there were no water in the bay. How would aquatic life survive?"

"It couldn't," Jonara said.

"An empty bay is like a desert," Johnny said. "A resource is expended until it's gone. It's much harder to bring the fish back when the bay is empty than when it's low. A desert is much the same way. Rains bring life, life holds water, but when the land is plundered, life fails, and water runs off or evaporates. The rains cannot restart that which has been destroyed."

"You're starting to sound like the Daddy I used to know," Jonara said.

"Life cannot thrive in an empty bay, nor can it thrive in debt," Johnny said. "Farmers work the land and reap the harvest, but they store the harvest to subsist until the following harvest. A farmer who borrows harvest from another farmer is no farmer at all. Savings, Jonara. Life thrives on savings— stores of water, stores of food, and stores of happiness. Misery thrives on loss and debt. These vitacepticals will force people to owe payment to the Church before they can bring life into the world. They'll always be indebted the Church. It's like—a regime. A regime of misery. The other timeline, Jonara. It's full of life, isn't it?"

"Yeah," Jonara said. "But it's full of death too."

"Life is always followed by death, but life follows anew. The only way to bring the other timeline around is to save up for it," Johnny said.

"Huh? What do I save?" Jonara asked.

"Before a farmer receives the happy harvest, the farmer must work the land and animals. The work is aligned with the seasons and stores of energy. Jonara—for the first time in my life, I regret the decision I made to have my ovary removed. It stole away my alignment with the Moissan Ruby."

"I don't understand. Alignment? What are you talking about?" Jonara asked.

"A farmer doesn't plant in winter," Johnny said. "And a farmer doesn't take from the land first. A farmer must give to the land first by planting seeds. A farmer must give food to the bull before the bull goes to slaughter. Jonara—the task falls upon you to change the timeline since I cannot. You must find the spring season in your soul and give something of yourself before you can receive into the other timeline."

"What do I give? How do I find a spring season in my soul?"

"You must be ready to receive sunlight, drink rain, and grow. Feeding off the death of old memories and past seasons is the winter in your soul," Johnny said. "It's the evil of dependence. Jonara—the secret to life is learning how to be independent of the winter in your soul. When you depend on absolute consumption without replenishment, your psyche takes a fast-track to death and in time becomes food for another winter-feeding soul. Do you understand what I'm saying, Jonara?"

"I have to grow up?" Jonara asked.

"Something like that. You must begin the spring season toward adulthood," Johnny said. "That means learning how to give in order to receive."

"I don't know what to give," Jonara said. "I can't give money."

"It's more of a giving of your psyche," Johnny said. "But don't go too far. A farmer does not plant herself in the ground, she plants one seed after another. And she plants it in the earth—not the road where others may trample it. Not all seeds grow to fruition. You must understand this. Don't expect all efforts to be fruitful."

"What can I give, what can I give?" Jonara repeated.

"Your attention," Johnny said. "Dip the Moissan Ruby into the bay water."

"My attention?" Jonara asked.

"You've been doing it all along," Johnny said. "Haven't you?"

"Is watching something an act of giving?" Jonara asked.

"It's the first seed of action," Johnny said. "You give attention to the misery of others, thoughts grow in your psyche, and you receive inspiration to act."

"Inspiration to act," Jonara said. "What inspiration?"

"You won't know until you complete the spring season of giving attention, and the summer season of growing thoughts," Johnny said.

Jonara dipped the Moissan Ruby into Corpus Christi Bay as she had done so on Sunday.

2007 Dec 8, Sat. The Caves of Healing. Carreña, Spain.

Jonara appeared in the Caves of Healing with Evanita, Shawna Johnny, and Geneva still in their chairs. Older Johnny did not appear with her.

"Daddy?" Jonara called. "Where are you?"

"I blocked him," Nekara said as she appeared out of nowhere.

"Why?" Jonara asked. "Are you afraid of him?"

"He annoyed me with his goody-farm-life stories," Nekara said. "Things are about to get more disturbing, and I don't need his temperance to spoil the occasion."

"Then Daddy's right," Jonara said. "Life needs stores of resources to begin. He mentioned sunlight, water, and earth, but he didn't mention another one—love."

"Life gets along just fine without love," Nekara said. "Look at me."

"No it doesn't," Jonara said. "It suffers from love depletion. And I *am* looking at you. Why do you think I say that? You have no stores of love left in you. They were siphoned away, weren't they? And now you're feeding off the leftovers of winter—the leftover misery after life died for the season. But there's a new season on the way! I can feel it!"

"You and your doomed delusions of hope," Nekara said. "I thought better of you at one time, Jonara, but now I see you're drinking the 'yellow cider' like the rest of the adults in your world."

"I can't be delusional," Jonara said. "Everything Daddy said makes sense."

"Like-minded people of delusions reinforce each other's paths of failure," Nekara said. "You and your father are of the same ilk. I once worshiped like my people, but in time, I saw the fallout of my fallow folly."

"You're the road my father warned me about. He said not to plant seeds on the road, for others will trample it," Jonara said. "You're trying to trample me. Begone, Nekara the Red! I have important attention to give!"

"Look at me, Jonara," Nekara said.

"There's something in this cave," Shawna Johnny said. "Something dreadful and desiring. It's like bacteria. It feeds on death and multiplies exponentially to the exclusion of all else until no life is possible."

"Pull your legs out of the water," Geneva said.

"Yes, but not me," Shawna Johnny said. "I must hold it off."

"He senses you!" Jonara said to Nekara.

"Your father is a fool in any timeline," Nekara said. "No male can stop me."

"But he has some femininity in this timeline. And my mother and Nanna Geneva are with him," Jonara said to Nekara. "Mommy, Daddy, Nanna—I'm here! I'll fight with you!"

"We have to put our legs back in the pool," Evanita said. "We have to fight this together."

"I must risk it alone," Shawna Johnny said.

"No you mustn't," Geneva said. "Evanita is right. All legs in the pool."

Jonara placed both of her legs in the pool too. Geneva read something from the diary, and for a moment it was 1492 again with the women converging in the Caves of Healing. The women held hands and spoke:

Miramish	**Translation**
Thoritho kapi dikoshiu	Hold hands together
Nui tesharafi.	My sisters.
Nuish e pilamefifa mahilu lonudo	Our friendship now enters
Dho meifu vemiana	A social winter
Tolu rialu denadi	Where low temperatures
Felito bushipu fioriki	Bring deep freezes
Dhaku shetito loreifu vilami	And test all bonds
Opeifu felausha.	Of life.
Hemeru shai waku kelifotu	Only the most hardy
Voifelaufoteio.	Will survive.
Hemeru shoshi lowei derapo	Only those who store
Tesh e voshara	Their love
Shupeio tilen okuanu.	Will find it again.
Loreifu mishi deriatheio	All others will perish
Ishu shai bushiki opeifu kupoga	In the depths of debt
Liufialotao haku lisha luvausho	Consuming what little remains
Opeifu kaifa dhaku burabolika	Of hatred and despair
Kivoanu shai ushethu shenakata	Before the last flicker
Opeifu kiata	Of death
Fiasho uilu ishetu fiorita.	Flames out into frost.
Thoritho kapi dikoshiu.	Hold hands together.
Nuish e pilamefifa lumioleio	Our friendship will renew
Ishu vorila.	In spring.

Nekara disappeared. Then Felifia and her women disappeared. The Caves of Healing returned as it was with Geneva, Evanita, Shawna Johnny, and Jonara.

"What did you read?" Evanita asked.

"It's a passage from the first page of my diary, a call to the beginning you could say," Geneva replied. "Shawna—is the dreadful thing still here?"

"No, it's gone," Shawna Johnny said.

"Very well," Geneva said. "Let's continue where we left off."

Geneva read from her diary, and the group journeyed back to 1989.

1989 Oct 6, Fri Afnoon 5 pm. MacNessi Dental. Portland, Oregon.

Valeria took Johnny to MacNessi Dental. The two waited for twenty minutes before Roberta called for Johnny.

"Come in, come in, Johnny," Roberta said.

Roberta led Johnny to a treatment room shared with another child. Johnny sat down in the dental chair.

"Today, I'm going to fill your roots with gutta percha and build up a post for the crown," Roberta said. "Some patients ask for novocaine, others don't need it."

"Will it hurt?" youngest Johnny asked.

"Most of the procedure won't hurt," Roberta said. "But I may have to perform a gingivectomy to remove a bit of the gum line. That would hurt. Let me take a look at your gums to see if you have gingivitis."

Roberta inserted a probe into Johnny's gum.

"Your gums are ones and twos, but unfortunately they bleed. I'll need to perform a gingivectomy."

"I'll take the novocaine," youngest Johnny said.

Roberta injected the novocaine.

"Rest there a moment," Roberta said.

Roberta attended the boy next to her by drilling the cavity, filling it, and finishing it.

"That's it, Ronny," Roberta said to the boy. "Your tooth is restored."

An assistant led Ronny out of the treatment room.

"Your turn, Johnny," Roberta said. "Are you numb?"

"Very numb," Johnny said.

"Good," Roberta said.

Roberta placed the rubber dam over Johnny's tooth. She scraped out the medicated filling and removed the paper points. She inserted new paper points to check for infectious material. The paper points came up dry.

"Good news, Johnny," Roberta said. "Your gums have completely healed. There's no evidence of infectious material."

Roberta cut and inserted lengths of gutta percha into the roots. She inserted a post and built up a core using composite.

"Your gum line must be trimmed away and heal for next week's visit," Roberta said. "We don't want any blood interfering with the cement when I attach the crown to the post."

Roberta trimmed the gum line around the molar. It bled a little bit. She rinsed and suctioned the blood away.

"Good," Roberta said. "The core should be hard enough to shape now."

Roberta shaped the core with the dental drill. Johnny felt himself travel through the dental chair into the floor and through the office walls. Roberta stopped the drill, rinsed with water, and suctioned.

"Ow," youngest Johnny said.

Youngest Johnny breathed heavily as if having just run around the building.

"Did that hurt?" Roberta asked. "Even without novocaine, that shouldn't have hurt."

"No, it wasn't that," youngest Johnny said. "I felt something. It wasn't you or anyone here. It was...a meeting next door. Doctor Carreña...she's in a meeting. She's upset. Something's changed. Marcus is yelling at people. He's angry. Very angry. Doctor Carreña is scared. She wants a drink. She wants...no, not amphetamine. She wants a painkiller. She wants morphine."

"Why?" Roberta asked nervously. "What's happening? Johnny—tell me what's happening?"

"I don't know. I'm too tired," youngest Johnny said.

"How did you see into the office next door?" Roberta asked. "I thought you could only see a woman's physiology and only when you're touching her and your skull is vibrating."

"Yeah, I know. This is the first time for me too," youngest Johnny said. "It happened when you drilled and rinsed. The drill vibrated my skull. I had an out-of-body experience. First I was in the office walls, but when you sprayed water in my mouth, I went through the water stream and followed it to the water pipe through the building to a water tank in a closet next to Marcus's office. The water tank was like a big ear, and I heard everything. But it was only for a few seconds. Maybe Doctor Carreña will tell you more."

"Hmm. She doesn't tell me anything," Roberta said. "I've got to find out what's happening with Marcus and his practice. I thought Eva was a little more agitated this week. But why? Johnny, would you be willing to try seeing into the office again if I rinse and send a vibration to your skull?"

"No," youngest Johnny said, still out of breath. "I'm too tired. I can't take it."

"We've got to find out what Marcus is doing—without him knowing we know," Roberta said. "I'm finished with your tooth for today. I'll fit the crown next week. Johnny—what do you know about computers?"

"Just what I've read in the encyclopedia and what my sister taught me," youngest Johnny said.

"Have you ever used one?" Roberta asked.

Roberta didn't wait for Johnny to finish. She removed the rubber dam, cleaned up Johnny, and led him to her office and showed him a DEC VT100 character-based monochrome computer terminal.

"This is a computer terminal," Roberta said. "It connects to a VAX 11/780 computer in the office next door—Cracbern Associates. Marcus has other clinics in other buildings that connect to the main computer next door. He uses the computer system to keep track of patients, accounting, inventory, and electronic mail. When I started handling part of his patient load, he had this terminal installed in my office. I can log in and keep my records up-to-date. I can send electronic mail. Johnny—I need the password to Marcus's account. How can I get it? Can you read through the communication cable like you did the water pipe?"

"I don't know," youngest Johnny said. "I've never tried. What about your other patients?"

"You're my last patient for the day," Roberta said.

"I'm afraid," youngest Johnny said. "It might hurt me. I'm still tired from the water trip."

"Okay," Roberta said. "I won't force you. I just wish I could get his password."

"There might be another way to get the password," youngest Johnny said.

"How?" Roberta asked.

"I don't know, but if I had a reference book on the computer, maybe I could figure something out," youngest Johnny said.

Roberta pulled a banker's box out of a closet and placed it on her desk. She opened it and revealed several books totaling thousands of pages.

"Wow!" Johnny said. "I'd hate to do a book report on these!"

"Would you be willing to look at them?" Roberta asked. "Marcus gave them to me as a joke. I don't think he expected me to read them."

"I could spend all weekend reading them," youngest Johnny said.

"Don't obsess too much on details," Roberta said. "Remember—we need to find a way to get Marcus's password. We don't need to plot rocket trajectories or teach the computer to play chess."

"Okay, I'll remember," youngest Johnny said.

Roberta called Valeria into her office and asked her to help Roberta carry the banker's box to Valeria's car.

"No—we shouldn't go out the front door," Roberta said. "We might be seen. Let's go out the back."

Roberta, Valeria, and youngest Johnny went out the back door with the banker's box and over to Valeria's car where the two women loaded it into the trunk.

"Some reading material for Johnny," Roberta said. "He's helping me with a special project."

"What kind of project?" Valeria asked.

"A computer project," Roberta said. "Johnny can tell you when you get home. If you'd like to help, I'd appreciate it."

"I'm good with computers," Valeria said. "I volunteer at the hospital when I'm not volunteering at Barnseed Baptist Church."

"You're a Baptist?" Roberta said. "I didn't know. I'm a Baptist too. Johnny—did you know I was Baptist?"

"No, I didn't," Johnny said. "I know you're a Christian believer, and that's good enough for me."

"That's good enough for me too," Valeria said. "Dr. MacNessi, if you'd like to attend service with us, you're more than welcome."

"I'd love to," Roberta said. "I've been meaning to find a good Baptist Church around here, but I haven't had time."

1989 Oct 8, Sun Morn 8 am. Roberta's Home. Portland, Oregon.

Eva did not return that night. Anxious about Eva, Roberta slept lightly. The sun rose, and still Eva did not return.

"Where did that girl go?" Roberta asked herself. "Should I go looking for her? No, I'll give her a little more time."

Roberta called Valeria on the telephone.

"Hi, Valeria, how are you?" Roberta said. "Yeah. Not so well. Eva went out last night. No, not yet. Of course I worry. I've been worried about her since she started drinking. Oh, I didn't mean to interrupt you. I should let you finish getting ready for Sunday service. Me, really? Yeah, that'd be great. How do I get there? West on Burnside Road toward Pittock Acres. Okay, got it. I'll see you at nine. Goodbye."

Roberta dressed up and drove to Barnseed Baptist Church. She saw a tall, barn-like building with a smiley face painted on one end. On top of the building at the center high points on both ends were two crucifixes fashioned as weather vanes. Roberta followed the line of people entering the church. She stood at the doorway and had an odd feeling, as if someone were breathing over her shoulder. Roberta turned around and saw no one behind her who could have affected her neck. She heard a door slam closed, and she looked across the way to the parking lot where she saw Johnny exit the passenger side of a car. Valeria exited the driver's side. Roberta walked toward them and met them halfway.

"Welcome to Barnseed Baptist Church," Valeria said. "Have you toured the church yet?"

"No, I just arrived," Roberta said.

"We have a few minutes before service starts," Valeria said. "Come on, let's go inside."

Valeria led youngest Johnny and Roberta into Barnseed Baptist Church.

"Look!" Evanita said. "The murals!"

"Yes," Shawna Johnny said. "In the early days, both walls had religious murals, not just the one."

"I remember the scene of Adam and Eve, and there's Noah and his Ark. And Jesus leading his people on horses," Evanita said. "I remember them too."

"The murals are beautiful," Roberta said.

"On the left wall," Valeria said, "is an opening to the daycare center. It's still under construction, but we hope to open it in a few months."

Roberta followed Valeria and youngest Johnny to the left wall.

"Look Shawna!" Evanita said. "The murals on the left wall! One shows Jesus holding his arm out as if telling his disciples to go somewhere."

"It's the scene where he's telling them to spread out to all parts of the earth and preach the Good News," Johnny said. "If you look closely, you'll see he's shaking the dust off his feet. Some towns will not accept you for who you are. He's saying not to dwell on rejection, but to go forth to the next town. It's really quite an interesting thing. You can look at it as a metaphor for your own life. The road to goodness is difficult and full of rejection. That rejection is an evil, like group pressure to conform to failure, and it can consume and destroy you. Jesus says to shake that evil off your feet. Some people—not Baptists—object to this mural."

"Why?" Evanita asked.

"I...hesitate to say in your grandmother's presence," Shawna Johnny said.

"Is it because of the verse regarding Peter being the rock of the Church?" Geneva asked.

"Yes, it is," Shawna Johnny said. "Some argue that Jesus never said that, that the phrase was inserted later to justify the consolidation of Christianity into a single power—the Roman Catholic Church."

"And what do you believe, Shawna?" Geneva asked.

"I don't know what was written when," Shawna Johnny said. "I always look for what I can apply in the Bible to my own life. Some things apply, some things do not. It's not rejection; it's just finding the help I need at the time."

"What's this other mural, Shawna?" Evanita asked.

"It's a scene of the disciples when they preach to people of different languages," Shawna Johnny said. "This is after Jesus has passed on to the next realm."

"I don't understand," Geneva said. "It appears the disciples are performing sign language."

"Yes, they are," Shawna Johnny said.

"That never happened," Geneva said.

"It's a stretch, I know," Shawna Johnny said. "It's supposed to be symbolic, that the message of Jesus transcends the particulars of languages and is universal to all."

"Sign language differs from one geographic region to another," Geneva said.

"I know," Shawna Johnny said. "But there's this perception by some that sign language could be a universal language without being weighed down by extra details found in spoken languages. It's metaphorical. It's not meant to be literal."

"Is that the Tower of Babel next to the disciple scene?" Evanita asked.

"Yes, it is," Shawna Johnny said.

"It's like the opposite of the disciple scene," Evanita said. "Look—there are clouds made of gold coins above the tower."

"You're right," Shawna Johnny said. "This scene is another metaphor, that an obsessive greed in a singular direction for quick reward divides people. Languages and cultures change until divisions are wide enough to set people against each other with enough hate and bigotry to launch wars. The message of Jesus crosses that great divide—his message is universal and is not limited to any particular language or culture. And his message is not part of any greed machine as the Tower of Babel was. Yeah, these three murals were special. Later, Pastor Ephram had them replaced with hunting scenes."

"Service will start soon. Let's take a seat," Valeria said.

Roberta followed youngest Johnny and Valeria to a pew just behind the deaf section. The pastor's wife, Patty Ephram, walked out from a side room and took her place behind a small podium in front of the deaf section. She was much younger and less careworn than the Patty Ephram who Evanita remembered. Shortly thereafter, the choir took its place. An organ started up in music, and the choir sang the opening hymn. The congregation joined the choir in song. Pastor Ephram appeared on stage and sang with the choir as well. He was also much younger than Evanita remembered, he was thinner, and he had a joyfulness to his step. The song concluded, the congregation applauded, and Pastor Ephram started the service. He began by thanking his wife, the organ lady, the choir, and the congregation for their devotion to Jesus. He led a short prayer before going into sermon.

"We are all children of God," Pastor Ephram said, "and we strive to keep Jesus in our hearts. Jesus is free and available to all people—no man or building may claim a monopoly on Him. Fellow members of our church, God speaks to all of us, and we encourage each of you to hear His voice and let His ministry flow through you. We at Barnseed Baptist Church encourage open exposition of His message in His faith, as such, I've asked one of our younger people to give today's sermon. Please give your support, attention, and a big round of applause to Valeria Pindus."

Roberta jumped in surprise. Valeria? Giving the sermon? Wow, Roberta's Baptist church in Texas didn't do this. Valeria stood up and walked to the stage. Pastor Ephram gave her the microphone, and Valeria started.

"Good morning, friends of Jesus," Valeria said.

"Good morning," the congregation replied.

"I...I'm just a little nervous," Valeria said.

Valeria pulled out a stack of index cards and flipped through a few to find the beginning, but the pack slipped out of her hands and spewed out everywhere. Patty rushed over to help her pick them up.

"Thank you, Patty," Valeria said.

Patty rushed back to the signing post.

"I spent all day yesterday working on my sermon," Valeria said. "But every time I recite it, it doesn't sound right. I guess I'm not as good as our pastor."

"Just do your best, child," Pastor Ephram said.

Valeria flipped through the note cards again and shook her head.

"I think I'll set these aside," Valeria said. "I want to speak to you today about what it means to bear fruit—spiritual fruit—and what happens when that ability is robbed. I hope I make sense. Maybe I should start with a reading. Okay? Okay. I want to read a passage about Jesus and the fig tree. From Mark 11:12, 'The next day as they were leaving Bethany, Jesus was hungry. Seeing in the distance a fig tree in leaf, he went to find out if it had any fruit. When he reached it, he found nothing but leaves, because it was not the season for figs. Then he said to the tree, *May no one ever eat fruit from you again.* And his disciples heard him say it. When evening came, they went out of the city. In the morning as they went along, they saw the fig tree withered from the roots'."

Valeria paused and took a sip of water.

"I know what you're thinking. The story of the fig tree is about faith," Valeria continued. "But I want to talk about my own interpretation of the fig tree. First, I want to talk about fig trees and seasons. A fig tree actually produces two fruits per year. The first fruit—the breba—grows in the spring from the prior year's shoot. It is small and sometimes destroyed by frost. The main fruit ripens in the fall from new summer growth. Now I've talked with our pastor and done some reading, and it's likely Jesus was looking for the breba fruit. This was out of season for the main crop, but still, a breba shoot would show that the old shoots are still alive. But he didn't find any breba fruits. That meant the old shoots were dead. The leaves were all that was left. Jesus 'cursed' the fig tree, but I don't think Jesus really did anything to kill the fig. Its shoots were already dead, so the tree was like a living shell. It was just a matter of time before the fig tree completely died."

"In my heart," Valeria continued, "I believe the old shoot is the tabernacle of Jesus in each of us. Through his love, he gives a part of himself so that we may bear fruit. The breba is our first innocence, our childhood of spirituality before we make an effort to grow spiritually in our own lives. It grows from the old shoot that God gave us, but the breba by itself is only a start. It's up to us to grow a new shoot of spirituality during the summer so that we may share in the main fruit at harvest time. My friends, the main fruit of harvest is the Great Harvest in Heaven, and the summer is our time here on Earth."

"The great sadness is that for some, the old shoot is ripped away. Without a beginning shoot, there is no breba, there is no new shoot, and there is no harvest of the main crop in Heaven. Friends—these are the lost souls we live with on this Earth. You see them all around you, and their old shoot has been hacked out for a variety of reasons—all of which means turning their backs on God. How does this happen? How can this be? It is because the lost soul attempts to harvest the old shoot before the breba is produced. The old shoot is hacked off and consumed. Technically, the fig tree is not dead. It has limbs, and it has leaves. It will not produce fruit, and so it will die without harvest."

"So you may ask what I mean when I say the old shoot is consumed in haste," Valeria continued. "I could say, 'sin'. And I'd be right. But so often, sin is disguised by fig leaves. From a distance, the fig tree looks healthy and whole. But Jesus sees the fig tree as it truly is from a distance. He knows the fig tree is barren. He sees the sin. No one can fool Jesus."

"Jesus is inside each of us. Our bodies are his tabernacle. Hold a spiritual mirror up before yourself, and Jesus will look upon from within you. He sees the sin that destroys the old shoot. You see it too. Jesus is hungry for the fig fruit, Jesus is inside of us, and so we are also hungry for the spiritual breba fruit too, but we can't find it, it's not there, because we've prevented it from growing."

"Pastor Ephram can tell you about sin and all the vices that are sinful," Valeria continued. "But hear me—think about what you do in the short term. Does it seem good? Now think about the same thing in the long term. Is it good? If the short term is good and the long term is bad, you are consuming the old shoot and destroying any future for the Great Harvest. If the short term is good and the long term is good, then you are consuming the breba, and you stand a good chance for summer spiritual growth of your new shoot for the Great Harvest."

"We see sin in ourselves, but often we see greater sin among others," Valeria continued. "What do we do about our fellow people? No doubt you've heard a phrase like, 'Prune the dead branches and burn them.' Is this the fate of a fellow person who has consumed his or her old shoots? I'm afraid the answer is 'yes.' Hell is real, the world would be much happier if it weren't. You may know someone you love who has thrown away the Great Harvest in exchange for the quick consumption of the old shoot God gave us. Drug addiction, sexual promiscuity, murder, deceit, and destruction are all such things that prevent the breba from growing. But these people deny the sins. They show you their beautiful fig leaves to hide their shame. But deep inside, they are suffering. If help does not arrive soon, they will perish."

"You know the sad reality of these people. Many do perish," Valeria continued. "And much destruction is pulled down with them. It is this loss of surrounding good that leads many to conclude that one must cut losses. That goes back to the pruning of dead branches and throwing them into the fire. Let the evil die in isolation. Even good Christians will give up in the vain attempt to help the lost ones. Didn't Jesus give up on the fig tree? Haven't the lost ones given up on themselves?"

"I have one last passage to read to you, and I hope it inspires you. Jesus tells a parable about another fig tree. From Luke 13:6, 'Then he told this parable. A man had a fig tree planted in his vineyard, and he went to look for fruit on it, but there was none. He said to the man who took care of the vineyard, *For three years now I've been coming to look for fruit on this fig tree and haven't found any. Cut it down! Why should it use up the earth?* The man replied, *Sir, leave it alone for one more year, and I'll dig around it and fertilize it. If it bears fruit next year, fine. If not, then I'll cut it down.'"*

"Sometimes," Valeria said, "it takes that one person making one last attempt to fertilize the fig tree in hopes of bringing the first breba fruit. It could be anyone—Christian, Jew, Muslim, Hindu, Atheist—anyone. It could be you. While the world seeks to cut down your lost friend, you are the last person to bring the old shoot back. You might fail, but you also might succeed."

"Friends, the breba fruit is baptism into faith—faith in oneself and one's God. Help your lost ones find their breba fruit. Help them find the spiritual life they destroyed. In God's name we pray. Amen."

The congregation applauded. Valeria thanked them and sat down. She returned to her place next to youngest Johnny and Roberta. Roberta wiped tears from her eyes. Valeria and Johnny hugged her. The service continued with more hymns and more prayer. At the conclusion, Pastor Ephram thanked everyone and invited them to brunch in the church hall. Valeria invited Roberta along, and Roberta accepted. The group donated a little money at the beginning of the line and filled their plates with eggs, bacon, fresh fruit, and breakfast rolls. The three sat down at a table next to a window overlooking the playground.

"This is a beautiful church you have here," Roberta said, "and that was a beautiful sermon you gave on fig trees, Valeria."

"Thank you," Valeria said. "I was terribly nervous. I hope I didn't mess up too much."

"You did fine," Roberta said. "The sermon made me cry."

"Because of Dr. Carreña?" youngest Johnny asked.

"Yes," Roberta said. "Her soul is in trouble. She has no breba fruit, and she fights me to keep it that way. But she wasn't always that way. Things didn't go bad until she came to Portland."

"So the city is to blame?" Evanita asked.

"No, of course not," Geneva said. "Listen."

"Has she been ensnared by vice?" Valeria asked. "No, I shouldn't pry."

"Normally I wouldn't either, but how can one repair the old shoot if one only looks at the fig leaves?" Roberta said. "Eva is caught in two traps—she has multiple drug addictions, and she gives up her freedom to a man named Marcus Cracbern."

"She worships him like a false god?" Valeria asked.

"I think so," Roberta said.

"They say the secret of life for a woman is that she should never become dependent on a man," Valeria said. "Once she does, she opens herself to abuse from him."

"It is the way with all false gods, isn't it?" Roberta asked.

"Yes, it is," Valeria said. "That's how we know the difference between a false god and the real God. He never abuses us."

"How I wish I could help her see this," Roberta said.

"She worships drugs as a false god too," Valeria said.

"And in turn, the drugs abuse her," Roberta said.

"A false god colors our vision—makes us see what the false god wants us to see so we'll continue worshiping the false god and block out those who love us—including the real God," Valeria said.

"I need to get her away from Marcus, too. I fear she worships him," Roberta said.

"Will she set herself up for abuse by this man?" Valeria said.

"I hope not, but this is not the first time she's worshipped a man. Her prior boyfriend, Simon, is wheelchair bound, and she did everything for him—I mean everything!"

"Out of the frying pan into the fire. Keep working with her, Roberta," Valeria said. "You are like the man tending the vineyard and fertilizing the fig tree that bears no fruit. There may yet be hope. Do you love her?"

Roberta paused.

"What is love?" Roberta asked rhetorically.

"Benevolent affection for another," youngest Johnny said as if reciting from a dictionary.

"If you affect her with benevolence, then you love her," Valeria said.

"Even if it hurts?" Roberta said.

"If you can ask the question, you already know the answer," Valeria said. "God loves his children, and he affects us with his benevolence. He also affects to share his benevolence with others who have cut off their old fig shoots."

"I wish I knew what I could do to share that benevolence," Roberta said. "I really do."

"While you're working that out, we have some benevolence to share with you," Valeria said.

Valeria pulled several sheets of paper from her purse and handed them to Roberta.

"What's this?" Roberta asked. "It looks like instructions or a procedure."

"It's DEC's Digital Command Language—DCL," youngest Johnny said. "It's script language for running programs on the VAX computer system at your dental office."

"What does it do?" Roberta said.

"It records login names and passwords," Valeria said. "Johnny and I worked on it together. Roberta—I feel guilty for having helped create this computer code. This is theft and invasion."

"Do you feel guilty too, Johnny?" Roberta asked.

"Naw," Johnny said. "It was fun!"

"Johnny doesn't see the possible long-term consequences," Valeria said. "But I do. For me, I'm endangering my summer shoot, but for Johnny, I'm encouraging him to endanger his old shoot."

"Well, a circle of earth must be dug up to add the fertilizer for the fig tree to bear fruit," Roberta said. "Some dirt must be displaced temporarily to achieve good. Will you help me?"

Valeria paused.

"Okay, but I won't run the program, and neither will Johnny," Valeria said. "It's your decision if you run the program."

"Fair deal," Roberta said. "Now then, how does this computer code work?"

"It simulates the login procedure," Valeria said. "You run the program, and it displays text suggesting the last person has signed off. The user hits the RETURN key a few times, and a fake login prompt appears. The user types in a login name, and the fake password prompt appears. The user types in a password. The program encrypts the login name and password and saves them to a file. Then the program displays a logon timeout error message, logs off silently, and the real logon prompt displays."

"There's a trick in doing this," youngest Johnny said. "Someone must log in to Marcus's terminal and run the program."

"Another thing—if the program crashes, or if he terminates it before it logs out, he'll know he was victimized by a fake login program, and he'll know whose login account ran the program."

"We can test the program on my terminal to make sure it doesn't crash," Roberta said. "But getting into Marcus's office will be more difficult. I don't have a key to his office, and I would think he'd be suspicious if I tried sneaking in during office hours. But if it works...I could get his password...except the log file will be encrypted. How am I supposed to read the log file if it's encrypted?"

Valeria pulled out another few sheets of paper with writing.

"Run this program against the log file, and it will unencrypt it," Valeria said. "You'll need to enter the encryption key to unlock the log file. But delete the program after you get the password. If Marcus sees it, he'll know what you're up to."

"What encryption key?" Roberta asked.

"A series of numbers and letters," youngest Johnny said.

"You'll enter a unique key when you first run the fake login program," Valeria said. "Remember the key, because there's no way to unlock the password log file without it. The encryption uses multiple cipher wheels like the enigma machine."

"You're quite the computer expert," Roberta said, "and I owe you an apology."

"Me?" Valeria asked. "What for?"

"I made the stereotypical assumption that since Johnny was a male, he would be better at computers. But it turns out you are," Roberta said.

"I have the advantage of being much older than Johnny. Someday he'll be just as smart as me," Valeria laughed.

The three traveled to MacNessi Dental followed by Evanita, Shawna Johnny, Geneva, and Jonara. Roberta and Valeria carried in the banker's box full of DEC reference manuals and placed the box on a stand next to the door.

"This is my terminal," Roberta said.

"I'll type in the code," Valeria said. "But I need a login."

"One moment," Roberta said.

Roberta logged into her account and relinquished control of the terminal to Valeria.

"This will take about ten minutes to type in," Valeria said.

Valeria began typing the code into the terminal.

"Now the trick is how to get into Marcus's office," Roberta said.

"Is there an air vent from your office to his?" Valeria asked.

"I know what you're thinking," Roberta said. "Johnny could crawl through the air vent. Unfortunately, there isn't. Marcus's office has its own specially-filtered ventilation system. He spent a lot of money on it. He wouldn't dare spend that money on the rest of the building."

"How close is his office to yours?" youngest Johnny asked.

"It's next door. You know that," Roberta said.

"Is there a secret passage between the two?" youngest Johnny asked.

"Oh, I see what you mean," Roberta said. "No, there isn't. Go ahead, Johnny, knock on the wall and look for a secret passage. That's only in the movies."

Johnny knocked on the walls and found nothing.

"You see?" Roberta said.

Johnny continued looking around the room. He drifted into the hallway and knocked on that wall. Roberta sighed.

"Will you need these reference books?" Roberta asked.

"No," Valeria said. "Oh, let me help you put them away."

"No," Roberta said. "Don't stop typing. I'll take care of it."

Roberta tried opening the closet where she had removed the banker's box on Friday, but it wouldn't open.

"That's strange," Roberta said. "The closet door is stuck."

"Is it locked?" Valeria asked, unable to see from her typing position.

"No," Roberta said. "I can turn the handle, but the door won't pull outward. It's like something is jamming it closed. I don't understand."

"Maybe a pry bar would help," Valeria said.

"That could damage the frame," Roberta said. "Wait—there's another way. I'll remove the pins from the hinges."

Roberta tapped the pins out and pried the hinges apart. The door opened outward approximately forty-five degrees before binding up at the door latch.

"What on Earth is all this?!" Roberta yelled in surprise.

To Roberta's shock, the closet was filled from floor to ceiling with boxes, books, and supplies. On hearing Roberta, Johnny returned to the room.

"Someone's been in my office," Roberta said. "And they stacked their things in here. This closet was empty on Friday. Marcus! He must have done this yesterday. Buy why this closet? There's a general storage room next to this room. He could have used that. He has a key to all rented space in the building. And look at the door latch. There's a board nailed on the inside of the closet from the door to the frame. How did he manage to do that?"

"The boxes are stacked backward," youngest Johnny said.

Roberta took a box and turned it around.

"You're right, Johnny. We're looking at the backs of these boxes," Roberta said. "Not only did Marcus fill my closet, he put the boxes in wrong. What is he smoking?"

In frustration, Roberta pushed on the pile of boxes. Something like a board moved in the very back.

"Did you hear that?" youngest Johnny asked.

"It sounded like a door," Valeria said.

"He's storing doors in my closet! He's absolutely lost it!" Roberta said.

Johnny walked to the closet and squeezed between two box piles.

"What are you doing?" Roberta said. "I don't have time for hide and seek."

"I want to see what's in back," youngest Johnny said. "Do you have a flashlight?"

"Johnny, this isn't the time," Roberta said.

Johnny walked deeper into the closet.

"I see a light at the bottom," youngest Johnny said.

"A light from the back of the closet? Johnny, come out of there right now," Roberta said.

Youngest Johnny came out of the closet.

"There's a door in back, a real door!" youngest Johnny said.

"He didn't," Roberta said.

"He did," Valeria said. "The boxes are piled in backward because we are at the back of the closet—his new closet!"

"That sneaky-ass bastard!" Roberta said. "He cut a hole through his wall into my closet! He filled it from his side! What kind of ogre does that?"

"A greedy ogre," Valeria replied.

"Doctor," youngest Johnny said. "I know how we can get into Marcus's office—through the closet."

Roberta paused for a moment then broke out into hysterical laughter. Valeria laughed too.

"It's perfect," Roberta said. "His own greed gives me access to his office!"

Roberta moved boxes from the closet to create a narrow passage into Marcus's office. She entered his office. Roberta attempted to open his desk and file cabinets, but all were locked.

"It was worth a try," Roberta said.

Roberta walked over to the terminal screen. It was on and displayed a message indicating Marcus's signoff.

"Don't touch the monitor," Valeria said as she walked in with youngest Johnny.

Valeria looked at the message on the monitor and wrote it on a pad of paper.

"The fake login program will display his signoff message. He'll think nothing has changed since he signed off. That will make him less suspicious," Valeria said.

"Is the program ready?" Roberta asked.

"Yes, it is," Valeria said.

"How do I run it?" Roberta asked.

"Log in to Marcus's terminal first," Valeria said.

"Wait!" youngest Johnny said. "Press Control-C and Control-Break several times, in case he's running a fake login of his own!"

Roberta and Valeria looked at youngest Johnny.

"Johnny's right," Valeria said.

Roberta hit Control-C followed by Control-Break. She hit the RETURN key.

"It looks like a real login prompt," Roberta said.

"It should be safe," Valeria said. "Go ahead and log in."

Roberta logged in to Marcus's terminal. The welcome message scrolled up, and the screen displayed a menu to the dental program.

"You need to break out of this program," Valeria said. "Press Control-C and Control-Break many, many times very quickly."

Roberta did as instructed. After six or seven times of pressing these keystroke combinations, the dental program exited to a shell prompt. Valeria and youngest Johnny clapped.

"Shh," Roberta said. "We don't want to be too noisy."

"Run the program from your home directory," Valeria said. "Here's the command."

Roberta typed in the command to run the program. It displayed a prompt requesting an encryption key.

"Type in a key—a combination of letters and numbers. Make sure it's something you'll remember."

Roberta typed in, "EVAISADRUNK" and pressed the RETURN key. Another prompt requested the initial logoff message.

"Type in this message that I just wrote down," Valeria said. "The program will display this first thing."

Roberta typed in the message and pressed the RETURN key. A prompt displayed, "Are you sure you wish to continue? (Y/N)"

"This is your last chance to back out," Valeria said. "If you press the Y key followed by RETURN, the program will run. Any other response will cancel the program. Johnny—face your back to Roberta. I'll do the same. Doctor—do what you will, but do not tell us what you've done."

"I understand," Roberta said.

Roberta pressed the Y key, paused for a moment of thought, and then pushed herself to press the RETURN key. The program displayed Marcus's signoff message and waited to trap the next victim's login password.

"We're done in here," Roberta said. "Let's go back through the closet."

The three walked through the closet passageway into Roberta's office. Valeria and Johnny helped Roberta return the boxes to the closet.

"Make sure the backs of the boxes face us," Roberta said. "We don't want Marcus suspecting we were in here."

The three finished placing the boxes in the closet correctly, and Roberta closed her closet door.

"I didn't type in the decryption program," Valeria said. "That you'll have to do yourself. Also, the fake login program encrypts itself before logging off. That way, you'll only have to unencrypt it if you want to run it again. The unencryption program is short, so it shouldn't take long to type in."

"Thank you," Roberta said.

1989 Oct 9, Mon 9 am. MacNessi Dental. Portland, Oregon.

Roberta finished up a treatment and entered her office. She closed the door and logged into her computer terminal. A menu for the dental program displayed. She pressed Control-C and Control-Break several times until the menu program exited to a shell prompt. Roberta displayed a directory listing of her home directory. No password file. Did the program work? Did it capture Marcus's password? Then a horrible thought hit Roberta.

"What if Milo or Frank logs in instead of Marcus?" Roberta said. "Then the trap will be sprung on the wrong person. I've got to get Marcus to log in. But how?"

An idea hit Roberta.

"I'll call his phone," Roberta said. "No, that won't work. Someone else could answer and log onto his terminal. Bad idea. Wait, I'll call his pager. That will get him to his desk."

Roberta called Marcus's pager and left a bogus number. She opened her closet door and listened as best she could to Marcus's office next door. She heard someone walk into his office and close the door. The person sat down and dialed a number on the telephone.

"This is Dr. Cracbern," Marcus's voice said. "What seems to be the problem? What do you mean? I have a pager number right here. You didn't? I see. It must have been a bad page, or someone playing a trick. Thank you," Marcus finished, and he hung up the phone.

Marcus's footsteps paced through his office. At one point he reached for his end of the closet. Roberta closed her closet door only just in time before Marcus opened his. He shuffled some boxes around restlessly, and he closed his closet door. Roberta breathed a sigh of relief. She opened her closet door again and listened. Marcus's footsteps took him outside of his office.

"Dammit," Roberta said. "He didn't log in. I need to get him in there again, but I can't call his pager—that didn't work. Wait, why didn't I think of it? I should have called his answering service to begin with. That's who he checks with."

Roberta got on the telephone and pretended to be a high-paying patient in need of emergency dental work. She left a bogus phone number with the attendant and completed the telephone call. Roberta went back to the closet and listened. Footsteps reentered Marcus's office, the person sat at the desk, and he dialed on the telephone.

"This is Dr. Cracbern," Marcus said. "Are you sending me a page, or is—oh, I see. Yes, I'll call her right away. Thank you."

Marcus hung up the phone and started dialing, but he stopped himself partway through the dial.

"I'd better look up the product first—I want to make the most money I can off this patient," Marcus said.

Marcus attempted to log in to his computer terminal.

"Damn computers," Marcus said. "Why are they always the slowest on Monday morning? Ack—it timed out. I'll try again."

Roberta closed the closet door quietly.

"I've got him—maybe!" she whispered to herself.

Roberta rushed to her terminal and requested a directory listing. The encrypted log file displayed with a file size greater than zero.

"Yes!" Roberta whispered.

Roberta entered Valeria's decryption program into the terminal and ran it against the log file. The program prompted for the decryption key. Roberta entered it, decrypted the log file, and read it—login: cracbernm password: newteeth1

"But will it work?" Roberta asked herself.

Roberta deleted the log file and the decryption program. She logged off and logged in as Marcus. The menu for Marcus was a bit different from hers, but many things were the same. She selected the option for Personal Calendar. To her surprise, Roberta saw many court dates beginning in September and running into the future—all against one person—Andrea Peddly.

"Where have I heard that name before?" Roberta asked herself. "Andrea Peddly, Andrea Peddly."

Roberta kept the name in the back of her mind. She continued looking through Marcus's daily calendar. She noticed a trend. Prior to September, Marcus had scheduled multiple weekly outings and evening parties. But around the time the first court appearance began, those outings and parties ended.

"If the parties are over, where has Eva been going this entire time?" Roberta asked herself.

Roberta exited the calendar program and selected the menu for personal notes. She opened up a file named, "todo-list.doc;84" and read it:

Cracbern's TODO List

New Motto: Reduce, Relink, Resurface

Goal: Raise additional revenue to cover civil suit costs

1) Increase productivity by exerting more control
   - Change one-on-one meetings to one-over-one. Emphasize the Darwinistic need for adaptation to changing office conditions.
   - Convince each employee that he is not pulling his weight.
   - Hold morning status meetings to check progress. Conference call with other offices. Emphasize need to support the team effort. Reiterate the privilege of working at Cracbern Associates.
   - Create offsite War Room for those not churning out patients quickly enough. War Room will be bare with no privacy and no comforts. Lack of privilege will encourage employees to step up productivity to get back the privilege of working in individual treatment rooms. Require War Room employees to "volunteer" on Saturdays.
   - Require use of Sargenti in all hot teeth to cut root canal/crown visits from three to two. Advertise Sargenti treatment as revolutionary but charge twice as much. Blame any permanent damage on preexisting conditions. Backdate memos and X-rays as needed for "proof".
   - Penalize underperforming employees by interrupting them during procedures to add workload. This will encourage underperforming employees to work harder to avoid penalties.
   - Create written agreements with employees requiring their increased productivity. Name them, "Personal Improvement Plan" and "Goals". Require them to read these, sign, date, and write, "I have read and agree with this document."
   - Change vacation policy. Allow no carryover from year-to-year. Use it or lose it.
   - Eliminate company-sponsored health insurance. Change to employee-funded cafeteria plan.
   - Force Milo to work in the War Room one week for each time he refers to Cracbern Associates as, "Strife, fiberty, and the pursuit of crappiness."

- Tell any lie necessary.

2) Increase fees
   - Charge patients for additional amounts not covered by insurance.

Goal: Find way to frame Andrea Peddly. Coerce her to drop paternity suit.

"Roberta, I have...what are you doing?" Kay asked as she stepped into Roberta's office.

Roberta jumped with a start and instinctively turned off the monitor.

"I'm sorry, I didn't mean to startle you," Kay said. "But I'm waiting for you to finish with Floyd."

"Let's switch the order," Roberta said. "Clean Floyd's teeth first, and I'll restore his tooth second."

"Okay," Kay said, and she left.

"Why did I turn off the monitor!?" Roberta asked herself. "I lost everything!"

Roberta turned the monitor back on. The screen was blank. She pressed an arrow key, and one line of text displayed. She pressed the page up and page down keys, and all text redisplay.

"Whew!" Roberta said.

Roberta sent the electronic document to a locally-attached dot-matrix printer. Once the printer finished, she went back into Marcus's calendar and sent a list of future court dates to her printer. With that printed, Roberta logged off Marcus's account, hid the printout in her briefcase, and went to work on her patients.

CHAPTER 12:

The Chase

Jonara walked all morning. She left Nanna Geneva's house after breakfast, saying she was going out for a walk. She didn't care anymore. She knew that in a day, her life would change forever. Any future for a family would be tied to the Church and the vitacepticals. She was sad. She was depressed. She needed a good walk to think. She missed her friends Cerafina and Almarita horribly—even with the fighting between the two.

Jonara wanted to walk straight to Corpus Christi Bay. She walked on Candlewood Drive northeast, but she was stopped by South Padre Island Drive. There was no nearby crossroad, no crosswalk, and it was too busy to cross on foot. She would have to walk along the edge of South Padre Island Drive one way or another. Which way to go—left or right? Jonara shrugged her shoulders, turned right, and walked southeast. After a bit, she reached Nile Drive, turned left, and walked northeast. She passed houses, fields, a little river, ponds, and a field with many baseball diamonds. She reached the end of Nile Drive and crossed Ennis Joslin Road into a wildlife refuge. She found a bird walk and traveled along the walk until she reached its end at Oso Bay. Oso Bay wasn't Corpus Christi Bay, but Oso was close to Corpus Christi Bay, and Oso was a large water body. For the moment, that was good enough for Jonara. She decided to pause at the end of the walk and think. The day was sunny and mild. She looked out and saw several different birds—gulls, ducks, pelicans, and herons.

"Oh to be a bird and free," Jonara said.

"They're not so free," Nekara said as she appeared out of nowhere.

"I thought Felifia and her women got rid of you," Jonara said.

"No one gets rid of Nekara the Red," Nekara said. "I'm the kind of person who should be with you."

"That's stupid," Jonara said.

"Is it?" Nekara said. "Look at the birds around you. Look at them! You wish to be free as a bird, but birds are not free. They never were."

"Your lies are getting on my nerves," Jonara said.

"Jonara—the one thing you must learn about your world is that truth is often uglier than deceit. That's why deceit is so popular. People will go to great lengths to deceive themselves so they don't have to face the ugly truth."

"What ugly truth? The only thing here that's ugly is your soul," Jonara said.

"The ugly truth is death," Nekara said. "Death! Every bird you see here fights from day to day to stay alive. Each bird must scavenge for food or die. But that's only part of the problem. Each bit of food scavenged by one bird deprives another of that food. This is the survival cost, and it affects every bird feeding off that food source. If food is in abundance, birds multiply to the balancing point where the food just barely supports the bird population. If food is scarce, some birds die off until the balancing point is reached between food and bird. Jonara—when that balancing point is reached, the birds form a spectrum of winners and losers. The winners eat well at the expense of losers, and the losers suffer at the dominance of the winners."

"That's wrong!" Jonara said. "The birds all look the same, they fly the same, and they hunt the same way."

"Ah, to an outsider it appears this way," Nekara said. "But there are subtle differences between the birds. The winners have an ever-so-slight edge over the losers, and the winners leverage this advantage to gain massive dominance. It is the way with all life on your planet. All life. Including humans."

"No. People aren't that evil," Jonara said.

"Yes. They are. You are young and idealistic," Nekara said. "If you are to become successful and survive as an adult, you must use all means of treachery to leverage advantage over your fellow human beings. If you don't, Jonara, if you decide to follow this narrow path of idealism, good character, and fairness for all, you will be on the tail end of the spectrum with the losers of your world—those who are caught in their internal miseries of vice and external miseries of oppression pressed down on them from the treacherous survivors. You will sink from the surface of strong daylight and clean water to the depths of darkness and never-ending excrement falling from those above who care only to step on you to elevate their positions. Even those who might call you 'friend' in the trenches of despair are doing everything they can to get out of their misery, and they'll readily sacrifice you to gain relief."

"No!" Jonara said. "You're trying to lure me into a trap like you did with Marcus."

"I enlightened Marcus when he was young," Nekara said. "And for the most part, he has prospered at the expense of others. Is this not success? Isn't this the survival strategy of the birds around you, those birds you wish to become for their freedom of flight? Freedom to exact downward pressure on the species so that you may enjoy the best food?"

"Felifia, come to me," Jonara said. "Felifia, help me in this moment of difficulty. Felifia, get Nekara out of my head!"

Felifia did not appear. Nekara laughed and laughed. Jonara looked over the edge of the walkway and observed Oso Bay.

"Go ahead," Nekara said. "Jump. Kill yourself now."

"What?! You're crazy!" Jonara said.

"Each species seeks to elevate itself above its current position. The drive is powerful—it cannot be stopped. When one falls to the bottom of the sea and can no longer ascend, then death itself becomes a form of elevating oneself," Nekara said. "You are at the bottom, Jonara. Even like-minded miserable people have abandoned you. You are now lower than them. There is nothing left. Elevate yourself through suicide. Do it now. Jump into Oso Bay and complete your journey. I welcome you into my Kingdom."

Nekara stretched out her arms as if welcoming Jonara. Jonara looked at the water and in Oso Bay. She looked back at Nekara.

"Come now, child. Come into Aunt Nekara's arms. I will help you kill yourself. I'll throw you into the water and baptize you into my Kingdom."

Jonara pulled out the Moissan Ruby and stared at it.

"Felifia, help me!" Jonara whispered into the stone.

"Where you're going, you won't need that," Nekara said. "Give it to me."

"If my life must end," Jonara said, "then I want to die holding this Water Ruby in my hand, as a remembrance of the people I love."

"No," Nekara said. "You must have no outstanding links with the living. You must bring closure to your life by jumping into the water freely and with no attachments. Give me the stone."

"No," Jonara said.

"Jonara—by rights the stone isn't yours. It's mine. Felifia gave it to me as a present," Nekara said.

"I want to keep it," Jonara said.

"It isn't yours! It's mine. Give me my moisharn stone!" Nekara demanded.

Nekara grabbed Jonara's hand—the hand holding the Moissan Ruby. Jonara passed the stone to her other hand. Nekara grabbed that hand instead, and Jonara passed it back to the first hand. Jonara and Nekara struggled for possession of the Moissan Ruby. Jonara was surprised at how well she was holding up against Nekara. Didn't Nekara have superior strength over her? But Nekara was not truly corporeal. She only appeared to her in ghostly form.

"No!" Jonara said. "You desire this stone to make yourself complete, so you can come into this world as a fully formed body. If I give you this stone and kill myself, you will use both to make your wish come true. I won't let you have the Water Ruby. I won't. And you can't catch me!"

Jonara popped the Moissan Ruby inbetween her teeth and dove into Oso Bay.

"NO!!!" Nekara screamed.

Nekara could not give chase to Jonara. Nekara's voice traveled both above and below water and sounded like the wailing of a large ocean liner bending and torsing while sinking. Jonara swam far and deep. She kicked her legs and paddled her arms until she was far from shore and deep into the bay. But there was something strange. She felt no need to breathe, no desire to replace the carbon dioxide in her lungs with fresh oxygen. It was as if the Moissan Ruby provided oxygen.

Jonara searched for large, underwater debris and found it— the remnants of an automobile that had plunged in years earlier unnoticed. The automobile was upright, but the windows had long ago shattered. She swam in through an opening and sat in the front passenger seat. This would be her final grave, she thought. No more worries about history, timelines, armies, institutions, and conflict. Just Jonara and the skeletal automobile. The water was warm, but Jonara felt a shiver course through her body, as if something had just swam through her body. The Moissan Ruby pulsed, as if it were being energized by the surrounding bay water. It pulsed and shook and vibrated Jonara's jaw. The water around her grew darker and darker until she could see nothing.

2007 Dec 8, Sat. The Caves of Healing. Carreña, Spain.

Jonara appeared in a cave, but she wasn't sure where. A blindingly white light obscured her vision. She placed the Moissan Ruby in her hand and spoke:

"Hello?" Jonara asked. "Am I dead?"

A voice spoke. Jonara recognized the voice as that of Felifia.

Miramish	**Translation**
Diato kapi boshu nau, Dzhonara.	Join hands with me, Jonara.
Kaish e zhuala mahilu lonudo	Your spirit now enters
Dho gaifiku vemiana	A bitter winter
Tolu rialu denadi	Where low temperatures
Felito bushipu fioriki	Bring deep freezes
Dhaku shetito loreifu borifi	And test all strengths

Miramish	**Translation**
Opeifu kaish e felausha.	Of your life.
Hemeru shetaushaola perinelita	Only enduring faith
Gerutheio kail e voifelaufota.	Will give you survival.
Hemeru ulu kail e zhupo	Only if you save
Kaish e voshara	Your love
Kokeio kail e shupeio tilen okuanu.	Will you find it again.
Mishefeluiku kail e deriatheio	Otherwise you will perish
Ishu shai bushiki opeifu kupoga	In the depths of debt
Liufialotao haku lishu luvausho	Consuming what little remains
Opeifu kaifa dhaku burabolika	Of hatred and despair
Kivoanu shai ushethu shenakata	Before the last flicker
Opeifu kiata	Of death
Fiasho uilu ishetu fiorita.	Flames out into frost.
Diato kapi boshu nau, Dzhonara.	Join hands with me, Jonara.
Kaish e zhuala lumioleio	Your spirit will renew
Ishu vorila.	In spring.

"I can't see," Jonara said. "I can't see!"

"Trust me!" Felifia said.

The light gradually dimmed. A woman with a long flowing robe in vibrantly changing colors of cerise, green, and white stood before her. She smiled and pointed to a pool of healing. The pool lashed around with tall waves and much splashing. Evanita, Johnny, and Geneva were nowhere to be seen.

"Go to the turbulence," Felifia said. "Go."

Jonara walked to the pool. A large wave crashed in on her and pulled her into a deep section of the pool. She fought to stay afloat, but the waves pounded on her. She ascended above the waterline then descended, like a lost bit of driftwood bobbing up and down. During one of her ascents, she saw Evanita, Johnny, and Geneva appear along the edge of the pool. Geneva read from her diary, and the group went back in time.

1989 Oct 13, Fri Afnoon. MacNessi Dental. Portland, Oregon.

"Welcome back, Johnny," Roberta said. "This way to the treatment room."

Roberta led younger Johnny back to the treatment room. He sat in the dental chair.

"I've cleared my appointment book so we don't have to share this room with an audience," Roberta said as she pointed to the empty dental chair next to her. "Today we finish restoring your tooth. Now—some patients ask for novocaine, but I don't think you'll need any. This shouldn't hurt a bit."

"Okay," Johnny said. "I trust you, Doctor."

"Open, please," Roberta said.

Johnny opened his mouth. Roberta cleaned off the core buildup and cemented the crown to the core. She inserted blue paper onto the crown.

"Tap your teeth together," Roberta said. "Tap, tap, tap."

Younger Johnny tapped his teeth.

"I need to do a little touch-up grinding," Roberta said.

"When you start grinding," younger Johnny said, "my skull will vibrate, and I'll read you again."

"I know," Roberta said. "But I have a better idea. I want you to read what's going on in Marcus's office next door. Now when you connected before, I sprayed water into your mouth. However, I'd like to try another method. I've hooked up this old rinse bowl next to you. In the old days, water would be sprayed into your mouth, and you'd be asked to spit out into the bowl. Nowadays we suction that out, but for you, I'd like you to hold your fingers in the running water while I do touch-up grinding on your teeth. Would you be willing to do that?"

"Okay," younger Johnny said.

"I'll put the drill on the lowest setting," Roberta said.

Younger Johnny held his fingers in the rinse bowl. Roberta drilled at a very low speed to finish off the blue-marked tips on the crown. Roberta drilled for only a few seconds, but in those seconds, younger Johnny felt himself travel through the water into Marcus's office.

"Johnny?" Roberta asked as she stopped drilling. "Johnny?"

"Yeah," younger Johnny said. "I'm back. I'm not as tired this time."

"Good," Roberta said. "The lower drill speed may have helped. Did you see anything?"

"I saw Dr. Carreña treating a female patient," Johnny explained. "I saw three female assistants helping with treatment, but I could not see who they were treating or the dentists they were helping. I saw three female hygienists, and I saw two of their patients—both female. I saw a receptionist. I saw two women in the waiting area. And I saw something else."

"You mean someone else?" Roberta asked.

"No—something," younger Johnny said. "It was small, like a pecan or hazelnut. It floated in the air."

"Where was it?" Roberta asked. "Was it on a shelf or table? Was it in Marcus's office?"

"No, no," younger Johnny said. "It was in one of the treatment rooms."

"How high in the air did it float?" Roberta asked.

"About as high as a belt buckle on an adult. Maybe a little higher," younger Johnny said. "Strange—I think I saw little pieces of something floating above the hazelnut thing, but I'm not sure."

"Johnny—you said you could only see women," Roberta said.

"Yes."

"Can you read yourself?" Roberta asked.

"Only my female parts—the ovary, fallopian tube, and primitive uterus," younger Johnny said.

"Did that floating thing look like an ovary?" Roberta asked.

"No," younger Johnny said. "It wasn't a body part. It looked like something someone made. I didn't get a good look at it."

"If I drill a little more, can you try to focus on—" Roberta started.

Younger Johnny jumped with a start and pulled his hand out of the rinse bowl.

"Ow!" he cried.

"What happened?" Roberta asked. "I wasn't drilling. There shouldn't have been a connection."

"I felt something like an electric shock," younger Johnny said. "No, it was more like something pinching my fingers. Yeah, the water became solid and pinched my fingers, and it tried to pull my fingers into the water stream."

"Did you get a sense of where it was pulling your fingers?" Roberta asked.

"Huh?"

"Could you tell what was pulling your fingers? Was it something in this room?" Roberta asked.

"Something in Marcus's office reached through the water," Johnny said. "This has never happened before. I don't know what to do."

"If someone had a stone like you do, what would happen if they received a vibration and touched water at the same time?" Roberta asked. "They could travel in here, couldn't they?"

"Yeah, I think so," younger Johnny said.

"Rest for a moment, Johnny. Let's check your crown," Roberta said. "Open."

Roberta inserted blue paper onto younger Johnny's crown.

"Tap, tap, tap," Roberta said.

Roberta removed the blue paper after he tapped his teeth.

"Bite down. Tap, tap, tap. How does it feel?" Roberta asked.

"It feels okay," younger Johnny said.

"Johnny, I don't need to do any more grinding, but I would like you to focus on that hazelnut-shaped object again. I'll hold the backside of the drill against your forehead while you hold your fingers in the rinse sink. I have a suspicion that object is similar to your stone. Someone could be spying on our office the same way we're spying on theirs. Johnny—I appreciate your help. Let's hope you don't get your fingers pinched again."

"Should I cross my fingers?" younger Johnny asked.

"Only on the dry hand," Roberta laughed.

"Okay," younger Johnny said.

Younger Johnny placed his fingers in the rinse bowl. Roberta placed the backside of the drill against his forehead and activated it. The drill bit twirled freely in the air, and Johnny felt himself travel through the water pipes into Marcus's office. He saw the female assistant. He could not see the patient. He saw the hazelnut-like object. It was

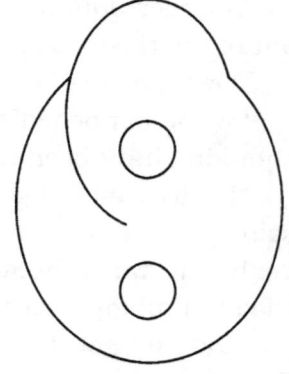

oblong with a smaller oblong sticking out of the top. One side was somewhat flat with a curving inward edge and two circles. Johnny looked above the hazelnut object, and at the level of someone's face he saw teeth floating in the air. Not haphazard teeth, but teeth arranged as if part of a skull. It was nearly a complete set, but it lacked the four canine teeth. The sight scared younger Johnny, and he hesitated for a moment, but when he regained his composure, he focused on the hazelnut-shaped object. As he concentrated, he moved closer to the object until he could identify its shape. Waves flowed from the object, waves that distorted the air like hot air from a fire. The waves encircled a human body with clothing. Younger Johnny focused more intently and sensed the outline of a man—a man performing dental work on a patient he could not see. The female assistant sprayed a mouth with water and suctioned. Younger Johnny felt a surge of power flow from the object through the man's body, the man's hand, the drill, the patient's mouth, the spray of water, the water pipes, and back to the rinse bowl in Roberta's treatment room. Younger Johnny withdrew his fingers as the water pinched his fingertips. Roberta noticed his reaction and withdrew the drill.

"It almost got me," younger Johnny said, "but I pulled my fingers out quickly."

"Did you see anything?" Roberta asked. "What happened?"

"The object," younger Johnny said. "It doesn't look like my stone, but it looks a lot like the symbol on my stone."

Younger Johnny showed the Moissan Ruby to Roberta and pointed out the symbol on his stone.

"It's attached to a man in his belly button," younger Johnny said. "He doesn't have an ovary. I saw his outline. He worked on a patient, and his assistant sprayed water. That's when a jolt came through the water pipe, and I pulled my fingers out."

"It was Marcus, Milo, or Frank," Roberta said. "But which one? Johnny—did you see anything unusual about the man? Anything at all?"

"I saw a lot of teeth," younger Johnny said.

"What do you mean, you saw a lot of teeth?" Roberta asked.

"I saw the hazelnut stone floating, I saw the outline of a man, and I saw teeth floating above the hazelnut stone—a lot higher, as high as someone's head."

"That's the first time you called the hazelnut object a stone," Roberta said. "But you saw teeth floating in the air, you say, and it was part of this man?"

"Yeah. It scared me," younger Johnny said.

"Did you see a jaw? Any other bones?" Roberta asked.

"No, no," younger Johnny said. "And teeth were missing."

"Which teeth?" Roberta asked.

"The canines," younger Johnny said.

"This is very strange!" Roberta said. "But I think I know which man it is—Marcus. The last few times I've seen him, I've noticed that his teeth are different, as if he's placed new crowns on them. Johnny—how much of the teeth could you see? Did you see only crowns?"

"No, I saw roots on every visible tooth. I saw nothing for the canines, no crowns or roots or anything," younger Johnny said.

"This doesn't make sense," Roberta said. "There's no such thing as female crowns. Crowns are inorganic. The only way you could see teeth is if they were female teeth, but that would only be possible if teeth were female, but again—it's impossible for a man to be born with female teeth. Incomplete female organs—maybe, but not teeth. The only way he could get female teeth in his mouth is if he put them there."

"Is that possible?" younger Johnny asked.

"It is if he does a tooth transplant, but the host must be alive. I can't believe he would do such a thing. It's criminal!" Roberta said. "Johnny, could you tell who the teeth were from?"

"Not exactly," younger Johnny said. "A woman's body has a unique signature. When I scan her, I learn this signature. It's like smelling a flower for the first time—it's hard to describe, but you know the flower if you smell the scent again. I don't know who the teeth belong to because I've never scanned those women before."

"What did you say?" Roberta asked. "Did you say *women*?"

"The teeth have different signatures," younger Johnny said. "They are from different women."

"He's a psychopath," Roberta said. "Somehow he's subverting women and stealing their teeth. No one in her right mind would donate teeth to him."

"Do we call the police?" younger Johnny asked.

"I can't—yet," Roberta said. "I don't have hard evidence. I doubt they would believe our story as-is. Imagine—a young boy with clairvoyance through water pipes."

"There was something else I saw," younger Johnny said. "And I don't understand it."

"What was it?" Roberta asked.

"The hazelnut stone...I don't understand...it was like...it had ...images...of people...of women," younger Johnny said.

"Did you recognize any of them?" Roberta asked.

"No, wait, just one image. It was you," younger Johnny said. "You were kissing a woman in front of a house. The image...the image...it's on paper. A photograph. Photographs of women."

"Now Johnny," Roberta said. "This is very important. Do you know where these pictures are?"

"I saw...no...yes...I jumped from one place to another. The photographs are not kept together," younger Johnny said. "Some are kept in a room...a bedroom...but it has a dental chair and equipment."

"What about the photograph of me," Roberta said. "Do you know where that one is?"

"I...I'm trying to remember...it wasn't in the bedroom. It was in...a safe with a combination lock," younger Johnny said.

"Where is the safe?" Roberta asked. "What is the combination?"

"I don't know," younger Johnny said. "That's all I remember."

"Johnny—it's important I get hold of that photograph of me," Roberta said. "I need to find the safe and its combination. Johnny—are you willing to risk traveling over to Marcus's dental office one last time?"

"One last time," younger Johnny said. "Because I'm getting tired."

"Okay," Roberta said. "I promise—I won't ask you to travel there anymore—today."

Younger Johnny dipped his fingers into the water. His eyes opened wide, and his body went rigid.

"Johnny?" Roberta called. "Johnny, do you hear me? Johnny? Blink your eyes if you can hear me."

Younger Johnny did not blink his eyes.

"Move your hands, fingers, or something if you can hear me," Roberta said.

No movement.

Roberta pulled younger Johnny's hand out of the rinse tub. Johnny remained motionless for a moment. Roberta checked his pulse—it was rapid and strong.

"Johnny, snap out of it," Roberta said as she shook him. "Johnny!"

Younger Johnny did not move. Roberta placed the backside of the drill against Johnny's head and turned it on. She placed her head against his. For a moment, she felt herself locked in a small room with Johnny, trying to help him escape while a large hand from above dove toward Johnny to grab him and squeeze him.

"Johnny, break free," Roberta said. "Johnny—concentrate on me. Concentrate on my voice. Read my biology. Ignore everything else."

In the vision of the box, younger Johnny dodged the gigantic hand and hugged Roberta. He scanned her organs and tissues and in doing so lost connection with the probing gigantic hand. The vision ended, and the two returned to Roberta's dental office. Roberta removed the drill and released her grip on Johnny.

"What happened?" younger Johnny asked.

"I was going to ask you the same thing," Roberta said. "You placed your fingers in the rinse bowl, and you went completely catatonic. I didn't get a chance to apply the drill while you were touching the water. I pulled your hand out of the water, but you remained catatonic. Only after applying vibration from the drill and holding your head was I able to connect with you. I asked you to let go."

"It worked," younger Johnny said. "I felt a person trying to get me. It was Marcus. He used his hazelnut stone to connect through the water. He saw me, and he tried to trap me. He wanted me to blab everything. I fought him. I didn't say anything."

"So he knows someone else has a stone similar to his," Roberta said. "He'll be on his guard. If we should try again, he'll trap us. Well, that ends our ability to spy on his office. Oh, I wish I knew where that safe was. Johnny, why are you smiling?"

"I know where the safe is," younger Johnny said. "Marcus revealed it to me without realizing it."

"Where is it, where is it?" Roberta asked.

"In his private office behind a fake panel in the wall," younger Johnny said.

"Oh, that's excellent," Roberta said. "But the combination. Johnny—please tell me you managed to get the combination!"

"10-14-8-9," Johnny said.

"That's a date, not a combination. Johnny—10/14/89 is tomorrow."

"But it's also the combination," younger Johnny said.

"Are you sure?" Roberta asked. "Why would he choose tomorrow as the combination?"

"I don't know," younger Johnny said.

"Could it be he has something planned for tomorrow?" Roberta mused. "Johnny—when you get home tonight, tell Valeria everything that happened here today between you and me. She's good with number riddles and ciphers. Maybe she has some ideas. I'll contact her later—after I finish a certain task here today. I need to stay late until a certain Mr. Marcus and his staff go home for the day."

Jonara returned to the Caves of Healing. She treaded water while Evanita, Shawna Johnny, and Geneva remained motionless on the water's edge.

"Felifia!" Jonara called. "Help me, I'm drowning."

"You're not drowning," Felifia said.

Felifia walked from the dry cave floor along the top of the water and pulled Jonara to her feet such that Jonara was also standing on the water.

"Felifia," Jonara said. "You're very beautiful and powerful. Make my life all better. Take me back to my life when Almarita was alive and Cerafina was my friend. Take me back."

"Jonara," Felifia said. "I cannot take you back to something that doesn't exist."

"What are you saying? Am I stuck in a world of vitacepticals?" Jonara asked.

Felifia smiled and patted Jonara on the shoulder.

"I am but an apparition before you. My full psyche is trapped in the duavisha," Felifia said.

"But you are strong. You are powerful. You're like a goddess," Jonara said.

"No, I'm not all-powerful," Felifia said. "I have some abilities, but so do you. I am trapped in a small place just as you are."

"Then is there no hope?" Jonara asked.

"There is hope," Felifia said. "To free yourself, you must first free a friend."

"What does that mean?" Jonara asked. "Who do I free? I have no friends left but you. I'm blocked off from everyone else."

"Then free me," Felifia said.

1989 Oct 13, Fri Eve. MacNessi Dental. Portland, Oregon.

Roberta's stomach growled. She stayed late and waited for all employees at Cracbern Associates and the cleaning staff to leave before she dared entering Marcus's office. She drank water from the bubbler, but the water did not stop the grumbling.

"I've got to get some food in my stomach," Roberta said, "or the combination of empty stomach and anxiety will make me throw up."

Roberta exited MacNessi Dental and strolled down the hallway of the Page Street Clinic building to a small alcove. She walked into the alcove, inserted fifty cents into a vending machine, and purchased a bag of chocolate candies. She wasted no time in popping several candies in her mouth.

"What would I do without chocolate?" Roberta said. "I'd better purchase a second bag in case I need additional therapy."

Roberta inserted another fifty cents, purchased a second bag of chocolate candies, and placed it in her pocket. She walked back toward her office and passed by Cracbern Associates on the way. The janitor finished vacuuming up the front lobby, exited through the front door, and locked it. Roberta followed the janitor as he entered MacNessi Dental.

"Late night, doctor?" the janitor asked to be friendly.

"Yeah," Roberta said. "Catching up on paperwork is easier when everyone's gone for the day."

"I hear you, I hear you," the janitor replied.

"Could you start with my private office today?" Roberta said. "I only need a light dusting and some trash taken away."

"No problem, be glad to," the janitor said.

The janitor cleaned Roberta's private office first. She didn't want an interruption from the janitor while in the middle of sneaking into Marcus's office.

"Thank you," Roberta said, and the janitor moved on to the next room.

Roberta closed her office door and locked it. She removed the pins from the hinges on her closet door and swiveled the door open.

"If I ever have a dental office in a shared building again, I won't put it next to someone I know!" Roberta said. "People you know think they can abuse you left and right."

Roberta moved several boxes out of the way and squeezed through to Marcus's closet door. She opened it up slightly. The room was dark.

"If I turn on the light," Roberta said to herself, "someone outside might see."

Roberta returned to her office, found a flashlight, turned it on, and went back to Marcus's office. She crept along the floor and tapped along the wall paneling in hopes of finding the safe. She crept about halfway around the room when some paneling gave in a little more than it should have. She pushed it several times, and as she did, a seam appeared between the regular wall and a secret door. Roberta edged her fingernails into the seam and pulled open the secret door.

"There it is," she said. "This is the safe!"

She entered the combination—10, 14, 8, 9. The safe opened. The safe was packed full of envelopes with photographs and negatives. Envelopes were labeled with names of people Marcus apparently knew.

One envelope had the word, "Milo," written on it. Roberta opened the Milo envelope and looked. The first few photographs showed Milo with an ordinary-looking woman his age and seven children. The fourth photograph showed Milo in a pub with a buxom, young hostess sitting in his lap and kissing him. The fifth showed Milo in a car with the hostess, and the sixth showed him in bed with the woman.

Roberta closed the envelope and opened one labeled, "Frank". The first photograph showed Frank holding an instrument and smiling in his dental treatment room. The second photograph showed Frank in a pub at a bar stool by himself. The third photograph showed Frank smoking a flat, blunt stick of marijuana. The fourth photograph showed Frank with a tourniquet on his upper arm and injecting something into his lower arm.

"This is the extortion safe," Roberta said.

Roberta returned the Frank envelope and opened one labeled, "Eva". The first showed Eva performing dentistry on a patient. The second showed Eva walking a dog in front of Marcus's house.

"She walks his dog?" Roberta asked. "She's enslaving herself to him."

The third photo showed Eva washing dishes in Marcus's house. The fourth showed Eva mowing his lawn.

"She's jumped from one subservient relationship to another," Roberta said. "Marcus is using her as an unpaid maid!"

The fifth showed Eva collecting dog feces from the ground next to Marcus's dog.

"Ugh," Roberta said.

The sixth photo showed Eva holding a bluish-gray pill (with a boxed letter M on the pill) upward with both hands as if she were a priestess holding up a Eucharistic host.

"The *divinity* of morphine," Roberta commented with disgust.

The seventh photo showed Eva saluting while popping a red-white-blue capsule into her mouth.

"A patriot marches on amphetamines," Roberta said with equal disgust.

The eighth photo showed Eva drinking from a beer bong and spilling much of the beer on her blouse. A ninth photo showed Eva passed out on a couch while clutching a partially filled wine bottle.

"My Eva. What happened to you?" Roberta said. "You've become a slave to men and drugs."

Roberta kept the photos and negatives of Eva and returned the empty envelope to the safe. She saw another envelope marked, "Roberta". Roberta opened the envelope and saw intimate photos of herself with Claudia. She kept those photos and the negatives but returned the empty envelope to the safe.

Something made a clunking sound in another part of Marcus's dental clinic. Fearful of being caught, Roberta closed the safe quickly, closed the secret panel, and withdrew to the closet with the photos and negatives of Eva and herself. She closed the closet door just as someone entered Marcus's office. She didn't have time to think. She tossed the photos and negatives on her desk and placed just enough boxes back in the closet next to Marcus's closet door to block the view of the path she created through the closet. She closed her closet door and kept her office light on. Roberta listened through her closet door. The person opened Marcus's closet door, paused, and closed it.

Roberta wanted to return the remaining boxes to the closet, but she didn't want to risk being caught. What if the person heard her making noise and opened the closet again from Marcus's side? Roberta decided the best thing to do was wait—at least five or ten minutes.

The telephone rang. Roberta jumped with a start. She rushed over to it, picked it up, and returned it to its cradle to end the call quickly. Roberta took several deep breaths.

"Maybe I should start drinking," Roberta said. "My nerves are shot."

Roberta reopened the closet and returned the boxes one by one. She closed the closet door and started placing a pin in the door hinge when the telephone rang again. The noise so badly startled Roberta that she dropped the pin, jolted the door, and the door flew open. Roberta rushed over to the phone and flicked it off its cradle like a hot potato on a grill.

"Hello, hello!" shouted a voice from the telephone. "Hello!"

Roberta returned the receiver to the cradle and ended the call.

"I'd better finish this up and get out of here before I'm discovered," Roberta whispered.

Roberta closed the closet door and placed the pins back in. She gathered together her things and proceeded to exit her clinic, but she paused at the doorway.

"What am I doing? I left the photos and negatives on my desk," Roberta said. "I have to dispose of them proper-like."

Roberta returned to her private office. She picked up the photos and negatives. The telephone rang, startling her again, and she accidentally tossed the photographs and negatives everywhere. Roberta picked up the telephone receiver again and dropped it on her desk.

"Hello, hello!" the same voice said. "Roberta! It's Kay. Are you there? There's been a terrible accident!"

Roberta stopped herself. She picked up the telephone and held it to her ear.

"Kay?" Roberta said.

"Roberta! I've been calling and calling. Thank goodness I found you!"

"What's happened? What's this about an accident?" Roberta asked.

"Eva's been in an accident," Kay said. "She was hit by a car while crossing the street."

"What?!" Roberta exclaimed.

"Don't worry, she's alive," Kay said. "I'm with her now at Lidian's Pub. Her injuries aren't too bad, but she needs to see a doctor. Roberta—if she goes to a hospital, they will—"

"I know," Roberta said. "What did the police do?"

"No one called the police," Kay said. "It was a hit and run. The driver obviously didn't want the police, and I scuttled Eva into the pub before anyone could call the police for her. I didn't think it would be good if Eva mixed with the law at the moment."

"You're very smart, Kay. And thank you for calling back," Roberta said. "I'm sorry I didn't answer sooner. Are you still at the pub?"

"Yeah. I'm calling from the pay phone inside," Kay said. "Roberta—Eva is in no condition to drive home. It's bad enough with...you know...her habit. But she's got a bump on the head."

"I completely understand everything," Roberta said. "I'll be right there."

Roberta rushed through the door but stopped herself yet again.

"I've got to remember these photos!" she said.

She pushed herself to pick up the photos and negatives as quickly as possible. She bundled them up with rubber bands and carried the package out of the office, out of the building, and into her car. She started the engine, backed out of her parking spot, and punched the gas pedal to the floor. The tires squealed, and Roberta's car careened out of the parking lot and down the road. A traffic signal turned yellow. Roberta intended to continue through the light even if red, but a car in front elected to stop at the light. Roberta slammed on her brakes, and the wheels wrenched the car to a stop.

"I've got to get on the freeway and bypass all these traffic lights," Roberta said.

The light turned green. Roberta navigated through traffic and reached the last traffic signal, but unfortunately it too was red. She waited.

"The fig tree bears no fruit," Roberta said tearfully. "I must fertilize it. I must help Eva."

Jonara returned to the Caves of Healing with Felifia. The two saw an image of Roberta in the water as if watching a movie.

"I must help Roberta, Felifia," Jonara said. "I must reach out to Roberta and give her hope and strength. Felifia—help me draw strength from this Water Ruby."

"It's dangerous," Felifia said.

"Please," Jonara said. "I must use the Water Ruby to help Roberta. She's a friend, too. I want to help a friend."

"Very well," Felifia said. "I will do what I can. But choose your words carefully."

Felifia placed one hand over her abdomen and the other hand on Jonara's Moissan Ruby. Jonara felt something like tingling in her abdomen—a tingling she hadn't had since she last used Miramish successfully. But she knew she had a reserve of energy to say a chant. Miramish words welled up in her throat, and she spoke:

Miramish	Translation
Nia fapo shaliniu dhaku felonapiu	I ask simply and humbly
Mafu teshunei:	For this:
Zhaipo borifa dhaku pereifa	Send strength and hope
Di Roberita	To Roberta
Rumaliu dhaku poshatiu	Gently and honestly
Boshuiliu bulirikao	Without descending
Ishetu bigaifota.	Into corruption.

The water swirled around Jonara's and Felifia's feet.

"Do not be distracted by the water," Felifia said. "Concentrate on Roberta."

"Think about Roberta, think about Roberta," Jonara said.

Jonara focused on the image of Roberta and the car in the water. A fin ascended through the water—a fin of a shark—and it continued circling Jonara and Felifia.

"This is scary," Jonara said.

"Do not be afraid," Felifia said. "Your ability to help Roberta depends on a calm heart."

Jonara continued concentrating on Roberta, her car, and the traffic signal. The traffic light turned green. The fin circled quickly, and an arm shot upward from the beast, grabbed Jonara, and pulled her under the waterline. Jonara traveled through the water. Then as strangely as she was pulled down, she found herself being pulled up onto the water surface of Oso Bay with Nekara standing next to her. Looking back into the water, she could see an image of Roberta and her car zooming away from the traffic light and onto a freeway entrance ramp.

"Nekara!" Jonara gasped.

"Did you think you could get away from me that easily?" Nekara said.

Roberta's car barreled down the entrance ramp and accelerated onto the freeway. She stabbed at the gas pedal, but the car wouldn't stop accelerating.

"What are you doing?" Jonara asked. "What have you done?"

"What have I done?" Nekara mocked. "It's what you've done. You wanted strength for Roberta. So her car has lots more strength."

"But gently and honestly, without descending into corruption," Jonara said. "You caused the corruption."

"I'm the consequence of your actions," Nekara said.

"You can't be!" Jonara said. "Felifia! Help me!"

The water in Oso Bay swirled around Jonara's and Nekara's feet. The fin of a dolphin surfaced and raced around the two while Roberta's car accelerated uncontrollably on the freeway. Roberta mashed hard on the brake pedal while she screamed and cursed. Jonara reached for the fin and latched onto the dolphin. The dolphin pulled her deep into the water and up through the pool in the Caves of Healing where Felifia pulled Jonara up onto the water's surface.

"Concentrate on Roberta!" Felifia emphasized.

Jonara focused on Roberta and her car, ignoring the circling shark's fin. Roberta continued pushing hard on the brake pedal with her left foot while stabbing the gas pedal with her right. The car stopped accelerating uncontrollably, and control of the gas pedal returned to Roberta—but only for a few seconds. Nekara's circling arm grasped desperately for Jonara. Roberta's car alternated between a state of sudden acceleration and full control.

"Help a friend, help a friend!" Jonara shouted.

"Shawna, what is it?" Evanita asked.

"Something troubles me about Roberta," Shawna Johnny said. "Something unnatural is happening to her car."

"Maybe the gas pedal is stuck to the floor mat," Evanita said.

"No, there are competitive forces at work," Shawna Johnny said. "She is caught in-between. I am compelled to act."

Shawna Johnny jumped into the pool.

"No, Shawna, your mascara will run!" Geneva shouted.

Shawna Johnny swam into the image of Roberta's car. He extended his arms toward the engine and said:

Miramish	Translation
Niai oi kiro beriku ilu yuanu,	We are not black or white,
Kufu ilu vozhaku.	Good or evil.
Niai kiro tharifotu, miroku,	We are diverse, angular,
Thuati opeifu shai valita.	Phases of the circle.
Leko shiami opeifu liukika	Let tangents of conflict
Piuferinifo dhaku berautho	Unhitch and flow
Ishetu shai valitata.	Into the circulation.

Jonara felt an electric shock from Shawna Johnny's Moissan Ruby to her own followed by an annoying beating sound of two very close frequencies—the frequencies of Shawna Johnny's Moissan Ruby and her own Moissan Ruby as the stones interacted, but with each stone slightly out of phase from the other. Roberta's gas pedal pulsed—slowly at first then progressively quicker until the gas pedal reached a state where Roberta seemed to have full control, but the gas pedal was more sensitive to her touch and accelerated more forcefully with less effort.

Jonara looked at Felifia, and for a moment she seemed to alternate between being Nekara, then Felifia, then Nekara and Felifia quicker and quicker until the two became one person—Felifia with more pink in her skin tone. The pink skin tone held firm for a moment, but gradually it faded, and as it did, the beating sound from Shawna Johnny's Moissan Ruby and her own Moissan Ruby also faded.

"This cheap car!" Roberta yelled. "I've got to trade it in for something new!"

Roberta managed to drive the rest of the way to Lidian's Pub without any additional automobile problems. She entered the pub. Kay flagged her down, and the three met.

"Well hello, Robbie!" Eva said in an inebriated condition.

"She's drunk," Roberta said, "and she has a slight concussion. I'd better take her home. I'll watch her tonight. If there's any sign of internal bleeding, I'll take her to the hospital."

"Do you need any help?" Kay asked.

"No thank you, Kay. We'll be fine. I'm going to start Eva on a new therapy, and it could get ugly," Roberta said.

"What *theraby*?" Eva asked. "I don't need no *ukly theraby*."

"Come on, Eva, we're going home," Roberta said as she helped Eva to her feet.

"But the *barty* is just *starding*," Eva complained.

"We're going home and having a nice, long chat," Roberta said.

On the drive from Lidian's Pub to Roberta's house, Eva fumbled restlessly with things. First it was the seatbelt, then it was the window, then the radio, then the air vent, and finally it was the seat position.

"Stop being so fidgety!" Roberta said. "You're driving me crazy!"

"Quit telling me what to do," Eva said. "You're not my mother."

"I simply can't believe I am sitting next to a medical professional who has the maturity of a two-year old!" Roberta said. "Eva! You've really hit bottom, haven't you?"

"Who are you to know?" Eva said.

Roberta begged her to stop being so fidgety, but Eva didn't like being told what to do. Roberta turned onto a side street leading to her house. At a stop sign, Eva suddenly opened the door to escape.

"Oh no you don't!" Roberta said.

Roberta reacted to Eva's maneuver by reaching over and yanking the door shut before Eva could get out, but in doing so, Roberta let her foot off the brake (to extend her reach toward Eva). The car idled forward, and a crossing car honked its horn and swerved around Roberta's car in a near-miss.

"You're going to get us killed!" Roberta said.

"You're the stupid driver," Eva said. "You're the one getting us killed."

Roberta rolled her eyes. She drove the car to her house, parked, walked to the passenger side, and opened the door for Eva.

"Come on, let's go inside," Roberta droned.

"No," Eva said, and she remained in her passenger seat.

"Eva, come on!" Roberta said.

Roberta extended her hand to Eva, but Eva shirked away.

"No," Eva said. "I'm going to a party."

"You're done for the night!" Roberta said.

Roberta grabbed Eva's arm and pulled Eva up. Eva grabbed the car frame with her free hand and held fast. Roberta tried undoing it, but Eva broke her first hand free and grabbed hold of the frame. Roberta grabbed Eva by the waist, but Eva maintained her grip on the door frame.

"Quit fighting me, Eva!" Roberta strained to say as she continued pulling on Eva.

"You can't make me do anything," Eva said. "Let me go."

"No," Roberta said. "I won't let go. You let go of the car."

"No," Eva said.

"Then I'll force you," Roberta said.

Roberta grabbed hold of Eva's wrists—one of Roberta's hands per wrist—and pried them off the door frame. Eva started kicking back, but Roberta avoided the brunt of Eva's attacks.

"I'm not a man," Roberta said. "I don't have a weak spot in the groin."

Roberta pulled Eva away from the car and managed to kick the passenger door closed. Eva gave Roberta quite a struggle and was strong from her dancing. Roberta breathed hard and was losing her grip on Eva. To prevent Eva's escape, Roberta pinned Eva to the ground by exerting her weight on Eva.

"If you put as much energy into straightening yourself out as you are in fighting me, you'll be sober by yesterday," Roberta said. "Now I don't have much more patience for this. I'm going to hold you here until you get some sense back in that stubborn head of yours and behave!"

"You wretched wench," Eva said. "You...you're making a scene!"

Several pedestrians paused on the sidewalk in front of Roberta's house and watched.

"Go on and mind your business," Roberta said.

"I should call the police on you," said a bystander.

"You keep your nose in your own business and stay out of mine," Roberta said. "Now all of you—scat!"

"Marcus was right," Eva said. "You like torturing women. You get off on that. I shouldn't have gone into *Dairy Duck* with you that one night. Are you getting a rise out of sitting on me?"

"Marcus is a big fat liar," Roberta said, "and I thought we had a stronger friendship than that. I'm here for you, not me. If I were selfish, I'd kick you to the street. But I'm not."

"You want to make love to me, don't you?" Eva said. "Marcus warned me."

"More lies!" Roberta said. "I'm your friend. I would never harm you."

"You're hurting me now! Get off of me!" Eva screamed.

Roberta let out a big sigh. She held Eva's arms behind her back, pulled her to her feet, shoved her to the house, in through the doorway, down the hallway, into Eva's bedroom, and pushed Eva onto her bed.

"Sleep it off," Roberta said.

Eva cried.

1989 Oct 14, Sat Morn 1 am. Roberta's Home. Portland, Oregon.

Roberta was sleeping lightly on the couch when Eva stumbled through the hallway. Eva was still drunk!

"Eva?" Roberta asked.

Eva mumbled something on the way to the bathroom. Roberta followed her into the bathroom. Roberta took a sniff of Eva's breath and recoiled from the stench.

"You've been drinking!" Roberta said. "You've got a bottle of booze in your bedroom, don't you?"

Eva ignored Roberta. Eva knelt on the bathroom floor, opened the cabinet below the sink, and pulled out a can of powdered cleaner.

"Eva, put that back. You're not fit to clean anything," Roberta said.

Oblivious to Roberta's surprise, Eva unscrewed the top of the cylinder.

"It's a fake can of cleaner!" Roberta said in amazement.

Eva pulled out a bottle of bluish-gray pills, opened it, dumped the pills down her throat, and swallowed.

"Dammit, Eva, what are you doing!?" Roberta screamed. "You just overdosed on morphine!"

Roberta ran to her medical bag and returned with syrup of ipecac. She forced two teaspoons down Eva's throat and chased the ipecac with a cup of water.

"Quit...treating me...like a child," Eva blabbered.

"You've crossed the line, Eva," Roberta said.

"What...do ya mean...Robbie-poo?" Eva asked.

Eva's face looked queasy and broke into a sweat. Roberta opened the toilet lid and positioned Eva's head into the bowl. The syrup worked its effect, and Eva vomited into the porcelain bowl.

"That's right," Roberta said as Eva continued to empty her stomach contents into the bowl. "Get it all out. You're very lady-like this weekend, aren't you?"

"Quit calling me a lady," Eva said. "I'm not a lady."

Eva puked again and again until her stomach had nothing left to throw up. Eva went into dry heaves. Roberta flushed the toilet several times and repeatedly offered toilet paper to Eva so she could wipe her mouth. After twenty minutes, Eva stopped vomiting.

"That's a good girl," Roberta said. "Now it's time to rinse your mouth and brush your teeth."

Roberta helped Eva to her feet and helped her clean her mouth and teeth.

"Good," Roberta said. "Merry Pumpkin would be proud. Let's get you to the couch."

"You're the best dentist," Eva said. "You keep my teeth clean."

Roberta was surprised by this sudden change of behavior, given how belligerent Eva had been the prior evening.

"Where would you be without me?" Roberta said.

"I have the best smile and the best teeth," Eva blabbered. "Marcus says so."

"Well I'm glad he thinks so," Roberta said. "And I have news for you, Eva. As your roommate and dentist, I'm ordering a new medication for you."

"I got plenty of meds," Eva said. "Pick one."

Eva put a hand in her pocket and pulled out a fistful of pills.

"Ugh," Roberta said. "This is despicable. Give me those."

Roberta took the fistful of pills from Eva's hand.

"You don't have to be so greedy," Eva said. "Get your own stash."

"There's not going to be any more stashing around here. I should have ended this long ago," Roberta said.

Roberta placed Eva on the couch. Roberta went to the kitchen for another cup of water and brought along a bottle of pills.

"Pills! Yay!" Eva cheered in her stupor.

"This is naltrexone," Roberta said. "You are to take a 50 mg pill once a day at bedtime. It won't get you high, drunk, or anesthetized. In fact, you won't even know you're taking it except for the side effects—it blocks the action of amphetamine and morphine, and it gives you a strong dislike for alcohol."

"Gimme pill. Gimme drug. Let's get high, Robbie. Get high with me," Eva said.

Roberta popped the naltrexone into Eva's mouth and washed it down with a cup of water. Eva swallowed it and passed out on the couch. Roberta placed a blanket over Eva.

"Goodnight, Eva. I hope you come to your senses this weekend," Roberta said, and she turned in for the night.

1989 Oct 14, Sat Morn 11 am. Roberta's Home. Portland, Oregon.

Eva rolled off the couch and woke up. Roberta—sitting in her easy chair—looked up from her crossword puzzle.

"Ugh," Eva said. "I've got this awful mucus tingling in my throat. What happened last night? I can't remember a thing."

"You never do," Roberta said.

"I need an amphetamine to wake up," Eva said.

"That won't work," Roberta said. "It'll be blocked."

"What are you talking about?" Eva said. "Never mind. I'll wash it down with a beer."

Eva went into her room and returned with two amphetamine pills. She retrieved a can of beer from the refrigerator, opened it, popped the pills in her mouth, and washed them down with a big gulp of beer.

"Yuck! This beer's gone bad!" Eva said.

Eva dumped the beer in the sink. She opened another can and drank it.

"This one too—it's gone bad," Eva said.

Eva threw that can in the sink and retrieved an imported German beer.

"Yuck! All right, Roberta, what's the game? Did you replace my beer with this junk?"

"No, I haven't," Roberta said. "The beer hasn't changed. You have."

"Impossible," Eva said. "I'm a wreck without a morning beer. Forget the beer—I'll have some nice, chilled, red wine."

Eva poured a glass and drank it.

"Disgusting!" Eva said. "What did you do—pour baking soda in my wine?"

"The wine is fine," Roberta said. "I told you—you've changed."

"Something strange is going on here. I should be waking up by now. Why am I still dragging? I need more amphetamines."

"Don't waste your time," Roberta said. "You don't remember last night how you emptied your guts into the toilet, do you?"

"No, I don't," Eva said.

"That will be the last time you do that. From now on, you're on naltrexone—my orders," Roberta said.

Roberta retrieved the prescription bottle of naltrexone and showed it to Eva.

"I'm a patient of Roberta MacNessi?" Eva asked. "Since when? Did you force medication on me? You violated me!"

"I'm putting my Celtic foot down, Eva Kelicacha Carreña. From now on, you're going to live a sober life," Roberta said.

"I can't live like this. I'm already feeling withdrawal symptoms," Eva said. "If you cared about me, you wouldn't have forced naltrexone on me."

"And I'll keep forcing it on you until you get your senses back," Roberta said.

"You bitch! What you're doing is criminal. I won't take it!" Eva said.

"I'll force you to, if it's the last thing I do," Roberta said. "And it's high time. I'm way past courtesy now, Eva."

"I'll move out. I'll move in with Marcus," Eva said.

Roberta rushed up to Eva and yanked her by the arm.

"You'll kill yourself if you move in with him. You'll die!" Roberta said.

Eva screamed. Roberta screamed back.

"Stop screaming when I'm screaming!" Eva screamed.

"I won't let you intimidate me!" Roberta screamed back.

"I'm getting out of here! I'm going crazy!" Eva screamed.

"No you're not! You're grounded!" Roberta screamed back.

"Arrrg!" Eva screamed.

Eva ran for the door, but Roberta ran quicker. Roberta put Eva in a wrestling hold. Roberta forced Eva to the kitchen and held her against the countertop while Roberta retrieved handcuffs from a drawer. Next, Roberta forced Eva to her bedroom and handcuffed one of Eva's wrists to the iron-wrought headboard of Eva's bed.

"This is kidnapping!" Eva said. "You can't hold me prisoner!"

Roberta left Eva's room and returned with a bedpan.

"Use this to relieve yourself," Roberta said coldly.

Eva took the bedpan with her free hand and threw it across the room with a loud bang!

"That was stupid," Roberta said, and she left.

"Let me go, you vicious bitch, let me go!" Eva screamed.

"Scream all day. I don't care," Roberta called back.

Roberta went into the other room and inserted ear plugs into her own ears. She sat in her easy chair and worked on her crossword puzzle. As the day progressed, Eva came down with severe withdrawal symptoms: abdominal cramps, nausea, sneezing, cold chills, and shakes.

"I'm sick!" Eva called after several hours. "I need to go to the hospital. I'm dying! Roberta! Help me!"

Roberta stood up for a moment. She felt badly for Eva.

"Should I give her something to ease the pain?" Roberta said quietly.

"Yes!" Evanita said. "Don't let Mama suffer!"

"No!" Geneva said. "Evanita—your mother must tough it out through her withdrawal. Giving in now will only make things worse, because Eva will go right back to taking drugs to 'solve' her problems."

Roberta removed the earplugs and walked to Eva's room.

"Roberta, Roberta!" an out-of-breath Eva pleaded. "I'm in pain! I can't stand it. I'll do anything. Give me a pain pill. Roberta, please!!!"

"Are you ready to talk?" Roberta asked.

"Talk? What's to talk about? I'm in pain! Give me a pain pill!" Eva begged.

"I won't," Roberta said.

"Arrrg!" Eva screeched.

"We have to talk about your lifestyle, Eva. We need to talk about your problems and how you're managing them," Roberta said.

"I...can't...cope...with...this...PAIN!" Eva said. "Just kill me and get it over. Kill me! Don't torture me with talk!"

Roberta was caught in a mixed state of anger and pity. Eva's behavior upset Roberta, but as a doctor, Roberta understood the nightmare of withdrawal symptoms.

"I've had to make a hard choice with you," Roberta said. "And I'm sticking to it."

Roberta left Eva's bedroom and reinserted the earplugs.

"No, wait! Don't leave me! Roberta! Help me! Roberta!" Eva screamed.

Later in the day, Marcus called on the telephone and asked for Eva.

"I'm sorry. She's sick today," Roberta said.

"May I speak with her at least?" Marcus asked.

"She's sleeping," Roberta said.

"I want to talk to her about work on Monday," Marcus said. "Wake her for me."

"She's very ill and can't talk right now," Roberta said. "Goodbye."

Marcus called back immediately.

"Hello?" Roberta answered.

"I demand to speak to Eva—now!" Marcus ordered.

"I've already given you the answer, Marcus. Goodbye," Roberta said, and she hung up the telephone.

The afternoon grew late, and Roberta started dinner. She prepared a simple chicken stew.

"Eat some dinner," Roberta said as she handed a plate of stew and a cup of juice to Eva.

Eva took the stew, sniffed it, and threw it across the room at the window.

"Oh Eva, try to sober up," Roberta said. "Here—take your naltrexone."

"No! You're trying to block my free choice," Eva said.

With much struggling and resistance from Eva, Roberta forced a naltrexone pill down Eva's throat with a glass of water.

"Ugh!" Eva wailed. "You're hijacking my body!"

The telephone rang.

"Not Marcus again," Roberta mumbled.

"What about Marcus?" Eva said, overhearing Roberta. "Did he call before?"

"Yes, and I told him you were unavailable," Roberta said from down the hallway as she made for the telephone.

"And you didn't tell me?" Eva shouted back. "I could use a stiff drink after what you've done to me."

"Hello?" Roberta answered in the living room.

Unknown to Roberta, Marcus appeared at Eva's bedroom window. Eva smiled. She dragged the bed toward the window so she could reach the lock.

"No, Simon, you can't talk to her. She's sick and sleeping," Roberta said.

Eva pulled the window open a bit, and Marcus opened it farther.

"Roberta handcuffed me to the bed frame," Eva whispered.

"What is she, your jailer now?" Marcus whispered.

"I know!" Eva whispered. "She's gone berserk! Help me out."

"Simon, I'm not going to argue with you," Roberta said.

"Don't go anywhere," Marcus said. "I'll be right back."

Marcus left momentarily.

"Where would I go?" Eva asked herself.

"Simon. Simon. Stop. Simon, listen to me. Simon!" Roberta repeated.

Marcus returned with a bolt cutter. He passed the bolt cutter to Eva through the window.

"Position the bolt cutters over the chain between the cuffs," Marcus said. "Good. Now steady one handle against the bed. Yeah, like that. Push the other handle."

The bolt cutter severed the chain. Eva returned the bolt cutter to Marcus, and Marcus helped Eva crawl through the window.

"What about the cuff on my wrist?" Eva asked.

"I'll help you get that off," Marcus said. "But first, let's get you out of here."

"I promise I'll let her know, Simon," Roberta continued. "Yes, I will. Goodnight. I said, goodnight! That means the end of conversation, Simon!"

Roberta hung up the telephone.

"Time to clean up Eva's dinner mess," Roberta said.

Roberta dampened a kitchen towel but stopped herself in the kitchen.

"Wait, why am I doting on her?" Roberta asked herself. "Let her sit in her mess. I'm going to relax and eat dinner out here."

Roberta placed a large helping of chicken stew on her plate, grabbed a soft drink, sat at the dining table, and enjoyed her meal. She had just finished her last bite and cleaned up when someone knocked at the door.

"Who could that be?" Roberta wondered.

Suspicious of Marcus, Roberta looked through the peephole. She saw Kay and Earl.

"Come in, come in!" Roberta said as she opened the door. "What a pleasant surprise! And what do you have in the case?"

"We thought you could use some cheering up," Kay said. "So I brought my *bendir* drum. It's a very old drum my mother gave me. It's a family heirloom really. No one knows where it came from, but some say it comes from Spain. I've mastered the bendir quite well, I think."

"That's great!" Roberta said. "I'll have to get my ancient oboe out. We'll have a musical party. Earl, do you play an instrument?"

"I play the violin," Earl said.

"I have Eva's mother's *viola de gamba* in the closet. I bet you could learn how to play it rather quickly," Roberta said.

"It would be an honor," Earl said.

"Speaking of Eva, how is she? May we see her?" Kay asked.

"Don't disturb her. She's quiet for the first time all day, for which I'm glad," Roberta said, not realizing Eva had snuck out the window with Marcus's help.

Roberta took up the ancient oboe from 1492, Kay the bendir from 1492, and Earl the *viola de gamba* from 1492. The group played a variety of musical selections. Kay's bendir provided a hypnotic rhythm, Earl's play of the *viola de gamba* gave harmonies, and Roberta's oboe the melodies. Evanita, Shawna Johnny, Geneva, Jonara, and Felifia watched this from the pool in the Caves of Healing, and something strange happened as the musical instruments continued playing—the vision split-screened into that of Roberta's home and Eva's adventure with Marcus.

"This is strange," Evanita said. "It's almost like watching a musical. My mother is the actress, and Roberta is in the background playing music with Kay and Earl."

"They are separate and together," Geneva said.

"Huh?" Evanita asked.

"That's the best I can explain," Geneva said. "Watch both."

"Oh Marcus," Eva said. "Thank you for rescuing me. I was going crazy in there."

Roberta's music continued in the background.

"You're welcome," Marcus said. "I heard you were in an accident last night."

"It wasn't bad," Eva said. "I got a bump on the head after a car ran over me."

"Ran over you!" Marcus said in surprise.

"Not really. I rolled onto the hood and hit my head on the windshield. But I'm okay, except I have this nasty headache today. I need something for it."

"Have you eaten dinner yet?" Marcus asked.

"No, and I'm starved," Eva said.

"Then I know just what you need. I'll prepare a nice dinner for you at my house," Marcus said, "and I have a bottle of aspirin if you need it."

"That sounds great," Eva said. "Maybe we can go dancing afterward."

"We'll be dancing," Marcus said. "I promise you that."

The two arrived at Marcus's house.

"I feel like I've been here before," Eva said. "But I'm not sure. I can't remember. Was I here?"

"If you don't remember, then you weren't," Marcus grinned.

Eva looked closely at Marcus's teeth. It was the first time in several months she'd seen them while sober.

"Your teeth look different," Eva said as the two exited the parked car. "Did you put veneers on them?"

"Something even better," Marcus said. "I'll explain in a bit. But first, let's get dinner."

The two entered Marcus's house. Eva spent time exploring the various paintings and relics in the large living room while Marcus prepared dinner. She noticed quite a number of stuffed animal heads mounted on the wall—a deer, a lion, a bear, and a gorilla. The gorilla head scared her, and she backed away, and away, and away all the while staring at the gorilla head. She bumped into something, turned around, and jumped in fright only to be relieved by the recognition of Marcus.

"There there!" he said. "I didn't mean to scare you. Here's a glass of water and aspirin."

"I'm sorry," Eva said. "It's me. I'm not used to seeing so many life-like animals."

"Well don't worry," Marcus said. "They can't hurt you. Come back to the dining room. Dinner is ready."

Eva took the aspirin and water. She handed the glass back to Marcus and thanked him. Marcus led her back to the dining room. She stood next to the window and peered out.

"Is something the matter?" Marcus asked.

"No...well...I was just checking," Eva said.

"This house is quite safe," Marcus said.

"I know. It's silly, but I keep thinking someone is following me," Eva said.

Eva sat down at the table.

"Liver?" Eva asked. "Are you serious?"

"You'll be surprised at how good it tastes," Marcus said. "I use a special recipe from my mother. It's called, 'Jelana's Cajun Liver'. I prepare the liver with bacon, peppers, and a special mixture of herbs. The liver tastes completely different once I'm through with it. Try it."

Eva took a piece of liver and placed it on her plate.

"Do you have beer or wine?" Eva asked.

"I'm sorry, I don't. My religion forbids it. But I have other things—juice, cola, coffee, and bottled water," Marcus said.

"I'll take a cola," Eva said.

Eva got up to get a cola.

"Please, sit down and be my guest. I'll get the cola for you," Marcus said.

"This is it," Geneva said. "This is where it all begins."

"Where what begins?" Evanita asked.

"Where your mother and Marcus...no, I shouldn't say anything. You must feel her emotions. Can you feel your mother's emotions, Evanita?"

"Yes, I can. She's cranky and paranoid," Evanita said.

"That's from her drug withdrawal," Shawna Johnny said. "And stopping cold turkey with alcohol is dangerous, too."

"Yes, it is," Geneva said. "But that's only one danger lurking in her future. Watch."

Marcus opened a can of cola from the refrigerator and placed it on the countertop. Outside of Eva's view, he quietly opened a cupboard door, removed a prescription bottle, opened it, selected a pill, and dropped the pill in the cola.

"He's spiking the drink!" Evanita said. "Shawna—what's he spiking it with?"

Shawna Johnny whispered a few words to himself and dipped his hand into the water.

"Flunitrazepam," Johnny said. "Also known by its trade name Rohypnol. It's a powerful sedative with short-term amnesia properties. Ms. Geneva—this drug is used for date rape."

"Oh my God, oh my God!" Evanita shouted. "Marcus is my father! He raped Mama! Oh how terrible! I'm half Marcus! Half worthless. I can't take it. Grandma Geneva! What am I going to do with myself? What am I going to do? I have to end it all. I'm jumping in the pool and drowning myself."

"No!" Geneva and Shawna Johnny shouted simultaneously.

"Shawna, grab Evanita," Geneva said.

Shawna Johnny placed both arms around Evanita and prevented her from jumping in.

"But I'm not a person. I'm a barbarian, a monster, a troglodyte," Evanita said. "I'll spare the world some misery by ending mine now."

"Stop it!" Geneva shouted. "Don't let an impulsive knee-jerk reaction draw conclusions beyond your ability to see all ends."

"You warned me, Grandma. You warned me that if you told me the story instead of showing me, I'd hate my mother," Evanita said. "Well it didn't work. I hate her. She should have aborted me. Rape does not deserve life or legacy."

"Evanita!" Geneva said. "Get hold of yourself. These waters show many things, and not all are pretty. I ask you to find within yourself the strength to continue. Will you be strong?"

Evanita shook in terror.

"I don't want to see Mama get raped," Evanita quivered.

"No matter what you see, you must be strong!" Geneva said.

"Felifia, I must help my Grandma Eva," Jonara said. "Even if she was hostile to me in the past. I have to help her."

"You tried helping Roberta," Felifia said. "Look what happened."

"I know, but I wasn't trying hard enough," Jonara said.

"Do you think that's what it was?" Felifia said. "The universe operates independently of what you desire or how hard you try. Jonara—you are caught between conflicts. A push one way pulls the other."

"I...I don't know...what conflicts?" Jonara asked.

"Don't you see them? They are everywhere," Felifia said. "There's the conflict between Nekara and me. There's the conflict between Marcus and Eva, between Eva and Roberta, between Marcus and Roberta. There was conflict on my home world of Eho Miriam when Dart collided with Seris—another conflict. You saw conflict in medieval Spain, conflict in Italy, conflict in—"

"Is there no end?" Jonara asked.

"No, there isn't," Felifia said. "Conflict never ends. Jonara—conflict may seem to end, but another sprouts up. Life is conflict, and conflict created life."

"What conflict?" Jonara asked. "What conflict created life?"

"The conflict of matter and energy," Felifia said. "Isn't it obvious?"

"No, it isn't," Jonara said. "Felifia—am I stuck watching my Grandma Eva getting raped by Marcus? Am I forced to watch this assault along with my parents and Nanna Geneva?"

"You are like your mother," Felifia said.

"I saw what my daddy did," Jonara said. "He jumped in the pool and performed a Miramish chant. That's what I'll do. I'll cast a direct chant and—"

"Be forewarned, Jonara!" Felifia said. "You performed a direct chant before, and look at the results."

"There's nothing else I can do," Jonara said. "I must chant."

"If you dare take this road," Felifia said, "cast not a direct chant, but an indirect one. Help a friend help a friend."

"Huh? Did you just stutter?" Jonara asked.

"I will say no more," Felifia said.

Jonara stared at the pool and watched the image of Marcus carrying the cola to Eva to drink.

"I must stop him," Jonara said.

"And you'll undo everything I've worked for," Felifia said.

"I thought you were done talking," Jonara said. "It doesn't matter. Marcus will just find another way. He has the duavisha, and Nekara is helping him. I'm doomed. And why do Roberta and her friends have to keep playing that music? Don't they realize how rude it is to be happy when my Grandma Eva is about to be mauled? Wait, she doesn't know. But what if she did? Roberta! Check the bedroom! Roberta!"

"She can't hear you," Felifia said, "and if you think of performing another Miramish chant—"

"I know, be forewarned," Jonara said.

Jonara jumped into the pool. Nekara's arm reached up and pulled her down and up through the surface of Oso Bay.

"Ah, Jonara. You've come to your senses," Nekara said. "That little stunt of your father's cost me an automobile accident. Fortunately, all is not lost. The best is yet to come."

"That's why I'm here," Jonara said. "I want you to warn Roberta about Marcus."

"Why would I do that? Marcus is doing such an excellent job for me," Nekara said.

"I know what your problem is, Nekara," Jonara said. "You're the fig tree without fruit."

"Oh garbage upon garbage," Nekara said. "Your Earth morality stories don't interest me. Are you so anthropocentric that you can't see the irrelevance of your culture beyond this little planet's atmosphere? You're no better than fish who believe life outside their ocean is impossible. Go back to your family history, Jonara. See what a real story is, not your feel-good-fast-track-to-philosophical-nowhere-fig-tree story."

Nekara pushed Jonara back into the water. Felifia's hand reached for Jonara, but Jonara resisted.

Miramish	**Translation**
Nia kilo nui Gereima Iva.	I am my Grandma Eva.
Roberita kilo Felifia.	Roberta is Felifia.

Miramish	Translation
Marikus e kilo Nekara	Marcus is Nekara.
Roberita—kelugo di Iva kaish e kapa	Roberta—lend Eva your hand
Yoshu Felifia kelugo di nau shash.	As Felifia lends me hers.
Nia gelorugo mafu Felifia,	I reach for Felifia,
Yoshu Iva gelorugo mafu kail	As Eva reaches for you
Idu Marikusanga kiafa/	At Marcus's house/
Idu Nekaranga shoita	At Nekara's side
Opeifu shai heidona.	Of the water.

Jonara reached for Felifia's hand at the water's surface of Oso Bay. As she did, she was simultaneously reaching for the cola from Marcus and pulling the oboe's reed toward her lips as Roberta. Jonara kissed the oboe as Roberta, sipped the cola as Eva, traveled through the water to the other side, and stood atop the water's surface in the Caves of Healing next to Felifia.

"Eva?" Roberta asked as she stared at the oboe.

Roberta lifted the oboe to her mouth as if she were drinking a tall glass. Kay and Earl stopped playing their instruments and stared at Roberta.

"Roberta," Kay said. "What are you doing? Are you okay?"

"I...I was somewhere else and someone else for a moment," Roberta said. "I was in Marcus's house. I was drinking a cola. And my hair was black, not red. I...was..."

The thought of Eva's presence in Marcus's house prompted Roberta into action. Still clutching the oboe, Roberta ran down the hallway and burst into Eva's bedroom.

"Eva!" Roberta yelled. "She's gone!"

Kay rushed into the bedroom.

"The window is open!" Kay said.

"The handcuff is still attached to the bed frame," Roberta said, "but the connecting chain's been cut."

"She got away. And she had help," Kay said.

"Marcus," Roberta said. "I saw him in a vision. She's at Marcus's house. I have to go get her. But my car! Something's wrong! The gas pedal sticks."

"Then let's go in my van," Kay said.

"What about Earl?" Roberta said.

"Let's work that out," Kay said.

Kay led Roberta back to the living room.

"Earl," Kay said. "There's trouble with Eva. She's gone. Roberta thinks she's at Marcus's house, but we're not sure. Would you stay here?"

"I should be with you, baby," Earl said.

"This is an emergency. Eva might come back, or she might call on the telephone. Would you wait here for us in case she does?" Kay asked. "Please, Earl, this is very, very important. And we're taking the van."

"You're taking the what?" Earl asked in shock.

"We'll be back," Kay said as she rushed Roberta out the door.

"Don't get a scratch on the van," Earl said. "We paid good money for it, and—"

Kay closed the door on Earl, and a few seconds later, she opened it again.

"You worry too much, Earl," Kay said. "I'll call soon."

Kay closed the door again and rushed Roberta to the van with Roberta holding the oboe. The scene changed back to Marcus's house. To her surprise, Eva enjoyed the liver. She finished drinking her cola, and Marcus went to work on his plan—a plan he had invoked many times before with other women.

"How do you feel, Eva?" Marcus asked. "Are you still edgy? Are you still afraid Roberta will nag you like a mother hen?"

"I feel better, thank you," Eva said.

"I thought you would," Marcus said. "Can you stand?"

"Of course I can stand," Eva said.

Eva stood up.

"Oh, I'm a little dizzy," she said.

"As you should," Marcus said. "Come this way. I want to show you something."

Marcus led Eva to the bedroom with the dental equipment.

"What did you mean when you said I should be dizzy?" Eva asked.

"It was an offhand remark," Marcus said. "I meant nothing by it. Do you remember this room?"

"No, I don't," Eva said.

"You were here once before," Marcus said. "You sat in this dental chair. Sit in this dental chair, Eva."

Reluctantly, Eva sat on the side of the dental chair.

"Is this a game? What about dancing?" Eva asked.

"We'll be 'dancing' very soon. And the game begins now," Marcus said. "Eva—when was the last time you had your period?"

"What?!" Eva asked. "What kind of question is that?"

"Oh, I meant nothing," Marcus said. "It was a joke really."

"A man shouldn't ask a woman that question in polite conversation," Eva said.

"Yes, of course," Marcus said. "A man would only ask that question to determine the best way to rape a woman."

Eva stood up in shock.

"That was another joke. Please, don't be alarmed," Marcus said. "I want you to watch a slideshow. That's all. Just a slideshow. You can trust me."

Eva hesitated and looked hard at Marcus. Marcus touched her shoulder and pushed her down into the dental chair gently. He dimmed the lights and turned on a slide projector.

"This is my first transplant patient," he said. "Her name was Lisa. I removed her molars. See? This is her before-picture, and her after-picture."

"What was wrong with her molars?" Eva asked. "They look fine. What kind of implant did you give her?"

"Lisa was a donor, not a recipient," Marcus said.

"I don't understand," Eva said.

"Look at the next slide," Marcus said.

"It's you!" Eva said.

"This is my before-picture with my own molars, now the middle picture with my molars removed, and the after-picture with Lisa's molars in my mouth," Marcus said.

A sudden pain of horror gripped Eva's face.

"This is some sort of sick joke, right?" Eva asked.

"No, it isn't," Marcus said. "Here's my next victim—her name was Julie. She donated incisors. See? Her before and after pictures. Now my before, middle, and after pictures."

Eva continued watching in shock. Julie's incisors were missing, and she was obviously heavily sedated in her photos.

"My third victim was Audrey," Marcus said. "She donated her bicuspids."

"This is criminal, Marcus," Eva said.

"Yes, I know," he grinned. "But I enjoy it. Having women's teeth in my mouth is exhilarating. When I place the plastic end of a permanent marker in my mouth and stroke my female teeth, I can taste the world as it was meant to be. Watch."

Marcus held his left hand to his abdomen. With his right hand, he retrieved a permanent marker from a desk. Keeping the cap on, he inserted the non-cap end into his mouth and stroked it across his teeth as if brushing, but his strokes were smooth and rhythmic. Marcus sighed. He shoved the plastic end into his upper palate and thrust upward. His eyelids pulsed open, and he continued thrusting the marker against his palate. Then he alternated between thrusting the pen against his female teeth, thrusting the pen against the gum line holding the female teeth, against his inside cheeks, and his upper palate. His head bobbed up and down like someone with an obsessive-compulsive disorder.

Eva stared in absolute shock. She had never seen a person perform the type of compulsive act that Marcus was now doing, and nothing in her medical training prepared her for Marcus's actions. He removed four loosely-fit bridges posing as his canine teeth. He probed his canine sockets with the capped marker. He probed, pushed, and added it to his collection of compulsive mouth explorations. He accelerated the thrusting, head bobbing, and eyelid pulsing all the while breathing harder and harder through his nose until he stopped suddenly. He squatted a bit as if preparing to defecate, his facial muscles contracted and contorted his face into a beet-red painful-like expression, and he held this pose for nine seconds until he sneezed rhythmically and regularly nine times at intervals of nine-tenths of a second per sneeze.

Marcus took a deep breath, exhaled, and returned the pen to his desk. Drops of blood flowed from his canine sockets.

"I'm primed for transplant," he said.

"Why are you showing me all this? The pictures, this epileptic act of yours—why, Marcus? You know I can report you to the legal and medical authorities," Eva said.

"Because I know you won't say anything," Marcus said. "I've drugged you with Rohypnol. The drug is coursing through your body, sedating you, and semi-paralyzing you. You'll do whatever I ask, and tomorrow you won't remember a thing. You are my number four donor, Eva. You'll donate your canine teeth to me. You'll do it gladly without reservation."

"No!" Eva said.

Marcus approached her, forced her mouth open, and took a photograph. Next, he grabbed a tool for extracting teeth and moved it toward Eva's mouth. Eva kicked him and jumped out of the chair.

"Something's wrong," he said. "You should be sedated, but you're not."

"I'm calling the police!" Eva said, and she leapt for the bedroom door to escape.

Marcus leapt after her and grabbed her arm.

"Let me go!" Eva yelled.

"Sit like a quiet girl so I can extract your canines!" he yelled.

"NO!" she yelled back.

Marcus pulled her to the dental chair and tried strapping her in, but she kicked and clawed and fought him with all her ballet strength. Each time Marcus tried strapping Eva down, she bit and clawed him. She tore at his face leaving bloody streaks on his cheeks, and she tore apart his shirt, revealing a glowing mass beneath a sewn-together belly button.

"What's wrong with your navel?" Eva shouted. "What have you done to yourself!?"

"You shouldn't have done that!" he shouted.

Marcus grew furious. He pinned Eva down with his weight and strapped her down. For that action, he received many welts from Eva's fists, knees, and feet.

"I don't understand," he said. "You should be sedated. Let's find out why."

Marcus placed his left hand over his belly button and said:

Dahmek	**Translation**
Fiurzbe Ivange shlarde.	Probe Eva's body.
Tulask shair biralautu gavert	Expose the blocking agent
Yarsh lutelirsk	That resists
Nui reilarku blirshk.	My chemical penetration.

Marcus touched Eva's head with his right hand. Eva moved her head back and forth to resist while thrashing her body and limbs about in hopes of escaping the straps. Marcus closed his eyes for a moment and opened them.

"Naltrexone!" he said. "So! You are taking an opioid receptor antagonist! But the solution is simple. I'll prepare a special chemical concoction just for you, Eva, to bypass your chemical block and render you unconscious."

"No, no!" Eva pleaded while Marcus prepared the syringe. "Marcus! You're making a terrible mistake. Marcus! I've helped you faithfully at the office. There's still time. I'll help you seek therapy. Don't end things this way!"

"Therapy?!" Marcus balked. "This *is* therapy!"

Marcus held Eva's arm firmly with one hand and injected the concoction into her arm with the other. Eva squirmed and screamed, but Marcus succeeded with the injection.

"How can you do this? How can you do this to me? We went dancing together! I thought maybe I could love you! Why, Marcus, why?!"

Marcus set the syringe aside and grasped the tooth extraction tool.

"Because I love you and your teeth," he said. "I must have them. I'll take good care of them. You'll be fine. We'll share this experience forever."

"NOOOO!" Eva yelled in agony.

Marcus attached the tool to Eva's first cuspid and tugged. Eva screamed in pain.

"It won't hurt much longer. The medication will put you asleep very soon," he said.

"Eva!" called Roberta's voice from Marcus's front door.

"Eva!" called Kay—also from the front door.

"You check the bedroom," Roberta's voice said.

Kay burst into the bedroom.

"Roberta, they're here! Help!" Kay called.

Marcus lunged into the hallway at Kay. Kay jumped to the side, but not before Marcus landed a punch in her shoulder. Roberta heard the ruckus and ran to help Kay. Roberta took a swing at Marcus, but he ducked and punched her in the back, sending her down the hallway. Kay found a vase and slammed it over the back of Marcus's head. Marcus fell to his knees, but he stood back up, turned around, swung his fist, and caught Kay in the side of the jaw. Dazed, Kay fell backward. Roberta got up, jumped on Marcus's back, wrapped her arms around his neck, and choked him. Marcus tried prying her arms off his neck, but she held fast. Marcus ran into the living room and turned around in hopes of swinging her off, but she didn't release her grip. Desperate, Marcus ran backward toward a wall and sandwiched Roberta in a collision between his back and the wall. He repeated this action several times. Roberta screeched in pain each time. She fought desperately to maintain her choking hold on Marcus, but the collisions weakened her stamina.

Hearing Roberta's screams, Kay shook off her daze, ran into the kitchen, and found an iron skillet. She snuck up on Marcus when he wasn't looking and tried to slam the skillet on his head, but he wouldn't stay still long enough to give her a good shot. More than once he nearly caught her between Roberta and the wall as he rammed backward. Roberta finally took the iron skillet from Kay and whacked it over Marcus's head. Marcus fell to the ground in a severe daze. He crawled slowly but could not get up.

"Kay—go help Eva," Roberta said.

Roberta held guard over Marcus in the living room with the skillet while Kay rushed to Eva's aid. Kay undid the restraints and helped Eva to her feet. Eva was groggy from the new medication and barely conscious. Kay walked her to the living room.

"Take her to the van," Roberta said.

"We need to call the police," Kay said.

"We will once you get Eva in the van," Roberta said.

Kay kept Eva's arm over Kay's shoulder and walked Eva to the van. Kay opened a side door and pushed Eva up the step into the van. The van had only two seats—the driver's and front passenger's. Behind the two seats was an open, flat area with carpet used for hauling equipment, but at that moment the flat area was empty. Eva collapsed onto the area and fell into a drug-induced sleep.

Kay returned inside. Marcus was face down with his left hand caught under his abdomen. Roberta kept a foot on his back.

"Call the police," Roberta said.

While Kay went for the telephone, Marcus mumbled something in Dahmek. Before Kay could dial a number, Marcus leapt to his feet and attacked Roberta. He punched her twice in the abdomen, she doubled over, and he punched her in the back. Roberta fell to the ground.

Kay dropped the telephone and rushed over to pick up the skillet, but Marcus blocked her, placed his hand to her neck, and lifted her. Kay struggled to free herself from his choking grip.

"It won't be you who calls the police but me," he said. "I could shoot you and Roberta for invading my house."

"You're choking me," Kay gasped. "You're choking your own sister."

"You'll have a harder time calling the police, won't you?" he laughed.

Marcus, while maintaining his grip on Kay, walked over to the telephone and began dialing. Meanwhile, Roberta—still in pain from his punches—crawled along the floor to the kitchen.

"Yes, this is Marcus Cracbern. I'm a homeowner at 1014 NE Fremont Street. I—"

Marcus screamed and dropped both the telephone and Kay. Roberta had stabbed Marcus in the thigh with one of two kitchen knives in her possession. Kay disconnected the telephone. Marcus reached behind his leg and pulled out the knife. Blood spurted onto the floor. Kay kicked Marcus in the groin and the head. Stunned, Marcus fell back. In a split second, Roberta cut open the stitches on Marcus's belly button with the second kitchen knife, inserted the knife below the duavisha, and flicked it into the air. Roberta caught the duavisha with her other hand and rushed Kay to the door.

"Let's go!" Roberta said.

"I'll kill you!" Marcus yelled as the two dashed out of the house and into Kay's van.

"Hit it!" Roberta yelled as the two took their seats.

Kay started up the engine, flipped the shifter into Reverse, and whipped the van backward out of the driveway with a turn into Fremont Street. Several cars Kay did not see honked at her and swerved to avoid hitting the van. Kay backed up too far, ran over a curb, and hit a tree. The collision jolted the three women back. Kay maintained her seat by holding onto the steering wheel, but Roberta slipped out of her chair and landed in the middle of the van on the floor with Eva.

"Sorry!" Kay said. "I'm nervous!"

"Get us out of here!" Roberta yelled.

Kay flipped the shifter in Drive and punched the gas pedal. The right rear wheel spun in muddy soil, and the van did not move.

"What's wrong? Why aren't we moving?" Roberta asked.

"We're stuck!" Kay said.

Kay kept pressing the gas pedal, but the tire only dug deeper. Marcus exited the house with a rag tied around his leg. He carried a baseball bat and hobbled toward the van with intent to inflict harm.

"Lock the doors!" Roberta said.

Kay locked the doors with the flick of a switch. Marcus reached the van and attempted to open a door, but he failed.

"Rock the van," Roberta said. "Put the van in Reverse, then Drive, and repeat."

Kay did as Roberta suggested. The van rocked back and forth but did not become free. Marcus swung the bat against the van and put dents in the body. Kay and Roberta screamed.

"Kay!" Roberta screamed.

"I'm trying!" Kay screamed back.

Marcus shattered the van windows on the non-driver's side. He reached in to open the side door. Kay and Roberta screamed again. Roberta leapt to the front passenger seat and beat Marcus's hand with her fist, but he responded by grabbing her hand. She fought to release his grip, but he wouldn't let go. He pulled her arm through the broken window, causing her head to hit the door frame and her shoulders to jam in the window glass. The glass—despite being safety glass—managed to gouge into her flesh. Kay rocked the van back and forth one last time, and the van gained traction. Kay punched the gas pedal, the right rear tire spun in the grass, and the van pushed to the street. The spinning tire squealed and the van took off west on Fremont—with Marcus holding onto the van and to Roberta— who by now had her head, an arm, and upper torso hanging out of the broken window. She tried beating Marcus off but without success. In desperation, she used her legs to pull her torso in with all her might. Marcus maintained his grip on her hand, and she pulled him closer to the opening. With her free hand, she grabbed for and found the oboe, stuck it through the window, and clocked Marcus on the noggin. Marcus let go and fell to the curb.

"Is Eva alive?" Kay asked.

"I'll check," Roberta said.

"I think we should take her to the hospital," Kay said. "Then we'll go to the police."

"Okay," Roberta said.

Roberta regained her composure and crawled from the front passenger seat to the floor. She checked Eva's pulse.

"Her pulse is getting weaker," Roberta said. "Take her to Legacy Emanuel. Take Fremont to Vancouver, and—"

"I know how to get there," Kay said. "Uh oh."

"Uh oh, what uh oh?" Roberta said.

"There's a car following us," Kay said.

"Do you see a car, Shawna?" Evanita asked.

"Yes," Shawna Johnny said. "It's a 1988 Chevrolet Caprice with a push bumper and a V8 engine. Marcus is driving it."

Roberta looked out the back window.

"It can't be," Roberta said.

The car accelerated rapidly, caught up to the van, drove alongside it, and plowed into the van's left side. The van swerved to the right. It took out a bench and newspaper stand before Kay regained control and directed the van back to the street.

"It's Marcus," Roberta said.

"I figured that," Kay said.

"He's trying to run us off the road," Roberta said.

"No kidding," Kay said.

"Just get us to Legacy Hospital," Roberta said.

"I can't get in the left lane," Kay said. "He's blocking."

"Push him out of the way," Roberta said. "The van has more mass."

Kay hit the brakes and clipped Marcus in the right rear corner. His Chevy veered in front of the van. Kay slowed more and veered to the left—avoiding Marcus and acquiring the left turn lane to Vancouver Avenue. The traffic signal was red, and Marcus gained enough time to get in the left turn lane behind Kay.

"He's right behind us," Roberta said.

"There's nothing I can do," Kay said. "I have to wait for the light."

Marcus crept up on the van until the Chevy's front push-bar bumper touched the van's rear bumper. Then Marcus hit the gas pedal and pushed the van into the intersection. A passing semi-truck trailer clipped the front bumper of the van and sent it spinning. Kay and Roberta screamed. Another semi-truck trailer locked its wheels to avoid hitting the van. It swerved and jackknifed in the intersection. The left turn arrow activated, and Kay turned the van around and headed south on Vancouver.

"Pull up to the curb at the hospital," Roberta said. "We'll carry Eva in directly."

Marcus caught up to the van again and cut into the front left corner. Kay spiked the brakes and turned right onto Cook Street to avoid him. She hit the gas pedal to the floor, but Marcus drove down Cook Street after them and performed the same maneuver—he cut in toward the front left corner to force the van into trees on the right side of the road. Kay spiked the brakes again, slalomed between trees into the American Red Cross parking lot, dodged parked cars, and exited the parking lot at the southwest corner onto the Interstate 405 entrance ramp. She attempted to drive the wrong way back toward the hospital, but traffic forced her to follow the one-way ramp onto the interstate. Marcus followed closely behind.

"Turn around," Roberta said. "Go back to Legacy Emanuel Hospital."

"I can't," Kay said. "I'll have to turn around somewhere else."

Kay picked up speed. She weaved through traffic with Marcus close behind, but traffic was such that Marcus could not get alongside or ahead of Kay. The two vehicles crossed the Willamette River on Fremont Bridge—the next bridge north of Broadway Bridge.

"Kay—I think there's another Legacy Hospital on this side of the river," Roberta said. "Take the ramp to U.S. 30."

Eva stopped breathing, and her heartbeat stopped.

"Dammit!" Roberta yelled. "She's in cardiac arrest!"

Marcus slammed his Chevy against the van, and the van scraped against the right-side barrier. Kay rammed back against Marcus.

"Kay—you've got to take the next exit off Highway 30 to 23rd Ave and turn south on 23rd," Roberta said as she pressed her hands on Eva's chest.

"What about Eva?" Kay asked.

"I'll perform CPR on Eva," Roberta said. "You deal with Marcus and take 23rd south to Legacy Good Samaritan Hospital."

Roberta pressed her lips against Eva's, forced air into Eva's lungs, and pressed Eva's chest. Kay reached the end of the ramp at the intersection of 23rd Avenue and Vaughn Street. The signal was red for Kay. Marcus barreled up from behind and showed no signs of stopping.

"He's going to force us into the intersection again!" Kay screamed.

"Then pull into traffic," Roberta screamed.

"I can't," Kay screamed back.

"Pull into traffic! Now!" Roberta screamed.

Kay ran the red light and dodged cross-flow traffic. A motorcycle slammed into the van's side. Kay pulled away. A car caught a back corner and loosened the bumper. Kay continued to pull away while the back bumper dragged on the road. She pushed the gas pedal to the floor and gained what speed she could south on 23rd Ave. Marcus followed but could not pass the van. He tried ramming the back, but the bumper caught his front wheel several times and misdirected his vehicle. She reached a traffic signal, it changed from green to yellow, and she raced through. Marcus stayed on her tail. Kay raced down 23rd with few additional stops. Side streets came to stop signs while Kay and Marcus blasted through. More than once, Marcus side-swiped cars parked on the side of the street while trying to clip Kay's van in the right rear.

"I can't get Eva's heart going on its own," Roberta said. "You must get us to Legacy Good Samaritan Hospital!"

"Tell Marcus that!" Kay said.

Kay caught up to a trolley in her lane. With the oncoming traffic and cars parked on the side, she could not pass it. Marcus slammed into the back of Kay's van and forced it into the trolley. The van's rear bumper came free and fell to the side.

"Kay!" Roberta said. "I'm trying to give Eva CPR!"

"Tell Marcus that!" Kay repeated.

Marcus continued slamming the van against the trolley. The trolley turned left onto Lovejoy Street toward Legacy Good Samaritan Hospital. Kay tried turning left to follow it, but Marcus slammed hard against the van and forced it south along 23rd Ave.

"You missed the turn!" Roberta said.

"Tell Marcus that!" Kay said again.

"Turn around, turn around!" Roberta said. "Or Eva will die! We've got to get into that hospital."

"I can't!" Kay said. "Marcus keeps slamming into me."

"Then pull away!" Roberta said.

Kay made a mad dash south on 23rd Ave. The street was too narrow to do a simple U-turn. Instead, Kay had the idea of turning around in a city block. She gained a bit of a lead by running a red light at Glisan Street forcing Marcus to wait for cross traffic to clear. She shot south of Flanders Street and turned left onto Everett Street.

"Why didn't you turn at Flanders Street?" Roberta asked.

"Because it's the next street," Kay said. "Marcus will expect me to turn there. This way I can lose him."

Kay took Everett Street east and turned north onto 22nd Ave. She reached Flanders Street just as Marcus crossed in front. He stopped short and blocked Kay's path.

"Turn right, turn right!" Roberta demanded.

Kay turned right onto Flanders Street. Marcus continued pursuit and clipped Kay's van in the left rear, but she managed to recover. Each time she slowed to turn left, Marcus caught up and attempted to force her off the road.

"I can't turn left," Kay said.

"You must. Eva's heart won't start, and CPR won't keep her alive forever!" Roberta said.

Kay took Flanders east until it ended at 16th Avenue. She turned left (north) and took it to Glisan Street, but she had to wait at the intersection. Marcus slowed down, touched the van's rear body, and timed his pushing of the van to collide with a passing truck. Marcus hit the gas and forced the van into Glisan Street. A truck hit the van and spun it such that it faced the wrong direction (east) of one-way west-bound Glisan Street.

"I can't wait!" Kay said.

Kay hit the gas and drove east on Glisan against traffic. Marcus followed closely. Kay narrowly missed several vehicles, and she turned left (north) onto 15th Avenue. Marcus followed the turn and rammed her hard in the left rear. The van turned sharply to the left and onto the entrance ramp to Interstate 405 north.

"Are you crazy?" Roberta said. "We can't get on the freeway now! We're out of time with Eva's life!"

"Marcus forced me!" Kay said. "I can't shake him!"

Roberta was now forced to consider the reality of Eva's condition. Eva was technically dead, but her tissues had not yet deteriorated, thanks to Roberta's CPR. But she had to get Eva's heart and lungs going again. There was no medical equipment in Kay's van. With Kay stuck on the interstate, there was no telling when or if they'd reach a hospital. Roberta stuck her hand in her pocket and felt the duavisha.

"I wonder," Roberta said. "No, it's superstition."

Roberta put the stone back. She hesitated, and she pulled the stone out.

"What the Hell, I'm at the end of my rope and Eva's," Roberta said.

Roberta placed the stone against Eva's belly button and continued CPR. Nothing. Roberta placed one hand on the duavisha and breathed into Eva's lungs. Nothing. Roberta placed a hand on the duavisha and another onto Eva's sternum and pumped Eva's heart. Nothing.

"Kay," Roberta yelled. "Take the 405 back across the Willamette and take the Legacy Emanuel Hospital exit ramp."

"Okay," Kay said. "I'll try."

"And don't let Marcus stop you this time," Roberta said. "I know, tell him that."

"You're picking up on me, Roberta," Kay said.

The van crossed the Willamette with Marcus in hot pursuit. Kay tried fending him off, but he continued slapping against the side of the van. Roberta continued CPR on Eva.

"Steady the van," Roberta said. "I can't do CPR like this."

"I'm doing the best I can," Kay said. "Yikes!"

Marcus slammed into the van and forced it sideways toward a center divider separating the forks to Interstate 405 north and Interstate 5 south. Kay fought and clawed with the steering wheel. She plowed through three water-filled barrels before regaining control, and she directed the van onto the ramp for Interstate 5 south.

"We missed the ramp for Legacy Emanuel," Kay announced.

"Dammit, dammit, dammit already!" Roberta said. "Wait, there's still hope. Take the next exit ramp. We'll go to Oregon State Hospital."

Marcus gained speed and zoomed along the left side of the van, but Kay hit the brakes and exited Interstate 5, taking the ramp to the intersection of Vancouver Avenue and Broadway Street. Smoke poured out of the van's front brake pads. Marcus hit the brakes and backed up until he could exit the freeway. With overheating brakes, Kay struggled to slow the van down at the end of the exit ramp for the red light.

"Hurry up, light, turn green!" Kay begged.

"Just go through!" Roberta yelled.

Roberta had the idea of placing the duavisha in her belly button as Marcus had done to his. Would this give her power? The idea was absurd, but she could think of nothing better. The light turned green. Kay hit the gas pedal and pulled away from the stop line. Roberta inserted the duavisha in her belly button. Marcus caught up to the van, passed it in the intersection of Vancouver and Broadway, and positioned the Chevy in front of Kay's van to block her.

"Turn left at the next street," Roberta yelled. "It's Weidler Street."

Kay swerved into the left turn lane, but Marcus swerved in the left lane ahead of her and brought his Chevy to a complete stop. Kay punched her brake pedal, the brake pads smoked, but the van wouldn't slow.

"The brakes are overheated!" Kay yelled. "Hold on!"

The van slammed into the back of the Chevy and hooked together, with the van's bumper riding atop the Chevy's rear-bumper push bar. Marcus pulled the van through the intersection and south on Vancouver as it became Wheeler. Kay did what she could to break free, but her brakes were overheated and wouldn't resist Marcus's pull. A horrible binding sound resonated through the van, like two gears out of sync with each other. Kay tried sheering left and right, but the Chevy's rear push-bar elevated the van such that the front wheels had little traction on the road. Kay tried accelerating the van, but that only helped Marcus's Chevy go faster and in doing so gave Marcus the extra power to pull the van through the intersection of Williams and Winning Way and onto the entrance ramp to southbound Interstate 5.

The binding and shaking of the two vehicles sent a shiver of horror through Roberta's body. The shiver activated the dua-visha and caused it to burrow and attach itself in Roberta's navel. The shiver crossed through barriers of space and time. Shawna Johnny shivered from the horror—this in turn activated his Moissan Ruby. Evanita, though only holding onto Shawna Johnny, shared in his apprehension. Jonara also felt the shivering, and her Moissan Ruby activated. The result was a collective vision by Jonara, Evanita, Shawna Johnny, and Roberta—a vision of two goddesses—the highest forms of life based solely on energy—coming together in an expression of love, donating the essence of themselves into an energy corridor of creation—a corridor which was in fact a toroid without beginning or end. These essences collapsed onto themselves into an infinitesimally small point. Roberta felt incredibly heavy and fell atop Eva. Evanita fell onto Shawna Johnny's lap, and Jonara fell onto the water's surface. The forces of Felifia's hand pulling on the back of Jonara's shirt and Nekara's hand pushing on Jonara's abdomen kept Jonara from falling into the water. The duavisha transferred a sense of love, benevolence, and life between Eva and Roberta, and Evanita and Johnny. Jonara felt herself caught in a conflict of love and hate between Felifia and Nekara.

Eva gasped for air, but just barely. Roberta's feeling of love for Eva gave just enough energy to twitch Eva's heart into a slow beat and nudge Eva's lungs into a slow breath. Evanita had a brief vision of her Coming-Of-Age ceremony at Broadway Unitarian Universalist Church, but it was a dual image of her initial failure and a later success.

Marcus pushed his Chevy up to freeway speed and continued pulling Kay's van behind him. The duo passed Steel Bridge. The three timelines of involved people (Roberta-Eva, Evanita-Johnny, and Jonara) saw the small point of light explode into blindingly white grains of light hyperspazzing out and across in all directions. Evanita had a brief vision of her visit to Saint Stellan Catholic Church while Jonara had a concurrent vision of the Castle Bravo nuclear explosion. Eva took another gasp of air, and the two goddesses succeeded in conceiving a cosmic zygote known as The Universe.

Marcus achieved freeway speed and swerved left and right such that the van slammed against the right-side barrier on the freeway. The van jumped and hopped and at times came off the Chevy's rear push-bar bumper, but it always returned. Shawna Johnny went into mild convulsions and shared visions with Evanita of seeing his sister die over and over again, and this vision alternated with a vision of Pastor Ephram hunting animals. Geneva saw a vision of her late husband escaping Franco's operatives with the help of Baptist missionaries. Jonara saw a vision of her first encounter with Cerafina in the altered timeline where Cerafina rejected Jonara and pushed her onto the walkway. The goddesses' zygote expanded and formed the first nebulas as the zygote descended into the one goddesses's cosmic uterus. Kay's van jostled around and flipped Eva and Roberta into the air such that Eva landed atop Roberta. Roberta was dazed from the impact and struggled to separate the visions from reality.

In one of the slammings against the side railing, the van came completely free from Marcus's Chevy. Kay hit the gas and accelerated past Marcus, but Marcus did not give up. He rammed the van from behind, and his push-bar front bumper caught into the body where the van's rear bumper was once attached. Marcus steered his Chevy from left-to-right-to-left and in so doing tore at the back of the van's body. Kay fought with all her might to keep the van steady. She hit the brakes, but again they failed. The duo passed Morrison Bridge. The cosmic zygote developed primitive galaxies. Eva gained some consciousness and with Roberta envisioned crossing an ancient land bridge from Israel to Egypt and back to Israel. Evanita relived her ride with Sharon in pursuit of a young male vandal who kidnapped Sheila. Jonara saw fast-forward images of Fantina and Axon getting married, Axon in battle, Axon's death, Fantina's flight to Palestine, and her flight to New Zealand. Geneva relived the moment where she and Aromani Pindos witnessed the self-immolation of Thích Quảng Đức in Saigon, South Vietnam.

Marcus hit his brakes hard. The inertia of the van pulled against the Chevy, and Marcus steered the Chevy back and forth. The Chevy pulled free. The van turned sideways abruptly and tilted with every desire of beginning a tumble, but Kay fought the van with the steering wheel. Instead of tumbling, the van went up on two wheels. Kay was pinned against her chair and driver's door while Eva and Roberta tumbled into the edge between the floor and left wall. Marcus accelerated, positioned his Chevy along the right side of Kay's van, and veered into the van, but Kay turned the steering wheel at the same time and sent the right-side wheels down. She landed the van on the Chevy's roof and nearly crushed Marcus. The duo passed Hawthorne Bridge. The cosmic zygote developed solar systems. Eva and Roberta saw a vision of each other when Roberta lectured Eva's class on tooth care with Merry and Glum Pumpkin. Evanita saw herself arguing with Sheila at Portland International Raceway. Johnny watched his mother go mad after his father died. Geneva witnessed her own birth from Margene. Jonara saw herself getting married to Cerafina.

Marcus hit the brakes. His Chevy fell back, and Kay's van drove over top his hood and onto the freeway. The two vehicles came to a brief stop before Kay hit the gas and pulled away. Marcus recovered from being dazed and followed Kay. The two vehicles continued on Interstate 5 as it crossed the Willamette on Marquam Bridge. The cosmic zygote developed into a cosmic fetus with highly developed galaxies and solar systems. The Damiriak solar system formed as did the human solar system of Sol, Earth, and companion planets. But there were no visions across Marquam Bridge except for Evanita's brief vision of the Arkham Atheist Group. Empty and devoid of imagination, feeling, and soul, Marquam Bridge was singularly used by Interstate 5 and was not a side road as the other bridges were. Evanita's vision faded quickly into bursts of alternating white and black without color.

The two vehicles crossed Marquam Bridge.

"Get off the freeway!" Roberta shouted. "We'll take Eva to the OHSU hospital."

Kay exited Interstate 5 at Hood Avenue. Marcus pulled up along the right side of the van, pinned it against the left-side barrier, and forced the van to a stop under Ross Island Bridge. The cosmic zygote was now a fetus, full of life but still developing. People developed on Eho Miriam, formed a civilization, and exiled the first criminals to Earth via an efferite sphere, thus spawning the first humans on Earth. Kay worked the van to escape the Chevy's barricade, but the van's engine stalled. Evanita and Johnny envisioned their prior visit to Cerossi Café when the flames moved quickly back and forth in nervous conflict. Roberta envisioned her trip to the ISIS meeting with her mother and the Studebaker's unique steering wheel design that mimicked a binary solar system she'd never seen. Roberta's vision quickly jumped to the moment Jane assaulted the unwelcome invader. In that moment, Marcus rushed the van, jumped in, pulled Kay out, and attacked her. Roberta—with the fresh image in her mind of her mother beating the male—jumped out of the van without hesitation and assaulted Marcus. Kay was freed from Marcus's grip and crawled into the van. Geneva envisioned Franco's troops assaulting innocent civilians. Evanita and Johnny envisioned Greg Applefoot's death in the River Wood and Battery factory fire. Jonara saw the men and women fighting on Eho Miriam followed by Fernando and the green-beam women fighting the Moors in Iberia.

A police cruiser pulled up to the scene. On seeing the cruiser, Roberta dropped her attack. A policeman exited the cruiser and raised his weapon against Marcus. Marcus rushed the policeman, and the officer fired. Marcus took the bullet in the shoulder but continued his rush and overpowered the officer. In that same moment, Kay managed to restart the van's engine. Roberta jumped into the van and checked on Eva.

"She's breathing on her own," Roberta said.

"But we might not be breathing pretty soon," Kay said. "Marcus is coming at us with the policeman's gun."

"Get us out of here!" Roberta yelled.

Kay backed up and hit Marcus. Marcus fell to the side. Kay put the van in Drive and pushed forward. She ran into the Chevy, causing a flat in the Chevy's tire. Kay drove the van south on Hood Ave, but Marcus jumped into the police car and pursued.

"We have to turn right for the hospital," Roberta said. "Ugh! My abdomen hurts! I'll need treatment too!"

With a fresh vehicle, Marcus pulled the police cruiser along the right side of the van and fired shots into the van's body. Two missed, but one grazed Eva's leg. She started bleeding lightly. Kay rammed the police cruiser, and the gun fell onto the pavement, but Marcus did not give up his position. He prevented Kay from turning right toward the hospital.

"Roberta," Kay said. "I think I damaged the radiator when I hit Marcus's Chevy. The van is blowing white smoke from the front."

"Dammit," Roberta said. "If it's not Eva's leg, it's the van's radiator. Can anything else go bad? Arg! My abdomen is killing me! I feel like I'm having a C-section!"

"You're in hysterics!" Kay said.

The pain in Roberta's abdomen came from the duavisha. It drew energy from Roberta, reenergized her ovaries, ripened an ovum from each ovary, and drew them painfully through tissue layers toward the duavisha.

"I can't turn right," Kay yelled. "But I can get back on Interstate 5."

"Don't get on the freeway," Roberta yelled.

The cruiser rammed the van in the back and clipped the left-rear corner just as the van passed under an Interstate 5 overpass. The van collided with the side barrier and came to a stop. Kay hit her head on the windshield and was dazed. Roberta and Eva slammed into the back of Kay's chair but were not seriously injured. The van's fuel line ruptured in the engine compartment and caught fire. Smoke filled the van's interior.

"Come on, we have to get out of here," Kay said.

"I have to bind Eva's leg wound first," Roberta said as she ripped cloth from her shirt and tied it around Eva's leg.

"No time," Kay said. "We have to get out—now!"

Kay helped Roberta lead Eva out of the van. Meanwhile, Marcus parked the cruiser behind the van. He stepped out, opened the cruiser's trunk, retrieved a shotgun, and walked deliberately toward the van.

"Marcus, stop," Kay said. "What you're doing is wrong. What would our parents say?"

"Your parents are not my parents," Marcus said. "They never were."

"They treated you like a son. They raised you!" Kay said.

"I'm here for two things," Marcus said, "the duavisha, and Eva's teeth!"

"What?!" Kay asked.

"You can't have Eva's teeth!" Roberta said. "But what is this duavisha thing you speak of?"

"You know exactly what it is," Marcus said. "You cut it out of my navel. See?"

Marcus lifted his shirt and exposed his bloody abdomen. He lowered his shirt and took aim at Roberta.

"The duavisha first," Marcus said. "Toss it here."

Roberta removed the duavisha from her belly button and held it out for all to see.

"That!" Kay gasped. "That's Mamma's! I haven't seen it since I was a little girl. You stole it from her!"

"It's mine," Marcus said. "It was always mine."

"She told me she found it in a cave in Africa," Kay said. "But it's cursed! Marcus! If you've been using it...why...no wonder you turned out the way you are!"

"What do you mean by that?" Marcus demanded to know.

"You're a rotten egg! A bad apple! A diseased tooth!" Kay said.

"You're wrong!" Marcus screamed, and he shot Kay in the leg.

Kay fell to the ground.

"You're next," Marcus said, "unless you cooperate. Give me the duavisha and Eva."

"No!" Roberta resisted.

"I'm warning you, MacNessi. Cooperate, and you'll live. Defy me, and I'll rain terror on you," Marcus threatened.

"You were powerful because of this duavisha," Roberta said. "But you don't have it now. I do."

Roberta placed the duavisha in her belly button. She held her left hand over her belly button and prepared to speak.

"Stop!" Marcus said. "You don't know what you're doing!"

As Roberta held her left hand over her abdomen, her bodily appearance changed. Her entire left side took on the appearance of Nekara the Red—dark hair, red skin, and fossilized flesh.

"Marcus!" Roberta's voice boomed.

Roberta stomped her left foot on the pavement, and the earth echoed with a deep thud. The van's fire stopped, and the smoke cleared.

"Aunt Nekara? Is that you?" Marcus quivered.

"Kay is bleeding!" Evanita said. "Shawna, do something!"

"Nekara," Shawna Johnny said. "Such an evil name."

"Shawna," Evanita said. "What are you saying? Help Kay!"

"We can't let Kay die," Jonara said to Felifia.

"Look!" Felifia said.

A whirlpool developed in the pool just in front of Jonara and Felifia. Jonara looked into the whirlpool and saw past crimes of humanity—wars, conquests, murder, assault, theft, deceit, and corruption. The many wailing hands of failure reached up for Jonara's Moissan Ruby. At the same time, Shawna Johnny felt the hands of failure beckoning him into the pool.

"Shawna," Evanita said. "What is it?"

Shawna Johnny jumped into the water as did Jonara. The whirlpool had attracted them, and the hands of failure pulled them under. The whirlpool shrank, and just before it collapsed into nothingness, Felifia dove into its center.

Jonara and Johnny stood together in the vastness of nowhere while a luminous image of Felifia approached. Felifia extended a hand to each of them and touched their Moissan Rubies, which was in fact the same Moissan Ruby in different times. Felifia exerted an energy and force upon Jonara and

Johnny—an energy force growing brighter and stronger until Johnny and Jonara merged into Felifia's body. Felifia, with Jonara and Johnny sharing her feelings and experiences, left the vastness of nowhere and appeared in front of the van, unseen by the others. She walked around the front of the van and knelt by Kay. Kay's body shook and jolted.

"Who are you?" Marcus said to Felifia.

Roberta's body turned around.

"Ack! Felifia!" Roberta's body said.

"Leave her body, Nekara," Felifia said as she repaired Kay's wound. "Marcus, drop your weapon. It no longer has power."

"Get away from Kay," Marcus said to Felifia. "Nekara—help me."

"I will help you Marcus," Roberta's body said, "as soon as I deal with Felifia."

"Are you such a coward that you must hide in the body of an Earth woman?" Felifia asked.

"I'm not afraid of anyone," Roberta's body said.

The Nekara half of Roberta separated from Roberta. Roberta returned to her full self, but she collapsed from the strain. She reached for the duavisha in her belly button, but it was gone.

"You no longer have the duavirt," Nekara said to Roberta. "It now belongs to me."

"I dealt with you on Montseny Mountain, and I'll deal with you again," Felifia said.

"Don't count on it, Felifia," Nekara said. "I am animated again, thanks to the duavirt that I now possess. But I have a bonus surprise. In this duavirt, I have two seeds of life."

"Nekara," Felifia said. "Do not tamper with life on this planet. It does not belong to you."

"Does anyone own a garbage dump?" Nekara said. "All life on this planet owes its existence to our sanitation department. Or have you forgotten how the everyday toxins of Eho Miriam were eliminated?"

"I know they were deposited on this planet, but that gives you no right to interfere with life here," Felifia said.

"I intend to prove something to you, Felifia. I have the power of life," Nekara said.

"I know what you are capable of," Felifia said. "You need not brag to me."

"Oh but I must. A creator of life should not be kicked out of the garden she created. I was forced out of the Damiriak solar system, but I will not be forced from the life I am about to create!"

"You're playing Goddess!" Felifia said.

"I am a goddess!" Nekara yelled back.

"This isn't how life should procreate!" Felifia said. "Independent choice—"

"Has never been a part of life. Life is driven by the need to consume energy. There is no choice in consumption. And now, consumption begins again."

Nekara touched the van. Dents, cracked glass, and mechanical damage healed themselves, including bumpers.

"Stop, Nekara," Felifia said. "The game is over."

"No, it's just beginning," Nekara said. "Behold! The dark vortex of humanity!"

A spiraling downward whirlpool-like funnel developed in the pavement before them. Marcus stepped to the edge of the vortex and knelt. Eva also knelt by the vortex. Marcus drooled and fingered his mouth, praying and begging for more female teeth. Eva clutched her temples and begged for more alcohol, amphetamines, and morphine. Kay walked toward the vortex, but Roberta held her back.

"No!" Roberta shouted. "This is some trick of Satan! He lures us with irresistible temptations!"

"There is no power that can overcome the vortex of combined human cravings on this planet," Nekara said to Felifia. "I have tapped into this power with my duavirt. I will use this power to create humans in my own spirit."

"You cannot succeed," Felifia said. "You are on a fast-track to destructive nowhere. Stop the vortex, Nekara. Stop it now and return to the Damiriak solar system with me."

"I didn't create the vortex," Nekara said, "and I won't let a bad thing go to waste."

"Torturing Eva with temptation is a waste, and I will fight to protect her," Felifia said.

"Eva I need most of all. I will not sacrifice the vortex of vice I have assembled for her," Nekara said. "Kay and Roberta—run for your lives. Marcus and Eva—enter the van."

The vortex shrank and disappeared. Marcus entered the van. Kay held her position, but Nekara changed shape into the most terrifying monster Kay could imagine. Kay ran alongside the road against the flow of traffic screaming for her life. Eva started for the van, but Roberta stopped her.

"I don't know who or what you are," Roberta said to Nekara. "But you have no right barking orders around here. For your information, Marcus was trying to kill us. He is not welcome in Kay's van. And you don't have the right to scare Kay like that. Now get out of here before I call the police!"

"You underestimate me, Roberta," Nekara said.

Nekara wiggled her fingers across her arm, pointed to Roberta, and squeezed her fist. Roberta fell into an uncontrollable fit—a fit where she scratched her skin to the point of tearing it open. Blood covered Roberta's arms from scratching.

"Go in the van, Eva," Nekara ordered.

With Roberta distracted by her scratching fit, Eva blindly followed Nekara's orders and entered the van, despite Roberta's calls to resist. Felifia shouted:

Mirsua	**Translation**
Derilakos e serotonina	Increase serotonin
Dis Roberitangas e sinenis	To Roberta's arms
Dhakus luripos e sases nizaolas	And relieve her itching.

Roberta's itching stopped. Nekara lifted her own foot, squeezed it, put her foot down, pointed to Roberta's foot, and squeezed her hand in the air to make a fist. Roberta fell to the ground in pain from a foot cramp. Felifia shouted:

Mirsua	**Translation**
Luderabos e semotatats	Restore balance
Dis Roberitangas loivis	To Roberta's nerves
Isus e sases posis.	In her feet.

Roberta's foot cramp stopped. Nekara punched her own abdomen, pointed to Roberta's, and squeezed her hand in the air to make a fist. Roberta doubled over with an intestinal cramp. Felifia chanted:

Mirsua	Translation
Ois biorisos Nekarangas lialitis	Do not drink Nekara's words
Ilus nietos	Or eat
Sases divurus terilosas.	Her melodic intonation.
Peiseis gerutheios kailes fikanikis.	Both will give you cramps.

Roberta's cramps subsided.

"How dare you make fun of my speech," Nekara said.

Nekara beat on her chest three times, pointed at Roberta, and clenched a fist. Roberta came down with a severe case of asthma and struggled to breathe. Felifia spoke:

Mirsua	Translation
Lekos maus Kelotikus e saradalas	Let no Celtic woman
Kauvutos lasipaolas butiapas	Suffer breathing deprivation
Veletus Nekarangas kauvaipas.	From Nekara's suffocation.

Roberta's normal breathing returned. Nekara pointed to her own eyes, wiggled her fingers toward her eyes, pointed at Roberta's eyes, and clenched her fist. A light flashed in front of Roberta's eyes six times per second. Felifia closed Roberta's eyelids and said:

Mirsua	Translation
Daikos tesunus ipidilokatus waibas!	End this bipolar madness!
Luderabos Roberitangas fiaisas.	Restore Roberta's vision.

The flashing cleared from Roberta's vision.

"Everything you do, I can counter," Felifia said to Nekara.

"Not everything," Nekara said.

Dahmek	Translation
Tuarsne Roberta ishte dhor noshk.	Change Roberta into a man.

"*Lusaikos!* (Revoke)!" Felifia yelled as she lunged at Nekara.

Felifia tackled Nekara to the ground and prevented the Dahmek chant. Nekara kicked Felifia off. Felifia swiped her foot at Nekara's head and connected with her jaw. Nekara's head jolted back in recoil, but Nekara would not stay still. She launched a hook punch into Felifia's shoulder and sent Felifia to the ground. Felifia jumped to her feet and swiped Nekara's leg out from under her. Nekara fell on her back, but she rolled backward, stood up, did a handspring, and caught her lower leg in Felifia's collar bone. Felifia's collar bone cracked, and she cried in pain. Felifia swung her fist at Nekara, but Nekara ducked—allowing Felifia's momentum to carry through, and Nekara backhanded Felifia in the side. Felifia fell to the ground. Nekara kicked Felifia in the head. Felifia's body jerked momentarily, and she remained on the ground.

"Nekara, my junior wife," Felifia said in a low voice. "I love you."

"I don't need love," Nekara said.

Roberta approached Nekara with intent to attack, but Nekara simply shoved Roberta to the ground.

"I don't need you anymore," Nekara said.

Nekara walked past Felifia and Roberta en route to the van's driver's door. Roberta stood up and started a lunge at Nekara, but Nekara turned around and backhanded Roberta across the face. Roberta fell to the ground in pain with blood running out of her nose and mouth. Nekara stepped in the van's driver's seat, started the engine, shifted the selector to Drive, punched the gas pedal to the floor, and sent the rear tires squealing as the van pulled away. The van merged onto and headed south on Macadam Avenue.

"Felifia or whoever you are," Roberta said, "we have to catch them. Felifia!"

Roberta grasped Felifia by the shoulders and lifted her with Johnny and Jonara still inside Felifia.

"Felifia, you have to drive the cruiser," Roberta said.

"You have an idea?" Felifia asked.

"Yes, but there's no time to explain," Roberta said.

Roberta hurried Felifia to the cruiser's driver's seat. Roberta ran around to the passenger seat and jumped in.

"What about Kay?" Felifia asked.

"Dammit!" Roberta said. "We have to pick her up first. Put the cruiser in Reverse. Hurry!"

Felifia moved the selector into Reverse and hit the gas pedal. The cruiser weaved backward under the Interstate 5 overpass and alongside the right shoulder on Hood Avenue. When the cruiser reached Lane Street, Roberta shouted for Felifia to stop.

"Kay! Get in!" Roberta yelled.

Kay sat on the edge of Lane Street and shook her head, "No."

"This is an emergency!" Roberta yelled. "Eva's been kidnapped! Get in!"

Kay hesitated. She stood up, sat down, and stood up. Finally, she darted into the back seat of the cruiser, and in that time, Felifia had moved the selector from Reverse to Drive, so when Kay closed the back door, Felifia hit the gas and sent the cruiser racing south on Hood Ave, back under Interstate 5, and southbound onto Macadam Avenue. Roberta stared to the left and saw the Willamette River and Ross Island.

"These vehicles are primitive," Felifia said, "and Nekara has a large lead."

"We must catch her," Roberta said. "When we reach the van, I want you to pull up next to the bumper. I'll crawl onto the hood of this cruiser and jump onto the van."

"That's suicide!" Kay yelled. "You'll fall off and die!"

"How else can we stop them?" Roberta said. "It's the only chance."

"We can't stop them," Felifia said. "It's too late."

"It can't be," Roberta said. "I refuse to believe it's too late."

Felifia continued accelerating south on Macadam Avenue.

"There are two southbound lanes," Roberta said. "If pulling behind doesn't work, we can pull alongside, and I can jump to the van that way."

"That's even worse," Kay said. "At least your first idea allowed you to fall back on this car. But jumping between vehicles with no safety behind is definite suicide. Roberta! It won't work."

"She's right," Felifia said.

"I have to try!" Roberta said.

The cruiser passed Willamette Park, raced past Butterfly City Park, and nearly reached Sellwood Bridge when the three heard a loud smash through concrete from the middle of Sellwood Bridge. The three looked and saw Kay's van plummeting off the north end of Sellwood Bridge into the Willamette River.

"Eva!" Roberta and Kay screamed.

"Turn around," Roberta said, "and pull into that boating center."

Felifia turned the cruiser around and pulled into Staff Jennings Boating Center, but the facility was closed.

"Dammit," Roberta said. "Go back north on Macadam Avenue. There's gotta be someone with a boat who'll take us on the water."

Felifia drove the cruiser north on Macadam Avenue. Roberta and Kay watched the Willamette River closely for the van, but the van suddenly sank.

"It's gone!" Kay said.

"Pull into Butterfly Park," Roberta said.

Felifia parked the cruiser, but not in Butterfly Park. She performed a U-turn and parked the cruiser on the shoulder of southbound Macadam Ave.

"What are you doing?" Kay asked.

"This is the point where Marcus hijacked your van," Felifia winked to Kay.

Kay and Roberta returned quizzical stares, but there was no time for explanation. The three ran across Macadam Avenue, rushed into the park, along a walkway, and onto moorage on the Willamette. Several people on the docks were standing and pointing to the place on Sellwood Bridge where the van had gone off. Two boats left the docks and headed to the spot where the van sank.

"Please sir," Roberta begged a boat owner, "take us on the river. My friend is in that van."

"Uh, I don't know you," the boat owner said.

"Please, it's an emergency," Roberta said.

"I can't help you," the owner said. "Even if I took you out, I got no equipment for diving."

"I'll dive in myself if I have to!" Roberta said.

The boat owner stopped talking and turned his back.

"This is an emergency!" Roberta screamed.

"Come," Felifia said. "I know someone who will help us."

Felifia led Roberta and Kay along the docks until they met a short, unattractive woman with thick glasses, thin hair, and oversized facial features. She sat by her small yacht and enjoyed a large mug of beer. Felifia approached the woman and whispered something in her ear. The woman jumped to her feet and dumped her beer in the river.

"Come aboard!" the woman said. "Hurry!"

Felifia, Roberta, and Kay boarded the woman's small yacht. The woman unhitched the little yacht from the dock, fired up the engine, and launched the foursome onto the river.

"Wow! This boat has good power!" Kay said.

"Did I not promise?" Felifia said.

"What did you say to her?" Roberta whispered to Felifia.

"I told her your wife was kidnapped and is drowning in the sinking van," Felifia said. "She understood completely."

"My name is Maggie," the woman said. "I have scuba equipment on board. Any of you dive?"

"Not me," Kay said.

"I do," Roberta said.

"There's gear in the cabin," Maggie said. "Suit up and get the gear ready. I'll dive with you."

"Don't go where the other boats are searching," Felifia said.

"Huh?" Maggie said. "Based on the river current and the van's entry point, it should be—"

"I know," Felifia said. "The kidnapper has ways of deceiving your instruments. Head directly to the bay at Ross Island."

"Okay," Maggie said. "I hope you're right."

While other search boats circled one another progressively north of Sellwood Bridge, Maggie pushed her yacht to full speed.

"Hold the wheel steady while I suit up," Maggie said to Kay.

"I don't know how to—" Kay tried to explain, but Maggie had already relinquished the steering wheel to Kay.

"Don't worry, I'll help you," Felifia said.

The yacht proceeded quickly to Ross Island Bay.

"Here," Felifia said. "Cut the engine."

"How?" Kay asked.

"Like this," Felifia said as she turned the engine off.

Maggie finished suiting up and dropped the anchor. Roberta, who had her suit and air tank, helped Maggie with her tank.

"Stay close," Maggie said. "Fresh water is notorious for low visibility. How many people are we talking about?"

"One," Roberta said.

"Two," Kay said at the same time.

"We're only concerned about Eva," Roberta said.

"You can't let Marcus die," Kay said, "even if he is evil. And what about that Nekara woman?"

"Three people?" Maggie asked.

"Don't worry about Nekara," Felifia said. "I'm sure she's already escaped."

"One or two?" Maggie asked.

"Two," Felifia said.

"We'll take an extra tank each," Maggie said.

The two grabbed extra tanks, stood at the stern of the yacht, and jumped into the bay.

"I want to know what's happening," Kay said to Felifia. "Can you tell me anything?"

"The van is at the bottom of the bay," Felifia said. "Roberta and Maggie are descending to the van."

"Are Eva and Marcus alive?" Kay asked.

"Barely," Felifia said.

"Is Nekara down there?" Kay asked.

Felifia closed her eyes and doubled over. She screamed in extreme pain. Johnny and Jonara divided from Felifia with Johnny returning to his chair next to Evanita and Geneva, and Jonara returning to a position standing on the pool-water's surface in the Caves of Healing.

"Felifia?" Kay asked.

Felifia faded from Maggie's yacht, but as she did, she said one last thing to Kay:

"Nekara is gone."

CHAPTER 13:

A Misunderstanding

2007 Dec 8, Sat. The Caves of Healing. Carreña, Spain.

"The vision stopped," Evanita said.

"Briefly," Geneva replied.

Jonara found herself standing atop the pool's surface. She looked for Felifia next to her, but the last traces of light outlining Felifia's body disappeared. Jonara fell into the pool with a splash. She swam out and stood on the dry cave just behind Evanita, Johnny, and Geneva.

"I'm confused. What just happened?" Evanita asked.

"Marcus tried stealing your mother's canine teeth," Johnny said.

"I know," Evanita said. "He drugged her."

"The naltrexone slowed the absorption of Rohypnol," Johnny said, "enough for her to resist. He gave her a strong chemical concoction to subdue her. Unfortunately, the brew was too strong and stopped her heart. Roberta gave your mother cardiopulmonary resuscitation. She was hoping Kay could get your mother to a hospital to save her, but Marcus was always in the way."

"He wanted her teeth that badly that he had to chase her?" Evanita asked.

"He was caught in the act, and he had to silence the witnesses," Johnny said. "But he also wanted your mother's teeth—even during the pursuit. I think if it weren't for that desire, he would have been more forceful in killing Kay, Roberta, and your mother."

"Shawna, for a moment I thought you weren't here," Evanita said.

"I wasn't," Johnny replied. "I was in the body of Felifia."

"Felifia—that woman in white. And what about that other woman?" Evanita asked.

"Nekara?" Johnny asked.

"Yeah."

"They seem to know each other. And they have powers. Miss Geneva—are you sure this really happened?" Johnny asked.

"This is what Kay and Roberta told me," Geneva said. "I suppose they could have embellished. But I tend to doubt it. Those two women—Felifia and Nekara—are almost symbolic representations of good and evil, don't you think?"

"If Felifia is good, then she failed. Good is supposed to triumph over evil, but Nekara beat up Felifia and kidnapped my mother," Evanita said.

"Evil often takes the first bite," Geneva said. "But if good perseveres long enough, good will overcome evil."

"Felifia left at the end of the vision," Evanita said. "She abandoned Kay and Roberta."

"Yes, I know," Geneva said. "There are times when good leaves us for no apparent reason. But we shouldn't stop striving for good. That's what life is really about, Evanita. Trudging along and harboring past evils in our hearts subjects us to the devil's desires."

"I don't believe in the devil," Evanita said.

"You don't have to," Geneva said. "The application is still the same. And so is the result. Evil begets evil, Evanita. It's contagious—like a disease. Good morals and ethics are like an immune system to fight against disease. When we compromise our bodies, our immune systems fail, disease takes over, and death is imminent. It is this way for our souls too, or our psyches if you're not religious. But you see—the application is the same."

"What happened to my mother in the van?" Evanita asked. "She couldn't have drowned. And why did Nekara order Marcus in the van? And what was going on with that—what was it called—a duavisha or a duavirt? And those foreign languages."

"Miss Geneva may be right about Felifia and Nekara being good and evil, but I also think they were or are real women from outside the United States—possibly from outer space," Johnny said.

"Aliens? Like Roswell?" Evanita asked.

"That was a weather balloon," Johnny said. "But back to the issue at hand—I've never heard languages like that before, except from this Moissan Ruby."

"This stone lets you hear a language?" Evanita asked. "Wait, I remember something. Little Voice used a language too, and she said the stone told her what to say. Is this true?"

"In a way," Johnny said. "The one Felifia spoke sounded almost identical to the one I've used with this stone. But Nekara spoke a different language that I do not understand."

"Do you believe your stone is from outer space?" Evanita asked.

"I do. I think the power in this stone is the same power Felifia and Nekara use," Johnny said.

"They said something about using Earth for a garbage dump. I thought evolution explained how life developed on this planet."

"There's also the story of creation," Geneva said.

"Apparently, Felifia and Nekara believe their people started life on this planet," Johnny said. "Who can know for sure how life started?"

"And how did my life start?" Evanita asked.

Johnny and Geneva fell silent.

"Did Marcus rape my mother in the van?" Evanita asked, almost in tears.

"Don't jump to conclusions!" Geneva said.

"Did she become pregnant in the van?" Evanita asked, still in tears.

"Should we tell her?" Johnny asked.

"She'll misunderstand," Geneva said, "but tell her anyway. One must dip a toe in the water before jumping in."

"Yes," Johnny said. "Your mother became pregnant with you while in the van—when it was underwater!"

Evanita let out a blood-curdling scream.

"Evanita!" Geneva called. "Evanita! Get a grip!"

Evanita jumped up and ran for the exit. Johnny ran after her and stopped her.

"No, no!" Evanita screamed. "This is too much to bear!"

"You must see the rest!" Johnny said.

"No!" Evanita said as she struggled against Johnny.

"Evanita," Geneva said. "Do not run away from the truth! You've always gone for a run in the past, but this time you must sit and witness the beginning. You must!"

"No!" Evanita struggled again.

Geneva stood up, walked over to Evanita, and hugged her.

"I'm scared, Grandma, I'm scared!" Evanita said.

"I know," Geneva said.

"What am I going to do?"

"You'll go on living like the rest of us," Geneva said. "Look for good in everything, Evanita."

"What good can there be in my creation?" Evanita asked.

"Someone who runs away from issues says that sort of thing," Geneva said. "To quit before trying is to plant a seed without watering it. You must stand up to rain and stormy weather for the plant to grow."

"I...I...know," Evanita said. "Are you going to tell me this is part of growing up?"

"You know what?" Geneva said. "No one completely grows up. Each year of our lives, we gain a little more experience about how the universe works. Harm comes our way—harm we never knew existed. When I was your age, I thought that when I reached eighteen, I was 'grown up,' and I'd have all the wisdom I needed to live a perfect life. But I was wrong. There are ups and downs to life as long as we live. If we work hard and have a little luck, we have more ups. But the challenges never go away. Never. Running away will bring back problems ten times as bad as before."

"My past...this pool...Marcus...the world," Evanita said. "They're all against me."

"We're here with you, Evanita. We won't let harm come to you," Geneva explained. "Come then. Let's sit down. It will be over soon enough."

Geneva led Evanita back to her chair, and the three sat. Geneva read from her diary, and the three (plus Jonara) returned to Ross Island Bay.

1989 Oct 14, Sat Eve. Ross Island Bay. Portland, Oregon.

Maggie surfaced with Marcus. Kay helped Marcus climb aboard Maggie's yacht, and he sat down. He spat out water and gagged, but he was otherwise conscious and semi-alert. Maggie dove back down.

"What happened?" Kay asked. "Where's Eva?"

"Happened?" Marcus asked.

"Yeah!" Kay said. "That woman drove my van off Sellwood Bridge! Don't you remember?"

Marcus rubbed his head.

"I have a really bad headache," Marcus said. "I don't remember anything. I was working on a patient, and now I'm here. Is today Wednesday?"

"No, it's Saturday. Saturday, October 14th, 1989," Kay said.

"That can't be. This is 1988," Marcus said in all honesty.

"You have amnesia?" Kay asked. "Are you telling the truth?"

"Kay—you're my sister," Marcus said. "You've always been able to read me. I'm telling the truth. To me, this is October of 1988. I don't know anything about a 1989."

Marcus looked directly into Kay's eyes.

"You are telling the truth," Kay said. "It's a rare moment, but you are. Most likely you hit your head when the van collided with the side barrier, and the concussion gave you this amnesia."

"My teeth feel strange," he said. "And my canine teeth are gone. Did I injure them?"

Kay looked inside Marcus's mouth.

"Yeah, your canine teeth are missing. The rest of your teeth look different somehow," Kay said. "So you don't know what happened to Eva?"

"Eva who?" Marcus asked.

"Eva Carreña!" Kay said.

"Never heard of her," Marcus said.

"She's one of your dentists," Kay said. "Now do you remember?"

"I remember Frank and Milo," Marcus said. "Kay—what are you doing in Portland?"

"I work here in MacNessi Dental," Kay said.

"Roberta? She's in Texas," Marcus said.

"I'll explain later," Kay said.

Marcus probed for the duavisha in his belly button, but to his surprise it was missing.

"I...I'm missing...where did..." Marcus stammered.

Marcus was caught by surprise regarding the missing duavisha, but he didn't want to admit anything to Kay.

"Look, they're surfacing!" Kay said.

Roberta and Maggie lifted Eva to the surface.

"Help me, Marcus," Kay said.

Marcus helped Kay lift Eva to the yacht. Eva was unconscious.

"We gave her oxygen, but she's not responding," Roberta said from the water.

Kay went to work on giving Eva CPR.

"What's going on?" Marcus asked.

Roberta climbed into the yacht, took off her tanks, and traded off with Kay.

"Come on, Eva, wake up!" Roberta said.

"Mama!" Evanita said. "Mama, wake up! Grandma—is she dead? She can't be dead! Mama! You can't die! You have to have me!"

Johnny gave Geneva a look as if to say, "A while ago, she didn't want to be alive. Now she's urging her mother to wake up."

Geneva nodded in affirmation as if to say, "Yes, a love for one's mother does strange things."

Eva coughed up water and awoke.

"Ugh!" Eva said. "That was one bad...what's everyone looking at?"

"You!" Roberta said. "You died twice on us."

"I did?" Eva asked. "I remember hitting the barrier on the bridge. And now I'm here."

"You remember more than Marcus," Kay said. "He's forgotten everything in the last year."

"I don't believe that for a moment," Roberta said. "Marcus has been known to lie before."

"Marcus!" Eva said.

Eva sat up and backed away in fear of Marcus. Roberta shushed and comforted her.

"Don't worry, he can't hurt you now," Roberta said.

"Are you sure there's no one else?" Maggie asked Roberta. "I can dive down and take another look."

"No," Roberta said. "There's no one else. We owe you too much already, and I won't have you dive down alone. Come on the yacht, Maggie. Let's return to the docks."

"All right," Maggie replied.

Maggie boarded her yacht and removed her tanks. She piloted the watercraft back to her dock and secured it from floating away.

"That's him," a uniformed officer said.

Several armed officers approached Marcus.

"You're under arrest for assaulting an officer and stealing his patrol car," said another officer.

"What? I didn't do anything!" Marcus protested. "Roberta, Kay—help me."

"I saved a bad guy?" Maggie said.

"Don't feel badly," Roberta reassured Maggie. "You didn't know. But at least Marcus will now receive fair treatment."

"This is an outrage!" Marcus said. "Somebody! Anybody!"

The police hauled him away.

"Officer," Kay said. "That was my van that Marcus drove into the river. It's in the bay by Ross Island."

"Can you come down to the station for a statement?"

"Sure," Kay said. "Eva—will you be all right?"

"I'll take her home," Roberta said.

Kay left with the officer. Eva and Roberta remained with Maggie.

"I don't know what's wrong with me," Roberta said. "I can't take Eva home. My car isn't here. I'll have to call a taxi."

"Let me take you home," Maggie said. "Or if you're hungry, I know this great restaurant down the way. It's called, *Dairy Duck.*"

Roberta rolled her eyes.

"What do you say to *Dairy Duck*, Roberta?" Eva laughed.

"Have you been there before?" Maggie asked.

"Yes, we have," Roberta said.

"Don't worry, Roberta, I won't drink," Eva said.

Roberta's eyes lit up in surprise. Maggie gave Eva a funny look.

"I'm a recovering alcoholic," Eva said. "I have Roberta to thank for treatment."

Eva winked at Roberta, and Roberta let out a sigh of relief.

"Congratulations," Maggie said. "We can visit the restaurant side. I'm buying."

"Oh no, no, no," Roberta said. "We owe you so much. I'll buy."

"Naw," Maggie said. "Let me buy. I never take advantage of people in the same day I help them. And afterward, I'll give you a ride home. No drinking in the bar."

"Deal," Eva and Roberta said.

Eva and Roberta joined Maggie in her car.

"It's a full moon tonight," Maggie said. "I used to have a girl-friend, but we broke up six months ago. How long you two love-birds been married?"

Eva looked at Roberta suspiciously.

"Only a very short time," Roberta said, and she held a finger over her mouth to Eva.

"Oh, newlyweds," Maggie said. "Well, the spark is always strongest when the relationship is young. I was with my girl-friend for ten years. I would have married her if the law permit-ted. But I must say, Denmark is the only country that recogniz-es same-sex marriage, well, they call it a 'registered partnership', but you know what I mean. Hey—you must have flown over there to get married, eh?"

"Yeah," Roberta said. "Denmark."

"Well good for you," Maggie said. "If enough of us push for our rights, we'll marry just as freely as breeders."

Eva felt queasy.

"Pull over," Eva said. "I feel sick."

Maggie pulled over, and Eva threw up on the side of the road.

"Thanks," Eva said.

"You sound sick," Maggie said. "Oh, Maggie, you silly sparrow. You can't just take people to dinner and forget the ordeal they've been through."

"No need to apologize," Roberta said. "But I am concerned. Eva—did you swallow river water?"

"Maybe," Eva said. "But I...no, it's impossible."

"What's impossible?" Roberta asked.

"This is going to sound silly," Eva said. "My symptoms resemble morning sickness."

Maggie laughed.

"That's a switch. A lezzie feeling like a breeder," Maggie said.

Roberta stared at Eva suspiciously.

"I'm not laughing," Roberta said.

"Oh, I shouldn't have said anything," Maggie said. "I'm so sorry."

"Don't worry," Roberta said. "But I am curious about my Eva."

"I'm not pregnant," Eva said.

"That she knows of," Geneva explained to Evanita.

"She has morning sickness?" Evanita asked. "But that's not normal! No one gets morning sickness that fast!"

"Your conception wasn't normal," Geneva said.

"Huh?" Evanita asked.

"You'll see," Geneva added.

The three women parked at *Dairy Duck* and walked inside. Claudia was their waitress again.

"Claudia, this is Maggie," Roberta said. "Maggie, Claudia."

"Nice to meet you," Claudia and Maggie said.

"Maggie is a heroine today," Roberta said. "She saved Eva's life."

"Oh my God!" Claudia said. "What happened?"

"It was nothing," Maggie said. "Roberta is the one who—"

"Don't be modest, Maggie," Roberta said. "Claudia—Eva was trapped in a van that sank in the Willamette River. A coworker of mine and I were on shore and looking for someone to help us fish Eva out. We came across Maggie here, and she took us on her yacht."

"You have a yacht?" Claudia asked. "I love yachts."

"It's just a little thing," Maggie said. "Nothing really to—"

"Maggie's yacht has more power than a vibrator," Roberta bragged.

"Roberta!" Maggie said sheepishly, but Claudia perked up with interest.

"I'd like a ride on your yacht," Claudia flirted with Maggie.

"Maggie took us to that little bay by Ross Island," Roberta continued. "She loaned me a wetsuit and tanks—"

"You scuba dive too?" Claudia said. "Do you dive in the Pacific?"

"From time to time," Maggie added. "But the real heroine is—"

"Maggie and I dove down while Kay commanded the yacht," Roberta said.

"Whatever happened to that other woman?" Maggie asked. "The one with the white outfit?"

"I don't know," Roberta said. "I just realized the same thing when you mentioned her. I'll have to ask Kay."

"What about the dive?!" Claudia asked with anticipation.

"Maggie can descend and ascend quicker than any diver I've ever met. I'd have the bends if I moved that quickly," Roberta said.

"You can go down that quickly?!" Claudia asked. "What are you doing later tonight?"

"Roberta!" Maggie said.

"Maggie is a little shy about such things at first," Roberta said. "It's been six months since she's had a companion, and—"

"Oh you poor thing!" Claudia said. "Let's get together after I get off work."

"But I—" Maggie said.

"You certainly need it," Claudia said, "and with you being a heroine and all, this calls for a celebration. I know the best clubs in town, that is if you have an inkling for something more than *Dairy Duck*."

"Roberta," Maggie said.

"Oh go on and accept," Roberta said. "And besides, I'm surprised at you. This *is Dairy Duck*, and you've been here before."

"But only with my girlfriend," Maggie said. "I never came here to...you know...find someone."

"Well you're missing out then," Claudia said. "Here's my number. What's yours?"

Claudia left her telephone number on a slip of paper for Maggie. Maggie looked for a slip of paper to write on but found nothing.

"Write on my arm," Claudia winked.

Maggie's eyes lit up. Roberta and Eva smiled. Maggie wrote her telephone number on Claudia's arm and liked doing so.

"It's a date," Maggie said.

Claudia took their orders and left.

"See, that wasn't so bad," Roberta said.

"I feel goofy," Maggie said.

"You weren't goofy when you helped me fish out Eva," Roberta said.

"That was different," Maggie said. "You had an emergency."

"And you responded with good will," Roberta said. "But your personal life is in need of resuscitation. You're allowed to pursue personal pleasure."

Maggie smiled.

"Thank you for hooking me up with Claudia," Maggie said.

"And thank you for the naltrexone," Eva said to Roberta. "You broke my dependency on those chemicals."

"You're welcome, both of you," Roberta said.

"Say," Maggie said. "If things go well with Claudia and me—"

"They will," Roberta said. "I can speak from personal experience."

Maggie's eyes nearly popped out of their eye sockets.

"Do you have an open marriage?" Maggie asked.

"Maggie," Eva said. "I'm going to be straight with you. I'm straight, and Roberta might be. We're not married. We're roommates and good friends."

"I don't understand. You treat each other like lovers," Maggie said. "And the woman in white—"

"Told you a fib to get your attention," Roberta said. "We approached a guy a few boats down who wouldn't lift a finger to help us."

"I think I know who you're talking about," Maggie said. "So no wedding in Denmark?"

"I'm afraid not," Eva said.

"Oh, what a shame. And I was just thinking about what sorts of children you two would have together—if science were advanced enough to provide for you," Maggie said.

Eva and Roberta laughed.

"There's no chance of that!" Eva said. "Ow, I had a little cramp."

"Do you need to go home?" Maggie asked.

"No, I'm fine now," Eva said.

"So what was your idea—before we interrupted you, that is," Roberta said.

"Oh yeah," Maggie said. "I was hoping the four of us could go out sometime—the two of you with Claudia and me. Or we could go to my place and play cards. Do you know how to play Sheepshead?"

"Sheepshead?!" Roberta exclaimed. "I don't believe it. My mother taught me that game. Are you from Wisconsin? No one plays Sheepshead outside of that state."

"I'm from Wisconsin, yes," Maggie said. "From Sheboygan, as a matter of fact."

"No kidding. I was a young child in Racine," Roberta said. "We both lived in port towns on Lake Michigan."

"Small world," Eva said. "I've always lived in Texas until I moved here."

"Aw, don't feel left out," Maggie said. "I've never been to Texas."

The three laughed. Claudia brought dinner, and the three women enjoyed a nice evening. Maggie dropped off Eva and Roberta at Roberta's house and wished them a pleasant evening. Roberta and Eva sat at the kitchen table, had coffee, and played Rummy.

"Roberta," Eva said. "I'm sorry about my addiction. You were right to force naltrexone on me, and I'm sorry about the Marcus thing. In my warped mind, I thought Marcus was doing me a favor when he snuck me out the window. Roberta—he drugged me with Rohypnol."

"That conniving parasite," Roberta said.

"Please, let me finish. The naltrexone inhibited the Rohypnol, so he injected me with a mixture of drugs and was about to pull one of my teeth when you and Kay arrived."

The telephone rang.

"One moment," Roberta said.

Roberta answered the telephone.

"Hello? Yes...I understand...I'm surprised too...I will...Thank you. Bye."

"Who was that?" Eva asked.

"It was Kay. She told the police that Marcus chased her in the van, forced her to the side of the road, and hijacked the van with you in it, and that he drove it off Sellwood Bridge," Roberta said. "The police believe her."

"She lied?"

"Yes," Roberta said. "Would you have done differently?"

"I don't know," Eva said. "I hate the idea of lying to law enforcement."

Roberta laughed.

"What's so funny?"

"This is from a person who was hiding a drug addiction," Roberta said. "Well, I guess this means you really have recovered. But I'm amazed—you recovered from your addiction quickly, and you recovered from Marcus poisoning you. It's almost as if you had outside help."

"She did," Johnny said. "Felifia helped her."

"How do you know?" Evanita asked.

"I felt it," Johnny said. "When Felifia vanished, I felt her purge the drugs and cravings from Mummy Eva's body."

"Is that supposed to be symbolic of a Savior?" Evanita asked.

"I don't know about that," Johnny said. "But it was a gift."

"We'll have to press charges against Marcus," Roberta said. "He assaulted you."

"Roberta, I think I'll let the issue go. I'm clean now. I'll quit from his practice," Eva said. "I'm thinking about returning to Texas."

"You can't let him get away with something like that," Roberta said. "It's wrong. Not to mention illegal."

"I don't want to challenge him," Eva said.

"What about me?" Roberta asked.

Eva was caught completely off guard.

"I...what? You? You'll be fine. You have your own intern," Eva said.

"Eva," Roberta said. "Is Marcus blackmailing you?"

"I...uh...no," Eva lied.

"One moment," Roberta said.

Roberta left the table and returned with photos of Eva popping pills.

"Are you afraid of these?" Roberta asked.

"How did you get these!?" Eva asked. "I...he used these against me!"

"I suspected as much," Roberta said.

Eva rushed over to Roberta and kissed her on the mouth.

"Thank you!" Eva said.

Roberta was dazed for a moment before she returned to her senses.

"You...kissed me," Roberta said. "Not just a little. You kissed me a lot."

"Oh, I guess I got carried away," Eva said. "It's just I'm so thankful you got the pictures away from Marcus. I'm ashamed of myself for what I did, and for letting Marcus photograph me like that. Maybe if I kiss you on the cheek like this..."

Eva kissed Roberta on the cheek.

"Well?" Eva asked.

"You're stirring something up inside me, Eva," Roberta said. "Something very real. I...oh, I can't believe this."

Roberta left the table and paced in the living room. Eva followed her.

"What? What is it?" Eva asked.

"I'm debating whether I should take you to the hospital and check for leftover mind-altering drugs in your system, or—" Roberta started.

"Or what?" Eva asked.

"Or take you in my arms right now and lose all control of myself," Roberta said.

Evanita gasped.

"Don't be too alarmed," Geneva said.

"You're a Catholic, Grandma. And you're telling me not to be alarmed?" Evanita asked.

"I am a Catholic, yes. But there are times when love transcends everything," Geneva replied.

"Are you saying what I think you're saying?" Evanita asked. "Do they...?"

"Do you love me?" Eva asked as she faced Roberta very close.

"Very much," Roberta said. "I've loved you for a very long time. I just don't know what to do with my love."

"Maybe Maggie is right," Eva said. "Maybe we are like a married couple. I didn't see it until now. I always go to men to fulfill a cheap craving, but I feel empty and cheated afterward. But with you, I feel like you give me something that sustains me. Even when I abused my body and defied your help by escaping with Marcus, you still cared enough to come after me. You could have cut your losses and kicked me out."

"I could have," Roberta said. "But I didn't. I love you."

Eva moved in very close to Roberta while staring her in the eyes. Then Eva felt something come over her. She and Roberta were like the two ducklings in the *Dairy Duck* sign. Eva was the shorter duckling but pressing forward toward Roberta, who was taller but a little standoff-ish. Eva hugged Roberta.

"Are you afraid to show your affection?" Eva whispered into Roberta's ear.

"I'm afraid of getting out of control," Roberta whispered back.

"You weren't afraid to experiment with Claudia," Eva whispered.

"I was scared to death," Roberta said. "I felt I had to find out about myself."

"Did you?" Eva whispered.

"I'm not sure," Roberta whispered back. "I'm not sure of anything. What about you?"

"I want to know what real love it," Eva said. "And I think I'm falling hard for you."

"Oh god!" Roberta whispered back.

Eva pulled her head back enough to look Roberta in the eyes. Roberta returned an expression of terror and exhilaration. Eva kissed Roberta gently on the cheek, then on the chin, the ear, and the neck.

"I'll never be the same if we take this all the way," Roberta whispered.

"Love me," Eva said. "Love me tonight."

Eva led Roberta to the bedroom and closed the door. The vision stopped.

"My mother and Roberta?" Evanita asked. "Then the photo on the desk...the dancing in front of her photo."

"Yes," Geneva said. "Your mother and Roberta were lovers. They consummated their love on that October 14th of 1989 with a full moon."

Evanita stared at Geneva then looked at Johnny. Then she saw Johnny not as a man dressed up as a woman named Johnny, but as a real woman. The fear that she too was a lesbian like her mother gripped her with anxiety. She slapped Johnny and ran for the exit.

"Evanita!" Geneva called.

Evanita stopped in her tracks with her back to Geneva.

"Come back here," Geneva said. "Come back and finish the vision."

"How can I?" Evanita said. "Marcus raped my mother, and as a result, my mother became a lesbian. I look at Johnny—"

"Shh," Geneva said. "You mean Shawna."

"No, Johnny," Evanita said. "I look at him dressed up like a woman, I've kissed him like this, and I wonder if I've crossed the line to the dark side."

"Is that what you think this is?" Geneva asked. "Evanita—come over here. Let's talk."

Evanita turned around, but she held her hand up.

"No, I don't want you spinning the truth," Evanita said. "My mother was addicted to Simon. Then she was addicted to drugs, and to Marcus. Now she's switched her addiction to Roberta. Isn't that the analysis? Isn't that what love really is? An addiction?"

"We love you," Geneva said. "Don't you remember what Shawna said about benevolence?"

"Can there be benevolence in a lesbian relationship?" Evanita asked. "It all seems like two women getting drunk with passion."

"Point well taken," Geneva said. "But remember this: passion is for the moment, but deep love—a love with an affect for benevolence—is long lasting and sustaining. Your mother said she felt such love with Roberta. You just said how your mother danced in front of Roberta's picture in later years. Is that a cheat?"

"It's a cheat," Evanita said. "Like all those poor people who delude themselves with religion. They worship nonexistent concepts and have 'personal relationships' with them. It's all a cheat!"

Geneva rolled her eyes. Johnny placed a hand to his forehead in dismay.

"There's also the other possibility," Geneva said.

"What possibility?" Evanita asked.

"That to deny love is itself a cheat," Geneva said.

"That's rhetorical trickery," Evanita said.

"Is it? Search deep within yourself," Geneva said. "Evanita—we are all human beings. We aren't robots. We have our deficiencies, yes, but to hack off every single element of our humanity in the name of 'cheat' is no better than Franco's regime to stamp out diversity and human expression. Are you imposing a cerebral regime on your humanity?"

Evanita froze in place. She didn't know what to say.

"You didn't expect that, did you?" Geneva said. "You know the truth, but you've isolated yourself from it. Come, Evanita. Sit down with us and watch the vision. This is for your benefit."

Evanita returned to her chair next to Johnny. Geneva read from her diary, and the vision of the past returned.

1989 Nov. Portland, Oregon.

In the days that followed, Roberta's and Eva's love for each other blossomed. They went to movies together, watched plays together, went jogging, played Sheepshead with Maggie and Claudia, and went bowling. Eva quit her practice with Marcus—who couldn't remember her being an employee—and worked with Roberta as another intern. Marcus lost his lawsuit with Andrea Peddly. Andrea won alimony and child support for her infant who Marcus fathered—Adrian Cracbern. Marcus also had to answer for his crime against the police officer. He managed to avoid prison time by paying a large fine. Due to these two fronts, Marcus's personal wealth disappeared, and he diverted funds from his business to pay for his decadence.

Seeing Marcus already in trouble, Eva did not push the issue of Marcus's crime over her. She joked with Roberta that justice was taking care of Marcus, and it was only a matter of time before he would disappear into the fabric of human failure.

Eva and Roberta worked late hours caring for the Title 19 patients. A month passed since Marcus chased Kay in her van, and Eva was late with her menstrual cycle. She threw up in the morning, couldn't do anything with her hair, and her breasts were tender. Eva knew she had the symptoms of being pregnant, but she couldn't understand how—she didn't have sexual intercourse with a man in recent months to her knowledge. Roberta noticed Eva's symptoms and became suspicious. More than once Roberta questioned Eva about having sexual relations with a man, and Eva denied the possibility each time. Roberta and Eva loved each other, but a tension set in over Eva's apparent pregnancy, and Roberta became edgy. It was this way then when Eva mysteriously disappeared from Roberta's home early in the morning, did not ride into work with Roberta, and showed up at MacNessi Dental just before noon.

1989 Dec 3, Mon. Page Street Clinic Building. Portland, Oregon.

Roberta had just finished an amalgam for younger Johnny Pindus and was cleaning up. Johnny left the treatment room and bumped into Eva in the hallway.

"Oh, I'm sorry," Eva said. "You're the Pindus boy, aren't you?"

"Yes," younger Johnny said.

When younger Johnny bumped into Eva, he sensed something different about her.

"One follows the other. One follows the other," younger Johnny repeated in reference to Eva's new physical condition.

"Are you here for a cleaning?" Eva asked.

"No, I just had a cavity filled," younger Johnny said. "My sister is waiting for me. She's taking me out for ice cream."

"Well don't let me keep you waiting," Eva said. "Go get your ice cream."

Eva stepped into Roberta's treatment room. Curious, younger Johnny stood just outside and listened.

"I was beginning to think you'd never show," Roberta said. "Where were you all morning? I've been running around doing double duty to cover for you."

"I just came back from the doctor," Eva said.

"Oh? Something wrong? You could have warned me this morning," Roberta said.

"I'm pregnant," Eva blurted.

"What!?" Roberta said.

"I'm pregnant. It's true, I'm expecting a child," Eva said.

"I knew it!" Roberta said. "Morning sickness and bad hair for the last two months. But how could you do it, Eva, after everything we've been through? You walk in here four hours late, make me bust my butt for you, and you have the nerve to say you're pregnant? What have you been doing? Sleeping with men behind my back? Well I guess it's over then."

"No, it's not like that!" Eva said, nearly in tears.

"Who do you think you're fooling? I know how the birds and bees work. Well? Who is he? Or don't you know? Too many to choose from? Or was it that Marcus Cracbern, as if he hasn't done enough already. Figures you would sleep with him. You worked for him and snuck out with him. You said you loved me. That was a lie, wasn't it? Wasn't it?!"

Eva slapped Roberta. Roberta slapped Eva back. Eva fell into tears, but Roberta's eyes went afire.

"So what do you want from me, Eva?" Roberta asked. "You want to determine the father? Go get a paternity test. Then sue the bastard for benefits. That's what your kind does. You want an abortion? Go get one. You want sympathy? Go look it up in the dictionary between *swastika* and *syndrome*."

"I don't know who the father is!" Eva cried. "I haven't slept with anyone!"

"You're pathetic," Roberta said. "Get out of my clinic. I never want to see you again, you lying breeder!"

Eva packed up her things and left MacNessi Dental. She returned to Roberta's house and packed her remaining things. Eva dialed a number on the telephone and held the phone to her ear.

"Hello?" a younger Geneva answered.

Eva opened her mouth to say something, but instead she hung up the telephone.

The vision stopped. Older Geneva broke into tears.

"I wish she would have told me," Geneva cried. "I would have run up to Portland in a heartbeat for my baby! But she held everything inside and took everything on the chin! My poor baby Eva! Eva! Call me on the telephone! Eva! Call your Mammma!"

Geneva closed the diary and buried her face in her hands. Evanita looked at her grandmother with a sudden shock and horror. Geneva was always the strong one, the one who gave lecture and wisdom on the world. She was a subconscious pillar of strength that Evanita had taken for granted without even realizing it until that moment. And in that moment, Evanita had a sinking feeling, like an ancient mountain that had been in existence longer than the earth itself was suddenly falling into a sinkhole.

"Grandma?" Evanita called. "Grandma?"

Geneva looked briefly at Evanita before looking away to hide her tears. She pulled a tissue out of her purse and blew her nose. She dried her eyes, put her tissue away, and straightened her hair.

"I shouldn't lose my composure in front of you, Evanita," Geneva said. "This is for you, not me."

"I...I'm sorry, Grandma," Evanita said. "Will you be okay?"

Geneva smiled.

"Your grandmother is a silly old woman," Geneva said. "But she'll be all right now. Whew! I get emotional sometimes with my Eva. And to think I had just one child. I can't imagine how parents raise four, five, or eight children! They must go insane!"

"Or gray," Johnny said.

"Or both!" Evanita laughed.

Johnny, Geneva, and Jonara laughed with Evanita.

"Well," Geneva said. "We are laughing together in a moment of strain. This gives me the strength I need to continue."

"Will I find out who my father is?" Evanita asked.

"Soon," Geneva said.

"Will my mother and Roberta make amends?" Evanita asked.

"I hope so," Geneva said.

"You don't know?" Evanita asked.

"Well, there's Eva's accident to deal with first," Geneva said.

"What accident?" Evanita asked.

"This accident."

CHAPTER 14

Early Birth

1990 Jun 14, Thu. Eva's Apartment. Portland, Oregon.

Eva took Thursday off from work. She had resigned her position at MacNessi Dental shortly after her argument with Roberta and took up a part-time lab-instructor position at Oregon Health and Science University. She also moved out of Roberta's house and took residence in a small apartment near the university.

Eva also started attending a Unitarian Universalist church—partly as a reminder of her times with Simon. She met Beverly Zyla, an instructor on the faith and a teacher at a local high school. Eva and Ms. Zyla enjoyed many Sunday coffees together after church. Eva mentioned the predicament with her pregnancy, the night of October 14th with Marcus's attempted assault and chase, her partial memory loss of that day, and how she suspected Marcus raped her. Ms. Zyla urged Eva to seek legal counsel with Jan Haughf to pursue charges of rape and paternity compensation against Marcus.

The case was slow. Eva submitted to a medical examination, but the exam was three months after the alleged assault, and there was no way to determine one way or another if Eva had been raped other than her pregnancy. Jan pressed the issue that they would order Marcus to undergo a paternity DNA test, but this required Eva's child to be born first, so again the case was slow. Marcus hired Viko Vastapo as his defense attorney.

Eva called Ms. Haughf to check on the case. There had been little development. Eva was eight months pregnant, and she had another month before the baby was due and the DNA testing could begin, plus another three weeks after the due date to learn the results of the testing.

"I don't know if I can wait a month for this baby to be born," Eva said to herself. "My legs are painful and swollen."

To relieve the swelling, Eva elevated her legs and rested on her side. To pass the time, she read a book. She had read perhaps ten pages of a new book when the telephone rang. Eva made the effort, got up, and answered the phone.

"Hello?" Eva said. "Oh hi, Kay, how are you? I'm doing okay—as well as an eight-month pregnant woman can do. Yeah, I took today off. My legs are swollen, and I need to get them down to size. Really? When? Oh I'd like to, but I really shouldn't drive. Earl will drive? Even better. Pick me up at my place. See you soon. Bye!"

Kay and Earl drove over to Eva's apartment and picked her up.

"I've never been to a professional basketball game," Eva said.

"Here, Eva," Kay said. "Sit in the back seat. I'll sit in the front, and you can elevate your legs on my backrest."

"Thank you," Eva said. "I see you have Earl driving. There's some good to having a man around after all."

"I'll be more than happy to let Kay drive," Earl said. "I'm a big believer in empowering women."

"The key is that women have the power to choose," Kay said. "And that may or may not mean driving."

Eva and Kay laughed.

"So who's playing?" Eva asked as Earl drove toward the basketball arena.

"You don't know?!" Earl said in amazement.

"Eva doesn't get out much," Kay said. "That's why we're bringing her along."

"Yeah, I've been a couch potato lately," Eva said. "I work, I go to school, I return home, and I sleep."

"That's not much of a life," Earl said. "But tonight is. The Portland Trailblazers are hosting the Detroit Pistons."

"You might not remember," Kay said, "but Earl is a big Pistons fan."

"And the Pistons are leading the series three to one. If they win tonight, they win the championship," Earl said.

"So Portland has a basketball team," Eva said. "I didn't know that."

"You really must have lived in a cave this year," Earl said.

"Don't pay attention to Earl," Kay said. "What he means is that Portland fans have been wild about their team making the finals. If Portland should win—"

"Which they won't," Earl bragged.

"But if they do, the town will go wild," Kay said.

"And if they don't?" Eva asked.

"The town will get looted," Earl joked.

"Oh Earl, you say the strangest things some times," Kay said.

The three arrived at Memorial Coliseum and found their seats. They sat and awaited the beginning.

"Are you still working at MacNessi Dental?" Eva asked.

"There is no MacNessi Dental," Kay said.

"What!? What happened? Where are you working? What about Roberta? And Cracbern Associates?"

"Whoa, whoa! One at a time. This could take all game to explain," Kay said, "but I'm not sure where to start. There's so much that has happened and so much that's going on."

"First, tell me where Roberta is working," Eva said. "Is she working?"

"Yes, she's working. At Legacy Emanuel Hospital in the ER," Kay said.

"The ER?" Eva said. "That's the bottom of the ladder."

"She said something about needing to get back to her roots," Kay said. "She's doing initial treatment on ER cases."

"But no dentistry?" Eva asked.

"No," Kay replied. "She said she needed a break from dentistry."

"Where do you work?" Eva asked.

"In the Page Street Clinic building. Once Roberta moved out, Frank and Milo knocked out a couple of walls and turned the two clinics into one. I work for Milo & Frank Dental now," Kay explained.

"How could they—wait, what happened to Marcus and his Cracbern Associates?" Eva asked.

"Too many lawsuits forced him into bankruptcy," Kay said. "He sold his part of the business and the Page Street Clinic building to Milo and Frank for a song. All the high-paying clients went away, so Milo and Frank are treating the Title 19 folk. I am too, but I was already doing that with Roberta. But the patient load is less now. It's actually pretty good. Pay is less, but the work is good."

"Well at least there's that going," Eva said.

"Why don't you come back?" Kay asked.

"I don't know," Eva said. "I just have this dark feeling Marcus will come back and haunt me."

"Unlikely," Kay said. "He's in and out of the hospital all the time. He's passing blood in his urine, and he won't say why."

"Kidneys?" Eva asked.

"Don't know."

"Bladder?"

"Not sure."

"Something else?" Eva asked.

"He won't say," Kay said. "Marcus is in pain and takes aspirin, but he's not allowed to take painkillers."

"How strange. Why won't he tell you?" Eva asked.

"Again, I don't know," Kay replied.

"Look, the game is starting!" Earl said. "Mariah Carey is singing the national anthem. Oh, she has the most beautiful voice in the universe. She can sing higher than dolphins, lower than lions, and make the world into the best tasting ice cream known to God."

"A-hem," Kay coughed.

"After you babe, of course!" Earl added quickly.

"That's better," Kay grinned.

Eva laughed.

"It's good to laugh, isn't it?" Kay asked.

"Yeah, it is," Eva replied.

The game started. Eva was shocked at how loud the crowd cheered after each basket was made and after each basket was missed. The crowd often jumped to its feet, but Eva wisely remained seated.

"Oh!" Earl complained. "Portland has an early lead. Go Pistons!"

"Go Blazers!" another fan yelled.

"Pistons!" Earl yelled back.

"Blazers!" the fan yelled again.

"Earl!" Kay said. "Don't fight with the home team fans."

The first period came to a close, and Detroit gained the lead.

"Yes!" Earl cheered. "We're winning!"

"Go home, Detroit!" another fan yelled.

Earl stood up and turned around to yell at the fan.

"Earl!" Kay said as she pulled him down. "Sit down!"

"So is that it?" Eva asked. "A team gets a lead and carries it to the end?"

"Oh no, no, no!" Earl explained. "No lead in basketball is safe. A team can go into a slump or get a run. Only if a really strong team plays a really weak team can a lead be 'safe'. But this is for the championship! These are both good teams."

The second period progressed, and Portland took the lead.

"No!" Earl said.

"Yes!" the other fan cheered.

"Come on, Pistons!" Earl said.

Portland missed some shots, and Isaiah Thomas made a deep shot.

"Yeah!" Earl cheered. "Isaiah is the best!"

The second period progressed.

"Yeah, go Pistons!" Earl cheered. "Work it, work it. Wow! Vinnie Johnson in the crowd!"

The second period continued and completed with Detroit maintaining the lead.

"Now it's time for things to get serious," Earl said.

"Weren't things already serious?" Eva asked.

The third period started. As it progressed, Earl cheered less and booed more as Portland overtook Detroit in points.

"Come on, Pistons!"

"Pistons are prissy," the fan yelled.

"Blazers are for women!" Earl yelled back.

"Earl," Kay said. "Behave!"

"Crap!" Earl said. "Portland stole it. Ooo, oo! Pistons stole it back, come on and score—what the—why didn't you score?"

As the third period drew to a close, Detroit closed in on Portland's lead. In the final few seconds, Portland and Detroit fought for control of a live ball hopping and bopping along until a jump-ball was called.

"Get the jump-ball," Earl called, but Portland took control and scored the last points of the period.

"So how serious is Detroit now?" Eva asked.

"Don't rub it in," Earl said. "It's early yet."

"It's *earl-y*, Earl?" Eva joked.

"Hah, hah," Earl replied sarcastically.

The fourth period started, and Portland expanded its lead.

"Crud," Earl said. "I was hoping we could watch the Pistons win the championship here. I don't know if I can get tickets in Detroit for another game."

"You're not going anywhere," Kay said. "You're staying here with me in Portland."

"Now if Mariah Carey sings at the next game—" Earl joked.

"She'd better not!" Kay said. "Or we'll be sleeping in separate beds for a month."

"Oh, baby, you know I'm only kidding. You're the only one for me," Earl said.

"Just keep pushing your luck," Kay said, "and see how far it gets you."

The fourth period progressed, and Detroit closed the gap to within one point.

"Come on, Pistons! Steal that ball!" Earl cheered.

"Come on, Blazers," another fan cheered, "and quit fouling us, Prissy-tons!"

Earl stood up and said, "Someone needs to be taught a lesson!"

"Sit down, Earl!" Kay said as she yanked him down again.

"He really gets into this, doesn't he?" Eva asked. "Is he like this during the season, too?"

"And then some," Kay said. "I can't tell you how many drinks he's spilled and how many tubs of popcorn he's scattered. And I always have to clean it up!"

"Oh, but I'm good for the entertainment," Earl said.

"Hah!" Kay retorted.

Detroit made two foul shots and took a one-point lead.

"Yes!" Earl bragged. "Domination!"

"Hmmph," Kay said. "One point ain't no domination."

But Earl's celebration was short lived. Portland outscored Detroit in the period until only two minutes and two seconds remained. Portland was ahead by seven points.

"That's it for the Pistons," Eva said.

"Don't count them out," Earl bragged.

"A seven point lead with two minutes left?" Eva asked.

"That's two minutes and two seconds," Earl said. "Anything can happen. Anything."

"The teams are going to Detroit," Kay said. "Detroit won't—"

"Two points for the Pistons!" Earl said. "And a foul! The foul shot is up—and it's good! Pistons down by only four!"

"Yeah, but the Blazers have the ball—" Kay started.

"They shoot, they miss!" Earl bragged. "Pistons have the ball back. Pistons shoot—it's good! Pistons down by only two points! Two! Two!"

"Okay, Mr. Owl, we hear you!" Kay said. "But the Blazers have the ball now. Look, here's an easy shot."

"It's a miss! A miss!" Earl cheered. "Pistons have the ball! Just a minute left. Oh! He almost threw it away! Come on, drive! Ugh! Jump-ball! Pistons win the jump! Long jump shot— it's good! Game is tied! Domination!"

"Why doesn't Portland score a basket?" Eva asked.

"They're choking!" Earl bragged. "It's the classic choke!"

"Well the Blazers have it again," Kay said. "Odds say they have to score here. There—he's going for the shot."

"Detroit ball! Detroit ball!" Earl said. "And with twenty seconds left! Pistons could win it here if they run the clock right! Ooh. Timeout, timeout!"

After the timeout, Earl continued his rant.

"Come on, Pistons, why are you taking so long? You're going to run out of time. Oh...my...Lordy in Heaven! Vinnie Johnson just made that shot with point seven seconds left. Point seven seconds! That's less than a second! And the Pistons lead by two! They lead!!!"

"I can't believe it," Eva said. "Portland was winning!"

"They choked!"

"Pistons cheat!" another fan said.

"I'm gonna settle this once and for all!" Earl said.

Kay held onto Earl and prevented him from standing up.

"Down, boy, down!" Kay said.

"And it's a timeout!" Earl said. "But there's not enough time!"

"Didn't you say anything can happen?" Eva asked.

"Did I say that?" Earl asked.

"Yes," the two women replied.

"Hmm. I—okay, here's the play—Blazers shoot—no good! No good! Pistons win! We did it! We did it!" Earl celebrated.

Earl did a little dance, and the Portland fans left in disgust.

"Let's celebrate! Let's celebrate!" Earl said to Kay and Eva.

"I hate to be a party pooper," Eva said, "but my legs are swelling badly. I need to go home and elevate them."

"Yeah, but the—" Earl started.

"Earl," Kay said. "We had this talk before we invited Eva. Let's take her home, and then we can celebrate."

"Oh, that's too bad," Earl said. "We're going out to a nice dance club I know."

"Do I look like I can live it up? I'm a fat goose!" Eva said.

"The woman needs her rest," Kay said. "Let's take her home."

"Okay, okay," Earl said.

The three waited with other people to exit the coliseum. On reaching the outside, the three were surprised to see angry fans running around and attacking whatever they wanted to blame for Portland's loss.

"We'd better hurry," Earl said. "I didn't count on the Portland fans behaving this badly."

Earl and Kay ran for the car, but Eva could barely hobble along. Kay turned around once and gave Eva a funny look before turning back forward and racing to the car.

"Wait for me!" Eva called, but it was no use.

A Detroit fan wearing a Pistons jersey ran past Eva with a Portland fan in chase. From a different direction, the same thing. Then it happened. A Detroit fan with a Pistons jersey ran up to Eva from directly behind. Eva saw nothing. An angry Portland fan wielded a stick, swung at the fan, and missed. Hearing something behind her, Eva turned around just in time to witness the missed swing land solidly and brutally against the front of her abdomen. Eva screamed in pain. Kay looked back and pulled Earl with her. Eva started to bleed and went into contractions.

"My baby, my baby!" Eva wailed.

"Did you see who did it?" Kay asked.

"I...I don't know. Everyone looks the same," Eva said.

"We have to get her to a hospital, Earl," Kay said. "Eva—can you walk?"

Eva moaned. Earl picked her up and held her face up. He carried Eva to his car as quickly as he could. Kay sat next to Eva, tore fabric from her (Kay's) shirt, and gave it to Eva to slow the bleeding. Earl jumped in the drivers's seat and drove the three away from the coliseum.

"Legacy Emanuel Hospital is the closest," Kay told Earl.

Eva moaned and wailed.

"Hang in there, Eva," Kay said. "Earl, punch it!"

Earl drove his car as quickly as possible to the hospital. He pulled up in front of the emergency entrance, parked, and carried Eva inside. Several technicians helped Earl and placed Eva on a gurney. Eva was wheeled immediately to surgery.

Jonara lost sight of the vision. She floated to the top of Oso Bay. It was dark, and no one was around—not even Nekara.

"She really is gone," Jonara said.

The hour was late—11:59 pm to be exact. Jonara stared at the stars in the sky as the last few seconds of Friday expired.

2023 Oct 14, Sat Morn. Oso Bay. Corpus Christi, Texas.

"Today is the fourteenth," Jonara said, "and I'm all alone in this water. I wonder if anyone even noticed my disappearance."

Jonara looked around but saw no one.

"I guess not," Jonara said. "The fourteenth—that's when Grandma Eva had her accident—her accidents. The first was October 14th, the second was June 14th. No—she had that accident on October 13th when she was hit by a car. Three accidents! But the one she had on October 14th was in the water. I'm in the water. Is there a connection? I don't know, but I feel like I'm close to the end—one way or another. I have to find out what happens now. Mommy is in the Caves of Healing, and Grandma Eva is in the hospital. But she's about to have Mommy, and maybe now Mommy and I will find out who Grandpa is."

Jonara dove down into Oso Bay, and she found herself in the Caves of Healing, standing behind Evanita, Johnny, and Geneva, and reconnecting with the vision of Eva in Legacy Emanuel Hospital.

1990 Jun 14, Thu Eve. Legacy Emanuel Hospital. Portland, Oregon.

Kay and Earl sat patiently in the waiting area. A doctor who had been working with Eva walked out to them.

"My name is Dr. Harvey," the doctor said. "Eva is in stable condition. We had to perform an emergency C-section. Her baby is alive, but—"

"But what?" Kay asked.

"Both mother and daughter lost a lot of blood," Dr. Harvey said. "We're giving Eva an infusion of blood, but the baby— well—if we don't perform an infusion soon, the baby will die."

"What are you waiting for?" Kay asked. "Look—I'll donate my blood."

"Me too," Earl said.

"The baby has a rare blood type. We've haven't found a histocompatible match yet. The odds of you having the same type are very low."

"We want to help," Kay said.

"Of course you do. Come this way. Let's see if either of you have matching blood."

Kay and Earl donated blood samples, and a quick lab result determined their blood unsuitable for the baby.

"I'm sorry," Dr. Harvey said. "We can't use your blood for Eva's baby."

"What about Eva's blood?" Kay asked.

"Her blood is not compatible," Dr. Harvey said.

"A mother can't save her own baby?" Kay asked. "I can't believe it."

"They aren't histocompatible," Dr. Harvey explained. "It happens. In fact, we've tested Eva's blood, and it appears she knows this already. She's been taking medication to protect her baby from being attacked by her immune system."

"Oh this is terrible!" Kay said. "We have to find a donor!"

"We're checking our internal medical records for a match," Dr. Harvey said. "We're also contacting the Red Cross and other blood banks. We'll do everything we can to save the baby."

"Thank you, doctor," Kay said.

"Now what?" Earl asked.

"We have to get Marcus in here," Kay said. "If he's the father, his blood might match."

"And if he's not?" Earl asked.

"Then we'll figure something out," Kay said.

Kay called Marcus's home telephone, but she reached his answering machine.

"Marcus," Kay said, "this is an emergency. Come down to Legacy Emanuel Hospital. Eva's been in an accident, and her baby needs blood. We think you might—Marcus, are you there?"

"I'm here," Marcus said. "I was in the bathroom passing blood again."

"You have to come to Legacy Emanuel now," Kay said.

"Why should I help someone who's suing me?" Marcus asked.

"This is a chance to redeem yourself," Kay said. "If your blood matches, you'll save Eva's and your baby."

"I'm not the father," Marcus said. "I got my own problems. I don't want anything to do with Eva."

"Marcus Cracbern!" Kay said. "Don't deny your parentage. Be a man and take responsibility. Our mother would be ashamed of you! She was a doctor, and so are you. You're sworn to help people and take care of your own. Well? Your baby needs help. Marcus!?"

"What happened?" Earl asked.

"He hung up," Kay said. "Now what?"

"Was she dating anyone else?" Earl asked.

"Not that I know of," Kay said. "She's convinced Marcus is the father. She's suing him for support."

Kay paced nervously in the waiting area.

"Stop pacing, you're making me nervous," Earl said.

"I'm pacing because I'm nervous," Kay said.

After another ten minutes, Mr. Vastapo walked into the hospital.

"Mr. Vastapo!" Kay said. "You're Marcus's lawyer. What are you doing here?"

"Marcus told me how you tried to entrap him," Mr. Vastapo said. "I'm here to gather evidence of such for my client's case."

"We're not entrapping Marcus," Kay said.

"No? You want him to donate a blood sample," Mr. Vastapo said. "Then you'll fabricate a story that his blood is compatible with Eva's baby. Eva will use that against him. Well, Marcus isn't going to fall for that, and neither am I."

"Why do lawyers have to get in the way of everything?" Kay asked.

Dr. Harvey rushed in and made an announcement.

"We've found a match! We've started the infusion. Eva's baby will survive!"

The doctor returned to Eva's room. Kay and Earl jumped for joy. Mr. Vastapo's eyes lit up, and a sneaky smile covered his face.

"This is very curious," Mr. Vastapo said. "This find could end my client's case in his favor by establishing the true father."

"Well if it does, I'm going to give a big hug to the man who donated his blood to Eva's baby," Kay said. "Life is more important than your court case."

Kay, Earl, and Mr. Vastapo watched as Roberta exited a small room. She held a white bandage over a vein on her arm.

"What's going on?" Roberta asked. "What are you two doing here? What's Marcus's lawyer doing here?"

"I'm here to gather any information helpful to my client," Mr. Vastapo said.

"Roberta!" Kay said. "Did you just donate blood?"

"Yeah," Roberta said. "I'm supposed to be working, but I got this weird request to donate blood. Something about saving the life of a newborn. My job gets all the strange ones."

Kay and Earl looked at each other in shock.

"She couldn't be," Kay said.

"She can't," Mr. Vastapo said, "and I'm disappointed, unless Roberta is in fact a Robert. Why do you dress like a woman, Roberta?"

"Huh?" Roberta asked. "What's your game? I dress like a woman because I am a woman."

"I don't think so," Mr. Vastapo said. "You just donated blood to save Eva Carreña's baby. That baby has a rare blood type. Not even Eva has the right blood. But you do. Now we know who the real father is."

"I saved Eva's baby?" Roberta pondered. "But you're wrong, Vastapo. I'm not a man! How dare you slander me!"

"A paternity test will show otherwise," Mr. Vastapo said. "I'll order Marcus to submit his DNA for analysis right away to establish his innocence. Will you submit your DNA?"

"I won't stand for this," Roberta said. "Marcus is the father—everyone knows that."

"Then you have nothing to fear," Mr. Vastapo said. "I'll have the courts order one for you. Good-day, Roberta—or should I start calling you Robert?"

Mr. Vastapo left.

"I don't understand," Roberta said.

"Neither do we," Kay said.

The doctor returned.

"Roberta," Dr. Harvey said. "Would you like to meet the mother of the baby you just saved?"

Roberta paused.

"I told her I never wanted to see her again," Roberta said. "She made a baby with Marcus."

"Roberta," Dr. Harvey said. "Eva doesn't know it's you. But she does want to meet you."

"Roberta," Kay said. "Eva was raped. You know that, don't you?"

"I wish I could believe that," Roberta said. "But the way she acted around Marcus last year, I'd swear she was having a consensual relationship with him."

"Please, Roberta, believe me. Eva told me she didn't have consensual relations with Marcus. Visit her. We'll go with you for emotional support."

"I don't know if I should do this," Roberta said. "Something very strange is going on."

Dr. Harvey led Roberta, Kay, and Earl to Eva's treatment room. Eva opened her eyes and saw Roberta. Eva shook and trembled with anxiety.

"No, no, no!" Eva said.

"Shh," Dr. Harvey said. "You're perfectly safe."

"But...Roberta...she doesn't want to see me," Eva said.

Roberta paused for a moment. She shrugged her shoulders and spoke.

"Dr. Harvey says I saved your baby," Roberta said. "I'm a doctor, and I help people. That's my job."

"Dr. Harvey said my baby has a rare blood type, and she would die without an infusion," Eva said. "I really appreciate your donation."

"Forget it," Roberta said.

"No, I can't forget it," Eva said. "I'm sorry about everything I've put you through. You've tried to help me, and I've always dragged you down. Now I've dragged you down again. But I'm more than grateful. I won't bother you again. When I'm better, I'll return to Corpus Christi."

Roberta placed her hand on Eva's shoulder and patted it. Eva reached for Roberta's hand and held it.

"I miss you," Eva whispered.

Roberta was afraid to respond. Something terrible welled up in her throat, and she could barely contain herself. She turned away from Eva and took a deep breath to clear her senses. She watched a nurse enter the room with an incubator on wheels. Roberta watched as the nurse wheeled the incubator up to and next to Eva's bed. The incubator contained Eva's baby. The baby had tubes in her mouth and nose and had probes attached to her chest.

"She's stable now," the nurse said to Eva. "Would you like to hold her?"

"Yes," Eva said.

The nurse handed the baby to Eva. Earl wanted to say something, but Kay nudged him.

"What is it, Earl?" Eva asked.

"Nothing," Earl said.

"Earl was about to say something rude," Kay said.

"No I wasn't," Earl said. "I just wanted to—"

"Ah-ah-ah," Kay said.

"But it's just," Earl continued.

"Oh let him speak," Eva said. "He's itching to say something."

Kay covered her eyes and looked down.

"I just wanted to say how much you white people look alike," Earl said.

"Oh?" Eva asked.

"Yeah," Earl said. "Your daughter looks like Roberta in the face."

"That's enough, Earl," Kay said. "Eva and Roberta, I apologize for Earl. Come on, Earl, we're leaving. Eva—we'll visit you later."

Eva looked at her daughter.

"Earl is right," Eva said. "She does look a little like you."

"Strange coincidence," Roberta said. "Have you picked a name yet?"

"Yes," Eva said. "Her name is Evanita Soledad Carreña."

"A nice name for a nice baby," Roberta said.

Little Evanita grew restless in Eva's arms. The nurse reached for little Evanita to place her back in the incubator.

"No, wait," Eva said. "Roberta, would you like to hold Evanita? Please?"

Roberta paused. She worried that her throat would well up again.

"I think she needs her incubator for—" Roberta started.

"Please?" Eva asked.

Roberta paused again.

"Very well," Roberta said. "I'm a doctor, and I'm sworn to do no harm."

Roberta held little Evanita in her arms. She sang a lullaby—mostly to calm her own nerves, but her voice soothed little Evanita, and Evanita settled into a light sleep. Roberta felt an unusually strong attachment to Evanita, though she didn't understand why.

"She likes you," Eva said. "She takes to you naturally."

"Is it customary for the people in your family line to take to strangers at such a young age?" Roberta asked.

"No," Eva said. "But Evanita doesn't think of you as a stranger. And that song. How did you know to sing it?"

"I haven't heard it in years. It was something my mother sang to me to help me sleep when I was younger," Roberta said. "I just felt like singing it. My nerves...I...maybe it's because I donated blood."

The nurse took little Evanita from Roberta's arms and returned her to the incubator.

"You should get some rest, Eva," the nurse said. "You've been through a lot today. You may have visitors tomorrow."

The nurse left with little Evanita. Roberta wrote a number down on a piece of paper and handed it to Eva.

"I work at this hospital," Roberta said. "If you need anything, call this pager number."

"Thank you," Eva said. "Roberta?"

"Yes, Eva?"

"I still love you," Eva said.

Roberta paused for a moment, opened her mouth to say something, and closed it. She waved goodbye, stepped out into the hallway, and put her hands over her face to cover her crying. She heard familiar voices—Kay and Earl arguing far down the hallway. Roberta wiped away her tears, blew her nose into a tissue, and walked down the hallway toward Kay and Earl.

"You know better than to talk like that," Kay said. "How many times do I have to tell you?"

"Ah, you two are still here," Roberta said. "You'll be happy to know the new baby's name is Evanita Soledad Carreña. She's sleeping, and hopefully so is her mother."

"That's wonderful," Earl said.

"I'm sorry about Earl, Roberta. I'm sorry, so sorry," Kay went on.

"Stop apologizing already," Earl said.

"You are the worst!" Kay retorted.

"Please!" Roberta said. "I think there's been enough excitement for the day. Perhaps you two should return home and get some rest yourselves."

"Not before we celebrate Detroit's win!" Earl said. "But I take back what I said about all white people looking alike."

"Good," Kay said. "Now we're making progress."

"Eva's baby doesn't look at all like Marcus," Earl said.

Kay punched Earl in the arm and pulled him by the ear out of the hospital. She turned around and said, "Goodbye, Roberta."

"Goodbye," Roberta replied.

CHAPTER 15

Paternity Court

1990 Jul 6, Fri. Multnomah County Courthouse. Portland, Oregon.

"All rise. Judge Jillian presiding," said the Court Clerk.

Jonara noticed there was no jury. There was Judge Jillian, a Court Clerk, a bailiff, a sheriff, Mr. Vastapo, Marcus in a wheelchair, Ms. Haughf, Eva, and several additional people including Roberta, Kay, and Earl. Ms. Haughf and Eva sat on the plaintiff side while Mr. Vastapo and Marcus sat on the defendant side.

The judge sat down as did everyone else.

"This trial is now in session. I will swear in the court reporter," Judge Jillian (The Court) said. "Do you swear that you will correctly record, to the best of your ability, all testimony given by each and every witness, counsel, judge, and all others attending this trial, and that you will keep secret these trial proceedings, so help you God?"

"I do," The Court Reporter said.

"This trial is a private matter to be kept in the strictest confidence and not to be discussed with anyone outside this courtroom," The Court said.

"I object, Your Honor," Ms. Haughf said.

"You object to confidentiality?" The Court asked.

"Your Honor," Mr. Vastapo said. "The plaintiff can't object before the trial starts."

"I do not object to the private nature of this trial. My client has a constitutional right to a trial by her peers," Ms. Haughf said. "We demand a jury."

"Your Honor," Mr. Vastapo said. "Precedence has been set for paternity suits."

"Objection is overruled," The Court said. "Paternity suits do not require a jury. This is to be a speedy trial. The hearing, evidence presentation, *voir dire*, pretrial, and everything else are to be incorporated into the trial. Court Clerk—read the complaint."

"The Plaintiff, Ms. Eva Kelicacha Carreña, seeks to establish the paternity of her daughter, Evanita Soledad Carreña. She posits that Marcus Cracbern is the father through nonconsensual sexual intercourse."

"How does the defendant plead?" The Court asked.

"Not the father," Mr. Vastapo said.

"Very well, we will begin. This trial's scope will focus solely on paternity. No rape charges will be pursued. Any charges of rape must be tried outside this trial," The Court said. "Is that clear, Ms. Haughf?"

"Clear," Ms. Haughf said.

"You may begin, Ms. Haughf," The Court said.

"I would like to call Eva Carreña to the stand," Ms. Haughf said.

Eva took the witness stand and remained standing.

"Raise your right hand, please," The Court Clerk said. "Do you solemnly swear that the evidence you shall give in this trial shall be the truth, the whole truth, and nothing but the truth, and that you will keep secret these trial proceedings, so help you God?"

"I do," Eva said.

"Please be seated," The Court said. "State your full name in the microphone, please."

"Eva Kelicacha Carreña," Eva said.

"Can you identify the defendant?" Ms. Haughf asked.

"Yes. He's Marcus Cracbern," Eva said.

"Do you believe he is the father of your child?" Ms. Haughf asked.

"Yes, I do," Eva said.

"Why do you believe he is the father?" Ms. Haughf asked.

"Because of what happened on October 14, 1989," Eva said. "He drugged me, and I have some memory loss for that day. I haven't slept with any men last year, and I got pregnant right around that date, so it had to be him."

"Objection," Mr. Vastapo said. "The witness is speculating."

"Your Honor, this trial is to determine paternity," Ms. Haughf said. "We must explore all witness testimony relating to paternity."

"Overruled," The Court said.

"You're kidding," Mr. Vastapo said. "This isn't testimony. It's wishful thinking."

"I said, overruled," The Court said. "Mr. Vastapo—unless you wish to take the witness stand, I suggest you refrain from offhand comments. Continue, Ms. Haughf."

"Tell us what happened on October 14, 1989," Ms. Haughf said.

"I was at home at the time," Eva started.

"Home being where?" Ms. Haughf asked.

"I was living with Roberta MacNessi in her house here in Portland," Eva said. "Marcus stopped by and picked me up."

"Could you describe your relationship with the defendant at the time?" Ms. Haughf asked.

"Marcus was my friend and my supervisor at Cracbern Associates," Eva said. "Cracbern Associates was a dental office, and I worked for him as a dentist."

"You were a subordinate under Marcus, then?" Ms. Haughf asked.

"Yes."

"Tell us what happened next," Ms. Haughf continued.

"He suggested we get something to eat, and I agreed," Eva said. "He invited me to his house for dinner, and I suggested that we go dancing later."

"Did you go dancing with Marcus prior to the 14th?" Ms. Haughf asked.

"Yes," Eva said. "We've been out dancing many times before."

"Continue," Ms. Haughf said.

"Well, he gave me aspirin for my headache, and he made dinner," Eva said.

"What did he make for dinner?" Ms. Haughf asked.

"Liver," Eva said.

The people in the courtroom groaned.

"It was actually quite good," Eva said.

"Did you have anything to drink?" Ms. Haughf asked.

"Yes. He gave me a cola," Eva said. "He spiked the cola with Rohypnol."

"Objection," Mr. Vastapo said. "The witness is jumping to conclusions."

"Sustained," The Court said. "Ms. Carreña—please try to describe what you actually witnessed, not what you think might have happened."

"How did the cola taste?" Ms. Haughf asked.

"What do you mean?" Eva asked.

"Did it taste like a regular cola? Did it taste flat? Did it taste like water? It tasted like Rohypnol, didn't it?"

"Objection," Mr. Vastapo said. "Leading the witness."

"Sustained," The Court said. "Ms. Haughf, please!"

"Did the cola taste like regular cola?" Ms. Haughf asked Eva. "Yes."

"What happened next?" Ms. Haughf asked.

"We finished dinner," Eva continued. "Marcus asked if I could stand. It was a strange question. No one asks a question like that. He was up to something, and I knew it, but I didn't listen to myself."

"Objection," Mr. Vastapo said. "The witness is jumping to conclusions again."

"Sustained. Ms. Carreña, please try to describe just the facts," The Court said.

"I'll try," Eva said who was now sniffling.

"Tell us what happened next," Ms. Haughf said. "You finished dinner, and then?"

"I stood up," Eva said. "I was dizzy from the drug."

"Objection," Mr. Vastapo said. "Jumping to conclusions."

"Sustained," The Court said.

"Miss Carreña, what is your profession?" Ms. Haughf asked.

"I am a dentist," Eva said.

"What training have you received to become a dentist?" Ms. Haughf asked.

"I have a Bachelor's degree in Pre-Dental studies from Wayland Baptist University. I have a Doctor of Dental Surgery degree from the University of Texas in Houston. I have dentistry licenses in Texas and Oregon."

"As a dentist, do you have enough medical training to determine cause and effect of medication?" Ms. Haughf asked.

"Yes," Eva said. "As a dentist, I am also a doctor. I can prescribe medication, and I understand its effects."

"For the record, I establish Eva Carreña as a medical doctor per *voir dire*."

"So noted," The Court said.

"In your professional opinion," Ms. Haughf asked Eva, "what was the cause of your dizziness when you stood up?"

"A sedative drug," Eva said.

"Did it surprise you that Marcus suggested you would be dizzy before you realized it yourself?" Ms. Haughf asked.

"Yes."

"What happened after you stood up?" Ms. Haughf asked.

"Marcus led me to an unusual bedroom," Eva said.

"How was it unusual?"

"It resembled a dental treatment room," Eva said. "It had a dental chair, light, drill, and other equipment. He asked me to sit in his chair, and I did."

"Why did you sit in the chair?" Ms. Haughf asked.

"I don't know," Eva said.

"In your professional opinion, was your judgment impaired?" Ms. Haughf asked.

"Yes," Eva said.

"How do you know it was impaired?" Ms. Haughf asked.

"I don't remember everything that happened. What I do remember is fuzzy. My decisions at the time were made without critical thought. I should have left there immediately. But I was scared of Marcus. I shouldn't have been, but I was," Eva said.

"What happened next—to the best of your memory?" Ms. Haughf asked.

"Marcus said I was in that room before," Eva said.

"Were you?" Ms. Haughf asked.

"I don't remember," Eva said.

"Eva—I'm going to ask you some personal questions, and I hope you can answer them," Ms. Haughf said.

"I'll try," Eva said.

"Do you monitor your daily flow in ways that would show if you have had sexual intercourse with a man?" Ms. Haughf asked.

"Yes."

"Based on the flow, did you have sexual intercourse with a man during the time you have known the defendant?" Ms. Haughf asked.

"Objection," Mr. Vastapo said. "Vague timeframe."

"Sustained," The Court said. "Please be more specific, Ms. Haughf."

"When did you first meet the defendant?" Ms. Haughf asked.

"It was last year—May 30th of 1989, I believe. Roberta and I had finished setting up her new office," Eva said.

"From the date you mentioned until just prior to your visit to Marcus's house on October 14, 1989, and based on monitoring your flow, did you have sexual intercourse with a man?"

"No," Eva said.

"Was there anything else to indicate you had had sexual intercourse with a man prior to October 14, 1989?"

"No," Eva replied.

"What happened next on the 14th?" Ms. Haughf asked.

"I asked if we would go dancing," Eva said. "He said, 'very soon,' in a way that sounded like he was lying. Then he asked a very odd question."

"What was the question?" Ms. Haughf asked.

"He said, 'Eva—when was the last time you had your period?' I was shocked and told him a man shouldn't ask a woman that question in polite company. He said, 'A man would only ask that question to determine the best way to rape a woman'."

The people in the courtroom groaned. Mr. Vastapo conferred rapidly with Marcus, and Marcus became defensive. Their voices became loud whispers and distracted the others.

"Your Honor," Mr. Vastapo said. "I request a short recess."

"Denied," The Court said. "This is a speedy trial. Continue, Ms. Haughf."

"What happened next?" Ms. Haughf asked Eva.

"Marcus showed me slides on a projector," Eva said.

"What did the slides show?" Ms. Haughf asked.

"They showed individual women with full sets of teeth, with Marcus removing teeth, and without certain teeth. Additional slides showed Marcus implanting these teeth into his own mouth," Eva said.

"What happened after he showed you the slides?" Ms. Haughf asked.

"He took a permanent marker...he...oh, it was disgusting!" Eva said, and she buried her face in her hands.

"Try to answer to the best of your ability," Ms. Haughf said. "Tell us about the permanent marker. What color was it?"

"It was black," Eva said.

"Did he write with the marker?" Ms. Haughf asked.

"No. He kept the cap on," Eva said.

"What did he do with the marker?" Ms. Haughf asked.

"He...he...inserted it into his mouth...he held onto the end with the cap and stuck the other end in his mouth," Eva said. "He moved it in and out. At first I thought he was pretending to brush his teeth. But he smiled, then he...he...the expression on his face...it was like...like...like he was stimulating his mouth for self-pleasure...like...a sexual response. His head moved up and down like he was engaged in sexual intercourse."

"What happened next?" Ms. Haughf asked.

"I...it...I don't remember much more," Eva said. "Everything went fuzzy after that. He attempted to subdue me physically."

"Did you resist?" Ms. Haughf asked.

"Yes," Eva said. "I remember telling him, 'No,' several times. I remember him sticking a needle in my arm. Other things happened. I just can't remember any more."

"No more questions," Ms. Haughf said.

"Do you wish to cross, Mr. Vastapo?" The Court asked.

"Yes," Mr. Vastapo replied.

Mr. Vastapo stood up from his bench and approached the witness.

"Not too close," The Court said. "You will not intimidate the witness."

"Oh, clumsy me," Mr. Vastapo feigned.

Mr. Vastapo took a few steps away from Eva and began questioning her.

"Miss Carreña, in your testimony you state that on the 14th of October, the defendant gave you an aspirin for a headache. Is this correct?" Mr. Vastapo asked.

"Yes," Eva replied.

"Why did you have a headache?" Mr. Vastapo asked.

"I bumped my head the day before, and it still hurt," Eva said.

"How did you bump your head, Miss Carreña?" Mr. Vastapo asked.

"I was hit by a car," Eva said.

"So you suffered injuries from a collision with a motor vehicle?" Mr. Vastapo asked.

"Yes," Eva said.

"Miss Carreña, did you stay at the scene of the accident for the police to arrive? Keep in mind you are under oath, and I can prove if you did or did not stay at the scene," Mr. Vastapo said.

"I left the scene," Eva said.

"You are correct. There was no accident report written up for Eva Carreña on the 13th of October," Mr. Vastapo said. "Why did you leave the scene? Were you under the influence of a drug such as alcohol? This is why you left the scene, isn't it?"

"Objection," Ms. Haughf said. "Relevance."

"Mr. Vastapo. This is a paternity trial. Unless you can demonstrate how a traffic accident adds to the volume of evidence for or against the defendant, I suggest you choose a new line of questioning."

"Your Honor," Mr. Vastapo said. "I intend to demonstrate that Miss Carreña fabricated a story regarding the events of October 14th. To do so, I must pursue questions that explore her mental stability prior to the day in question."

"I'll allow the leeway," The Court said. "But don't push too far. Keep your focus, Mr. Vastapo, and remember that everything here today is to be kept strictly confidential. No discussion outside the courtroom."

"I understand, Your Honor," Mr. Vastapo said. "Miss Carreña, did you consume drugs of any sort prior to your accident on October the 13th? I remind you again that you are under oath, and I have evidence to confirm or challenge your answer depending on what you say."

"I object," Ms. Haughf said. "If Defense has such evidence, he should present it first. If he's bluffing, he's in contempt."

"He is only in contempt if he perjures himself while on the stand or if he acts against the order of The Court," The Court said. "He is not. The question of Mr. Vastapo's evidence for the moment may remain in question. But Mr. Vastapo, you must bring forth any evidence you wish to use for your defense. You cannot present vapor evidence."

"I only ask for the witness's answer," Mr. Vastapo said.

"Miss Carreña, you may answer the question," The Court said.

"I consumed drugs on October the 13th prior to my accident, yes," Eva said.

"What drugs were they?" Mr. Vastapo asked.

"I took amphetamine, morphine, and alcohol," Eva said.

"Miss Carreña, or should I say, Dr. Carreña—in your professional opinion, what was the medical value of taking the drugs you listed?"

"There was no medical value," Eva said.

"Why did you take the drugs you listed?" Mr. Vastapo asked.

"I took them to cope with stress," Eva said.

"Stress from your personal life?" Mr. Vastapo asked.

"No."

"Stress from your professional life?" Mr. Vastapo asked.

"Yes."

"What was your profession on October the 13th?" Mr. Vastapo asked.

"I was practicing dentistry," Eva said.

"Where?" Mr. Vastapo asked.

"Here in Portland," Eva answered.

"Let me rephrase," Mr. Vastapo said. "In whose office did you practice dentistry?"

"Marcus's," Eva said.

"The defendant's office?" Mr. Vastapo asked.

"Yes," Eva said.

Mr. Vastapo took a few steps away from Eva then moved toward her suddenly and spoke quickly.

"Isn't it true, Miss Carreña, that you resented the defendant for the professional stress he placed upon you to the point you took pain-killers, speed, and booze to cope? Isn't it true you resented the defendant? Isn't it true you did anything to relieve that stress? Isn't it true the concussion you suffered on October the 13th caused you to hallucinate the events at the defendant's home on October the 14th, that you had a grudge against the defendant and subconsciously decided to seek revenge by claiming he raped you? Isn't it true the reason you didn't go to the police or hospital immediately after your visit to the defendant on October the 14th was because there was no evidence of rape in your vaginal secretions?"

"Objection, Your Honor, objection!" Ms. Haughf repeated throughout Mr. Vastapo's accusations.

"Sustained!" The Court said. "Strike Mr. Vastapo's questions from the record."

"No further questions," Mr. Vastapo said.

"You may step down," The Court said to Eva. "I remind you to keep secret these trial proceedings, and do not divulge its contents to anyone outside this courtroom."

"I call Marcus Cracbern to the stand," Ms. Haughf said.

"The defendant?" Mr. Vastapo asked. "Your Honor, the defendant invokes his 5th Amendment right. I'm surprised at Prosecution for making the request."

"The defendant has a right to refuse testifying against himself," The Court said. "Ms. Haughf, choose another witness."

"I call Dr. Harvey to the stand," Ms. Haughf said.

Dr. Harvey took the witness stand and remained standing.

"Raise your right hand, please," The Court Clerk said. "Do you solemnly swear that the evidence you shall give in this trial shall be the truth, the whole truth, and nothing but the truth, and that you will keep secret these trial proceedings, so help you God?"

"Yes," Dr. Harvey said.

"Please be seated," The Court said. "State your full name in the microphone, please."

"Doctor Harold Harvey."

"Dr. Harvey," Ms. Haughf said. "Do you recognize the plaintiff?"

"Yes," Dr. Harvey said. "That's Eva Carreña."

"And how do you know the plaintiff?" Ms. Haughf asked.

"I treated her at Legacy Emanuel Hospital for injuries," Dr. Harvey said. "I also delivered her daughter."

"Can you state the name of Eva's child?"

"Yes. Evanita Soledad Carreña."

"Doctor, are you in charge of the DNA testing to determine paternity of Evanita?" Ms. Haughf asked.

"Yes."

"Would you share those results with the courtroom, please?" Ms. Haughf asked.

"I object," Mr. Vastapo said. "All evidence gathered by the plaintiff must be shared with the defense first."

"Your Honor," Ms. Haughf said. "Mr. Vastapo has a short memory. It was agreed that paternity results would be revealed to no one until now."

"Overruled, Mr. Vastapo," The Court said. "Please, Dr. Harvey, let the courtroom know the results."

"After taking and processing DNA samples from the plaintiff, from Evanita, and from the defendant, we have determined there is a sixty-percent chance the defendant is the father," Dr. Harvey said.

"Can you be more precise, doctor?" Ms. Haughf said.

"No, I can't," Dr. Harvey said.

"What I mean is this—is the defendant the father of the plaintiff's daughter?" Ms. Haughf said.

"There's a sixty percent chance."

"Yes or no?" Ms. Haughf pressed.

"I can't say with any certainty," Dr. Harvey said.

"Why not?" Ms. Haughf said.

"DNA testing is time-consuming and at times complicated. In this particular case, Evanita has certain mutations that make paternity determination more difficult," Dr. Harvey said. "I've never seen these types of mutations before."

"But the odds favor paternity for the defendant?" Ms. Haughf asked.

"Slightly," Dr. Harvey said.

"No further questions," Ms. Haughf said.

Dr. Harvey stood up as if to leave.

"A moment please," Mr. Vastapo said. "I wish to cross-examine."

"I thought I was done," Dr. Harvey said.

"Please remain seated and answer all questions put to you by the defense attorney," The Court said.

"Dr. Harvey, since the plaintiff did not establish your credibility through *voir dire*, I will," Mr. Vastapo said. "What is your occupation and assignment?"

"I am an Emergency Room surgeon at Legacy Emanuel Hospital," Dr. Harvey said.

"How long have you been assigned at Legacy Emanuel?" Mr. Vastapo asked.

"Twelve years."

"What is your education that qualifies you as an Emergency Room surgeon?" Mr. Vastapo asked.

"I received a Bachelor of Science degree in biology from the University of Oregon. I received a medical degree from Oregon Health and Science University," Dr. Harvey said.

"What is your experience in blood testing and DNA testing?" Mr. Vastapo asked.

"Object," Ms. Haughf said. "Dr. Harvey is here to answer for DNA testing only."

"Your Honor, since this is a speedy trial, any evidence we wish to submit is fair game. I am simply establishing credibility of the witness for both blood and DNA testing. I will demonstrate relevance as new evidence is submitted," Mr. Vastapo said.

"Make sure you do," The Court said. "Objection overruled. Dr. Harvey—please answer the question."

"I do not personally perform blood tests or DNA tests. Blood tests are performed in the lab at Legacy Emanuel. We send out for DNA testing. I am qualified to read and interpret the results," Dr. Harvey explained.

"What is the percent probability that the plaintiff is the mother?" Mr. Vastapo asked.

"I don't understand," Dr. Harvey said. "The plaintiff is the mother."

"And how was that established?" Mr. Vastapo asked.

"Objection, Your Honor," Ms. Haughf said. "Are we to debate the color of the sky and the texture of the earth?"

"Mr. Vastapo, unless you have a good reason for wasting The Court's time on the obvious," The Court said.

"I'm getting to it, Your Honor, if you'll give me a little more latitude," Mr. Vastapo said.

"Only a little more," The Court said. "Dr. Harvey, please answer the question, and quickly."

"I removed the daughter, Evanita, from the plaintiff's uterus, Eva," Dr. Harvey said. "This makes her the mother."

"Now using the DNA results, what is the probability the plaintiff is the mother?" Mr. Vastapo asked.

"Object. Maternity is already established. Mr. Vastapo is wasting time," Ms. Haughf said. "This is a paternity trial, not how-many-ways-can-we-establish-maternity trial."

"Sustained. Mr. Vastapo—do you have a learning impediment?" The Court asked.

"Your Honor, I am attempting to establish the reliability of DNA testing. My question regarding probability of the plaintiff being the mother is for comparison against the sixty percent already established for paternity probability."

"Then rephrase your question, and move on," The Court said.

"For comparison against the DNA paternity test, what did the DNA test show for maternal probability?" Mr. Vastapo asked.

"One hundred percent," Dr. Harvey said. "And zero percent. But that is for mitochondrial DNA."

The court murmured in confusion.

"Dr. Harvey—I think we are all a little confused here. Could you expand on your answer?" Mr. Vastapo asked.

"Certainly," Dr. Harvey said. "Maternity DNA tests tend to focus on mitochondrial DNA. This is because mitochondrial DNA is passed down directly from mother to child. A father's mitochondrial DNA is never passed down to the child. Now paternity DNA testing uses cellular DNA. This is not the same as mitochondrial DNA. Maternity DNA tests should be straightforward and easy; paternity DNA tests require some work because a father's DNA combines with a mother's DNA to form the child's DNA."

"And as to the testimony you gave regarding one hundred percent and zero percent maternity match—what did you mean by that?" Mr. Vastapo asked.

"As I said, typically, a child inherits his or her mitochondrial DNA from the mother and only the mother," Dr. Harvey said. "This means all mitochondrial DNA in the child match those of the mother. In Evanita's DNA testing, we determined that half her mitochondrial DNA match those of the mother. The other half do not. So the one-hundred-percent match is for the matching half of mitochondria, and the zero percent is for the other half."

"Did you examine these mitochondria?" Mr. Vastapo asked.

"Yes. Both types of mitochondria are perfectly healthy," Dr. Harvey explained.

"In your opinion, why does Evanita have mitochondria that do not match her mother's DNA?" Mr. Vastapo asked.

"I don't know."

"Did you test these nonmatching mitochondria against the defendant's mitochondrial DNA?" Mr. Vastapo asked.

"Yes."

"What were the results?"

"Inconclusive."

"How can the result be inconclusive?" Mr. Vastapo asked.

"The defendant's mitochondrial DNA is damaged for an unknown reason," Dr. Harvey said. "We are unable to properly test his mitochondrial DNA against the plaintiff's daughter."

"Your Honor, at this time I would like to introduce new evidence," Mr. Vastapo said. "Dr. Harvey will now discuss blood typing of the plaintiff's daughter against the plaintiff and the defendant."

"I object," Ms. Haughf said. "I called this witness."

"Overruled," The Court said. "Ms. Haughf—you have the right to re-direct if you wish to challenge this new evidence. Please proceed, Mr. Vastapo."

"Dr. Harvey, can you determine paternity based on blood type?" Mr. Vastapo asked.

"Not precisely," Dr. Harvey said. "The best we can do is to eliminate paternity."

"Eliminate? What do you mean by that?" Mr. Vastapo asked.

"A mother's and father's combined blood types will yield only certain possible blood types. If the child's blood is not one of those possible types, the alleged father cannot be the father," Dr. Harvey said.

"Did the defendant submit a blood sample to you for paternity testing?" Mr. Vastapo asked.

"Yes, he did," Dr. Harvey said.

"What was the result?" Mr. Vastapo asked.

"According to the blood tests on the defendant, the plaintiff, and the plaintiff's daughter, the defendant cannot be the father," Dr. Harvey said.

The people in the courtroom gasped.

"Dr. Harvey, you testified that you delivered the plaintiff's daughter, is that correct?" Mr. Vastapo asked.

"Yes."

"What was the daughter's medical condition?" Mr. Vastapo asked.

"She was in critical need of blood," Dr. Harvey said.

"Did you succeed in treating the plaintiff's daughter?"

"Yes."

"How did you accomplish that?"

"We found a blood donor and infused Evanita with the blood," Dr. Harvey said.

"Was the donor the defendant?"

"No."

"Could the defendant have donated blood?"

"Yes he could have donated, but we couldn't use his blood in the plaintiff's daughter without killing her. The two bloods aren't compatible."

"Doctor—you testified that you found a donor and infused this blood into the plaintiff's daughter."

"Yes, that's correct."

"Based on the donor's blood type, could the donor be a parent?" Mr. Vastapo asked.

"Yes, but that doesn't prove—"

"A 'yes' or 'no' please," Mr. Vastapo said. "Could the donor be the parent based on blood type?"

"Yes."

"Dr. Harvey," Mr. Vastapo said. "Who is the donor?"

"Doctor Roberta MacNessi," Dr. Harvey said.

The courtroom erupted in excitement.

"Order, order!" The Court gaveled.

"No more questions," Mr. Vastapo said.

"Ms. Haughf—do you wish to re-direct?" The Court asked.

"No, but I reserve the right to recall the witness," Ms. Haughf said.

"So ordered. You may step down, Dr. Harvey," The Court said. "I remind you of your oath to maintain trial confidentiality."

"I call Johnny Pindus to the stand," Ms. Haughf said.

Nine-year old Johnny Pindus took the stand and remained standing.

"Objection, Your Honor," Mr. Vastapo said. "What is a child doing as a witness?"

"Mr. Vastapo," The Court said. "Is that the best you can do? Don't answer. Overruled."

Younger Johnny took the witness stand and remained standing.

"Raise your right hand, please," The Court Clerk said. "Do you solemnly swear that the evidence you shall give in this trial shall be the truth, the whole truth, and nothing but the truth, and that you will keep secret these trial proceedings, so help you God?"

"I do," younger Johnny said.

"Please be seated," The Court said. "State your full name in the microphone, please."

"Johanidan Reginald Pindus," younger Johnny said.

"Hello, Johnny," Ms. Haughf said.

"Hello, Ms. Haughf."

"Are you nervous?"

"A little."

"Well try to relax."

"Okay."

"The first thing we need to do, Johnny, is prove you are a clairsentient," Ms. Haughf said.

"A what?" Mr. Vastapo asked.

"Objection," Judge Jillian said.

"You can't object," Mr. Vastapo said. "You're The Court."

"I know who I am," said The Court. "Do you? Now please, wait your turn."

"Your Honor, I intend to conduct a *voir dire* on the witness to establish his expertise in the field of clairsentience," Ms. Haughf said.

"This is highly unusual," The Court said. "Are you mocking The Court with supernatural gobbledy-gook?"

"No, Your Honor," Ms. Haughf said.

"Are you pulling a Vastapo?" The Court asked.

"I object, Your Honor," Mr. Vastapo said.

"Your Honor, I take my work quite seriously, unlike Mr. Vastapo," Ms. Haughf said.

"I object to that too," Mr. Vastapo said.

"Both objections overruled," The Court said. "But Ms. Haughf—I do not take kindly to courtroom games."

"No courtroom games, Your Honor. I can prove Johnny's credibility."

Judge Jillian paused. Mr. Vastapo opened his mouth to say something, but before he could speak, Judge Jillian spoke.

"Please proceed," The Court said. "But do not waste the courtroom's time."

"Thank you," Ms. Haughf said. "Johnny—we are going to prove to the courtroom you have the ability to read human female biology. Your Honor, when Johnny incurs a vibration to his skull and touches a human female, he can see her biology as if performing a computer aided tomography scan."

"Impossible," Mr. Vastapo said.

"Mr. Vastapo, please!" The Court said. "Ms. Haughf—how do you intend to prove Mr. Pindus's alleged ability?"

"I will need a volunteer—a woman—who has a birthmark or other special feature that is not visible to the courtroom at this moment. When she lifts a selected piece of clothing, she will reveal this mark—within reason of modesty of course."

"I will volunteer," The Court said.

"Your Honor, please extend your hand to Johnny," Ms. Haughf said. "Johnny, please touch Judge Jillian's hand."

Younger Johnny touched the judge's hand.

"Your Honor—what sort of feature should Johnny describe?" Ms. Haughf asked.

"A birthmark," The Court said.

"Thank you. I will now wind up this vibrating toy and hold it to Johnny's head," Ms. Haughf said. "Johnny, I want you to concentrate on Judge Jillian's biology and tell the courtroom about her birthmark."

Ms. Haughf wound up the toy and held it to Johnny's head. The toy vibrated, Johnny closed his eyes, and he concentrated.

"I see a body, a shape," Johnny said. "No, it's blurry. Now it's clear, no, I'm seeing double. I've never had this problem before. I'm seeing double. I can't focus on an image. Wait, there's something on a foot. The right foot. Not the big toe, but the toe next to it. It's an ingrown toenail. It's infected."

"That's not a birthmark, that's a medical condition," Mr. Vastapo said.

"I'm sorry, Ms. Haughf, but I have no ingrown toenail," The Court said.

"Uh, I think I know the problem," Ms. Haughf said.

"The problem is, the witness is a phony," Mr. Vastapo said.

"No, he's not," Ms. Haughf said.

Ms. Haughf removed the toy from younger Johnny's head. She removed her right shoe and ripped open her nylons at the toes and showed the courtroom her ingrown toenail.

"Johnny reads women," Ms. Haughf said. "He read Judge Jillian and me at the same time. This explains the double vision. He saw my ingrown toenail. Johnny—I will give you this toy. You wind it up and hold it to your head with one hand while holding Judge Jillian's hand with your other hand."

"Okay," young Johnny said.

Ms. Haughf gave Johnny the toy. He wound it up and held it to his head. He touched Judge Jillian's hand, closed his eyes, and concentrated.

"Judge Jillian has a mole on her upper left shoulder," young Johnny said.

The Court reacted with surprise. She lifted her left sleeve to reveal a mole.

"She also has a red patch on her back just below her neck," young Johnny said.

"I do?" Judge Jillian said.

"If I may, Your Honor," Ms. Haughf said.

Ms. Haughf helped Judge Jillian by turning the judge around and pulling the back of her judge's gown down in the back of the neck. Judge Jillian's back revealed a red patch. The courtroom clapped.

"I guess I do have a red mark," The Court said as she turned around and sat down.

"Judge Jillian has a tattoo that looks like a snake. It says, 'Don't tread on me,' and it's next to her—"

"*Voir dire* is over!" The Court said. "The witness is hereby certified a clairsentient!"

"Thank you, Your Honor," Ms. Haughf grinned. "Johnny, do you see Doctor Roberta MacNessi in the courtroom?"

"Yeah."

"Could you point her out?" Ms. Haughf said.

"Right there," he said.

"Let the record show Mr. Johnny Pindus is pointing to the only woman with red hair in this courtroom, Doctor Roberta MacNessi."

"So noted," The Court said.

"Johnny, do you know the difference between men and women?" Ms. Haughf said.

"Yes."

"In the most polite way you can, please tell us the difference," Ms. Haughf said.

"Men are stocky and strong, women are smooth and curvy," young Johnny said.

"Can you read male biology as you did with Judge Jillian and me?" Ms. Haughf asked.

"No."

"Have you used your clairsentience on Doctor Carreña?"

"Yeah."

"Were you able to read her?"

"Yeah."

"I would like you to read her now," Ms. Haughf said.

"Okay."

"I request Eva Carreña stand by the witness for a demonstration," Ms. Haughf said.

Eva walked up to and next to young Johnny.

"Now we'll do as before," Ms. Haughf said. "Johnny—wind up the toy, hold it on your head, and touch Eva's hand."

Young Johnny did as instructed.

"What can you read about Eva?"

"She just had a baby," Johnny said.

The courtroom laughed.

"She can bend her elbows backward," Johnny said.

Eva bent her elbows, and indeed they bent a little backward.

"She has a scar around her belly button," Johnny said.

Eva lifted her shirt and revealed the scar.

"Is Eva a woman?" Ms. Haughf asked.

"Yeah," Johnny said.

"Thank you, Eva. You may sit down," Ms. Haughf said.

Eva returned to her seat.

"I request Doctor Roberta MacNessi stand by the witness for a demonstration," Ms. Haughf said.

Roberta walked up to and next to young Johnny.

"We'll do as before," Ms. Haughf said. "Johnny—wind up the toy, hold it on your head, and touch Doctor MacNessi's hand."

Young Johnny did as instructed.

"What can you read about Doctor MacNessi?"

"She has damaged ovaries as a result of X-ray overexposure as a child. She has a scar around her belly button. Her monthly flow—"

"That's enough, young man," Judge Jillian said.

"Is Doctor MacNessi a woman?" Ms. Haughf asked.

"Yeah," younger Johnny said.

"No more questions. Thank you, Doctor MacNessi. Thank you, Johnny."

"Mr. Vastapo?" The Court asked.

"Yes, thank you. Johnny—why did Ms. Haughf ask you those questions?"

"Objection. Subjective," Ms. Haughf said.

"Your Honor, if Mr. Pindus is a clairsentient, then he also read the thoughts of Prosecution. I simply wish to prove his ability."

"Logical. Overruled," The Court said.

"She wanted to prove that Doctor MacNessi is a woman," young Johnny said.

"Why?" Mr. Vastapo asked.

"To prevent you from suggesting Doctor MacNessi is the father of Evanita," young Johnny said.

"What other strategies does she plan?" Mr. Vastapo asked.

"Objection, Your Honor. Prosecution's game plan is confidential to Prosecution's team. Mr. Vastapo is soliciting this information illegally from a minor."

"Mr. Vastapo. You are not to question the witness about Prosecution's game plan," The Court said.

"No further questions."

"Then I recall Dr. Harvey to the stand," Ms. Haughf said.

"Johnny," The Court said. "I remind you not to speak of this trial outside of this courtroom."

"Yes, ma'am," Johnny said.

"You may step down, Johnny," The Court said.

Johnny stepped down, and Dr. Harvey sat in the witness stand.

"Dr. Harvey," The Court said. "I remind you that you are still under oath. Please proceed, Ms. Haughf."

"Thank you, Your Honor. Dr. Harvey—based on blood type, can the plaintiff be the mother?" Ms. Haughf asked.

"Yes."

"You also testified that based on blood type, the blood donor to save Evanita's life could also be a parent."

"Yes."

"Dr. Harvey—given that my adversary has asked absurdly simple questions, I am about to do the same. What types of people must come together to conceive a child?" Ms. Haughf asked.

"I...any sort of people—white, black, Asian, Hispanic—as long as the couple has reached puberty, they can conceive."

"No, no, let me rephrase," Ms. Haughf said. "What genders of people must come together to conceive?"

"A male and female?" Dr. Harvey seemed to ask.

"Yes. Which gender is the plaintiff?" Ms. Haughf asked.

"Female."

"What gender must the other parent be?" Ms. Haughf asked.

"Male."

"On what gender must this paternity trial focus?" Ms. Haughf asked.

"Objection. Out of expert's scope," Mr. Vastapo said.

"Sustained," said The Court.

"Who donated the winning blood?" Ms. Haughf asked.

"The winning blood? I don't understand," Dr. Harvey said.

"The winning blood. The blood donor who saved Evanita's life. Who donated the blood?" Ms. Haughf asked.

"Doctor Roberta MacNessi," Dr. Harvey said.

"Is she in this courtroom?" Ms. Haughf asked.

"Object," Mr. Vastapo said.

"What now?" Ms. Haughf asked.

"Mr. Vastapo—what on Earth can you object to now?" The Court asked.

"She."

"Are you objecting to Doctor MacNessi?" The Court asked.

"Doctor MacNessi was asked to attend this trial," Ms. Haughf said. "Defense has no right to object to trial procedure."

"Mr. Vastapo, you can't object to trial procedure. If you do, I will hold you in contempt," The Court said.

"I object to the use of the pronoun 'she' in reference to Doctor MacNessi," Mr. Vastapo said.

The courtroom burst into laughter.

"Order, order!" The Court gaveled. "Mr. Vastapo—are you blind? Are you ill?"

"No, Your Honor. This trial is to establish paternity. I intend to do just that," Mr. Vastapo said.

"Your honor, Defense is on the defense. His role—" Ms. Haughf started.

"Is to defend my client. The best defense is a good offense. I intend to prove my client's innocence by establishing correct paternity," Mr. Vastapo said.

"Then please wait your turn," The Court said. "You will be permitted to re-cross if you like. Ms. Haughf—please continue to re-direct."

"Thank you, Your Honor. Dr. Harvey, is Doctor Roberta MacNessi in this courtroom?" Ms. Haughf asked.

"Yes."

"Would you identify her verbally, please?" Ms. Haughf asked.

"She is sitting in the first row behind the plaintiff. She is the only woman with red hair," Dr. Harvey said.

"Dr. Harvey—you just testified that Doctor MacNessi is a woman," Ms. Haughf said.

"Yes."

"Can she be the father of the plaintiff's daughter?" Ms. Haughf asked.

"Given that a father is a male, and Doctor MacNessi is female, the conclusion is—no, she cannot be the father."

"No more questions."

"You may re-cross, Mr. Vastapo," The Court said.

"Dr. Harvey, you testified that Doctor MacNessi is a woman," Mr. Vastapo said.

"Yes."

"Is that a professional evaluation?" Mr. Vastapo asked.

"No, it's common sense," Dr. Harvey said.

"Dr. Harvey. You are under oath to give the truth and nothing but the truth. Now based on your profession, can you tell us if Doctor MacNessi is a woman?" Mr. Vastapo asked.

"To do so I would have to perform an examination, and even that is questionable. The only sure method is a DNA test," Dr. Harvey said.

"With The Court's permission, I request a DNA test for Doctor MacNessi," Mr. Vastapo said.

"Object. Totally irrelevant," Ms. Haughf said.

"Your Honor, I intend to prove that Doctor MacNessi is male, that Doctor MacNessi engaged in sexual intercourse with the plaintiff, and Doctor MacNessi is the father of the plaintiff's daughter," Mr. Vastapo said.

Judge Jillian let out a big sigh.

"This is the most ludicrous, far-fetched, and pathetic attempt at defense, Mr. Vastapo. Why not simply proclaim me the father?" The Court asked.

"If you were a man, I might," Mr. Vastapo said.

"Ms. Haughf, Mr. Vastapo—approach the bench," The Court said.

Ms. Haughf and Mr. Vastapo approached.

"Mr. Vastapo—this is not a circus, this is not a comedy show, this is not a political convention!" The Court said. "I am this close to having your bar license revoked in this state. Try me one more time, and I'll have the bailiff throw you out to the street in disgrace!"

"But Your Honor, I have every reason to believe—" Mr. Vastapo started.

"Of what?!" The Court asked.

"If I could just get your permission to perform a DNA test on Doctor MacNessi, I'm confident I can show she is both a male and the father. The fact that her blood saved baby Evanita, and the fact that the defendant's blood is incompatible leads me to believe Doctor MacNessi is the father," Mr. Vastapo said.

"Doctor MacNessi is a woman, dammit!" The Court said. "This is a speedy trial. We don't chase geese by sampling Doctor

MacNessi's tissue and waiting another three weeks only to find out she's a woman! We already know she's a woman!"

"But this goose could be the one. And we don't have to wait three weeks. The DNA test has already been performed," Mr. Vastapo said.

"Your Honor! This was obviously done without Doctor Mac-Nessi's knowledge. It's no wonder he sought your permission first."

"Yes, this is highly unusual," The Court said. "Mr. Vastapo—do you have anything else to pursue in your defense?"

"No," Mr. Vastapo said. "I stand by the results of Doctor MacNessi's DNA tests. Once revealed, defense will rest without any further questioning."

Judge Jillian grinned. She was delighted with the idea of a speedy trial.

"Then we will admit the evidence to complete this speedy trial," The Court said.

"Your Honor, I object!" Ms. Haughf said. "This is a bad poker game with Doctor MacNessi as the wild card."

"Doctor MacNessi is a woman. There's nothing to fear, Counsel," The Court said.

Judge Jillian waved the two attorneys back to their places.

"Proceed, Mr. Vastapo," The Court said.

"Dr. Harvey, please give us the results of the paternity test against Doctor Roberta MacNessi," Mr. Vastapo said.

"WHAT!?" Roberta yelled.

The courtroom reacted in an uproar.

"Order, order!" The Court gaveled.

"This is insane!" Roberta yelled. "I never submitted my DNA for a paternity test!"

"Please, Doctor MacNessi, return to your seat and be silent," The Court said.

"No! This is in violation of my civil rights to privacy!" Roberta said.

"Your Honor," Mr. Vastapo said. "When Doctor MacNessi donated her blood to save baby Evanita, she yielded certain rights for blood analysis."

"But not for a paternity suit!" Roberta yelled.

"No more outbursts!" The Court yelled as she pounded her gavel.

Roberta tried to say something else, but Judge Jillian pounded her gavel each time Roberta did.

"Jan, what's going on?" Eva whispered to Ms. Haughf.

"Some stupid attempt by defense before he loses the trial," Ms. Haughf said. "Don't worry—this will all be over soon."

"Dr. Harvey, please present the results," The Court said.

"According to the DNA test, there's a sixty-percent chance Doctor MacNessi is the father," Dr. Harvey said.

Mr. Vastapo stood in disbelief.

"Are you sure, doctor? Only sixty-percent?" Mr. Vastapo asked.

"Yes."

"But MacNessi is the father!" Mr. Vastapo blurted.

"Object. Supposition," Ms. Haughf said.

"Sustained," said The Court. "Mr. Vastapo, do you have any additional questions?"

Mr. Vastapo stared at the floor and motioned his fingers as if rethinking something.

"Mr. Vastapo?" The Court demanded.

Mr. Vastapo remained deep in thought.

"Mr. Vastapo! Speedy trial!" The Court said.

"Give me a moment, I'll think of something," Mr. Vastapo said.

Ms. Haughf threw her papers into the air in disbelief. Judge Jillian pounded her gavel to get Mr. Vastapo's attention.

"Bailiff, have Mr. Vastapo take a seat," The Court said.

The bailiff forced Mr. Vastapo to his seat.

"You may re-re-direct, if you wish," The Court said to Ms. Haughf.

"Dr. Harvey," Ms. Haughf said. "Does the DNA test of Doctor MacNessi indicate gender?"

"Yes, it does," Dr. Harvey said.

"According to DNA testing, what is Doctor MacNessi's gender?" Ms. Haughf asked.

"Female."

"No more questions," Ms. Haughf said.

"You may step down, Dr. Harvey. I remind you to keep secret these trial proceedings, and do not divulge its contents to anyone outside this—"

"Wait!" Mr. Vastapo shouted. "I wish to re-re-cross!"

"Is there no sanctity left?" Ms. Haughf said. "Your game is over, Defense. The dinner bell has rung."

"Your Honor, please!" Mr. Vastapo said. "Prosecution had the opportunity to re-re-direct. By right I am allowed to follow with a cross."

"This had better be the last cross-examination of this witness!" The Court said. "Make it fast!"

"Dr. Harvey," Mr. Vastapo said. "Was there a mitochondrial DNA test performed on Doctor MacNessi?"

"Yes."

"Does it match that of baby Evanita?" Mr. Vastapo asked.

"I don't know. I didn't check," Dr. Harvey said.

"Can you check now?" Mr. Vastapo asked.

Dr. Harvey reviewed his papers.

"Your Honor, Doctor MacNessi is a proven female. She cannot be the father. This paternity trial seeks a male," Ms. Haughf said.

"This paternity trial seeks a human parent who is not the child-bearing mother," Mr. Vastapo said. "I may have been wrong about gender. But no one can ignore the blood test! Doctor MacNessi must be the other parent!"

"Absurd! Haven't we entertained the taxpayers' money enough?" Ms. Haughf asked.

"I have it," Dr. Harvey said.

The courtroom grew silent and hung onto Dr. Harvey's next words.

"Doctor MacNessi's mitochondrial DNA does...NOT match baby Evanita's."

The courtroom breathed a sigh of relief and broke into laughter. Some joked about the silliness of a woman being paternal.

"What would you call her?" one asked.

"A paterna?" another asked.

"That's all, Dr. Harvey," The Court said. "You may step—"

"No, wait!" Mr. Vastapo said.

"No more no-waits," The Court said. "I want to hear closing arguments."

"But Your Honor, I did not phrase the question correctly," Mr. Vastapo said.

"What's to phrase? Roberta isn't the father. Cracbern is! And he's going to pay!" Ms. Haughf said.

"Dr. Harvey, one last question—the most important question of the trial—which mitochondrial DNA of Evanita's did you compare against Doctor MacNessi's?"

"They're all the—" Dr. Harvey said.

"The same? No, you testified baby Evanita has two types of mitochondrial DNA. Which one did you compare against for MacNessi?"

Dr. Harvey looked at the papers again.

"Oh," the doctor said.

"Oh?! What do you mean, Doctor?!" Mr. Vastapo asked.

"I compared Doctor MacNessi's mitochondrial DNA against baby Evanita's type A mitochondrial DNA. Evanita's type A mitochondrial DNA matches her mother, the plaintiff Eva Carreña," Dr. Harvey said.

"Compare against the other type, please!" Mr. Vastapo begged.

Dr. Harvey studied his papers again. The courtroom fell into a more intense hush than when he first examined his papers.

"I...don't know what to say," Dr. Harvey said with an expression of realization.

"Say it," Mr. Vastapo said. "Say it!"

"Baby Evanita has two types of mitochondria—type A and type B," Dr. Harvey said.

"Yes, we know this!" Mr. Vastapo said.

"Type A matches Eva Carreña," Dr. Harvey continued.

"Yes, yes! You testified this already!" Mr. Vastapo said.

"Type B matches...Roberta MacNessi."

The courtroom remained in silence. Eva looked at Ms. Haughf. Ms. Haughf gave Mr. Vastapo a dirty look. Mr. Vastapo looked at Judge Jillian with a canary-swallowing grin. Marcus looked confused. Roberta looked at Eva, and Eva turned back to look at Roberta. Eva smiled a little. Roberta looked back and covered her mouth.

"We have a conflict," Ms. Haughf said to break the silence. "Judgment of paternity can only be satisfied with the selection of a male."

"I object," Mr. Vastapo said. "There is nothing in the Paternity Acknowledgment Form stating gender of paternity."

"Mr. Vastapo is correct," The Court said. "It is generally understood that only men can satisfy paternity, but it is not specifically documented as such. Dr. Harvey—are your test results notarized?"

"Yes, Your Honor."

"Hand them to me, please," The Court said.

Dr. Harvey handed his documents to Judge Jillian. She added them to a bundle of other papers. The courtroom fell silent again. Judge Jillian tapped her fingers on her desk and paused in thought.

"This is a speedy trial," The Court said. "As such, and in light of this latest evidence, we will not hold closing arguments. I will render my decision now. The law does not create fantasy or delve into the supernatural. That is left to novels and religions. Nor does the law attempt to explain things when no evidence is available. Evidence is presented, and judgment is made on this evidence. Based on the evidence presented here, Doctor Roberta MacNessi passes the paternity test. The plaintiff has no further claim against the defendant, and the defendant is excused."

Mr. Vastapo shook Marcus's hand in congratulations.

"Given this, it is up to the plaintiff to determine what options she wishes to pursue. She may seek financial compensation from the paterna, the paterna being Doctor Roberta MacNessi, and the paterna would be required under the law to pay."

"The paterna must be required to pay," Mr. Vastapo said. "The plaintiff stipulated this in the pretrial paperwork. Had the defendant been found the father, he most certainly would have paid."

"Mr. Vastapo has a point. Ms. Haughf—you did request financial compensation in this paternity trial," The Court said.

"Your Honor...my client...one moment," Ms. Haughf said.

Ms. Haughf whispered to Eva. Eva whispered back. The two argued back and forth.

"Your Honor," Roberta said as she stepped forward. "May I say something?"

"You have not been called, but I so recognize you now," The Court said.

"Am I right in understanding that baby Evanita's biological parents are Eva and myself?" Roberta asked.

"According to this court, yes," The Court said.

"And there's a possibility I will be required to support Eva and baby Evanita financially?"

"The pretrial paperwork says so, yes," The Court said.

"If the biological parents should marry..." Roberta suggested.

"In all cases prior to this one, a marriage ends any special financial support as it is assumed the spouse of the mother will provide live-in support," The Court said.

"Then I have this to say," Roberta said.

Roberta walked over to Ms. Haughf's and Eva's bench, knelt before Eva, and said, "Eva—will you marry me?"

The courtroom erupted in hysteria.

"Order, order!" The Court gaveled. "Doctor MacNessi—the state does not provide for same-sex marriage."

"But it provides for biological parents to marry," Roberta said.

"No," Mr. Vastapo said. "It only allows for opposite-gendered people to marry."

"The state does not define marriage based on biological parents, it defines marriage based on gender," The Court said.

"But shouldn't the biological parents of a child be allowed to marry? They have already made a commitment unto science and unto God," Roberta said.

"I would caution you on your reference to God. Not all who believe in God believe two biological mothers are a part of God's Plan. The state does not set law based on discipline or disciple, it sets law based on the will of the people—regardless of cosmic reality. I appreciate your position, Doctor MacNessi, and I wish I could help, but I am bound by the will of the people. I cannot provide any special marriage treatment in this trial. I will establish paternity, however. Ms. Haughf, does your client wish to seek financial support from the paterna?"

Ms. Haughf spoke briefly with Eva.

"My client does not wish to seek financial support," Ms. Haughf said.

"Miss Carreña," said The Court. "Do you understand that by waiving your right to seek financial compensation from the paterna, the paterna will be under no obligation to support you or your daughter financially?"

"I understand," Eva said.

"Do you still wish to waive this right?" The Court asked.

"I do," Eva said.

Judge Jillian finished the paternity paperwork and handed it to the bailiff. Eva and Ms. Haughf signed one part while Roberta signed another.

"Mr. Vastapo—congratulations," The Court said. "Your client is exempt from paternity. Ladies and gentlemen of the courtroom, please give a round of applause to the first female biological parents in the world."

The courtroom clapped. Eva stood up and hugged Roberta. Roberta hugged back. The two exchanged kisses and hugs with the courtroom cheering. All cheered except for Mr. Vastapo and Marcus. Marcus became irritated, and as the cheering continued, he stood up from his wheelchair defiantly.

"Get back in your wheelchair, Marcus," Mr. Vastapo said.

"No, no, no!" Marcus said to the courtroom. "This is all wrong. This is all wrong. Two women can't have a baby. It's impossible."

"This trial says otherwise," The Court said.

"There must be a mistrial here. There must be. It isn't fair to men. It isn't fair to me. Men are hunters, fighters, lovers, and protectors. We are the breadwinners. Women should manage the home, have our children, and raise them. We fight hard, and women respect us. That's the way of the natural world. Not this travesty today. Women aren't designed to have children with each other."

"Marcus, sit down," Mr. Vastapo said.

"No, I won't sit down. Not until I've been heard. Does anyone understand what is happening here? Anyone?"

"It's just a paternity trial, Marcus," Eva said. "That's all."

"No, it isn't all. This is precedence—precedence for women to exterminate men. It's gendercide. Doesn't anyone see this? Women won't need us anymore. They'll have babies with each other. What will we do? Dr. Harvey—can two women have boys?"

"No, they can't," Dr. Harvey said. "They can only have girls."

"Doc, please, don't encourage him," The Court said.

"Yes, encourage me," Marcus said. "Someone encourage me. Because I speak for myself and all men when I say we will become discouraged. We will be excluded from parenting until the last of us dies of old age. This is the thanks we get for millions of years of taking care of our women. Gendercide. Gendercide!"

Marcus's blood pressure increased significantly. His face turned beet-red. He waved his arms around violently as he repeated the word *gendercide*. Mr. Vastapo attempted to help him sit in his wheelchair, but Marcus beat back. The bailiff and a sheriff worked to subdue Marcus. Marcus resisted and resisted until suddenly something broke loose in his groin, and blood poured onto the floor. He screamed in pain before collapsing. People screamed at the sight. An ambulance was called and carried Marcus to Legacy Emanuel Hospital.

"So Roberta's my father?" Evanita asked Geneva.

Geneva held silent.

"Johnny, I mean Shawna, is it true?" Evanita asked. "Is Roberta my father?"

"How can she be your father?" Johnny asked back. "She's a woman. Only men can be fathers."

"But...it's impossible," Evanita said. "Two mothers? But Mama said I had no father. Was she telling the truth? All these years I thought she was lying. Tell me, Grandma, tell me!"

"Eva and Roberta are your mothers," Geneva said. "Judge Jillian referred to Roberta as the paterna. I like to think of Roberta as the Wanda—the wandering person, or the Wather—the wandering mother."

"But how, Grandma, how? Women can't have children together," Evanita said.

"I'm not quite sure," Geneva said. "But I think we will find out soon."

CHAPTER 16

Cracbern's Demise

1990 Jul 14, Sat. Legacy Emanuel Hospital. Portland, Oregon.

Eva stood in the neonatal intensive care unit where baby Evanita was sleeping.

"She's so beautiful," Eva said to the nurse. "Earl was right. She looks like Roberta."

"Evanita is doing very well," the nurse said. "She's ready to go home with you."

The nurse removed baby Evanita from her incubator, wrapped her in a blanket, and gave her to Eva.

"My sweet little Evanita," Eva said to her baby, "I never want to let you go."

"May I hold her for a moment?" said a familiar voice.

Eva turned around quickly. It was Roberta.

"Oh, Roberta! Of course!" Eva said with tears of joy.

Eva handed baby Evanita to Roberta.

"I remember when I held you before, little Evanita," Roberta said. "I felt a little strange then, and I didn't know why. Now I know why. I'm your second mother, your paterna."

"Roberta," Eva said. "I...we...I wish we..."

"Would you like to raise her together?" Roberta asked.

"I would very much like that," Eva said.

Kay interrupted their meeting.

"Kay! What are you doing here?" Eva asked.

"It's Marcus," Kay said. "He's here as a patient. He's dying."

"It is his time," Roberta said.

"Please," Kay said. "I know he's had a troubled life."

"That's an understatement," Roberta said.

"But he's still a human being. I'm his stepsister. I've known him his entire life. It hurts me to see him in pain," Kay said.

"What do you want from us, Kay?" Eva asked.

"I want you to stand with me and with Marcus. He only has hours, maybe minutes left," Kay said.

"I don't know if I want to," Eva said. "I've moved on, and I don't need to think about him."

"Please," Kay said. "You could bring closure to your life. I don't like doing these things alone."

"It would give us the satisfaction of seeing him die in pain," Roberta said.

"Roberta, you're a doctor. So am I," Eva said.

"I'm human too. And so are you," Roberta said. "Let's see justice prevail."

"Nurse!" Eva called.

The nurse walked over to Eva.

"Please watch Evanita for a moment. I have something to take care of. I'll be back for my baby shortly," Eva said.

Kay led Roberta and Eva to Marcus's room. Marcus writhed in pain. A nurse led young Johnny Pindus to the room.

"Johnny!" Eva said.

"Kay asked me to come," he said.

"Kay?" Eva asked.

"Johnny has a special gift," Kay said. "He can sense things about women no one else can."

"Nurse," Marcus called. "I'm in pain. I need a painkiller."

"Sorry, no controlled substances," the nurse said.

"But I'm in pain, and I'm dying," Marcus said.

"I'm sorry, but you can't have any. Good-day," the nurse said, and she left.

"Interesting," Eva said.

"Kay," Roberta said, "why is Johnny here?"

"I want Johnny to scan us, all of us, and tell us what happened that night on October 14, 1989."

"Is that a good idea?" Roberta asked.

"I don't want to relive that day," Eva said. "What little I remember is sheer horror."

"I don't like it any more than you," Marcus said. "But I'm dying, and I want to know how a fetus lodged itself in my prostate gland."

"What!?" Roberta and Eva replied in shock.

"It's true," Kay said. "This is why Marcus has been sick."

"You mean he has prostate cancer, right?" Eva asked.

"No, he has a real, living fetus in his prostate," Kay said.

"That's impossible," Roberta said.

"Yes, it's impossible," Marcus said. "It's also impossible you're a mother, Roberta. But it's true. And they won't give me a painkiller. They say it's bad for the fetus. So I suffer!"

"You've let us down, Marcus. You've let us all down," Roberta said. "A little over a year ago you were helping me set up a dental practice, but things went downhill quickly after that."

"I've had problems including memory loss, I know that," Marcus said. "I got a former girlfriend pregnant, and she had a boy she named Adrian. She's got my money, now. Did I deserve that?"

"Yes," Roberta said. "Men must take responsibility for their actions. And as for your current illness which I still don't believe, you should have taken responsibility for that too and gone in for surgery when it first became a problem instead of waiting until it was too late."

"I didn't wait! I went to a specialist right away!" Marcus said. "He'd never seen a fetus in a prostate gland before. Never!"

"Marcus, removing the prostate gland is a routine procedure. Why didn't you have it performed?" Roberta asked.

"The technology is there, but that pesky law got in the way," Marcus said.

"What law?" Eva asked.

Marcus's face turned red as a beet. He wanted to speak, but he couldn't.

"Abortion," Kay said.

"What?!" Eva asked.

"Abortion?" Roberta asked.

"Yes! Killing a fetus is abortion!" Marcus said. "Any surgery to my prostate would result in abortion. And the law does not allow for it."

"Marcus," Roberta said. "Roe vs. Wade established abortion rights in this country back in 1973."

"Yes, for women. But not for men," Marcus said. "It's ridiculous. Men can do whatever they want with their bodies. Whatever. The government has no say in what we do. We can have vasectomies, our prostates removed, our testicles removed—anything to our reproductive tract. Anything! Until now! I've been tied up in court for the last six months over this issue, and the legal system is stalled. But the fetus continues to grow, and it won't stop. My body isn't designed to carry a fetus to term. It simply isn't!"

"Is it possible that for the first time in human history, a man is undergoing the same invasion of rights that we women have endured from men since the beginning of time?" Roberta asked.

"I'm being murdered by the legal system!" Marcus said. "Murdered!"

Marcus yelled in pain.

"How long has he had this fetus?" Roberta asked Kay.

"The doctor says his fetus is three months old," Kay said. "There's something else, too. Look."

Kay pulled up Marcus's shirt and revealed a scar around his navel.

"That looks like my scar," Eva said.

"And mine," Roberta said.

"The doctor says an ovum entered Marcus's body through his navel and traveled through his tissues for six months until it combined with Marcus's spermatozoa in his prostate gland."

"But why the prostate?" younger Johnny asked.

"The prostate is the male equivalent of the uterus," Roberta said.

"Yes, that's what the doctor said," Kay said. "It's as if something is backward with Marcus."

"Why?!" Marcus groaned. "Why?!"

"That's what we're here for, Marcus. We're going to find out why," Kay said.

"Wait—then the way Marcus got pregnant," Eva started.

"Could be the same way you got pregnant," Kay said to Eva.

"I'm still not sure how that happened," Eva said.

"Neither am I," Roberta said.

"Well, that's why I have Johnny here. Hopefully, we can find out," Kay said. "Please—sit around Marcus's bed and join hands with each other. We will link with Johnny. Johnny, I made this special helmet for you. It contains a device inside that will send vibrations to your skull."

Roberta, Eva, Kay, and younger Johnny gathered around Marcus's bed and held hands with one another and Marcus. Younger Johnny placed the helmet on his head and pressed a button. Younger Johnny closed his eyes and concentrated.

"I see Roberta," younger Johnny said. "The myelin sheaths on her nerves are weakening. I see Eva—she is lactating. I see Kay. She has a recessive marker for sickle-cell anemia. And I see an outline. The outline has teeth where a skull should be, and there's a little fetus in the middle of the outline."

"Then the fetus is a girl," Roberta said. "Johnny can't pick up men."

"Johnny," Kay said. "Concentrate on the fetus in Marcus. Concentrate."

"I see it. It's a little girl," younger Johnny said.

"Can you see how she came to be?" Kay asked.

"I...don't understand," younger Johnny said.

"Concentrate on the fetus—her blood, her cells, and her cells' movement. Focus on every fetal cell," Kay said.

"I see them," younger Johnny said. "She's beautiful."

"Now, can you predict how the fetus will develop?" Kay asked.

Younger Johnny paused. He shook his head.

"Yes. She is suffering too. She will break through the walls of Marcus's prostate gland and cause lots of bleeding. She'll die," younger Johnny said.

"Now run that in reverse," Kay said. "Run the bleeding backward until you reach the present, and keep going into the past."

Younger Johnny's head shook and twitched.

"She's getting smaller," younger Johnny said. "She has a tail. She looks like a tadpole. Now she's spherical with thousands of divided cells. The cells are undividing. Now just a dozen cells. Now two cells. Now an egg surrounded by sperm. No sperm. The egg is in something—it's in something oblong, like a little nut. It's traveling very slowly up. Up. Up. It's in the belly button. It's...it's...two wheels rolling in a circle, one follows the other. Another two wheels following each other. Push and push the rear wheels drive the van forward. Nekara drives the van. Marcus and Eva asleep. The van enters Sellwood Bridge. Sellwood Bridge. The middle. Crash through the side wall into the river. Willamette River. The van sinks into the river. A little water comes into the van. Nekara dips the duavisha into the water. Two eggs are in the duavisha—two eggs from Roberta. They were pulled from her when she wore the duavisha on her belly button. Nekara is placing the duavisha on her belly button. Something is happening. Heat, light, vapor. The duavisha is creating a copy of itself known as a *pelepa*. An egg is transferred into the pelepa. Nekara is removing the pelepa from her skin. She applies it to Eva's belly button and places the backside of the duavisha against the pelepa and Eva's belly button. The pelepa is pushed into Eva's belly button. It's traveling through Eva's flesh. It's shrinking. It's finding its way into Eva's uterus. It waits. Some of its genes are changing. They are changing to become compatible as if the pelepa egg is a spermatozoon. It waits. An egg is released from Eva's ovary. It travels. It combines with the pelepa egg. It divides."

Younger Johnny paused and took several deep breaths.

"Nekara is pleased. She is the catalyst, the goddess. She has combined life between two Earth women. But she is not done. She wishes to prove she has no limits with fertility. She takes the duavisha and presses it against her belly button. Another bit of tissue is created, another pelepa. The second egg migrates to the pelepa from the duavisha. Nekara takes the pelepa and applies it to Marcus's belly button. She presses the duavisha against the pelepa, but only briefly. Divers have reached the van. The divers are Maggie and Roberta. Nekara takes the duavisha away. Nekara disappears with the duavisha. The pelepa on Marcus's belly button goes into his flesh, but very slowly. The duavisha wasn't on long enough. The pelepa is slow. It is slow."

"Johnny," Kay said. "Concentrate on the pelepa in Marcus. Follow it. Tell us what happens."

"It's shrinking. It's descending. Its genes are unchanged. They will not change. It's descending very slowly. Six months. It enters a tube running through the prostate. Marcus has a relation with a woman. He...it's disgusting. He fertilizes the pelepa. The pelepa dissolves into the prostate. The egg becomes a zygote. It attaches to the inside of the prostate. It grows. It's cramped. Bleeding. Bleeding."

"Okay, Johnny, stop," Kay said.

"Bleeding, bleeding," younger Johnny said.

"He's stuck," Roberta said.

"Everyone, let go," Kay said. "Johnny, stop! Stop!"

Kay removed the helmet from younger Johnny's head. She threw it across the room.

"Bleeding. Bleeding," younger Johnny continued.

"Stop!" Kay said, and she hugged him and shook him.

Younger Johnny stopped. He breathed heavily.

"I'm okay," he said. "I'm very tired."

"Then...the fetus," Marcus stammered. "Roberta is the mother?"

"How does that work?" Eva asked. "Is the mother the one who supplies the egg, or the one who carries the fetus to term?"

"Arrrgg!" Marcus screamed in the final agonies of his life.

Marcus's heartbeat and respiration increased. Doctors and nurses rushed in and forced Kay, Eva, Roberta, and younger Johnny out of the room. Marcus thrashed around violently. They strapped him down but were careful not to give him medication. Marcus writhed in agony, his heartbeat increased dramatically, and his blood pressure skyrocketed. His groin ruptured, his innards thrust outward, and blood spewed everywhere. Marcus gave one last scream, and he fell silent. The heartbeat and respiration monitors fell silent. The bleeding stopped. Marcus was dead.

1990 Jul 15, Sun. Broadway Unitarian Church. Portland, Oregon.

"Thank you for helping me, Eva," Kay said. "Our Mosque wouldn't host Marcus's funeral service."

"You're welcome," Eva said.

Eva, Roberta, Kay, and younger Johnny stood in front of Marcus's casket. The funeral service had not yet begun, and the foursome were paying what respects they could manage to Marcus.

"Such a waste," Roberta said. "He was a medical professional, yet he pursued the wrong things."

"Where's Evanita?" Kay asked.

"With a sitter," Eva said. "She's too young for these things."

"It seems like a dream," Kay said. "The chase last year, the trial, and now this funeral. I hope we have some normal time ahead."

"So do I," Roberta said.

"Do you think anyone will find out that Roberta is Evanita's—"

"Shh," Eva said. "Don't you remember what Judge Jillian said? You can't discuss it outside of court. People may hear."

"Eventually these things get around," Roberta said.

"Well let's hope society matures enough so that when it does get out, it's no big deal," Eva said.

"I hope you're right," Roberta said. "Let's take a seat."

The funeral service began. Kay sat in the front row with Dr. Jelana, Quadri Dakari, Andrea Peddly, and one-year-old Adrian Cracbern. Roberta, Eva, and younger Johnny sat in the second row and were joined by Milo and Frank. Other people sat in other rows.

The service was rather ordinary. Adrian swung his legs restlessly, and younger Johnny fell asleep. The church leader focused on the good things in Marcus's life. Nothing was said of his pregnancy, only that he died from a sudden hemorrhage.

Roberta twitched with nervousness. She heard whispering from behind, but when she turned to look, she saw people staring forward with silent, solemn expressions on their faces. Roberta faced forward, but when she did, she heard the whispering again. She had a nervous feeling as if a person were planning some sort of action.

"What's wrong?" Eva whispered to Roberta.

"I feel like someone's watching us," Roberta whispered.

"Everyone behind us is watching us," Eva whispered.

"I know, but it's more than that. Must be the funeral," Roberta said.

"Death is full of anxiety," Eva said. "The service will end soon."

The service continued. Younger Johnny slept pleasantly and leaned next to Roberta. Roberta had a momentary chill travel through her body, and she trembled. Younger Johnny woke up and looked around.

"What is it?" Roberta whispered to him.

"I read something in your body," Johnny said. "I...oh, it's not true. That's strange."

"What's strange? What did you expect?" Roberta asked.

"I thought you had a gunshot wound in your neck," Johnny said.

"Here?! In this church?!" Roberta asked.

"Yeah," Johnny said.

Roberta turned around and looked back. The church was peaceful.

"Bang!" echoed a rifle.

The church erupted in panic. A gunman jumped down from a balcony and stormed out the door. Some gave chase to him, others fled, and others (including Eva and Roberta) dropped onto the floor to hide.

"Roberta," Eva said. "We have to get out of here. Roberta?"

Eva tapped Roberta, but Roberta didn't move. Eva turned Roberta over, and she'd been shot in the neck. Eva screamed.

1990 Jul 30, Mon. Portland International Airport, Oregon.

"I wish you wouldn't go," Eva said. "We can move to a place where no one will recognize us."

"No," Roberta said with a bandage on her neck, "I can't stay in this country. I almost died when a religious fanatic shot me. And for what? Because I was the first female paterna—the first female father. They said it was an attack against God, that I was evil, and I had to burn in Hell. I can't live in a country with that type of ignorance."

"Then take me with you," Eva said.

"No. It's too dangerous," Roberta said. "Wherever I go, I represent a risk, and someone may seek to kill me. Why? People don't like change or the threat of change. You could get caught in the attack. I won't risk that."

"But...I'll miss you terribly!" Eva cried.

The two embraced.

"I know, I know. If we didn't live in such barbaric times, we could enjoy a wonderful life together. As it is, we must live in separation. I've made arrangements to live in New Zealand. I'll write. And perhaps I can risk a visit from time to time. In the meantime, here is a gift to remember me by."

Roberta handed Eva a small box with a bow. She gave Eva a deep kiss, and Eva returned the kiss.

"I'll love you always," Roberta said. "Goodbye, Eva."

Roberta turned and headed toward the tunnel to the aircraft. She paused for a moment, turned around, and said, "Tell Evanita about me someday."

"I will," Eva said.

Roberta turned to the tunnel and disappeared from view. Eva opened the box and touched a locket of Roberta's red hair.

"Goodbye," Eva cried.

Of Age

2007 Dec 8, Sat. The Caves of Healing. Carreña, Spain.

Geneva stopped reading from her diary. The vision stopped.

"That's it," Geneva said. "Now you know."

Evanita paused. Her throat welled up into a lump, and she burst in tears.

"Why didn't my mama tell me?" Evanita asked with a shaky, sobbing voice. "All she had to do was explain it."

"It's easy to accept truth once you understand," Geneva said. "But reaching truth is difficult sometimes. Do you really think you would have been so accepting of her had she simply told you that Roberta is your other parent? Look at what happened when she told you that you have no father. You resented her."

"But I'm different," Evanita said.

"Yes, you're the only person in the world whose biological parents are both women," Geneva said.

"My mama always said I was special, that I'm unique. What a brat I've been all these years," Evanita confessed.

"Yes," Geneva said.

"I didn't even try to understand," Evanita continued. "I just ran away from everything."

"Yes," Geneva repeated.

"She's not perfect. She's human. She can only do the best she can, given the situation," Evanita admitted, still tearful.

"You see, then, you see," Geneva said. "Most children don't reach your point of realization until they start their own family. Then they learn—painfully—how difficult parenting can be."

"I owe her a big apology, the biggest in the world," Evanita said. "I hope she accepts it."

"Oh Evanita. Your mother will be thrilled. It's amazing how little contrition is needed to fill a mother's heart with joy. She is so tormented by her past. She feels isolated and alone. She can't be with Roberta, she didn't feel she could talk with you, and she doesn't trust me."

"And she's alone now. How terrible. And to think I wanted to die," Evanita said.

"She would have been devastated, as would I. Carreña women are a special lot. We have suffered much over the ages. We don't die easily," Geneva said.

"I want to go home," Evanita said. "And I want to redo my Coming-Of-Age ceremony. My mother was right—the Unitarian faith is the best one for me. I have more exploration to do, and the Unitarian faith will help me do so. Shawna, I mean Johnny—thank you for being with me. Thank you for helping my family in the past. You're...you're...like no other man in the universe. It's like you belong to our family in some way. I don't want you to leave me."

"I won't," Johnny said.

"Johnny, I know I'm underage and all, and I know what I'm about to say is against tradition," Evanita started.

"The Carreña family always finds ways to go against tradition," Geneva said.

"Well this is a big one. Johnny, when I'm old enough, will you marry me?"

"This is a surprise!" Geneva said.

"I...I...I'm a little nervous," Johnny said.

"We're meant for each other, Johnny. We are. There's only one of me, and there's only one of you. You have the gift of clairsentience. You read women. No other man has the respect for women that you do. Johnny—I want to be your wife," Evanita said.

Evanita kissed Johnny deeply on the lips. Johnny trembled in nervousness. The Moissan Ruby activated, and he read her thoughts. Evanita finished her kiss.

"Well?" Evanita asked.

"You're sincere," Johnny said. "Every cell and cellular component has attuned itself to me. It will find no satisfaction with another. I...I...I can't ignore reality."

"Then you'll say 'yes'?" Evanita asked.

"It's my fate," Johnny said. "I will marry you."

The three finished their visit in Carreña, Spain. They checked out of Carreña Hotel, drove the rental car back to Castrillón, and hopped on an EasyJet to London where they transferred and flew to New York. Another flight from New York to Portland, and Eva picked up the three.

"Mama, Mama!" Evanita yelled with delight.

Evanita hugged and kissed Eva.

"I missed you so, so, so very much! I'm so glad you're my mother! I'm so glad!" Evanita said.

"Wow! Well, I'd say the trip went well then?" Eva asked.

"You have no idea!" Evanita said.

"Good. Let's get going. I can't stay parked by the curb all night," Eva said.

The company jumped into Eva's car. Evanita originally got in the back seat with Johnny, but Geneva pulled her out.

"You should sit next to your mother," Geneva said.

"Why?" Evanita asked.

"It's important," Geneva replied.

Eva drove the car out of the airport and onto a highway toward home.

"Mama," Evanita said. "I know about my father."

"You don't have a father," Eva said.

"I know. I know! Roberta MacNessi is my other mother," Evanita said.

Eva slammed on the brakes and pulled to the side of the road.

"You told her?" Eva asked Geneva.

"It's all right," Geneva said. "Your daughter learned the full circumstances surrounding her creation. You need not worry about a thing."

"But it's private," Eva said. "I was going to tell her someday."

"You can't," Evanita said. "You don't have the courage. You love Roberta too much to risk having her name circulate outside our family that she's my second mother, my paterna. I saw the paternity trial, Mama. I saw the chase and the van going into the Willamette River off of Sellwood Bridge. I understand what was going on in Cerossi Café too. My journey from one church to another followed the bridges across the Willamette from Broadway to Sellwood. I was going back in time, Mama. I was going back to your past, to my beginning. Because I'm your daughter and Roberta's too. Your past and Roberta's past is my past too. I'm both of you. I'm your love for each other. And I'm sorry for everything I've put you through. I should never run from you. I should have never run into that abandoned factory. I wish children could absorb the experiences of their parents like a sponge absorbing water. But it doesn't work that way. We have to grow up slowly, painfully, and make lots of mistakes. I love you, Mama, and I love my entire family. Mama—I want to finish my Coming-Of-Age at Broadway Unitarian. I'm a Unitarian. That's where I belong. That's where we—you and I—belong. Mama!"

Eva burst into uncontrollable tears. She wailed. Evanita hugged her, but Eva cried all the harder.

"Oh, you don't know how long I've waited for this moment," Eva cried. "And I wish to God Roberta could be here with us. I...we've suffered so much without her. Evanita—I'm sorry I held back the full truth for so long. I'm sorry for being so authoritative. I try to protect you from the world of cruelty, but that only makes you want to experience it all the more. Oh Evanita, I love you more than anything. Please don't fail me. Please!"

"I won't, Mama, I won't," Evanita said. "I feel like I died and came back from the dead. You're my first mother!"

Eva and Evanita cried on each other's shoulders. Geneva shed a few tears. The sadness and joy carried vibrations through the car, Johnny sensed it, and he became sad too, but it was sadness with a sense of relief. Johnny let out a wail with such volume that it sounded comical. Eva, Evanita, and Geneva laughed. They wiped their faces dry, and Eva took them home.

Johnny visited for another hour before returning to his own home.

*2007 Dec 14, Fri. Broadway Unitarian Universalist Church. Port-
land, Oregon.*

Jonara watched as her mother attended her Coming-Of-Age ceremony. Evanita was the only one attaining Coming-Of-Age—others had already completed theirs earlier in the year. The piano lady played several classical pieces, including Beethoven's Seven Bagatelles, Op. 33, No. 4 Andante. Several church leaders spoke about the meaning of reaching a spiritual adulthood, including Ms. Zyla. Evanita also talked about her spiritual journey.

"My name is Evanita Carreña. First I want to thank everyone here for attending my Coming-Of-Age ceremony. I was supposed to do this over a year ago, but...well...things didn't go so well then. Coming-Of-Age seemed like a scam to me—just read a document and earn a gold star. For a time, I left the Unitarian church. I wanted to see what other churches were like. I went to Saint Stellan Catholic Church, I attended a funeral at Barnseed Baptist Church, I saw Morris Synagogue being vandalized, my friend went to a Zoroastrian church, and I met with people from the Arkham Atheist group. Each group of people had their own beliefs—even the atheists. I wanted to find a sense of belonging in one of the groups, and for a time I think I was an atheist, but things never felt quite right."

"I've made some bad decisions," Evanita said. "I went into a factory, and a boy died accidentally. I hurt my legs and went to the hospital. I was blamed for the boy's death and went to jail at the Elrod 402. I spent a year there and got out just last month. When I got out, I felt empty. I felt like nothing. I was still an atheist, but being an atheist doesn't give you anything—it takes away nourishment for your psyche, your soul."

"My grandmother, bless her heart, took me on a trip to Spain with my boyfriend," Evanita said. "My grandmother used to live in Spain before she lived in America. She showed me a place where she lived in an abbey. I can't tell you much more about the visit, but I'll say that I learned a lot about my family and what they suffered through to bring me into this world, and for that, I'm thankful."

"I woke up early this morning," Evanita continued. "I couldn't sleep. I walked outside and looked at the stars. I wondered how many people since the time of the ancients looked up at those stars and questioned the nature of the universe. Then the stars faded into dawn. The colors in the sky were orange and violet and pink. I couldn't believe such a beautiful thing was coincidence. It's no coincidence, for I have seen God. She is that first moment in the dawn before the sun's rays warm the earth, when the sky is filled with the hues of creation and all its infinite beauty. Beyond that is our universe, a metaphor of her beauty. As we live throughout the day, we sometimes forget the morning beauty to the point where we say, 'There is no God.' But when we do so, we distance ourselves from her, seeing only the extrapolations of our desires instead of what she has created—a creation she celebrates every day with her beautiful dawn."

"People can become slaves to this universe, blinded by the solitary rays of daylight," Evanita said. "Only when the sun sets, and the stars of our memories and ancestors' memories take hold, can we come to realize how precious is the gift of life. Before the stars completely fade and daylight makes us forget, she shows us her moment of love and kindness she gave us, with fantastic hues and colors dancing in the sky, the beauty and magic of our universe, her wondrous creation."

Evanita's audience clapped. Evanita grasped a candlelighter and approached an unlit chalice inside two concentric circles.

"As I light this chalice," Evanita said, "I light the love between my two parents who came together as two circles of interlocking love, like two stars revolving around each other. Planets are like children. I am a planet of life. I am my parents' child."

Evanita lit the chalice. The audience clapped again. Johnny walked up to Evanita and presented her with a gift.

"I made something for you," Johnny said. "Before we left for Spain, I spent a week making this gift for your Coming-Of-Age."

"But how did you know I would go through with Coming-Of-Age?" Evanita asked. "I had not decided it yet."

"I knew," Johnny said, and he pulled out the Moissan Ruby and showed Evanita.

Evanita smiled. She opened the envelope and pulled out several sheets of paper.

"Why, it's sheet music," Evanita said. "It's a waltz, the *Patchwork Waltz*."

"I thought maybe we could dance at your Coming-Of-Age ceremony," Johnny said.

Evanita handed the sheet music to the piano lady.

"Mr. Pindus, I accept," Evanita said.

Evanita motioned to the piano lady for the song to begin. The waltz started, and the coupled danced.

Patchwork Waltz

The waltz ended. The piano lady turned to Evanita and gave her the sheet music.

"A very unusual waltz," the piano lady said. "There were moments when my thumbs pressed the same note."

"It was by design," Johnny said. "I wanted the left and right hands to touch."

"As you and I touch now," Evanita said to Johnny. "Thank you, Johnny."

Evanita kissed him, and the audience clapped. Evanita requested the piano lady to play more dance music, and Evanita invited everyone to dance and make merry.

CHAPTER 18

Eclipse

2023 Oct 14, Sat Morn. Oso Bay. Corpus Christi, Texas.

"Jonara!" shouted a voice. "Jonara!"

Jonara surfaced. The sun was rising, and a familiar figure stood at the edge of the bird walk where Jonara once stood. The figure was Johnny.

"Jonara!" Johnny called.

"Daddy!" Jonara called. "I'm here."

"Oh, praise Jesus!" Johnny said. "You're alive. Alive! Come out of the water, sugar! Hurry!"

"I'm swimming to you, Daddy. I'm swimming," Jonara said.

"Hurry, Jonara, hurry!" Johnny said.

Jonara swam to Johnny, and he pulled her up to the walkway.

"My sweet daughter," Johnny said. "Everyone is looking for you. We thought you killed yourself by jumping into one of these water bodies. Did you try to kill yourself?"

"No, Daddy, no," Jonara said as she hugged Johnny.

"Then what?" Johnny asked.

"This," Jonara said, and she held up the Moissan Ruby to Johnny.

"The Water Ruby?" Johnny asked.

"I saw things in the Water Ruby, Daddy. I saw my past. I saw how Mommy overcame her doubt when she was younger to complete her Coming-Of-Age."

"Oh, Jonara, don't obsess on the past," Johnny said.

"But I had to know. I had to know who I am, who my parents are, and who the women are in my family."

"There's no time to get you into dry clothes," Johnny said. "The Whitebird leaves Portland at eleven-twenty this morning and will reach us—along with the full eclipse—at noon. That leaves us one hour to get to North Beach."

"Why do I need to see this, Daddy? Why?" Jonara asked.

"Your mother and I have been given special positions to watch the eclipse, and so have you," Johnny said. "Come on, Jonara."

Johnny led Jonara back to the car. As he did, he telephoned Evanita and informed her of the good news—Jonara was found. Evanita in turn relayed this information, and preparations were made to receive the threesome at North Beach. Johnny took the highway, reached North Beach, turned southeast on Burleson Street, and drove to the end of the street where it met the beach on Corpus Christi Bay. A platform had been erected—much like a podium for the top three medal winners at the Olympics—but with the first-place/center podium significantly higher than the outer two podiums. Evanita was already standing on one of the outer podiums. Johnny took his position on the other outer podium, and Jonara was lifted up to the center podium.

"Your attention please, your attention," a loudspeaker called. "The eclipse has reached Eugene, Oregon. The Whitebird of Freedom is now following the eclipse and will arrive here with the eclipse in forty minutes."

Jonara looked around. There were many, many people gathered along the beach both for Corpus Christi Bay and Nueces Bay. But she was the only person standing on such a tall platform.

"Why am I here?" she asked. "Isn't this event about the vitaceticals and control over fertility?"

"Yes, that's part of it," said Nekara as she appeared out of thin air.

"Nekara the Red!" Jonara said.

"I see you remember me," Nekara said.

"I thought you were gone forever. Didn't Felifia get rid of you at Ross Island?"

Nekara let out an evil laugh.

"Oh Jonara, when will you learn that evil takes no vacation?" Nekara asked.

"I...I..." Jonara stammered.

"You are here because I want you here," Nekara said. "Unlike you shallow Earthlings who live for the moment without a care for tomorrow's consequences, we Damiriak women work and plan across hundreds of years. I orchestrated your mother's birth. I put your father's father in harm's way in Vietnam so Agent Orange would mutate any children he had. Your father's one testicle and one ovary are my doing."

"But why?" Jonara asked.

"I'm in the fertility business," Nekara said. "That's what I do. I woo women into having children with each other. I cause men to become pregnant—like Marcus. I knew he would die, but the data was valuable. I can now cause men to become pregnant anytime I wish. But you, Jonara—you are a product of my female fertility experiments—your mother, and my male fertility experiments—your father. You are the numero uno, the primary one, the alpha female Earthling. You will lead my new race of subordinates on this planet. I have encoded my instructions into your genome. You have no choice. Your fate is indurated."

"Indurated?" Jonara asked herself.

"Like celestial bodies in the cosmos," Nekara said. "Their mass precludes the insignificance of human intervention. So it is with you. In comparison to me, you are a human, and I am a giant planet."

The minutes passed. The sunlight faded gradually into twilight from the occluding moon, and the SR-71 Whitebird blistered across the United States along the path of the full eclipse.

"Your light is fading, Jonara," Nekara said. "My darkness is penetrating this world and yours. In mere moments, the eclipse will be full, and the aircraft overhead will complete its conversion of this planet from yours to mine."

Jonara stared at Nekara in horror, and then in a brief moment, Jonara saw not Nekara but Felifia.

"Felifia!" Jonara screamed.

"There is no Felifia, just me," Nekara laughed.

"I saw her! I did!" Jonara said.

Jonara continued watching Nekara and saw the image of Felifia for another brief moment.

"I saw her again! Not you, but her!" Jonara said.

"Your mind plays tricks on you in your final moments before spiritual death," Nekara said.

"No! You're in conflict with her—even to this very last moment! She's fighting you! She's trying to get out!"

"No!" Nekara said.

"Yes!" Jonara said. "Felifia—hear me now! Give me a chance to undo the induration I created. Send me back to the Montseny Mountains in 1970! Send me back!"

Jonara hugged Nekara.

"Quit hugging me! This is my moment of triumph. You should hate, not love me!" Nekara said.

"I love the Felifia in you! Felifia! I love you!" Jonara said.

The image of Felifia flickered for a moment over Nekara's body, and as it did, it pulled Jonara from the podium and sent her to the Montseny Mountains.

1970 Jul 3, Fri. Dan-Air Flight G-APDN. Spain.

Jonara was back on the De Havilland aircraft headed for Barcelona, Spain.

"Cerafina, wake me up!" Jonara said.

Nothing.

"*Peliko!*" Jonara said, but again nothing. "*Peia elifa lerifa ilofa keia orifa!* (P-e-l-i-k-o!)"

No change. Jonara shook the Moissan Ruby.

"Show me Cerafina," Jonara said.

An image of Cerafina at home playing a piano duet with her boyfriend appeared in the airplane's window.

"Just as before," Jonara said. "Everything is happening the same way."

"Show me Mommy," Jonara said. "Show me Evanita Carreña Pindus."

The airplane window swirled with grays. Jonara spoke again:

Miramish	Translation
Feifo nau	Show me
Ivanita Karenya Pinedosa!	Evanita Carreña Pindus!

The windows continued to swirl in grays.

"Dammit again!" Jonara said, and she spoke:

Miramish	Translation
Feifo nau Iva Karenya!	Show me Eva Carreña!

The window showed six-year-old Eva with Geneva in the freight box at the rear of the airplane.

Miramish	Translation
Feifo nau Iva Karenya	Show me Eva Carreña
Ishu shai kelosha	In the year
Avu-dint avuda-iri!	Two-thousand twenty-three!

The window showed a sign for Arbúcies Municipal Cemetery in Spain, followed by two tombstones—one with Geneva's name and the other with Eva's—both with death dates of July 3, 1970.

"Dead today. Going back to this event accomplished nothing. Nothing!" Jonara cried.

"The path is indurated," Nekara's head said as she appeared for a moment and disappeared.

A stewardess heard Jonara shouting and came over to check on her.

"We have to stop this plane," Jonara said.

"I'm sorry. Is there a problem?" the stewardess asked.

"We're going to crash!" Jonara said. "We have to turn around and return to Manchester."

"Is this your first flight?" the stewardess asked. "I can tell it is. Children often get frightened by airline flight. Here, I'll bring you something to drink. It will help you sleep."

"No, I don't want to sleep," Jonara said. "You're not paying attention, just like last time. Please! Turn around now!"

The stewardess signaled to another stewardess who picked up the plane's phone and spoke with someone. After a moment, the stewardess hung the phone on the switch hook and joined the discussion with Jonara.

"We have a nice place for you to rest in back," the second stewardess said. "There are no windows and nothing to see that can frighten you. You'll be perfectly safe. I assure you."

"You did that before, and it didn't help!" Jonara yelled.

Jonara jumped out of her chair and bolted for the pilot's cabin, but a third stewardess blocked her path and grabbed hold of her arms. Jonara struggled and nearly got through, but the two stewardesses behind caught up with her and helped drag her to the back. A fourth stewardess opened a bathroom door. The first three pushed Jonara into the bathroom, and the fourth one locked it.

Jonara lifted a fist to pound on the wall, but she remembered how it didn't help before. The stewardesses left her and returned to work. Jonara looked at herself in the mirror. Her eyes were red with dark patches under them. She turned on the water and held her hands below.

"I ask again, please, someone help me. Felifia?!" she said.

"Did I hear someone call me for help?" Nekara said as she appeared in the mirror.

"I don't want your help," Jonara said. "I didn't want it before, and I don't want it again."

"Real evil has a way of repeating itself," Nekara said. "You rejected my perfect world of controlled fertility. Now you will meet your end as originally intended."

Jonara watched again as an image of the De Havilland Comet plowed through a grove of beech trees on a mountain slope, exploded into fireballs, and disintegrated on impact. A 125-acre swath of leveled trees was all that remained.

"There must be another way," Jonara said.

"Evil has no other way," Nekara said. "The straight and narrow path of obsession neither desires nor seeks alternatives. All roads lead to destruction."

"I'm going to die? But everything is supposed to have a happy ending!" Jonara said. "My mother got through her problems. Why can't I?"

Jonara beat her fists against the floor.

"You and your family had much promise, Jonara Carreña Pindus," Nekara said. "But you've thrown it away. I will have to start with another family. So it is with fertility experiments. The cultivator tries a new hybrid, it fails, and she moves on to the next hybrid. Goodbye, Jonara. I'm sorry you couldn't support my fertility program. Your death is imminent, and I must move on. Evil doesn't wait for the unproductive."

Nekara disappeared.

"Help me, please!" Jonara cried.

Nothing.

"This is your pilot speaking," called a voice over the intercom. "We will be arriving at Barcelona in about thirteen minutes. Please attach your seatbelts, and thank you for flying Dan-Air."

Jonara stared at the mirror.

"I'm the unproductive," Jonara said. "Why am I unproductive? Because I didn't produce? No, because my Grandma Eva didn't produce. Fertility, Jonara, fertility. Nekara wants to control fertility. Be she won't. She's given up on the Carreña family. What now? Someone's gotta take over. Felifia? No, she never did fertility projects. That leaves just me. Me. I have to save Nanna Geneva and Grandma Eva. I have to save me. I have to save us Carreña women. But I can't indurate the aircraft. That changed everything. Not the aircraft. But I must protect the family. The family. Machines mean nothing, family means everything. I have been exiled from the family. I must return. I must return!"

Miramish	Translation
Lukaima nau, Dzhonara Pinedosa	Return me, Jonara Pindus
Di shai kunaola	To the beginning
Opeifu nui teferapa	Of my development
Opeifu nui malishanga teferapa	Of my mother's development
Ishu shai keluapua	In the ovary
Opeifu Gereima Iva.	Of Grandma Eva.
Boshu nui lukaima	With my return

Miramish	**Translation**
Nia yadito nui borifa	I yield my strength
Dhaku felaushu viuka	And life force
Di Gereima Iva	To Grandma Eva
Dhaku di shelaibaolu felianua	And to surrounding family
Hishei igeruto	Which includes
Kelauku-Gereima Dzheniva.	Great-Grandma Geneva.
Nia ferugo boshu nui felausha	I pledge with my life
Dzhonara Karenya Pinedosa.	Jonara Carreña Pindus.

Jonara's final Miramish words overlapped with the pilot's last communication with Air Traffic Control. Jonara felt herself shrinking and traveling across what seemed billions of miles to a place with two stars orbiting each other—two stars that could be a mother and daughter, or one female lover and another. The stars were both white. She was pulled into a star, the star became Seris, and male life on a planet died. Jonara was pulled into Eva's ovary and melded with an ovum—the ovum that would someday become Evanita.

1802	ATC:	"DN. Turn now left heading 140."	
	Pilot:	"Left onto 140 leaving 85 for 60."	
	ATC:	"Confirm passing Sabadell now."	
	Pilot:	"In about 30 seconds."	
	Pilot:	"Barcelona. DN. Passing Sabadell."	
	ATC:	"DN Roger. Radar contact. Continue descending down 2800 feet, altimeter 1017, transition level 50."	
1803	Pilot:	"Roger. Cleared further down to 2800 feet on 1017, transition level 50."	
	Pilot:	"Barcelona. DN requests the duty runway."	
	ATC:	"DN. Duty runway 25."	
1805	ATC:	"DN. Altitude."	
	Pilot:	"DN is passing 4000 feet on 1047."	
1807	ATC:	"DN. Confirm if on course."	
		Static.	
	ATC:	"DN. Confirm if on course."	
		Static.	
	ATC:	"DN. Do you read?"	
		Static.	

The aircraft plowed into trees and broke apart into a fireball killing all but two people. Geneva's and Eva's crate was thrown clear into the snow, broke open, and tossed Geneva and Eva down the mountain slope into a slide. The two were hurt but otherwise alive. The fire raged but fell behind as the Evas continued descending the mountain. Jonara felt herself falling, falling, and falling.

CHAPTER 19:

Delivery

2023 Oct 14, Sat Morn. Corpus Christi Hospital, Texas.

Jonara rolled off a hospital bed and crashed into a stand holding her intravenous bags. An instrument measuring her vital signs went berserk, and nurses rushed in.

"I'm okay, I'm okay," Jonara said.

Cerafina rushed in a moment later.

"Shnuki! You're alive! You're alive!" Cerafina cried.

"Cerafina!" Jonara said. "You called me Shnuki!"

"Of course! You're my Shnuki! I'll always love my Shnuki! We thought you were brain-dead. You've been in a coma for a week!"

"What?!" Jonara replied.

"Take it easy," a nurse said.

"What's today?" Jonara asked. "What's the date?"

"October the 14th," Cerafina said.

"No! It can't be! We've run out of time!" Jonara said.

Jonara pulled the tube out of her arm and the electrodes off her chest. She rushed down the hallway and into Evanita's treatment room.

"Mommy!" Jonara said.

Johnny was already by Evanita's side, and Eva sat nearby. Cerafina caught up and stood in the doorway—in shock. Eva walked over to Cerafina, escorted her into the room, and consoled her. One of Jonara's nurses entered the room.

"You're not well," the nurse said to Jonara. "You should be in bed."

"I want to be with my mommy!" Jonara said. "My mommy!"

"Please," Evanita said. "Let her stay with me. She's my daughter."

The nurse left.

"Mommy?" Jonara asked. "Are you awake? Are you alive?"

"I'm both," Evanita said. "But I'm very tired. Very tired. And my legs. Ow, my legs!"

"Try to relax, Evanita," Eva said.

"What's wrong with my mommy?" Jonara asked.

"It's like the second accident," Johnny said. "When she and Adrian—"

"What second accident?" Jonara asked.

"When your mother was nineteen years old," Johnny said, "she took a trip to Spain with Adrian Cracbern. She showed him the Caves of Healing. It didn't go well. She's had nightmares about it ever since."

"We must help Mommy," Jonara said. "We must help her like we helped Grandma Eva with her thyroid."

"I've tried," Johnny said. "I could never help her."

"Did you try with the Water Ruby and the Aromani Candleholder?" Jonara asked.

"No. Just the Water Ruby," Johnny said. "But there's metal in your mother's legs. Metal causes problems."

"What if we don't try? What will happen to Mommy?" Jonara asked.

Johnny looked at Eva then looked at Jonara.

"Jonara, I must prepare you for what is about to happen. Your mother will not survive childbirth. She will die," Eva said.

"No!" Jonara said. "NO! NO! NO!"

Eva walked over to Jonara, held Jonara's head, and looked straight into her eyes.

"This is life, Jonara. Doctor Reegen can't save her. No one can. The baby boy is killing her. Doctor Reegen has waited as long as he can. This is the day. Doctor Reegen will perform a C-section to deliver the new baby boy. His name is already selected—Robert. But when he's delivered, your mother will die."

"We can't let her die!" Jonara yelled.

"There's nothing we can do!" Eva yelled back.

"Daddy! Daddy!" Jonara yelled.

Johnny looked back at Jonara fondly and with tears in his eyes. He embraced Jonara.

"We can't let Mommy die! Don't let her die!" Jonara said.

"I can't stop it!" Johnny said. "I've tried for years with the Water Ruby to prevent this event. But the result has always been the same. Jonara—I have no power over reproduction. Life and death are beyond my ability."

Jonara cried in Johnny's arms. Cerafina cried a little, but an unexpected visitor appeared in the doorway.

"Leo!" Cerafina said. "What are you doing here?"

"I want to make sure you are all here," Leo said. "I can tell him now."

Leo left Evanita's room. Shocked, Cerafina followed him.

"Tell who? What's going on?" Cerafina asked.

Leo laughed with such smugness and satisfaction that he felt no reservations about bragging.

"You and your friend think you're hot stuff. But you're nothing. As we speak, a friend of mine in Portland, Oregon is powering up the fastest airplane in the world."

"Who?"

"Adrian Cracbern," Leo laughed.

Jonara heard the name echoing through the hallway. She stepped out of Evanita's treatment room and joined up with Cerafina.

"Adrian?!" Jonara asked. "Leo—what have you done?"

"Adrian and I are good friends. And he's been very interested in following your mother's progress," Leo explained. "He's preparing to fly an SR-71 Whitebird from Portland to Corpus Christi to follow the eclipse. The aircraft is specially modified with a mineral from Africa to focus solar coronal light onto a terrestrial path from Portland to Corpus Christi. You see, we discovered there are mineral remnants of spacecraft wreckage on that path, and by activating it, we can control the act of conception in the world."

"What?!" Cerafina asked in surprise.

"It's happening again," Jonara said. "Shlifa—what time is it?"

"It's eleven o'clock," Cerafina said.

"In twenty minutes, he departs," Leo laughed.

"We have to stop him," Jonara said.

"You can't," Leo said. "You're powerless."

"We can use the Water Ruby and the Aromani Candleholder," Jonara said.

"To stop a military jet?" Cerafina asked. "How?"

"I don't know how," Jonara said.

"What about your mother?" Cerafina asked. "She's dying."

"Yes, your mother is dying," Leo said. "As expected."

When Leo said, "As expected," another voice spoke with him in unison. Leo suddenly changed shape and became Nekara the Red.

"Nekara! Here! Impossible!" Jonara said.

Nekara laughed.

"You're such a simpleton, Jonara. You delude yourself into thinking that you have defeated evil. You can never defeat me. When you complete one thing, I return with greater might. I will complete my plans of fertility control after all. And with you here trying in vain to save your mother's life, I'll be unopposed. The Earth will be mine."

"No! It's not fair. Why must you do this now? Why?" Jonara asked.

"Because that's how evil thrives," Nekara said. "Create conflict, tear the good people into little pieces, and succeed. Divide and conquer. You won't leave your mother's side, will you? You would be throwing away your own humanity. How could you live with yourself after that?"

"Don't listen to Nekara," Cerafina said. "This talk of controlling the world is a trick, a deception. It's garbage talk."

"Oh no it isn't, my little Cerafina. I have already proven to Jonara that my plans are quite real. Aren't they, Jonara?"

"Yes, they are," Jonara said.

"I have a special plan for you, Jonara. It's an escape from all responsibility. I've arranged for a platform in North Beach at the end of Burleson Street on the beach of Corpus Christi Bay. I'll take you there. You can hold your arms up to the heavens as Adrian flies overhead to seal the fate of women everywhere. You can absorb the last of those rays. You'll be enabled with special powers to lead and control the fertility program here on Earth. Take Cerafina with you as your consort. She can be your deputy administrator. We'll build vitacepticals along the shoreline around this bay and bays around the world. No need to involve the Church on this one. You're all I need. What do you say? You can leave all this wretched family responsibility behind and take on a new role, a new life."

"Jonara, don't listen to her," Cerafina said.

"I can't save my mother," Jonara said. "And I can't stop the jet. What else can I do?"

"No!" Cerafina said. "No!"

"Yes," Nekara said. "Yes!"

"Take me to the podium," Jonara said.

"Then take me too," Cerafina said. "I want to be with you."

"Yes, Cerafina should be with you. She will be your deputy," Nekara said.

"No," Jonara said. "I want to do this alone. Cerafina—stay with my mother."

"As if she has a choice," Nekara said. "The deed is done."

Nekara placed her left hand over her abdomen, and the three traveled through the ether until they reached the podium at the end of Burleson Street.

"I don't want you to suffer with me," Jonara said.

"But I do want her to suffer with you," Nekara said. "You two remind me of Felifia and me."

"That's a horrible comparison. Neither of us is evil like you," Jonara said.

"There's time enough to remedy that," Nekara said. "Behold, the time is eleven-eleven. I must leave you. I have a plane to catch—an SR-71 Whitebird to be exact."

Nekara disappeared.

"Don't worry, Jonara, everything will be fine," Cerafina said. "This is just some stupid trick of hers. Let's go back to the hospital and see your mother."

"No, it's not a trick," Jonara said. "Cerafina—when I was in the coma, I lived in another timeline. I saw what happened when the SR-71 Whitebird flew over the United States from Portland to here. It really did trigger a chain of events. Women couldn't get pregnant unless they used these special vitaceptical booths provided by the Catholic Church."

"That was a dream," Cerafina said.

"Was it? I think the Water Ruby showed me that other time-line so I'd be ready for this one. Cerafina—Nekara is a fertility expert. She pioneered female fertility on her planet, she's done experiments on this planet, and now she wants to control the planet—through fertility."

"So your plan is to stand here and wait for the jet to fly over?" Cerafina asked.

"No, I'm going to connect to the jet and force it to land," Jonara said.

"I won't risk you going in a coma again," Cerafina said.

"Then help me. Take the Aromani Candleholder and press it against your belly button. I'll press the Water Ruby against my belly button. We'll hold onto each other and use our together-ness to force the jet down," Jonara said. "But we must start now!"

"Okay, I hope this works," Cerafina said.

Cerafina held the Aromani Candleholder to her navel, and Jonara held the Moissan Ruby to her own navel. The two joined hands.

Miramish	Translation
Gethiko omei aulekafipa	Track an aircraft
Boshu beroteiru keliegi	With crystal wings
Fuifao veletu Poritelanuda, Origona	Flying from Portland, Oregon
Di Koripusha Kerishuta.	To Corpus Christi.

Jonara held her eyes closed.

"Do you see anything?" Cerafina asked.

"No, nothing," Jonara said. "What's wrong? I can't connect with the jet."

"Can you connect with Adrian?" Cerafina asked.

"He's a man. This Water Ruby doesn't work well with men, but I'll try," Jonara said.

Miramish	**Translation**
Shinafo boshu	Connect with
Aderian e Kerakuberin	Adrian Cracbern
Ishu aulekafipa	In aircraft
Boshu beroteiru keliegi	With crystal wings
Fuifao veletu Poritelanuda, Origona	Flying from Portland, Oregon
Di Koripusha Kerishuta.	To Corpus Christi.

Jonara shook the Moissan Ruby.

"Nothing," Jonara said.

"Nekara is the only woman on board," Cerafina said.

Jonara's eyes lit up.

"Now wait!" Cerafina said.

"I have to. It's the only way," Jonara said. "I have to connect with Nekara."

"She'll corrupt you! You'll be enslaved by her forever," Cerafina said. "I won't let you. Give me that Water Ruby!"

"No!" Jonara said. "I have to connect with Nekara, and now!"

Jonara shoved Cerafina off the podium. Cerafina fell to the sand. She looked up and searched frantically for a way to reach Jonara, but the podium was too high and there were no steps. The best she could do was watch her girlfriend.

"Miramish is no good—that's Felifia's language. I must use Nekara's language—I must use Dahmek," Jonara said.

Jonara held her arms up to the sky and yelled:

Dahmek	**Translation**
Shnarsf borsh Nekara shair Fiesht	Connect with Nekara the Red
Ishe aulkarfp	In aircraft
Borsh britar kliergyek	With crystal wings
Fuirsfaut velt Portelanurd, Origorn	Flying from Portland, Oregon
Dir Korpus Kristi.	To Corpus Christi.

"Jonara!" Cerafina called from the ground.

Cerafina watched. The wind picked up and howled. The sun was high in the sky, and Jonara—with her last Dahmek words still echoing from her mouth—disappeared.

"Jonara!" Cerafina cried.

She was gone.

Jonara appeared inside the SR-71 Whitebird. It accelerated along a runway at Portland International Airport—spilling JP7 jet fuel from its fully-loaded fuselage. Adrian Cracbern piloted the craft with Nekara riding as passenger. Both wore dark brown pressure suits and helmets. Jonara was melded with Nekara's body and experienced everything Nekara did.

"So, you have decided to join me after all," Nekara said. "Even Felifia would not meld her body with mine as you have done. I'm impressed, Jonara."

The SR-71 gained altitude and flew into the eclipse. The earth below the craft turned dark.

"Do you see the ground?" Nekara asked. "If you look closely, you can see a path of cerise light reflecting back. The light is coming from minerals deposited by my spacecraft when I first landed on this planet. This aircraft is reactivating those minerals."

"I'm not here to bask in your glory. I'm here to stop you," Jonara said.

"You cannot stop me. I have full control," Nekara said.

"I will do everything in my power to stop you," Jonara said.

"You Carreña women think you're something special, but you're not. Adrian robbed your family of the very essence of female fertility that I needed to modify this aircraft."

"What are you talking about?" Jonara asked. "More lies?"

"In the Caves of Healing—where Felifia's spacecraft came to its resting place," Nekara said. "Your mother showed Adrian the caves in hopes of showing him the failures of his father, but instead, Adrian got the best of Evanita."

"What?!" Jonara asked. "That can't be."

"Didn't you know?" Nekara asked. "I would have thought that with all your journeys back in time with the assorted Damiriak artifacts, you would have tapped into that event."

"I...didn't," Jonara said.

Nekara let out a hearty laugh.

"Well, I'll send you there," Nekara said. "Consider it a parting gift from me before we reach the end of the world as you know it."

2009 Jul 11, Sat. Castrillón, Asturias Province, Spain.

"Thank you for taking me to Spain, Evanita," Adrian Crac-bern said.

"Thank you for paying the fare," Evanita replied.

"It's the least I can do," Adrian said. "I hope you're right about these Caves of Healing."

"It will help you learn all about the past and your father," Evanita said. "I know it helped me. Here—let's drive along the coastline of the Bay of Biscay."

Evanita drove the car along the shoreline.

"I'm glad I got my international driver's license. Isn't the bay beautiful? It's part of the Atlantic Ocean connecting northern Spain to western France."

"I'm more interested in you," Adrian said.

"You know I have a boyfriend," Evanita said. "We're getting married on January 1st of next year."

"That's not what I mean," Adrian said.

"You're not making a pass at me, are you?" Evanita asked.

"No. I'm more interested in your birth, your parents," Adrian said.

"Let's walk on the beach," Evanita said.

Evanita parked, and the two walked on the beach.

"I heard that your biological parents are women," Adrian said. "Is it true?"

"Yes, it's true," Evanita said. "Now look at these rocks. See all the layers? They're pointing up. Don't you wonder about the years of buildup with a final upheaval?"

"Evanita—I have a transcript of the paternity trial—the one that determined your father," Adrian said.

"I don't have a father," Evanita said.

"I know! It's a breakthrough! We must explore it!" Adrian said.

"Let's go somewhere else. This beach is not helping as I hoped it would," Evanita said.

The two returned to the car.

"Maybe we should eat some fresh fish and drink local wine. I'll stop at the next restaurant," Evanita said.

The two entered a restaurant and sat down to eat. Evanita ordered in Spanish and helped Adrian with his order. Within a moment, their food was prepared and their wine served.

"I love fresh food," Evanita said. "It's tough finding fresh food like this in the States."

"My father said that your conception by two women marked the beginning of the end for men," Adrian said.

"Can you stop talking about my conception and enjoy your food?" Evanita asked. "We're in Spain, Adrian! Spain! Think of the rich history around here. The people who slaved and suffered for hundreds of years—the plague, conquest of one kingdom over another—it's all here."

"My father died because of a fetus in his prostate," Adrian said. "I owe it to him to advance the state of human fertility."

"Adrian—that was the end of your father's life. I thought you wanted to know about the rest of his life. Didn't you?" Evanita asked.

"Oh yeah, yeah," he said.

"I don't feel like drinking wine anymore," Evanita said.

Evanita and Adrian paid the bill and continued on a path eventually leading to Carreña. Evanita followed the same winding paths up and down hills that Geneva had followed a year and a half earlier. Evanita parked the car and led Adrian to the first waterfall.

"Isn't it a pretty waterfall?" Evanita asked. "My grandmother showed this waterfall to me. Look at how the plants cling to the rocks so precariously."

"Evanita—I must know how your mother became pregnant with you," Adrian said.

"You're missing the point. Look at the waterfall. It's like life. See how it forms a delta? That's when life becomes bland and flat before it empties into the ocean. The ocean is death."

"I'm talking about a new sort of genetic engineering," Adrian said. "People wouldn't have to suffer from congenital defects. We could orchestrate the fertilization of embryos. If a couple wants a boy with blue eyes and blond hair, we could provide that baby for them."

"The waterfall doesn't look right," Evanita said. "It's not the same as I remember. Come on. Let's go."

Evanita drove the car to Bricias and followed highway AS-115 as Geneva had done.

"Isn't the countryside beautiful?" Evanita asked.

"You know, we could make a lot of money together—you and I. If you help me with my research, I'll split the profits with you," Adrian said. "I bet there are lots of couples out there—rich couples—who would pay well to have their own children exactly the way they want—with no physical problems, no mental illnesses, and no vices. Superior human engineering."

"You're scaring me," Evanita said.

Evanita turned east on highway AS-114.

"Have you ever been to the Peaks of Europe?" Evanita asked.

"I've been on lots of mountains—mostly in Oregon," Adrian said.

"You might want to know that we're passing Carreña," Evanita said. "That's also my last name—Carreña."

"The first thing we have to do is figure out how your mother conceived you. Two ova can't mix together—the genes aren't right. The sperm has certain genes flipped to make it compatible with an ovum," Adrian said.

Evanita turned south on highway AS-264 and continued to Bulnes where she parked.

"Aren't the mountains beautiful?" Evanita asked.

"Do you know what's beautiful? Coming up with a product and selling it for millions in profit," Adrian said.

"Don't you feel a sense of awe and respect for these magnificent mountains?" Evanita asked.

"I have more respect for a mountain of money," Adrian said.

"Come on. Let's take a walk along this river," Evanita said.

The two walked past ancient buildings next to the river.

"At one time, the river was everything to people. It sustained life. The river provided power to grind grain, water to drink, and it was used for washing," Evanita said.

"Municipal water is much superior," Adrian said. "Regulated, sanitized, and pressurized."

"At one time, there were Celts everywhere," Evanita said. "I'm part Celtic. My second mother is Celtic. Her name is Roberta."

"Yes. Roberta is the paterna. If only I could get some tissue samples from her. What force altered her ovum's genes to make it combine properly with Eva's ovum? That's the million-dollar question."

"The Celts lived off the land. They were a hardy folk whose spirits dwelled strongest in the mountains," Evanita said.

"Do you think that's it? Something in the genes of Celtic people that mutates their eggs?" Adrian asked.

"Please, stop it!" Evanita said.

The two walked a little farther.

"Look! It's the second waterfall," Evanita said.

"Are you obsessed with waterfalls?" Adrian asked.

"It's symbolic. You're born in the mountains, the waterfall is a turbulent event, and the river is life afterward," Evanita said. "Maybe I didn't say it right."

"It's just a river. It doesn't mean anything," Adrian said. "But the potential for profits does mean something."

"Forget the waterfall," Evanita said. "Let's go to Carreña."

Evanita drove the car west until the two reached Carreña. She parked in front of Carreña Hotel.

"I'll reserve two rooms for us," Adrian said. "No sense in putting each other at risk of bacterial infection by sharing one room."

Adrian disappeared and returned with two hotel keys.

"That was rude what you just said," Evanita said.

"You wanted to share a room?" Adrian asked.

"Well no, not really, no," Evanita said. "I thought I'd have to fight you to get two rooms. I thought you'd make another pass at me and insist on sharing a room. I never dreamed you'd accuse me of giving you a bacterial infection! What do you think I am, some subhuman wretch who never takes a shower?"

"I didn't mean it like that," Adrian said. "I just have to make sure I stay perfectly clean."

"You know, your father had this thing about shaving his hair off. He had an obsession with keeping clean too," Evanita said. "Are you covering up some sort of guilt?"

"What? No," Adrian said.

"Sigh," Evanita said. "I give up. This trip was supposed to give you insight about your father. But so far you've completely ignored everything I've explained to you."

"There are waterfalls and mountains back in America," Adrian said. "I don't have to fly halfway around the world to see them in a little-old Spanish-speaking country."

"This little-old country is the home of my ancestors! I hail from these hills!" Evanita said.

"Whatever," Adrian said. "I'm going to take a nap."

Adrian disappeared into his hotel room.

"He's going to take a nap?" Evanita asked herself. "What about a Carreña point and all that? This is supposed to be his moment of realization! Oh, Evanita, this was a mistake. He doesn't realize a thing. He's obsessed with my conception so he can make money. What a dork!"

Evanita took a little walk through Carreña. She smiled and waved to several passersby.

"He has no sense of past or future. He's just stuck in this narrow-focused line of vision," Evanita said. "I should have brought Grandma Geneva along. She would have known what to do. Now I'm stuck with him. Well, there's one last chance with the Caves of Healing. Oh, I almost forgot! I have to get his disguise ready."

Evanita returned to her hotel room and made final preparations for Adrian's disguise. She knocked on his hotel door and woke him.

"Wake up, Adrian," Evanita called. "It's time to visit the castle."

Adrian opened his door and rubbed his eyes. He closed the door behind him and followed Evanita to her hotel room.

"I had the strangest dream," Adrian said. "I dreamt I was putting two hard-boiled eggs in a blender with ice, fruit juice, and vodka. I hit the button, and the blender made some sort of strange alcoholic beverage."

"The abbey doesn't allow men or boys, so we have to dress you up in a disguise," Evanita said.

"As a woman?" Adrian said. "I shouldn't have to dress up as a woman. The sisters should let me walk right in."

"Well they won't, so let's get you dressed up," Evanita said.

Evanita had Adrian change clothes, throw on a wig, and place his feet in high-heeled shoes.

"These shoes are terrible," he said. "I can't walk in these."

"You'll have to," Evanita said. "Come over here and sit down. I need to work on your makeup."

Evanita did her best to apply makeup to Adrian, but he shifted and moved around in discomfort.

"Hold still. I can't do anything with you fidgeting like this," Evanita said.

Evanita did the best she could to apply makeup. She attached plastic fingernails to Adrian's fingers.

"Take a look in the mirror," Evanita said.

"Yuck," Adrian said.

"Yeah, I don't know what happened," Evanita said. "I'm not having much luck with you. Well, let's give it a try. Maybe the sisters will let you in as-is."

Evanita drove the car to St. Renata's Abbey and parked. She led Adrian across the drawbridge and rang the doorbell.

"So," Nekara said to Jonara as Nekara appeared out of thin air. "We are here again at the abbey. Isn't it ironic that you were aboard the Whitebird when your father dressed up as Shawna and entered this front gate?"

"I thought you'd leave me alone for this last journey," Jonara said. "Don't you at least owe me that?"

"Owe? Owe!" Nekara protested. "I'm the queen of debt and desire. All misery of the world comes from a lack of something. I owe nothing, but I make people owe me. That's how I trap them, as I have trapped you."

Nekara disappeared. Sister Charlene answered the door.

"Evanita," Sister Charlene said. "This is a surprise. Where's your grandmother?"

"She's back in the States," Evanita said. "I came here with my friend."

"Oh?"

"Yeah. Her name is...is...Adriana," Evanita said.

Sister Charlene stared intently at Adriana.

"Evanita. This is all very strange. I wish you or your grand-mother would have called ahead," Sister Charlene said.

"I'm sorry," Evanita said. "You're right. I was hoping I could take Adriana to the Caves of Healing."

"You know we're not a tourist resort," Sister Charlene said. "We don't make it a habit of letting the public troll through our abbey."

"I know," Evanita said. "Adriana has some problems with her past. We're hoping the caves will help."

"The caves cure or corrupt," Sister Charlene said. "I'm hesitant about letting you in with your friend."

"We won't be in very long," Evanita said. "Maybe ten or fifteen minutes. This will be very quick."

"Very well, if it's only ten or fifteen minutes, I will allow it. But no more!" Sister Charlene said.

Sister Charlene led Evanita and Adriana through the abbey to the Caves of Healing.

"You know where the towels are," Sister Charlene said. "Call me if you need anything."

"I will," Evanita said.

Sister Charlene exited the caves. Adrian wasted no time in kicking off his shoes and removing his wig.

"What are you doing?" Evanita asked. "Put that wig back on."

"I can't stand it," he said. "It's uncomfortable."

"But we could get caught. We'll get kicked out! I'll never be able to return," Evanita said.

"So? I don't care about these caves," Adrian said. "But if it helps me figure out how to get my fertility business going, I'll throw the wig back on."

"It's not like that," Evanita said. "There are no secrets to life in these caves."

"Then why are you wasting my time? I want a competitive edge! Give me superior knowledge!" Adrian commanded.

"Come over here," Evanita said, "and bring a chair with you. We'll sit at the edge of the pool and dip our feet in the water."

"You're kidding. Why?" Adrian asked.

"Because that's how the pool works," Evanita said. "Bring a chair. Come on, now."

Adrian sighed and brought a chair with him to the edge of the pool. Evanita did likewise and placed her chair next to his.

"Sit in the chair," Evanita said.

Adrian sat in the chair. Evanita sat in her chair next to him.

"Place your feet in the water," Evanita said.

"They're already in the water," Adrian said.

"Now we should start seeing things," Evanita said. "Pool of healing, take us to the past of Marcus Cracbern. Show Adrian what his father's life was like."

The pool remained calm and dark.

"Nothing's happening," Adrian said. "I knew this was a waste."

"What am I forgetting?" Evanita said. "Think, Evanita, think! I was sitting here. And Grandma Geneva said something. Okay, but what else did she do? She read from her diary. Oh no, I don't have the diary."

"The diary? What difference does a diary make?" Adrian asked.

"It makes all the difference. We were able to go back in time with that diary. She read a passage from a date, and we saw what happened on that date."

"Hogwash," Adrian said. "That's superstition."

"But it worked," Evanita said. "Oh, this is a disaster. There's no way to show you your father's life. I don't have the diary. And I don't have Johnny's Moissan Ruby. That might have been worth a try, but I don't have it. Now what do I do?"

"It's time for an intervention," Nekara said, who now appeared standing on the water's surface in the middle of the pool.

"Nekara!" Jonara cried.

Nekara waved her arm, and Jonara stood next to Nekara.

"Look," Adrian said. "There are two other people in here. Who's the little girl?"

"I've seen you before, little girl. You claim to be my future daughter," Evanita said.

"I am," Jonara said.

"And you," Evanita said. "You were driving Kay's van. You kidnapped my mother. Your name is Nekara."

"That's correct," Nekara said.

"I don't get it," Adrian said. "What's going on?"

"You two—Adrian and Evanita—are here at my request," Nekara said. "I kidnapped your parents—Marcus and Eva—and forced a fetus on each of them. You have a common link. Adrian—your father was impregnated with Roberta's egg. Evanita—your mother was also impregnated with Roberta's egg. Adrian—your father died because his male body could not harbor a fetus. Evanita—your first mother survived because her body *could* harbor a fetus. Evanita and Adrian—I intend to make you two my next experimental subjects."

"This is wrong!" Evanita said. "This is all wrong! I didn't call you up."

"No, but your daughter in here was meddling with Damiriak power, and she called me up," Nekara said. "There is a price to be paid—and I'm here to collect. Further, two men is too many in the Caves of Healing. These are sacred waters created by my senior wife, Felifia of Eho Miriam. It was fouled once with the flesh of Johnny Pindus. Now it is twice fouled with Adrian Cracbern. I seek cause of vengeance. You, Adrian, will lead my cause to convert the world to a fertility plan of my choosing. You, Evanita, will in some future time give birth to a boy who will also become a part of my world fertility plan. But to accomplish this, I must balance things out. Marcus, a male, died as part of my experiment. Now I need a female's death to offset his death. You, Evanita, are that female."

"You're some kind of she-demon or something," Evanita said. "If my grandmother were here—"

"But she's not, nor is your boyfriend Johnny Pindus," Nekara said. "And unlike the River Wood and Battery factory, you can't run away from me in a scrap chute. I have you bound to these caves as I have Adrian bound."

"Stop!" Jonara said. "Stop this madness!"

"Go ahead, invoke a chant. You'll draw more Damiriak power and inversely supply me with more power. It's that simple," Nekara said.

"I'm getting out of here," Adrian said.

Adrian jumped out of the pool and ran for the door, but Nekara pointed at him. His legs froze in place, he turned around slowly, and he walked into the pool until he reached knee-deep.

"Now it is your turn," Nekara said.

Nekara pointed at Evanita. Evanita fought Nekara, but she couldn't stop her legs. She walked into the pool until she also reached knee-deep.

"My legs are on fire!" Evanita screamed. "My legs are on fire!"

2023 Oct 14, Sat. Corpus Christi, Texas.

"My legs are on fire!" Evanita screamed from inside her hospital room.

"Her heart is racing," Eva said.

Doctor Reegen and several nurses rushed in.

"Clear out, clear out!" a nurse said.

The nurse forced Eva and Johnny out of Evanita's room. Evanita wrenched her legs in pain.

"Hold her down," a nurse said.

"She's dying," Doctor Reegen said. "We must deliver the baby now!"

Doctor Reegen and nurses hastily prepared Evanita for a C-section. Evanita screamed.

2009 Jul 11, Sat. Carreña, Spain.

Evanita clutched her abdomen in the Caves of Healing and screamed.

2023 Oct 14, Sat. Portland, Oregon/Corpus Christi, Texas.

Jonara rode in the SR-71 Whitebird as the engines screamed at Mach 4. The eclipse was full, and the craft left Oregon en route to Corpus Christi.

Cerafina stood on sand next to the platform in North Beach and heard screams echoing—one from Corpus Christi Bay, and another from Nueces Bay.

"Help!" Cerafina yelled. "Help!"

2009 Jul 11, Sat. Carreña, Spain.

"I will teach you the secret of female fertility," Nekara said to Adrian while in the Caves of Healing. "You will become a soldier of Nekara."

2023 Oct 14, Sat. Corpus Christi, Texas.

Evanita screamed as the knife cut through her abdomen. Blood spurted everywhere despite Doctor Reegen's attempt to clamp the bleeders.

"Help!" Cerafina called as she stood next to the platform.

Cerafina looked at the Aromani Candleholder, and she remembered how Jonara had chanted in another language for power. Cerafina held the Aromani Candleholder to her abdomen, rubbed it, and concentrated. Miramish words came to her mind, and she said:

Miramish	Translation
Nia voshavovo nui Dzhonara.	I love my Jonara.
Ferilopo, Felifia, ilu zhinonei	Please, Felifia, or someone
Veletu shai Damiriak beresha	From the Damiriak place
Gailo nau gailo dho pilama.	Help me help a friend.

A glowing white figure appeared on the podium. She held out her hands, and Cerafina floated in the air from the sand to the podium next to the figure. The glow dimmed, and an outline formed into the figure of a woman dressed in clothing from the 1940s.

"I am Doctor Alina Zavuski," the woman said.

"You? But how? You're from Jonara's past," Cerafina said.

"I from many past histories of many people. I help with ISIS group. I help women in Korea," Dr. Alina Zavuski said.

"Are...are you human? You have supernatural powers," Cerafina said.

The shape changed from Alina Zavuski to Antonina Zavuski.

"I also her granddaughter, Doctor Antonina Zavuski. I help at Evanita's trial. I help Carreña family. I help many families. I at Caves of Healing in 1492. I help Niessa of MacNessi family, I help Karla of Karrano and later Pindus family, I help Nariva of Carreña family, I help Ziana of Dakari family, and I help Sarina of Ancona family. You, Cerafina Ancona Vagatti—I help you and your family. I help you now. I help because—"

The woman's shape changed again, and she became another woman.

"Because I am Felifia of Eho Miriam," Felifia said. "I have been watching my families for hundreds of years. And I will not abandon them now. Come."

Felifia held her arms out to Cerafina, and Cerafina embraced Felifia. The two disappeared and reappeared wearing flight suits and helmets inside a MiG-31 Russian aircraft with Felifia as pilot and Cerafina as passenger.

"There are many advantages to posing as a Russian woman," Felifia said. "For one, I was able to acquire this MiG-31 Foxhound and upgrade its engine and fuselage. Hold on!"

The MiG-31 launched from the Corpus Christi naval base.

"This is a Russian aircraft?" Cerafina asked. "Aren't you worried about people noticing?"

"They are frozen in time and place," Felifia said. "They will not notice until we are gone."

The MiG-31 with Felifia and Cerafina ascended to an altitude of 80,000 feet.

"Where are we going?" Cerafina asked.

"Toward Portland, Oregon," Felifia said. "But we will not make it. This is an interceptor aircraft, and we will intercept the SR-71 Whitebird that Adrian and Nekara are flying. Your friend, Jonara, is fused with Nekara's body."

"Is she in danger?" Cerafina asked.

"Great danger," Felifia replied. "She is on the brink of losing her immortal spirit to the lowest ethereal bowels of the cosmos."

The MiG-31 broke the sound barrier, and as it did, a momentary water vapor encircled the aircraft.

"What was that?" Cerafina asked.

"Water vapor," Felifia said. "We are now traveling supersonic. We will continue to accelerate until we reach Mach 4."

"Mach 4!" Cerafina exclaimed.

"Yes!" Felifia said. "The same speed as Nekara's SR-71 Whitebird. We must stop her craft from converting your planet into a fertility regime!"

"Then you know! You know!" Cerafina said.

"I knew all along," Felifia said. "But I could not act until this moment. Nekara has focused all her energy on the Carreña and Dakari families—including Marcus and Adrian. But in doing so, she ignored the Ancona family. That means you, Cerafina. I waited until the moment became yours, because Nekara would not see it, and I could act without her detecting me. This is the moment, Cerafina, where I will stop Nekara's plans for the fertility regime!"

The aircraft reached Mach 4.

"There's a halo around us," Cerafina said.

"Yes," Felifia said. "It is a hypersonic shockwave. It engulfs us like an oval. The same shockwave is engulfing Nekara's SR-71. We are both like eggs on a collision course—two aircraft from opposing superpowers, two women from the Damiriak Empire, and two young women from Earth. We will meet and collide."

"You're going to kill us? All of us?!" Cerafina said. "This can't be!"

"The only way to defeat hate is to love your enemy, or your friend. We will join in love," Felifia said.

"This isn't the kind of love I had in mind," Cerafina said. "Felifia—tell me this is a joke. Tell me you have another plan."

2009 Jul 11, Sat. Carreña, Spain.

Nekara orchestrated two, small, water spouts atop the pool in the Caves of Healing. As she did so, Jonara also saw an image in her mind—the image of two stars revolving in opposition to each other clockwise with two orbiting planets in resonance with each other counterclockwise. It was the Damiriak solar system with stars Seris and MacNesi, and planets Eho Miriam in a rounded box orbit and Eho Dahma in a double-spoon-shaped orbit.

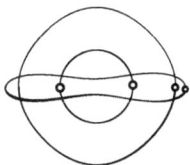

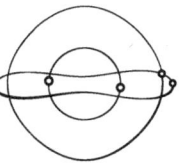

"Adrian—you are to step in the first water spout. Evanita, you are to step in the second," Nekara said. "Then I will join the water spouts to each other."

"This is wrong!" Jonara said. "I am Johnny's daughter, not Adrian's!"

"This is your imperative birth," Nekara said. "I'm attuning their bodies to my command. Their future offspring will bend to my will. And you will be one of those offspring, Jonara. Look at you."

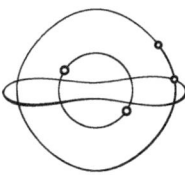

2023 Oct 14, Sat. Over Western United States.

"You are bending to my will," Nekara continued from inside the SR-71 Whitebird. "You are part of my flesh. I programmed this into you from the two waterspouts in the Caves of Healing."

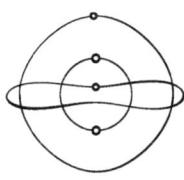

2009 Jul 11, Sat. Carreña, Spain.

Adrian entered one waterspout and Evanita the other. Evanita cried out in pain.

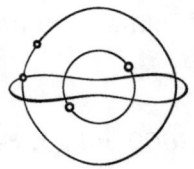

2023 Oct 14, Sat. Corpus Christi, Texas.

Doctor Reegen finished cutting open Evanita. She cried out in pain.

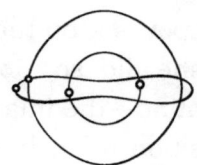

2023 Oct 14, Sat. Over Western United States.

The American and Russian aircraft made their final approach on a collision course with each other. The engines on both planes screamed in pain.

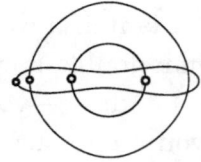

2009 Jul 11, Sat. Carreña, Spain.

The waterspouts began merging. The water thrashed with explosive sheer force. Nekara chanted something in Mirsua ending with "*Miaras felaufikaras. Dosikos!* (Ocean deliverance. Execute!)"

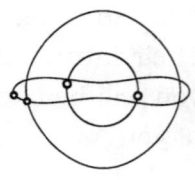

2023 Oct 14, Sat. Corpus Christi, Texas.

Doctor Reegen removed baby Robert with his umbilical cord still attached.

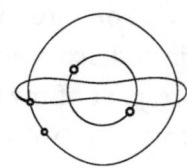

2023 Oct 14/2009 Jul 11, Sat. over Western United States/ Corpus Christi/ Carreña, Spain.

Doctor Reegen cut the umbilical cord, and at the same time, the two waterspouts merged and the two aircraft collided. Evanita screamed in the Caves of Healing as the merged waterspouts physically destroyed the Caves. The two aircraft ensnared each other into a colossal fireball. Evanita died while delivering Robert. Evanita and Adrian were ejected from the rubble of the Caves of Healing and beyond the castle of St. Renata's Abbey. Nekara and Felifia merged spirits while in the air, but Adrian (the pilot) died. Jonara and Cerafina briefly merged spirits from the aircraft collision, and the Water Ruby and Aromani Candleholder merged and 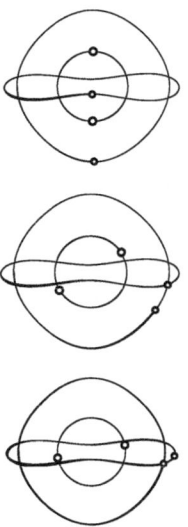 fused into Jonara's navel. Halos of cerise light encircled the two girls' bodies and traveled up and down. One traveled to their feet and dissolved while the other traveled to their heads, reversed direction, traveled to their abdomens, and dissolved. Jonara separated from Cerafina. The two parachuted to the ground with the Water Ruby and Aromani Candleholder still fused in Jonara's navel.

A nurse took baby Robert away and cleaned him up. Doctor Reegen went to work on reviving Evanita. Sisters at St. Renata's Abbey scrambled from the explosion in their facility while some went to the aid of Adrian and Evanita. Evanita was alive, but her memory of all past events was gone.

Jonara and Cerafina reached the ground and removed their parachute gear.

"My abdomen feels strange," Jonara said.

Jonara lifted her own shirt, and indeed, her navel looked different, as if the Moissan Ruby had fused to her navel in the shape of the Aromani Candleholder. Surrounding her navel were nine symbols tattooed to her skin.

"I'm a High Priestess!" Jonara said. "I can invoke High Priestess power."

Jonara embraced Cerafina and shouted in the language of the high priestesses of Eho Miriam:

Mirsua	Translation
Gokos raus dis Ivanitas	Take us to Evanita
Tolus e sas geruthos valesas	Where she gives birth
Dis nuis deidus kelufotas.	To my baby brother.

The two returned to the hallway outside Evanita's room in Corpus Christi Hospital as if they'd never left. Jonara tried entering her mother's room, but a nurse prevented her. She watched in horror as Doctor Reegen applied defibrillation paddles to Evanita's chest. Evanita's body jumped in the air, but she did not return to life. Doctor Reegen tried and tried, but Evanita did not return. Doctor Reegen and nurses called the time of death. Evanita was dead.

"NO!" Jonara shouted.

Jonara held her left hand to her abdomen and shouted repeatedly:

Mirsua	Translation
Felitos Malisas	Bring Mother
Veletus e sais kiosatas!	From the dead!

Evanita did not return from the dead.

"All the world and my priestess power in exchange for my mother's death is too high a price to pay!" Jonara cried.

Cerafina took Jonara in her arms and comforted her.

"The price is too high! The price is too high!" Jonara cried. "I wish I could blow all misery to the four corners of the earth and start over! Blow all misery away!"

Images flew through Jonara's mind as Cerafina comforted her. Two aircraft from two superpowers, two women from another solar system, two stars in another solar system, two planets in crossing orbital paths, two women conceiving a child, a daughter losing her mother to childbirth, Jonara and Cerafina...

Two candles stood on a birthday cake—one shaped like a "1" and the other like a "3". Jonara was growing up, and that meant two candles instead of thirteen. She had closed her eyes to wish for something—thirteen candles—but instead, she received a vision that spanned three books. She opened her eyes, and the two candles burned brightly. She blew them out, and her family clapped in applause.

"Mommy! You're alive!" Jonara said.

"Is that what you wished for?" Evanita asked.

"And I thought you'd wish for a career choice," Grandma Eva said.

"I wish you would stay my little girl forever," Johnny said.

Jonara looked around. Yes, she was in her home. Yes, everything seemed normal. Yes, yes, yes!

"We have a special surprise for you," Grandma Eva said. "She flew all the way up from Corpus Christi to celebrate your thirteenth birthday and your first day as a teenager."

An older woman entered from the hallway.

"Happy birthday, Jonara," her familiar voice said.

"Nanna Geneva!" Jonara cried.

Jonara ran from the table and gave Geneva the biggest hug she could muster. Jonara wouldn't let go. Instead, she jumped up and down with Geneva while maintaining the hug. Jonara started singing a children's song, and Geneva sang it too. Evanita and Eva joined in with the hugging, the jumping, and the singing. Johnny reached for his camera and took photograph after photograph of the four generations of Carreña women. The women finally settled down long enough to sit at the table and enjoy cake, but that didn't stop Johnny. He continued taking photographs of the celebration. Jonara cut cake and handed it out, but before anyone took a bite, Jonara's three Evas gathered around Jonara as she sat at the head of the table with her birthday cake. They embraced Jonara. Johnny photographed them.

The celebration continued long into the evening. The four generations laughed, cried, played card games, board games, and even rushed out of the house several times and yelled whatever they felt like to the world and the sky above. Eva had taken a day off from her naltrexone treatment and enjoyed red wine as if tasting it for the first time. Geneva read from her diary, Evanita played the *viola de gamba*, and Jonara played the oboe. Jonara wished the night would never end, but the night grew late, and even Jonara grew sleepy. Johnny printed out several photographs from the evening's wildness, and Jonara paged through them. She picked a particular one for the wall next to her bedroom window, and after the others had gone to bed, Jonara taped the photo to the wall just as the last stars of the night faded into dawn. Jonara watched the dawn and stared at the photo of herself before her birthday cake surrounded by her mother, grandmother, and great-grandmother—the four generations of Carreña.

2110 Dec 29, Mon 7 pm. 376 Grey Road, Hamilton, New Zealand.

"It was all a dream!?" Kristi asked. "Of course!"

"It was a vision," Jonara said. "In that brief moment where I made a birthday wish, I had a vision of my family past, the present, and an alternative timeline. But once the vision was complete and I returned to my senses, I knew what I had to do. I had to give women everywhere the opportunity once and for all to liberate themselves from men totally and completely—if they wished—by providing them the means to create their own families together without the need of spermatozoa. The secret of life—do you remember? It's that a woman should never become dependent on a man. She must always have her legs."

"I threw myself into learning as much as I could about biology, chemistry, and technology when I was a teenager," Jonara continued. "While my classmates took pills, smoked marijuana, got drunk, and engaged in random, unprotected sexual intercourse, I locked myself away from society as much as possible, because I knew time was precious, and no one else would do it—they were too busy 'hanging out' and wasting their lives away. Instead of being belligerent and fighting my female ancestors as my classmates did at that age, I sought out my female ancestors for knowledge and guidance. They were happy to give me all the support I asked for. It was a rare gift—to have such strong bonds with one's mother, grandmother, and great-grandmother, but I worked my butt off, and I made my family relationships yield the sweet fruits of reward. I went to university and graduated with top honors, but I didn't care about the honors. I cared about the work. Cerafina was a real person, however, and she did live in Corpus Christi. She and I were lovers—you probably guessed that. We married and had several children together, but she was killed by an anti-lesbian extremist while we were at church—very much like Roberta's attack, only Cerafina died. That was in 2050. After her death, I realized I couldn't stay in the United States any longer. There would always be ignorant extremists who would commit murder to advance their mindless agendas. So I followed my vision of Roberta and my Pindus ancestors and came to New Zealand."

"Wow!!" Kristi said. "I don't know what to say, except thank you! You're like the female Newton or Einstein or something."

"Well, I just chipped away at the problem. No one's a goddess," Jonara said.

"I beg to differ," Margaret said. "When the light is right and the mood overtakes me, I look at my wife, Kristi, and to me she looks like a goddess."

Kristi smiled. The two women embraced and kissed.

"There's nothing sweeter than the love between two women," Jonara said.

The two finished kissing.

"Mamma Maffet," Kristi said. "That Damiriak solar system—we would like to do a graphic on it. Do you have any notes on how those planets orbit?"

"Kristi, come on! It was just a vision," Margaret said.

"Or was it?" Jonara asked.

"What are you saying, Mamma Maffet?" Margaret asked.

"The lines between vision and reality are often blurred," Jonara said. "One moment."

Jonara disappeared and reappeared with a paper.

"You may keep this," Jonara said. "It's a copy. I came up with some numbers off the top of my head one day and gave them to Cerafina. She put together a book about the Damiriak Empire—their languages, a little on their culture, and a bit of astronomy. I have a copy of the book somewhere around here, but I'll have to look. Meanwhile, keep this copy with my compliments."

Margaret and Kristi looked at each other in shock before looking at the matrix of numbers.

"Back in the day," Jonara said, "Cerafina had an astronomy simulator computer program. She entered these numbers into the simulator, and it showed the stars, planets, and moons in motion. These are crude numbers, but they should give you a start."

"Thank you!" Kristi said. "I'd like to read Cerafina's book someday. I'm interested in those Damiriak languages."

"I'll look for it," Jonara said.

"You mean...the Damiriak women...they were real?" Margaret asked. "Did Cerafina meet them? But how? It was just a vision!"

Jonara winked.

"We've got to find that book," Margaret said. "The one Cerafina wrote."

"Suddenly," Kristi said, "my Margaret lights up with great interest."

"But it could be true," Margaret said. "I never thought I'd hear myself say it, but I believe Damiriak women really exist!"

"It's the power of the mind," Jonara said.

"And the power of the clock," Kristi said as she looked at her watch. "We have to go."

"Oh, I so enjoyed your company today," Jonara said. "You're welcome here anytime you like."

"We enjoyed our visit," Margaret said. "And it'll be an honor to visit you again. I still want to read that book."

"I learned a lot," Kristi said. "I never thought I'd say that, but it's true. A person just doesn't learn these kinds of things reading the news or watching television."

"I'm glad I was of help," Jonara said. "I'm Mamma Maffet. I help."

"Thank you again," Margaret said.

"Please, one more thing," Jonara said. "I would like to send a gift for the baby. May I have your address?"

"With pleasure," Margaret said, and she wrote down the couple's address on a pad of paper.

"Thank you," Jonara said.

Jonara placed her left hand to her abdomen, and with her right hand, she touched Kristi's shoulder.

"You will give birth to a healthy girl during the first minute of the New Year," Jonara said.

Margaret and Kristi were stunned with the prediction, but they realized it had to be a joke, and they laughed. The girls laughed all the way to the door, and Jonara laughed with them as she gave them a last wave of goodbye. Margaret and Kristi headed back to Hamilton and finished their editing while Jonara relaxed to a cup of tea. She looked out her window and saw green lights flashing. She smiled.

2110 Dec 31, Wed 11:55 pm. Hamilton, New Zealand.

"Push, Kristi, push!" Margaret urged.

Kristi was delivering her baby in a Hamilton hospital with Margaret at her side.

"Jonara was right!" Kristi said. "How could she know?"

"Don't talk, just push!" Margaret said.

"Ugh! I thought childbirth is supposed to be easier with Jonara's fertility methods!" Kristi said.

"Her methods helped you get pregnant. They don't help with childbirth. The pain is the same," Margaret said.

"Well I've been robbed somehow," Kristi said. "Everyone else is out celebrating New Year while I'm in here laboring with a baby!"

"It's just like Jonara's life!" Margaret said. "While her peers wasted away their lives with parties, she struggled in near isolation working on her creation. Think of it, Kristi, you're like Jonara."

"Well, I think I'd rather be like Eva and enjoy a tall glass of red wine!" Kristi said. "Arg! This is it!"

With a final push, Kristi delivered a healthy, baby girl, just as Jonara predicted.

"Congratulations," the doctor said. "Your baby is the first of the New Year!"

Kristi pushed out the afterbirth, and the doctor cleaned her up. A nurse checked the baby girl, cleaned her up, and placed her next to Kristi.

"Have you decided on a name?" a nurse asked.

"Are you still thinking of Marci?" Margaret asked.

"Special delivery for Kristi Fernandez," said a delivery boy.

"Sorry, that will have to wait outside," said a nurse.

"No, wait—who's it from?" Kristi asked.

"A Doctor Jonara Pindus," the delivery boy said.

"Please—bring it to me!" Kristi said.

The delivery boy handed the gift to a nurse who handed it to Kristi. Kristi opened the package.

"Well I'll be," Margaret said. "It's one of those communication devices used by the greenbeam women."

"How did she...I wonder...was it all real?" Kristi asked.

"Jonara has an impressive mind, if she could build such a device out of a vision she had when she was thirteen," Margaret said.

"Unless the vision is real," Kristi said. "We saw those green lights when we were visiting her house. There could be Celtic women in our mountains—here—in New Zealand!"

"It wouldn't surprise me," Margaret said. "Hamilton is the antipodal city of Córdoba, Spain. Doctor Jonara's house is very likely an antipodal point of Verda's and Raya's house."

"I never realized that!" Kristi said.

"It's like the furthest two points on the planet coming together," Margaret said. "We're like that too."

"Have you decided on a name?" a nurse repeated.

"What should we name our girl?" Margaret asked, and Kristi replied:

"Carreña McAleese Fernandez."

Characters

Kristi Fernandez

Television journalist for Channel-A news interviewing Dr. Jonara Carreña Pindus in 2110 at Jonara's home. Kristi is nearly nine months pregnant with her wife's child. She is married to Margaret McAleese.

Margaret McAleese

Television camerawoman capturing video and audio of Kristi's interview with Dr. Jonara Carreña Pindus. She is married to Kristi Fernandez and is the other biological mother of Kristi's unborn baby.

Jonara Carreña Pindus/Jonara Cracbern Pindus/John-Error

Daughter of Johnny Pindus and Evanita Carreña. Jonara is the primary character in book three. She struggles to find a way back to her own timeline after Nekara the Red forces her into a world of strict compliance.

Evanita Soledad Carreña Pindus/Evanita Cracbern Pindus/ Eve Carson

Jonara's mother. Daughter of Eva and wife of Johnny. In the altered timeline, Evanita is never in the hospital and never has the growing up problems the Evanita of the regular timeline has. Despite this, Jonara is able to use the Moissan Ruby to see her mother as she was in the regular timeline—she finishes her sentence at the Elrod 402, she visits Spain, and she comes to a sense of self-realization about her ancestry and herself. Evanita delivers a second child, Robert Pindus.

Eva Kelicacha Carreña/ Eva Carreña Cracbern

In the altered timeline, Eva is married to Marcus Cracbern, who did not die. The altered Eva is a devout Roman Catholic and believes women should be subservient to men—all contrary to the Eva in Jonara's regular timeline. Eva's past in the regular timeline regarding her conception of Evanita is explored in book three.

Geneva Carreña/ Nanna Geneva

Eva's mother. In the altered timeline, she is in the hospital. In the regular timeline, she is dead and buried. Geneva helps Evanita discover herself after Evanita's time spent in the Elrod 402.

Margene Carreña

Geneva's mother. Gives birth to Geneva in Girona, Spain.

François Vallan

Margene's husband. Dies shortly after marrying Margene.

Johanidan (Johnny) Reginald Pindus/ Shawna

Johnny Pindus is Jonara's father and the husband of Evanita. In the altered timeline, he is fat and has no power with the Moissan Ruby. In the regular timeline, Johnny helps Roberta and Eva during the paternity trial. Later when he is older, he accompanies Evanita to the Caves of Healing with Geneva, and he dresses as a woman named Shawna to gain entry.

Anna

Anna is Geneva's housekeeper in both timelines. She is a Latina.

Marcus Cracbern/Marcus Cracbern Dakari

Marcus is the son of Theodore and Alice Cracbern. He is adopted by Dr. Jelana after birth and grows up with the Dakaris. He drops his Dakari last name when he becomes an adult.

Marcus is married to Eva in the altered timeline and is Jonara's step-grandfather. In the regular timeline, he has a conflict with Roberta, seeks to woo Eva, and chases the two and Kay along Portland streets resulting in an accident in the Willamette River. He dies of a ruptured prostate gland in the regular timeline.

Adrian Cracbern
Son of Marcus Cracbern and Andrea Peddly. Adrian is the pilot of the SR-71 Whitebird in both timelines. He and Evanita go on a trip to Spain in the regular timeline with hopes he can uncover the secret of her female-couple conception.

Cerafina Vagatti
In past books, Cerafina was Jonara's friend, but in the altered timeline, Cerafina wants nothing to do with Jonara. She accuses Jonara of being a lesbian. Cerafina has a boyfriend in the altered timeline, Tony.

Davino Vagatti
Cerafina's father. He's married to Marina Ancona.

Leo Vagatti
Cerafina's half brother.

Greg Dannerstadt
Cerafina's classmate of ill repute. Claims to be the boyfriend of Jonara in the altered timeline.

Tony
Cerafina's boyfriend in the altered timeline.

Bishop Tárrega
Bishop of Corpus Christi, Texas. Coordinates the vitaceptical implementation.

Karl
Project manager under Marcus Cracbern. Karl prepares the SR-71 Whitebird for flight from Portland, Oregon to Corpus Christi, Texas.

Sonja, Dorsia
Greg Dannerstadt's girlfriends. Sonja is a blonde while Dorsia is a brunette.

Dr. Reegen
Evanita's doctor while she's in the hospital with preeclampsia. Dr. Reegen delivers Evanita's baby boy, Robert.

Iberia in Middle Ages

Rabbi Nachmanides
Jewish scholar from Girona who answers the Disputation of Barcelona in 1263. In the indurated timeline, he never reaches the Disputation.

Friar Raymond of Penyaforte
Confessor of King James I of Aragon. Mentor to Friar Pablo Christiani. Coordinates Disputation of Barcelona.

Friar Pablo Christiani
The lead Christian advocate in the Disputation of Barcelona in 1263. In the indurated timeline, Friar Christiani goes on to educate Prince Fernando de la Cerda of Castile and become his confessor. Friar Christiani negotiates with the greenbeam women in the mountains such that they help Prince Fernando in battle against the Moors.

King James I
King of Aragon. Presides at Disputation of Barcelona in 1263. Father-in-law to King Alfonso X of Castile.

King Alfonso X
King of Castile. King James I's son-in-law. Father of Prince Fernando de la Cerda. He along with King James work to expand their kingdoms southward in Iberia against the Moors.

Master William
A royal judge at the Disputation of Barcelona in 1263.

Pope Clement IV
Banishes Rabbi Nachmanides from Iberia.

King Ferdinand III
Alfonso X's father who reconquers most of Andalusia, Iberia.

Infante Prince Fernando de la Cerda
Son of King Alfonso X of Castile. Is heir to his father's throne. Dies in summer of 1263 either from illness or in battle. In the indurated timeline, he survives and leads Iberia into quick victory over the Moors, accelerates the Reconquista into early completion, creates a navy, has a naval route to the Far East established, and conquers the New World.

Princess Blanche of France
Prince Fernando de la Cerda's wife.

Sancho IV
Fernando de la Cerda's younger brother who in reality took over the throne of Castile from their father after Fernando's and Alfonso's death. In the indurated timeline, Fernando does not die, and so Sancho never takes command of Castile.

Alfonso de la Cerda
Prince Fernando de la Cerda's son and disputed heir of Castile after Fernando's death.

Sultan Abu Yusuf Ya'qub
Leads Moorish invasion from Morocco into Andalusia in the summer of 1275 causing a setback in the *Reconquista*.

Atina of Tarragona
Celtic woman of late 1200s. Lives in Collserola Mountains northwest of Barcelona with her lover, Sarita. In the indurated timeline, Atina and Sarita raise an army with the greenbeam women and help Prince Fernando defeat the Moors in 1275.

Sarita
Atina's lover and roommate. She leads a greenbeam army along the Guadalquivir River to attack the Moors.

Tinta
Atina's black Asturcon pony.

Polilla
Sarita's white Galician pony.

Verda, Raya
Lovers and inventors of the greenbeam device. The two live in the Morena Mountain foothills north of Córdoba.

Luis, Vimaro
Musicians who with Atina play music at *La Taberna del Rey* in Villarreal, Aragon in 1275 for Prince Fernando de la Cerda and his men.

King Fernando II of Spain
In indurated timeline, King Fernando II sends Amerigo Vespucci to the New World to put down a rebellion for New World independence. In appreciation for Vespucci's success, the New World is renamed from Fernanica to America.

Amerigo Vespucci
Often credited in both timelines for lending his name to the New World, "America". In the indurated timeline, Vespucci puts down a rebellion in the New World within five years time.

Felifia's Sapphic Women

Karla Karrano
Fantina's, Aromani's, and Johnny's female ancestor who attends Sapphic meetings with Felifia and others in Alhama and

Carreña, Iberia. Karla is Jewish and receives a special two-position candleholder from a craftswoman in Carreña as a gift.

Niessa
Female ancestor of Jane MacNessi and Roberta who attends Sapphic meetings with Felifia and other women in Alhama and Carreña. Niessa receives an oversized flute-like instrument from a craftswoman in Carreña that later becomes an oboe. Niessa is Celtic.

Nariva
Female ancestor of Geneva Carreña who attends Sapphic meetings with Felifia and other women in Alhama and Carreña. Nariva receives a stringed instrument from a craftswoman in Carreña that becomes a *viola de gamba*. Nariva also receives a blank codex book to use as a diary. Nariva is Roman Catholic.

Ziana
Ziana is a female ancestor of Dr. Jelana who attends Sapphic meetings with Felifia and other women in Alhama and Carreña. Ziana receives a *bendir* drum as a gift from a craftswoman in Carreña. Ziana is Muslim.

Sarina
Female ancestor of Marina Ancona and Cerafina Vagatti. Sarina also attends Sapphic meetings with Felifia and other women in Alhama and Carreña. Sarina is Zoroastrian. She receives a chalice and a blank codex book as gifts from a craftswoman in Carreña.

Damiriak Women

Princess Felifia of Miriam
Princess of planet Eho Miriam. She is a senior wife and is married to Tanina, Teluna, and Nekara. She works to save her

planet after star Seris changes solar output. Eventually, she leaves Eho Miriam to pursue Nekara on Earth. Felifia's efferite spacecraft crashes along a stretch from Eritrea, Africa to Carreña, Spain. Felifia forms secret societies to aid women—most famously in Spain circa 1492. Felifia has a major battle with Nekara in the Montseny Mountains in Spain. Felifia's native language is Miramish.

Countess Nekara/Nekara the Red/Nekara Redding
Felifia's third junior wife. Nekara researches methods for women to have children with women. She perfects such methods on Eho Miriam but runs into conflict with the Miramish priestesses over her methods. She leaves Eho Miriam and begins a colony of women on Eho Dahma where she takes Dahmek as her native language. She is expelled from Eho Dahma in an efferite sphere. The sphere lands on Earth leaving a trail from Corpus Christi, Texas to Portland, Oregon. Nekara enjoys watching Earthlings suffer. She forms a special relationship with Jonara and is often finding ways to cause misery for Jonara.

High Priestess Vadafa
Officiates at Felifia's and Nekara's wedding. She is a High Priestess and is Felifia's mentor.

Anba, Biorna
Vadafa's first and second junior wives respectively. Both are priestesses. Anba is a women's activist while Biorna runs the observatory.

Tanina, Teluna
Felifia's first and second junior wives respectively. Both are priestesses.

Nelaga
Nekara's grandmother. Nelaga proposes that a woman should have the right to procreate as she chooses. She warns that male-female procreation without options for women to procreate

with other women is dangerous since an accidental elimination of men leaves the remaining women powerless to perpetuate the species. Nelaga also invents a robot, but it is destroyed.

Nelasha

Nekara's mother. Nelasha is an archaeologist. Believing that ancient women had the power to procreate with each other, Nelasha attempts to rediscover their methods by searching for and studying remnants of their civilization.

Noryat

Passenger on a spacecraft of pilgrims leaving Eho Miriam for Earth. Princess Felifia gives him a locket with three seeds—one for a Norway Crimson King Maple, one for a Norway Spruce, and one for flax. Noryat's spacecraft lands in a region to be known as Norway, Rogaland County, in a bay known as Boknafjord. Sami people of Norway help Noryat and his people survive. Eventually, Noryat leads a group to the Iberian peninsula.

Representative Haubar

Assumes dictatorial powers on Eho Miriam after star Seris undergoes massive solar changes.

Andoranka

Ancient Damiriak woman who creates a man from a bone in her leg. She raises an army of these men in a failed *coup d'état*. After she is overpowered, her male army is set free. These men form unions with women resulting in male-female marriages and reproductive bondings. In time, the ability for women to have children without men fails.

Eva's Youth

Simon Tsarovsky

Eva's boyfriend from dental school. Simon is an atheist existentialist who at times favors a little Marxism. He is a paraplegic but manages to earn a Master's degree in Clinical Informatics from the University of Texas at Houston. Simon is clingy and micromanaging in relationships. He seeks to have others do things for him as much as possible and makes little effort to do things for himself. Simon introduces Eva to existential philosophy and the Unitarian Universalist church.

Roberta MacNessi

Jane MacNessi's daughter. Roberta is a dentist. She divorces Richard Brack, moves to Portland, Oregon, and starts MacNessi Dental. She rents a house and shares it with Eva.

Richard Brack

Roberta's husband.

Jane MacNessi O'Leary (Janna, Janie)

Jane is the mother of Roberta MacNessi. She plays professional women's baseball in Wisconsin before traveling down south and becoming a military pilot.

Sally

Young mistress of Richard Brack who bears a child with him.

Kay Margo Dakari

Dr. Jelana's biological daughter and Marcus's stepsister. Kay is a dental hygienist and works at MacNessi Dental. She dates Earl Jackson.

Earl Jackson

Kay's boyfriend. Earl is a Detroit Pistons fan.

Milo, Frank

Dentists practicing under Marcus Cracbern.

Andrea Peddly

Former romance of Marcus's. She gives birth to Marcus's son, Adrian Cracbern.

Claudia

Waitress at *Dairy Duck*. Claudia and Roberta make love two nights in a row.

Donna

A patron at *Dairy Duck* and Claudia's ex-girlfriend.

Valeria Pindus

Johnny Pindus's older sister.

Amber, Ronny, Floyd

Young patients at MacNessi Dental.

Pastor Ephram

Pastor at Barnseed Baptist Church.

Patty Ephram

Wife of Pastor Ephram. She performs signing for the deaf at Baptist church services.

Lisa, Julie, Audrey

Victims of Marcus's tooth obsession. Marcus extracts teeth from these women and transplants the teeth into his own mouth.

Maggie

Yacht owner on the Willamette River in Portland, Oregon. She helps Kay and Roberta fish Marcus and Eva out of the river.

Jan Haughf

Eva's prosecuting attorney during her paternity suit against Marcus.

Viko Vastapo

Marcus's defense attorney during Eva's paternity suit against him.

Mariah Carey
Singer at the Detroit Pistons-Portland Trailblazers championship game.

Isaiah Thomas, Vinnie Johnson
Basketball players for the Detroit Pistons.

Dr. Harvey
The doctor who delivers Eva's baby—Evanita—via Caesarean section.

Judge Jillian
The judge at Eva's paternity trial against Marcus Cracbern.

Evanita's Youth

Oxia
Chief of security at the Elrod 402 detention campus.

Ox-One, Ox-Two
Security guards at the Elrod 402.

Ms. Zyla
Evanita's religious mentor from Broadway Unitarian Universalist Church.

Ms. Nordekter/O Grammeni
Chief administrator of the Elrod 402.

Calico Shepherd/Fiori Sheppe
Evanita's roommate at the Elrod 402. Calico has Turner's syndrome. She is of stocky build and very strong.

Mac-Two
Real name is Tara Tushenne. Cafeteria employee at Elrod 402. Evanita's roommate for a time. Has a lesbian interest in Evanita.

Baria
Medical chief at the Elrod 402.

Bar-One, Bar-Two, Bar-Three, Bar-Four, Bar-Five
Medical employees at the Elrod 402.

Dialytika
Head of sanitation at the Elrod 402.

Ben Boolet
Movie actor of a horror film O Grammeni wishes to see.

Riggs, J. Smith, Barnett, C.T. Jones
Dead detainees transported by Evanita on her electric truck.

Sister Rosa
Former administrator at St. Renata's Abbey.

Sister Charlene/Chalina Darconejo
Geneva's friend at St. Renata's Abbey.

Garcia Delgato
A witness at Margene's and François's wedding.

Father Mendez
The priest who marries Margene and François.

Timeline

4101 BCE
Felifia's and Nekara's wedding day. Seris undergoes massive solar changes from a white star to a cerise star. Noryat leaves Eho Miriam for Earth and settles in present-day Norway. Nekara becomes fossilized and ultrapowerful. All men on Eho Miriam die.

1263 Jul 15
Jonara and Rabbi Nachmanides witness the duel between Felifia and Nekara in the Montseny Mountains, Iberia.

1263 Jul 20–24
The Disputation of Barcelona.

1263 Aug
In the altered timeline, Friar Christiani meets Atina and Sarita in the Collserola Mountains in the Kingdom of Aragon, Iberia.

1268
Fernando de la Cerda marries Princess Blanche.

1269
In the altered timeline, Friar Christiani introduces plan of trading directly with the Far East to Alfonso X. Shipbuilding for this purpose begins. Greenbeam women begin using ships.

1275 Jun 1
In the altered timeline, Fernando de la Cerda eats dinner with troops at *La Taberna del Rey* in Villarreal, Valencia, Iberia. Fernando avoids the poisoned fish and survives.

1275 Jun 8

In the altered timeline, Atina and Fernando de la Cerda arrive in Córdoba, Iberia and meet up with Sarita and the greenbeam army.

1275 Jun 9

In the altered timeline, Atina and Sarita along with Fernando de la Cerda begin westward march from Córdoba to meet the Marinids in combat.

1275 Jun 20

In the altered timeline, Fernando de la Cerda greets Abu Yusuf Ya'qub in Tarifa—a port controlled by Fernando.

1275 Jul 24

In the regular timeline, Fernando de la Cerda eats dinner with troops at *La Taberna del Rey* in Villarreal, Valencia, Iberia. He dies from food poisoning after eating an enlarged fish.

1292

In the altered timeline, all of Iberia is unified into Spain. Jews are expelled. The Americas are conquered and named *Fernanica*.

1482 Feb 27

In the regular timeline, Felifia holds the Spa of Alhama's last Sapphic meeting in Granada, Iberia.

1492 Jan 1

In the regular timeline, Felifia holds last Sapphic meeting in Carreña, Iberia. She instructs craftswomen to make various gifts for her followers.

1970 Jul 3 Fri

Geneva and Eva crash with the De Havilland Comet aircraft on Montseny Mountains in Spain.

1970 Jul 4 Sat
Geneva and Eva recover from their airline accident in an Arbúcies hospital.

1973 Oct 31 Wed
Roberta instructs Eva's elementary school class on proper hygiene using Merry and Glum Pumpkin.

1988
Jane MacNessi dies.

1989 May 20 Sat
Eva graduates from dental school at the University of Texas at Houston.

1989 May 21 Sun
Simon proposes marriage to Eva.

1989 May 29 Mon
Eva goes for a jog with Roberta after eating breakfast and discussing Simon.

1989 May 30 Tue
Roberta, Eva, Kay, Earl, and Marcus go out to Page Street Pub for drinks.

1989 May 31 Wed
Marcus shows Eva his tooth collection. Eva learns of Simon's infection and flies to Houston to visit him.

1989 Jun 2 Fri
Eva visits her mother, Geneva, in Corpus Christi. She goes dancing with Marcus. Eva breaks up with Simon.

1989 Jun 3 Sat
Eva returns to Portland, Oregon from Corpus Christi. Eva and Roberta visit *Dairy Duck* for the first time. Marcus takes Eva to his home and makes an impression of her teeth.

1989 Jun 5 Mon
Marcus announces plans to Milo and Frank regarding dentistry for high-income clients only. Marcus convinces Eva to go along with his plan for doubling up patients in Roberta's treatment rooms.

1989 Jun 30 Fri
Eva passes out in the lab at MacNessi Dental due to alcohol abuse. Eva quits working for Roberta and takes a dentistry job under Marcus.

1989 Sep 29 Fri
Eva meets Johnny Pindus for the first time. Johnny is kicked out of Cracbern Associates and has his infected tooth treated by Roberta at MacNessi Dental. Roberta lends Johnny a reference manual for the VAX 11/780 computer.

1989 Oct 6 Fri
Johnny's second visit for restoring his infected tooth.

1989 Oct 8 Sun
Roberta attends church service at Barnseed Baptist Church with Johnny and Valeria. Roberta, Johnny, and Valeria set up a fake login program on Marcus's computer terminal.

1989 Oct 9 Mon
Roberta hacks into Marcus's computer account.

1989 Oct 13 Fri
Johnny's third visit to finish his root canal and crown restoration. Roberta sneaks into Marcus's office and opens his safe. Eva is hit by a car.

1989 Oct 14 Sat
Roberta starts Eva on naltrexone for drug abuse and handcuffs Eva to her bed. Marcus helps Eva escape and takes her to dinner at his house. Marcus attempts to steal Eva's canine teeth.

Marcus chases Kay, Roberta, and Eva in Kay's van. Nekara and Felifia have a fight. Nekara drives the van and crashes it through a side barrier from Sellwood Bridge into the Willamette River with Eva and Marcus inside.

1989 Dec 3
Eva and Roberta have a falling out in their relationship over Eva's pregnancy.

1990 Jun 14
Eva attends the Portland-Detroit championship game in Memorial Coliseum. After the game, Eva is attacked by an angry fan and is rushed to Legacy Memorial Hospital. Eva's baby—Evanita—is delivered through emergency Caesarean section.

1990 Jul 6 Fri
Eva's paternity trial against Marcus Cracbern.

1990 Jul 14 Sat
Eva takes Evanita home from the hospital. Eva, Roberta, Kay, Marcus, and Johnny learn how Eva became pregnant. Marcus dies.

1990 Jul 15 Sun
Marcus's funeral. Roberta is injured.

1990 Jul 30 Mon
Roberta leaves the United States for New Zealand.

2007 Apr 8
Evanita is visited by Ms. Zyla in the Elrod 402.

2007 Apr 9
Evanita's first day of work as a health assistant in Cafederijet.

2007 Nov 13
Evanita is released from the Elrod 402 detention center.

2007 Dec 5 Wed

Evanita, Geneva, and Johnny leave Portland, Oregon for a visit to Spain.

2007 Dec 6 Thu

Evanita, Geneva, and Johnny arrive in Castrillón, Spain en route to Carreña. The party visit the Bay of Biscay shoreline and two waterfalls.

2007 Dec 7 Fri

Evanita, Geneva, and Johnny visit the Caves of Healing in St. Renata's Abbey in Carreña, Spain.

2007 Dec 8 Sat

Geneva and Evanita return to the Caves of Healing with Johnny dressed as a woman.

2007 Dec 14 Fri

Evanita completes her Coming-Of-Age ceremony at Broadway Unitarian Universalist Church.

2009 Jul 11 Sat

Evanita and Adrian arrive in Castrillón, Spain. The two enter the Caves of Healing.

2010 Jan 1

Evanita Carreña marries Johnny Pindus.

2023 Oct 3

In the regular timeline, Jonara and Cerafina visit Evanita in Corpus Christi Hospital.

2023 Oct 8 Sun

Jonara wakes up in the altered timeline where the Roman Catholic Church dominates the United States. Evanita is not in the hospital with preeclampsia, Eva is married to Marcus, and Cerafina has a boyfriend. Jonara travels with her family to Corpus Christi Bay to hear Bishop Tárrega's speech about the new fertility plan. Jonara takes a boat ride on Corpus Christi Bay with Johnny.

2023 Oct 9 Mon
Jonara visits the park, looks through the Moissan Ruby, and sees animal life as orange and plant life as blue.

2023 Oct 10 Tue
Jonara—on crutches from leg cramps—goes on a walk with her family. Later, her family attends Daily Mass.

2023 Oct 11 Wed
A squirrel gnaws at Jonara's bedroom window. Adrian flies the SR-71 Whitebird to Corpus Christi as part of a dry-run test. Jonara rides as a passenger in an SR-71 flight over the city.

2023 Oct 12 Thu
Jonara goes on another boat ride with Johnny in Corpus Christi Bay. Johnny speaks of Jonara giving something in order to return to the other timeline.

2023 Oct 13 Fri
Jonara walks to Oso Bay in Corpus Christi and jumps in.

2023 Oct 14 Sat
In the altered timeline, the SR-71 Whitebird flies from Portland to Corpus Christi to prepare the world for the Catholic Church's control over fertility. In the regular timeline, the SR-71 Whitebird flies from Portland to Corpus Christi to alter world fertility—independent of the Catholic Church. Evanita delivers her son, Robert.

2110 Dec 29
Kristi and Margaret return for their third day of interviewing with Doctor Jonara Pindus.

2110 Dec 31

Kristi goes into labor with Margaret's child.

2111 Jan 1

Kristi gives birth to a healthy girl.

www.ingramcontent.com/pod-product-compliance
Lightning Source LLC
Chambersburg PA
CBHW070533030726
47505CB00001B/23